Praise for *Dust and Shadow*

"Lyndsay Faye has crafted an elegant, suspenseful thriller that feels right at home on Baker Street. Sherlock Holmes is in good hands."

—Daniel Stashower, author of *The Beautiful Cigar Girl*

"*Dust and Shadow* is fast-moving fun. Lyndsay Faye has done a great job of combining the romance of Sherlock Holmes's London with the menace of Jack the Ripper."

—Phillip Margolin, author of *Executive Privilege* and *Proof Positive*

"A well-written and atmospheric adventure, Lyndsay Faye's excellent tale of the Victorian period and the clash of archfoes Jack the Ripper and Sherlock Holmes makes for exciting reading. Journey back in time to the gaslit London of the 1880s in search of the Whitechapel murderer. Come—the game is afoot!"

—Stewart P. Evans, coauthor of *Jack the Ripper: Letters from Hell*

"Lyndsay Faye's *Dust and Shadow* is a rare gem: a never-told story about Sherlock Holmes that rings true! The voices are near perfect, her research impeccable—all in all, a feast for fans of the Great Detective and the Good Doctor and for those thrilled by the hunt for Jack the Ripper!"

—Leslie S. Klinger, editor of *The New Annotated Sherlock Holmes*

"Sherlock Holmes is Jack the Ripper's mortal enemy, and never more so than in Lyndsay Faye's *Dust and Shadow*. This first novel has bags of atmosphere. With a great deal of skill, the fictional Holmes and Watson are carefully woven into the weft and woof of the true-life Ripper story."

—Donald Rumbelow, coauthor of *Jack the Ripper: Scotland Yard Investigates*

"A brilliant piece of work, a first novel, and one that smoothly captures the moods of late Victorian London and those fictional characters first given life by Doyle. . . . If history does not know for sure who the Ripper was, readers of this fine novel do."

—Charles Stephen, *Lincoln Journal Star* (NE)

"[Faye] uses a convincing Watsonian voice to present versions of Holmes and his chronicler faithful to the originals. . . . Sherlockians will hope to see further pastiches of this quality from Faye."

—*Publishers Weekly*

"Faye displays a superb grasp of the known facts about the murders, and she effectively captures the vibrancy and squalor of the underclass in late-nineteenth-century London. . . . Mystery aficionados, especially those with an interest in the Ripper murders, will find this work a worthy revisiting of the case."

—*Booklist*

"Faye's debut novel faithfully captures period flavor. . . . Her greater achievement is using the Ripper case to present a more complex portrait of Holmes and his world."

—*Kirkus Reviews*

"Writing effectively in Watson's voice, Faye is faithful to both the Holmes oeuvre and the Ripper case, and she successfully evokes 1880s London. The secondary characters are interesting and believable."

—*Library Journal*

AN ACCOUNT OF THE RIPPER KILLINGS
by Dr. John H. Watson

DUST AND SHADOW

Lyndsay Faye

Simon & Schuster Paperbacks
NEW YORK • LONDON • TORONTO • SYDNEY

Simon & Schuster Paperbacks
1230 Avenue of the Americas
New York, NY 10020

First Simon & Schuster trade paperback edition December 2009

Simon & Schuster Paperbacks and colophon are registered trademarks
of Simon & Schuster, Inc.

For information about special discounts for bulk purchases,
please contact Simon & Schuster Special Sales at
1-866-506-1949 or business@simonandschuster.com.

The Simon & Schuster Speakers Bureau can bring authors to your live event.
For more information or to book an event contact the Simon & Schuster
Speakers Bureau at 1-866-248-3049 or visit our website at www.simonspeakers.com.

Manufactured in the United States of America

3   5   7   9   10   8   6   4

Library of Congress Cataloging-in-Publication data is available.

ISBN 978-1-4165-8330-1
ISBN 978-1-4165-8331-8 (pbk)
ISBN 978-1-4165-8362-2 (ebook)

For Jim LeMonds
and his Five Easy Pieces

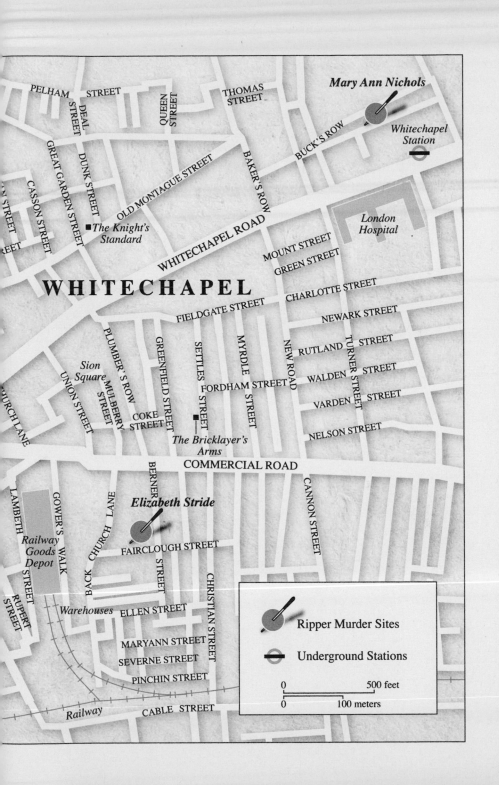

PELHAM STREET
DEAL STREET
QUEEN STREET
THOMAS STREET

Mary Ann Nichols

BUCK'S ROW

Whitechapel Station

GREAT GARDEN STREET
DUNK STREET
CASSON STREET

OLD MONTAGUE STREET
BAKER'S ROW

■*The Knight's Standard*

WHITECHAPEL ROAD

London Hospital

MOUNT STREET
GREEN STREET

WHITECHAPEL

CHARLOTTE STREET

FIELDGATE STREET

NEWARK STREET

PLUMBER'S ROW
GREENFIELD STREET
SETTLES STREET
MYRDLE STREET
NEW ROAD
RUTLAND STREET
TURNER STREET
WALDEN STREET

Sion Square

UNION STREET
MULBERRY STREET

COKE STREET
FORDHAM STREET

VARDEN STREET

CHURCH LANE

NELSON STREET

■*The Bricklayer's Arms*

COMMERCIAL ROAD

BERNER STREET
BACK CHURCH LANE

Elizabeth Stride

CANNON STREET

LAMBETH STREET
GOWER'S WALK

Railway Goods Depot

FAIRCLOUGH STREET

STREET

CHRISTIAN STREET

RUPERT STREET

Warehouses ELLEN STREET

MARYANN STREET

SEVERNE STREET

PINCHIN STREET

Railway CABLE STREET

Ripper Murder Sites

Underground Stations

0   500 feet
0   100 meters

At first it seemed the Ripper affair had scarred my friend Sherlock Holmes as badly as it had the city of London itself. I would encounter him at the end of his nightlong vigils, lying upon the sofa with his violin at his feet and his hypodermic syringe fallen from long, listless fingers, neither anodyne having banished the specter of the man we had pursued for over two months. I fought as best I could for his health, but as a fellow sufferer I could do but little to dispel his horror at what had occurred, his petrifying fear that somehow, in some inhuman feat of genius, he could have done more than he did.

At length, though never for publication, I determined that in the interests of my own peace of mind I should write the matter down. I think only in my struggle to record the Reichenbach Falls business have I borne so heavy a weight as I laid pen against paper. They were evil days for me, and Holmes more than once, up and about as the cases flooded in with more force than he could practically avoid, leaned against my desk and remarked, "Come see about the Tarlington matter with me. You needn't write this, my dear fellow. The world has already forgotten him, you know. One day we shall too."

However, as was very seldom the case, Sherlock Holmes was mistaken. The world did not forget him. It has not forgotten him to this very day, and it is a brave lad indeed who does not experience a chilling of the blood when an elder sibling invokes the frightful phantom of Jack the Ripper.

I finished the chronicle, as much as possible in that measured biographical tone which had become my habit. I did so many years ago, when Holmes's part in the matter was still questioned. But our role in the Ripper murders soon ceased to be a topic of any interest save to a select few. Only the cases visibly solved by my friend drew the accolades of a grateful public, for a story without an end is no story at all, and for London's sake, as well as for our own, the solution to the Ripper affair had to remain absolutely secret.

Though I may act against my own best interests, I cannot now bring myself to burn any records of the cases Holmes and I shared. I intend to leave my papers in my solicitor's capable hands, with this particular missive resting upon the very top of my dispatch box. No matter how vehemently I may insist upon it, however, I cannot be certain that my desire to leave this account unpublished will be obeyed. This tale throws into stark relief the most distant margins of man's malevolent capacities, and I will not stand accused of embellishment or of sensationalism. Indeed, by the time anyone lays eyes on these pages, I pray that Jack the Ripper will have faded into a mere memory of a less equitable, more violent time.

My sole intent in setting the story down at all was to applaud those indefatigable talents and high-minded purposes which I hope will ever single out my friend of more than fifty years. And yet, I am gratified to note, even as I write—beset with tidings of new war and of new grief—posterity in her kindness has already singled out a place in history for the great Mr. Sherlock Holmes.

Dr. John H. Watson, July 1939

Prologue

FEBRUARY 1887

"My dear Doctor, I fear that I shall require your services this evening."

I looked up quizzically from an article on the local elections in the *Colwall Gazette*. "With pleasure, Holmes."

"Dress warmly—the barometer is safe enough, but the wind is chill. And if you don't mind dropping your revolver in your pocket, I should be obliged. One can never be too careful, after all, and your revolver is a particularly businesslike argument."

"Did I not hear you say at dinner that we would return to London by the morning train?"

Sherlock Holmes smiled enigmatically through the gauzy veil of pipe smoke which had gradually enveloped his armchair. "You refer to my remarking that you and I would be far more productive in the city than here in Herefordshire. So we shall be. There are three cases of variable interest awaiting us in London."

"But the missing diamond?"

"I have solved it."

"My dear Holmes!" I exclaimed. "I congratulate you. But where is it, then? Have you advised Lord Ramsden of its whereabouts? And have you sent word to Inspector Gregson at the inn?"

"I said I had solved it, not resolved it, my dear fellow." Holmes laughed, rising from the damask chair in our elegant guest sitting

3

room to knock his pipe against the grate. "That work lies ahead of us. As for the case, it was never a very mysterious business, for all that our friend from the Yard appears to remain bewildered."

"I find it just as inexplicable," I admitted. "The ring stolen from a private vault, the absurd missing patch of lawn from the southern part of the grounds, the Baron's own tragic past . . ."

"You have a talent of a sort, my dear Watson, though you make shockingly little use of it. You've just identified the most telling points in the whole affair."

"Nevertheless, I confess myself all in the dark. Do you intend this evening to confront the criminal?"

"As it happens, no actual lawbreaking has yet been committed. However, you and I shall tonight don as much wool as we can lay our fingers on in order to witness a crime in action."

"In action! Holmes, what crime can you mean?"

"Grave robbing, if I have not lost all my senses. Meet me upon the grounds at close upon one o'clock, if convenient—the staff will be largely abed by that time. I would not be seen exiting the house, if I were you. Needless delay could prove very unfortunate indeed."

And with that, he disappeared into his bedroom.

At ten to one I quit the manor warmly bundled, for the night was bitter indeed, and the stars were mirrored by frozen moisture upon the grass. I spotted my friend with ease as he wandered down a stately path groomed with an almost Continental exactitude, apparently engrossed by the prospect of Nature's constellations strewn across the sky with perfect clarity. I cleared my throat, and Holmes, with a nod, advanced in my direction.

"My dear Watson!" he said quietly. "So you too would prefer to risk a chill than to miss the Malvern Hills by night? Or so the housekeeper must assume?"

"I do not believe Mrs. Jeavons is awake to assume anything of the kind."

"Marvelous. Let us see, then, what a brisk walk can do to combat this frigid weather."

We followed a path which at first pointed toward the gardens but soon banked to trace the curvature of the nearby bluffs. It was not long before Holmes led us through a hinged gate of moss-covered wood, and we left the grounds of Blackheath House behind us. Feeling at a severe disadvantage regarding our intentions, I could not help but inquire, "You have somehow connected grave robbery with a recently stolen heirloom?"

"Why recently? Remember, we have very little evidence as to when it disappeared."

I considered this, my breath forming ghostly miasmas before my eyes. "Granted. But if there is any question of grave robbery, should we not prevent rather than discover it?"

"I hardly think so."

Though I was entirely inured to Holmes's adoration of secrecy at the closing moments of a case, on occasion his dictatorial glibness grated upon my nerves. "No doubt you will soon make clear what a bizarre act of groundskeeping vandalism has to do with the defilement of a sacred resting place."

Holmes glanced at me. "How long do you suppose it would take you to dig a grave?"

"Alone? I could not say. Given few other constraints upon my time, a day perhaps."

"And if you required utter secrecy?"

"Several more, I should think," I replied slowly.

"I imagine it would take you nearly as long to undig a grave, were the need to arise. And if it were imperative that no one discover your project, I presume your native cunning would suggest a way of hiding it from public view."

"Holmes," I gasped, the answer suddenly clear to me, "do you mean to tell me that the missing patch of sod—"

"Hsst!" he whispered. "There. You see?" We had crested the top of a wooded ridge perhaps half a mile from the estate and now peered down into the rough depression forming one of the boundaries of the nearby town. Holmes pointed a slender finger. "Observe the church."

In the vibrant moonlight, I could just make out through the trees of the cemetery the stooped figure of a man laying the final clods of dirt upon a grave graced with a diminutive white headstone. He wiped his brow with the back of his hand and started directly for us.

"It is Lord Ramsden himself," I murmured.

"Back below the crest of the ridge," said Holmes, and we retreated into the copse.

"He is nearly finished," my companion observed. "I confess, Watson, that my sympathies in this matter lie squarely upon the side of the criminal, but you shall remain behind this outcropping and judge for yourself. I intend to confront the Baron alone, and if he proves reasonable, so much the better. If he does not—but quick, now! Duck down, and be as silent as you can."

Settling onto a stone, I lightly grasped my revolver within the pocket of my greatcoat. I had just registered the hiss of a vesta being struck and caught a whiff of Holmes's cigarette when muffled footsteps all at once thudded against the incline. I found that Holmes had chosen my hiding place with great care, for though I was concealed in the lee of the rock, a crack between it and the adjacent boulder afforded me a contracted view of the scene.

The Baron came into sight as he crested the ridge, perspiring visibly even in the frosty air, drawing his breath in great gasps. Glancing up into the woods before him, he stopped in horror and drew a pistol from his fur-lined cloak.

"Who goes there?" he demanded in a rasping voice.

"It is Sherlock Holmes, Lord Ramsden. It is imperative that I speak with you."

"Sherlock Holmes!" he cried. "What are you doing about at this hour?"

"I might say the same to you, my lord."

"It is hardly any business of yours," the Baron retorted, but his words were brittle with panic. "I have paid a visit. A friend—"

Holmes sighed. "My lord, I cannot allow you to perjure yourself in this manner, for I know your errand tonight dealt not with the living but with the dead."

"How could you know that?" asked the Baron.

"All is known to me, my lord."

"So you have discovered her gravesite, then!" His hand wildly trembling, he waved his pistol at the ground in small circles as if unsure of its purpose.

"I paid it a brief visit this morning," Holmes acknowledged gently. "I knew you, upon your own confession, to have loved Elenora Rowley. There you thought yourself wise, for you reasoned that too many trysts and too much correspondence had occurred between you for utter secrecy to be maintained after her death."

"I did—and so I told you all!"

"From the instant your family realized the ring was missing, you have played the game masterfully," Holmes continued, never moving his hypnotic grey eyes from the Baron's face, though I knew his attention as well as my own was firmly fixed upon the pistol. "You summoned Dr. Watson and myself to aid the police; you even insisted we remain at Blackheath House until all was settled. I extend my compliments to your very workmanlike effort."

The Baron's eyes narrowed in fury. "I was forthright with you. I showed you and your friend every imaginable courtesy. So why, then, did you do it? Why would you ever have visited her grave?"

"For the very simple reason that you claimed not to know where it was."

"Why should I have?" he demanded. "She was the entire world to me, yes, but—" He took a moment to master himself. "Our love was a jealously guarded secret, Mr. Holmes, and I abased myself once already by mentioning it to a hired detective."

"Men of your station do not venture upon painful and intimate subjects with strangers except out of dire necessity," Holmes insisted. "You gambled that employing complete sincerity at our initial conference in London would terminate my interest. Your candour would indeed have bought you time enough to complete the affair had you been dealing with a lesser investigator. Even your tale of rebellious village boys vandalizing the grounds by night was a plausible fabrication. Much was revealed to me, however, by the condition of your clothes last Sunday evening."

"I've told you already—my dog went after a pheasant and was caught in one of the villagers' snares."

"So I would have thought if your trousers alone had been muddied," Holmes replied patiently. "But the soil was heaviest on the back of your forearms, just where a man rests his elbows to pull himself out of a hole in the ground nearly as high as he is himself."

With a crazed look, Baron Ramsden leveled the pistol at Holmes, but my friend merely continued quietly.

"You loved Elenora Rowley with such a passion that you removed your grandmother's wedding ring from the family vault, which you knew to be secure enough that it is scarcely ever inventoried. You then bestowed the gift on Miss Rowley, fully intending to marry a local merchant's daughter whose beauty, or so I have been told, was matched only by her generosity of spirit."

Here the Baron's eyes dimmed and his head lowered imperceptibly, though the pistol remained trained on Holmes. "And so I would have done had she not been taken from me."

"I had a long conversation with Miss Rowley's former maidservant this morning. When Elenora Rowley fell ill, she sent you word she had departed with her parents to seek a cure on the Continent."

"The specialists could do nothing," the Baron acknowledged, his free fist clenched in his misery. "When she returned, the strain of travel had only hastened the course of her illness. She sent a note through the channels we'd created, telling me she loved me as she ever had—since we were both children and she the daughter of the dry-goods supplier to our household. Within three days she—" A spasm seemed to shake him and he passed a hand over his brow. "Any fate would have been better. Even my own death."

"Be that as it may, the lady died," my friend replied compassionately, "and before it could occur to you in your grief that she had kept your token sewn into the lining of her garments, it had been buried with her. When you regained your senses, you realized, no doubt, that the heirloom had passed beyond your reach."

"I was ill myself then. I was mad. For the better part of a month I was the merest shadow of the man I had been. I cared for nothing and no one," the Baron stated numbly. "Yet my brother's many follies follow each other like days upon a calendar, and our family is not as wealthy as my mother would have us suppose."

"A matter of accounting, then, brought the missing jewel into the public eye."

"I would never have taken it back from her else—in life or death. God help me! All the woes my brother has brought upon our heads are as nothing compared to my own. What will the appellation 'grave robber' do to the name of Ramsden?" he cried. Then, calming himself with all the reserve he could muster, Lord Ramsden drew himself up to his full height, his blue eyes glimmering eerily. "Perhaps nothing," he continued, with a new and chilling precision to his speech. "Perhaps the only other person who knows of the matter will perish this very night."

"It is not a very likely circumstance, is it, my lord?" my friend remarked evenly.

"So you may think," his client snarled, "but you have underestimated my—"

"I am not so foolish as to have arranged this meeting in total solitude," stated the detective. "My friend Dr. Watson has been good enough to accompany me."

I emerged cautiously from behind the stony outcropping.

"So you have brought your spies!" cried the Baron. "You mean to ruin me!"

"You must believe, Lord Ramsden, that I have no intention of causing you the slightest harm," Holmes protested. "My friend and I are prepared to swear that no word shall be breathed of this business to any living person, provided the ring is returned."

"It is here." The Baron placed his hand over his breast pocket. "But do you speak in earnest? It is incredible."

"My little career would soon enough suffer shipwreck if I neglected my clients' best interests," my friend averred.

"Not the police, nor my family, nor any other person will ever hear of the matter now I have retrieved the ring? It is far more than I deserve."

"They shall not on my account. I give you my word," Holmes declared gravely.

"As do I," I added.

"Then that is enough." The Baron's head fell forward as if in a daze, exhausted by his grief.

"It is not the first felony I have commuted, and I fear it is unlikely to be the last," confessed my friend in the same calming tones.

"I shall be eternally grateful for your silence. Indeed, your discretion has been unimpeachable throughout this affair, which is far higher praise than I can apply to my own."

"There I cannot agree with you," Holmes began, but the Baron continued bitterly.

"Ellie died alone rather than betray my trust. What have I offered her in return?"

"Come, my lord. It is hardly practical to dwell on such matters. You acted in the interests of your family, and your secret is safe, after all."

"No doubt you are right," he whispered. "You may proceed to the house, gentlemen. It is over. I shall be more silent hereafter, you may trust."

I had turned to go, but suddenly an inarticulate cry from Holmes swung me round again. The pistol fired just as Holmes, in a desperate leap, reached the Baron. My friend caught him round the torso and laid him on the frozen ground. I was beside them in an instant.

"Quick, man! He breathes—can you not—"

But Lord Ramsden had already passed beyond the aid of any man. As I loosened his collar, he emitted a low, shuddering sigh and was still.

"Holmes, he—"

"He is dead." My friend passed a hand over the Baron's eyes, his suavity of movement dulled in the shock of the tragedy. "If only I had— but Lord Ramsden would surely have revealed himself otherwise! No, no, Gregson is an ass, but he can see a brick wall when it is in front of him. Only I could have returned it in safety." He descended quickly and removed a glittering band from the upper waistcoat pocket of the dead man.

"What he must have seen to retrieve it," I muttered in horror.

"God help us, Watson." My friend, though outwardly serene, was as shaken as I had ever before seen him. "I would not wish his history on any man."

We knelt in silence under the black shadows of the trees, slowly growing cognizant once more of the piercing cold.

"What are we to tell them?"

"There, at least, our course seems clear," Holmes considered. "You and I heard a shot from just beyond the grounds and, considering the hour, went to investigate. We found the Baron already beyond assistance. That is all."

I nodded. "I suppose the pressures of financial ruin could account for suicide in a man of sensitive nature, but what of the ring?"

"As for the ring, I am prepared to go rather further," Holmes replied softly. "The Baron thought his life a threat to his secret, and I have no intention of allowing his death to be one likewise."

The grief which seized the household when we returned with our sad burden and raised the alarm was pitiable to behold. The lady of the house, in the loss of her eldest son, seemed to forget her mother's ring had ever existed. Finding ourselves quite useless amid the chaos, we arose early the next morning to stop at the inn and bid farewell to Inspector Gregson and the constable he had brought from London to aid in the investigation; they had taken over a suite of rooms, using the simple parlour as an office. The inspector, in his own unique way, expressed considerable distress at our sudden departure.

"Well, well, you're quite right, I suppose. Once you know a thing is over your head, you may as well act the man and own up to it. I intend to play the game to the end, though, Mr. Holmes. Simply not capable of leaving a case half finished with so much to go on."

"You've unearthed fresh leads, then?" my friend responded coolly.

"Well, there's that brother of the late Baron's—a gambler and a rake, if you listen to my sources."

"I hardly think it likely that—"

"And now this suicide!" Inspector Gregson proclaimed. "Under the circumstances, very black indeed."

"How so?"

"Why, guilt! What does a man have to kill himself over if not guilt? Really, with all these developments, Mr. Holmes, if you remained, you might yet get a hint of what's going on."

"I have word of the gem in London." Holmes shrugged one shoulder dismissively. "A stonecutter friend of mine has given me reason to return to the city, and I find the evidence meager enough here in Colwall to justify following this fresh lead."

"Excuse me, sir," interjected a voice from the side of the room. "Surely there is a great deal of evidence."

Holmes swung his head to regard the young constable who had ventured this remark. "Do you think so?" he queried dryly. "I call solving a crime a near impossibility when one cannot even fix the date of occurrence within a twelvemonth."

This retort elicited a chuckle from Gregson, who added, "Now, now, my boy, I brought you down so that you could watch a true professional in action. And Mr. Holmes here may have the odd tip as well. But you'd do better to listen, I think, and keep your opinions mum."

The officer appeared unperturbed. "But what of the vandalized grass plot?"

"The grass plot?" Gregson laughed. "What can you see in that? As if gardening had anything to do with the matter!"

"I thought it rather queer myself, before I met the boys responsible," Holmes said swiftly. "Yesterday a brief walk through your inn's stable yard brought me into personal contact with young Fergus MacArthur and his several associates. They were busy rubbing the guests' saddles with tallow while the groomsman lay snoring. If creativity alone ensured success in this world, that young gang would soon enough rule the Commonwealth."

My friend rose gracefully and retrieved his hat from a small bench by the door. "I shan't hesitate to forward you any news I may manage to unearth in London."

"Ah, well. I have no doubt but that we'll have solved the whole matter by the time we hear from you again, but despite that—my thanks."

"Farewell, Inspector Gregson, and farewell to your staff. They are more promising than you realize." Holmes gave a final nod and shut the door firmly behind us.

"Back to London," I mused.

"Yes, Herefordshire has no further use for the two of us," my friend replied. "However, I have every confidence of locating the ring through its mysterious buyer." He patted his own breast pocket and the ghost of a smile appeared on his somber face.

We had not been long in London before Holmes telegraphed Lady Ramsden with the news that her mother's ring had been found. Not only was the household's joy at the ring's return buried under their misfortune, but to my friend's evident satisfaction, so was their curiosity at its initial disappearance. Gregson's case thus remained regrettably inconclusive, but once the ring had safely arrived via Scotland Yard escort from London at Blackheath House, the good inspector's spirits had risen enough to compliment the private detective on his "extraordinary luck."

Stretched upon the settee two weeks later, I was engaged in a medical journal when I heard Holmes's familiar step bounding up the stairs and into the sitting room. He held a letter to the lamp bemusedly, then with a motion of indifference tossed it onto a formidable stack of documents near the bookshelf.

"Holmes, I do believe you've Irregulars* who are shorter than that monstrous pile," I observed.

"Mmm?" he queried distractedly. "Oh, I hardly think so. Little Graves has had an extraordinary bout of growth since you saw him last."

I smiled. "What was it, then?"

"The letter?" Holmes stretched his sinewy arm to retrieve it, paused over it for a moment longer, and passed it to me. It was written in vivid red ink in an oddly erratic script, and it read:

Mr. Holmes,

You are a clever one. Arent you? No matter that you may be devillish clever you may be the very devil, but not so clever that Mr. Nobody doesn't see you. Yes, I see you clear enough, and I may also

See you in Hell

Sooner than you think, Mr. Holmes.

I looked up in chagrin. "Holmes, this letter is an outright threat!"

"The tone is rather unfriendly," he conceded, digging for tobacco in the depths of his Persian slipper.

---

* The group of street urchins often employed by Holmes to elicit information.

"What do you intend to do?"

"Do? Nothing. Your correspondence is not, perhaps, quite as vivid as is my own. When I inspect the mail, desperate for a case worthy of my time and my talent, I all too often find instead the ramblings of the fanciful spinster or the lyricism of the bored newlywed. I'd a priceless example from Brighton last week which I must show you—"

"You have not the slightest interest in this bizarre missive?"

"To my deep discredit, I've known far too many criminals not to expect this sort of thing occasionally," Holmes countered irritably. "It is written on cheap foolscap, posted in the East-end of London, no marks of fingers or other identifying features. What am I to do with it? Queer enough hand, though. I've hardly seen one like it." He scrutinized the page.

"What steps can you take?" I asked once more.

"The best of all steps, my dear Watson—to throw it in the dust-bin." He tossed the paper in the general direction of his desk and forcefully steered the conversation to Richard Owen's work in the realm of philosophical anatomy.

It was only the next afternoon, when I noticed Holmes's commonplace book open on his desk, that I realized the letter had not been discarded but pasted carefully under "Miscellaneous Posts." I meant to inquire of Holmes whether he had discovered any clue to the matter, but my fellow lodger's abrupt arrival with an urgent appeal from Camberwell drove the matter from my mind entirely.

CHAPTER ONE

Two Crimes

It has been argued by those who have so far flattered my attempts to chronicle the life and career of Mr. Sherlock Holmes as to approach them in a scholarly manner that I have often been remiss in the arena of precise chronology. While nodding to kindly meant excuses made for me in regards to hasty handwriting or careless literary agents, I must begin by confessing that my errors, however egregious, were entirely intentional. Holmes's insistence, not to mention my own natural discretion, often prevented me from maintaining that exactitude so highly prized in a biographer; I have been forced to change the dates of marginal cases to disguise great ones, alter names and circumstances, all the while diligently preserving the core truth of the events, without which there would have been no object in writing anything at all. In this instance, however, any obfuscation would be absurd, as the facts are known not only to the people of London but to the world. I shall therefore set down the entire truth, as it happened to Holmes and to myself, omitting nothing that pertains to the most harrowing series of crimes my illustrious friend and I were ever called upon to solve.

The year of 1888 had already proven significant for Mr. Sherlock Holmes, for it was in that twelvemonth that he performed valuable services for one of the reigning houses of Europe and continued forestalling the activities of Professor James Moriarty, whose hold over London's underworld grew ever more apparent to my friend. Several highly publicized investigations that year displayed Holmes's remarkable skills to the public, including the appalling affair of the faulty oil lamp, and the matter of Mrs. Victoria Mendosa's mysteriously vanishing thimble and its consequences. My friend's talents, which had once languished in obscure specialism, in that year flamed into the most gratifying notoriety.

Despite the busyness that accompanied Holmes's ever-increasing reputation for omniscience, we found ourselves at home on that evening in early August, the day after Bank Holiday, Holmes performing chemical analyses of an American snake venom which had recently proven itself a nearly untraceable poison, and I engaged in a perusal of the day's papers. To my delight, the skies above the buildings burned with that most elusive of all elements, the London sun, and a brisk breeze fluttered about the windows (one of which I'd opened as a safeguard against Holmes's chemical efforts), when an item in the late edition of the *Star* caught my eye.

"I cannot begin to understand," I said to no one in particular, "what could drive a murderer to such total desecration of the human body."

Holmes, without looking up from his work, remarked, "An argument could be made that the ultimate desecration of the human body is to end its earthly usefulness, which would imply that all murderers share equally that specific charge."

"This is rather beyond the pale. It states here that some poor woman, as yet unidentified, was found stabbed to death in Whitechapel."

"A deplorable, though hardly baffling occurrence. I imagine that she worked the area for food, drink, and daily shelter. Such pitiable unfortunates are particularly likely to inspire crimes of passion in the men with whom they associate."

"She was stabbed twenty times, Holmes."

"And your unassailable medical assessment is that once would have been enough."

"Well, yes," I faltered. "Apparently the villain continued to slash at her long after she was dead, or so the pattern of blood indicates."

The detective smiled. "You are a gentleman of the most sympathetic character, my dear Watson. While you would possibly—for I have seen you do it—condone a crime of passion committed in the throes of despair or of vengeance, you can see nothing permissible about such morbid abuse."

"I suppose that expresses it."

"I confess I cannot imagine myself in such a rage as to batter my victim beyond all sense either," he admitted. "Is there anything further?"

"The police know nothing yet."

Holmes sighed and pushed aside his scientific materials. "Would you and I had the power to make all of London safe, my good man, but for the moment, let us leave our musings upon the depths to which our fellow citizens can sink and instead explore whether or not we have time to make a seven-thirty curtain for Brahms's Symphony No. 4 in E Minor at the Royal Albert Hall. My attention was directed to the second-chair cellist by my brother Mycroft, and I should be grateful for your company while I observe the gentleman in his natural habitat."

It took Sherlock Holmes exactly five days to complete the affair of the second cellist, and once concluded, my friend had the thanks of the premier branches of the British government, of which his brother Mycroft was a pivotal member. My own knowledge of Mycroft Holmes's exalted occupation was at that time a closely kept secret, for he occasionally engaged his brother upon nationally vital inquiries about which neither Sherlock Holmes nor I ought to have had the slightest inkling. I regret to say, however, that when nothing but the most pedestrian of wrongdoing took place in the following weeks, my friend lapsed into that melancholy torpor which made my own life, not to mention that of our landlady, Mrs. Hudson, taxing in the extreme. Holmes ever maintained the opinion that we should abandon him entirely when such a fit was upon him, but as a medical man, I dreaded the sight of his tiny, impeccably kept hypodermic syringe and that momentous stop at the chemist's which promised that my friend would commence to ruin himself for a matter of days or weeks if I did not take any steps to circumvent him. In vain I scanned the papers, and in vain I attempted to convince Holmes that a woman ought not to be stabbed so very many times, Whitechapel or no. At length I found myself longing, fleetingly and against the dictates of my conscience, for the advent of some sensational misfortune.

I rose early that fateful Saturday, the morning of September the first, and as I sat smoking a pipe after breakfast, Holmes strode into the sitting room, fully dressed and in the process of reading the *Daily News*. The warmth of his pale complexion announced he had been out, and I noted with relief that his keen gaze betrayed no glimmer of the drug I had come to despise. His chiseled brow furrowed in concentration, he laid the open paper on our dining table and within moments had opened seven or eight other editions to which we sub-scribed, quickly locating the same story in each and then draping the paper over an article of furniture.

"Good morning, Holmes," I remarked, just as our sitting room seemed in danger of disappearing under the crackling storm of news-print.

"I've been out," he replied.

"Yes," I returned dryly.

"I hope you have already broken your fast this morning, Wat-son."

"Whatever do you mean?"

"It appears that the defilement of corpses is a growing industry in Whitechapel. They've found another one, my dear fellow. Abdomen apparently slashed after she was murdered."

"What was the cause of death, then?"

"Her neck was nearly severed."

"Good heavens. Where was she found?"

"In Buck's Row, it seems, which arrested my interest immediately. I imagined the other matter a bizarre aberration, but here is another on its heels."

"The first was bad enough."

"That girl's name was Martha Tabram, and the early report had it wrong: she was stabbed a grand total of thirty-nine times," he stated dispassionately. "Yesterday morning's victim, whose name was apparently Mary Ann Nichols, by all accounts was partially eviscerated."

"Dare I hope you shall look into the matter?" I asked.

"It is hardly within my purview to do so when no one has consul—"

At that moment, Mrs. Hudson entered and surveyed our newly adorned furnishings with silent cynicism. Our landlady was not in the best of spirits, for Holmes in his devil-may-care humour had used the berry spoon to dissolve chemical elements over his burner, and the disagreement this activity had caused had not yet resolved itself to her satisfaction.

"Gentlemen to see you," she said from the doorway. "Inspector Lestrade and one other. Will you be requiring aught from my cupboards, Mr. Holmes, or have you everything you need?"

"Ha!" Holmes exclaimed. "Lestrade occasionally evinces the most impeccable timing. Indeed no, Mrs. Hudson, I've sufficient cutlery for my purposes. I shall ring if I want anything in the way of a pickle fork. Do show up the inspector, if you will."

With studied dignity, Mrs. Hudson exited. A few moments later Inspector Lestrade and an associate entered the room. Holmes often had occasion to bemoan the intellect of our hatchet-visaged friend, the lean and dapper little inspector, but Lestrade's diligence commanded our respect even when his utter lack of imagination strained the independent investigator's nerves. On this occasion, Lestrade looked as rumpled and anxious as I had ever seen him. His companion was dressed in dark tweeds, his beard modestly trimmed beneath a more impressive moustache; he had a pale, retiring aspect, and his eyes darted shyly between Holmes and myself.

My friend took them in at a glance. "How are you, Lestrade? We should be delighted to offer you both coffee, or something stronger if required. I am pleased to make your acquaintance, Doctor . . . ?"

"Llewellyn. At your service, sir," our visitor replied with evident disquiet.

"Dr. Llewellyn, I assure you I am at yours. You will excuse my use of your prefix—you have recently sustained some slight injury to your right hand, and the way in which the dressing is fastened leads me to believe it was secured entirely by the aid of your own left appendage. And yet, the cloth is not of a variety to be found outside a medical facility. I should be shocked to learn our local surgeons have grown so slovenly as to require a gentleman to secure his own bandages."

"You are correct on all counts, sir—how very extraordinary."

Holmes nodded briefly. "This is my friend and colleague Dr. Watson."

"I am glad to meet you. I am glad to meet anyone willing to get to the bottom of this horrid affair."

Holmes waved Lestrade and our nervous new acquaintance to their seats, the backs of the furnishings still entirely wreathed with newsprint. My friend then threw himself into his own armchair.

"You are here about Buck's Row, I imagine," he remarked. "You were knocked up yesterday, Dr. Llewellyn?"

"My surgery is at one fifty-two Whitechapel Road, some few minutes' distance," he acknowledged. "I was summoned at slightly before four yesterday morning. I completed a postmortem examination just now."

"One moment, if you please. Lestrade, while I am delighted to see you, as ever, why in God's name have you waited an entire day to consult me?"

"I've only just been reassigned two hours ago!" Lestrade protested. "Inspector Spratling began it, then Helson. I wasted no time in bringing Dr. Llewellyn round."

"My abject apologies, Inspector." Holmes smiled. "Your haste was not lax; it was unprecedented."

"No more unprecedented than the corpse. If you had seen what I did at the morgue this morning, what Dr. Llewellyn here saw yesterday . . ." Lestrade shook his head. "Your methods may be unconventional, but we need an end to this case as quick as is possible. There's something about it that's very queer, Mr. Holmes, and correct me if I've the wrong end of the stick, but that's where you tend to come in."

Holmes settled back in his chair, half closing his eyes. "Very well, then. The story, as it happened to you, Dr. Llewellyn."

"Well, Mr. Holmes," Dr. Llewellyn began hesitantly, "as I have said, I hold a medical practice in Whitechapel Road which I obtained after I finished my studies at the University of London. That main thoroughfare is quite respectable, and to a great extent, the same ailments parade across my consulting room from day to day—influenza, rheumatism, agues—the most peaceful of maladies. However, living in London's East-end as I do, I occasionally find my work to be of a more unsettling nature. A regular patient of mine once burst into my offices with a nasty knife wound, as he'd forgotten himself and wandered into a corner where some roughs thought his pocketbook worth trying for. I suppose that the immediate proximity of the slums would be all too obvious if I ever had cause to treat any of my poorest neighbours, but I fear they haven't the means. In the case of disease, they consult quack street doctors for penny compendia of gin or of laudanum. And in the case of injury, as their wounds were often got through misadventure, many deem it safer to suffer in anonymity than to risk dealing with police.

"That terrible murder in George Yard Buildings three weeks ago left a strong impression on my mind. We all were shocked by the ferocity of it. I cannot convey to you my horror at what I was called upon to witness yesterday."

Holmes held up a cautionary hand. "Please," said he, "everything just as you saw it."

"Buck's Row is one of those sordid pitch-black byways of which Whitechapel boasts so many once the main road is abandoned. The body was situated at the entrance to a stable yard beneath a decrepit gateway. I saw nothing out of the ordinary save the body, but the inspector may have more to say on that subject."

"I wish I did," sighed Lestrade. "As you say, the body was the only thing out of the ordinary, as it were."

"And the body?" prompted Holmes.

"Something over thirty years of age," said Dr. Llewellyn, mopping his brow with a handkerchief. "She had brown hair and was missing several of her front teeth, but that characteristic did not seem to be a recent development. Nearly all of her was still warm, save her extremities. Her throat was savagely slashed two times. She may as well have been decapitated. Apart from her throat, I found her upper body to be completely intact, but the lower—she was ripped apart, Mr. Holmes. Her skirts were raised up to reveal the torso, and savage cuts penetrated her lower abdomen, exposing the internal organs."

I regarded the doctor with dismay, but for Holmes, shock remained secondary to professional absorption. "Her chest was unharmed, you say? Surely her garments, at least, were soiled with blood?"

"She was wearing a brown frock, and I assure you it was entirely free of stain."

"If that is the case, she was prostrate before the wound to her neck was administered. Where is she now, Lestrade?"

"At the morgue. Name of Mary Ann 'Polly' Nichols, identified by a friend from Lambeth Workhouse who calls herself Mary Ann Monk. Mark of the workhouse was on the petticoats, which led us to seek identification there. Shabby clothing, black bonnet, and she had on her person a comb, pocket handkerchief, and a piece of mirror. More than likely it's all she had to her name."

"What do you imagine the time of death to have been, Dr. Llewellyn?"

"I arrived at three fifty a.m. She could not have been dead more than ten minutes."

"And the gruesome discovery was made by whom?"

"One Charles Cross, a carman on his way to work," said Lestrade as he consulted his notes. "In my opinion, he's merely a passerby. Poor chap was terrified. Constable Neil arrived on the scene shortly after and sent for Dr. Llewellyn here, hoping to save her. It was too late by that time, of course."

We sat silent as the wind picked up. I wondered briefly whether Polly Nichols's family knew of her hideous fate, and then whether she had any family to tell.

"Lestrade," Holmes said finally, "has the force had any luck in clearing up the murder of Martha Tabram early this month?"

Lestrade shook his head perplexedly. "The inquest has just been reopened. I was not myself working on the case, but we're all of the mind it was a tryst gone terribly wrong. Good Lord, Mr. Holmes, you don't think these events could have been connected in any way?"

"No, certainly not. I've merely the professional certainty that two such outrageous crimes committed ten minutes' walk apart from each other is remarkable enough to note."

Dr. Llewellyn rose and reached for his hat. "I am very sorry I have not more to tell you gentlemen. I'm afraid I must return to my practice, as my patients will be wondering what has become of me."

"Be so good as to leave your card, Dr. Llewellyn," said Holmes, shaking his hand absently.

"Of course. The best of luck to all of you. Do let me know if I can be of any further assistance."

After Dr. Llewellyn's departure, Lestrade turned a grave face to Holmes.

"I don't like your harping on Martha Tabram one bit, Mr. Holmes. Surely the same man couldn't have fallen out with both these women? More likely Polly Nichols was killed by a jealous lover, or a gang, or one of her clients who'd fallen into a drunken rage."

"You are probably right. However, I beg that you will humour me far enough to fill me in on the details of both crimes."

Lestrade shrugged. "If Tabram is of interest to you, of course I've no objection. It shouldn't be difficult for me to gather up the papers. I can have them for you this afternoon."

"I shall cast an eye over the evidence immediately."

"You have full access, Mr. Holmes—just mention my name at the morgue or at the crime scene. I shall see you both at the Yard." The inspector nodded and made his way out.

My friend crossed to the mantelpiece, shook a cigar out of an empty bud vase, and commenced smoking with the deepest absorption. "This Tabram murder is a very curious affair," he commented.

"You mean the Nichols murder?"

"I mean precisely what I say."

"You thought little enough of it before, Holmes."

"I expected every morning to read that they'd solved it. Men do not often stab helpless females thirty-nine times and then disappear into the ether. The motive behind such an outrageous act would necessarily be sensational."

"And such women necessarily have a great many associates, most of them untraceable," I pointed out.

"That is obvious," he retorted. "It is also obvious that the district of Whitechapel offers a great many natural advantages to the predator. Once the sun has fallen, you can hardly see your hand before your face, and the slaughterhouses allow blood-spattered men to pass without remark. What is less obvious is whether we have anything to fear from the proximity, in place and in time, of the two deaths."

"It is certainly a distressing coincidence."

Holmes shook his head and reached for his walking stick.

"One viciously maimed corpse is distressing. Two is something else entirely. I fear we have not a moment to lose."

CHAPTER TWO

The Evidence

The body of Polly Nichols clearly demanded our immediate attention, so we at once made our way by cab to the mortuary shed at Old Montague Street Workhouse Infirmary. As we clattered roughly toward the East-end of London, the buildings grew steadily smaller, their façades coated with decades of sooty atmosphere. When we reached Whitechapel Road, however, I was struck as always by the headlong commotion of the place. A preacher stood shouting at a knot of jeering locals, fighting to wrest their attention from a gin palace on the one side and an equally vociferous peddler of men's work shirts on the other. Light and dust sparkled from the backs of loaded hay-wains, and dead cattle swung from hooks above carts filled with fresh hides. But despite the thriving dynamism of its widest thoroughfares, I never failed to be shaken by the misery evident as we turned off the main road into narrow, shop-lined byways and passed snarling youngsters fighting over a street corner from which to sell matches, and staggering drunks of both sexes propped against doorframes in the early afternoon.

The mortuary shed was by its very nature a dismal place, frequented only by those whose sole recourse was to indenture themselves to the parish disposing of human remains, and characterized by its utter unsuitability as a medical facility. Lestrade had sent warning of our imminent arrival, so immediately upon locating the hodge-podge of wooden slats, we witnessed firsthand the sight that had so upset Dr. Llewellyn.

Across the crude wooden slab of an examining table lay a woman slightly more than five feet tall. Though her face was small-featured with high, merry cheekbones and a sensitive brow, it was etched deeply with the coarseness of care and toil. Her neck was indeed nearly severed and her abdomen opened in bestial, purposeless lacerations.

I began to inquire whether anything stood out to Holmes's sharper eye, but suddenly he dived toward the corpse with a cry of impatience.

"We have arrived too late after all! It has been washed, Watson," he exclaimed. "Most obtusely and effectively washed."

I nodded. "It is a common enough practice, as you know. Some even argue one cannot see the wounds effectively otherwise."

Holmes practically snorted. "I tell you, Watson, if Scotland Yard were to reimburse my time for retrieving every clue lost due to negligence or hysterical hygiene, I could no doubt retire this afternoon. As it is, I am forced to glean the leavings. Do you observe anything Dr. Llewellyn may have missed, being less intimately acquainted with the criminal element than you yourself?"

"Really, Holmes."

His eyes glinted wickedly over my shoulder. "Come now, my dear fellow. Expertise is none the less admirable for being of an unsavoury variety."

I looked her over. The poor wretch had come to a sorry end; a blessing indeed if her killer saw fit to cut her throat first, leaving the remainder of his rage for a lifeless shell.

"Her neck has been slashed nearly to the vertebrae, lacerating the two major arteries, and there are seven senseless cuts through her abdominal tissue. She does not appear to have been victim of any other indecencies, for I see no sign of recent connection, and the cuts are smooth-edged and deliberate. What do you make of it, Holmes?"

The detective hovered over her pensively. "Notice the discoloura- tion near the jaw; he robbed her of consciousness, then slit her throat upon the ground, for she exhibits no bruising on the arms consistent with fending off her attacker, and it would explain the lack of blood upon the upper torso that Dr. Llewellyn mentioned. From the clean- liness of the other cuts, which you noted so astutely, we may also deduce that she was dead, drugged, or in some other way incapable of struggle when they were performed, else they would be jagged or torn. I believe all these injuries were made with the same weapon, that is to say, a six- or eight-inch knife kept well sharpened, possibly with a double blade. He killed her, cut her apart in near total darkness—at a serious threat to his own safety, if we consider the surplus time required—and then made his escape."

"But why? What could possibly have occurred between Polly Nichols and her killer to enrage him so?"

"Why, indeed. Come, Watson—off to Buck's Row. If we are mirac- ulously lucky, we may find something the police have not already either trampled on or swept into the rubbish bin."

When we arrived at the scene of the murder, the bustling cacoph- ony of Whitechapel Road faded, replaced by the headlong rushing of the Northern Railway Line. Mean two-story houses, hastily con- structed and poorly maintained, crept along one side of Buck's Row, while the blank faces of austere warehouses stood like sentinels on the other. Holmes leapt down from the hansom and approached a knot of reporters and policemen while I paid the driver and elicited a promise to await our return.

"Certainly, Mr. Holmes," a young constable replied as I approached, tipping his rounded hat. "We were about to scrub down the whole area, but we can give you ten minutes if you like. We've found noth- ing out of the ordinary."

Holmes, every sinew of his slight frame alive with that nervous energy only apparent within the boundaries of a crime scene, set to work. The detective was as avid in his pursuit of a case as he was lethargic at the lack of one, and no patch of the surrounding roads or stable yard escaped his steely scrutiny. After nearly twenty minutes, he struck his stick impatiently against the stable yard fence and returned to where I stood.

"Any progress?"

Holmes set his thin lips and shook his head. "From the blood upon the ground, I believe she was not moved from another site, which is a point worth knowing. The quarrel ended here. Apart from that, I can only tell you that the apothecary over there was recently the victim of a robbery, that two gentlemen of leisure came to blows over a bet near that patch of mud, and that the police constable immediately to your left is a bachelor who owns a terrier. And thus, friend Watson, we finish no better off than we began." He waved to the constables to proceed about their business.

"I suppose the points you've mentioned can have nothing to do with the crime itself, but how did you deduce them?"

"What?" His grey eyes were busily scanning the upper stories of the surrounding buildings. "Oh, yes . . . Old door with new lock near broken window, a costly variety of the jack of spades torn in half near obvious signs of a struggle between square-toed male boots, and Constable Anderson's truly appalling trouser legs. No, they are not related to our investigation. And yet, we may still find ourselves employment. The angle of that window is ideally positioned for our purposes."

I looked up in curiosity. Behind us stood the Brown and Eagle Wool Warehouse and Schneider's Cap Factory, both constructed with that wholehearted devotion to industry that sullies the word *architecture*. The window Holmes indicated, belonging to a tenement, was almost immediately above us. My friend lost no time but strode forward and rapped upon the door.

At first I thought his mysterious intentions would be denied, for there was no answer. Then the detective smiled in his ironic fashion.

"Slow footsteps . . . a woman, I think. Yes, and slightly lame in one foot. Naturally, I cannot yet tell you which foot. My apologies. Ah, here is the lady herself."

The door flew open, revealing a wrinkled, forward-thrusting face wreathed with a nimbus of wispy white hair, a face resembling nothing so much as a mole emerging from its burrow. Her spectacles were so dirty that I could hardly see the use of them. She peered at us as if at two scabrous street dogs and tightened her grasp on her cane.

"What do you want? I don't let rooms, and if you've business with my sons or my husband, they work for a living."

"What miserable luck," Holmes exclaimed. "I was informed that your fellow knew a man with access to a cart."

"Yes, sir," she replied, her eyes narrowing still further, "but my youngest won't be back until seven."

"By Jove! No rest for us today, Miles," said Holmes with a wry face. "I was prepared to meet nearly any price, the goods being what they are, but we'll simply have to inquire elsewhere."

"Now, wait. You've need of a cart today?"

Holmes bent his aquiline face toward the old woman and replied, "I've certain . . . materials which need transporting. I'm afraid it's rather a man's business, Mrs. . . . ?"

"Mrs. Green."

"Of course, you're his mother. And you're sure Mr. Green will be out for some time? Well, it is a pity. I don't imagine you've any experience with such matters?"

She pursed her wrinkled mouth and, reaching some private conclusion, beckoned us inside. We were led into a small, dimly lit parlour, which featured not one iota of furnishings more than was necessary, and sat down.

"I must admit," Holmes began, "I've been set on my guard by recent events."

Mrs. Green's eyes lit like tapers. "Oh, you mean the murder, do you? Begging your pardon, what was your name?"

"I am Mr. Worthington, and this is my associate Mr. Miles."

She nodded sagely, replying, "A nasty business."

"But how terrifying! You must have heard something, living so near at hand."

"Not I, sir. Though I am, I may tell you, a very light sleeper. I was once awoken by nothing more than my cat leaping onto the downstairs balustrade."

"Dear me. But you sleep downstairs, surely, to have heard such a thing?"

She shook her head proudly. "No, indeed. My daughter and I sleep on the first floor. I am very sensitive, nocturnally speaking, sir."

"Then you must certainly have been disturbed! Your window overlooks the very spot."

"Would that I had seen something, or heard it, but I slept peacefully through till morning. It's eerie, that's what. But what time shall you be needing the cart?"

"In all honesty, Mrs. Green, I should not like to discuss my goods with anyone other than your son. I cannot convey to you my absolute trust in his discretion except to offer my warmest compliments regarding his upbringing. We shall return at a later time." Holmes bade a cordial farewell to the woman, who limped appreciably on her right foot as she showed us to the door.

"You were quite effective at gaining an entrance," I noted as we returned to the cab.

Holmes smiled, but his gaze was distant. "It goes without saying in this community that, given even a single male member of the household, any resident will be acquainted with a man who has access to a cart. You can hardly fail, provided your pronouns are vague enough."

"It is a pity she could tell us nothing."

"On the contrary," my friend replied softly, "she told us a great deal."

"How do you mean?"

"I had hoped, despite its cool execution, that this was some monstrous crime of passion. Mrs. Green's room overlooks the scene of the assault, and I know for a fact that Nichols was not moved. If Mrs. Green is a light sleeper, and if Nichols was not moved, and Mrs. Green heard nothing, then there was no quarrel. If there was no quarrel . . ."

"Then the murder was premeditated," I continued. "And if the murder was premeditated—"

"Then it is worse than I thought," Holmes concluded grimly. "Whitehall, please, driver! Scotland Yard."

We entered the Yard's headquarters through the rear of the building and hastened up the familiar staircase to locate Inspector Lestrade. Our associate's office was hardly a shrine to organization at the best of times, but that afternoon we found the windowless room could hardly be glimpsed beneath its litter of notes, maps, and memoranda. He looked up from his chair with a decided smirk.

The inspector appeared to have recovered a deal of composure within the haven of the Yard, along with the officious manners which were wont so often to chafe the considerable vanity of my companion. I had watched the pair collaborate over crimes both trivial and momentous over the years, and despite their mutual love of justice and regard for each other's talents—tenacity on Lestrade's part and innate brilliance on the part of Sherlock Holmes—I had never yet witnessed a meeting when the two friends failed to pique one another's temper, either deliberately or incidentally. The fact that both would end up nettled and self-important was a foregone conclusion, even if Holmes religiously delivered full credit to Lestrade in all their mutual cases, and Holmes was Lestrade's first and last defense against the incomprehensible.

"Well, Mr. Holmes, the notion we'd a homicidal maniac on our hands was a bit rich, don't you think? I've put together the evidence regarding the Tabram case for you, and I think you'll see it's hardly the work of the same man."

"I do not recall stating that the crimes were perpetrated by the same individual, only that they are both singular and similar."

Lestrade proceeded to rummage through his papers primly.

"Very well, Mr. Holmes. Lecture as you like. I will confine myself to the facts. Deceased, one Martha Tabram, an unfortunate, found in George Yard Buildings on August the seventh stabbed thirty-nine times. Took us a full week to identify the body, finally confirmed by Henry Samuel Tabram, her former husband. They had two sons, but she seems to have been more interested in gin than in children, so she deserted him. He cut off her maintenance money when he discovered how she was supplementing her income. One can hardly blame him." Here the inspector coughed discreetly before continuing his report. "She was last seen in the company of a drunken sergeant, and whoever he may be, the case is black against him. Tabram ducked into an alleyway with the chap and that's the last we know."

"To whom are we grateful for this information?"

"Constable Bennett, whose beat includes George Yard Buildings, and a Miss 'Pearly Poll.' Miss Poll and Mrs. Tabram fell in with a pair of guardsmen at the Two Brewers public house sometime before midnight. When they had finished at the pub, they parted ways into dark corridors in pairs. I'm sure you can deduce why that might be."

"Thank you, the matter is indeed within my powers. What says this Constable Bennett?"

"That he approached a young grenadier guardsman at two o'clock in the morning just north of George Yard Buildings. Fellow told Bennett he was waiting for a friend who had gone off with a girl. Almost three hours later, one John Reeves came running up to Bennett with the news that he'd found a body. Bennett said that the corpse was placed in a disheveled and provocative position, and the time of death was estimated at close upon two a.m. So you see by now, it can have nothing to do with the other business."

"Lestrade, you really must lead me through the steps which brought you to that conclusion, as they are dark to me," Holmes murmured.

The inspector puffed up noticeably. "I am disappointed you don't see it. Martha Tabram ducked into the shadows of George Yard with this sergeant, intending to ply her trade. The young grenadier waited for his comrade to return. He did not return, however, as he was engaged with Tabram, fought with her, and killed her, leaving her body on the landing of George Yard Buildings."

"It is becoming more clear," Holmes laughed. "In fact, I have very few questions to pose. First, have you any notion of what they quarreled about?"

"Certainly, Mr. Holmes. He was a young soldier on holiday but very likely to have been a rogue. She had no money on her person when she was discovered, therefore it is clear to me that they fought over a question of payment."

"Dear me. He could not pay?"

"They had been frequenting public houses, and he had probably run through what scant coin he had. When Martha Tabram demanded recompense, and he could not deliver, she would have grown very insistent."

"I understand she was jabbed nearly forty times with a common pocketknife."

"Yes, so we think. But one wound, the cause of death, was inflicted to the sternum with a bayonetlike blade, which implicates the soldier yet again," declared Lestrade triumphantly. "Finally, her death occurred at very close to two in the morning, which shows that Tabram had not the time to make any new acquaintance before she was killed."

Holmes steepled his two index fingers before his lips. "Lestrade, I must congratulate you, for your hypothesis does not directly oppose any known facts. Unfortunately, it abysmally fails at covering all of them, but you have done worse, my good Inspector, and this theory shows some salient points."

"And what, if you don't mind telling me, is wrong with it?" demanded Lestrade.

"I will do you the courtesy of elucidating the benefits straight off.

For one, it is indeed extremely suspicious that Tabram was found in the alley she entered with the soldier; very likely she was occupied there until the time of her death."

Lestrade looked as though he was about to say something self-congratulatory but was prevented by my friend.

"I have not quite finished. It is also of the greatest interest to me that Tabram was mutilated with a different variety of knife than that used to end her life. I suppose a bayonet would not allow a very effective range of motion for such a free-form exercise, but I have not yet made up my mind on that point. And now, inevitably, to your theory's flaw. Murders motivated by money are immensely practical crimes, of the most transparent motivation and prosaic execution. You suggest that this guardsman killed Martha Tabram in order to silence her demands for money, and rather than flee the scene, he put away his bayonet, pulled out his pocketknife, and proceeded to stab her chest, groin, and abdomen, presumably because he wasn't sure he'd finished the job."

"I challenge you to show me another explanation that so closely covers the facts," cried Lestrade. "We know nothing of this soldier, after all. For all we know, he may be an extremely perverse individual."

"Ha! You are right. He may indeed be. Can you tell me the whereabouts of the other witnesses, this so-called Pearly Poll and the second guardsman?"

Sulkily, Lestrade shuffled through his file. "As far as Pearly Poll is concerned, not only is her address hardly permanent, but we've put her through two police lineups and she's proven an utter waste of our time. As for the private—well, he has disappeared into thin air."

"One more question, if I may."

"Yes?" Lestrade replied, looking as though his good nature had been sorely tried indeed.

"The constable did not happen to note the colour of stripe on the soldier's cap, did he?"

"It was white," he snapped, "so of course he was a member of the Coldstream Guards. And now you'll have no difficulty whatsoever in identifying the suspect that the entire force has had their eye out for.

Just wire me when he's found the culprit, will you, Doctor? Good day to you, Mr. Holmes."

When the door had slammed testily behind us, Holmes set off down the hallway which led to the front exit of the Great Scotland Yard building. Though few policemen were present with the leisure to stop and speak to each other, those who could spare the time were muttering in hushed tones as they attempted to make sense of the events. I little knew what my friend was thinking, but Lestrade's explanation seemed to me to fall far short of the mark.

"Holmes, surely Martha Tabram's murder was an act too brutal for a brawl over a few pence?"

"Agreed," replied Holmes as we regained the street, surrounded comfortingly by leafy trees and solid red brick. "I haven't the slightest doubt that whoever is responsible was in the grip of a powerful emotional force."

There was a brisk wind flowing through the Yard's open spaces, and I welcomed its invigourating influence as Holmes hailed a cab and we made our weary way back to Baker Street.

"I cannot make it out yet, Watson," my friend mused, drumming his long fingers against the side of the hansom, "but I would not have missed it. It is a far queerer matter than it appeared on the surface. As Lestrade has been at pains to remind us, these murders are in no way linked. But consider that in the case of Nichols, we have a killer who is exceedingly eager to cut women apart after they are dead, and in the case of Tabram, a killer so dedicated to the idea that he puts away his murder weapon to begin coolly stabbing his victim."

"What can we do?"

"I must consider the options at hand. After all, we do not yet know these women. Speaking with their friends and loved ones may prove very profitable indeed."

"We will at least learn more than we did this morning."

Holmes nodded. "It was most peculiar. We unearthed no immediate alleys which demand investigation. I suppose I shall have to invent my own."

CHAPTER THREE

Miss Mary Ann Monk

The next morning I completed my ablutions quickly, as I could just make out voices emanating from downstairs. When I entered the sitting room, I found Holmes leaning against the sideboard with his hands in his pockets as he conversed with a man whose general appearance spoke of neither good hygiene nor good spirits.

"Ah, Watson," cried my friend. "I was about to fetch you, as we have an important caller. May I present to you Mr. William Nichols of Old Kent Road, a repairman of printer's machinery, if his fingertips had not already declared as much to you."

Our guest was a weathered fellow of middle height with sly blue eyes and bushy grey side-whiskers. A tremor in his strong, ink-stained hands informed me he was quite disturbed by recent events.

"Do be seated, Mr. Nichols, and accept our condolences regarding your wife's death. I have no doubt but that, despite the earliness of the hour, Dr. Watson would be happy to prescribe you something fortifying. You have had a most trying ordeal."

I poured Mr. Nichols a brandy and led him to the settee. He drank slowly from it, then turned back to Holmes.

"I've not tasted a drop in years," he confessed, "for I knew the ill of it. Polly Walker was a sweet girl in her youth, and no one knows it better than I do. But as for her drinking, and her other vices . . . Polly

Nichols turned into a bad sort, gentlemen, make no mistake about
that."

Holmes shot me a look and I located my notebook. "Mr. Nichols,
if it would not be too terribly painful for you, I should like you to tell
me all you can about your late wife."

He shrugged. "There's nothing I can say as will do any good. I
hadn't seen the woman in over three years."

"Indeed? You were utterly estranged?"

Mr. Nichols pursed his lips, considering his words. "I'm no angel,
Mr. Holmes, and I've my own mistakes to pay for . . . There was
another woman, and Polly took on about it to the point of packing
up her things and running off. I'll say as much only because you're
said to know things you oughtn't. But it was good riddance, so far as
I was concerned. Polly more often than not had a drop in, and when
she did, the children and I suffered for it. We had five, Mr. Holmes,
and I think sometimes it was a strain on her. She wasn't the mother-
ing kind. When she left for good, I supported her for a year, but I cut
off her allowance when I learned what she'd become."

"I see. But what of the children?"

"Oh, I've care of the little ones, Mr. Holmes. I'd not let her lay one
filthy hand on them once she'd set her course in that direction."

"So you dissolved all contact with her, being yourself a man of
unimpeachable moral character?"

I worried lest Holmes's dig might offend Nichols, but our visitor
merely answered gruffly, "She contacted me, all right, Mr. Holmes.
She tried to cozen the authorities into forcing her maintenance money
out of me. But they saw I didn't deserve the keeping of her, common
baggage that she was. She went from man to man and workhouse
to workhouse. None of them kept her long. I'm sorry to say it, Mr.
Holmes, but her death was less of a shock than it should have been."

Holmes raised a single eyebrow coldly as he lifted the tongs and
lit his pipe with an ember from the fire. "I should at least have thought
the manner of her death would give pause to her kith and kin."

At this, Nichols paled slightly. "Yes, of course. I've seen her. I would not wish that end on anyone."

"I am very gratified to hear it."

"It's a hard push for me, though. I daresay it will cost me for the funeral, her dad not being well off and she without a penny to her name."

"Yes, yes, I am sure it is a very trying time for you. You know of no enemies, nor of any further information which might aid us in our inquiries?"

"Polly's only enemy so far as I could see was gin, Mr. Holmes," replied Nichols with a knowing look.

"However, as I am sure you will agree, gin unfortunately was not responsible for her death," returned Holmes with some asperity. "And now, Mr. Nichols, I must devote my entire energies toward my thoughts and my pipe, so you will forgive me if I bid you good morning."

After I had shut the door upon Mr. Nichols, my friend exclaimed, "A nice spouse, Watson. He has at least absolved himself as a suspect. Crimes of jealousy require a measure of regard for the victim."

"He seemed more shaken by the cost than by the death of his wife."

Holmes shook his head philosophically. "It is not difficult for me to envision Polly Nichols's flight from his establishment. If she was everything he says she was, they must have made a charming pair." He set his lit pipe on the mantel and made for his bedroom.

"And what is the agenda for today?" I called out, helping myself to the egg and tomato Mrs. Hudson had sent up on the silver breakfast tray.

Holmes emerged donning his frock coat and adjusted his collar in the mirror above the fireplace. "I shall devote myself to Lambeth, my boy, and the pursuit of those who were actually acquainted with the deceased at the time of her death. Miss Mary Ann Monk identified Nichols, and so to her we must appeal. Have you any appointments?"

"I have canceled them."

"Then finish your eggs while I call for a cab. The undiscovered country of Lambeth Workhouse awaits."

As we rattled up to the front gates of Lambeth Workhouse, I had the distinct impression our destination was a prison, not a charitable facility to aid the plight of London's poor. The autocratic structure, with its grey façade and absence of any grounds whatever, silently proclaimed its total devotion to severity and order. We were shown in by the angular Miss Shackelton, who informed us that Miss Monk was indeed availing herself of the shelter afforded by the workhouse, that she was far too given to drink, that she gave herself airs, that she was clever enough when she wished to be, that she would come to a bad end if not careful, and that she was to be found picking oakum in the common room down the hall.

As we walked down the featureless corridor, I caught glimpses of row upon row of cots suspended from poles in the common sleeping areas. We eventually reached a wide room filled with women young and old dressed in cheap workhouse-issue uniforms who were pulling apart old ropes to reuse what hemp fibers could be salvaged. Holmes made inquiries, and an overseer soon delivered to us Mary Ann Monk, with instructions we were to take her into the front parlour for questioning.

"Here, then. What do you toffs want me for?" demanded Miss Monk, upon our arrival in a cramped but well-furnished sitting area. "If it's to do with Polly, I ain't seen nothing more than what I said already."

Far from the downtrodden creature I had expected to encounter in those hateful surroundings, we were confronted by a diminutive young woman whose radiant eye and smooth neck led me to think she could not be above five and twenty. She was very slim, though she appeared even thinner in the ill-fitting clothing issued her, her hair escaping its bounds in thick black spirals and her hands raw from the chafing of the rough rope she'd been picking apart. Her skin was greatly freckled with the effects of our brief London summer, and she had such an air of readiness about her, of good humour in her green eyes mixed with open challenge in her set shoulders, that I could not help but think that her friend's killer was lucky not to have chosen Miss Monk as his victim.

Holmes smiled sympathetically. "Do sit down, Miss Monk. My name is Sherlock Holmes, and this is my friend and partner, Dr. Watson. We are aware of our imposition, but we would very much appreciate your recounting the details of your relationship with Mrs. Nichols." The detective offered her his hand to help her into a chair.

Miss Monk laughed outright at this display of courtesy. "Well, if you don't mind sitting down with a girl of my character, I've no objection. You're no cops . . . I can tell by your shoes. All right, then, lads. What are you on to, and what the devil have I to do with it? I chummed about with Polly for a year or more, but that don't mean I can tell you who done her in."

Miss Monk's careless manner did not shield from me her obvious regard for her friend, for as she finished, her eyes meandered over the worn Persian carpet beneath our feet.

"When was the last time you saw Mrs. Nichols before her death, Miss Monk?"

"I was out of the workhouse last week for four days and saw her at the Frying Pan. We had a drop or two, she met a gent, and I went on my way."

"Do you know where she was living at that time?"

"She'd used to live in Thrawl Street, but two of the judies she shared digs with couldn't cough up ha'pence between 'em for three nights running, so of course they were chucked out. Polly had slept rough before, but she knew if the law caught her in a park, she'd wind up back here straightaway, so she took a berth at the White House on Flower and Dean. They don't take exception if a woman brings a friend home with her, if necessary."

"What sort of woman was Mrs. Nichols? Did she have enemies you are aware of?"

Miss Monk sighed and tapped her severely abused man's work boot against the chair leg. "Not a one. Polly weren't the sort to have enemies. She swept her doss room and she kept herself tidy and she always had a kind word when she was about. She was a real good sort, Mr. Holmes, but you may as well know she was in the drink as often as she was out of it. Couldn't bear the workhouse for more than a week at a time before the lack of gin and lack of food got to be too much for her. I don't suppose you know it, but Polly took up as a maid in Wandsworth not long ago. She had her room and board all settled like and thought she'd get on well enough. But they were religious types, Mr. Holmes, and by the time she'd been without a drop for two months, she finally cut clear of the place."

"You learned this from Mrs. Nichols?"

"It was plain enough to see," she answered. "She'd a new frock, but no doss money. I soon had it out of her. She vamped the togs the next day."

"When she had run through the money from pawning the dress, she then returned to the workhouse?"

"The workhouse," Miss Monk returned amusedly, "as well as other means of employment what every woman has at her disposal."

"Quite so. And, to your knowledge, there is no reason why anyone would have wished her death?"

At this our companion flushed vividly and replied, "Wish her death? That ain't the way of it, Mr. Holmes. We all of us takes our risks to keep aboveground in the Chapel. 'Twon't be long before I've had enough of Lambeth and shoved off myself. We're not allowed so much as a match, gents, nor a scrap of cloth or mirror, nor even our own water for washing, begging your pardon. I'll take to the streets again soon, same as Polly did. And when I does, I'll take the same chances. There's blokes in these parts would kill you soon as kiss your hand."

Holmes replied gently, "Should you ever in the future encounter such a man and wish to be rid of his company, I hope you will contact me. I only meant to inquire whether Mrs. Nichols was ever molested by a particular person, or if there was anyone of whom she was afraid."

My friend's words and the sincerity with which he spoke them soon had the desired effect upon his subject. Releasing a laboured breath and twisting her hands in her lap, Miss Monk replied, "I don't know nothing about it, Mr. Holmes, but Lord knows I wish I did. Killing Polly wouldn't serve no one. Only the devil would do such a thing."

I found myself inexplicably moved by Miss Monk's words, even jagged and rough as they were. There was something in the line of her jaw which demanded respect even as it defied judgment.

"Here is my card, Miss Monk," said Holmes as he rose to leave.

"What use is it to the likes of me?"

"Tut, tut, you can read as well as I can, Miss Monk. When you entered the room, your eyes skimmed that deeply inspirational quote so delicately embroidered and mounted upon the wall. Verse three of the Beatitudes, if I am not mistaken. The eyes of an illiterate are never drawn to text."

"Very well," she acknowledged, smiling, "and what shall I do with it?"

"If any detail returns to your memory, or if you find yourself worried over anything to do with the matter, please let me know."

She laughed, following us as we moved out into the hall. "Shall I send my man round with the message? Or come myself in the carriage and four?"

Sherlock Holmes put a finger to his lips and tranquilly handed her a crown. "If you manage to hide this from the matron," said he, opening the heavy outer door and descending the steps into the open air, "and fail to spend it upon any other diversions, you'll have the ability to wire me whenever you feel it necessary. Good afternoon, Miss Monk." So saying, he extended his hand.

"You're a strange one, you are," she declared as she shook the detective's hand. "You're a private 'tec, ain't you? I've seen your name in the papers. Well, as you've naught else to go on, I'll leastways tell you who we spend our days avoiding. Goes by the name of Leather Apron. I'd not be caught in a dark alley in his company, make no mistake."

When we had passed beyond the forbidding ironwork dividing the workhouse from the road, I could not help observing, "She seems a very intelligent young woman."

I had expected Holmes, who regarded females solely as unpredictable and vexing factors in his criminal equations, to dismiss my remark entirely. Instead he replied with an amused look, "You are the connoisseur of femininity, my dear fellow. Still, she has an eye for trivia and a memory to repeat it. In addition, she has an intimate knowledge of the neighbourhood, and associations which could aid us if she decides to make use of them."

"Is that the reason you enabled her to contact you?"

"Her natural talent for observation could prove very useful. I would rather have ten of her than fifty of Scotland Yard."

"I should not like Lestrade to hear you say that." I laughed.

"My dear fellow, I assure you I meant no offense." Holmes chuckled in return. "The good inspector has many fine qualities to recommend him, as does Miss Monk, it seems clear. However, I would venture to say that it is unlikely that any of them overlap."

The funeral of Polly Nichols took place at Little Ilford Cemetery, on the afternoon of September sixth. The day was a fittingly inclement one, the skies mourning the dead with a profusion of rain. I learned that Mrs. Nichols's father, children, and estranged spouse attended, though few other people presented themselves: as many mourners who had known the deceased as members of the public who had come solely to remark upon the lurid manner of her death.

Minor business matters required my presence at my bank that day, though it was only with the greatest reluctance that I left the comforts of our sitting room. I returned to Baker Street thoroughly soaked to find Holmes at our table, a newspaper at his fingertips and a cup of tea in his hand.

"There is an air about you which positively cries out for refreshment, my dear Watson," he hailed me. "Allow me to pour you a cup. There are developments upon the Leather Apron front. Miss Monk was by no means wrong in her expectation that suspicion would fall upon this rascal."

"Yes, I spied a description of him in yesterday's *Star.*"

"I have it here. Hum! Short, thickset, late thirties, black hair and moustache, thick neck. The remainder hardly rests upon a firm bed of fact: silent, sinister, and repulsive. You can see that the press are already indulging in gleeful and inventive adjectives. Half the article is unmitigated conjecture."

"Do you lend any credence to the matter?"

"Well, even given the natural hysteria of the journalistic world, it bears investigating. I may as well own, Watson, that my other lines of inquiry have proven quite barren. Polly Nichols was turned away from her doss house upon the night in question but seemed confident of earning her pennies, as she had a new black bonnet. She went from pub to pub and was last seen, very drunk, at two thirty in the morning. An hour later, she was discovered."

"And Martha Tabram's case?"

Holmes threw up his hands in resignation. "Pearly Poll, the lady's intimate companion, has gone underground. The soldiers have likewise disappeared. It will be a job to find them, but I have initiated inquiries."

"What are your plans?"

"I shall just cast my eye over him of the menacing leather apron, as Miss Monk appears to consider him dangerous. I've worked out his identity, though the force are still mulling over it—he is a bootmaker by the name of John Pizer. I fear he is not the most sophisticated of criminals, Watson. He has mastered the rather crude technique of accosting helpless women and demanding their pennies if they wish to avoid bodily harm. The scoundrel was convicted last year to six months' hard labour for stabbing the hand of a fellow boot finisher who dared to operate in the same neighbourhood."

"You think him capable, then, of Mrs. Nichols's murder?"

"I require more reliable data. I intend to pay him a call this afternoon."

"Are you likely to need assistance?"

"No, no, my dear fellow, finish your tea and I shall regale you with the story upon my return—it is hardly an errand worthy of both our energies."

My friend returned that evening spattered with sleet but nevertheless laughed silently as he stretched his long legs before the fire. I passed him the cigar box with an inquisitive glance.

"You have enjoyed your afternoon?"

"It was in many ways remarkably refreshing. A lower species of the thug genus I've never before encountered. I called upon Mr. Pizer and expressed my condolences that he was shortly to be named the first definite suspect in the Nichols case. I believe I may have startled him, but he has apparently been holed up in his house since the crime occurred, so he must have had some inkling that the local tide was against him. We had a very absorbing conversation about his boot-making income and the ways in which he supplements it. I think one or two remarks of mine may have offended him, for he took a swing at me, and I was forced to consign him to his wooden floor. He protested an alibi, and I expressed doubts as to its veracity. I then quit his establishment and wired Lestrade immediately his full name and address."

"Then you think him guilty?"

"No, my dear Watson, I'm afraid I believe him innocent. Consider: John Pizer is a coward whose notion of commerce is to rob destitute women. Is he likely to commit an audacious murder? Further, if John

Pizer makes a living threatening those with considerably smaller musculature than his own, would he endanger that living by endowing
them with a mortal terror of dark alleys and sinister strangers? Pizer
had only his own income to lose."

"Then why did you wire Lestrade?"

"Because I can hardly recall the last time I disliked a man quite so
vigourously. If we are lucky, he will be arrested for some few days,
which will at the very least prevent him from roaming the streets. I am
not sorry to have seen him, though," Holmes continued thoughtfully.
"He clarified a valuable opinion of which I was hardly aware before."

"What opinion?"

"Pizer and his ilk demand attention wherever they go. I would
venture to suggest that any man who performs such acts as we have
observed upon Polly Nichols's corpse, and then walks off into densely
populated streets without exciting remark, is of a far more colourless
mien. Merely an indication, but entirely against the tack Scotland
Yard and our beloved press have set themselves upon. And now, with
thanks to Miss Monk for an engrossing afternoon, let us devote our
entire attention to the cut of beef upon the sideboard. Cold weather,
when mixed with thuggery, does try a man's resources so."

CHAPTER FOUR

The Horror of Hanbury Street

Two days after my friend's encounter with Leather Apron, at half past six in the morning, my sleep was disturbed by a whimpering cry, far off yet terrible in its intensity. The next instant snapped me into wakefulness and I left my room with a hastily lit taper in my hand, anxious to determine the source of such pitiable sounds.

Nearing the bottom of the stairs, I heard, with all the drowsy confusion of the startled sleeper, the sound of Holmes's voice intermixed with that of the unnerving siren. I threw open the door to our sitting room, and there sat Holmes, likewise hastily clad in shirtsleeves and dressing gown, holding both the hands of a ragged child who appeared to be six or seven years of age.

"I knew you to be blessed with great strength of character," Holmes was saying to the boy. "You behaved splendidly and I am very proud of you. Ah! Just the thing. Here is Dr. Watson. You remember Dr. Watson, do you not, Hawkins?"

The ill-fed vagabond swiveled his head in alarm at the introduction of another's presence, and I at once recognized the pale features and dark Irish curls of Sean Hawkins, one of the youngest members of Holmes's band of street urchins, the Baker Street Irregulars.

"Hawkins," said Holmes softly, "it is extremely important that you tell me what has happened. You wish me to help, do you not? There,

now. I thought so. And I must have all the information at your disposal, yes? I know it is very difficult, but I only ask you to try. Sit
next to me upon this chair—no, no, strong back, like your father, the
prizefighter. Now, tell me all about it."

"I found a woman who was killed," said little Hawkins, his lips
trembling all the while.

"I see. That is just the sort of thing I am able to solve, is it not?
Where did you find her?"

"In the yard of the building next to my own."

"Yes, you live in the East-end. Twenty-seven Hanbury Street, is it
not?" said Holmes, his grey eyes meeting mine with grave urgency.
"So you saw a woman who had been killed. I know you are frightened,
Hawkins, but you must pretend that you have come back from enemy
territory to give intelligence."

The lad drew a deep breath. "I quit our room this morning to see if
there were any leavings on the shore. When you've no cases to hand,
I tries my luck as a mudlark. I keep a sharp stick hidden in the back
yard on a hook, and I climbed up to get at it. When I looked over the
fence to the next yard, I saw her. She was all in pieces," cried the child.
"Everything meant to be inside was outside." Hawkins then burst into
a fresh assault of tears.

"There now, you are perfectly safe here," said Sherlock Holmes,
sending a hand through the boy's hair. "You were very brave to come
all the way to Westminster on the back of a gentleman's hansom, and
very clever not to be caught. I am at your service. Shall I go to Hanbury Street?"

The youth nodded feverishly.

"Then Dr. Watson and I shall leave at once. On my way down,
I'll speak to Mrs. Hudson about your breakfast, and I shall tell your
mother you are sleeping upon my sofa. Oh, come now. Mrs. Hudson
will be only too glad to see you as soon as I inform her she is playing host to the hero of Hanbury Street. Well done indeed, Hawkins."
Holmes shot me a significant glance and ducked into his bedroom. I
was dressed not half a minute after my friend, and away we rushed in

the first cab we could find, after informing Mrs. Hudson that our tiny houseguest was to be treated in every way as if he had just returned from near-fatal conflicts abroad.

Our cabman delivered us to Hanbury Street, with all the haste our equine allies could muster, by the streaks of dawn's skeletal fingers. We strode without hesitation toward a cluster of police constables, distraught residents, and ardent reporters, who veiled their enthusiastic questions under a thin veneer of shock. Their eyes lit up when they glimpsed my friend's singular profile, but he brushed through them as if they were so many chickens.

A clean-shaven young constable guarded the greying wooden entrance to the building's yard. "Sorry, gentlemen, but I can't allow you through. There's been a murder done."

"My name is Sherlock Holmes, and this is my associate Dr. Watson. It is the event you speak of which brings us here."

The constable's relief was palpable. "Right you are, Mr. Holmes. Step through this doorway and down to the yard. Inspector Lestrade will see you're shown the . . . the remains, sir."

We hastened along the dark route through the building to the yard beyond. Holmes pushed open the swinging door at the end of the musty passage, and we proceeded down a few uneven steps into an open space paved with large flat stones, grasses pushing up through every fissure. At our feet, her body lying parallel with the short fence young Hawkins had described, was the head of the murdered woman. I saw at a glance that the lad's mortal terror had been more than justified.

"Dear God, what has he done," Holmes muttered. "Good morning, Inspector Lestrade."

"Good morning!" cried the wiry inspector. "Good morning, he says! What in the name of God and the devil brings you here? Murphy! Blast it all, where are you going? Never mind about that telegram. Mr. Holmes here is some kind of clairvoyant."

"My methods are worldly enough, I assure you. As it happens, we've a colleague in the neighbourhood."

"Of all the confounded—all right, then, Murphy, you can leave us to it. See that Baxter has everything under control."

When the constable had gone, Lestrade shook his head incredulously. "Mr. Holmes, there's something about you that isn't entirely natural, if you'll pardon my saying it. But for the love of heaven! Thank God you're here. Dr. Watson, see what you can make of her, if you've the stomach for it. The surgeon hasn't arrived yet, and I am at my wits' end."

Steeling myself with the reminder that I had never been a victim of dissecting room nerves, I advanced toward the poor wretch lying supine upon the cracked flagstones and tried to make some sense out of what had been done to her. She appeared the victim rather of the slaughterhouse than of murder.

"Her head has been nearly detached. There are bruises on her face, which is swollen and may indicate she was choked before her throat was slashed. Rigor mortis has just begun; I should say she was killed at approximately half past five this morning. Her abdomen has been opened entirely, and her small and large intestines detached from their membranes. You see he has lifted them out of the abdominal cavity and placed them over here upon her shoulder. Her other wounds . . ." Here I believe I must have trailed off at the revolting realization which struck me. As I peered more closely down at the body, an icy stab of alarm shot through my spine. I stumbled to my feet to gaze numbly about the yard.

"What's the matter, Watson?" I heard Holmes's precise, forceful tenor as if from across a great chasm.

"It isn't possible . . ."

"What isn't possible, Watson? What has he done?"

"Her womb, Holmes." I am afraid I could not quite keep my voice from catching at the words. "Someone has taken it. It's gone."

All was silence save for the rumble of carts upon the road outside and the twitter of a sparrow perched high in the tree in Sean Hawkins's adjacent yard. Then Holmes, passing a pale, distracted hand over his high forehead, advanced to see for himself. After a moment's scrutiny, he straightened, as stoic as ever, but his deep-set eyes betraying—perhaps only to me—his revulsion at my discovery. Handing me both his hat and his stick, Holmes began his systematic examination of the scene.

Lestrade emitted a slight choking sound and sank down upon a rotting crate, his slender profile stricken. "Gone?" he repeated. "It can't be gone, for heaven's sake. He's completely gutted her, Dr. Watson. Surely you overlooked it?"

I shook my head. "The entire uterus, as well as a good portion of the bladder, have been taken."

"Taken! Taken *where*? It is preposterous. Surely it is here somewhere? Under that bit of scrap lumber, perhaps?"

"I believe not," called Holmes from across the yard. "I see no trace of it."

Lestrade's shoulders collapsed still further at this dire revelation.

It was not long before my friend had finished his intent perusal, but to Lestrade and to me it seemed an age had passed since we had first set foot into that terrible pen, open to the sky but closed off from every vestige of the human decency we had been raised to cherish. Finally, Holmes approached us.

"The body is that of an as yet unidentified unfortunate of approximately fifty years of age. She entered the yard voluntarily in the company of her killer, who approached her from behind and took a moment to grapple with her before slitting her throat. After he had delivered the fatal wound, he looked over the fence between the yards to ascertain that there was no one nearby. Before he began mutilating the remains, he removed the contents of the deceased's pockets: one piece of muslin and two combs. Then he proceeded to dissect his victim with a very sharp, narrow knife. When he had finished, he somehow managed to escape the way he had come without leaving the slightest drip or mark from his . . . trophy."

"It is horrible," Lestrade murmured. "It is positively inhuman."

"Lestrade, my dear fellow, don't look so cowed. We have progressed significantly since the Nichols case."

"The Nichols case? Then you think it the same man?"

"We would be deeply foolish to suppose it were otherwise," Holmes replied impatiently.

The inspector groaned in despair. "The Yard has not the slightest lead even in those murders, let alone—" He stopped abruptly. "By George! But we do! That terrible bootmaker with the leather apron! Mr. Holmes, you yourself gave me his address."

"Lestrade, it would be very ill-advised to—"

"Here's the surgeon! Good morning to you, Dr. Phillips. I'm afraid I must be off upon official business."

"Stop a moment and I shall save you a deal of trouble," Holmes cried heatedly.

"Inspector Chandler is outside, should you need anything. Right, then. I must take immediate action. Mr. Holmes, Dr. Watson—good day to you." The inspector, looking for all the world as if he had stared evil in the face directly, scurried away to pursue his new lead.

"Come, Watson," said Holmes. "It's quite hopeless. We must see if we can make any progress with the neighbours. Good morning, Dr. Phillips. We have left all as it was, I am afraid."

We exited to the sound of a muffled oath uttered by the surgeon and hurried back down the passage. "Holmes," I hissed, "please tell me you can see some light in all this. Who would be capable of such an act? A vicious gang? A new incarnation of Burke and Hare?* I begin to think that the act of murder has grown secondary to the defilement of the corpse."

Holmes stopped to light a cigarette as we emerged from the other side. "Let us see whether the residents of twenty-nine and twenty-seven have anything relevant to convey."

---

* William Burke and William Hare sold the corpses of their seventeen victims to Edinburgh Medical College between 1827 and 1828. The murders led to the legalization of obtaining cadavers by other means.

It proved a punishing task to interview all the frightened inhabitants of Hanbury Street without dwelling upon the particulars of the crime, which were so enormously sensational, and so scintillating to the pressmen, that the details had already spread like a plague. Holmes and I were forced to field almost as many questions as we posed. My friend's granite gaze brightened subtly only twice: first, when he learned there was a cat's-meat seller upon the ground floor of number twenty-nine; and second, when a young man named Cadoche related that he had heard a cry of "No!" and a thud against the dividing fence at approximately five thirty, which corresponded to my estimated time of death. Our last business was to relate, briefly but gratefully, news of Hawkins's actions and whereabouts to his anxious, quivering mother.

Finally, in early afternoon, we set foot once more on the pavement, my friend making off in a direction both unambiguous and inexplicable. Holmes displayed all the energy of his uniquely unflagging will, but I felt shattered and weak, and scarcely able to stomach much more uncertainty than I had endured already.

"Holmes, if I may, where are we going?"

"I have seen enough penniless women hacked apart in a month's time. We require assistance."

"From whom?"

"A renovator of music halls by the name of George Lusk."

"Is he an acquaintance of yours?"

"He is a businessman who resides in Mile End. I was once of some use to him. He is about to return the favour."

Mile End, so named for its position precisely one mile east of the ancient City's boundary, had grown up considerably in the latter half of the nineteenth century. New roads, buildings, and courts gave birth to one another continually in London, but Sherlock Holmes was master of every street and byway. There was one occasion in particular, the incident involving Fenchurch the weaver and his now-infamous needle, when Holmes's knowledge of a secret alleyway undoubtedly saved both our lives. I was not surprised, therefore,

when Holmes led me down a series of labyrinthine corridors east-
ward out of Whitechapel only to emerge on a tree-lined thoroughfare in front of a respectable white-columned house.

My companion strode up the stone steps and knocked at the
polished door, cocking an eye back at me and beckoning me to
join him. "You must help me keep the conversation on topic," he
whispered. "Mr. Lusk is an articulate gentleman, whose opinions are
wont to flow as freely as the Thames." With that, a young servant
girl admitted us, ushering us into a well-appointed, palm-dotted sitting room, occupied only by a regal orange cat. We sat down to
await our host.

He was not long in coming. Mr. George Lusk threw wide the
doors and exclaimed, "Why, if it isn't Mr. Sherlock Holmes. By
Jove, but it's good to see you! I don't mind telling you, sir, had you
not been on hand to discover what those lumbermen were really
about, I should be a poor man today. And you must be Dr. Watson. It gratifies me tremendously that someone has undertaken to
record Mr. Holmes's exploits for the world at large. A pleasure to
meet you."

Mr. Lusk was a man of open, expressive features, and perceptive
brown eyes, though the bags beneath them taken in conjunction
with his coat's somber cut and sable colour led me to believe he
had recently lost someone dear to him. He wore a plentiful moustache, which descended nearly to the jawline, and held himself
with the confidence of an established entrepreneur. His hair was
slicked back upon his head, revealing a sensitive brow, and I was
impressed immediately by his alert manner and his general air of
ready assurance.

"It was a very simple problem," said Holmes, shaking the hand of
our host. "I was delighted to be of assistance."

"Simple! It was nothing of the kind. In any event, it did me a world
of good, Mr. Holmes. But do sit down, gentlemen, and tell me to what
business I owe this pleasure."

"Mr. Lusk," my friend ventured kindly, once we had seated our-selves, "I fear our condolences are in order. You must feel the loss of your wife keenly after so short a time."

Our host exhibited no surprise that Holmes had deduced the sad event, though he indicated with the sudden contraction of his brow that he wished not to speak of it. "Susannah was a wonderful woman, Mr. Holmes, and a finer mother I've never yet seen. But we shall over-come, the children and I. Now, Mr. Holmes, do tell me what brings you here."

"You are aware of the recent string of murders in the neighbouring streets of Whitechapel?"

"Why, of course, Mr. Holmes. And may I profess myself heart-ily ashamed of the values this nation continues to countenance. The poor must be seen to, or they will fall upon each other in the streets, as they have always done. If the greatest empire on earth cannot be trusted to meet the needs of its lowest classes, Mr. Holmes, I do not know what the world will come to in the end. Why, if one considers the wealth—"

"I have no doubt but that, given free rein, you would do much to solve the problems of humanity at large, Mr. Lusk," Holmes inter-jected smoothly. "However, I appear before you in regards to specifics. Another tragedy occurred this morning, near Spitalfields Market."

Mr. Lusk appeared genuinely distressed. "You cannot mean there has been another murder?"

"Early this morning, in fact, at twenty-nine Hanbury Street. The circumstances surrounding the killings are worsening."

"You shock me, Mr. Holmes. I am afraid almost to pose the ques-tion, but how can that be possible?"

Holmes briefly recounted the particulars of our morning's inves-tigation. Mr. Lusk's eyes grew ever more large, but when my friend had concluded the deplorable tale, he quickly absorbed the facts laid before him.

"So," he stated firmly, "what are we to do about it? I am not a man to stand idly by with such a ruthless fiend at large. It is against the very fabric of the social contract. You shall direct me, Mr. Holmes. What is to be done?"

Holmes's pale countenance gained a touch of colour at this remark, and he shot me a look of triumph. "I knew you could be counted upon, Mr. Lusk. I require men of action, and you have not disappointed me. Mr. Lusk, you must without any hesitation whatsoever form a committee."

"A committee?" queried the startled businessman.

"I require you to pluralize yourself, Mr. Lusk. Find others like you, who are horrified by these crimes and wish to put an end to them. In addition to our intrepid constables, I need a band of plainclothesmen to patrol the streets and report their findings directly to me."

"I see, I see," our host replied eagerly. "We shall man Whitechapel with organized citizens whose only thought is to extend the arm of British law to the slums. By Jove, but Susannah would have supported this! That ruffian Sir Charles Warren* has trodden upon the poor with the approbation of the middle class for long enough. This committee will balance the scales of justice. It will serve the women whose only crime has been to suffer—"

"Those are precisely our thoughts, Mr. Lusk," I interrupted him. Holmes nudged my arm in silent gratitude.

George Lusk, who was nodding vigourously, an action which caused him rather to resemble an active sea lion, began to pace the carpet with the decisive step of the self-made man. "I shall call upon Federov, that is clear," he said, ticking candidates off on his left hand. "Harris and Minsk will be great assets, as will Jacobson, Abrams, and Stone."

Holmes laughed, that staccato exclamation which only emerged when he was both amused and gratified. "Mr. Lusk, the Doctor and I shall leave you to devise a list as you best see fit. I propose you assem-

---

* At the time, the Metropolitan Police Commissioner, whose actions during the "Bloody Sunday" riot in Trafalgar Square in 1887 were much deplored by liberals.

ble your candidates, present the plan, and in due course find yourself their natural and apposite leader."

"I shall call upon them at once! It may take me a matter of days to fully sort out our committee, Mr. Holmes, but once formed, you may be absolutely certain of our devotion to your cause."

We took our leave, and Mr. Lusk bade us farewell, clasping our hands and assuring Holmes in fine terms of his enthusiasm. We found ourselves out of doors once more on the quiet, sun-dappled street, with nothing to distract us from the unholy spectacle we had witnessed early that morning. I could tell from his measured tread that Holmes's mood was withdrawn as we descended the steps, and the set of his shoulders said more than words how very much our experience had affected him.

"Your plan seems to imply you fear more killings."

"Let us hope that my fears are outstripping the facts."

"They never have, in my experience," I pointed out.

"Then I should be most gratified if this were the first time."

"Engaging Mr. Lusk was an inspired notion. You could hardly justify use of the Irregulars in such a case."

"Indeed. They would discover much, perhaps, but to what ill effects? Even as lucky and profitable as it was, having been informed so quickly by little Hawkins comes at a high cost. All too high. I would have preferred we'd learned of it by telegram and he had never laid eyes on such a miserable sight."

"I could not agree more."

"I only hope," said he, as we suddenly turned down a wide avenue, "that we ourselves are up to the challenge. It is a fundamental principle of my methods that there is nothing new under the sun, yet I confess I cannot fathom what in the world could possibly give rise to such hysterical monstrosities."

I ventured no reply to this half-posed question, for no more could I. We made our way back to Baker Street with the deaths of three women revolving silently through our minds.

CHAPTER FIVE

We Procure an Ally

We arrived home in time to witness young Hawkins's final victory over the most abundant cold luncheon I had ever seen the good-hearted Mrs. Hudson produce. After entrusting him to a hesitant but financially approachable cabbie, we sat down to a comparable feast ourselves, which Holmes picked at for perhaps three minutes before allowing his fork to dangle momentarily between his slender fingers and then tossing it in disdain upon the china.

"It is like trying to build a pyramid out of sand," he stated contemptuously. "The dashed bits won't hold together. I cannot believe that London has suddenly generated three separate and equally brutal killers, all roaming about Whitechapel having their way. No more is it possible that a gang of roughs could perform their perverse acts secretly within such a densely populated terrain, not to mention fit within the confines of the Hanbury Street yard. The odds against such notions are simply astronomical." He rose abruptly. "I am going out, Watson. If these crimes are linked, then the women are linked. We do not even know the identity of our latest victim. It is ludicrous to theorize in such an abyss."

"When shall you return?" I called as he disappeared into his bedroom.

"The answer to that conundrum, friend Watson, I could not even begin to guess," came his reply.

"If you should need me—"

"Never fear. I'll scale a tree and raise the flag. England expects that every man will do his duty." With a nod and a wave, the unofficial investigator departed; I did not see him again that day.

The events in question left me in such a state of unease that I spent much of the night staring at my ceiling. When morning at long last lifted her golden head above the brickwork of the neighbouring houses, I was seized with an irresistible urge to get out of doors. Thankfully, I had given my word to a young medical friend that I would look in on an invalid patient of his, as he had left London for the weekend and would not return until Monday. I am quite certain that old Mrs. Thistlecroft was taken aback by my strenuous advice on no account to allow castor oil through her bedroom window, nor to forsake her daily dose of cold draughts. Mercifully, I did her no harm, as she brooked no traffic with the foolish or distracted, and I very narrowly avoided being thrown out on my ear with the ringing declaration that my friend Anstruther should soon hear of her treatment at my hands.

Making my way back up Oxford Street, I stopped for a copy of the *Times*, to see what progress Holmes had made. I swiftly found the column, as the papers were concerned with little else:

Annie Chapman, *alias* "Sivvey"—a name she had received in consequence of living with a sieve maker—was the widow of a man who had been a soldier, and from whom, until about 12 months ago, when he died, she had been receiving 10s. a week. She was one of the same class as Mary Ann "Polly" Nichols, residing also in the common lodging houses of Spitalfields and Whitechapel, and is described as a stout, well-proportioned woman, as quiet, and as one who had "seen better days." Inspector Lestrade, of Scotland Yard, who has been engaged in special inquiries surrounding the murder of Nichols, at once took up the latest investigation, the two crimes being obviously the work of the same hands. A conference with Mr. Sherlock Holmes, the well-known private consulting detective, resulted in the experts' agreement that the crimes were connected, and that, notwithstanding many misleading statements and rumours, the murders were committed where the bodies had been found, and that no gang were the perpetrators. It is feared in many quarters that unless the culprit can speedily be captured, more outrages of a similar class will follow.

Suppressing a smile at Lestrade's new views, I tucked the paper under my arm and dashed upstairs to see whether my friend was at home. He was not, but affixed to the mantelpiece with my letter opener was a note he had left for me:

My dear Watson,

Investigating the fascinating inner workings of the cat's-meat trade. Might I suggest that you await the arrival of Miss Monk.

SH

I must admit to some surprise at Holmes's afternoon appointment, and no less intrigue. I spent an hour organizing the notes I had made at Hanbury Street into some coherence, and just as I laid down my pen to stretch my legs, Mrs. Hudson peeped into the room.

"A young person to see Mr. Holmes, sir. Are you expecting her? She gives her name as Miss Monk."

"Send her straight up, Mrs. Hudson. She is an associate of ours."

Lifting her brows delicately, Mrs. Hudson departed. A minute later, the door burst open to reveal the petite frame of Miss Mary Ann Monk, clad this time in her own attire: a dark green cotton bodice fastened with seven or eight varieties of carefully salvaged buttons, a skillfully altered man's vest, and a midnight blue figured coat which hung to the knee, revealing a profusion of skirts, the outermost an ancient green wool so much abused that it had deepened nearly to black. Her riot of hair was pinned and then tied back over the crown of her head with a narrow strip of cotton fabric, but it nevertheless showed signs of impending escape. She approached me and extended her hand.

"Very pleased to see you again, Miss Monk. Do sit down."

She did so, with a poise implying that she had not always been in her present circumstances. However, she was soon up again, perusing the assortment of curiosities above the fireplace and tossing an ancient spearhead nervously from hand to hand before speaking.

"I can't say as I know why Mr. Holmes asked me to tea, nor how he come to know I was lodged at Miller's Court. Though," she added, smiling, "I think Mr. Holmes does what he likes and knows a great many things he oughtn't."

"What you say is very true. I am afraid I cannot answer any of your questions just yet, though it is certainly within my purview to ring for tea."

At the mention of this precious article, a gleam appeared in her eye, which she quickly buried beneath studied nonchalance. "Well, if Mr. Holmes won't be offended. He did say four o'clock in the telegram, and I'm before my time. First wire in British history to be delivered to Miller's Court, like enough, and I'd still his money in my boot for paying the shoful. Don't know the last time I've ridden *inside* a cab. You could have knocked my pals down with a feather. I waved out the window as I left." Miss Monk laughed at the thought, and I could not help but join her.

"As Mr. Holmes has charged me with keeping you comfortable until he arrives, I think immediate refreshment is in order, don't you?" I inquired, ringing the bell.

"Tea," she said languorously. "Served in good china, I'd wager. Maybe even with cream. Oh, I am sorry, Dr. Watson," she exclaimed, embarrassed. "Here, then, I've some tea in my pocket—just enough for three, I'd say. I had a run of luck last night. Should you like some?"

Miss Monk produced a small leather pouch stuffed with dusty brown tea leaves, obviously an item of immense value to its owner.

"I am sure Holmes would prefer not to accept such a courtesy when you are a guest in our home, Miss Monk. Here is Mrs. Hudson now."

Our landlady had indeed arrived, hefting a tray loaded with far more than the usual sandwiches required by Holmes's erratic appetite and my discretion.

"It's just as it was when I was a girl! I remember trays like these—tiered, ain't that the word? Shall I pour, Dr. Watson?"

"By all means." I smiled. "But do tell me, if you are not offended by the question, where were you born, Miss Monk?"

"Here in England," she replied readily, making surprisingly elegant work of pouring the tea. "Mum was Italian, and Dad convinced her to throw her own family over and put her hand in with him. We had land once, but there was a disputed will . . . I was seven, if I remember rightly. Lord knows but it's been ages since they both died. Cholera struck 'em down, one right after t'other. So here I am. Staggered at the sight of a decent tea."

Though she smiled, I could not help but feel I had awkwardly broached a painful subject, and I had just opened my mouth in hopes an appropriate reply would emerge when Sherlock Holmes entered our sitting room.

"Halloa, halloa, what have we here?" he cried. "Miss Monk, you are most welcome. I have spent my time—well, perhaps I had better just splash some water on my face and be with you directly. I have been in a most pernicious environment." He disappeared for a brief period but returned looking quite his orderly self again and plunged a lean hand into the slipper which held his tobacco.

"You will excuse me, I am sure, if I light my pipe. Did this spearhead interest you? It is a very ancient object, recently the instrument of death in a very modern crime."

All of Miss Monk's nerves, which I flatter myself had been largely dispelled, returned at the sight of my friend. "Thank you kindly for the tea, Mr. Holmes, but I've already answered all the questions I could, honest I have."

"Undoubtedly. However, I did not invite you here to interrogate you. I brought you here to ask you plainly, Miss Monk, do you feel as if you could play a part in bringing the Whitechapel killer to justice?"

"Me?" she exclaimed. "How do you expect me to help? Polly's cold in her grave, and the other lass had her innards mucked all over the parish."

"And I fear I must inform you, Miss Monk, that I suspect this man may continue killing until the very day that he is caught," replied the detective. "Though it is undoubtedly in all our interests to find him quickly, I imagined your feelings for Polly Nichols might encourage you to take a more active role."

"Really, Holmes, I cannot imagine what sort of role you mean," I countered.

Holmes drew upon his pipe languidly, always a sign of concentration rather than of relaxation. "I propose that you enter my employment, Miss Monk. I could spend the lion's share of my days building connections in the East-end, keeping the pulse of fresh rumour ever at my fingertips, but I am afraid I cannot afford to stretch myself so thinly. You, however, are placed in an ideal position to go unnoticed, hearing and seeing everything."

"You'd pay me to nose? Nose on what?" Miss Monk asked incredulously.

"On the neighbourhood itself. There's no more lucrative cover for flushing a bird than the local alehouses at which you are already known and trusted."

Miss Monk's emerald eyes widened considerably at Holmes's remarkable suggestion. "But why ask a ladybird like me to spy on the Chapel? Why not use some jack or other, what's trained to sniff about?"

"I do not think I need employ other detectives. You, Miss Monk, see more than those fellows do already. As for terms, here is an advance of five pounds for expenses, and I imagine you would do well enough on a pound a week, is that not so?"

"Would I!" cried Miss Monk, her pointed chin descending at the generous figure. "But if I'm to pitch over my daily work, how am I to explain the chink?"

Holmes considered the question. "I imagine you could tell your companions that you have arrested the attentions of a poetic and passionate West-end client who has determined to engage your services under more exclusive terms."

This suggestion elicited a ringing peal of laughter from Miss Monk. "You're mad, you know. I'll be rubbish—who am I to help hunt down the Knife?"

"Is that what they're calling him?" My friend smiled. "Miss Monk, I can think of no one better suited to assist me."

"Well," she said stoutly, "I'm all for it if you are. If I can help lay a hand on Polly's killer, it's a job well done. No more smatter hauling for me this month, gents."

"Income garnered through theft of handkerchiefs," Holmes murmured under his breath.

"Ah, yes," said I. "Quite so."

We settled that Miss Monk would confine her investigations to the neighbourhoods of Whitechapel and Spitalfields, taking note of all local speculation. She would then report to Holmes twice weekly at Baker Street, under the pretext of paying calls upon her gentleman suitor. It was a determined Miss Monk, I noted, who descended our stairs to the cab waiting at the street corner.

Holmes threw himself upon the settee as I cast about for a means to light my pipe.

"She'll prove useful, Watson, mark my words," he declared, tossing me a matchbox. "*Alis volat propriis,** if I am not very much mistaken."

"She'll come to no harm, Holmes?"

---

* Latin, "She flies with her own wings."

"I should hope not. Alehouses are safe as churches by comparison with the murky alleys of her usual vocation. By the way, I came by a spot of success this morning."

"I meant to inquire. What the deuce has cat's meat to do with the matter?"

"Although I have not yet ascertained whether Annie Chapman, for so I have discovered she was called, was tied in any way to Polly Nichols or Martha Tabram, she was nevertheless ill-starred enough to fall victim to the Whitechapel killer, who made off with possibly the most repellent token I have ever heard spoken of."

"I recall as much."

"Well, then. What does that aforementioned token suggest to you?" Holmes's eyes shone and the twitch of his brow gave me every hope that he was onto something.

"Do you mean to tell me you have found a clue?"

"My dear Watson, flex your mental musculature and see if you can make note of the remarkable fact which Lestrade, in his horror at the proceedings, has seemingly not yet grasped."

"Every one of these vile facts is remarkable enough to me."

"Oh, come, Watson, do make an effort. You are the killer. You dispatch your victim. You open her up, and remove her womb."

"Well, of course!" I exclaimed. "What the devil did he do with it?"

"Bravo, Watson. The blackguard certainly did not amble down the lane with it in his trouser pocket."

"But the cat's meat?"

"This morning I found, because I was looking for it, a quantity of cat's meat hidden beneath one of the stones in the yard of number twenty-seven, which must make all clear for you. You recall my interest in whether Mrs. Hardyman of twenty-nine Hanbury Street, ground floor, front room, had done a brisk business that morning?"

"I see! He purchased a package of cat's meat."

"Excellent, my dear Watson. You make me feel as if I were there."

"He then hid the cat's meat, placing the organ in the bloody package and making off down the street, free of suspicion."

"You shall master the deductive arts yet, my boy."

"But who is he?"

"Mrs. Hardyman's riveting description was as follows: 'A sort of regular-looking chap, middle-sized, very polite in his ways.' She thought she had seen him before but could not recall where or whether she had ever previously sold him cat's meat. You see our earlier inference is confirmed; he is apparently not a man who imposes himself upon the senses. And this cat's-meat business indicates premeditation yet again, which is more than a little disturbing to my mind."

"What the devil could he have wanted with such a gruesome prize?"

"I cannot begin to tell you. Well, at any rate, it is certainly the best lead we've dug up, and while Miss Monk pans the silt, we shall see if we cannot add some fresh particulars to this shabbily dressed fellow, whose taste in souvenirs is as indecent as it is incomprehensible."

CHAPTER SIX

A Letter to the Boss

The next morning, I was interrupted whilst stoking the fading morning fire in our sitting room by a resounding exclamation of disgust from Sherlock Holmes, who sat transfixed with a newspaper upon the breakfast table in front of him and an arrested coffeepot in his hand.

"Confound the man! Well, if the fool wishes to waste his labour on squaring the circle, as it is said, we can do nothing about it."

"What has happened?"

"Lestrade has arrested John Pizer, against all tattered remains of rational thought."

"At your suggestion, surely," I reminded him.

"I wired him there was nothing in it!" Holmes protested. "Even the *Evening Standard* cannot credit his having anything to do with the matter."

"And what more have the gutter press to say on the subject?"

Snapping the paper emphatically, he read, "'It would seem that there is, haunting the slums and purlieus of Whitechapel, some obscene creature in human guise, whose hands are stained with the "gory witness" of a whole series of butcheries' . . . ha! . . . 'shocking perversion of Nature . . . bestial wretch . . . unquenchable as the taste of a man-eating tiger for human flesh.'"

"For heaven's sake, my dear fellow."

"I didn't write it," he said mischievously.

A brief knock at the door heralded the approach of our pageboy. "You've a telegram, Holmes." I could not help but smile as my eyes scanned the correspondence. "Mr. Lusk is now the acting president of the Whitechapel Vigilance Committee. He sends his allegiance and his warm regards."

"Capital! Well, I am gratified to see that some of these active fellows are actually applying their energies in a beneficial direction. We shall follow their example, my good man—we must learn more about this purchaser of cat's meat, and with all possible haste."

But throughout the week that followed, Holmes met with only the most limited success. Despite all our efforts, as the killer had left no physical trace, we could not identify the man who had vanished that morning into the cold September air. The Vigilance Committee, a truly robust organization from the start, swiftly organized neighbourhood watches and nightly patrols, but they encountered few hazards beyond the outbreaks of vicious antiforeign mobs, who took it upon themselves to beat any hapless immigrant whose "sly looks" or "crooked demeanour" proved his degenerate nature. Every citizen of Whitechapel from the most devout charity worker to the lowest cracksman cried out in chorus that no native Englishman could ever have killed a poor woman so.

Annie Chapman was buried secretly on Friday the fourteenth of September, at the same paupers' cemetery where Polly Nichols had been given back to the infinite little over a week before. *"Pulvis et umbra sumus,"* Holmes remarked that night, staring into the fire with his long arms cast thoughtfully about his drawn-up knees. "You and I, Watson, Annie Chapman, even the revered Horace himself—dust and the shadow cast by it, merely that and nothing more."

Though Holmes lamented during the weeks following Annie Chapman's death that the trails grew colder with every nervous twitch of the clock, I knew he was gratified that at least his investment in Miss Mary Ann Monk had proven fruitful. As Holmes followed slender leads to their barren conclusions, we anticipated eagerly our meetings with Miss Monk, who appeared to relish her new occupation. My friend, whose casual charm all too often masked cold, incisive professionalism, seemed genuinely pleased to see her, while I looked forward warmly to the boisterous air of enthusiasm with which she infused our discouraged sitting room.

On the twenty-third of September, the Polly Nichols inquest ended in resounding ignorance. Upon the following Wednesday, the selfsame coroner concluded the Annie Chapman inquest with the novel suggestion that a rapacious medical student had killed her and stolen the organ, intending it for sale to an unscrupulous American doctor. This news, reported earnestly in the *Times* the next day, resulted in Holmes's raving silently at the ceiling before locating his hair trigger, falling despairingly into his chair, and tattooing a small crown in bullets above the previously rendered intertwined *VR* to the left of our fireplace.

"My dear fellow, might I suggest that any further adornment of Her Majesty's initials would be disrespectfully garish?" Carefully orienting myself behind Holmes, I opened the windows in anticipation of Miss Monk's imminent arrival.

"You question my loyalty to the Crown?"

"I question your employment of firearms."

Holmes sighed ruefully and replaced the gun in his desk. "Miss Monk is due any moment. Perhaps she brings further evidence against the diabolical American purveyor of female reproductive organs."

"Really, Holmes!"

The detective smiled briefly by way of apology and then, catching the unmistakable tread of a slightly built woman ascending a staircase in heavy work boots, crossed our sitting room and threw open the door.

"Lor', what's this, then? A fire?" Miss Monk demanded, coughing. She had indulged part of her weekly pound in a bit of silvery ribbon to line the bottom of her coat, I observed. I also noted, not without some satisfaction, that her tiny frame had taken on a decidedly less skeletal appearance.

"Holmes occasionally mistakes our sitting room for a firing range," I replied wryly. "Do sit down, Miss Monk."

"Had a drop of the lush, have you?" Miss Monk nodded. "I'd a friend once was known to shoot at naught when he'd made himself good and comfortable with a bottle of gin. You've something better, haven't you—whiskey, I suppose?"

I hid my own smile by clearing some newspapers off the settee, but Holmes laughed outright and strode to the sideboard for glasses.

"Your remark seems to me absolutely inspired. Whiskey and soda for all concerned is, I think, very much in order."

"Bollocks to this cold," Miss Monk said contentedly when she had been seated by the fire clutching her glass of spirits. "Could freeze the eyes out of your head. At any rate, gents, I've earned my billet this week."

"How so?" queried Holmes, leaning back and closing his eyes.

"I've traced the soldier, that's what."

Holmes sat up again, the picture of zeal. "Which soldier do you mean?"

"The pal. The cove what lost his mate, like enough to have stabbed that first judy, Martha Tabram."

"Excellent! Tell me everything. You may well have wired me over a discovery of this magnitude, you know."

"Happened this morning," she replied with pride. "Dropped by the Knight's Standard for a cup of max* to open me eyes as I do every morning, earning my keep all the while as you know. It's a right thick, smoky place, and near empty at that time, but there's a soldier I could barely make out, off in the corner. I begin to think I'll wander over and chat him up a bit, but before I can shift, he's spied me, seemingly, and gets up to join me at the bar. He's a well-built chap, strong jaw, dark moustache turned up at the ends, with blue eyes and sandy brown hair.

"'Hullo there,' says he.

"'Hullo yourself,' says I. 'Share a glass of gin with a lonesome girl?'

---

* A glass of gin.

"'I can't imagine you're ever lonesome for long,' says he, smiling.

"I think to myself, if that's all he's after, he can move straight along, for I've no need of his business. But he must have seen I weren't pleased and says quick and eager, 'It was only meant for a compliment, Miss.'

"'That's all right, then. I'll let you sit here till you've thought of a better one.'

"'A very generous offer,' says he, and sits.

"The conversation starts out slow, but seeing as we're drinking max and he's a proper flat, soon enough he's chattering his nob off. 'Got discharged just last week and came straight back to London. The whole lot of us were in town last near two months ago,' says he. 'There's a pal of mine I'm keen to find.'

"'Your mate owes you something?' I ask.

"'Nothing like that. But I have to lay my hands on him all the same.'

"'But why?'

"'He's committed murder, you see.'

"Well, you can bet your last tanner I wasn't letting him out of my sight now until I'd heard the whole tale. I look as shocked as I can, which is no hard lay seeing as I'm fairly staggered.

"'Murder! What'd he do it for, then? Lost his head during a caper? Or was it a fight?'

"'I'm afraid it's far worse. My friend is a very dangerous fellow.'

"'What, one of a gang?'

"He shakes his head and peers down his nose thoughtfully and says, 'He acted alone, so far as I know.'

"I sit and wait for him to go on, and when he sees I'm hanging on his every word, he says, 'You see, when we were last here, a woman was killed. My friend did it, or so I believe. And I'm very sorry to say that he got away.'

"'You gave me a turn!' I gasp, for I can't help but think he's talking of Martha Tabram, and suddenly I feel cold all over at the sight of him. 'You ought to be ashamed of yourself, telling such stories when every judy in the Chapel's fair sick over rumours of the Knife.'

"'You don't believe me, but every word of it's true,' says he. 'I had a friend in my regiment. Never knew a better mate than him. He was a fine chap all round but had a temper like you've never seen. He met a girl here when last we were in town. It all began harmlessly enough. We went from pub to pub—but then he took her into an alleyway with him. I waited. I knew something was wrong when they weren't back in a few minutes, but I waited all the same. I've already told you the end of it, anyway. Since that terrible night, I've not laid eyes on Johnny Blackstone, but I am going to find him if it's the last thing I ever do.'

"Then he's quiet for a spell. Soon enough he comes back to himself and notices me sitting there. 'I haven't frightened you, have I? I've no wish to burden you, but it's heavy on my mind. My duty's clear enough: he has to be found, and found quickly.'"

"One moment," Holmes interrupted. "This guardsman—he believes his missing comrade to be responsible for the other murders as well?"

"Seemed troubled enough by the question," replied Miss Monk calmly. "So I tries to draw him out, but I must have looked so rattled that he thinks he's said enough and shuts it. Keeps telling me he's sorry to have upset me. Had the devil of a time after that to even get his name. I says to him, looking a mite faint, 'I must go home . . . ,' and he takes my arm and leads me out. I stagger on the doorstep and clutch at his jacket, and he helps me up like a proper gentleman, but by then I'd tooled the reader straight from out his gropus."

"You lifted his wallet?" Holmes repeated incredulously. I must confess that I was grateful for the interjection.

"I beg your pardon," she blushed. "Been at it so long, it's a job not to voker Romeny.* That's right—I pinched it. His name is Stephen Dunlevy," she finished.

---

* To "voker Romeny" was to speak the language of London's destitute, also known as Thieves' Cant, which Sherlock Holmes would likely have employed very often in a professional capacity.

Holmes and I looked at each other in amazement. "Miss Monk," said my friend, "you have done splendidly."

She smiled, a little shyly. "It was a ream job right enough, and I'm proud of it."

"However, I fear that you may have burned a significant bridge by stealing this fellow's wallet."

"Oh, never fear for that, Mr. Holmes," she replied, laughing. "I put it back."

At that moment we detected the sound of a muffled argument on the ground floor. Before we could guess as to its source, the singular sound of two feet accompanied by two crutches approached our sitting room at an alarming speed, and seconds later one of Holmes's most peculiar acquaintances tore into the room like a winter's gale.

Mr. Rowland K. Vandervent of the Central News Agency was approximately thirty years of age and exceptionally tall, nearly on par with Holmes himself, but he appeared much less so as he was bent at the waist from a crippling bout with polio when he was a child. He had an unruly mop of shockingly blond, virtually white hair, and I fear that this combined with his frail legs and crutch-assisted gait gave me the perpetual impression that he had just fallen victim to electric shock. He had once watched Holmes spar, I believe, when a spectator at an amateur boxing match, and Mr. Vandervent, who held my friend in the highest regard, occasionally sent wires to inform Holmes of stories which had just been broken to the agency. Nevertheless, I was startled at the sight of the man himself, wheezing after his rapid ascent of the stairs. His right arm, clad as always in a shabby pinstriped frock coat, held aloft a small piece of paper.

"Mr. Holmes, I've a matter to discuss with you which can brook no delay. However, I encountered serious impediments downstairs. You've a most uncouth and tenacious landlady. By the Lord Harry! Here she is again. Madam, I have explained that it is a matter of profound indifference to me whether he is engaged or no."

76 ❈ Lyndsay Faye

"It is all right, Mrs. Hudson," cried Holmes. "Mr. Vandervent has had scant exposure to polite society. Do excuse us, if you will."

Mrs. Hudson wiped her hands upon the tea towel she was holding, regarded Mr. Vandervent as she would a venomous insect, and returned downstairs to her cooking.

"Mr. Vandervent, you never call upon me but you upset the fragile balance of our household. Dr. Watson you know, of course. May I introduce our new associate, Miss Mary Ann Monk. Now, whatever it is you've got there, let us have a look at it."

We all crowded around the table and examined the curious missive Mr. Vandervent had brought with him. I read the letter aloud, which was penned with vivid red ink and went in this manner:

Dear Boss

I keep on hearing the police have caught me but they wont fix me just yet. I have laughed when they look so clever and talk about being on the right track. That joke about Leather Apron gave me real fits. I am down on whores and I shant quit ripping them till I do get buckled. Grand work the last job was. I gave the lady no time to squeal. How can they catch me now. I love my work and want to start again. You will soon hear of me with my funny little games. I saved some of the proper red stuff in a ginger beer bottle over the last job to write with but it went thick like glue and I cant use it. Red ink is fit enough I hope ha. ha. The next job I do I shall clip the ladys ears off and send to the police officers just for jolly wouldnt you. Keep this letter back till I do a bit more work, then give it out straight. My knife's so nice and sharp I want to get to work right away if I get a chance. Good luck.

Yours truly

Jack the Ripper

Don't mind me giving the trade name

Wasn't good enough to post this before I got all the red ink off my hands curse it. No luck yet. They say I'm a doctor now—ha ha

"It is hardly the natural correspondence of our readership, as you can see," stated Mr. Vandervent, collapsing unceremoniously into a chair. "A bit more about repealing the corn laws and a bit less about clipping off ladies' ears, and I should not have troubled you."

Holmes lifted the object by its edges and took it to his desk, where he commenced a meticulous study through his lens.

"Any envelope?"

"Thought you'd say that. Here it is."

"Postmarked September twenty-seventh, eighteen eighty-eight, receipt same day, mailed from the eastern side of the metropolis. Address straggling and unbalanced—you see, he has no regard for uniformity of line."

"What's got me concerned," continued Mr. Vandervent, "is not the compelling style of the note itself. It's that the mad bastard—my apologies, Miss Monk, to your delicacies—should ask us to hold it back until he 'does a bit more work.' I am in the position, for quite the first time in my life, of not knowing what to do."

"You amaze me, Mr. Vandervent."

"Indeed! Yes. It is a very disquieting sensation. But as I understand it, rum notes and dark plots are quite your arena, Mr. Holmes. You've traced his whereabouts by now, no doubt."

"I think I would do well to exchange my actual powers for Mr. Vandervent's imagined ones," the detective replied. "In fact, I cannot make out his game at all."

"His game is clear enough. States it right there—fourth sentence, I believe: 'down on whores.'"

"No, no, the note itself. You've called attention to the key oddity already: why should this man, if he is not the killer, ask that the letter be held back until after he has killed again? The casual prankster would wish the letter to be published immediately, seeking only to frighten the public and see his handiwork in print."

"Is there anything that could help us to trace the author?" I asked.

Holmes shrugged. "The man is moderately educated. The irregularity of the baseline, as well as the downward-slanting script, indicate he is moody and unpredictable. His *t*s are determined, his *r*s intelligent, and the confidence in his capitals is troubling. The envelope reveals nothing aside from origin, and the Moncton's Superfine watermark is clear but certainly not a clue by which we could trace a man."

"Moncton's Superfine watermark. You don't say. But let us address the real problem, Mr. Holmes," drawled Mr. Vandervent. "What am I to do with it? I've done my civic duty in bringing it here, but I fear the citizenry might be nonplussed at reading it over breakfast."

"May I keep this document for further study?"

"So you advise me to hold it back for the time being? A very roundabout way you have of putting it too. Very well, Mr. Holmes, I shall leave the thing in your hands, to be retrieved the day after tomorrow, at which time I shall forward it to the Yard. Make good use of it. I have no doubt but that it would prove excellent kindling." Mr. Vandervent, with a supreme effort, raised himself from his chair and descended the stairs.

Holmes drained his glass thoughtfully. "Miss Monk, would it be at all possible for you to see this Dunlevy fellow a second time?"

"We've fixed Saturday evening to meet at the Queen's Head. Nine o'clock sharp," Miss Monk replied innocently.

"Brava! Miss Monk, you are of inestimable help. Dr. Watson and I will be on hand in Whitechapel to provide support. Meanwhile, I intend to study this letter until it can house no secrets from me. The author may not be our man, but this 'Jack the Ripper,' whoever he is, certainly bears investigating."

CHAPTER SEVEN

A Whitechapel Rendezvous

Holmes was absent for much of the next day, revealing when he returned only that we were to meet Miss Monk in the East-end on the following evening. No more would he say regarding either the case or the mysterious letter, and when, against my better judgment, I pressed the subject, he embarked upon a discussion of architecture as a reflection of national ideals, steadfastly refusing to be led astray from that intriguing though irrelevant subject.

The following afternoon proved an arena for the wind to strew showers against windowpanes and blow gusts of cold, wet air through timidly cracked doorways. My friend arrived for supper in high spirits, and we sat down over a bottle of Bordeaux before embarking upon our journey east.

"I have been returning Mr. Vandervent's property," said Holmes as he poured me a glass. "I was not thanked for my trouble. That poor misanthrope has no patience for his own kind, but he's a decent enough sort, and as you have seen, occasionally invaluable."

"What do we intend to accomplish this evening?"

"We shall stay a reasonable distance behind Miss Monk and see whether this mysterious soldier has had any luck in tracing his friend Johnny Blackstone. I have not yet had a look at the fellow, after all, and he has piqued my interest enormously."

"In what way?"

"Surely it is apparent that Dunlevy is not all that he seems."

"Is it?" I inquired. "We have never laid eyes on him."

"Yes, but she has, and if what she says is accurate, he is a slippery fish, this Mr. Dunlevy. Consider: a woman has been brutally murdered. You were present at the scene. You know who has done it, or you think you know. You never say a word about it to anyone and you fail to inform either the police or your superiors what has happened."

"He claimed they were fast friends."

"Even more baffling. Rather than request a leave of absence to seek out your fallen brother, or even go so far as to place an ad in the agony columns, you leave the city and only upon your return develop a burning desire to find him. He cannot be both fiercely loyal and glaringly negligent. Now, look here, Watson, we haven't much time. It is nearly seven. We shall finish this excellent vintage, and then into evening dress."

"Evening dress? In Whitechapel?"

"We'll be far less visible that way, and we shall incorporate, beneath our coats, your revolver and my bull's-eye lantern. I assure you that evening dress is the best possible measure to avoid undue attention. Better for us to appear swells of dubious morals than gentlemen of mysterious purposes. Besides, Watson," he added, with a glint of humour in his grey eyes, "you, after all, are a man of the world. We must put your skills to use, for there is no greater tragedy on God's green earth than that of untapped talent."

Thus, attired as elegantly as if our destination were the opera and not the East-end, we set forth into the glittering streets as the evening deepened into night. The freshly lit gas lamps flung yellowed light across the rain-streaked windowpanes but grew ever more scarce as we drove east. At length, when we had left the vast tracts of brick dwellings behind us, our cab turned onto Whitechapel High Street.

Light poured from the doorways of the gin palaces, illuminating the fruit peddlers who laboured at the end of the day to sell their remaining wares. An organ-grinder with his chattering simian companion stood before a music hall upon a crumbling street corner. Everywhere men leaned in doorways puffing at cigars, and everywhere women strolled about, some housewives with hair in loose buns gossiping with their neighbours, some ladies of more mercurial design who kept in constant motion to avoid the attention of the local constabulary. Gentlemen of leisure too, weary of concerts and of dinner parties, lounged from temptation to temptation with cynical aplomb. The place was a veritable hornet's nest of whirring activity, illicit and otherwise, and the rawness of it reminded me less of London than it did the heaving markets of Calcutta and of Delhi I had encountered during my time in service.

At length we turned north onto Commercial Street, where pools of water stood in front of the narrow shops illuminated from within by greasy tallow candles. Rats scurried from under our clattering wheels, and doors leading to derelict stairwells stood yawning in the rain. I peered into them, but to no avail; the glow and bustle of Whitechapel High Street had been replaced by pervasive darkness. It was a black so heavy that its weight appeared only to be deepened by the efforts of the meager lamps, and I wondered aloud to Holmes what deeds might with impunity be committed in such a realm.

"To live in these houses, one cannot survive without either condoning or incorporating the criminal element," my friend replied. "See here—this street we are passing, Flower and Dean—it is one of the most dangerous places in the known world, and it is not in the wilds of Africa but mere miles from the place where you and I so peaceably hang our hats."

One glance down the road he had indicated sufficed to prove his point. The air was heavy despite the recent rain, and there was hardly a window which had not been smashed in, then vainly patched over with paper or scraps of cheap cloth.

"Here is our destination. I thought it best to establish our connection early in the evening. Follow me, and please try not to draw attention to yourself."

Holmes has, as I have remarked elsewhere, an air of self-importance about him which occasionally tries the patience of his few friends. However, upon entering the establishment called the Queen's Head, on the corner of Commercial and Fashion Streets, I at once took his meaning. The place was populated by gentlemen—if one could stretch the word to its outer limits—of the roughest character; by rouged women awkwardly holding babies in their arms, pausing for a glass of gin before returning home; and by Miss Mary Ann Monk, who sat at the bar near the doorway and shot an eye at us as we entered.

"How about that one, Middleton?" Holmes said brightly after surveying the room. "She looks likely enough, and that glorious hair. You won't do better than that, my friend, not in these parts."

My look of dismay must have registered with many of the patrons, who chuckled quietly at Holmes's words.

"Oh, come off it, man, we haven't got all week. See here," he said to Miss Monk in a lower tone. "My friend is about to leave London for the Australian colonies, and—well, it would be pleasant to remember England as a welcoming land, if you understand me. You are not engaged at the moment?"

Miss Monk regarded us appraisingly and made no reply.

"Well, well, it is no matter," said Holmes suavely, passing her a half-sovereign. "Now, I expect this is more than you make in a month, and I further expect you to earn it. We shall stay here for a drink, then continue on to the Bricklayer's Arms down the road apiece. A thicker* when all's said and done ought to persuade you to meet us there, I think? Many thanks, my dear girl."

After purchasing two glasses of beer and two glasses of gin from

---

* A sovereign; Holmes is offering her as much again if she meets them at the rendezvous point.

the proprietor, we sat down on a bench near the back of the room. We sipped the beer, leaving the gin untouched.

"I suppose that we intend to grant Miss Monk an ironclad justification for giving Dunlevy the slip when she feels it necessary," I remarked dryly.

"Precisely so. My apologies, my dear Middleton, but apart from an assignation, I could not devise any excuse that would so effectively ensure her safety."

"Your vaunted imagination fell so short?"

"Come now, my dear fellow! It is a dark enough investigation without a touch of sport to lighten it. But I say, what have we here—no, do not look toward the door, I beg of you," he stopped me softly. "The reflection in that excellently placed mirror should serve you every bit as well."

Stephen Dunlevy, his face slightly distorted by the ageing of the mirror, was casting an affable blue eye about the crowded room. He was a genial fellow with a modest, upward-tilting moustache set over a pleasant mouth and a square jaw. Holmes looked him over in his careless, languid fashion, but I knew that he was recording every salient detail as the ex-guardsman strode further into the room and hailed our diminutive friend. On their way to sit down, Miss Monk nodded once in our direction, which immediately prompted her companion to question her.

Holmes smiled. "Now that Dunlevy has seen us, let us take our leave." We exited the bar and the air hit our faces in damp gusts as he continued. "You see, my dear fellow, the only way I could feel absolutely sure of Miss Monk's security was if she had an appointment—not a fabricated one, mind you, but an established fact—that her companion discovered as if by accident. Should she not appear, she will be missed, and Dunlevy knows it."

We walked slowly down Commercial Street as the skies began to clear. "I have no doubt but that you are aware of every possible eventuality," said I, recovering my equanimity outside the close confines of the Queen's Head. Falling into a more comfortable silence, we drifted in the direction of our meeting place with Miss Monk.

By the time we had reached Whitechapel High Street once more, all the revelry and apathy of a hedonistic Carnevale permeated the smoky atmosphere. Had Holmes or I wished to lose any of the money in our pockets, every corner boasted either a cardsharp, skittle sharp, or some other variety of bold-faced cheat. As we passed the intersection into the morass of Commercial Road, I confess that I should have doubted the safety of our route had Holmes not so clearly known precisely where he was going. Indeed, I believe that only my friend's air of total self-assurance prevented us from harm as we strolled down the jaggedly cobbled street.

While I cannot vouch for the history of the Bricklayer's Arms, it had likely once served as a local guildhall, for it boasted the banner of its trade name above the low-linteled door. It was perhaps eleven o'clock by the time Holmes and I arrived, as we had more than once been forced to extricate ourselves from the attentions of inquiring ladies of the evening. I will be pardoned, therefore, for having expressed a degree of relief when we at last entered the crowded tavern.

A stranger to all, my companion was within half an hour the intimate confidant of every unhappy sot within the premises. Though seeped through with tallow smoke and careless splashes of gin, the atmosphere grew less unpleasant as I realized that Holmes was as at ease in our present environs as he was in our own rooms, and thus I settled back in my chair and tried my own hand at observation. Close upon my right was an elderly fellow, clearly a sailor, I thought, from his tattoos, who declaimed to a curly-headed boy that he had more women at his beck and call in Asian ports than any other seafarer he had either seen or heard tell of. Directly in front of us sat a woman who I imagined to be in mourning owing to her dark garments, then remembered that the denizens of that neighbourhood possessed at the most one entire set of clothing.

When over an hour had passed without a sign of our comrade,

I began to shoot Holmes worried glances, only one of which he responded to by pressing my arm reassuringly. My friend was lifting his glass once more in the direction of the barkeep's daughter when Miss Monk at last appeared at the doorway. Upon spying us, she rushed over, leaping into the nearest chair.

"I'd bet my life that bloke's onto summat," she declared delightedly, drawing Holmes's half-sovereign out of her garments and tossing it back to him. He placed it in his waistcoat pocket and then quite inexplicably glanced down at her shoes.

"Well, then," he prompted, raising his eyes, "pray report. What did he tell you?"

"Wouldn't talk about that soldier friend of his for nigh on an hour. Just asks what I've been about and who you lads are, and I tells him some stories so everything's warm and comfortable. Finally he lets on that he thinks he's found a way to trace Johnny Blackstone."

"This gentleman grows ever more enthralling," Holmes remarked. "Did you discover anything further?"

"Only where he lives!" she whispered.

"How on earth did you accomplish that?" I exclaimed.

"Well, when I left him to meet my swells, I'm off with a peck and a nod, but I ducks into an alley to see which way he goes. When he comes out, he walks straight down Commercial Street and ends up on Ellen Street, down a passage or two and into a doss house. I spies a woman at the front entrance, and I offer her a shilling to let on what sort of callers he has. 'No one,' says she, 'but he's out all hours, and only the devil knows what he's about. He's true enough to you, so far as I know.' Well, I weren't about to wait around for him to come out again. But I'll show you his digs, and the woman what keeps the entrance will tell me for a few pence if he's there, like as not."

"It is a sterling idea, Miss Monk. I may have a mind to follow him myself tomorrow. Quietly now, and so as not to cause any curiosity over our departure, do take my friend Middleton's arm and lead us out of the bar."

CHAPTER EIGHT

In Pursuit of the Killer

Heading in a southwesterly direction, we were soon avoiding heaps of debris and rivulets of sewage on our way to Dunlevy's abode. Miss Monk, freed from the gaze of our fellow bar patrons, let go of my forearm with a comradely squeeze and we traveled three abreast. We had passed a board school, and were nearing a two-story barn housing what sounded like a gentleman's club in the midst of a celebration, when a pony-driven cart blocked our path as it approached an open gate. The workman sitting upon the small seat of his costermonger's barrow, a stooped man with spectacles and fingerless gloves, called out impatiently to his animal. To his surprise, his pony shied backward with a nervous neighing sigh. Another attempt to enter met with the same resistance, and as a result, our party trod into the street to cross to the other side.

We had continued for several more paces when Holmes cried, "Wait! The reins, Watson! The reins in that man's hand, they were slack, were they not?" Without awaiting a reply, he turned on his heel and flew back toward the gate and the fretfully pawing pony, whose owner had temporarily abandoned the project and gone inside the club.

Miss Monk turned a quizzical eye toward me. "They were slack, right enough. But what could that mean?"

I intended to reply, but some instinct instead caused me to run with all my speed after Holmes into the long space between the two buildings. The walls rose at an impossible angle for any light to penetrate from the street beyond, and I could barely make out my friend's tall form against the opposite mouth of the corridor.

"Holmes!" I called, proceeding forward with one guiding hand on the cold wall. "What is it, Holmes?"

The spark of a lit vesta flared out, revealing my friend's thin hand and a patch of stone wall. "It is murder, Watson."

When Holmes lit the bull's-eye, the sight which had been invisible to my duller senses caused me to gasp in alarm. There lay the very gaunt, sable-clad woman I had noted in the Bricklayer's Arms not two hours previous. Her eyes were now open and staring, seemingly in disbelief at the rivulets of blood which ran from the gaping gash through her neck onto the ground.

I immediately knelt to see what could be done, but she had breathed her last mere seconds before our arrival. At this observation, a new thought struck me, and I looked urgently up at Holmes as I drew my service revolver, indicating the enclosed yard beyond. He nodded once. Lantern in hand, the detective cautiously advanced the remaining fifteen feet down the end of the corridor until he reached the edge of the threshold and stepped into the shadowy yard.

The attack happened so quickly that it was difficult for me to know exactly what occurred. A dark figure, who had clearly been waiting flat against the wall beyond, focusing all his senses upon our movements, darted behind Holmes and dealt me a powerful blow near the left eye, momentarily stunning me as he tumbled out the street side of the passageway. My next memory, which could only have been a split second later, was of Holmes shouting, "Remain here!" as he left the lantern and took flight after the murderer of the unidentified female, whose eyes, though my own were still painfully blurred, I gently closed as I leaned against the wall.

After bitterly regretting my own stupidity in allowing myself to be assaulted in such a manner, I reflected that the terrain had been far from in our favour—to walk from a narrow entrance into unknown landscape is to invite ambush—and I soon left off cursing my ill luck to ponder what use I could be where I was.

Upon approaching the gate, I nearly collided with the workman from the pony cart, which remained where we had left it, the animal still tossing its head in indignation at the proceedings. The driver had evidently gone inside and brought back with him a few lit candles and several of his comrades, many of foreign appearance, all respectably dressed and glaring at me suspiciously.

"My pony was afraid, and I stop to see why," he began in slightly accented but perfectly comprehensible English. "He is not usually this way, and I saw a dark shape. You—you were hiding? In the yard?"

"No," I replied, "but a terrible event has occurred there. We must summon the police at once."

The knot of men exchanged worried glances. "I am Mr. Louis Diemschutz," declared the cart driver. "We are members of the International Workingmen's Educational Club, through that door. My house, my wife—they live off this yard. I must see what has been done."

I nodded and stood aside. Mr. Diemschutz approached the body and gave a small exclamation at the pool of blood surrounding the victim's head.

"This is not my wife," he cried, "but another woman has been killed! This man is right. We must find help."

Fortunately, that task required negligible effort, for before we had traversed ten yards of the street, Miss Monk rounded the corner in a visible rage with an exceedingly recalcitrant police constable in tow.

"You'll leg it sharp, or I'll begin screaming and I won't stop till you've done what's right. Bloody hell, do you think I spend my time chatting up every crusher I see trudging along his little circle?" She stopped short at the sight of me. "Oh, Dr. Watson," she cried, leaving the policeman and flying to my side. "Your eye is bleeding. I knew summat was wrong. What's in that alley? What's happened to Mr. Holmes, then?"

"There has been another murder, and Holmes has gone after the killer," I replied, half for the benefit of Miss Monk and half for that of the bewildered constable. As I uttered those words, I wondered with a sudden stab of fear whether it was remotely possible for Sherlock Holmes to be outmatched, and I lamented even more keenly that I was not with him.

"You saw the man what's done it?" Miss Monk questioned. I nodded. "And there's—there's another woman in there? She's dead, you've said as much, but is she—?"

"We interrupted her killer. Nothing of the sort that was done to Annie Chapman has happened here."

"That's a blessing, then." Miss Monk exhaled. "Right. You want me to see her? The poor soul. I may know her, after all."

I considered this suggestion and, knowing that time was of the essence, reluctantly gave my assent. The startled policeman likewise had no objection. I had left the lantern by the corpse, so together we approached the harsh halo of illumination delineating the arm and head of the body. Miss Monk bit her lip in distress at the sight of the victim but slowly shook her head. I took her arm and led her away.

"Are you all right, Miss Monk?"

"I'm like to be fine in a moment, Doctor."

"Perhaps one of the men associated with the Educational Club will escort you inside."

I had expected words of protestation either from Miss Monk, who looked stalwart but very pale, or from the club members, each of whom appeared to be attempting to work out my exact relationship with the shabbily clad young woman. No dispute was forthcoming, however, and a thin fellow with a pince-nez offered Miss Monk his arm and led her into the light and noise of the club.

"You're Dr. Watson?" demanded the policeman. He was a ruddy-faced youth with a blond moustache and weak chin. "I am Police Constable Lamb. The area must be secured, and no one is to leave the club until we've settled this matter. Pray God Mr. Holmes has caught the fiend by this time."

His words echoed my fervent hopes. I informed Constable Lamb I'd seen the dead woman two hours previous at the Bricklayer's Arms, and Mr. Diemschutz, who was much distressed, then described his pony's fright and his subsequent foray into the men's club for assistance. By this time many of the neighbours had been roused, and word of the fresh crime spread rapidly from house to house as other policemen arrived on the scene.

After twenty minutes had elapsed, I was anxious; twenty minutes beyond that saw me fretfully pacing the pavement, wondering whether it would be possible for one man, in the dead of night in an unfamiliar and tortuous setting, to find another man when his initial trajectory had not even been observed. At nearly a quarter to two by my watch, feeling vaguely ill, I made up my mind simply to cast about the adjacent streets and had just set off when an unyielding hand on my shoulder stopped me.

"I'm sorry, Dr. Watson, that Mr. Holmes has not returned," said Constable Lamb firmly, "but it is in direct violation of police procedure to allow you to exit the scene of a crime you . . . well, discovered, sir."

"Sherlock Holmes is at this very moment attempting to bring in the man responsible for these vile acts, and I mean to help him in whatever way I can."

"With respect, sir, you can't find Mr. Holmes without even a notion of where to look."

"He may be in desperate need of our assistance!"

"We can hardly provide him that without any idea where he is."

"I can at least determine he is not nearby."

"Not without violating the Yard's procedure, sir."

"I do not think that, even at this dark eleventh hour, we need entertain any notion of violating the procedure of the Yard," said a familiar sardonic voice.

"Holmes!" I cried, whirling around in relief. There he stood, not five yards away, holding himself in a peculiarly stiff manner as he slowly advanced. "The killer—did you encounter him? Did he disappear?"

"I am afraid the answer to both questions is yes," my friend replied, and then, taking another step, he seemed to suffer a loss of balance and staggered slightly.

"Dear God, Holmes, what has happened?" I rushed to his side and grasped his arm, and was all the more troubled when he did not protest but leaned on me heavily.

"Help me get him inside," I ordered the constable.

"Thank you, Watson, I believe you and I can manage it. Although, perhaps, the 'inside' to which you refer ought to be somewhat private."

One glance through the windows of the boisterous men's club, confined to their quarters for questioning and gesticulating wildly, was enough to convince me Holmes was right, and I led my friend instead to the building on the south side of the enclosure, which I had come to understand was called Dutfield's Yard. In the hallway between two families' living quarters, Holmes lowered himself onto a filthy stoop, and in the better light I finally caught sight of the massive bloodstain seeping across his right shoulder.

"For the love of God, Holmes, if I had seen this, I should not have allowed you to walk under your own power more than two paces," I cried, carefully pulling off his overcoat and his evening jacket, both of which were saturated with blood.

"I'd anticipated as much," he murmured, wincing only occasionally as I furthered my attempts to expose the actual wound. "I am relieved to see you well, by the way. You were dealt a considerable blow."

I threw off my greatcoat and began tearing apart my own dinner jacket, which I knew to be relatively sanitary, with Holmes's pocket-knife. "It was nothing. My own carelessness. Drink this," I directed, handing him my flask.

Holmes took it from me with an unsteady hand. "I have seldom myself encountered so fleet or agile an opponent."

"I wish to hear no explanations, nor do I wish you, in strict point of fact, to speak at all." I marveled at the forceful injunctions I was laying upon my friend, whose total authority, outside of a medical emergency, I would never have challenged.

"No doubt you are right, Doctor. But allow me to enlighten the constable here, whose testimony may be called upon by the Yard in our own absence."

"Briefly, then," I growled. "What happened?"

"This fellow couldn't hold a candle to the devil when in a tight corner. He ran off in the direction of some deserted warehouse byways, I imagine to prevent my shouting to any passersby to help me stop him. He knows these streets like the back of his hand, and I admit he had the advantage of me, for it has been months since I had a case here and one or two new gates and boarded-up alleys caught me by surprise. We had gone perhaps a quarter of a mile when he darted into a maze of passages. I made every effort to keep him in sight, for we both knew that once he had shaken me off, I would never regain the trail. Finally I did lose the culprit, or thought I did."

"Brace yourself a moment," I directed, pressing a hastily constructed compress to Holmes's shoulder. He turned even a shade paler but made no sound.

"I came to a very narrow crossroads of dripping stone corridors," Holmes continued. "He appeared to have turned a corner, and as both the east and the westerly branches turned yet again within a few yards, my only option seemed to be mere guesswork."

"You never guess."

"No," he acknowledged, with the hint of a smile, "nor did I in this case. I listened. I could no longer hear him running. Soon I realized that the creature could have made his escape through a door and out the back entrance, which would explain the lack of audible footsteps. In any event, I could not wait indefinitely, so after a brief perusal of the area, I grudgingly turned back the way I had come.

"It was as I passed the lintel of a deep doorway that the glint of a knife caught my eye, and the unfortunate incident occurred which you are working to correct. He'd stopped just before the crossroads, not after, and I curse my own stupidity for not having noted the absence of footfalls a moment before. I am possessed of quite rapid defensive reflexes, however, and diverted the blow effectively."

"You are very seriously injured, Holmes!"

"As the knife was aimed at my throat, you will concede I could have done worse. In any event, before I could rally, he was off again. I followed him, then began to feel I was not at my best and made my way back here."

"Indeed, you are hardly at the top of your form," I agreed, finishing the final knot of a makeshift brace and thanking my stars that in Afghanistan I had frequently done without proper medical supplies. "That is all I can construct for the moment. Slip your arm into this sling and we are off to hospital."

"Yes to the former and no, I think, to the latter. There is work still to be done. Have you any cigarettes about you? I've lost my case."

I opened my mouth to protest and closed it again, knowing I could no more drag Sherlock Holmes away from a murder investigation than command the world to spin in the opposite direction. Constable Lamb, who had been taking notes, rose to his feet as I passed my friend a cigarette and struck him a match.

"By the way, Mr. Holmes, how came you to suspect something was amiss?"

"Watson did not tell you? A pony on the street reared up and refused to approach the passage."

"Many ponies are skittish and dislike entering new territory if it is dark."

"Yes, but this pony was going home. Its master's reins lay slack in his lap; therefore, the pony stopped upon seeing something unusual which it did not like."

"I see," said the constable, somewhat dubiously, I thought with irritation. "And the murderer—would you describe him?"

Holmes closed his eyes and leaned back against the wall. "The damnable luck is that I never once caught a glimpse of his face. He had wrapped himself about the neck and mouth and ran with his head down. He wore an overcoat, British cut, dark material, heavy shoes, and a worn cloth hat. He was clutching a parcel wrapped in newspaper, not heavy, under his left arm. Did you see him clearly, Watson?"

I somberly indicated I had not.

"So, Mr. Holmes, you and your friend here maintain that, although you confronted this fellow on two separate occasions this very night, you would be unable to identify him? I mean to say, it seems very unlikely, does it not?"

"Well, Officer," my friend replied, crushing the remainder of his cigarette underfoot, "I suppose I must ask whether you find it likely that a man would take up tearing apart street women as a hobby. We appear to have quit the realm of likelihood, have we not? Come, we are losing time. Where strength has failed us, let us see what we can accomplish through reason alone."

CHAPTER NINE

The Double Event

It must have been well past two by the time we approached the grimy passageway where the body remained. Holmes looked ghastly but frenziedly determined. The constable frequently attempted to catch my eye, I suspected with the idea of removing Holmes from the scene, but he met with a stony and unflinching profile.

"Has anything been touched?"

"We have searched the surroundings for accomplices. The scene remains as it was when the Yard took possession."

It is perhaps irrelevant, however pressing it seemed to me at the time, to say I had developed a headache the likes of which I had never before experienced. In my dazed state, I failed to observe my companion's machinations with any exactitude until he approached the constable with fiery resolve in his slate grey eyes.

"The deceased is between forty and forty-five years old, though hard living has made her age more difficult to ascertain. She is a smoker, she went with her killer willingly into this byway, she makes occasional use of a padlock, she is not an absolute drunkard, she had experienced more than her share of violence before this event, and she consumed a bunch of grapes with the man who killed her. He, by the by, is right-handed, five foot seven, intimately acquainted with the district, and an Englishman."

Constable Lamb blinked once and then narrowed his eyes. "In the absence of my superiors, I must record the evidence behind your . . . assertions, sir." He rested his case, seemingly pleased by his own propriety.

"Must you indeed?" Holmes said lightly. "She is a smoker, because she retains in her hand a packet of cachous.* She went with her killer willingly because she would have dropped them had she fled. In addition, I happen to have seen this woman some little time ago at a pub, and she was not then wearing a red rose with white maidenhair fern pinned to her jacket. The killer courted her briefly—you may observe the grape stalk yourself just beside the body—and led her into this alleyway. She or someone she knows must own a padlock, for what other lock could possibly fit the key I have discovered upon her? She once before was the victim of a violent individual who tore an earring from her lobe, and were she an utter drunk, she would doubtless by now have pawned one of her two combs."

"I don't see what's so dashed clever about any of that," muttered Constable Lamb, jotting down notes as quickly as he was able.

"Yes, I would be very much surprised to learn you could see anything at all."

"Er . . . ," faltered the constable. "Yes, Mr. Holmes. If you would just wait for my superiors—"

"I should be all too gratified if you had any, but I fear—"

"They are approaching, I think, sir."

Constable Lamb was correct. A very distraught Inspector Lestrade bore down upon us, nearly at a run. Behind him stood a hansom cab as well as a police carriage emitting further reinforcements from the Yard.

"Sherlock Holmes himself!" the trim inspector snarled, clearly delighted at the opportunity to vent his fury. "I have no reason to question why you are here. I am grateful—indeed, deeply grateful.

---

* Lozenges used to freshen the breath.

For if you were not here, how would I go about explaining two murders in one night? Two murders, all within the space of a half mile! Who could explain such a thing if not Sherlock Holmes, the crack private theorist?"

"Two murders certainly demands an explanation," my friend replied, but I would be guilty of perjury were I not to report that he started visibly at the news, while I inhaled an unabashed gasp of amazement.

"What the devil has happened to your arm?"

"Return, if you will, Lestrade, to the scintillating topic of double murder," Holmes shot back bitingly, his deeply rooted nonchalance shattering beneath the force of his alarm.

"Oh, it is of considerable interest, without a doubt," sneered Lestrade. "Two murders certainly, to the minds of the official force, grow in consideration if they are committed within an hour of each other, not to mention a bloody twenty minutes' walk!"

"Oh, yes?" was all my friend managed to stake upon a reply.

"You may 'oh, yes' all you like, Mr. Holmes, but you must know perfectly well that the murder you are presently investigating is neither the more revolting nor the more pressing of the two."

Doubting my companion's capacity for speech, I interjected, "We discovered this crime in progress. What has the killer done since we interrupted him?"

Lestrade looked as if he were about to swallow his own head, such was his confidence in Sherlock Holmes's omniscience. "Don't set yourselves against my nerves," he snapped. "You mean to tell me you've heard nothing of the second victim this evening? Nothing of the evisceration, nor the cutting of her face, not to mention the intestines smeared all over her," he continued, with ominous calm, "nor the other atrocities visited upon her person, which so help me God I will wrest from you the truth of if it is the last thing I do!"

"Lestrade," my friend protested, "I promise you I know nothing of which you speak, but I will immediately place myself in a cab in the hopes of assisting you. Where did this second event take place?"

"Holmes, I cannot allow—" I began, but at that very instant, as my friend set off toward the vehicle, his iron strength at last failed him and he clutched at the window of the cab for support.

"We are taking you to hospital, and I will not hear another word on the subject," I swore.

"Hospital! Confound it all, what has happened to him?" begged Lestrade.

"He pursued the killer and was the victim of a murderous attack. I do not like to think what will happen if he exerts himself an instant longer. Driver, you are to proceed to London Hospital!"

"I believe that Baker Street would be preferable, driver," Holmes called out, as I half lifted him into Lestrade's hansom. I made as if to join him.

"You are forbidden to accompany me."

"Why on earth should I be?" I demanded, wounded to the quick.

"You are going to the site of the second killing. You are taking Miss Monk, whose eyes are invaluable. The two of you will record everything you see, and you will tell me of it when we meet again. See that Miss Monk comes to no harm." During these instructions, he paused intermittently to gather the fortitude to speak, which did nothing to calm my fears.

"I am to safeguard Miss Monk while you may be—"

"Of course not. You are to lead a murder investigation whilst I am recovering. All caution, Watson. Drive on!" he cried, and I stood there as the hansom cantered off into the darkness, leaving only myself, a hysterical inspector, various constables, and the intrepid Miss Monk, who had just emerged from the men's club composed and resolute.

"Is that Mr. Holmes?" she asked as his cab pulled away.

"Yes," I said shortly. "He is not well. There has been another murder."

Her hand flew to her mouth, but she immediately recovered her self-possession. "Then you and I had best leg it over or there'll be hell to pay."

As distraught as I was, I had no doubt that Miss Monk was in the right. "Lestrade, where is the other crime scene?"

"Just west of here in Mitre Square," Lestrade replied, still gazing with an expression of ill-disguised panic at the point where Holmes's hansom had disappeared. "Inspector Thomas has arrived, so I can take you there myself. I must warn you, however, the Yard has no jurisdiction. The murder was committed within the City of London."

The central pivot of the eastern metropolis, mirrored by the City of Westminster in the West-end, the City of London was limited to a single square mile of ground, safeguarded not by Scotland Yard but by their own small company of police under the authority of the Corporation of the City of London. However many individuals within that force Holmes had dealings with, I knew not a soul, and I gratefully accepted Lestrade's offered escort.

"Let us be off," said I, with the roughness that is born of deep apprehension. "We cannot lose any more time."

"One moment," replied Lestrade with a wondering glance toward Miss Monk. "Who the devil is this young person? Do you live in these buildings?"

"My name is Mary Ann Monk, sir," she stated. "I am in the employ of Mr. Sherlock Holmes."

The inspector raised his eyes heavenward and shook his head, but to his credit he did no more. "No doubt you are, miss. No doubt you are. But I warn you, Doctor—this young lady is to be presented as an associate of Mr. Holmes, not of Scotland Yard, if she's presented at all. My head would be in a basket by morning. Very well, into the carriage all, and back to Mitre Square. I hope you've the stomach for it, Doctor: there's a level of hell made especially for this bastard, or there's no justice in Creation. Of that, at least, I'm sure."

We drove westward along Commercial Road and then down Whitechapel High Street to the ancient core of Her Majesty's wide realm.

No one spoke a word, for Holmes's absence had cast a greater pall even than the news of the second murder. Setting aside my severe anxiety for my friend, the Whitechapel killer had proven himself to be the most fearsome menace ever to strike terror into the hearts of the populace. What powers could we expect to set against him without Holmes? I had never in my life been placed in such a false position, but I set my teeth and determined to do my utmost, whatever was required.

We none of us had long to worry, for it was a mere five minutes' journey. Stopping the carriage on Duke Street, we descended and passed the Great Synagogue, ducking into a small, covered opening. When we emerged in the wide square, we found a somber group of City Police surrounding the body, obscuring it from our immediate view. She lay in front of a row of empty cottages, with blank gaping windows and the creeping tendrils of weeds hastening their decay.

A tall, actively built man with sharp eyes and a military bearing, dressed in fashionably cut plain clothes, turned at the sound of our footsteps.

"This is a murder investigation," he proclaimed. "You must step outside the square to avoid disturbing evidence."

"I am Inspector Lestrade of the Metropolitan force." Lestrade proffered his hand rather uncertainly. "Major Henry Smith, is it not? To tell the truth, sir, we are investigating another murder committed on Berner Street, with all signs of it having been the work of the same party."

Major Smith emitted a low whistle. "By George, Inspector, you astonish me. And you are?" he asked, turning to me.

"Dr. John Watson. I was there when the event occurred."

"Your name is known to me, Dr. Watson. You say you were there— you interrupted the murderer at his work?"

"That is correct."

"Then the man is in custody?"

"We believe he escaped to commit the second atrocity you discovered in this square."

"Your tale is quite fantastical, sir. Forgive me, but considering your own presence here, Dr. Watson—where, in this extraordinary array of characters, is Mr. Sherlock Holmes?"

I hesitated. "He met with the killer and suffered an attack on his own person. He has been taken to seek aid." Gesturing to Miss Monk, I added, "This is an associate of Mr. Holmes and myself who has been helping with the investigation."

"Mary Ann Monk, sir. Pleased to meet you."

"The pleasure is mine. Well, then, now that we are acquainted," Major Smith continued, evidently not wishing to dwell upon the propriety of Miss Monk's presence, "Police Constable Watkins discovered the deceased while on his beat. His full circuit takes him approximately thirteen minutes to traverse, and he assures me the body was not in the square when he looked in at one thirty. Constable Watkins immediately engaged the aid of the night watchman from yonder warehouse to send for reinforcements and has not left the body since. You are welcome to make your own observations, Dr. Watson, before this poor creature is taken to the morgue."

"Miss Monk, if you would be so good as to look about the square for anything out of the ordinary," I suggested with a significant glance.

As she did so, Lestrade and I advanced through the cluster of officials. The inspector, one hand poised to take notes, clapped the other to my shoulder and nodded his head. I knelt beside the victim.

"Her throat has been cut from ear to ear. There is serious damage from a knife to both eyelids, both cheeks, and the tip of the nose. Abdomen has been laid entirely open and her intestines drawn out of the body and draped over the right shoulder. Severe injury to the pancreas, the lining of the uterus, the colon . . ." I stopped to draw a deep breath. "We must wait for the postmortem to determine the full extent of it. I can tell you that the pattern of her blood suggests the mutilations occurred after the poor woman's death."

A short silence punctuated my speech. Lestrade tucked his notebook in his coat with a sigh. "It seems clear that after he met Mr.

Holmes, the beast inflicted his filthy urges on the first candidate. I know the last murders were ugly, Doctor, but this—the monster was in a blind frenzy."

I was pulled out of my dark reverie by a delicate hand on my shoulder.

"Her ear, Doctor."

There was Miss Monk, peering down at the desecrated remains. Her high tone of voice gave the only clue as to the strain she was under. "You see her ear?"

"Yes. A small part of the right ear has been cut off."

"You remember the letter?"

Miss Monk's words brought it flooding back to me as if it were before my very eyes. "Of course!" I cried. "Just such a mutilation was mentioned. Do you recall the exact wording, Miss Monk?"

"'The next job I do I shall clip the lady's ears off and send to the police officers just for jolly wouldn't you,'" she replied rapidly, under her breath.

"I think I should be most gratified to learn who received this letter," said Major Smith evenly.

"It was sent to the Central News Agency last Thursday," I replied. "The letter references clipping off the next victim's ears, if possible, and sending them to the police, as Miss Monk has said."

"Does it indeed! The missive has not been published, as I understand you?"

I shook my head. "Holmes returned it to the Central News. The letter was signed with the name 'Jack the Ripper.'"

"It's true," Lestrade said through his teeth, "but we supposed it a hoax. Now it seems this lunatic is not merely running about ripping whores to shreds, he's appointed himself a pen name and mailed his agenda to the national press."

"It would on the surface appear so."

Lestrade struck his head gently with the flat of his hand. "I cannot be expected to endure much more of this. We've been torn to pieces in the papers for weeks, and now he gets away with two murders in one night? The whole country will be in an uproar!"

"Calm yourself, Inspector," Major Smith reproved. "Both these deeds have been freshly committed. It is impossible that a man could perform such acts without leaving a trace of his own identity. We may well have this 'Jack the Ripper' in our hands this very night."

Miss Monk, I realized, had wandered off of her own accord. She now arrived at my elbow again wearing a look of puzzlement. "I can't seem to find it here."

"Find what, Miss Monk?"

"Her apron," she replied, pointing. "She couldn't rightly have worn it so. I'd not a' been half surprised if it had a ruddy hole in it, but the ties have been cut clean through where the piece is missing. She'd have mended it, surely, or used the cloth for scrap."

Major Smith advanced to see for himself. "You are entirely correct, Miss Monk. Constable Watkins," he called out, "spread the word that a piece of apron has been taken from the body, most likely by the killer." He then turned and engaged in a quiet, businesslike conversation with Inspector Lestrade.

It was by now past three a.m. I had neither the implements nor the right to begin the postmortem, and surely Holmes realized that I was no more capable of crawling about on my hands and knees scrutinizing cigar ash and footprints than I was of returning the stiffening corpse before me to life. The City Police had no doubt already completed their investigation, it seemed with scant enough results, and a crushing feeling of inferiority swept over me as I wondered whether they had missed the key to the entire matter, and if it were now my responsibility to find the piece of twig, scrap of paper, or smear of mud that would make all clear to Holmes.

Just as Miss Monk and I had resigned ourselves to the conclusion of a long and unspeakable night, we heard the heavy, thudding boots of a running policeman.

"There's been a discovery, Major Smith!" he managed, his chest heaving. "That missing apron piece—a Metropolitan constable encountered it on his beat and told the Leman Street station, who wired Sir Charles Warren. Our man Daniel Halse is on the scene, sir, but the message is on Metropolitan ground. Goulston Street. Sir Charles wants it rubbed out!"

"What message, my good man? Pull yourself together."

"Left by the murderer, sir. He used that scrap of apron to clean his knife. It was found on the ground beneath a note he'd scrawled on the wall."

"By George—we must have a look at it at once."

"Our men in Dorset Street have also found a clue, Major. There is a bloody basin where the killer may well have washed his hands."

"Then I shall accompany you immediately to Dorset Street," replied Major Henry Smith promptly. "Inspector Lestrade, we enter your territory as regards Goulston Street. If you would be so good as to take your companions and see what may be found there, communicating any fresh finds to our man Halse, I should be obliged to you. Dr. Watson, please convey my regards to Mr. Holmes," he added as he turned abruptly and exited the square.

Lestrade's close-set, ferretlike eyes glinted with the light of hope. "I'll be damned if Sir Charles, Commissioner or no, destroys any evidence before I've had a look at it. And you, Doctor, shall take note as well. When he recovers, Sherlock Holmes will want to know of it, whatever it may be."

CHAPTER TEN

The Destruction of the Clue

I experienced a thin thrill of anticipation on our journey as I realized we were now taking the very path used by the killer in his flight. A walk of ten minutes was reduced to a drive of three, and before we knew it we had pulled up to the aptly titled Goulston Street. The culprit had evidently fled up Stoney Lane, crossed Middlesex Street, and proceeded a block up Wentworth Street before ducking into the more secluded Goulston Street.

When we reached the doorway where Detective Daniel Halse stood guard in the starless darkness like a gargoyle over a turret, we met with a curious sight. There stood a Scotland Yard inspector smiling indomitably, holding a large piece of sponge, and there also stood a quantity of both Metropolitan and City constables, saying nothing but clearly awaiting the arrival of a superior to judge a hostile dispute.

"I still say, Inspector Fry," declared Detective Halse, as if repeating the crux of his earlier argument for our fresh ears, "that the idea of destroying evidence against this fiend is contrary to every notion of scientific inquiry."

"And I maintain, Detective Halse," said Inspector Fry doggedly, "that the civil unrest which allowing this message to remain in view would foment is against the principles of conscience and of

British decency. Are you against the principles of British decency, Detective?"

The two appeared as if they were about to come to blows when Inspector Lestrade interposed his lean frame between the antagonists. "For the moment, I shall decide what course we will take in this matter. If you would be so kind as to step aside."

Lestrade lifted the lantern in his hand and directed its beam at the black bricks. The remarkable riddle, chalked upon the wall in an oddly sloping hand, went in this way:

The Juwes are
the men that
will not
be blamed
for nothing

"You see the trouble, Inspector Lestrade—it is Lestrade, is it not?" inquired Inspector Fry placidly. "Riots on our hands, that's what we'll have. I'll not be the one caught in the middle of them. Besides, there is no evidence the killer wrote these words. More likely the hand of an unbalanced youth."

"Where is the piece of apron?" Lestrade questioned a constable.

"It has been taken to the Commercial Street police station, sir. The dark smears upon it followed exactly the pattern produced by wiping a soiled knife blade."

"Then surely he left it deliberately," I remarked to Lestrade. "As in the past he has left no traces, there is every likelihood he dropped that bloody cloth in order to draw attention to this disquieting epigram."

"I'm of your mind, Dr. Watson," Lestrade replied in low tones. "We must prevent them destroying it, if we can."

"I beg your pardon, sir?" demanded Inspector Fry.

"It must be photographed!" Detective Halse shouted. "And the City Police given an opportunity to examine it."

"I have my orders from Sir Charles, sir," said the infuriatingly dignified Inspector Fry.

"Instead, the message might be covered over with a piece of dark cloth," remarked a constable.

"An excellent notion"— Lestrade nodded—"permitting us to preserve a clue."

"Respectfully, I do not think that would be in accordance with Sir Charles's wishes."

"You could take a sponge to the top line only, with no one the wiser for it," said Miss Monk.

"What if," I suggested, "the oddly spelled word 'Juwes' only be erased, and the rest remain?"

"By Jove, the very thing!" cried Lestrade. "Better and better—no danger, then, of the sense of it being glimpsed."

"What if," replied Inspector Fry in the same maddeningly courteous tone, "we were all to construct daisy chains and drape them so as to shield the words from public view?"

"With all respect, sir," snarled Detective Halse, "in another hour it will be light enough to photograph. The sun will begin to rise at any moment. We can cover the bloody thing with whatever you like until then, but I beg of you not to throw such a clue as this away."

"This difficult decision is not mine to make."

"No indeed, it is mine," called a forceful, ringing baritone, and there to my astonishment stood Sir Charles Warren himself, the decorated war veteran of the Royal Engineers and the Colonial Office, who had once attempted to relieve a hero of mine, the matchless General Gordon, when he had been hopelessly outnumbered at Khartoum. He was as methodically dressed as if he had not been awoken in the middle of the night with bitter news, and the determined curve of his high, rounded forehead, the authority of his impeccably combed walrus moustache, and the obdurate resolve behind his monocle led me to believe we were in for trouble.

"I have come from Leman Street police station," he declared, "and

I am displeased with the news I have had from that quarter. You are under orders to destroy this monstrous blot of anti-Semitism before the traffic to Petticoat Lane Market is disturbed by it."

"If you'll pardon my saying so, sir," interjected Inspector Lestrade, whose presence I was beginning to welcome with enthusiastic gratitude, "there are, perhaps, less radical possibilities open to us."

"Less *radical* possibilities? The only radical sentiments being expressed here are written upon that wall and are about to be permanently expunged."

"This detective, sir, has sent for a photographer—"

"To what purpose?"

"That the message might be made available also to the City force, sir."

"I do not care two figs for the photographers of the City of London Police. They do not answer to the Home Office over riots, as I undoubtedly will should that absurd phrase remain."

"Perhaps if we were to cover it, Sir Charles, only for half an hour—"

"I will not be coddled, nor will I be bargained with," the former military commander averred. "What is your name?"

"Detective Inspector Lestrade, Sir Charles."

"Well, Inspector Lestrade, you show an admirable passion for police work. You seem to me to have the very best interests of the populace at heart. You will therefore now take this sponge from your colleague and erase that vile scribbling so that we may return to real detective work."

Inspector Lestrade's lips set into a forbidding line while Detective Halse, rage twisting his knotted brows, slammed his palm against the wall and stepped aside. Lestrade took the damp sponge from Inspector Fry and approached the writing, stopping to shoot me a significant glance.

"No fear, Doctor," Miss Monk whispered, "I've copied it down during all that racket."

I nodded to Lestrade, who then proceeded to erase the curious clue. When finished, he shoved the damp sponge against Inspector Fry's chest and turned to his Commissioner.

"It has been done, as you ordered, Sir Charles."

"You have averted what could have been a powerful spark to the kindling of social unrest. I've business elsewhere. My thanks, gentlemen. As you were." With that, Sir Charles Warren strode off in the direction of the station and the men began to disperse.

Lestrade regarded the blank wall with pained disquiet. "Dr. Watson, Detective Halse, a word with you please."

The three of us strolled toward the waiting cab, Miss Monk trailing three or four feet behind.

"I'm not ashamed to say that was a bad business," began Lestrade, with a dignity I had never before observed in the quick-tempered, rat-like investigator. "Dr. Watson, I expect you to forward copies of that message to both the Metropolitan and the City of London Police."

"It shall be done immediately."

"I had never met Sir Charles, you know," he reflected. "I'm not anxious to repeat the experience—though he is right in that little good it would do us to plunge the entire district into chaos."

"Surely that is not the point," I began angrily, but Lestrade held up a hand.

"I'm no spinner of fanciful theories, Dr. Watson, and there are times when, sharp as he is, I think Mr. Holmes would be as well off in Bedlam as in Baker Street. But I am a believer in facts, and that chalked writing was as sound a fact as I've ever seen. Good night to you, Detective Halse. You'll tell your superiors, no doubt, that we were given no choice."

The City detective, still visibly suppressing his fury, bowed to us and left.

"Lestrade," I ventured, "I cannot tell you how glad I have been of your presence, but I'm afraid we must leave at once. We have a great deal to report to Holmes, and I fear very much for the condition in which we are likely to find him."

"Believe me, Dr. Watson, it has been heavy on my mind. I must return to Dutfield's Yard, but I'll leave you the cab. This night would have gone a sight differently had Mr. Holmes been here to the end. Next time our police commissioner takes it into his head to expunge a clue, I'd give fifty pounds to have Sherlock Holmes in my corner. I should be grateful if you would tell him so." Lestrade tipped his hat to us both and strode off into the first brightening light of dawn.

It was then I noted that Miss Monk had grown singularly pale and drawn. I took her arm.

"Miss Monk, are you quite well?"

"It ain't nothing to speak of, Doctor," she replied. "Queer stroke of luck that led us to be so in the thick of it, but oh, Dr. Watson—did you ever in all your life even think on a deed so horrible as what he's done?" She quickly hid her face in her hands.

"No, I have not," I said quietly. "I feel just as you do, my dear. Get into the cab with me and I shall return you to your lodgings at once. You've found better ones, is that not so?"

"If you could drop me at Great Garden Street, Doctor, I'd be grateful. I've taken rooms there. Mr. Holmes will want to know everything, and make no mistake we'll tell him plain what we saw, but not now. I couldn't rightly bear it now."

I shook my head as I helped her into the four-wheeler, searching for words of comfort, which rose to my lips and died there in mute sympathy. Miss Monk had been out all night in the cold, pursuing a creature whose great impulse was to brutally slay women exactly like her. She buried her head in the lapel of my greatcoat and we spent the short journey in silence. We soon reached her street, and I saw her to the door.

"You require complete rest for the remainder of the day. Come to Baker Street when you are able. I haven't words to express my admiration for your courage, Miss Monk, and I know Holmes would say the same." I left her, returning to the hansom heartsick and defeated as the first true rays of sunlight stole along the cracks of the paving stones.

• • •

I had hardly crossed the three shallow steps leading to our front door, nor breathlessly turned my key in the lock, when the door flew open to reveal Mrs. Hudson's kind, familiar face, spectacles perched upon her head, and oddly done buttons upon her left sleeve.

"Oh, Dr. Watson!" she cried, grasping me by the shoulders. "When I think of what you must have been through! And Mr. Holmes! Seeing him as he was a few hours ago when he arrived here—oh, Dr. Watson, who has done this to him? He wouldn't speak a word on the subject. I've only just finished scrubbing the blood from the kitchen." The brave woman then dissolved into a brief sob of long-suppressed tears.

"Mrs. Hudson, you shall know all about it," I returned swiftly, taking her hand. "But first, tell me, is Holmes in any danger?"

"I can't say, Doctor. I was awoken in the night by a terrible banging. When I saw Mr. Holmes, I thought he had lost his key, but he leaned on the doorframe in such a peculiar way, his arm tied up in black rags, that I knew something was terribly wrong. I let him in at once, but he had hardly walked two steps before he fell against the balustrade and looked up the stairs to your rooms as if they were the side of a mountain. He said, 'Kitchen, Mrs. Hudson, with your permission,' and once inside, he fell straight into a chair. 'Go at once and fetch a doctor,' he said, in that masterful way of his. 'Watson cannot be the only one in the neighbourhood. There is that chap at two twenty-seven—mass of dark hair, boots thrice mended, coming in and out and leaving a trail of iodoform—knock him up, if you will be so kind.' Then he leaned his head back in a kind of faint. I was in such a panic at leaving him that I sent the pageboy instead, and Billy soon enough came back with the fellow. His name is Moore Agar, and he is indeed a doctor. Between them they took Mr. Holmes to his room. Billy has been up and down the stairs four times to fetch the water I heated. But that was hours ago, and Dr. Agar has not come down at all."

I took the seventeen steps up to our sitting room two at a time and found a tall, handsome, round-featured young man with a determined jaw, a generous shock of wavy brown hair, and deeply set, thoughtful brown eyes checking our mantelpiece clock against his watch. He was dressed as a perfect gentleman in dark tweeds, and I noted an elegantly styled bowler hat thrown carelessly upon the settee, but the elbows and knees of his garments had worn nearly through, and the edges of the hat were beginning to fray. He looked up at my hurried entrance.

"Dr. Moore Agar at your service," he said earnestly. "I had the honour of stitching up your friend in the next room. He has lost a considerable amount of blood, I am afraid, but I believe he will come out of it all right."

"Thank God for that." I exhaled in relief, collapsing into the nearest chair. "That is the very first piece of good news I have had this night. Forgive my exhaustion, Dr. Agar, but I have been taxed in every way possible. Mrs. Hudson tells me we are neighbours."

"And so we are! I am quartered a mere two doors down. I am just beginning in practice, which is a black mark against me, but you will corroborate my findings, no doubt, and ensure that all will be well with your friend. You are the celebrated Mr. Holmes's physician, Dr. Watson, no doubt?"

"Merely his biographer. Sherlock Holmes is elaborately uninterested in the state of his own health," I replied, warmly grasping the hand before me.

Dr. Agar laughed. "It is of no surprise to me," he replied. "Men of genius are often cavalier about physical trifles. This injury could hardly be termed trifling, however. No fear of muscular impairment, but the tissue damage is quite extensive and the blood loss, as you know, severe."

"My friend will be very grateful."

"Mr. Holmes has no reason to be. Perhaps when you have both recovered, you can relate to me more of these extraordinary circumstances, but for now I will leave you in peace. I have injected morphine, but if it is convenient to you, Doctor, I'll not leave any of my own supplies behind. I imagine you have access to fresh bandaging and so forth; poverty compels me to be rude. Or practicality has trounced my manners. Whichever it may be, I apologize. A better morning to you, Dr. Watson," the young physician said as he saw himself out and down the stairs.

I made my way quietly into Holmes's bedroom, where I was peered at malevolently from every angle by the images of infamous criminals carelessly tacked to the walls. My friend, though deathly pale, was breathing regularly and at last, blessedly, unconscious. I swung the door to but did not shut it and returned downstairs for a soothing word with Mrs. Hudson. Then finally, retrieving a quilt from my bed and a generous glass of brandy from the sideboard, I made my home on the sofa within easy call and fell asleep just as the sunlight poured over the windowsills and struggled to flood the room in defiance of the closely drawn curtains.

CHAPTER ELEVEN

Mitre Square

When I awoke, I was startled to discover that it was nearly night once more. I sat up groggily and beheld at my feet a tray, laden with a few meats and a cup of cold broth, which did wonders for my state of mind. Supposing my own exhaustion had prompted me to sleep through the day, I at once chastised myself for failing to look in on Holmes. Peering into his chamber, I was comforted by the presence of a candle and another tea tray, partially used, and evidently provided by the conscientious Mrs. Hudson. I made my way upstairs in hopes a wash and change of clothes would restore my energy, but upon my finishing, the dizzy ache in my head revisited me with a vengeance. I tended to Holmes's bandages and then collapsed once more upon the sofa in hopes that we both would be capable of more upon the morrow.

The birds were still singing, but the quality of light told me it was midmorning when my eyes fluttered open for the second time. For a moment I was harrowed by the disoriented dread one experiences when too much has occurred to be immediately recalled, but a minute's further repose brought it all back to the forefront of my mind, and I hastened to Holmes's bedroom.

The sight which greeted me upon my throwing open his door brought a smile of relief to my face. There sat Sherlock Holmes, his

hair all awry, telegrams scattered over his lap, the bed literally covered with newsprint, a cigarette held awkwardly in his left hand as he
attempted to sift through his considerable correspondence.

"Ah, Watson," he saluted me. "Don't bother to knock. Do come
in, my dear fellow."

"My apologies," I laughed. "I had heard rumour you were an
invalid."

"Nonsense. I am a pillar of strength. I am, in strict point of fact,
quite disgusted with myself," he added more quietly—with a tweak of
one eyebrow that told me more than his words of his profound dissatisfaction, "but no matter. Up until this moment, Mrs. Hudson and
Billy brought me everything I required. Now you must sit in that armchair, my boy, and tell me the whole ghastly mess."

I did so, omitting nothing from our universal dismay at his misfortune, to the state of the second girl's ears and the dispute between
our good Lestrade and his own Commissioner. A solid hour must have
passed, Holmes's eyes closed in concentration and my mind straining
for each and every detail, when I arrived at Dr. Moore Agar and my
own homecoming.

"It is unforgivable that we have lost Sunday! The police no doubt
have swept both crime scenes of any useful evidence in my absence,
and this business of the chalked message is altogether tragic. I cannot remember anything at all," Holmes confessed bitterly, "from the
time I alighted the hansom until this morning at around nine o'clock.
Of course I deduced the profession of two twenty-seven Baker Street
months ago, but the business of the summons Mrs. Hudson related to
me is merely a painful blur."

"I was at a continual loss whether to come after you or remain in
the East-end."

"Your sentiments do you credit, as ever, Doctor, but were you not
present, how would you explain to me the seven urgent messages I
have received so far this morning?"

"Seven! I am all attention."

"Let me relate them to you in the order I read them. First, a note from the doughty Inspector Lestrade, with well-wishes, requesting a facsimile of the curious inscription you fought fruitlessly to preserve."

"Miss Monk has given it to me. I shall send copies immediately."

"Next, President George Lusk of the Whitechapel Vigilance Committee, with compliments, informs me he has written the Queen demanding a reward be offered."

"Good heavens! London will be a madhouse."

"My sentiments echo your own. Here we have a very considerate note from Major Henry Smith, who has enclosed the results from the postmortem of the City victim. We shall return to that in a moment. If you would be so kind as to pour me another cup of coffee, my dear fellow, as my usual motility has been greatly hampered by our neighbour two doors down. Much obliged. Fourth, a telegram from brother Mycroft: 'Will visit at earliest possible convenience—great uproar in Whitehall. Mend quickly; your death would be most inconvenient at this time.'"

"I heartily agree."

"Fifth, Miss Monk asks that we wire her a convenient time to meet."

"She has proven herself to be a woman of extraordinary fortitude."

"For which I am exceedingly grateful. Item the sixth, calling card of Mr. Rowland K. Vandervent, who likewise begs an audience. Finally, there is a preposterous missive from a reporter who claims to know more than he should demanding an interview in the interests of public awareness."

"Hardly worthy of your immediate attention."

"I am inclined to be as dismissive, although there is an ominous tone to his wording. See for yourself."

The paper was typewritten on a single sheet of cheap off-white paper, with some dark smudges near the margins.

Mr. Sherlock Holmes,

In the interests of the public and of your own reputation, I strongly suggest you meet me at Simpson's in order to address some serious questions. I shall await you at ten o'clock this evening, alone.

Mr. Leslie Tavistock

I turned the inexplicable summons over in my hands. "Holmes, the author mentions nothing of being a pressman."

"He needn't, for it is all too obvious to any specialist in typewriters. Observe the characteristics of this particular machine. Mr. Tavistock ought to be deeply ashamed, if for nothing else, of the nearly nonexistent tail of the *y*s, the ramshackle upstroke of the *d*s, and fully nine other points indicating nearly continuous wear."

"Surely other professions than journalism are hard on typewriters?"

"None that brings one's fingertips into such intimate congress with cheap newsprint ink. There are several other points I might make, but I fear we must return to the bloody business of Saturday night and leave our mysterious reporter to his own devices. Here is the autopsy report writ brief by Major Smith. Read it aloud, would you, Watson, so that I may be sure of my facts."

"'Upon arrival at Golden Lane, a piece of the deceased's ear fell from her clothing. There were three incisions in the liver of varying size, a stab to the groin, and deep cuts on the womb, colon, lining membrane above the uterus, the pancreas, and the left renal artery. I regret to say that the left kidney was taken entirely out of the body and retained by the killer.' But this is despicable, Holmes!" I exclaimed in disgust. "He has taken another grisly memento."

"I had anticipated as much."

"But Holmes, the kidney is lodged behind several other significant organs, not to mention shielded by a membrane. He must not have feared interruption to have absconded with the kidney of all objects."

"Hum! That is indeed remarkable. Pray continue."

"'The lack of clotting from the abdominal region indicates that she was entirely dead when these acts occurred. Enclosed is a complete list of the deceased's belongings and attire at the time of her death.' It is signed with respects from Major Henry Smith, and with regrets that you could not yourself have been in attendance."

"I can assure the major his regrets are entirely dwarfed by my own." Holmes sighed. "I've made an unspeakable hash of it, I don't mind telling you."

"Are we really no further along?"

"Well, I would hardly say that. We know that this 'Jack the Ripper' letter may well be the work of the killer, for a detail like notched ears is very unlikely to turn up in both jest and in fact. We know that he has an iron nerve to locate and remove a kidney. We know that one effective method of carrying off organs is to cart about an empty parcel, for I have no doubt but that the package I observed under his arm was later used to transport a very sinister object indeed. And I have my reasons for suspecting that this 'Jack the Ripper' has taken a very strong dislike to your humble servant."

"What on earth do you mean?"

"Watson, do you recall the letter I received in March of last year just after we returned from Colwall?"

"After the affair of the Ramsden heirloom? I seem to remember something of the kind."

"I have been looking over the handwriting. Though disguised, I am certain that it was the work of the same man; the hooked end-strokes are indicative, but the pressure on his descending lines concludes the matter. Which means he wrote to me—"

"Before a single murder had been committed!"

"Precisely." Holmes looked pensively at me for a moment. "If you would go so far against your conscience as to prepare a dose of morphine, Doctor, I shouldn't refuse it. I'll do it myself if you prefer, but . . ."

I located his bottle on the mantel amongst a litter of pipe cleaners and reflected, as I was readying my friend's pristine little syringe, upon the oddity of the situation. When I turned back to Holmes, I saw with dismay that he was attempting to extricate himself from the bedclothes with no very great degree of success.

"Holmes, what the devil do you think you are doing?"

"Readying myself to go out," he replied, using the nearest post of the bed to steady himself as he rose.

"Holmes, have you completely taken leave of your senses? You cannot possibly expect—"

"That any evidence will remain to be found?" he lashed out in vexation. "That is one damnable fact, Watson, of which I am all too well aware."

"Your condition is—"

"Of the utmost irrelevance! In any event, I do myself the honour of assuming I shall be accompanied by a skilled physician."

"If you imagine that I have any intention of allowing you to leave these rooms, you are delirious as well as badly injured."

"Watson," he said in another voice entirely. To my immense surprise, it was not a tone I had ever heard from him before. It was far quieter than his usual measured voice, and far more grieved. "I have maneuvered myself into an intolerable position. Five women are dead. Five. Your intentions are commendable, but take a moment to imagine what it would be like for me to receive news of the sixth."

I stared at him, weighing considerations both medical and personal. "Give me your arm," I said at length. The sight of innumerable tiny scars scattered like miniature constellations pained me as it always did, but I made a sincere effort not to show it as I administered the injection.

"Thank you," said he, starting haltingly for his wardrobe. "I will see you downstairs. I advise you to wear your old army coat if you do not wish to look hopelessly out of place."

Hesitantly, I donned an old astrakhan and the heavy coat I had needed so seldom in actual service, and dashed down the stairs to procure a four-wheeler. If Holmes was determined to visit the crime scene, best it be done immediately, for the sake of his health more than of any evidence remaining.

Cabs were plentiful, and Holmes himself was seated on the front steps of 221 when I returned. He wore the loose-fitting attire of a disengaged naval officer, complete with seafaring cap, heavy trousers, a rough work shirt, cravat, and a pea jacket through which he had managed to pass his left arm, the other side draped over his sling.

"You wish to remain anonymous?" I remarked as I helped him into the hansom.

"If there are any neighbours willing to communicate useful gossip, they'll do so far more readily to two half-pay patriots." He added ruefully, "In any event, the garb of the British gentleman is well-nigh impossible to achieve with one arm."

On our route to the East-end, as Holmes appeared to doze and I gazed out the window in uneasy contemplation, I saw that London had changed since I had last set foot out of doors; a veritable snowstorm of papers printed in bold block capitals was pasted to every ready surface. I soon discerned the leaflets were all identical appeals from the Yard to the citizenry, urging the public to come forward with any helpful information.

We had turned north on Duke Street and approached one of the entrances to Mitre Square when the cabbie stopped abruptly and began to grumble sotto voce about "thrill seekers" who evinced "all the human decency of vultures." When he saw the denomination of coin I offered him, he grew more acquiescent, however, and agreed to wait until we had finished in the square.

Sherlock Holmes leaned heavily on his stick as we traversed the long passage, but he scanned the floor and walls of the alley as a hawk seeks prey from on high. Mitre Square, far from being the sordid cul-de-sac my memory had painted it, was an open space, well kept by the City but surrounded by featureless buildings, few of which proved to be tenanted. Those warehouses which were occupied were also guarded, for a small knot of men chatted earnestly where we had viewed the body two nights previous.

"I take it the poor woman was found in that southwest corner?" queried Holmes.

"Yes, the City constable discovered her there. I don't like to think of the condition she was in."

"Very well. I shall search the rest of the square and surrounding passageways first, for it doesn't seem likely we can peruse that area without inciting unwelcome conversation."

I followed the detective as he made an exhaustive study, exiting the square by means of the constrictive Church Passage, which led to Mitre Street, and returning through the one corridor left to be explored, which passed by St. James Place and the Orange Market. Though Holmes had been at work for only perhaps half an hour, the strain of simply remaining upright had already begun to take a visible toll upon his haggard countenance.

"As far as I can make out by memory," said he, "the path I followed after leaving you at Berner Street took me north via Greenfield Street, Fieldgate Street, then Great Garden Street and thus to the small maze surrounding Chicksand Street, which is where I encountered our quarry. I then made my way back to Berner Street, whilst he, inexplicably, proceeded here to a largely emptied commercial district. I imagine he traveled down Old Montague Street, which becomes Wentworth Street, then narrows again into Stoney Lane, which finally led him straight to where we stand. Then, and here we are blessed, for the extraordinary is always of use to the investigator, he did something positively absurd. He killed a woman, then disemboweled her in an open square with three separate entrances and any number of guards within—but we have visitors, Watson. It was only a matter of time. Let me do the talking, if you don't mind."

A middle-aged man with greying muttonchop whiskers, a shabby bowler hat, and the physique of a dray horse approached us, a tentative smile fighting for supremacy with his suspicious and hooded eyes.

"Excuse me, sirs, but I can't help but notice that you've been in this square and out again more times than is natural. I wonder if you might be good enough to say what your business is here."

"Tell me who's asking," my friend replied with a surly glare and, I noted with amusement, a perceptibly Welsh turn of phrase.

The man crossed his powerful arms expectantly. "That's no more than your right, I suppose, though I'm under no obligation to tell you with the Ripper still at large. My name is Samuel Levison, and I'm part of a group organized to keep the peace in these parts. The Whitechapel Vigilance Committee we go by, and if you're reasonable, you'll tell me your business before I call a policeman to do my work for me."

Holmes's eyes lit up eagerly. "I've heard of your men," he cried, "and you're just the help I've been wanting. Yesterday, it was—I'd been to a few more pubs than I should, I don't mind telling you, and close toward morning someone told me I was but a quarter mile from the spot where another poor creature was killed. Sounds absurd in the light of day, but I'd a terrible urge to see the place. I'd hardly entered the square when I heard someone behind me. A rogue and a rascal if I ever saw one, and he flashed a blade, saying he'd have my money or my blood. Well, I've never been one to back down from a fight, so I pulled out my knife, but drink had the better of me and the bloody scoundrel cut me straightaway—here, in the shoulder. By the time I'd dragged myself home, I never realized I'd dropped my pipe in the scuffle. It's been with me for many a voyage, and I wasn't easy in my mind until I'd had a look round. Stem was burnished wood, with designs I'd carved—birds and such."

"Lads?" Mr. Levison called to his companions. "Seen anything on the ground that might belong to this fellow? I am sorry, sir, but like as not someone's pawned it by now."

"Ah, more's the pity. I'd little enough hope as it was." Holmes squinted at the murder site. "You've more important things on your minds than my pipe. The body was in front of those houses?"

"Yes, opposite Church Passage."

"And what did the neighbours hear?"

"Unfortunately, the buildings are unoccupied."

"Ah, that's a shame, it is. Seems an empty enough place, to be sure."

"Kearly and Tonge's Warehouse yonder is guarded by night, and a police constable lives just there, but no one heard a thing."

"Police just on the other side of the square?" Holmes whistled softly. "I might never ha' lost my pipe if I'd known that."

"Don't see how you could have known—not unless you were Sherlock Holmes, that balmy cove."

The men laughed heartily at this incomprehensible jest, and Holmes flashed a ready smile in return. "What, that unofficial 'tec? Don't tell me you know him."

His question provoked another bout of merriment. "Know him!" chuckled Mr. Levison. "That's rich. I think Lusk, our president, knows him, but if he's a careful man, he'll steer clear of Sherlock Holmes. I know I would, if I were him."

Torn between burning curiosity and the sight of a colourless Holmes leaning ever more urgently upon his stick, I ventured, "Hadn't we best return home?"

"Yes indeed, see your friend home, my good man," agreed Mr. Levison genially. "I'm right sorry about your pipe, sir, but you're a good deal too peaked to be out of doors."

"There's days I've felt better, and that's certain," Holmes replied. "My thanks for your help, such as it was."

We slowly, for my friend grew steadily more faint, passed back through the narrowest of the entrances. Holmes made no protestation when I took him firmly by the arm.

"What in the world could that fellow have meant?"

My companion shook his head. "I haven't the first idea," he answered, "but I fear that we shall soon enough find out."

CHAPTER TWELVE

Dark Writings

By the time I got Holmes up the stairs, he was so drained of all energy that I lost no time in administering a fresh injection of morphine before consigning him to his bed. Afterward I felt compelled to clear my thoughts and, with no immediate object in mind, ambled toward Regent's Park where a hailstorm of brown leaves lay strewn over the spacious grounds.

Our visit to Mitre Square appeared only to have raised still more mystifying obstacles. Why should our quarry have killed again when he knew the alarm had been raised? Why should he have done so where at any moment he may have been interrupted from one of three directions? Above all, I dwelt upon the bizarre remarks the committee man had made about my friend. For all the Yard's reticence to consult a self-labeled amateur, there was scarcely a more respected figure in the layman's eye, and with each successive case Sherlock Holmes solved—in the rare instances he received full credit—he was compelled by his natural Bohemian reticence to turn down countless congratulatory invitations proffered by rich and poor alike. What extraordinary rumour could possibly have run him afoul of public opinion?

I must have wandered for an hour, lost in pointless speculation. I had just turned the corner, my steps leading back down Baker Street, when I observed from half a block's distance an angry altercation taking place upon our doorstep.

"It is undoubtedly a sad circumstance which brings harm to the faultless health of the great Mr. Sherlock Holmes," growled Mr. Rowland K. Vandervent, "but I will be damned, my good lady—and I use the word *damned* only in the presence of those it will affect—I will be damned if his condition prevents me from saving his character!"

"Good afternoon, Mr. Vandervent," I said sternly. "I should like to have a word with you in private. Your gross disregard for both courtesy and Holmes's frail state of health has been well noted, I warn you. Mrs. Hudson, I will deal with this person."

Thanked with surreptitious glances of gratitude from both parties (neither of whom, providentially, observed the other), I proceeded with Mr. Vandervent up the stairs. I roused the coals into a blaze as he finished the few laboured steps required to propel him into our sitting room.

"I say, she isn't a distant extraction of any of the Borgias, is she? I've never had such adjectives trowled in heaping mounds upon my person. What I mean to say is, Doctor," continued Vandervent, suddenly lowering his raspy voice and glancing toward Holmes's door, "the gawky fellow isn't about to die on us, is he?"

"By no means!" called the detective's piercing tenor from his bedroom.

"It is common enough knowledge," declared Holmes when we had entered the room and Mr. Vandervent had cast himself into the armchair, "that spoken low tones, provided that the *s* consonant is disguised, are far more easily masked than a whisper."

"So it's true, then?" returned Vandervent, running his hand through his frenzied hair. "You were knocked about by Jack the Ripper?"

"I am at death's door," my friend replied acidly. "Therefore, I beg of you to come to the point."

"I only mean to tell you that I am sorry about the late edition of the *London Chronicle*. I had nothing whatever to say about it."

"How fascinating. I have barely finished the early morning editions. Look it up, would you, Watson?"

I cast about the chaotic room for some moments in search of the periodical in question, finally extracting it from the vortex of newsprint. The article was titled, in the usual gaudy capitals, "A MURDEROUS STRUGGLE," and read as follows:

It has been brought to the attention of this publication that further circumstances pertaining to the infamous double event, which may enhance our knowledge of the killer whose savage acts have brought terror to our streets, have recently come to light. It was not well known before today that Mr. Sherlock Holmes, the eccentric and reclusive consulting detective, was in the area upon the night of the double murder. We have learned that his time was spent in dalliance with a number of ladies of questionable vocation, consorting in the dens of vice so prevalent in those dark streets. It is also evident that it was Mr. Holmes who "discovered" the murder in Dutfield's Yard during its very execution, and that in pursuit of an unknown suspect, he then disappeared during the time the second victim met her own hideous demise. Whether those lost minutes point the finger of suspicion at one of London's most cloistered characters remains to be seen, but it is an established fact that Mr. Holmes returned to the site of the first murder in a state of bloody disarray. In addition, Mr. Holmes arrived without prior summons by the police at the scene of Annie Chapman's brutal slaying three weeks ago, and the peculiar gentleman offered no satisfactory explanation of his being there. To suggest that Mr. Holmes's self-imposed mandate to combat crime in all its forms has taken a turn against the destitute would be the lowest form of conjecture; however, we can state with greater positivity that the unconventional vigilante must be questioned to the closest degree regarding his activities and his strange foreknowledge upon the nights in question.

To my immense surprise, at the conclusion of this trash, Sherlock Holmes threw his head back and laughed heartily in his inner, noiseless fashion until he had entirely exhausted himself.

"I fail to see the humour you have, in your greater wisdom perhaps, detected," remarked Mr. Vandervent.

"As do I, Holmes."

"Oh, come, Watson! Really! It is quite too preposterous."

"It is libelous!"

"It is superb. It clears up a small mystery, for this piece was written by the enigmatic Leslie Tavistock. However, it presents a fresh one, for the article is factually irreproachable. Where could Tavistock have obtained these particulars? Before the press even learned of the first murder, I had been carted off like a sack of oranges and you had left the scene. Do you imagine Miss Monk was interviewed about the events of the evening?"

"It seems very unlikely."

"Or perhaps the regular Yarders spread the word that their peculiar amateur reinforcements frequent pubs of ill repute?"

"Even less probable."

"I don't imagine you've forgone your usual custom of appallingly florid biography and gone straight to the gutter press?"

"You may put the thought from your mind."

"There is something about this article I do not understand," Holmes confessed. "It is peculiarly malignant."

"I don't see anything so peculiar about that. Journalists rarely worry about malignancy," Mr. Vandervent corrected him. "They are far too concerned with selling papers, you see."

"I cannot help but think that the business of journalists is to report the news, and not to sell newspapers," Holmes returned dourly. "Be that as it may, I cannot imagine any newsman would take it upon himself to write such rubbish without cause."

"You have more faith in my industry than do I, perhaps because you have suffered from less prolonged exposure. Nevertheless, you are right in thinking he has a clever source. Apart from your friends and the Yard, who are diligently shutting as many open mouths as they can, it is difficult to know who could have dogged your movements that night. Speaking of your allies, I don't suppose any of them are false?"

"I don't suppose they are," my friend stated flatly.

"Quite right. In that case, I believe we have exhausted the subject of your delightfully rendered portrait in the local press. Consider, then, a postcard we received the morning after. It doesn't make for pleasant reading, but I am clearly no judge as to what will amuse you."

Holmes's face changed swiftly when he viewed the card, betraying his eager interest. After scrutinizing it, front and back, he tossed it to me.

I was not codding dear old Boss when I gave you the tip, youll hear about saucy Jacky s work tomorrow double event this time number one squealed a bit couldnt finish straight off. had not time to get ears for police thanks for keeping last letter back till I got to work again.

Jack the Ripper

"Curiouser and curiouser," mused Holmes. "The hand at first appears to differ, but on closer examination, it is merely very hastily and agitatedly written. What do you intend to do with this beauty?"

"The papers will be falling over each other to publish it. That previous letter has already been printed in facsimile by the *Daily News*. Every man, woman, and child is referring to the mad devil as Jack the Ripper."

"So I observed. What do you hope to accomplish?"

"We shall sell newspapers, no doubt. In addition, I have not despaired that the handwriting may be recognized."

"You have been of immense help."

"Well, it was my duty to warn you and warn you I did. I was also determined to absolve myself of blame, and I congratulate myself on both counts. I shall see myself out, thank you. It would be a waste of ten minutes to accompany me, Dr. Watson. Good day to you both."

Holmes lit a cigarette at the candle by his bedside. He then glanced at me with a shrewd smile. "You see the significance of these taunting missives?"

"Do they furnish any tangible clue?"

"No, but they indicate a trend. In the first case, they are localized; both are postmarked from the East-end, which is further confirmation that our man knows Whitechapel intimately, perhaps lives there. But more interestingly, these letters will accomplish a very specific purpose upon their publication."

"What purpose, Holmes?"

"Terror, my dear fellow. Abject terror. I will be very much mistaken if the colour of this investigation, black as it was before, will not have darkened by this evening."

CHAPTER THIRTEEN

Miss Monk Investigates

I knew better than to think Holmes had been exaggerating for the purpose of effect, and soon word arrived from George Lusk that riots had flamed up in various East-end neighbourhoods, none of them fatal yet each an outpouring of impotent rage. A creeping fear now gripped half of London, and geographically speaking, the hysteria was spreading. Proposed solutions flooded into the Yard from all quarters and included, as I recall, dressing up male constables as female unfortunates, and spreading alarm wires throughout Whitechapel to serve as electric warning buttons.

On the following morning, at Holmes's request, I set out for the East-end to retrieve Miss Monk, whose presence was required in order to lay out our plans. What these plans included the detective omitted to tell me, but I was easier in my mind merely knowing such existed.

When I knocked at the ground-floor room Miss Monk had taken for herself upon her improvement in fortunes, I half expected to find her still the victim of a morose nervous reaction. Instead, when the door opened, I discovered her neatly dressed, with a pot of tea on the stove and the gleam of fresh intelligence in her green eyes. She bid me sit with her usual blend of imitative elegance and habitual coquetry, then threw herself into the other of the two chairs flanking her roughly sanded table.

"And wouldn't you love to hazard at what I've been about." She grinned, pouring me a cup of tea. I assented with an encouraging smile.

"I've been out on the town with the likes of Stephen Dunlevy, that's what."

I started forward in some disquiet. "Miss Monk, surely you know how dangerous his company may be. We were in pursuit of Mr. Dunlevy when last we encountered . . ."

"Jack the Ripper?"

"Indeed, for want of a better name. Miss Monk, I don't like to think what could happen."

"Aye, I know," she assented gravely. "It's a funny thing, Doctor—I thought I'd be too terrified to set foot out of doors again. Spent half of Sunday starting at every creak and whisper. But now even when I am frightened, the devilish thing is that I'm too angry to notice."

She looked me square in the face, and in that moment, Miss Monk and I understood each other. I had traveled through lands that she had never dreamed of in her most elaborate imaginings; she had lived a life whose sufferings I could not begin to guess at. Still, we understood each other, and I knew that whatever was asked of her in our increasingly desperate venture, she would perform to her utmost ability.

"Very well. You saw Stephen Dunlevy. You are far too pleased for the errand to have been fruitless."

"You recall how his landlady let on he goes out more than he should, but never with any woman in mind?"

"Yes, she reassured you of his total devotion."

Miss Monk laughed. "He don't care ha'penny for me, Dr. Watson. But this tale he has, about his mate Johnny Blackstone killing that girl while he stood by—it's true as gospel so far as I can tell, for after we'd had an afternoon pint yesterday, I doubles back and follows him again, and he walks straight over to—"

"I beg your pardon, Miss Monk, but how did you come to meet with him in the first place?"

"We'd arranged it when I left him to find you and Mr. Holmes. How is Mr. Holmes, then, Doctor?" she added apprehensively. I assured her that he would soon mend and requested she go on with her story.

"We'd set on two o'clock to have a glass of beer just round the corner, and after what happened I was fair sick over whether he'd show up at all, for there's something in this business he knows more about than he tells. But at two there he is, sure enough, and when he sees me he smiles right out and calls my name. The Knight's Standard is a right den of fighting cocks now, the ladies all huddled together, whispering over what's to be done—the hop picking's good as spent, so even the judies what prefer to leave the city won't have any means to buy bread and tea. So there they are, wondering just as everyone is what's best to do, though with a sharper interest than most.

"Well, we'd stowed ourselves in a corner when he says, with an odd look, 'I'm glad you're all right, for you must have seen by now what has happened.'

"'The whole Chapel's well-nigh set on fire over it,' I says back.

"He looks at me right close and then asks if I've been putting myself in any sort of careless danger. Of course I says no, though I can't think why he should ask, and we're back to the question of finding Blackstone before the worst happens again. He allows as he's sure he's on the trail. 'But,' he says, 'I'll not hear of you running around in dark alleys and corridors.'

"Now I'm wondering what cause he could have to warn me special when every ladybird this side of the City is shivering at the thought of a knife 'cross her neck, so I asks him whether I've any choice but to take a plunge into the dark every now and then.

"He grabs my hand and then he says, 'Rely on your income from this West-end benefactor. I have high hopes of success, but I beg that you will keep low until I can manage to set things right.'

"Well, that couldn't help but strike me as queer, and when he'd left the pub with a promise to meet again, I duck out of sight into a tobacconist's and wait until he's a fair ways off afore I follow him. He goes into the same crib he'd done before, comes out in fresh togs— not the uniform he sometimes wears, but dressed like a toff—and then sets off again. I follows at a safe distance until he turns into a passage what leads to a few rookeries. I waits a good piece before dogging him down the corridor, and when I does I've a story to tell him about knowing he's after another woman if my luck runs out and he spies me. When I reach the end of it, I watch as he goes into a set of digs there on the ground floor.

"I figure the chances a window or a door is open enough for me to hear are long odds considering the London particulars* we've had of late, but I creeps up to the house to be certain. And when I does, I hear something, so I duck around the side. Would you believe it— the window's clear cracked and all broken at one edge, as half of them are thereabouts, not covered by anything more'n a scrap of paper, and if I sets my ear to the broken part careful enough, I can hear every blooming word.

"'You are certain he stayed here for the duration of his leave?' Dunlevy asks.

"'Oh, yes,' says a woman's voice. 'It was but a few days shy of the Bank Holiday and both my daughters away with their aunt in Yorkshire. Naturally I hadn't the heart to leave the attic room empty when I knew there'd be visitors to the city, and soldiers on leave.'

"'Indeed not. But the day after the holiday, he disappeared without warning?'

"'It was the strangest thing,' says she. 'My Joseph is naught but ten, and that Blackstone swore he would show him the right way around a pistol the next morning. Then we come to find he was clean gone. Though he did leave his money all laid out on the table there. It's a shame he left no trace of himself, for as you know he's a charming fellow and was very well spoken to the children.'

---

* Heavy, polluted fog.

"'Quite so, ma'am. If I should discover his whereabouts soon, I shall be glad to give him your regards.'

"And on they go, but I've heard a fair piece and've always had rum enough luck without tempting it, so I legs it back here. I thought best to leave all to Mr. Holmes."

"Undoubtedly, Miss Monk!" I affirmed. "Back to Baker Street and Holmes will sort this out. Stephen Dunlevy was right about one thing—we must exercise all necessary caution."

Holmes was awake when we arrived but still ashen of countenance, leaning heavily against the sitting room mantelpiece in his shirt-sleeves and mouse-coloured dressing gown. He had swept all objects from the ledge and replaced them with a hastily sketched map of Whitechapel covered in scrawled markings and obscure street references. Its legibility was not aided by the fact that my friend was right-handed, and unable to make use of that particular limb. Disheveled as he was, staring fixedly at a jumble of erratically scribbled byways, he could as easily have been an escapee from an asylum as the final court of appeal in criminal detection.

"Miss Monk, where does Stephen Dunlevy keep his pocket hand-kerchief?"

"In the lining of his coat, if I recall."

"Hum. I thought as much."

She was staring at my friend despondently. "Lor', Mr. Holmes, I knew you was bad off that night from the doctor's dinner jacket, but to see you like this—"

"You have been considering going into business, I see."

"How do you know that?" she gasped.

"The same process which informs me you got very drunk recently and have a young female acquaintance, possibly a neighbour, whose happiness is of some import to you."

"Of all the rotten cheek," cried Miss Monk, her chin up and her eyes blazing. "You'll talk that way to the carpet if you like, for I'll be damned if I stay to hear it."

As she made her way to the door, Holmes, employing perhaps the last of his resources, leapt after her, catching her gently and easily by the wrist. "My sincerest apologies, Miss Monk. Dr. Watson will tell you that my powers have not the charm of tact to recommend them. Pray sit down."

Miss Monk peered suspiciously at Holmes, but her temper waned as quickly as it had sparked. "Well, then. I'll not say you were wrong, just a mite . . . *forward*. I'm that glad to see you alive, at any rate. There, I oughtn't to have flared out so, but I thought the whole thing a slum."

"My dear Miss Monk, I would never dream of using trickery to gain special knowledge," sighed Holmes as he made his laborious way toward the settee, lying down and passing his operative hand through his hair. "Though you are not the first to think so, and if I am lucky you shall not be the last."

"How d'ye do it, then?"

He leaned his head back, shutting his eyes. "That you are thinking of going into business is obvious from the four separate varieties of rag doll peeping at various angles from your pockets. Impoverished mothers make them, leaving it to their young offspring to hawk the wares. If you can provide materials with your new capital, you may well manage to ease the lives of all your acquaintances, at least those with rudimentary sewing skills."

"What of the girl?"

"You've already examined and formed an opinion of each design. They are now well within your income, have no actual value, and yet you carry them about with you. They are a gift. What sort of person would be likely to enjoy such a gesture?"

"They are for Emily. She's not yet four, poor little mite. And?" Miss Monk prompted, not willing to employ any further syllables.

Holmes winced gallantly and replied, "Your shoes."

"My shoes?"

"The right shoe."

She looked down quickly and glanced up again at Holmes.

"You recently replaced your worn boots with new ones, and thus when I last saw you, they were relatively unmarked. There is now a significant marring of the leather, in more than one place, on the right boot: you have been kicking something heavy, and quite violently." The clinical tone in an instant gave way to easy charm. "I congratulate you that, while it is the nature of drink to compel one to lash out physically, it is the nature of a thinking person to confine her rage to one foot."

"I'll own up to it. Saturday night gave me a turn, and I was finding a bit of ease at the bottom of a glass."

"My dear Miss Monk, I cannot tell you how—"

"Oh, bollocks to you both! I've had my fit, don't you see, and all that's left is a scuffed boot, and what's a scuffed boot to the likes of us?" she cried, and sat quite naturally on our sitting room floor, Indian-style, next to Holmes's head. "So what are we to do?"

"Wait a moment." He laughed. "I have not all my data about me. You continue to meet with Private Dunlevy, do you not?"

"How the devil did you—"

"You do, then."

"Well, yes."

"Then if you would be so kind as to make me aware of any recent developments."

Miss Monk did so, omitting nothing she had told me, although her narrative had smoothed through repetition.

"There it is, Mr. Holmes," she concluded at length. "What am I to do with the blighter?"

Holmes considered briefly. "Have you any objection to continuing in his company?"

"No objection, save that I know what I'm in for."

My friend rose with an effort and crossed the room. "Nothing perilous, I assure you, provided you keep to public areas and take no risks once the sun has set. Carry this somewhere about your person— disguised, mind." He produced from a drawer in his desk a small collapsible blade and tossed it to Miss Monk.

"Bloody hell," she muttered, then remembered herself and replied, "Right then. I'm to gad about with Dunlevy looking for staring, mad soldiers, eyes glazed over and trousers covered with dried blood, and report back to you, shall I?"

"If you would be so kind. Dr. Watson and I can cover most lines of inquiry, but it is essential that someone remain in the field."

"Seems best, with Blackstone on the lam," she returned lightly. "Hope we find him soon, at any rate. Wouldn't want to wander the Chapel with Dunlevy wi'out a specific agenda. Poor lad might get the wrong idea."

"By the way, Miss Monk, do any of your companions, in your experience, carry pieces of chalk about with them?"

"Chalk? Like what that batty message about Jews was written with?" She reflected. "The girls I know might carry a stub of pencil, but it's long odds. Half of them wouldn't know the use of it. Chalk would be used to mark lengths, I suppose—a bolt of cloth, maybe, or a piece of lumber?"

"One more thing, Miss Monk," Holmes added as she made her way to the door. "I discovered a stalk of grapes near the dead woman. If you would be so good as to look further into the matter, I should be grateful."

"What sort were they?"

"The stem was consistent with black grapes."

"There ain't but a few merchants in that area who'd be selling black grapes. I'll ferret 'em out, never fear."

"Thank you, Miss Monk. Please be careful."

"That I'll be, make no mistake," she called over her shoulder, already halfway down the stairs. "I may work for you, Mr. Holmes, but I'm not entirely daft just yet."

I closed the door and turned on Holmes as he lit a cigarette. "Are you quite certain you know what you're doing, old man?"

"You mean to ask whether I am certain I know what Miss Monk is doing," he shot back, and I was once more made aware of just how excruciating it must have been for a man of his active nature to find himself restrained by his own body. "For the moment, I am rendered physically inert. Do you imagine it possible for you to saunter into Dunlevy's digs and demand Blackstone's whereabouts? She'll play the game nearly as well as I could, and one mystery, at any rate, will be solved."

"The whereabouts of Johnny Blackstone?"

"The intentions of Stephen Dunlevy."

"Did we not venture into Whitechapel in the first place to safeguard Miss Monk from him?" I queried bluntly.

"I know far more now than I did then."

"That is very gratifying. But in any event, there are key discrepancies surrounding the Tabram murder. What if the thread leads us nowhere?"

"You regard the matter from the wrong angle entirely, which hardly surprises me," Holmes replied caustically. "This thread cannot lead us nowhere, for wherever it leads, it exposes more of Stephen Dunlevy, who interests me in no small degree. And now, Watson, you are going out."

"Indeed?"

"You are to meet with one Leslie Tavistock, in the offices of the *London Chronicle*, that shining beacon of ethical journalism. You've an appointment at half past three. And on your way back from Fleet Street, do stop by our tobacconist's for a fresh supply of cigars," he finished, nudging their receptacle with his foot. "The coal scuttle, I am afraid, has run entirely dry."

CHAPTER FOURTEEN
Lestrade Questions a Suspect

I was made to wait for a quarter of an hour after my designated time in the bustling antechamber of the *London Chronicle*'s headquarters, rife with shabbily appointed journalists and far too short on both light and coal. From the moment I stepped into the office of Mr. Leslie Tavistock, I knew that the experience would not be a pleasant one. The man himself sat in his desk chair with a mixture of calm insouciance and deliberate irony on his clean-shaven, calculating features. I introduced myself, and before I could utter another word, he had half raised his hand in a gesture of amiable protest.

"Now, Dr. Watson," he began, "I have no intention of insulting either your natural loyalties or your good sense by asking what brought you here. That story is already the talk of London, and I've followed up with my original source in order to furnish the public with a few more salient details regarding the unconventional Mr. Sherlock Holmes. But in the meanwhile, I am delighted you are here. I should like to pose a few questions, if you don't mind."

"I most certainly do. Mr. Holmes has already been shamefully abused at your hands, and my sole mission this afternoon is to determine whether you would prefer to reveal your source or defend yourself against charges of libel."

If Tavistock was surprised at my words, I had hardly expected myself to engage in a frontal attack so suddenly and so soon. He arched his brows as if greatly disappointed.

"I have my doubts as to whether that course of action would be open to you, Dr. Watson. Mr. Holmes must resign himself to the glare of public scrutiny if he wishes to continue his extraordinary exploits. The facts behind my article are entirely true; if the particulars are couched in terms you dislike, perhaps you would care to clarify Mr. Holmes's uncanny prescience."

"Sherlock Holmes has always been the scourge of the criminal element. His motives in this case should be abundantly clear," I seethed.

"Does he hold himself responsible for apprehending the culprit?" Tavistock asked casually.

"He intends to do everything in his power to—"

"How does Mr. Holmes feel about having failed to capture the Ripper that night, possibly enabling further killings?"

"Come, sir! This is really intolerable."

"My apologies. Dr. Watson, considering the terrible mutilations that have become the overriding feature of these crimes, is it possible that a doctor could be responsible for them?"

"I beg your pardon?"

"I mean to say, speaking theoretically, as a medical man, you would no doubt be aided in such work by your own skills and training?"

"The Ripper's 'skills' are the merest butchery. As for my own medical abilities, I have so far confined their use to healing the sick, both practically and theoretically," I replied coldly.

"No doubt, no doubt. Now, Mr. Holmes, though not a doctor, possesses a very workable knowledge of anatomy. I believe I may have read so in your own account of his work—that very engaging piece in *Beeton's Christmas Annual* from last year. In your opinion—"

"In my opinion, you are guilty of the most outrageous perversion of the truth I have been witness to in the public print," I exclaimed, rising from my chair. "Rest assured that you will hear from us again."

"I have no doubt of it, Dr. Watson," Leslie Tavistock smiled. "May I offer you and Mr. Holmes the same assurances? A very pleasant day to you, I am sure."

The sun had etched long shadows across the brick walls of Baker Street before I arrived home once more. Though the crimes of Jack the Ripper had sickened me beyond words, this lesser grievance infuriated me in a much more personal fashion. My arrival in our sitting room must have been more violent than I intended, for Holmes, who appeared to have appointed the sofa as his base of operations, awoke immediately upon my entering.

"I see you've exchanged pleasantries with Mr. Tavistock," he commented wryly.

"I am sorry, Holmes. You ought to be resting. How do you feel?"

"A bit like the misaligned pistons of an unbalanced steam engine."

"I shall prepare some morphia if you like."

"Dear me. Best have it out at once, Watson." He smiled. "It can't be as bad as all that."

I related, with a deal of disgust, the conversation which had passed between me and Mr. Tavistock. When I concluded, Holmes's piercing gaze settled into an unfocused reverie as he reached for a cigarette. It was near ten minutes before he spoke again.

"It is the most confounded nuisance to be unable to light one's pipe effectively."

I could not help but smile at this non sequitur. "It is always trying to lose the use of an appendage, however temporary. I ought to know."

"I have my pick of annoyances today, to be sure. Tavistock mentioned nothing that would give away a clue as to his source?"

"Nothing."

"And he does not appear to you to be approaching a state of penitence."

"That would be understating the matter."

Our conversation was interrupted by the distant ringing of the bell. "That will be Lestrade." Holmes sighed. "He purports to inform us of the new victims' identities and habits. His call, however, was preceded by a reply-paid telegram asking after my degree of fragility, a kindly meant sentiment that you will agree does not bode well."

Lestrade's dogged, inquisitive features had sagged into an expression of resigned determination to see a bad business through no matter the cost. His persistence was an admirable distinction but, I now realized, a trying one as well, for he seemed not to have slept more than six hours since I had left him in Whitechapel.

"Mr. Holmes," he said, a smile briefly quickening his features, "I've brought respects from your friends at the Yard."

"Convey them my thanks, if you would. Have a seat, and regale the infirmatory with tales of the latest victims."

"Well," Lestrade declared, drawing out his official notebook, "we do at least know who they are. Though that does us no positive good at all. First victim of the evening was one Elizabeth Stride, a widow who may or may not have had children."

I nodded. "The unhappy woman dressed all in black. By chance, we caught a glimpse of her in the neighbourhood just before she was killed."

"Did you?" Lestrade responded eagerly. "Who was she with?"

I had already shrugged my shoulders in apology for my imperfect memory when Holmes replied, "A brewer who resides in Norwood with his domineering mother and has absolutely no bearing upon the matter at hand."

"Ah. In any case, her habitual mourning was supposedly for her husband and children, all of whom she claims died in the *Princess Alice* steamship collision, but we have records stating her husband, John Thomas Stride, died from heart disease in the Poplar Union Workhouse; she must have meant to elicit more charity by it. She was born in Sweden, according to her local Swedish Church clergy, who tell us she was a wreck of a woman and lucky to have lived so long. We've also interviewed her live-in man, Michael Kidney. He apparently used to padlock her indoors."

"Charming. Well, it explains the duplicate key."

"As for the other poor creature," continued Lestrade with a shudder, "her name was Catherine Eddowes, and she had three children by a man named Thomas Conway of the Eighteenth Royal Irish. No suggestion they were ever married. Just wandered from place to place hawking gallows ballads. She lost touch with him and the children after she took to drink, and had recently returned from hop picking with her man when she was killed. Name of John Kelly—took us a mite longer to find him than we would have liked, but they were sleeping separate on the night of the murder. Hadn't the money for a double bed."

"Lestrade, does any evidence lead you to believe that Eddowes and Stride, or Nichols and Chapman, or any combination of the victims accrued thus far were known to each other?"

The inspector shook his head. "Seemed an idea worth having to me as well, Mr. Holmes—they all may have been members of some heathen cult, killed for betraying the society, that sort of trash. Better still, that they'd all an old flame in common. Nothing of the sort has turned up. They may have spoken to each other, but they were none of them friends."

"Then I am very much afraid I may be right," Holmes murmured.

"Right about what, Mr. Holmes?"

"I must iron out my theory a bit more, Lestrade, and then you can be sure to learn of it. Have you any leads in your own investigation?"

"Well, Mr. Holmes, the truth is, there are some at the Yard who think we do have a lead," Lestrade admitted.

"You're of the opinion they are mistaken, then?" my friend suggested knowingly.

"Well, I am. Mind you, it's not many of the inspectors, but they're a damn sight louder than they ought to be."

"You have my full attention."

"Bearing in mind, Mr. Holmes, in my opinion, this line of questioning is the worst sort of wild goose chase."

"So this fruitless lead is emphatically not one that you espouse?" the detective prodded with uncharacteristic good humour. "Perhaps your firsthand experience of the case sets you against it. Or perhaps even your own special knowledge of the suspect."

"Well, I don't intend to waste my time on it, that I'll swear to. So have Gregson, Jones, Wickliff, Lanner, Hawes . . ."

"I should be delighted to look into the matter in your stead," my friend offered.

"I don't intend to squander your energies, Mr. Holmes."

"Nonsense," he scoffed. "I suspect I could confine my inquiries to this very room."

Lestrade looked as if our carpet had been pulled out from under him, but he soon rallied and clenched his fists in frustration. "Confound it all, I'm that ashamed to tell you, but you've brought it on yourself, haven't you?" cried the exhausted inspector. "All this 'you will find the gun in the third stable on the left,' and 'the letter was posted by a man in a wideawake hat.' Knowing things you shouldn't, appearing magically at crime scenes! Bennett was in my office this morning and said it's a miracle this hasn't happened before."

"Ha! You do suspect me, then! This really is most gratifying."

"Mr. Holmes, I assure you—"

"No, please, I shall just sketch the outline of this little theory for the sake of argument," announced Holmes with an air of exaggerated deliberation. "So, to retrace my own steps, the night of Bank Holiday, I stabbed Martha Tabram thirty-nine times in a mad frenzy. Dr. Watson may assert that I passed a quiet evening restringing the bow for my fiddle, but—"

"I never said—"

"When you knocked me up the morning after the Nichols killing, did I betray myself with any suspicious behaviour?"

"Mr. Holmes—"

"I am just working out how I managed to kill Elizabeth Stride moments before I discovered her body," he continued ruthlessly. "But if the Doctor lied about my activities the night of Bank Holiday, why should he not do so again? I really must apologize to you, my dear Watson, for ever having asked you to maintain this vile charade. After killing Stride, I dashed off to the City to slay Eddowes, then returned to the scene of my earlier crime covered in her blood. What could be simpler?"

"Now, see here," cried the red-faced inspector. "I've not come here in person to present you with all the evidence we've gathered because I think you've anything to do with the matter! Your character was never even questioned before that wretched article turned everything on end yesterday. We've been hung out to dry in the press, and there's one or two who had a dark laugh that you'd been put to it as well. Soon enough, some of our number started asking awkward questions about the article's contents, and there you are."

"Men have been hanged for less, that I'll grant you."

Lestrade calmed somewhat when he saw that Holmes was more amused than outraged. "Very good, then, if I could just take your statement back with me to the Yard, we'll avert some unpleasantness. Just the bit before I arrived, if you please."

"Dr. Watson and I happened upon a woman who appeared only very recently to have died. We commenced a search for the culprit and all too quickly found him."

"I see," said the inspector, jotting down notes. "Time?"

"Close upon one in the morning."

"There was a constable we encountered who was privy to the whole story," I interjected. "Constable Lamb, I believe."

"Yes, well," replied Lestrade sheepishly, "we have his report. But as he arrived after Mr. Holmes disappeared, I've volunteered to get the story from your own lips. I turned up soon after you came back, Mr. Holmes, and saw you enter the cab. You proceeded directly to London Hospital?"

"No, I returned here."

The inspector looked crestfallen. "Did you?"

"What difference can it make?"

"Oh, none, none. Save that . . . well, a particularly idiotic suggestion was made that once you departed in the cab, Mr. Holmes, you wrote the chalked lines in Goulston Street."

Holmes and I must have looked as stunned as we felt, for the inspector hastened to assure us, "The timing of such a caper would be extremely difficult, but you see how I am obliged to set the record straight."

"The handwriting was as unlike Holmes's as I can possibly imagine," said I, growing angry in spite of myself.

"I know that, don't I? I saw it. But as you'll recall, Doctor, there's nothing left for a comparative sample. And taken in conjunction with the equally wild idea that the blood was not his own . . ."

"If my own word is not good enough for the Yard, you need only apply to a Dr. Moore Agar of two twenty-seven Baker Street to confirm whose blood it was!"

"Or have a look for yourself," Holmes added merrily. "Watson? Have you any medical objection?" Throwing his tie to the ground, he undid the first two buttons of his shirtfront.

"Heavens no, no, thank you, I have quite enough material," said the inspector in an agony of professional embarrassment.

"Good evening, then, Lestrade. A pleasure to see you," tossed Holmes over his shoulder as he strode toward his room.

"There is just one more thing, Mr. Holmes! Gregson and Lanner wanted me to tell you that it may be best not to be seen in Whitechapel for some short time—until after all this ugliness is cleared up."

"They are far more likely to encounter me in Whitechapel with greater and greater frequency, until such time as one or all of us put a stop to this Jack the Ripper's reign of terror," replied my fellow lodger, leaning defiantly against his doorframe.

I imagined our colleague would take umbrage with my companion's declaration. However, once more I had underestimated Inspector Lestrade, and to my regret, for I realized suddenly that Holmes had no better friend in all Scotland Yard. Far from appearing surprised, he only smiled with wearied satisfaction.

"Oh, I've no doubt of that, Mr. Holmes. Not a doubt in the world. But I was bound to tell you, wasn't I? Mend well. Good day to you, Dr. Watson."

CHAPTER FIFTEEN

The London Monster

Holmes remained in his room for some time after Lestrade had made his way out. The sun had set entirely when he emerged, asking, "Care to pay a call guaranteed to be more civil than your earlier endeavour?"

"I am at your service, Holmes."

"Then help me into my coat and we shall settle a problem that has been plaguing my mind."

"Certainly. Where are we going?"

"To consult a specialist."

"A specialist?" I repeated in surprise. "But you are the world's foremost specialist in crime detection."

"I do not dispute it," he replied smoothly. "We shall consult a specialist in another field entirely."

"But are you strong enough for a journey tonight?"

Holmes tucked one of his commonplace books under his good arm with a slightly puckish smile. "I appreciate your solicitude, Doctor. However, in this instance, I fear it is misplaced."

Once out of doors in the bracing cold, Holmes turned and proceeded down Baker Street. He had passed two houses when he stopped abruptly. "If you wouldn't mind ringing the bell, Watson. You are better acquainted with the fellow than I, I'm afraid."

Suppressing a smile, I did as he asked. We had not long to wait before the door flew open to reveal Dr. Moore Agar with a pair of not unbecoming spectacles perched on his nose.

"Oh, I say!" he exclaimed delightedly. "I thought you a client, but this is even more gratifying."

He escorted us into a cheerful, well-appointed chamber with a striped Venetian carpet on the floor, an economical fire in the grate, and more bookshelves than there were bare walls. Dr. Agar insisted that Holmes take the entire settee, deposited me graciously in an armchair, then stood before the fireplace in unabashed pleasure.

"Your uncle is a kind gentleman to have set you up in practice," said Holmes.

"Is he, now!" Our host laughed, clapping his hands silently in approval. "I had hardly ventured to hope for a demonstration. If I were a less thoughtful man, I might have guessed that I mentioned my Uncle Augustus to you on Saturday night—or was it Sunday morning? But I did no such thing, and you must trot out your reasoning before a devoted admirer."

Holmes smiled ruefully. "You may be amused to learn that I cannot recall the smallest detail of your visit."

"My apologies, Mr. Holmes. Dr. Moore Agar, at your service," he replied, extending his left hand to shake my friend's unharmed limb. "Now, how did you deduce that Uncle Augustus financed this operation?"

"Certain indications suggest that you are forced to employ economy in your practice. However, your library is extensive, a few of your books quite rare, and your rooms well appointed. You have a benefactor, but not one from whom you receive regular sustenance. A single endowment, then, from a party whose fortunes do not permit more frequent aid. In my experience, the only folk in this world who donate large sums without fortunes to back them are close relatives. The box photograph on the mantel clearly depicts your own parents, who are dressed very simply. An unlikely source, then, for setting a young doctor up in practice. However, I observe a framed document behind your desk certifying one Dr. Augustus Agar a licensed physician. Your uncle, upon his retirement from practice, made you a gift of monies and, I daresay, a significant portion of his library. His medical license you retain as a keepsake."

"It is marvelous! But how did you know Augustus Agar was my uncle and not my grandfather?"

"The date on the certificate, not to mention the typeface and the colour of the paper, rather precludes that notion."

Dr. Agar shot me an appreciative glance. "I admit that I wondered whether your account of Mr. Holmes had embellished his powers, but I am now prepared to believe Mr. Holmes a genius, and yourself a man of unimpeachable honesty."

"It is merely a matter of drawing inferences based on the visible data," Holmes demurred with his usual withdrawn composure, but I could see he was flattered by the young doctor's approval.

"Tush! There is nothing 'mere' about it. You are a pioneer in your field, a characteristic I wholeheartedly admire. I am also guilty of a unique course of study, which you have noted has not yet made my fortune."

"You are engaged in an unusual branch of medicine, then?" I queried.

"And not a very popular one, I am afraid," he smiled. "We tend to run the gamut from pathological anatomy to mesmerism, with all manner of phrenology, craniometry, and neurology thrown in. I am a psychologist."

"Are you indeed?" I exclaimed.

"I studied in Paris for a year under Charcot at the Salpêtrière Hospital.* If Uncle Augustus had possessed the funds, he would certainly

---

* Jean-Martin Charcot was a French neurologist whose work in the fields of hypnosis and hysteria broke new ground in the burgeoning field of psychology. Sigmund Freud studied under him in 1885.

have set me up in Cavendish Square, and my expertise would thus be certified geographically. I am afraid Baker Street is the revered locus of criminal detection, not of the cure of mental disease. At present I subsist on referrals: the nervous, the hypochondriacal, and the merely sick. And of course, the occasional stabbing comes my way."

"Yes, well," coughed Holmes, "as it happens that is just the matter in which I require your assistance."

"That is wonderful news!" Dr. Agar grinned. "I was burning with curiosity, but as a gentleman, I could hardly ask. What sort of assistance may I render?"

"Dr. Watson's Medical Directory informed me you were a specialist in nervous disorders, and a glance at your shelves tells me you may be just the expert I require. *Textbook of Brain Disorders, Mental Pathology and Therapeutics, Psychopathia Sexualis**—if you are the doctor your library proclaims, you could be of the greatest use."

Holmes related briefly the circumstances which led to his grisly introduction to Dr. Agar. When he finished, the doctor nodded with an expression of deepest interest.

"I have, of course, followed the Ripper's crimes very closely. I had an inkling from the press reports that it was his work I stitched up the other night. But let me understand you, sir—do you seek aid that is in some way psychological?"

"I do," confirmed Holmes. "I am a consulting detective, Dr. Agar, and as such many branches of study come within my sphere, the majority of which deal with gathering and interpreting hard evidence. However, I believe the Ripper may be a variety of criminal I have never before pursued, and one against whom hard evidence is of alarmingly little use. My practice is based upon the fact that, although a given crime may appear unique, to the connoisseur of criminal history, it nearly always follows an established pattern. In this case, the

---

* Penned by Carl Wernicke, Wilhelm Griesinger, and Richard von Krafft-Ebing, respectively.

template was so very rare that it took me some time to identify it. But since the events of the thirtieth, I begin to know this fellow better. The double murder eroded his mask in a profound fashion. It appears we must understand that slaying these women is a pleasure second only to afterwards ripping them to pieces."

I felt a growing revulsion at the conversation, but Dr. Agar appeared profoundly intrigued. "He seeks out women who have wronged him and enacts these terrible crimes out of sheer hatred?" I questioned.

Holmes shook his head. "I do not believe he knows them. It is my working hypothesis that this man kills perfect strangers. In fact, I have been led to believe that we are on the trail of a complete madman who is for all appearances an ordinary person."

I stared at him aghast. "I could well believe that the fiend is mad," I protested, "but what you suggest is impossible. There must be another motive behind the deaths of these women. The mad do not walk among the sane unremarked."

"Do they not?" he queried, one brow tilted toward the ceiling.

"No," I insisted irritably. "The merely eccentric are as sane as you or I, but as for a man who butchers the most pitiable of our populace without reason or foreknowledge—can you seriously believe such malice could go about the business of day-to-day life without exciting alarm?"

"Do not ask me. That is what I wish to inquire of Dr. Agar," Holmes replied, turning the force of his steely gaze upon the psychologist standing before the dwindling fire. "Is it possible, in your professional opinion, for a madman to enact a faultless pretense of rational humanity?"

Dr. Agar moved to his bookshelf and selected a slim volume. "I begin to guess at your meaning, Mr. Holmes. You refer to the London Monster."

Holmes swiftly indicated a passage from his commonplace book. "I refer not only to the London Monster, although he plays a telling role. Nearly a century ago—April seventeen eighty-eight, London: first appearance of the London 'Monster.' Approximately fifty women knifed on the streets between the years of eighty-eight and ninety. Suspect never caught. Mark that, Watson. Moving to the Continent; Innsbruck, eighteen twenty-eight: multiple women approached and stabbed with a common pocketknife. Case never closed. Bremen, eighteen eighty: a hairdresser slashed the breasts of no fewer than thirty-five women in broad daylight before he was apprehended. All are examples of what I believe could be termed a deeply morbid erotic mania."

"Your chain of reasoning is rather terrifying, sir," said Dr. Agar.

"What chain of reasoning, Holmes?" I questioned apprehensively.

"If I can discover a link connecting the victims—shared knowledge of a secret is an excellent example—the hypothesis will, blessedly, shatter," he returned. "But I have repeated to myself *Cui bono?* until I can feel the words burned upon my brain, and the only answer is *No one.* For now, it is clear that any man committing so many *motiveless* crimes must necessarily be mad. And yet, in order to continue freely committing them . . ."

"The culprit cannot have appeared to be mad," finished Dr. Agar.

"So I put it to you, Dr. Agar," Holmes concluded grimly. "Is such a thing possible?"

"It is a very difficult question to answer with any degree of assurance," he replied carefully. "After all, is mental illness a sickness of the soul, degeneracy of stock, or a defect of the brain? What you propose is an entirely new form of madness—a monomania lurking beneath a rational mind, aiding itself and disguising itself. Your idea comes closer to the classical definition of pure malevolence than any maniac who lashes out with a frenzied knife. You speak of a complete moral degeneracy, assisted by an affable exterior and a shrewd intelligence."

"Precisely," said Sherlock Holmes.

"I'm afraid I think it entirely possible," Dr. Agar replied.

"Then there is nothing for it," said my friend. "My thanks for your assistance. If you will excuse me, I have a deal of work ahead of me. Payment for your past services is there, on the table."

Dr. Agar quickly attempted to return the notes. "Mr. Holmes, as your neighbour, I would not dream of exacting payment over an emergency."

"Then consider it a consulting fee," my friend smiled. "This way, Watson. We'll not intrude further upon Dr. Agar's time."

"Thank you, Mr. Holmes," said the affable young fellow at the door. "If you should feel the need to intrude again, I beg that you will not hesitate! I treated three patients this afternoon—two for insomnia, and one for an ill-disguised preoccupation with opiates. Your visit has quite redeemed the day."*

We waved to Dr. Agar and strolled the few steps back to our own door.

"You appear disturbed, Dr. Watson," Holmes remarked.

"I cannot readily believe such men exist outside the realm of fiction designed to horrify the reader," I admitted, casting about for my key.

"It is difficult to fathom, I know, for I required weeks to even consider such a nightmare possible."

"And you are sure our man is of a kind?" I persisted as we made our way up the stairs.

"I have no doubt of it."

"I cannot begin to think what steps you will take. It is a monster you describe, Holmes."

"He is neither a monster nor a beast, but something far more dangerous. I fear that men, when possessed of both utter depravity and absolute conviction, are far more deadly than either. And I begin to fear that such men are nearly impossible to find. But I'll do it, Watson. I shall have him. I swear to you it shall be done." Holmes nodded a good night and then, without another word, vanished into the confines of his room.

---

* It is gratifying to note that Dr. Watson is able to describe him in "The Adventure of the Devil's Foot" (dated 1897) as "Dr. Moore Agar, of Harley Street," suggesting his practice later met with considerable success.

CHAPTER SIXTEEN

The Problem of Whitechapel

The following morning, I descended from my bedroom to discover Holmes had already finished his breakfast. He had then, I gathered, occupied himself by amassing all our cushions, piling them beneath the settee, supplying himself with an unholy reserve of cigarettes, and then draping himself on the floor with all the incense-shrouded dignity of a heathen god. My greeting went unanswered, so between the hours of eight and nine I devoured an egg and several rashers of bacon over a slow perusal of the *Times* and *Pall Mall*.

"A word with you, Watson, if you can spare the time," Holmes called out as he discarded the stub of a cigarette in a teacup situated within easy reach.

"Certainly, Holmes." I quit the breakfast table and, selecting a cigar from the coal scuttle, settled myself in my armchair.

"I shan't tax your patience for longer than is necessary, but it is the curse of the solo investigator that he has no confederate to bend an ear when a problem grows too unwieldy for private conjecture. You have surely realized that our case proceeds upon three lines. The primary—and may I say least fruitful—investigation is that surrounding the Ripper's actual crimes, which have afforded us shockingly little physical evidence. Although our conference with Dr. Agar last night aids us in a general sense, our quarry still has allowed us no details which could possibly lead to a residence, name, or arrest. The next line of inquiry concerns the proposition that Jack the Ripper, who-ever he may be, takes a deal of pleasure in tormenting us. This idea is based on the letter I had in February of last year. It seems he takes nearly as much pleasure in penning taunting notes as he does in com-mitting horrific murders; however, this thirst for correspondence may well prove very dangerous for him, for the slightest physical clue could point to a place of origin and thus prove his ultimate undoing. Am I clear thus far?"

"Perfectly."

"Finally there is the matter of the Martha Tabram murder."

"You still believe it to have been the work of the Ripper."

"I do indeed, but there is another puzzle tied to Tabram's stabbing, and that is this abstruse tale of Stephen Dunlevy and Johnny Blackstone. Miss Monk had barely been in our employ a week when a strange man approached her claiming to know all about Tabram's death. Granted, Whitechapel is not a large district, although it is densely populated, and thus it is perfectly possible that she should have instantly met a man connected to the Ripper. But is it probable?"

"How do you mean?"

"Is it not odd that within a few days of our forging an associa-tion, Miss Monk should discover a colossal lead quite by accident? The circumstance grows even more inexplicable when one takes into account the source, Mr. Dunlevy himself. I must confess to you that our glimpse of him in the pub that terrible night was not the first time I laid eyes on the man, but it has taken me days to place where I'd seen him before. I saw him the very day we met Miss Monk, as we exited Lambeth Workhouse."

My mouth fell open at this revelation. "You are certain?"

"Entirely. Yet another reason, you see, for Miss Monk to keep a close watch on the fellow."

Though I had often noted the peculiarly scientific way in which Holmes at times directed people like pieces on a chessboard, custom

had not inured me to it. I shrugged coldly, exasperated by his glibness. "Perhaps Dunlevy and Miss Monk are engaged in a conspiracy
against you."

My friend only smiled. "You imagine I had not considered that
alternative. Rest assured, Miss Monk is not in his employ, or she was
not when I engaged her assistance."

"Barring any personal bias from the question, how can you be
sure?"

"Because of the scuffed new boots which caused such a fracas last
night."

"I do not understand."

"Her old men's boots had two small symmetrical holes just in the
instep where the foot breaks the arch, an almost unbearable condition at this time of year when the wet and the cold are conjoined
against one. And yet she did not, for two weeks after I had been paying her, purchase new boots. No, she presumed I was joking when I
took her on as a colleague, and she clearly had no competing source
of income from Dunlevy. She imagined if I came to my senses and cut
off her payments, she would still be ahead by a pound or two, which
is enough to keep out of the workhouse."

At that moment we detected a slow, lumbering tread upon the
staircase. The door swung open to admit the enormous personage of
Mycroft Holmes, the elder brother of the great detective, whose high
position in government office was as unknown to the public as it was
vital to the realm. While his formidable acumen could hardly be exaggerated, neither could his martial adherence to habit, which made
sightings of him outside the vicinity of Whitehall, his own lodgings in
Pall Mall, or the Diogenes Club exceptional indeed. I at once offered
him a chair, but he stood peering down at his brother upon the floor
from his own formidable height with profound concern and displea-
sure mixed in his cutting grey eyes.

"I was most unpleasantly alarmed about you Sunday when a circulatory from the highest levels was posted directly to my home,"

Mycroft Holmes announced. "I trust he will come to no lasting harm?" The latter query was addressed to me, and I shook my head. "Well then, Sherlock, what the devil have you been playing at? You have been pursuing the Whitechapel killer in an egregiously foolhardy manner."

"Do sit down, brother Mycroft, you'll exhaust yourself. You are already exhausting me," my friend replied, both amused and annoyed by his sibling. "As it happens, we came upon the murder scene entirely by accident."

Mycroft Holmes accepted the chair grudgingly, his eyes focused as always upon some vacant middle ground, a gaze which in both men looked like distraction and was in fact the most powerful con- centration of thought. "I had wondered. Clever of you to pursue him unarmed, in the dark. I suppose you continued the chase even after the first time you collapsed."

I must have looked confused at this remark, for Holmes, with a satirical flourish, pushed up his cuff and further exposed the opposite wrist, which, I had not even noticed, had been more than once bruised and scraped in a fall. "I thought to limit his future activities, but as you can see, rather the opposite has occurred," he said to his brother.

"My dear boy, you must take this matter more seriously, really you must."

Holmes's mouth twitched impatiently. "Mycroft, if you imply that I consider the gruesome murders of five helpless women a frivolous concern—"

"You deliberately misunderstand me." Mycroft's expression was as fond as his tone was dry. "It is of immense practical interest, not to mention of course immense sentimental interest to your only sibling, that you leave off rushing single-handedly after dangerous madmen. More is at stake here than has been made clear to you. Whitechapel is a very minor fraction of a vast metropolis, but the effect these crimes are having on the entire nation . . . Sherlock, surely you see the con- sequences of failure?"

"An ever-increasing number of ritually disemboweled prostitutes."

"Your morbidity is misplaced," the elder Holmes sniffed. "Did you see the report on the double murder in the *Star?*"

"I looked over it. They are calling for the dismissal of Sir Charles Warren."

"Occasionally those zealots hit near to the mark of public opinion. Whitechapel will smash the Empire, they say—a hyperbolic slander, but one which worries us exceedingly. Though I know it doesn't interest you in the slightest, my boy, the problem of Whitechapel is being amplified to symbolize the problems of an entire nation. Even as we pray for progress, we are beset by anarchists and agitators."

"Surely a dilemma more worthy of your attentions than of mine," my friend observed. "I do not pretend to be the incarnate central clearinghouse of the British government."

Mycroft Holmes merely pursed his lips sternly. "You would be shocked, perhaps, to learn of the woes currently assailing Her Majesty from all sides. I am not at liberty to discuss such matters with you, but perhaps you will do me the honour of trusting me. It all looks very bad, Sherlock, and getting worse all the time. The question of Irish autonomy alone has so splintered Parliament that this madman at large among the destitute could plausibly fuel incendiary actions rather than incendiary words. And now I hear rumours that a provocative message was scrawled upon a wall directly implicating the Jews."

"I heard the same rumour," Holmes drawled. "Your Sir Charles erased it, you see."

Mycroft sighed with an expression of sorely tried patience. "Can you imagine I do not appreciate your frustration? Perhaps you will be more disposed to consider the political side of this affair when I say that though I have been most anxious to call upon you, I was also asked to do so by an individual whose importance can hardly be exaggerated."

Holmes's eyes softened, but his brow lifted quizzically. "My dear brother, what do you wish me to say? I can offer you nothing but assurances."

"On the contrary, you can answer key questions. Mr. George Lusk has sent a petition to Her Highness directly, asking that a reward be offered."

"Yes, he has an excellent grasp of the concept of chain of command."

"I should like to hear your thoughts."

My friend shook his head decisively. "No. The game would hardly be worth the candle: to say nothing of the official force, who are already in it to their necks, I should be required to sift through great masses of useless detritus."

"We are in agreement, then. No reward. What other forms of assistance would prove functional?"

Holmes drew a deep breath. "I need unquestioned access to the evidence held by the City Police and the Yard, no matter what the *London Chronicle* is inclined to print about me."

"I shall ensure the fact."

"I need an increase in Whitechapel patrols and a guarantee that they will be manned by competent men."

"I'd already anticipated that requirement. The new men were diverted from other districts yesterday. You've glanced into the history of the London Monster, I imagine?"

"My dear Mycroft, what a very novel idea."

"Have you any further needs?"

Holmes looked suddenly very weary. "I need time. If that is all, Mycroft, I wish you good afternoon. I must resume my threads of inquiry."

My friend's elder brother heaved his considerable frame out of our chair. "Sherlock, I know very well that our respective fortes are at cross-purposes. You revel in the minutiae, and I, the macrocosm. You reason backward from the smallest details, while I predict the great events which arise from the soil of the trivial. I rely now entirely upon your own specialty; be active, Sherlock. Come to me immediately if you find yourself in need of aid."

"You may report back to that gracious personage that I will shirk at nothing to stop this man."

"Indeed, Sherlock, well said. And nor will I. Once you have a case, I shall see to the rest. Mend quickly; I am pleased beyond words you aren't lying dead in a ditch somewhere."

"My thanks. I quite share your view on that point."

"Farewell, then."

I saw Mycroft Holmes out. As he stepped from our dwelling onto the street, he turned and grasped my arm with one of his sizeable hands. "Look out for him, Doctor," he said. "I am dismayed to see my younger brother embroiled in this wretched business, but he can leave no stone unturned. He must act, and act quickly! We all of us depend upon it."

As his portly yet erect frame lumbered its slow way down Baker Street toward the neighbouring Dorset Street cab stand, I stood for a moment to breathe in the crisp draughts of the autumn afternoon. Mycroft's exhortation had lifted my spirits more than any false assurances could have done. My friend possessed remarkable powers of recovery when his mind was set upon it; the same man who had lain ill with nervous prostration for over a month following an arduous case would stop at nothing whilst in the midst of one. I silently vowed that when Sherlock Holmes set himself once more in the path of Jack the Ripper, I would be there beside him.

CHAPTER SEVENTEEN

A Man in a Uniform

Close upon four o'clock the following afternoon Mrs. Hudson appeared at the door.

"Miss Monk is here to see you, Mr. Holmes. She's brought a man with her as well."

"Capital, Mrs. Hudson. Send them up!" With a display of energy that surprised me, Holmes leapt to his feet. "We progress, Watson, despite the odds. Miss Monk, how are you?"

She must have taken the stairs at a run, for we heard the slower steps of her companion still plodding upward. "I've brought him!" she whispered excitedly. "I've followed the grape trail ever since you put me onto it, and strike me dead if I haven't found him. Took a shilling's worth of persuading to do it, but he came round in the end."

The man who walked through our doorway was grey and wizened with a prominent nose, deeply furrowed jowls, and an expression of permanent chagrin which we soon learned could shift toward resigned disappointment or deep disdain depending upon immediate circumstance. Just then, his watery blue eyes and obstinate chin seemed to indicate he was even more displeased than was usual.

"My name is Sherlock Holmes," said my friend cordially, "and this is my associate, Dr. Watson."

"I know who you are," he snapped, "and I know what you do. What

I don't know is why I've been dragged across London to assure you of it."

"This is Mr. Matthew Packer," Miss Monk put in hastily. "He lives across town, right enough, on Berner Street as it happens. Mr. Packer's digs have a very nice front window to 'em and he uses it to sell fruit out of. Don't you, Mr. Packer?"

"Never said I didn't."

"Mr. Packer, I am very gratified to meet you," said Sherlock Holmes enthusiastically. "Would you care to sit here, by the fire? I find the cold troubling at this time of year, and your rheumatism must render it well-nigh intolerable."

"Never said I had rheumatism. But I don't care how you know it, so don't bother to tell me," said Mr. Packer as he made his way to the basket chair.

"Dr. Watson," said Holmes, hiding his amusement beneath a mask of perfect innocence, "have I not heard you remark that there is nothing better for rheumatism than a glass of good brandy?"

"Many times, Holmes. Might I pour you a glass, Mr. Packer?"

"You might, and then this young woman can start explaining why an old man can't be left in peace to tend his shop of a morning."

"You see, Mr. Holmes," obliged Miss Monk, "there I was walking down Berner Street when I sees that Mr. Packer has a mess of fresh black grapes in his window. Then it comes to me—that poor woman what was killed near the club! She'd a stalk of grapes in her hand. The same kind you sell, Mr. Packer," she added with a radiant smile. "Black ones, if you please."

"I suppose you mean to say I killed her," sneered the old scoundrel, "and you have brought me to these gentlemen for interrogation."

"Nothing of the kind, Mr. Packer," said Holmes sadly. "In fact, I'm afraid it's nearly an impossibility that you may have seen anything of use."

"That's what I've been telling this young madwoman."

"Our only hope of success would hinge upon your having seen

a woman with a flower pinned to her jacket on that evening. Red, backed by white fern. But as I've said, the situation is quite hopeless. This Jack the Ripper seems far too clever for any of us."

Mr. Packer's face shifted slowly from contempt to condescension as he sipped his brandy. "You say a red flower pinned to her jacket?"

"Yes," sighed the detective. "Futile, is it not?"

"Funny thing is, I do seem to recall having sold grapes to a woman with a red flower; the man paid for them, of course, but she was standing there the whole time."

"Really? That is a strange coincidence. I don't suppose you recall anything else about her face or figure?"

"She was a sad sort," Mr. Packer replied, "fair-complected, dark curls, and dressed all in black—black skirt, black bonnet, dark bodice—with fur trim on her jacket."

"Indeed?" Holmes replied coolly.

"She had what I might call a strong face—square-jawed, high cheekbones, if you understand me."

"And her companion?" Holmes appeared as nonchalant as ever, but I could see he was entirely engrossed.

"He was a plain fellow—not thin, of healthy build, I suppose, average height. Simply dressed, like a clerk or a shopkeeper. And he wore no gloves. A frock coat and hat but no gloves."

"You interest me exceedingly, Mr. Packer." My friend's zeal was beginning to infuse his tone. "And his face? Can you describe the fellow?"

"He had regular features, clean shaven, wearing a cloth hat. I'd seen him before, to be sure."

At this Holmes could not help but start forward. "Oh, indeed?"

"Must live in the neighbourhood, for he seemed that familiar."

"Can you recall where you had seen this man before?"

"Somewhere about. Could have been in a pub or a market."

"But you have no clue as to his occupation or place of residence?"

"Said I'd seen him before. Didn't say I knew him, did I?"

Holmes clenched his fist in frustration, but his voice remained even. "What time do you imagine you sold them the grapes, Mr. Packer?"

He shrugged. "Close to twelve, I should think."

"And have you spoken to the police?"

"The police!" he snorted. "Why should I speak to the police, I wonder. They spoke to me right enough—knocking on my door, demanding to know what I'd seen. Well, of course I told them what I'd seen when I closed shop at twelve thirty. Nothing."

"You failed to tell the police you had seen anything suspicious?"

"I saw nothing suspicious. What in God's name is suspicious about folk buying a bunch of grapes?"

"Quite so. Well, Mr. Packer, is there anything further you can recall about that night or the man you saw?"

"Well, for the sake of the brandy I'll say one more word on the matter," Mr. Packer deigned to reply. "This gloveless fellow, then— they may not have been friends, but the woman had seen him before, sure as I had."

"Why do you say that, Mr. Packer?" asked Sherlock Holmes.

"He's buying the grapes when the woman says, 'They won't be missing you tonight, then?' 'Who won't be?' he says, irritated. 'Oh, I see the game,' she says. 'Right enough, no offense meant. But you do look splendid in those clothes.'"

"She mentioned his attire specifically?"

"That she did," Mr. Packer assented, downing what remained in his prodigious snifter. "Can't think why, for it was nothing to speak of. Shame she seemed so taken with the bloke, if what you say is true. An hour later she was dead."

Holmes made no reply, for his mind was elsewhere. Our guest made a studied harrumphing sound and arose. "In any event . . . that's all the time I'm willing to give you gents, for I don't see what good any of you have done so far."

"I beg your pardon, sir!" I exclaimed.

"Five women dead and not a suspect to show for it. I don't call that a good average, do you? Well, let me know if anything comes of it, which doesn't seem likely. I'm off to my shop."

"Excuse me, Mr. Packer, but I do not believe you can deny us your company just yet," said Holmes casually.

"Is that so? And why in hell not, might I ask?"

Holmes advanced toward the elderly man and stopped at a distance of no more than two inches. My friend towered over the irascible fellow, and even pallid of complexion with one arm in a sling, his physical presence was daunting in the extreme.

"While I am grateful for your call, you may well have heard that Scotland Yard is also pursuing Jack the Ripper. And while you may not have realized you possessed valuable evidence before, I believe we have now made your position abundantly clear to you. You and I will take the cab downstairs directly to Scotland Yard, where you will tell a friend of mine named Lestrade precisely what you told me. Do not for one instant make me suspect, Mr. Packer, that you have the Ripper's best interests at heart."

Mr. Packer struggled in vain for a reply.

"Very well, then. Watson, my coat, if you would be so kind. Miss Monk, I have greater respect for your time than to suggest you accompany us. You have my warmest congratulations for having managed to get him here in the first place. After you, Mr. Packer."

So began a day that proved enjoyable for us only insofar as it was inconvenient for Mr. Packer. Lestrade eagerly took his statement, then required him to visit the morgue, where he was shown the face not of Elizabeth Stride but of Catherine Eddowes. At his adamant refusal that he had ever laid eyes on her, he was shown Stride, whom he confidently proclaimed to be the girl with the grapes. Evening drew near when, as a reward for his correct identification, he was taken to see Sir Charles Warren and deliver his statement a third time, at which point we gratefully took our leave of him.

"I must say," I remarked to Holmes in the cab, "your tip to Miss Monk bore fruit swiftly enough."

"It narrows our search exceedingly," drawled my friend, as he leaned his head against the side of the hansom. "Rather than exert ourselves looking for a five-foot-seven Englishman, we shall set our caps for a five-foot-seven Englishman who is 'clean shaven,' with 'regular features.'"

"Then what have we gained by Packer's account of the man?"

"Well, two features of interest present themselves."

"The lack of gloves?"

"Excellent, Watson. The glove detail narrows the social sphere, for I do not believe the lowest denizens of Whitechapel would balk at eating with gloves on. And the other feature?"

"That Packer recognized him from the neighbourhood?"

"My dear chap, surely we have not so soon forgotten that this man's intimate knowledge of Whitechapel hints at his having been there before."

"The odd remark about his clothing, then, if Packer heard aright?"

"Watson, you really do improve all the time. Yes, that remark interests me exceedingly. The fellow seemed to think that by wearing the apparel of any innocuous Britisher, he would be less recognizable."

"I cannot imagine why."

"Can you not?" he smiled. "You surprise me, my boy. Let us take you as an example. Now, I could, if pressed, deliver a very detailed description of you indeed. However, if you were a stranger to me and I had not made it part of my vocation to recognize traits of human physiognomy, I might describe you as having 'regular features,' for what does the term mean if not symmetrical and evenly spaced?"

"I fail to see what I have to do with Stride's recognition of the man who would be the death of her."

Holmes laughed suddenly. "Very well—your friends in London, they are astute enough to recognize you when they see you. If you were dressed to the nines as a common seaman, would they still recognize you?"

"I imagine so."

"Do you? Dressed as you are now, if you were suddenly trans-ported to India, would your acquaintances there know you?"

"Some would. Possibly some would not," I granted.

"Why not?"

"My appearance has changed significantly. And I was always in uniform."

"And there I rest my case," said Holmes with his habitual far-off expression. "If your colleagues might not know you in a crowd when out of uniform, why should a stranger be expected to do so? There are people in this world with an eye for faces, and Elizabeth Stride was one of them. While most would not have recognized an unex-ceptional face without its context, she did so. Sadly, she would not live to tell of it."

"You are right, Holmes," I reflected, my friend's idea now perfectly clear to me. "The garb of a civilian would significantly alter a man's appearance if he were perpetually in uniform."

"I am currently devoting all my resources to locating this Johnny Blackstone," Holmes replied. "Whenever we do so, it will be not a moment too soon."

CHAPTER EIGHTEEN

Trophies

The morning of October sixth dawned misty and chill, with tendrils of fog making concerted, sinuous efforts to penetrate chimneys and windowsills. It must have been nearing eight o'clock when a brief knock at my door presaged the appearance of Sherlock Holmes with a cup of coffee in his hand.

"What is it, old man?"

"Elizabeth Stride is to be buried today," said he. "I wondered if you might wish to accompany me to the East London Cemetery, for I gather she'll be interred there."

"I can be ready in ten minutes."

"Good. The cab will be here at half past the hour."

I finished dressing quickly and after a brief repast mounted a four-wheeler with Holmes. "What do you expect to happen?" I inquired.

"I haven't the slightest notion, my dear Watson, which I might add is why we are going."

"But you suspect something?"

"Look—there is the new vegetarian restaurant on the corner of Marylebone Road. I have heard it said that the spread of such establishments is due in large part to the influence of our Indian colonies, but the practice has a long British history as well. Sir Isaac Newton harboured an absolute horror of black pudding."

I stifled my curiosity, for nothing on earth would induce Sherlock Holmes to proffer information against his will. We huddled into our overcoats, Holmes deep in his own thoughts and I cursing the thin walls of cabs, which were never adequate proof against the weather. As I watched the streets fade into one another, the damp frost soon set my leg to aching.

An iron fence separated the East London Cemetery from the road, and beyond the gate an expanse of grass edged with alder, field maple, and young wych elm trees shimmered in the mist. The fog hung in the air like a spectral presence, and I drew my muffler tighter about my throat.

"Holmes, where is the chapel?"

"There is none. This cemetery is hardly more than fifteen years old. It was built by professionals of the district to provide a resting place for locals. One of the overlooked consequences of a city doubling in size to four million in fifty years' time, Watson—what to do with the dead?"

A group of ten or so men and women waited near a low shack, clustered around a cart holding a long bundle wrapped in torn burlap. A police constable stood a few yards away observing the Dr. Moore Agar proceedings.

"Good morning, Officer," Holmes greeted him. "What brings you here?"

"Good morning, sir. Inspector Lestrade thought it best that there be a representative of the force at the victims' ceremonies, sir."

"Very thorough of him too."

"Yes, Mr. Holmes, though whether it's to keep the peace or simply be visible to the public I can't say."

Holmes laughed. "I suppose even the appearance of work is of some use to the Yard."

"Well, I didn't say that, sir," the constable replied judiciously, adjusting his collar. "But there are expectations of us, if you take my meaning."

"Assuredly. The chaplain has arrived. Shall we join the procession?"

An employee of the parish, with the white collar of a clergyman just discernible beneath his overcoat, came puffing up the path toward the cart, slick-faced and scowling darkly. We followed the body at some little distance, far enough to avoid comment but close enough that I could catch some of the mutterings of the other mourners. I doubted not that Holmes, with his keener senses, heard still more.

"Not much of a showing, eh?" said a blond fellow who even from yards away smelled sharply of fish.

"You know well enough Liz had no kin," replied a young female in a black straw hat and shawl.

"Never had much of anything. She always was unlucky."

"At least she weren't slit up like the other girl. I call that lucky enough."

"If I could take my mind off who'll it be next for half a moment, I might sleep again," came a gentler voice, heavy with tears. "A rat jumped out of an alley last night and set me screaming."

"Not I. You won't catch me in a dark corner with the Knife on the loose."

"Aye, true enough for today, but tomorrow you'll be wanting a drop of gin, and then where'll I find you?"

"Back of White's Row with her skirts over her head."

"Leave off Molly, Michael."

"He's right enough. Molly no more than any of us can keep off the streets for long."

We arrived at an area which more closely resembled the efforts of enormous moles than of any gravediggers. Much of the earth was overturned, the freshest of it piled next to a hole in the ground six feet long and six feet deep. I could see no monuments of any kind, and the scene reminded me piteously of the hasty burials I had witnessed all too often in the war.

"This is it, then, Hawkes?" asked the chaplain.

"Here she'll stay," growled the undertaker. "Number one-five-five-oh-nine."

The chaplain lost no time in beginning a rapid recitation of the prayer for the dead while Hawkes and one of the male attendants lifted the shrouded body from the cart and dropped it in the grave.

"Elizabeth Stride was penniless," my friend remarked quietly, "and the cost of her burial thus deferred to the parish. Still, it is heartless to think that a fellow creature who had already suffered so cruelly should end like this."

Shortly thereafter the mourners, such as they were, began to disperse. Soon the only one remaining was a rust-haired, dark-eyed man of middle age, who had all along appeared more enraged than grieved by the proceedings. At length he picked up a stone and hurled it in the direction of Hawkes the undertaker, crying out, "That woman was like a queen to me, and here you're shoveling dirt as if she weren't of no more consequence than a dead dog to throw in the river!"

"Move along, you," Hawkes barked in return. "I'm doing my duty, for I'm paid for naught else. Bury her yourself if you've a mind to."

Passing the three of us, the wild-eyed fellow caught sight of the constable's rounded helmet and striped armlet* and slowed ominously, cursing under his breath, "If I'd been a bluebottle patrolling the Chapel that night, I'd lose no time killing myself for the shame."

"You'd best shove off, mister," answered the officer. "We all of us do what we can."

"Take a knife to your own worthless throat, and lose no time about it!"

"I'll have you for public drunkenness, if you insist."

"Better still, find him as killed Liz or you can go to the devil," the man sneered.

"And who might you be, sir?" queried Sherlock Holmes.

---

* The striped band around a policeman's cuff was for many years a mark of identification.

"Michael Kidney," said he, drawing himself up with an effort, for balance seemed to be largely eluding him. "I was her man, and I mean to find her killer while you pigs sniff about in the mud."

"Ah, he of the padlock," Holmes commented. "Tell me, did she come to love you after you imprisoned her, or before?"

"You sly devil!" Kidney snarled. "It was only when she drank she ever thought to leave me. Who are you, then, and how do you come to know aught of it?"

"My name is Sherlock Holmes."

"Oh, Sherlock Holmes, are you?" This information incensed Kidney all the more. "From what I hear of you, you're as likely as anyone to be the Ripper yourself."

"So I have been given to understand."

"What in blazes do you think you're doing at her funeral, then?"

"Nothing which need trouble you. Take my advice, Kidney, and keep out of it."

"Come to see what you've accomplished, have you?" he screamed. "Gloating over her funeral, before God and all who loved her!"

Kidney, disheveled and frantic, swung a fist at Holmes, but the blow was easily avoided by my friend, who sidestepped deftly. I dived to restrain Kidney's arms, and the officer stepped in close with his truncheon under the ruffian's nose.

"If you make so much as another sound," he said, "I will see to it your own mother won't recognize you. Now come with us, and remember—one more word gives me license to do as I please with you."

Between us we dragged the struggling brute down to the street, where good fortune blessed us with a second constable patrolling his beat. I left Kidney in their capable hands and returned to where Holmes remained on the grass, adjusting his sling thoughtfully, rotating his arm in tiny circles.

"That constable appears to have a temper," I remarked.

"No more than Kidney," Holmes returned wryly. "I am grateful that he made no serious effort to fight me. He would have gotten hurt."

"You are a formidable match even when injured, and I am very pleased to point out that you are looking less injured every hour. But Holmes, I must know—did you find what you expected?"

"I suppose dragging you out in this wretched damp demands some degree of explanation," he conceded as we walked back to the open road. "Strange as it may sound, I had the same idea as Michael Kidney. These murders—their glory in excess, their delight in the press— have been conducted in the most public manner conceivable. And what could possibly be more public than the victim's funeral?"

"Surely the Ripper would be very obtuse to show himself."

"I did not imagine that he would, but there is a streak of vanity about his correspondence which had invested me with hope. He is growing ever more sure of himself and will soon enough bluff his way into a corner," my friend predicted. "I only hope he will do so before anyone else is killed."

The following Monday, I returned from a game of billiards at my club to a curious spectacle in our sitting room: Holmes was stretched out upon the settee, feet propped on its arm and head supported by pillows, with the neck of his violin wedged into the cloth of his sling and his left hand scraping the eerie, vagrant chords which I associated with his most melancholic levels of meditation. I made for my bedroom, for his more abstract musical efforts were keenly disquieting to my nerves and I did not relish hearing them played left-handed, but he stopped me with a question.

"And how is your friend Thurston?"

I turned to regard Holmes with an expression of utter bewilderment. "How did you know I was with Thurston?"

He set his violin on the side table and sat up. "You are returning from your club. You declared in some distress eight months ago that you did not intend to play billiards at your club anymore because your opponents were no match for your prowess. You and I have only played once, but I found you to be a daunting challenger indeed. A month later, you returned from your club only to confess that you had been bested at billiards by a new member named Thurston. Since that happy occurrence, you have neither given up billiards nor bemoaned your proficiency."

"But how did you know I was playing billiards?"

"You lunched at home, and there was no rugby match yesterday to discuss with your fellow sportsmen."

"Am I so transparent?"

"Only to the trained observer."

"You have been devoting the afternoon to music, I see."

"So it may appear, but in fact I attended Catherine Eddowes's funeral. It was a study in opposites, my dear fellow; there were close to five hundred people in attendance if my calculations were correct. Polished elm coffin, open glass conveyance, mourners lining the streets—immigrant, native, rich, poor, East-enders, West-enders, both the City and the Metropolitan police forces, and one independent consulting detective. You see what a little money can get you."

I had hardly begun to reply when a brusque knock at the door interrupted me and Mrs. Hudson entered with a small package.

"This was left for you downstairs by the last post, Mr. Holmes. I thought to bring it up with your tea, but the cat won't leave off the thing, as it's been smeared with Lord only knows what."

Holmes, with all the galvanized energy of a hound on the scent, leapt to his feet and hurried to his chemical table, where a powerful lamp provided better light for study. He had regained most of the strength in his right appendage and could make use of the hand while keeping the arm motionless. Slitting the paper with a jackknife, he commenced to peruse the wooden box itself with his lens. Uttering a few murmured exclamations of satisfaction, and twice removing with tweezers small indications and placing them carefully on a piece of blotting paper, he worked until I was beside myself with curiosity over what the box actually contained.

At long last, he cautiously lifted the lid. Revealing only straw, he grasped a slender letter opener and with it disturbed the hay until he finally revealed a glint of silver.

Holmes frowned, covered his hand with a cloth, and reaching in, pulled out a small cigarette case. Turning it over under the light, he looked for traces on the surface of the metal, but the case appeared to be brand new. He tossed it on the table and drew out a short note, which read:

Mr. Holmes,

Sorry you've lost your case I didn't have time to monnogram this one but you could always have it done of corse if you wish it. I have a deal of work to do sharpening knifes (they have been so much used of late) but never to busy to wish you and your frend the Doctor my compliments. Back to it then, I hope you don't think I've finished, for there's much work still to be done.

Yours,

Jack

PS—Had no time to clean my knife between you and the last girl what a jolly red mix that was.

I stared in disbelief. "You lost your cigarette case when you encountered the killer! I distinctly remember your asking for mine."

He did not answer.

"My dear Holmes, this is nonsensical. Why should he return you a cigarette case which is not your own?"

"Page torn from a notebook, standard pocket size, black ink, and with any luck . . ." He fetched a piece of graphite and ran it lightly over the surface of the note. He gave a cry of delight when a pattern revealed itself.

"What have you found?"

He passed me the scrap of notepaper with evident satisfaction and I squinted at the writing he had revealed:

245	— 11:30
1054	— 14
765	— 12:15

"Holmes, what could this possibly mean?"

"It is an impression from the previous page. I confess I make nothing of it at the moment, but that surely does not mean it is beyond human imagining. No finger marks on either the paper or the case, which is very odd indeed and means he either wore gloves from its moment of purchase or else wiped it carefully. He is a collector of trophies, fair-haired, meticulous, and I doubt not that there is a stable very close to where he lives, for this hay has recently been in the immediate vicinity of a horse. He was in attendance at Catherine Eddowes's interment today. And when he packed this box," Holmes concluded triumphantly, "he was smoking a cigarette. The ash has fallen in the hay." Scraping a flake of fluffy white ash onto another piece of blotting paper with the jackknife, the detective held up his lens.

"I can see the hair follicle you discovered between the paper and the box, and the postmark no doubt revealed he was in the vicinity of the funeral. What of the ash? Will it help us to trace him?"

My friend dropped his lens in deepest disdain, crushed the paper in his fist, and drew a very deep, very slow breath before replying, "Afraid not, my boy."

"But why not?" I inquired hesitantly.

"Because he was smoking my cigarettes."

I could think of no reply to this repulsive piece of information and thus attempted none.

"As for the trophies," Holmes continued more evenly, lifting a glass test tube from its holder and switching on his blue-flamed burner, "he has amassed, so far as we know, a womb and a kidney. And now my cigarette case is certainly in his possession, for how else would he know it was monogrammed?"

"Holmes, what are you doing?"

My friend fixed me with a sly glance as he set a container of water on the burner and drew a vial of snow white crystals out of a small leather case. Reaching for the soiled paper and cutting the dark stain free of the rest, he tossed it into the steaming water. "What do you imagine this stain to be, Watson? Ink? Mud? Dye?"

"I hardly like to think of what it—oh, but Holmes—of course!" I cried, as he drew drops of various liquids from their jars and carefully combined them in a test tube. "How could I forget? At the very moment I met you, you were quite incoherent over your discovery."

"That is because the Sherlock Holmes test for hemoglobin represented an incalculable breakthrough in criminal science, and may I add it took me nearly four months to perfect," he returned airily.* He unstopped the vial and shook a few pale crystals into the water in which the dark paper was beginning to break down, switching off the burner as he did so. "It was an historic day, friend Watson, in more ways than one, in celebration of which I invite you to do the honours."

I took the clear liquid he had prepared and hesitantly tipped a few drops into the water. Before our very eyes, it turned from transparent to a menacing maroon.

"Blood it is," he said evenly. "I thought as much. Well, share and share alike. I'm off to the Yard. It would be pretty miserly of me to keep this to myself after all Lestrade's tribulations on our behalf. Do me the favour, my dear fellow, of waiting up for me? It is just remotely possible that I may require a friend to post bail."

---

* Sherlock Holmes perfected his formula for identifying the presence of hemoglobin on the same afternoon that he was introduced to Dr. Watson by their mutual acquaintance Stamford. Holmes was at the time searching for someone to go halves with him on a suite of rooms in Baker Street.

CHAPTER NINETEEN

What Stephen Dunlevy Had to Tell

Sherlock Holmes was not detained at the Yard, although he remarked that night that more than one officer of the law had eyed him in barely suppressed suspicion. "The joke of it is," he mused, "that if I were indeed engaged in any sort of nefarious activity, there's not a man among them who'd work it out. I am under no delusions regarding my chances of success should I ever shrug off the constraints of civilization, my dear fellow. I fear I would prove entirely unstoppable."

My notes indicate that the eleventh of October saw the completion of the inquest into the murder of Catherine Eddowes, which I attended in hopes of extracting any relevant medical knowledge which may have come to light. However, apart from assuring the coroner that removing a kidney required at least a rudimentary anatomical education, and that such a kidney could have no value whatever on the open market, little was said about the Ripper's second "trophy." The verdict returned, as all the others had been, was that of "willful murder against some person or persons unknown."

I returned to Baker Street in the evening disheartened by the proceedings and was donning my slippers when I heard the violent ringing of our front door bell. Hastening to the bow window, I drew the curtain and peered down, but our caller had either disappeared or already entered. I had just turned back toward the sitting room door when Miss Monk flew through it and slammed it shut behind her.

"Where is he, then?" she demanded furiously.

"Holmes? I could not say. My dear Miss Monk, whatever is the matter?"

"If he's played me the crooked cross, he'll answer for it! He'll not charm himself out of it either, the slang cove. I'll do him down, mark my words. I'll not spy for him and be kept in the dark, not for a pound a week, not for a pound a day, nor yet a pound a minute!"

"Miss Monk, I beg of you, sit down and tell me in plain English what has happened."

"I am being followed!" she cried.

"Good heavens! Have you any idea by whom?"

The door opened and Holmes entered, a brooding look upon his face, which cleared to pleased surprise upon seeing our guest.

"By Stephen Dunlevy!" she nearly screamed.

"You were followed," said Holmes.

"Christ," she snarled, "I thought as much. You can go straight to the devil, the pair of you." She attempted to shove past him through the door, but he took a quick step back and forced it closed while deftly pulling a scrap of paper from one of Miss Monk's pockets.

"This is an underground ticket from the Metropolitan District Railway. You have never once used the underground in your visits to Baker Street. Cabs are highly visible conveyances, particularly in Whitechapel; therefore, you wished to appear less conspicuous and to lose yourself in a crowd. Why would you take such a step if you were not being followed?"

She opened her mouth to reply, but Holmes stepped around her and strode to the window. "Were you successful?"

She closed her mouth and nodded.

"Tell me from the beginning. When did you realize you had been followed?"

Miss Monk walked numbly to a chair and collapsed into it. "I'm sorry, Mr. Holmes," she whispered. "I didn't know what to think." To my great shock, her eyes filled with tears and she emitted an over-wrought sigh before burying her face in her hands.

"My dear young lady," Holmes exclaimed, placing a hand on her shoulder, "I had not the slightest idea you were so distressed."

She looked up a moment later and dashed the water from her cheeks with a scowl. "The sooner you tell me what it all means, the better."

"You mentioned Stephen Dunlevy as I entered. Was it he who fol-lowed you?"

Miss Monk nodded. "I saw as it was growing late and I left the cot-tage to buy some tea and see what had become of a few of the girls I'd used to pal around with."

"Go on."

"I've taken lodgings in Great Garden Street, Mr. Holmes, and I'd thought to look in on a girl what lives over Mount Street way. The evening was clear enough and I was in no hurry, so I thought I'd head t'other direction first off and redeem a book I'd pawned when I'd nary two ha'pence to rub together. I walks down Old Montague Street toward the pawnshop, but before I've passed two streets, I realize I'd clean forgot the ticket and turn around.

"There's a chap passes me on the street dressed all in rags, hat pulled down close and a muffler over his face, and over the top of the muffler you can just see two eyes looking out from a great tract of dirt. He was walking the way I'd been before I remembered my ticket. I don't think twice of him but leg it quick to the lodging house and find the ticket in a tobacco pouch I'd stuffed under a floorboard.

"Now I'm off again down Old Montague Street to the jerryshop, and I picks up the book, and I'm back outside quick as anything. The dirty muffled chap's still there, but people's always thick as fleas in the Chapel, and I turns back toward the hospital without thinking much of it.

"I'd got a few more paces along when I'd a queer feeling that the dirty fellow hadn't just been there begging, or waiting, or standing, or sleeping, or anything he's a perfect right to do. I might have left off stewing over it if there hadn't been something familiar about the blighter, but I makes up my mind to duck into a doorframe when I'm a bit further ahead. For by now I'm walking back, and as I've passed my own street going the opposite way, if he's still behind me, I'll know he's on my tail.

"I sees a likely deep entrance, there's a pack of the Salvation Army behind me, and I cuts away into the shade of the door. Soon enough the muffled chap passes, but he's looking around like he's lost sight of summat, and when he turns his head just as he passes me, I see that it's Dunlevy, sure as I'm sitting here."

"Lor', but it gave me a turn, Mr. Holmes. If I hadn't turned back, I might never have seen him, and who knows but that he's been follow-ing me ever since I've met him? It ain't right for a cove you've been following to follow you that way. I dived out of that doorway with my heart pounding in my ears and the chiv you gave me in my hand, and I cut across Great Garden Street to Whitechapel Road, and I didn't stop running till I'd reached that great mob riot of a station across from the hospital."

My friend pulled a telegraph form out of a drawer. "Miss Monk, does Stephen Dunlevy know where you reside?"

"He's seen me go in often enough."

"Has he ever caught sight of you tailing him, to your knowl-edge?"

"I'd have sworn he hadn't this morning, but I'd sound a proper flat, saying such a thing now."

"Miss Monk, I give you my word that I never expected Dunlevy to do anything so precipitate as to dog your movements, but I admit that I have long suspected him of being more than meets the eye."

"Well, that's clear enough!" I scowled. "What business would a common soldier have trailing Miss Monk?"

"He's no soldier," said Holmes and Miss Monk, very nearly at the same time.

"What?" I cried. My companions eyed each other warily.

"Well, one or the other of you is going to have to make clear to me why he is not a soldier," I declared in exasperation.

The replies, "His stride" and "His pocket handkerchief," once more vied for my attention.

Holmes cleared his throat. "Every serviceman who's been in more than a fortnight's time carries his pocket handkerchief in his sleeve, not in his coat pocket," he explained. "You do so yourself, my dear fellow. You were saying, Miss Monk?"

"Oh, I—that is to say, I noticed where he kept his billy when you asked after it, Mr. Holmes—but in any case soldiers don't walk that way. Least none I've ever laid eyes on. Not even orderlies."

"Very well, then," I said testily. "Leaving aside what Stephen Dunlevy is not, may I inquire what he, in fact, is?"

"You will both know as much as I do tomorrow," Holmes stated firmly. "This telegram will settle the matter for good or ill. I am happy to say that few shadows remain to confound us, but if you would both agree to meet here at three o'clock tomorrow afternoon, all will be made clear to you then. Miss Monk, have you any objection to continuing your use of the underground just for the day?"

"I may have a pound a week, but I'm not such a lady as all that."

"And would it trouble you to sleep away from your rooms tonight? I've an address where you will be well looked after." Holmes handed her a card. "It is entirely a matter of precaution, but I would prefer if you weren't left to fend for yourself. My friend has an amiable housekeeper and an extra room."

"'Mr. George Lusk, One Tollet Street, Alderney Road . . . ,'" she read. "It's all one to me. Nearly everything I need's in my pockets. But what happens tomorrow?"

Holmes smiled as he led her to the door. "I look forward to tomorrow with the greatest interest. In the meanwhile, Miss Monk, you'll be in safe hands. I'm terribly sorry you were startled, but I've the greatest respect for your fortitude throughout this inquiry, you must know."

Miss Monk flushed slightly pink at his words. "If I'm to suffer no more than a few trips on the underground, it's worth my time. Until tomorrow, then, gents. I suppose this Mr. Lusk will be surprised to see me? Well, no matter. I'll make him used to the idea soon enough."

The following afternoon at half past two, I sat alone smoking a cigar with an issue of the *Lancet* on my knee, attempting with negligible success to follow the thread of reasoning in an article concerning parasitic ailments. At ten to the hour, I stoked the fire and peered out the bow window for signs of life. Finally I heard Holmes's catlike tread upon the stairs, and my friend entered, laughing silently to himself.

"It is quite too perfect," said he. "I could never have imagined it falling into place so—mind you, I'd no notion he was dogging her before yesterday, but it plays into our hand beautifully. Halloa—there's the bell! Miss Monk has arrived."

Miss Monk appeared in far better spirits than she had the day before. She greeted us cheerfully and, catching sight of her hair in the reflection of the sideboard, feigned a scowl and attempted to wrest it into submission.

"Them small ones Mr. Lusk is left with are a sight too much for one girl to take on," she remarked contentedly, pulling a pin out of one of her pockets. "Though the older four don't plague you half as much as the younger three. I've been a princess, a maharaja's slave girl, a genie, and a pack horse since I arrived last night, so if I can stay awake long enough to—" She interrupted herself at the ringing of the downstairs bell.

"Miss Monk, if you would take the basket chair," Holmes suggested. "Dr. Watson, in your usual place, and we'll leave the whole expanse of the sofa for our guest's comfort."

I do not know what I had expected when the door swung open, but the tall, fair, broad-shouldered young fellow, dressed in quiet check trousers and a coat of dark grey, appeared in the worst state of contained agitation. His pleasant features, clean shaven save for an upturned moustache, were marred by a terrible apprehension. In the gleaming light of afternoon, for an instant I was unable to place him, but in a flash I recognized the young man Miss Monk had met for drinks at the Queen's Head on that night of abominable memory.

"Mr. Stephen Dunlevy, I presume," the detective declared. "My name is Sherlock Holmes, although I flatter myself you are already aware of it. Dr. Watson you will likewise recall, and I know you have had the pleasure of Miss Monk's company on numerous occasions."

Stephen Dunlevy, who had appeared not in the least surprised to see Sherlock Holmes awaiting him, gave an unabashed cry of relief at the sight of Miss Monk, whose expressive brows were aloft in surprise.

"What ho, Dunlevy," she said at length. "You've had a wash since last I saw you, at any rate."

Our guest appeared deeply taken aback by this remark, but Holmes, as ever, was in control of the room.

"Pray sit down, Mr. Dunlevy," my friend requested. "I am pleased to say your presence here confirms the opinion I had formed of you. Perhaps you would be so good as to answer any little questions we may care to pose."

"Certainly, sir. Since your summons, I hardly know what has happened."

Sherlock Holmes smiled enigmatically. "I fancy I can describe the chain of events to you. There are, of course, one or two trifling details I require you to supply."

"I am at your service, so glad am I to see Miss Monk here at Baker Street."

Miss Monk and I exchanged puzzled looks at this, but Holmes continued unperturbed.

"I am glad to hear it. At the outset I was unsure whether you were a City plainclothesman or a private detective, but I am now pleased to introduce you to Miss Monk and Dr. Watson as one Stephen Dunlevy, journalist at the *Star*, that seething hotbed of liberal disaffection."

I drew a sharp breath in surprise. "A journalist! Then what of this tale of the lost cohort and the murdered girl?"

"Ah, there's the crux of the matter," said Holmes, lighting a cigarette complacently. "I shall begin at the beginning, and just interrupt me if there are any points which are not clear.

"Stephen Dunlevy, for he has been using his real name, earns his bread and cheese by writing those incendiary social articles that my brother recently had reason to bemoan in these very rooms. There is a living to be made by exposing the shambles of British civilization known as Whitechapel, and for the more audacious members of the press, it is not unheard of to investigate in disguise if a better story is to be gained.

"The day before Martha Tabram's murder was a Bank Holiday, and an already tumultuous metropolis was thus flooded with the idle, the curious, and the hedonistic. The promise of street markets and fireworks rendered the day a special one for the working classes, and any keen journalist would have been wise to attend. You, Mr. Dunlevy, rented the attire of a grenadier private for a few shillings, hid a notebook somewhere on your person, and sallied forth in hopes of garnering a compelling story.

"As they are a sociable set and inclusive of their own, it was not long before you fell in with a group of soldiers recently granted leave. Their failure to see through your ruse can be explained only by your being very cautious or their being very drunk, and I believe a combination of both factors enabled you to succeed. Together you stumbled from public house to public house, and as the evening drew on, you found yourself nearly as intoxicated and venturous as they.

"By all accounts, the most gregarious fellow of the regiment was one Sergeant Johnny Blackstone, known to all his fellows as a good sort when on duty but an absolute hellion when drunk. Not knowing anything of his character, you continued in his company long after his closer comrades thought it best to quit him, for he was notorious for starting brawls at the slightest provocation.

"At the Two Brewers public house, you made the acquaintance of Martha Tabram and an associate of hers, Pearly Poll. Pearly Poll has disappeared into the netherworld of London, but Martha Tabram has the distinction of having been the first woman Johnny Blackstone ever killed in a violent rage. Or at least, the first we know of. I've a good approximation of what led up to his bloody deed, but perhaps you could provide more precise, firsthand information."

Stephen Dunlevy had grown more and more agitated during this narrative. At Holmes's suggestion, he mopped his brow with his pocket handkerchief and nodded resolutely. "You astonish me, Mr. Holmes, for everything you've said is perfectly true. Knowing what you do already, I can hardly fail to oblige you; by the time we arrived at the Two Brewers, we were both in the drink, and we fell to chatting with a few of the girls. Blackstone was everything you've said—a very dashing, dark-haired fellow, who'd fought at Tel-el-Kebir in 'eighty-two with the Coldstream Guards. He was near to thirty, so far as I could tell, and very popular with all around him.

"I saw past the fog in my head that we'd stayed too long when a brawl broke out at the next table and Blackstone smashed a bottle against a man's hand. We left the pub in a disgraceful state, at perhaps ten minutes to two, walking down the road with the girls for a short distance. Blackstone soon enough excused himself so he could duck into a dark crevice with Martha, and I made as if to do the same, but I'd recovered a fraction of my senses by then and sent Miss Poll on her way with a shilling for her trouble. I thought to stake out the entrance of the alley and wait for Blackstone to reappear.

"Five minutes passed, then ten. I returned to the pub to see if he'd changed his mind as I had, for the men we'd fought had gone, but as there was no sign of him, I retraced my steps. It must have been a quarter after two o'clock when a police constable coming out of the dark alleyway nearly walked right into me. I was so startled, I couldn't think of a thing to do but maintain my charade, knowing that any admission I was not a soldier would lead to awkward questioning. I said my friend, a fellow guardsman, had gone off with a girl and that I was awaiting their return. The constable said he'd keep an eye out for any other soldiers and told me to be on my way."

"And you took his advice, I believe. It was not until the next day, as you nursed your head and perused the papers, that you learned a woman had been stabbed thirty-nine times."

Stephen Dunlevy nodded gravely, darting an occasional glance at Miss Monk. "It was as you say, Mr. Holmes."

"Now we come to the more raveled thread. You determined that, no matter how important your evidence might prove to the Yard, not only were you uncertain about the role Blackstone may have played in Tabram's death, but your own masquerade put you in such a false position as to make it impossible to consult the police. Not a very manly decision, Mr. Dunlevy, if I may say so."

"I have these two months been working to redress my mistake," cried Dunlevy.

"Indeed you have, for when Polly Nichols was killed nearby in a similarly violent manner, you took it upon yourself to discover Blackstone's whereabouts."

"He returned to the company barracks the night Tabram was killed—early in August, the seventh, I believe. But he complained of a number of ailments, behaving most irrationally, and soon fell into a low fever. He was relieved of his duties within the week and found himself free of all obligation."

"And you very astutely decided that he may well have had something to do with the second murder, so you mounted your own investigation. By doing so, you could not only appease your conscience but further your career, for if you managed to discover Jack the Ripper, you would have made a journalistic coup never before equaled.

"It took time to contact Blackstone's regiment. It took time to locate his friends. Indeed, you went so far as to seek out Pearly Poll to determine if she had any prior acquaintance with Blackstone. This inquiry took you to Lambeth Workhouse, Miss Poll's occasional address, and there, through a very odd twist of fate, you observed us with Miss Monk. I must deduce that you recognized me and questioned why I was shaking hands with this young lady on the workhouse steps, for I can supply no other reason for your approaching her in a public house with a tale of murder most foul."

"Mother of God!" exclaimed Miss Monk.

"I did recognize her," Dunlevy conceded, flushing with colour, "and I had heard of your practice of employing . . . East-end associates, Mr. Holmes. Dr. Watson has written of such things. I freely admit I hoped she was an ally of yours and that I might learn something from her. But I wasn't certain of your collaboration until after I realized she'd taken the extraordinary measure of stealing my wallet and then returning it."

"You never did!" she gasped.

"It is no reflection on you, Miss Monk; it was expertly done. I always make certain I've my valuables about me when I leave a pub. I was about to demand its return when you very kindly replaced it."

"And is that when you took to tailing me?"

"No, no!" he protested. "It was only after the night of the double murder! There you all were, in the thick of it—I thought you must have known something I did not. It was a far simpler proposition, Miss Monk, for me to follow you through the throngs of Whitechapel than to tail Mr. Holmes in the West-end. And when I learned that your only habitual destination was Baker Street, I stopped altogether, unless—that is to say, excepting certain circumstances."

"When you'd read all the papers, or when you'd naught to do after tea," she fumed.

"In any event," Holmes continued, "Miss Monk was adroit enough to discern your pursuit yesterday, and I wrote you a telegram that I fancied would assure your presence here this afternoon."

"And the contents of the telegram?" I prompted.

Stephen Dunlevy pulled a crumpled piece of paper out of his pocket and handed it to me with a wry countenance.

"'Miss Monk has disappeared under dark circumstances; meet me at Baker Street at precisely three p.m.—Sherlock Holmes,'" I read aloud.

The lady in question stared in disbelief, at a total loss for words for the first time since I had known her.

"I am sure you will forgive me for having played a small trick on you. Your concern for Miss Monk's well-being does you credit, Mr. Dunlevy, for all your shortcomings," Holmes said, swinging his calculating gaze back to Dunlevy. "However, I must be satisfied on one point. You have been in correspondence with your employer throughout your stay in the East-end. Did you inform any members of the press of my own movements?"

"You refer to the article by that dreadful bounder Tavistock. I did mention your involvement to several colleagues, to my lasting regret," Dunlevy owned with a pained expression, "but only insofar as to say your genius had anticipated the fiend's attack."

"And to my lasting regret, your assumption was utterly vacuous," Holmes retorted coldly.

"Holmes, he could not possibly have—"

"Of course not, Watson. Mr. Dunlevy, excuse me for saying that I asked you here to determine whether you intend to be a help or a hindrance to this investigation henceforth."

"I am your man, Mr. Holmes," Dunlevy declared earnestly. "I fear my only real discovery was of his original lodgings, but immediately following the night in question, he abandoned them entirely. I should be overjoyed to offer you any assistance it is within my power to provide."

"Splendid! Then I bid you good afternoon," my friend said curtly, throwing open the door. "You may expect to hear from me within the week."

Mr. Dunlevy shook my hand and bowed to Miss Monk. "I heartily apologize for the deception I've practiced," he said, turning to Holmes. "I will think more carefully before engaging again in any undercover work. Good day to you all."

When the door had shut, I ventured, "I do hope you intend to tell us how you worked it out, my dear fellow, for the sake of our mental health if nothing more."

Holmes was tossing newspapers about to make room for other newspapers he prized more highly. "It is a simple enough chain, once one observes the incongruities. As I have said before, why should an army friend only mount a search a month after a traumatic event has passed? And why should a confidant take two months' time merely to pinpoint his comrade's lodgings on the night in question? On the other hand, why should a man harp upon the least sensational murder in a series of such crimes unless he truly was involved somehow? The rest was mere painstaking research. He had no acquaintance at Lambeth Workhouse, yet he questioned its inmates; he had no acquaintance with me, and yet he approached Miss Monk with a scintillating account of Tabram's death. However, nothing proved so fruitful as my habitual scouring of the papers. I draw your attention to the *Star*, morning edition of September fifth, and again the fifth of October: they are pasted in my commonplace book, there on the desk."

The volume lay open, weighted with a box of hair-trigger cartridges. I rose and examined the articles in question. "'The City of Night; A Continuing Journal of the East End,'" I read. "'By S. Leudvyn.'"

"A most informative diary of an undercover reporter. I've unearthed several others. The anagram was simple enough, but I consulted the offices to be sure I had my man."

"You are certain that journalism was his only consideration?"

My friend dropped the editions he had gathered with an angry flourish. "I grow weary of the accusation that I have arranged a series of rendezvous between Miss Monk and London's vilest criminal dregs, Doctor," he exclaimed severely. "I can assure you that—"

"Begging both your pardons, but I slept poor enough with one little one's hand in my hair and another's foot in my gut. It were a right well-populated guest room, and I'm clean done. Oh, no," Miss Monk assured us, rapidly making her way to the door, "the bed was intended for one, but the natives are that clever. I'm off home. I'll see you at the usual time, gents. Keep to it, Mr. Holmes."

When the door had shut, I turned back to my friend. "My dear chap, if I implied you held Miss Monk's safety lightly, please believe that I am sorry for it," said I.

Though my apology fell upon stony ground, I determined to carry on in spite of the rigidly set shoulders and deliberate complacency of London's finest sleuth. "Is it not odd that Blackstone, if he is a cunning murderer, should enact a crime while still in Dunlevy's company?"

"Hardly odd when one considers that Dunlevy had been plied with drinks the entire evening, perhaps purposefully, then packed off into the loving arms of Miss Pearly Poll. Blackstone would have imagined him entirely out of the way."

"I see," I acknowledged. "He did not know Dunlevy is a journalist, after all. Yes, that is very plausible. But Holmes—"

"What is it, Watson?" he demanded, snapping shut the edition he held.

"Dunlevy said he only continues to tail Miss Monk during special circumstances."

"Of course he does." Holmes pulled out a notebook and began to jot down cross-references. "He no longer tails her on the usual days, when she hails a cab and makes for Baker Street. He only tails her when she wanders, on foot and unescorted, through the labyrinthine darkness of Whitechapel." My friend cocked an ironic eye at me and added, "Why he would do such a thing I leave to your unparalleled imagination."

CHAPTER TWENTY

The Thread

As Holmes's investigations continued, I grew ever more certain that I knew next to nothing of what he was investigating. However, to my intense private satisfaction, every day he grew more visibly active, until, on Monday the fifteenth, he threw his sling into the fire in a fit of impatience and declared, "If Dr. Agar's work and yours combined, my dear Watson, have not had their effect by now, then God help the British public, who are plagued with new ailments every day."

The following morning, soon after I had dressed, I heard Holmes's footsteps approaching my bedroom, and a brief knock preceded the man himself.

"How soon can you be in a cab?"

"Instantly. What is the matter?"

"George Lusk requests our aid in the most urgent language. Make haste, my dear fellow, for he is not a man to trifle with our time!"

When we arrived at Tollet Street, Holmes was out of the cab in a moment, bounding up the stairs and leaning against the bell. Immediately we were shown in to the same pleasant sitting room, occupied by the same palm fronds and self-important feline.

"I am very glad you both have come," George Lusk declared, shaking our hands firmly. His lively brow was clouded with anxiety and the downward sweep of his moustache emphasized his unease. "The thing is a repulsive hoax, of course; I have no doubt it is merely a boon for those vultures of the popular press, but I thought it best to call you in." He gestured to the rolltop desk.

Holmes reached it in an instant and lifted the slats. A strong smell, which I realized had faintly infused the room all along, permeated the atmosphere. I recognized it at once as spirits of wine, which was everywhere employed as a medical preservative and which I had often used myself during my years at university.

My friend seated himself at the desk, surveying a small box of plain cardboard, resting on the brown paper in which it had arrived. Mr. Lusk and I crowded round either shoulder to witness him open the receptacle. Inside sat a mound of glistening flesh.

"Well, Doctor?" said Holmes, glancing up at me. He pulled a pocketknife from his frock coat, opened it, and passed it to me along with the sinister box. I probed the object carefully.

"It is a portion of a kidney."

"Nearly half, I would say from the angle of the cut and the arc of this side. Human?"

"Undoubtedly."

"Gender? Age?"

"I could not tell you. If it is half, as you say, then the kidney is adult, but beyond that, further identification is impossible."

"It does not appear to be injected with the formalin* used for dissection organs. Tissue preserved only in spirits of wine would inevitably deteriorate without a fixative and grow quickly useless in the classroom, so we can rule out a prank by an undergraduate. However, the ethyl alcohol it has been resting in is easily obtained."

"This letter accompanied the organ," Mr. Lusk indicated.

My friend first inspected the container itself, followed by the paper wrapping, before reaching for the document which explained, in the most vile terms and debased calligraphy I had ever laid eyes on, the contents of that horrid box.

---

* More commonly, formaldehyde.

From hell

Mr Lusk

Sor

   I send you half the
Kidne I took from one women
prasarved it for you tother piece I
fried and ate it was very nise I
may send you the bloody knif that
took it out if you only wate a whil
longer.

   Signed Catch me when
You can

   Mishter Lusk

"Black ink, cheapest foolscap, no finger marks or other traces," Holmes said softly. "'From hell,' indeed! What sort of frenzied imagination could be capable of constructing such trash?"

"It is a hoax, surely," Mr. Lusk insisted. "Everyone knows Catherine Eddowes's kidney was taken, after all, Mr. Holmes. It is the organ of a dog. Oh, I do beg your pardon, Dr. Watson—if human, as you say, perhaps it is a prank enacted by a roguish medical examiner."

"It is possible," said Holmes. "I do not think it likely. Look at this script: I detect key similarities to other samples from our quarry, but what a state he was in to pen this dark epistle! I have made a special study of handwriting, or graphology,* as it is now called by the French, but I have never seen anything so debauched as this specimen."

"The script alone leads you to think this her kidney?"

"This scrap of flesh came from no school or university, and neither did it come from the nearby London Hospital."

---

* Term originated by Jean Hippolyte Michon, 1871. Graphology would not be studied in England for many years to come.

"How can you be sure?"

"When necessary, they preserve organic materials in glycerine."

"Well, then, but it need not have come from the East-end. Surely in the West-end, many establishments—"

"The postmark, if one regards it with a lens, reveals the barest smudge of a 'London E.' It originated in Whitechapel."

"Still, any mortuary could have supplied the thing."

"Whitechapel possesses no mortuary!" Holmes snapped, his patience failing him. "It possesses a shed."

Mr. Lusk's features were suffused with complete astonishment. "But the crime rate in Whitechapel! The sickness, the disease . . . Only half the children ever grow up, Mr. Holmes. No district has greater need of a mortuary!"

"Nevertheless."

"God in heaven, if the world knew the troubles of this district . . ." Mr. Lusk calmed himself through a visible effort of will and regarded us with a touching sadness.

"Watson, we have work ahead of us," the detective declared shortly. "Mr. Lusk, may I entrust to you the task of reporting this matter to the Yard?"

"Of course, Mr. Holmes. Oh, and please do give my regards to Miss Monk!" Mr. Lusk exclaimed as we turned to leave. "I fear she may have been tormented to some degree by my offspring, but I trust she came to no lasting harm."

Holmes was already halfway down the street before I reached him, the length of his stride more than making up for any residual weakness of constitution. Knowing him as I did, I had not expected him to proffer a single word, but to my surprise, speech fairly exploded from his gaunt frame.

"I will not be toyed with in this manner! As if we'd not already suffered intolerable lows, the sending of a preserved organ through the London Royal Mail quite strikes the final quivering nail into the coffin of this investigation."

"My dear fellow, whatever can you mean?"

"Here we are furnished with clue after clue, missive after blood-soaked missive, and the villain has no further revealed his identity than he did when he plunged a knife in my chest," he spat out in disgust. "Apart, of course, from its being a six-inch double-bladed dissection knife."

"Holmes," I protested, alarmed, "you have done all that could be expected of—"

"Of Gregson, or of Lestrade, or any of the other farcical simpletons who joined the Yard because they weren't strong enough for hard labour or rich enough to buy a decent army commission."

Shocked at his vehemence, I could only manage, "Surely we have made progress."

"We are surrounded by quicksand! No footmarks, no signal traits, no traceable characteristics, merely the assurance he is enjoying his purloined organs and my cigarettes!"

"Holmes, where are we going?"

"To settle a debt," he snarled, and not one word more did he say for the twenty minutes it took us to walk from Mile End to the throbbing artery of Whitechapel Road and then down a series of streets to a green door in a begrimed brick wall. Holmes rapped brusquely and then fell to tapping the head of his stick against his high forehead.

"Who resides here, Holmes?"

"Stephen Dunlevy."

"Does he indeed? You have been here before?"

His answering glare was so exquisitely pained that I resolved to postpone further queries for better days.

A slatternly creature of advancing years in a meticulously preened bonnet opened the door and regarded us with the primness of the long-ruined. "How may I help you gentlemen?"

"We are here to see your lodger, Mr. Stephen Dunlevy."

"And who are you, sir?"

"We are friends."

"Now, this is a private establishment, gents. I can't just allow any man from the street to harass my lodgers, if you understand me, sir."

"Perfectly. In that case, we are here to bring charges against you for brothel keeping under Section Thirteen of the Criminal Law Amendment Act. That is, of course, unless you manage to remember we are friends of Mr. Dunlevy."

"Why, of course!" she exclaimed. "The light must have dazzled my eyes. This way, if you please."

We ascended a staircase draped in layers of cobweb and silt and crossed the hallway to an unmarked door. The landlady knocked.

"Come along, now, for there's men to see you. Friends of yours, or so I'm told." She favoured us with a sparingly toothed smile before descending out of sight beyond the staircase.

Without waiting for a response, Holmes gripped the knob and plunged inside and had seated himself in a nearby chair before our startled host, standing next to his open door, could venture to greet us.

"Though slowed by the thankless task of ascertaining your identity, Mr. Dunlevy, I have traced Johnny Blackstone back to his birthplace, his parents' country farm, his primary school, his initial regiment, his transfer, his Egyptian service, and his disappearance. What I want to know is where he is. His regiment, his parents, and his dear sister are quite as eager to find him as I am. You are about to tell me every detail of your first encounter with Blackstone, omitting no microscopic facet no matter how trivial. I invite you, in fact, to glory in the trivial." Holmes lit a cigarette and exhaled slowly. "This agency runs on minutiae, Mr. Dunlevy, and you must furnish me with fuel."

So began an interrogation which lasted the better part of four hours; however, it seemed to me (and, I have no doubt, to Stephen Dunlevy) to have gone on for days. Over and over again Holmes demanded he recount his story. Dunlevy somehow managed to retain his good humour, but I watched him grow increasingly angry at himself that his indiscretions that night had so far impaired his observation.

I was leaning against the door smoking, Dunlevy sunk in an armchair with his chin in his hand, and Holmes draped across another chair with his feet propped on the low mantelpiece, when my friend resumed a line of questioning I thought had been exhausted long before.

"From the time Blackstone met Martha Tabram to the time you left the Two Brewers, how much of their conversation were you able to catch?"

"Only what I have told you, Mr. Holmes. Everyone was shouting and no one taking heed of a word."

"It is not good enough! Cast your mind back. You really must try, Mr. Dunlevy."

Dunlevy screwed his eyes shut in concentration, rubbing a weary hand along the bridge of his nose. "Blackstone complimented her bonnet. He called it very becoming. He insisted on paying for drinks for her, and she knew they would be fast friends. They fell to tormenting one of the other fellows—an edgy private who'd had his eye on a girl for an hour and still hadn't spoken to her."

"And then?"

"He talked of the Egyptian campaign."

"The words he used?"

"I cannot recall exactly. He used exotic language, vivid pictures . . . There was a tale about three cobras that seemed to amuse her very much. I could barely manage to—"

Holmes sat up in his chair with an expression of burning interest. "Three cobras, you say?"

"That's what it sounded like."

"You are sure of the number?"

"I would be prepared to swear it was three. Remarkable he should have encountered so many at once, but I confess I know nothing of Egyptian terrain."

Holmes leapt to his feet and steepled his fingers before his lips, his countenance frozen but his entire posture vibrating with barely contained energy. "Mr. Dunlevy, the question I am about to pose is of paramount importance. Describe to me, as precisely as possible, Blackstone's eyes."

"They were blue, very pale in colour," Dunlevy faltered, attempting to rearrange his features so that they did not imply my friend was out of his senses.

"Did he seem troubled at all by the light?"

"There was little enough light in the lairs we visited. One bright lamp in the White Swan, I believe. I remember he sat with his back to it, but they never lost their colour. Even in the darkest of the gin shops you could see his pale eyes shining out at you."

Holmes let out an exclamation of unparalleled delight. Rushing forward, he began to wring Dunlevy's hand. "I knew you could not have been thrown in our path merely to torment us!" He retrieved his hat and stick and made a theatrical bow. "Dr. Watson, our presence is required elsewhere. Good day to you, Mr. Dunlevy!"

I raced after my friend and caught him up at the corner.

"*Nihil obstat.** It is a great stroke of luck. Stephen Dunlevy has just told us everything we need."

"I am heartily glad of it."

Holmes laughed. "I'll own I was in a bit of a fit this morning, but surely you'll overlook it if I tell you where we shall find word of Johnny Blackstone."

"I confess that I cannot imagine any link between a man's eyesight and his Egyptian exploits."

"You, like Dunlevy, think the reference to three cobras a relic of foreign wars, then?"

"What else could it possibly mean?"

"As a medical man, the constriction of his pupils even during levels of very low illumination ought to suggest something to you."

"On the contrary—cobra venom is a neurotoxin working on the

* Latin, "Nothing stands in our way."

muscles of the diaphragm and could have nothing to do with photo-sensitivity, or indeed any ocular symptom."

"As usual, my dear fellow, you are both correct and misled." He whistled stridently for a fortuitous hansom which had just rolled into view. "It will all be clear to you in a few minutes' time, when I have introduced you to the Three Cobras, possibly the least savoury opium den in the whole of Limehouse."

CHAPTER TWENTY-ONE

A Narrow Escape

It was not a long journey down Commercial Road from Whitechapel to the tiny dockside realm of Limehouse, but the latter's total dependence upon all things nautical made it a vastly different topography. Here the carmen were replaced by sailors, the market porters became dockside labourers, and the races as we approached the river grew ever more diverse. As the sun began to set over the lumbering Thames, I glimpsed from the window Welsh dockworkers, African stevedores, and Indian porters, all drifting in the general direction of hearth and home with a stop at the pub and two or three glasses of gin to sustain them on their way.

We turned abruptly onto a street, and all around us Chinese men and women, dressed immaculately in the British style, ducked in and out of shops marked only with the delicate slashes which served as writing in their native land. One young fellow, his pigtail tucked under a neat cloth cap and his fingerless gloves affording slight protection in the chill wind, pushed a child about in a tea leaf box which had been fitted with two front wheels, a back prop, and sanded handles.

Holmes rapped the ceiling of the cab with his stick, and the driver halted before a storefront identifying itself only by a crude picture of a steaming bowl. My friend leapt down with agile enthusiasm, tilting his head to our left toward the dampest, most soot-encrusted archway

I'd ever laid eyes on. The businesses on either side, whose commerce I could not even hazard a guess at, boasted broken windowpanes patched with greasy brown paper.

"It's just this way. Thank you, driver. And now, Watson, we would do best to keep our wits about us."

Under the arch, we came upon a flight of mossy stone steps which led steeply down, under wooden slats and walls of grim brick, to a grotesque courtyard some three stories below the street at the level of the river. Seven houses sat in a semicircle, all constructed of rotting grey timber. My friend approached the sagging doorframe belonging to one of these and rapped three times.

When the door opened, a stoop-shouldered Chinese man with tufted silver brows and a peculiarly detached expression made a polite bow.

"I wonder, is this the establishment known as the Three Cobras?" Holmes ventured deferentially.

The proprietor, or so I assumed him to be, nodded his head. "There are several berths if you wish to smoke, sirs," he said in near-perfect English.

"What a stroke of luck," Holmes smiled.

"I am Mr. Li. Please step this way."

The outer door opened into a hallway, which after a flight of three steep steps became a narrow passage with beds built into the walls like berths on a ship, six pallets arranged in a rectangular formation on each side of the corridor. One old woman, with eyes set deep as wells and a long braid of lead-grey hair, looked to have just enough life in her to continue smoking the vile substance.

"Holmes, how on earth did you come to know of this pit?" I murmured.

"I make it my business to acquaint myself with a great many particulars," he whispered.

Mr. Li waved us onward, for the corridor ballooned at its far end into a larger common room with a bed pushed against the wall and grass mats lining the floors. Gauzy hanging strips of tattered cloth, which had no doubt once contributed to an air of mysticism, now hung slick with smoke like the mud-soaked sails of a shipwrecked vessel. I could see other Englishmen in this chamber—two soldiers, lounging with elongated pipes dangling from their limp fingers, and a slack-jawed naval officer, whose hand traced lazy patterns in the thick air above him.

Mr. Li waved us over to a pair of grass pallets cloaked by the decrepit drapery. Holmes indicated we had time only for a four-penny smoke, and Mr. Li retreated to the stove, where a great mound of shredded opium simmered in a sieve set over a pot of shallow water.

"My dear Holmes, assure me that we have no intention of actually smoking this dross," I mouthed as softly as I could.

"Never fear, Watson," he returned equally quietly but with a mischievous grin. "You know my taste in self-poisoning to run quite in another direction."

When Mr. Li had toasted two tiny portions of resinlike amber material and loaded it into pipes, he handed them to us and vanished. Holmes, to my dismay, placed the pipe between his teeth, but I soon saw he merely sought to free his hands and unfasten his watch chain. A gold sovereign dangled from the end of it, a relic of an earlier adventure,* and in a trice he had scooped the smouldering lump out of his pipe, dropped it to the floor, returned the stem to his mouth, and held a hand out for my own. This process he repeated with my pipe, and then he pulled out his pocket handkerchief and methodically restored the Queen's golden visage to her former spotlessness. Finally, he picked up the cooled pieces with his handkerchief and deposited them in his pocket.

"I fancy that will do the trick. Care for another pipe, Doctor, or shall we call an end to this reconnaissance?"

"The latter, if you have seen all you need."

---

* Dr. Watson records these circumstances under the title "A Scandal in Bohemia."

"Then let us be on our way. Ah, here is the man I want. May I have a brief word with you?" Holmes asked Mr. Li, heavy-lidded and reserved.

Our host nodded, and we followed him to a side room off the entrance chamber where books and ledgers scribbled with cryptic characters covered the single small table.

"You see, sir," Holmes began languidly, "our friend can hardly stop praising your business, and his words were more than justified. You do quite a commerce with soldiers, do you not, Mr. Li?"

"As you saw."

Holmes placed a five-pound note on a yellowed ledger page. "In fact, while we settle up with you, I wished expressly to mention that our friend is being pursued by some very unsavoury characters—moneylenders, you understand—and is in hiding. I would like very much to help him if only I knew where he was. I wonder if, when he next drops in, you might find a moment to notify me? You would be rewarded, of course, for your time and trouble."

"Your name, sir?"

"Basil. I was once a shipping captain, but I now own a small fleet," Holmes said as he jotted down his address on a scrap of paper.

"And who is your friend?"

Holmes described Blackstone in detail, failing to mention any name.

Mr. Li scratched more notes upon his sheet, then straightened with a sigh. "Your friend does come here from time to time. Always alone. Always very popular once he arrives. Captain Basil, I make a great effort to help my customers. I make one request only, and that is truth. This business with your soldier friend—there is a possibility of violence?"

"That possibility exists," Holmes assented, smiling briefly.

"I see." He made another note. "In that case, Captain Basil, I must warn you that any violence occurring upon my property makes you liable to me." He smiled at my friend in return. "I do not think you wish to be liable to me."

•   •   •

I had not gone many paces up the dripping stairs to the street when Holmes remarked, "You dislike our new associate."

"If you must know, I think the whole business proved him to be cunning and mercenary."

"Oh, to the uninitiated, of course. However, I know that whole discussion of violence to have been entirely genuine. He is quite an eccentric character, Mr. Li. I have had dealings with him, though never in person, several times. He is a philanthropist, an opium purveyor, a Buddhist, and a tenacious enemy. The man was a renowned scholar in Peking. There was a little girl killed in this area not four years ago; Mr. Li found the culprit, a member of the Limehouse Forty Thieves gang, and I don't like to tell you what became of him. He has done more in five years to relieve the area of gangs than Scotland Yard could do in twenty."

"He is an ally, then? Why the absurd rigmarole with the pipes?"

"Business, my dear Watson, business! I'd never met the fellow in the flesh. There is a great deal of brotherly feeling amongst followers of that particular vice. If I am a client, I am on even footing with Blackstone. Otherwise, I am merely a swell or a plainclothesman. In any event, I wished a glimpse of the patrons."

We reached the street just as the lamps were being lit, though I noted distressingly few in that locale.

"We had better trudge back to that portion of London populated by hansoms," Holmes said. "I ought to have paid that fellow to wait. Your leg can manage it?"

"Certainly."

"Then quick march, my dear fellow, spurred on by home, hearth, and the taste of future victory."

The detective's infallible sense of direction soon led into territory which, though unfamiliar, boasted English characters upon the sides of buildings. Holmes, deep in thought, strode forward with his aquiline profile straying neither to the left nor to the right, but I, as a man will do when he is in unknown terrain, looked about with curiosity at the deserted warehouses, which soon gave way to ramshackle tenements and the smells of a hundred suppers being prepared behind boarded windows.

I must have been so preoccupied with the scene that the first weary news vendor, hawking the last of his wares in a hoarse shout, failed to impress himself upon my consciousness. However, the second fellow, a taciturn youth with the face of a bulldog, held the front page up so determinedly that I glanced at the headline. With a cry of astonishment, I halted and fumbled through my pockets for a coin as Holmes broke from his reverie and returned to see what had startled me.

SHERLOCK HOLMES AT LARGE

While the police force in the district of Whitechapel has more than doubled since the discovery of Jack the Ripper's grisly "double event," it is regrettably still possible to fault the Metropolitan Police on one glaring miscarriage of public safety. As shocking as the citizenry will no doubt find it, the foremost suspect (and indeed, the only likely perpetrator identified thus far), the self-professed "consulting detective" Mr. Sherlock Holmes, is still at large and all too frequently to be found in the East-end. The reader ought not to feel guilty of a suspicious nature when he considers that Mr. Holmes attended the funerals of both the deceased, and is the subject of an active Scotland Yard investigation into his whereabouts on the night in question. These circumstantial matters appear black indeed when taken in conjunction with the discovery of a seemingly unrelated knife a few streets away from the depraved Eddowes murder. It is well known that Mr. Holmes was wounded in some manner on that night, and the discarded knife—clearly not the killer's own, as it could not have inflicted her gruesome injuries—gives rise to the suspicion that Eddowes may well have concealed a weapon on her own person and was able to strike a blow to her assailant before finally succumbing to his evil designs. While no doubt the police are handling the inquiry around Mr. Holmes with due diligence, one cannot help but feel that the streets would be safer if his freedoms were more stringently curtailed.

"Curse the scoundrel!" Holmes exclaimed, folding the poisonous print out of sight. "What a tortuous argument, to be sure! A delusive pressman gives rise to a police investigation, then cites a police investigation as a further cause for alarm."

"But how could he know that you attended the funerals?"

"If Stephen Dunlevy had a hand in this, so help me, I will wring the truth out of his miserable neck."

He set off again down the street, his pace redoubled.

"What are we to do, Holmes?"

"We are going to get inside as quickly as possible."

I realized with a quick stab of apprehension what he meant; every day we read news of mob activity in the East-end, directed with barren fury against any handy immigrant or meandering pedestrian. There had been multiple reports of near lynchings. If any suspicious-minded citizenry identified Holmes abroad by night in Whitechapel, I dared not imagine the consequences.

"This is Tavistock's doing, I trust?"

"Whose else?"

"Oh, if I had him here!" I cried. "I would make him regret he'd ever set foot in a news office!"

"The wretch prints what is true in such an inverted fashion that every fact stands on its head," Holmes growled. Suddenly he stopped. "Look here, my boy, odd as it may sound, the danger at the moment is in crowds."

He turned into a pathway which must officially have been termed an alley and I would have better characterized as a crevice. The only beings we encountered at first were vermin and half-crazed dogs who stared at us with baleful hunger in their yellow eyes.

"Holmes, what do you intend to do?"

"Your idea of expressing ourselves with our fists was attractive but sadly untenable. We must determine where the insolent wretch is getting his information."

We had gone halfway down a block marred everywhere with eroding stone when I realized that the clatter of trains to our left had mingled with another sound; footsteps now echoed our own. I knew better than to look behind me, but a glance at Holmes told me that he too had heard our shadowy companion.

My friend ducked into a side street, changing our direction, but still the curious trudge followed us in the gloom.

"We are walking north on Mansel Street, and any second should pass the railway depot," he murmured. "We have to take Aldgate High Street, and in a moment we'll be in the City."

"I'd prefer Westminster."

"Baker Street is but a cab fare away from us."

As we emerged onto Aldgate High Street very near the place where it became Whitechapel High Street, it seemed for a moment as if our troubles were over. Then the man behind us began to make his presence more keenly felt.

"Is that Mr. Sherlock Holmes?" he cried out.

The better-lit, better-populated expanse of road seemed at once a hostile landscape, for every head within hearing distance swiveled round to confront my friend's justly famous countenance.

"Here now!" the man yelled. "That's Sherlock Holmes, it is! Strolling down dark alleys wi'out a care in the world!"

A few bystanders, men with surly faces and no better occupation, joined our unwelcome associate and marched along behind.

"Hey! You! You've a great deal to answer for in these parts!"

An inauspicious grumble of assent erupted from the gathering crowd.

"Turn around and tell us all what the devil you think you're doing in the Chapel, you bleeding pig!"

Holmes rolled his eyes at this equation of him with a Scotland Yard detective but otherwise made no sign.

"You think," screamed the fellow, whose voice I was beginning heartily to loathe, "that you'll get away with it? Knifing all those beauties, you think there's no one of us with a knife for you?"

"Watson, if you happen to lay eyes on an officer before I do, just signal him, will you?" Holmes remarked, his right hand in his pocket and the other tightening its grip on his weighted stick.

"So help us, we protect our own, don't we, lads?" cried our antagonist.

"How is your arm?"

"Good for a blow or two at best. I would welcome your revolver."

"You'll have to make do with my fists." Though my eyes searched the streets for police, by a great stroke of misfortune I could see none.

"We are close enough to the Aldgate underground stop," Holmes noted.

"What are our chances at running?"

"Poor, with your leg to consider. We've already walked—"

"Holmes, they don't want me."

"If I knew that to be true, I might take to my heels. As matters stand, you'll have to endure my company a while longer."

Just when we reached a crossroads, several of the gang behind us burst forward and encircled us from the front. I turned slowly round. To my dismay, nearly thirty men had joined the preposterous procession, and ten more lined up to prevent our progress.

"I don't suppose we could have a word with them?" I asked in as easy a tone as I could manage.

"We'll serve them as they served Catherine Eddowes!" shouted the odious little devil.

Holmes at last turned with a look of deadly resolve in his iron-grey eyes. "It is not a scheme which is likely to work, you realize."

"Still, for lack of a better one . . ." I hissed.

"Gentlemen," Holmes announced, "I have no notion of what you are pursuing, but as it appears to mean a great deal to you, I am prepared to offer my wholehearted assistance!"

This remark did not soothe the mob, but it had the distinct virtue of puzzling it. One or two people chuckled morbidly, and others raised their fists.

"You know what we're after right enough, or you'd ha' been walking a good deal slower, you bloody 'tec."

"It appears that you are pursuing *me*," Holmes replied pleasantly. "But I can think of no reason for doing so unless you meant to procure my help. I am known for my skills in the art of detection. I will say this once, and once only: I have been seen in the vicinity of the Ripper because I have been striving with all my might to rid your neighbourhood of him."

Several members of the crowd regarded Holmes with fresh interest at this defiant declaration, but their sympathy proved to be short-lived.

"You were seen!" mocked a club-wielding ruffian, starting forward. "What good is the word of a cold-blooded killer?"

"You, sir, are from West Yorkshire, I observe."

The brute stopped in his tracks. "Here now! How in hell d'ye know that?"

"You have hunted rabbits in your time, I suppose?"

"So what if I have done," he scowled.

"You were very near them when you did so. Have you ever been mistaken for one?"

The metaphor, apt as it was, drew laughter from several patches of the assembly while others, sensing an oblique insult, tightened their grips on their makeshift weapons and advanced spitting curses at the pair of us.

"Perhaps something a shade more conciliatory," I suggested.

"You truly imagined I could argue our way out of this?" Holmes demanded, sidestepping so that we were back to back.

"No," I replied quietly, turning my head, "but they have now allowed a slight gap. I am going to tackle that pockmarked lad with the shovel. When I've knocked him down, I fully expect you to run like the devil."

We pivoted slowly, our eyes fixed on the hostile circle. "You are mad," Holmes hissed, "if you think I am—" Then all at once, arresting both his speech and his movement suddenly, he caught me by the sleeve and inexplicably smiled in delight.

"Man Jack!" he cried. "What possessed you to join this misguided lot?"

I stared in astonishment. A man with an enormous frame and a livid scar running straight from his temple down across his nose and deep into his cheek stepped forward through the crowd.

"Now, I know for a fact," he said in rumbling baritone, "that this is no night for Sherlock Holmes to be abroad in the Chapel."

"Man Jack, I am overjoyed to see you."

"I can't say as I feel the same, Mr. Holmes."

"The papers say he's the Knife!" bellowed a surly youth.

"We'll send him to hell this very night!"

"And what say you, Man Jack?" my friend asked. "It's quite a little work of fiction."

"You know as well as I do it's the boy as can read," he growled dismissively. "Now, be off. Or I won't spend so long talking the next time."

"There he is safe as a lamb," called the villain who had started it all. "We've jawed long enough. I've a knife here, will serve him!"

"And I!" cried another.

"You're none of you fit for proper policing," Man Jack said calmly, but his voice reverberated through buildings. "You there! Let these fellows pass. Be off, now, Mr. Sherlock Holmes. They obey me when they've a mind, but when they don't, God help the man they take a grudge against."

"My thanks. This way, Watson."

Though their faces were scowling, and a few, including the burly

Yorkshireman, ventured to spit in our direction, our opponents parted as if a curtain had been drawn.

"Who in God's name was that fellow?" I asked in amazement.

"Man Jack? He is a prizefighter."

"You know him from the ring, then, I suppose?"

"No indeed, my dear fellow. You're sporting man enough to know my weight class and his ought not to intermingle."

"He saved us from a terrible brawl for no reason I can see."

"That is because you do not know his full name. Man Jack Hawkins has a family member in my immediate employ. I must confess, my dear fellow, when I amassed the Irregular force all those years ago, I never imagined that any of their parents would be called upon to vouch for my good name. Though God knows few enough of them have any parents." Holmes sighed, as a wave of exhaustion seemed to pass over him. "Little Hawkins has just earned another sizeable bonus. There is a cab, my dear fellow, and if we make a dash at him, I think he shall just see us."

CHAPTER TWENTY-TWO

The Disappearance of Sherlock Holmes

I saw nothing of my friend the next day until nearly eight o'clock, when an exceedingly disheveled character wearing the filthy oilskins and the high boots of the men who risk their lives raking the sewers for coins saluted me and disappeared into Holmes's bedroom. In half an hour he emerged again in grey tweeds, collected his pipe, and sat down at the table with the look of a man who relishes the work ahead of him.

"And what has that scavenger been doing today?"

"He has set foot in realms where Sherlock Holmes, temporarily at least, dares not tread. What is for supper?"

"Mrs. Hudson spoke of lamb."

"Admirable woman. Just ring the bell, my dear fellow. I haven't thought of food since early this morning, for there was a great deal of work to be done."

"You have been in the East-end?"

"Well, for part of the day. I had other errands. I've stopped by the Yard, for instance."

"In that getup?" I laughed.

"I demanded to see Inspector Lestrade. I revealed I had pressing information to relate, which would profit him immensely. His colleagues hesitated. Then I was forced to admonish them that if I went with my information to the papers instead, they would look rather foolish. This suggestion altered their mood, and I was in Lestrade's office a moment later. I revealed my identity, much to the good inspector's irritation, and I asked him some key questions."

"Such as?"

"In the first place, the force are very put out by this Tavistock mongrel's theorizing but are also anxious to avoid accusations of favouritism. Some of the more active fellows have suggested arresting me in the interests of thoroughness and public opinion."

"On what evidence, in God's name?"

"Incredibly, there really was a bloody knife found discarded a few streets away from Catherine Eddowes, but Lestrade never bothered to mention it to us because it was so unlike the double-sided blade which the Ripper used. Its discovery was a complete coincidence, but the villainous mind of either Leslie Tavistock or his foul source hit upon the happy notion that Eddowes could have wielded it in defense. In such a state of panic, it counts for nothing that any British jury would dismiss the whole tale in the blink of an eye. I can't even bring charges of libel, for he hasn't penned an untrue word."

"Surely he has gone too far!" I protested.

"Watson, if the newspapers could be punished for speculation, every publication in England would soon enough be bankrupted. After I quit the Yard, I made my way to Whitechapel and looked in on Stephen Dunlevy. He proclaims his innocence in the strongest terms."

"No doubt that is to be expected," I said tightly, while privately thinking that if Dunlevy continued to operate under false pretenses with us, all the while endeavouring to enter the good graces of Miss Monk, I would have scant choice but to throw him in the Thames.

"I am inclined to believe him," Holmes mused. "Indeed, I feel ever more certain that there is a malevolent force at work determined to impede my progress. Perhaps my mind detects conspiracy where none exists, but these small persecutions play directly into the Ripper's hands by tying mine."

"I should hardly call them small persecutions."

My friend waved his pipe dismissively. "I've nothing further to report on the subject, for we can hardly know more until we have seen Tavistock."

"We intend to see Tavistock?"

"We are to meet him at Simpson's for cigars at ten."

"You will then be able to claim acquaintance with the lowest form of life in London other than Jack the Ripper," I stated dourly.

Holmes laughed. "Well, well, we go into it with the comfort of a good day's labour behind us."

"But what else have you been doing, Holmes? You left early this morning."

"My time has not been wasted, I assure you. Ah! Here is Mrs. Hudson, and I beg your permission to confine my attentions to the tray she carries with her."

That night, as many others had been that October, was shrouded in pungent fog, and we wrapped our mufflers tight about our faces and ducked our heads as if we walked against a strong wind. Despite the company which awaited us there, I was heartily glad to finally discern, nearly five yards in front of us, the façade of Simpson's glimmer through the murk of the atmosphere.

The polished mahogany and gentle clink of crystal and silver improved my spirits, at least until we found ourselves in a private salon with a fire in the grate and stately palms in the corners, for it was then I laid eyes once more on Leslie Tavistock. In his office I had hardly taken notice of his physique, but now I saw he stood rather below average in height, with sharp, alert brown eyes which bespoke cunning rather than intellect. His light brown, slicked-back hair and expressive hands enhanced the impression of a man who had ascended to his current position by whatever means he had thought necessary.

"It is an honour to meet you in person, Mr. Holmes," he cried, approaching my friend with a hand outstretched, which my friend studiously ignored. "Ah, well," he continued, turning the failed greeting into a flourish of understanding with a flick of the wrist, "I can hardly blame you. Public figures grow so accustomed to hearing their praises sung by the adoring masses that any censure can be most disconcerting."

"Particularly when said masses take it into their heads to kill you," Holmes replied dryly.

"By Jove!" Tavistock exclaimed. "You didn't venture into the Eastend again, did you? It isn't a safe neighbourhood, you know. But how you interest me, Mr. Holmes. Would you care to elaborate on what you were doing there?"

My friend smiled the slow, frigid smile of a bird of prey. "Mr. Tavistock, beyond the facts that you are a bachelor, a snuff user, a union advocate, and a gambler, I know nothing whatever about you. However, I do know that if you refuse to reveal to me your source for these damning articles, you will very soon come to regret it."

While I was familiar enough with Holmes's methods to note the disheveled attire, the fine dust on his shirt cuff, the discreet pin, and the two open racing periodicals upon the table, the journalist was not. A twinge of fear crossed Tavistock's features, though he attempted to hide his chagrin with a laugh while he poured three glasses of brandy.

"So you can make clever guesses about people. I thought that an invention of Dr. Watson's admirable style."

"The guesses, as you term them, are in fact the very least stylistic aspect of the good doctor's literary efforts."

Tavistock handed us two snifters of brandy, which we accepted, though I have never been less inclined to share a drink with anyone in my life. "Mr. Holmes, you seem to have got it into your head that

I have done something terribly wrong. I assure you, though my humble pieces may have afforded you some temporary inconvenience—which, believe me, I heartily regret—my responsibility is to inform the public."

"Do you really wish to act in the public interest?" Holmes asked.

"Without question, Mr. Holmes."

"Then tell me who approached you."

"You must understand that is impossible," the insufferable man replied smugly, "for his interests are also those of defending the populace, even if it means defending them from you."

"If you dare to imply to our faces again that my friend is capable of such barbarities, you will answer for it to me," I could not help but interject in fury.

"We are going," Holmes said quietly, setting his glass down untouched.

"Wait!" Tavistock called out, anxiety clouding his clever features. "Mr. Holmes, I am a fair man. If you were to grant me an interview, I assure you our next publication would present you in a very different light indeed."

"Mr. Tavistock, it should not shock you to hear that you are the very last person in London to whom I would entrust any words on that subject," my friend replied icily.

"Forgive me, Mr. Holmes, but that is absurd. You have the opportunity to emerge from the mud a figure of the purest intentions."

"You are dreaming."

"It is the most compelling story in decades!" he cried. "Sherlock Holmes, noble sentinel of justice or perverse scourge of carnality? All you have to do is provide me with a few salient details."

"If you will not reveal your source, you are not of the slightest use to me."

Tavistock's eyes narrowed slyly. "Do you really think your investigation stands any chance of success if the residents of Whitechapel consider you the killer?"

Holmes shrugged, but I could see from the tightening of his jaw that the same thought had crossed his mind.

"Come, now." The reporter pulled a notebook out of his coat pocket. "Just a few statements, and we'll make the most stirring headline you've ever set eyes on."

"Good night, Mr. Tavistock."

"But your career!" Tavistock protested desperately. "Can't you see, it doesn't matter to me, so long as the story is mine!"

Holmes shook his head, disgust at the pressman's admission clouding his brow. "I think the air is cleaner out of doors, Watson."

Outside, the acrid atmosphere remained viscous and faintly sickening. Cabs could not operate in such weather, so we walked toward Regent Street in silence, each lost in uneasy reflections. I could not help but agree with Tavistock's taunting declaration: if feelings against Holmes continued to run as high as they had the night before, not merely his investigation but his very life was in danger.

We had nearly reached Baker Street when Holmes broke the silence. "You are entirely correct, my dear fellow. I cannot hope to act with impunity in Whitechapel while Tavistock's slanders still retain their power. In the last five minutes, you have glanced at my profile four times; you are right in observing that the *London Chronicle's* illustration was disturbingly accurate, and we both suffered the results last night."

I smiled in spite of myself, and Holmes sighed ruefully. "It's a lucky thing I have only one confidant. Explaining myself only knocks little holes in the masonry of my reputation."

"Your reputation—"

"Has greater problems just now, to be sure. I am glad I have laid eyes on Tavistock, in any event. I was willing to take your word he was a scoundrel, but there is nothing like exposure to the genuine article. He let one curious phrase drop."

"Did he?"

"He said his source wished to protect the populace. If he thinks the populace will be any better off without me, he is either a lunatic himself or a—" I waited hopefully, but soon Holmes shook his head and continued. "We can discard one hypothesis—that this Tavistock cur has some reason to persecute me. He made it nauseatingly clear I could be inducted as prime minister or be drawn and quartered with my head on a pike just so long as he is allowed to write it up."

"Is there anything I can do, Holmes?"

We had reached our own door, though it was barely discernible through the gloom. "No, no, my dear fellow. I fear that it is I who must act. And act I shall."

That night Holmes folded himself into his armchair with one knee drawn up to his chin, staring fixedly at the numbers on the torn page from the Ripper's gift of a cigarette case. For more than an hour he remained in the same position with his eyes nearly closed, as still and solitary as an oracle, smoking endless bowls of shag, until I retired to bed and my own ruminations about the trials before us.

The next morning I found a note in my friend's clear, fastidious script wedged under the butter dish.

My dear Watson,

It is just possible that my investigations will not allow me to return to Baker Street for some brief while. You will appreciate that time is of the essence, and my inquiries in the East-end are of such a nature they can be conducted far more effectively alone. Do not worry, I beg, and do not stray too far afield, however sordid London has grown, for I hope very soon to have need of your assistance. Letters will reach me if directed to the Whitechapel Post Office branch, to be left until called for by Jack Escott.

S. H.

P.S.—As my new researches have taken a more dangerous turn, you will be delighted to learn I have directed Miss Monk to take a paid hiatus.

I need hardly state that the postscript rather worked against Holmes's prior instruction not to fear for his own safety. While acknowledging to myself that he could indeed work more efficiently alone, and had done so during many of our shared cases, unbidden thoughts also flew into my mind of occasions when the danger had proven too great for one man, even if that one man was Sherlock Holmes.

Mrs. Hudson poked her head round the edge of the door. "It's Miss Monk to see you, Dr. Watson."

Our colleague's expressive features were weighted with concern. She pulled off a new pair of gloves and concealed them in a pocket.

"Good afternoon, Miss Monk."

"Mrs. Hudson's just offered tea, though it ain't my usual time. She is a dear one, isn't she?"

"Please sit down. I am delighted to see you, considering—"

"Considering I've been sacked?" she asked with the trace of a smile.

"Good heavens, no!"

I handed the note to her, and her eyes flew back to mine in alarm. "What's he up to all alone, then?"

"I am afraid that Sherlock Holmes is the most solitary man I have ever encountered in my travels on three separate continents. I have no more idea what he is doing than you do."

Biting her lip, she approached the fire I'd allowed to die down and stabbed it combatively with the fire iron. "I've had a telegram from him this morning before breakfast. I ain't getting paid for sitting in pubs chatting up drunken judies," she declared, straightening. "What can we do?"

"Your sitting in pubs certainly led us to some intriguing results last time."

"It's a gift, I'll own. But the well's run a mite dry. Thought I'd hit a good line t'other day, but her idea the Knife can transport himself by electricity sort of threw a wet blanket on the rest of her story. Poor Miss Lacey. It's the laudanum, I promise you. What else?"

"Miss Monk, as much as may be dark to us, I've learned that most of it is generally clear to Holmes," I pointed out. "It may be foolish to take any precipitate steps."

"I'll be damned if there isn't *something* we could do, even if it's to patrol the streets with little striped wristbands."

"Well," I replied slowly, "it would certainly profit Holmes to have Leslie Tavistock discredited."

"The journalist? I'd give a good deal to see his face in the mud." My companion shot up again and took a turn around the carpet, her freckled brow tense with concentration.

"Miss Monk?"

"It may not wash. But if it worked . . ."

"My dear Miss Monk, what is it?"

"Doctor, it would do Mr. Holmes a world of good if we could discover where Tavistock digs up his trash, wouldn't it?"

"I should think so indeed."

"I know I can do it."

"What precisely do you have in mind?"

"I don't rightly like to tell you, as it may come to naught. But if it works, it might be a ream flash pull. It'll take a bit of conniving on my part, perhaps, but if he can get it . . ." She came to a breathless halt. "Tell you what, I'll bring it here to you and you can decide." She retrieved her black gloves and waved them at me from the door.

"My dear Miss Monk, I absolutely forbid you to take any risks in this matter!" I called out.

It was to no avail. A moment later she was halfway down the stairs. I could just hear her good-natured apologies to Mrs. Hudson over the tea things as she lilted out the front door into the fog like a melody on the breeze.

CHAPTER TWENTY-THREE

The Fleet Street Enterprise

As it happened, I did not see Miss Monk again until Tuesday, the thirtieth of October, during which heart-wrenching period I heard not a single word from Sherlock Holmes. According to Lestrade, the men of the Yard were greatly discouraged. Rumours of mad kosher slaughtermen and deranged doctors ran so wild in the district that it was all they could do to keep the peace. And as if it were not enough that they suffered defamation from every quarter for their failure to locate the Ripper, they now faced the burden of diverting a significant portion of their force to police the Lord Mayor's resplendent annual procession on Friday, the ninth of November.

It may be imagined that, with the weight of the Whitechapel problem bearing down upon me, not to mention the disturbing absence of Holmes, I spent my days endeavouring to relieve my tumultuous state of mind without straying too far from Baker Street should matters come to a head. Novels were intolerable, and the atmosphere of my club stale and wearisome. On that sleepless Tuesday night, while attempting to defy all my friend's injunctions against recording a case I had filed under "The Adventure of the Third Candle," I had just determined that a glass of claret would do me more good than harm when I heard the avid ringing of the downstairs bell.

Knowing Mrs. Hudson to be long abed, I hurried down the stairs, fully dressed, for I had not yet entertained any thought of sleep. When I unlatched the door, I discovered, to my great surprise, Miss Monk and Stephen Dunlevy.

"Forgive the lateness of the hour, Dr. Watson," Dunlevy began, "but Miss Monk was determined not to let the matter wait."

"You are most welcome. I have been expecting Miss Monk, in any event."

Once upstairs, I opened the claret and located two more glasses. Dunlevy sat in the basket chair, while Miss Monk stood proudly before the fire with the air of an orator who has been asked to make a statement. When I had seated myself, she set her glass upon the mantel and drew a small object out of her garments.

"It's a present for you, Doctor." She grinned broadly as she tossed a piece of metal through the air and I caught it, turning it over in my hand.

It was a key. "All right," I said, laughing, "I'm game. What does it open?"

"Leslie Tavistock's office."

"My dear Miss Monk!"

"I'd a mind to see whether Dunlevy here was good for anything apart from shadowing decent folk," she said happily, settling herself upon the arm of the sofa. "But I know you was worried about taking any steps wi'out Mr. Holmes, for good reason too, so once we'd got it, we legged it straight here to turn it over."

"Mr. Dunlevy, would you care to elaborate how this came into your possession?"

The young man cleared his throat. "Well, Miss Monk did me the honour of appearing at my door the Thursday before last, and explained to me her belief that, as I am a journalist and journalists are a clubbish sort of folk, always rubbing shoulders to be apprised of the latest developments, it was inconceivable to her that I would not have an acquaintance at the *London Chronicle*. Miss Monk's conjecture was not entirely correct, but it may as well have been, for I've a friend at the *Star* who has a very close connection with a chap by the name of Harding, who is employed there."

"I see. And then?"

"The young lady's idea, and a very clever one if I may say so, was to coerce Harding into taking an impression of Tavistock's key. As it happens, no coercion proved necessary."

"Tavistock's a complete rotter," Miss Monk interrupted. "We might have known as much, the way he went after Mr. Holmes."

Dunlevy quickly suppressed what appeared to be the beginnings of a fond smile and went on. "As Miss Monk says, there is no one so universally reviled at the *London Chronicle* as Leslie Tavistock. It took a couple of days' management, but I met with Harding in the company of our mutual friend for a glass of beer, made the suggestion, and was instantly heaped with praise for my idea of playing a prank on the most friendless man in journalism."

"A prank," I repeated, beginning to see the inspired simplicity of their plan. "What sort of prank do you intend?"

"Oh, I daresay we could accomplish something nice with paint, and there's always dead rats to consider," Miss Monk remarked with an air of delighted nonchalance. "There's a horse slaughterer not far from Dunlevy's East-end digs. And of course, once we were in the office—"

"This little pleasantry may take us considerably more time than one would think," I finished.

"With all his papers just lying about, it would be a shame not to glance through them, eh, Doctor?"

"Wait a moment. We know nothing of Tavistock's hours, or indeed, those of the building itself."

"Harding has proffered very eager cooperation," Dunlevy explained. "It seems he was once investigating a story which Tavistock got wind of, and had it stolen right out from under him. He took an impression of Tavistock's office key, and this duplicate was in my hands a day later. There is no getting into the building undetected during the week, for as you must know the press keeps all hours. Saturday night is the only clear time, for as they have no Sunday publication, Harding says that the lot of them scatter to pubs in the area or go home to their families."

"What of security when the building is locked?"

"Harding is prepared to lend us his own outer door key in light of the nobility of our mission. As for security, the offices have not seen fit to employ a night guard. There will no doubt be a beat officer of some kind nearby, but that is easily ascertained."

"It will put us in a monstrous position to rifle through his office in such a manner," I cautioned.

"That may be, but the cause is righteous and the quarrel just. Mr. Holmes has a right to know who has invented these aspersions, and though he seemed to accept my protestations of innocence, I would be very glad to see it proven."

"It is alarming to consider what steps Tavistock could take if we are caught."

"I know, Doctor," said Miss Monk sympathetically, "but if you'll just reread those two articles what weren't fit for dead fish to be wrapped in, it'll shore up your nerve right quick."

I may say without undue pride or fear of contradiction that I have never been a man to back away from danger where a comrade's interests are concerned. "Saturday," I mused. "It gives us three clear days to perfect our plans."

"And who knows but that Mr. Holmes may be back by then!" Miss Monk exclaimed. "But if we've still seen no sign of him, we can at least try to clear up one dark spot in this bloody mess."

"Miss Monk, Mr. Dunlevy," said I, rising from my chair, "I congratulate you. Here's to the health of Mr. Sherlock Holmes."

In such a depth of numbing uncertainty, it was impossible not to feel uplifted at the mere idea of a mission. Still later that night, when I at last blew out my bedside candle, I began to wonder if—for a mind as incandescent as that of my friend—perhaps inaction could truly be so torturous that a syringe and a bottle of seven-percent solution seemed the only tolerable recourse.

Our schemes developed quickly. Miss Monk was kind enough to hawk some handkerchiefs in the vicinity of the building until she was warned off by a policeman, after which she quietly pursued him and found that his route took him directly past the entrance: a cause for anxiety, perhaps, for a callow housebreaker, but hardly of any concern for one possessed of a set of keys. Moreover, the enthusiastic Harding informed us that Tavistock's office did not look out upon the street, so that a lamp could be lit there and never be noticed in the darkness of the surrounding building.

There was initially some discussion regarding who would attempt the endeavour itself, but Miss Monk would not hear of being left behind, and as Dunlevy's presence was deemed likewise necessary, I faced breaking into Leslie Tavistock's place of employment as part of a courageous band of three. We met on Friday to work out a story in case of emergency, the following evening at eleven fixed as the start of our nocturnal enterprise.

At a quarter after ten that Saturday night, I walked as far south as Oxford Street, then hailed a cab, for the air had cleared considerably and the last traces of fog swirled about the windows as playfully as a child's toy ribbon, tempting faceless passersby further into the night. We approached the Strand by way of Haymarket, and I alighted from the hansom with ten minutes to spare. Turning onto a side street, I descended the steps of a tiny public house and hailed Miss Monk and Mr. Dunlevy, who had engaged a small corner table lit by an oil lamp which I do not think had ever been cleaned.

"Ladies and gentlemen," declared Stephen Dunlevy, a smile tugging at the corner of his moustache as we raised our glasses, "I give you Mr. Alistair Harding, a man who holds a grudge with vigour and enthusiasm."

"Miss Monk, have you the bag?" I inquired.

She tapped a small burlap sack with the toe of her boot.

"In that case, let us be on our way. Miss Monk, we will see you in ten minutes."

Leaving Miss Monk in the pool of light at the table, Dunlevy and I strolled past the last stately buildings of the Strand, through the demarcation of the Temple Bar where the great stone archway had once stood, and thus entered Fleet Street, that strident nucleus of British journalism. The area was calm so late on a Saturday, and the general impetus of the pedestrians seemed that of departure rather than arrival.

Dunlevy approached the front door of 174 Fleet Street, stolid block lettering declaring it to be the home of the *London Chronicle,* and inserted Mr. Harding's key in the lock. Seconds later, we were within the vestibule, Dunlevy pulling a dark lantern from within his voluminous coat.

"I see no sign of occupation," he mouthed cautiously.

"We will know for certain once we have reached the upper floor."

With painstakingly silent tread, we advanced up the stairs to the first floor, where no more light met our eyes than the beam of our own lantern. I knew my way, and passing through the common room, we proceeded directly to the second office, secured with one simple lock. I withdrew the key from my pocket and opened the door.

Dunlevy fully unshuttered the eye of the dark lantern and the room flooded instantly with light. Papers lay strewn across the desk, and files sat upon bookcases and lay open over reference volumes. We began shuffling through the scattered texts, careful to keep them in order lest the true reason for our nocturnal visit be revealed. We had been reading every scrap of paper we could lay our hands on for several minutes when a low whistle from Dunlevy arrested my attention.

"Hullo! Here is something."

I abandoned the disjointed jottings of my own chosen page and focused instead upon Dunlevy's, which read:

There have been no murders since Holmes was wounded, which is very likely not a coincidence.

Has expressed contempt for police in past cases.

Continues to frequent the East-end.

Then, scrawled at the bottom of the page:

Holmes has disappeared. An admission of guilt?

"Good lord, Dr. Watson, I never anticipated there may be more of this garbage in the works."

"I confess I feared as much, but this is uglier than the others combined."

"But see—this page could not have been written by Tavistock. The handwriting is different." From down the stairs, I heard the creak of the outer door.

"What sort of papers are those?" I asked.

"This is the beginnings of an article, and here is a letter, signed by Tavistock, not yet sent. These are in the same hand as most of the documents on the desk. The note about Mr. Holmes must be suggestions from the rascal's source."

Miss Monk entered and shut the door behind her. "What's up, then?"

"This note seems to have been penned by the cause of all this trouble," said I.

She looked over my shoulder. "A man's writing. Mr. Holmes would make something of it."

"I would take it to him, but there cannot appear to be anything missing," I considered, copying the noisome text into my pocketbook.

"Is there an envelope?" Miss Monk asked. We cast about for one in the basket full of crumpled scribblings. Soon she emerged from under the desk with a flush of triumph.

230 🏶 Lyndsay Faye

"Dated Saturday the twentieth. Paper matches the envelope, addressed to Leslie Tavistock, *London Chronicle*. It's in the same hand! We can take the envelope, for it won't be missed."

Our search brought to light more documents but no new information. The same man had written three other letters to Tavistock, once to arrange an appointment and twice to forward fresh news of Holmes, but as they had already resulted in calamity, they told us nothing. At length, as the hour approached one o'clock in the morning, I suggested we depart.

As Dunlevy and I cast a final glance over the room to ensure we had not left any identifying traces, Miss Monk picked up the burlap sack she had propped against the wall, and, with an air of courtly ceremony, deposited its contents upon the desk, dropping the bag in the dustbin with a final toss of her head.

We made our way downstairs. As I reached my hand toward the door handle and the outside world beyond it, I started at the sound of approaching footsteps. I signaled my companions to step back. Scarcely breathing, I prayed silently to hear the same tread depart, but to my dismay, the handle of the door was tested and then pushed carefully open.

In an instant, Stephen Dunlevy opened the shutter of the dark lantern and sprang before the door, his hand raised as if to open it when a grey-whiskered police constable entered with his truncheon in hand.

"Oh, I say! How you startled me, Officer," Dunlevy exclaimed.

The stout fellow returned his truncheon to his belt but regarded us with suspicion.

"Do you mind telling me what the three of you are doing here? There's never a soul in the building at this time on a Saturday."

"To be sure, my good man. I admit, though, you gave us a fright."

"No doubt," he replied tersely. "You have a set of keys, do you?"

"Indeed, yes. I must say, sir, I admire your thoroughness in policing, if you always check locked doors while on your beat."

"I string the locked doors, as most of us do. The string was broken."

"Aha! Very workmanlike, Constable . . . ?"

"Brierley."

"Well, then, Constable Brierley, my colleague and I required absolute secrecy in order to interview this young woman."

"And why might that be?"

"She claimed to hold very valuable information about the Ripper murders."

Miss Monk nodded shyly, half hidden behind my shoulder.

"And why was it necessary to meet in the dead of night in a deserted press building?"

"It's very dangerous information, Officer," she whispered.

"Well, if you've information about the Ripper murders, miss, you must tell me what it is that you know."

"Please, sir," she said, shuddering, "they'll come after me, I know it."

"Who will come after you?"

"His friends—they'll murder me in my sleep."

"Come now, my dear," the constable said serenely. "If you are in any danger, we will provide you with protection."

"You don't know them! It's as much as my life is worth to gab to the Yard."

"Nevertheless, I must insist upon it."

"Very well," Miss Monk replied in an agony of distress. "I know who the killer is."

"And who might that be?" the patient constable demanded.

"Prince Albert Victor."

I did my best to regard Miss Monk with the air of an abundantly disappointed and exceedingly irritable newsman. It was difficult to achieve.

Constable Brierley sighed heavily. "Is he indeed? I will pass that startling piece of news on to my superiors. And now, the three of you had best go on about your business. I strongly suggest that your business take you home without delay."

Our return journey to the Strand was a silent one for some three blocks, until we had left all trace of Constable Brierley behind us and Stephen Dunlevy threw his head back with a peal of relieved laughter.

"Prince Albert Victor?"

"I'm sure he would be glad to know his name came in handy," Miss Monk remarked.

"Miss Monk, you are absolutely unparalleled. Well, Dr. Watson, I dearly hope that the envelope will be of some use to Mr. Holmes."

"You may be sure I will keep you apprised."

"In any event, the evening has been most enormously satisfying. Miss Monk, I beg you will do me the honour of sharing a cab with me back to the East-end."

"The honour is granted. Oh, Dr. Watson, I do hope we've helped Mr. Holmes."

"We have helped Alistair Harding, in any event," Dunlevy proclaimed gaily. "I'm to return his keys in the morning. I have not a doubt but that when he hears the news, he will be the happiest man in London."

CHAPTER TWENTY-FOUR

The East-end Division

As I sat at the breakfast table next morning, feeling not a little self-satisfied, I turned the envelope over in my hands pondering the best way to get it to Holmes. No doubt he had made excellent arrangements, for he was continually darting off to the country or to the Continent and never had I seen him without prompt postal service. However, perhaps from a sense of innate pride in our accomplishment and perhaps from a certain leery caution, I found myself in midafternoon with the hard-won object still resting in an inner pocket and realized that I had grown irrationally determined to deliver it to my friend in person. How I could go about that task I had barely begun to surmise, but circumstances soon occurred which lifted the burden of ingenuity from my shoulders entirely.

The frail light had begun to fade and the combative autumn winds come to blows with the last of the dry leaves when the pageboy arrived with a hand-delivered note from Holmes. The message was addressed to Dr. John Watson and read:

> *Am on our quarry's scent. Meet me at the corner of Commercial Street and Brick Lane at once, on foot, and bring your medical bag, as I fear we may have need of it.*
>
> *Sherlock Holmes*

I need hardly say that not only my black bag but my cleaned, loaded revolver were at hand in an instant, and I bounded into the street to hail a cab. It was just past seven o'clock in the evening as I set off, and the stolid, pastel houses passed by me in a darkening blur. Descending from the hansom just as night officially triumphed over day, I cast about for the correct orientation.

To my complete dismay, almost instantly, my direction grew twisted and confused due to the bizarre fact that the streets Holmes had indicated ran parallel to each other. After some deliberation, I determined to follow Brick Lane to see whether it intersected any roads of a similar name to Commercial Street, for often the names of London thoroughfares repeated themselves, and after turning off Stoney Street, one would hardly be surprised to find oneself in Stoney Lane. It was not a mistake typical of Sherlock Holmes's exhaustive memory, but I could account for it in no other way and so determined to find the true cross street even if it took me all night.

I fell victim to nothing more than a few haphazard jeers for the first half hour, but as I retraced my steps down Brick Lane past Hebraic fellowship halls and the smell of frying sausages, sick at the thought I might have failed Holmes at the culmination of his labour through a simple misdirection, I became aware that the shouts of the locals were increasing in frequency as they narrowed in scope.

"Oy, you doctor! Out to sew up a whore?"

"Looking for a fresh one to patch together, are you, or will you do it yourself?"

These gibes soon became so antagonistic that I ducked down a quiet alley to think of a way to contact Holmes, if that were even possible. I had not been there two minutes, however, leaning against a barrel and straining to recall every detail of Whitechapel's topography, when a group of five men approached me from the left, their mean figures silhouetted by the single jaundiced lamp. Even had I not been accustomed to the advent of sudden danger, my instincts would have alerted me to their postures and the cudgels they carried in slack, cavalier grips.

Initially I hoped they had some other object in mind and would pass me by, but the leader of the gang, a heavyset man with bristling hair and weighty jowls, nodded to the others to stay back and advanced toward me, tapping his stick against a meaty palm.

"Good evening," I began. "Is there a problem?"

"Well, lads? What say you? I believe Underhill thought there might be a problem, is that not so?"

His four footpads laughed, slapping a thin, evil-eyed man with a wicked gash for a mouth upon the back. "That's it! Underhill! He's not easy in his mind, he isn't," one of them chuckled.

"Look here, sir," I attempted, "I am—"

"Wait just a tick, guv. These is dangerous times we find ourselves in. So let's say it comes to our attention that there has been sighted a bloke, a medical type of bloke, what's pacing the area as if he's . . . well, he has a prowling manner about him, if you understand me."

"Now, see here, my good man—"

"And let's further suppose that I, Ezekiel Hammersmith, being a chap of upstanding character, let's say I calls me lads from the pub so as to get a better look at this medical bloke what's lying in wait in a dark alley ten yards from me sister's lodging house." The brute smiled evilly and glanced up at a dingy hellhole of red brick.

"No, no, guv'nor," he continued sadly. "Folk of your type need a powerful reason to be in these parts after dark." He dropped his voice to a gravelly undertone. "By God, you'll wish you'd never seen a whore before we're done wi' you."

I reached for my revolver in an effort to deter them from five-on-one hand combat, but a swarthy fellow missing the majority of his left ear leapt forward and hacked my arm away with a cane. He had attempted two more solid blows, one narrowly missing my forearm and a second aimed at the neck that I managed to take on the shoulder, when his proximity afforded me the opportunity of delivering the left-handed hook which had many years previous granted me total freedom of movement at my rough-and-tumble grammar school.

Just then a very slender man entered the alley behind me, whistling softly to himself and carrying a long-handled brush over his left shoulder. His face and all his dark clothing were obscured by soot, and I saw at once that he was a chimney sweep returning home from an engagement. In a far-off corner of my mind, I noted in confusion that the tune he whistled was from Wagner's *Parsifal*, but all my thoughts were suspended when the fellow stopped short at seeing so many rough characters wedged into the narrow corridor.

"What's the trouble?" he asked.

"Be on your way, if you don't want a piece of it for yourself," Hammersmith replied, stepping aside to let him pass. "This gentleman here is down on whores, and we are helping to make his peace with them."

Fate, as I have often had cause to reflect, is a fickle entity. At one moment, five armed brutes bore down upon two guiltless men harbouring no wish to fight. The next moment, two of the five lay on the ground howling in pain, their ribs victimized by the long-handled tool of the chimney sweep. Hammersmith, who had narrowly escaped the assault, roared with rage, threw his club to the ground, reached under his trouser leg, and charged me and my new ally with a vicious short-handled knife.

Though I at last drew my revolver, I was ultimately spared its use. The sweep dealt him a crushing jab to the solar plexus, then hissed, "Down the passage and keep at my heels." Sherlock Holmes then took my arm and we flew through the alleyway into a series of mews, over a low fence, and into the windswept autumn night.

Though we ran for perhaps ten minutes, I had the impression we did not get very far. Holmes executed a few simple dodges and once stopped to listen intently for our pursuers, then led me through a series of interconnected alleys littered with wood and broken shipping crates before finally, to my great surprise, he ducked into a low doorway and ushered me inside.

Hastening up the dark stairway with more regard for speed than for caution, I would likely have plummeted through to the floor below had not Holmes pulled me back just in time to prevent my falling down a rotting gap. At last, after two positively archaeological flights of stairs, we reached a door at the end of a brief hallway. My friend flung it open with a flourish, so far as such a rude assemblage of slats can be said to be flung.

"May I present, with all attendant welcome and ceremony, the Baker Street Private Consulting Detective Agency, East-end Division, the pulsing nucleus of the Ripper investigation."

Sherlock Holmes maintained, so far as his fortunes permitted, no fewer than five and more probably seven secret lairs throughout London. Some boasted no more comforts than a basin and a trunk of clothes, but he often employed these nooks when a disguise or pursuit necessitated immediate private rooms. In all my many years of partnership with Holmes, I was introduced personally to a total of three such dwellings, as my friend's native passion for secrecy prevented me from ever so much as laying eyes on the others.

This startling Whitechapel refuge consisted of a rectangular room, slightly longer than it was wide, with no windows, walls entirely papered with maps and news clippings, and two new, stout inner bolts of differing builds which Holmes proceeded efficiently to lock, finally fastening me with a look of inquiring concern.

"I should have liked to introduce you to our secondary branch under more relaxed circumstances, my dear fellow, but in any event you have immediately seen its usefulness. We are now on Scarborough Street, just south of Whitechapel Road. You will note that we have as much relevant information as possible at our fingertips, that we are fully equipped to maintain every requirement of hygiene and civility, and that a rather fine brandy rests upon the corner table. Pray help yourself to any amenities you see fit."

The "corner table" referred to an upended water barrel adjacent to a straw mattress and a pile of clean, if worn, grey wool blankets. The room had no other rugs or furnishings save a dangerous-looking stove next to the fireplace, a battered desk, and two chairs, one of which appeared in a former life to have been an orange crate.

"Holmes, what exactly have you been doing in this cave?" I asked, advancing without hesitation toward the spirits on the makeshift side table and shaking my head at my friend's considerable eccentricities. Holmes sat down upon the orange crate, removing his coat and vigorously applying a damp cloth to his blackened visage.

"I have been making the acquaintance of a great many members of Her Majesty's army who have fallen under the spell of *Papaver somniferum*.* In fact, I've every hope of discovering Blackstone's lodgings tomorrow." Though jubilant, freed from its mask of soot, my friend's face showed clear signs that he skirted the edge of complete exhaustion.

"But that is marvelous, Holmes!" I exclaimed. "By the by, I suppose I mistook the instructions, but however did you happen to find me?"

Holmes's expression of perplexity, so rarely in evidence, only increased. "Finding myself without occupation for the evening, I was patrolling the streets, and I flatter myself with more discernment than your acquaintances of the alley. My dear Watson, I believe that there is not a soul in the world I should be happier to see just now, but may I ask what on earth you were doing wandering about Whitechapel with a medical bag and a sinister expression?"

"You summoned me here. Is this not your message?"

After casting an eye over the brief letter, Holmes looked at me in dismay.

"I corresponded with no one this afternoon."

"Then you did not send for me?"

"Not I. When did you receive this?"

"Half past five in the afternoon."

"It did not come through the post."

"No, it was delivered."

---

* Opium poppy.

"Did you ask Billy what sort of man he got it from?"

"I thought it immaterial once I had seen your signature."

"You know nothing of this note's origin, then?"

"Nothing whatever."

At length he cried out, "I cannot imagine what object you had in mind to follow these instructions, but this epistle is certainly penned by an adversary."

"What object I had in mind?" I retorted readily. "You required my help!"

"No, no, Watson, it is all wrong. These certainly are my *t*s, *y*s, and *m*s, and the capital *A* is very good, but what on earth induced you to obey a note with such a manifestly inaccurate *q*?"

"My training as a doctor of medicine, I regret to say, was deficient in handwriting analysis," I returned with greater asperity. "I supposed it written under some duress."

"A thousand small clues should have given this away! For example, you and I have known each other for over seven years, yet in this brief note, I somehow see fit to include your prefix, given, and family names."

"Surely not surprising if the conveyor of the message did not know me."

"The paper, then! My stationery—"

"Is irrelevant as you were not at home," I shot back heatedly. "However, if you wish, in the future I shall treat all your emergency summonses with suspicion and disbelief."

Holmes softened with a visible effort. "It is only your safety which worries me, after all. I regret that little business back in the alley, but now that we have it, this note . . . this note is of immense interest. Its author has done a very workmanlike job of my signature; however, the remainder of the lettering was formed very slowly, which is a sure indication of forgery. Still, it is quite obvious that whoever penned this message to plague us has had access to a genuine sample of my handwriting."

"Where on earth could he have obtained such a thing?"

"Ah, but we may draw still more conclusions: the document he has in his possession, while featuring a signature at the end, evinces fewer examples of my other characters. A short note, then, and I would wager fifty pounds one lacking the letter *q* entirely."

"Some villain has access to your correspondence?"

"I hardly see how."

"Your bank?"

"The Capital and Counties is renowned for its trustworthiness."

"Well, then, you may have dashed off a note to your solicitor or penned a response to a client. It is impossible to know where the sample was obtained."

"I will not say that you are wrong," my friend replied abstractedly, "but surely the balance of probability is enormously against an agent of evil happening upon my handwriting by chance. It is far more probable that he stole a missive from some party who could be assumed to possess a sample of my script. At once the field is narrowed considerably. There is yourself to consider, my brother, several inspectors of the Yard, and those agencies to which you have already so shrewdly alluded, such as my bank or solicitor."

"But stop a moment, Holmes—forgive me, but it was for good reason that I was particularly eager to meet with you this evening."

My friend indicated his interest with a tilt of his head, and I proceeded to tell him all that we three had accomplished in his absence. I am still delighted to recall that, when I had concluded my narrative, Sherlock Holmes himself appeared astonished in no small measure.

"And your tracks are entirely covered?"

"It will be thought a childish pleasantry enacted upon a particularly rank example of British journalism."

Holmes's eyes narrowed impishly. "What pleasantry?"

"An inspired whim of Miss Monk's devising. Rest assured it was entirely anonymous and that he will come to no lasting harm by it. The only thing of any interest was the note. It came in this envelope."

To my great shock, my friend's wan face paled still further.

"Holmes, whatever is the matter?"

He rushed to the wall, where notes were tacked in jagged rows, and pulled down perfect facsimiles of the last two letters we had received purportedly from Jack the Ripper.

"I knew he had motive, but it seemed too fantastic to contemplate. Surely I was within the bounds of reason to think it a paid mercenary or a political opportunist . . ."

"My dear fellow, what is it?"

"Look at it!" he cried, holding up a letter next to the envelope. "They are disguised, yes, but there cannot be a doubt in the world that these are penned by the same hand!"

"Do you mean to tell me that the man who has been tracing your movements, the blackguard who has set this journalist against you, is none other than Jack the Ripper himself?"

"Identical unmarked stationery to the kidney package," my friend murmured. "Dated only two days after I quit Baker Street. Postal district E one—Whitechapel, Spitalfields, and Mile End."

"Holmes, what can this possibly mean?"

My friend's eyes met mine with a hunted expression I had never seen there before. "It means that the Whitechapel killer is determined to see me blamed for his crimes. It also means that my movements, in any event those before I left Baker Street, were as open to him as the pages of a book. It is not a pretty thing to contemplate, Watson, but I very much fear the author of these murders has taken it upon himself to ruin me."

I stared at him aghast. "I am heartily sorry not to have furnished you with better news."

"My dear fellow, I am eternally grateful."

"Then what can we do?"

"We can do nothing yet. I must think," said he, sitting on the edge of the bed and drawing his knees into his wiry frame.

I nodded. "In that case, I shan't dream of interrupting you."

Holmes eyed me suspiciously. "You are not staying."

"Nonsense," said I. "I am assisting you in your work."

My friend leapt to his feet. "That is entirely out of the question," he cried. "Whatever nightmare it was before, this has developed into an extraordinarily dangerous undertaking."

"Precisely so," I agreed, helping myself to a woolen blanket.

"I categorically forbid it! You could fall prey to the gravest possible consequences if I am discovered."

"Then we must do our best to remain incognito." It was near impossible to ignore Holmes at his most imperious, but I had never been so set on a course of action in my life.

"Watson, you are the very least apt dissimulator it has been my privilege to know: in fact, I have hardly met anyone in my life whose mind is on more open display."

I felt my colour rise at these remarks, but then I thought of Holmes undergoing the same threats I had faced in that dark corridor, but every day and without an ally.

"Holmes, give me your word as a gentleman I could not possibly be of use to you here in Whitechapel."

"That is not the point!"

"Given your reputation for superior mental faculties, I should have thought you'd have grasped that it was."

After a glare of considerable acrimony, Holmes smiled in resignation.

"Well, well, if I cannot dissuade you, I suppose I must thank you."

"It will be my pleasure."

He returned to the pallet, spread himself across it, and crossed his feet upon the water barrel. "I daresay you'll find the surroundings a difficult adjustment."

"I served in the second Afghan war, Holmes. I imagine I shall be comfortable enough."

At this my friend sat bolt upright again with an exclamation of glee. "You have hit upon the very thing! And doubtless without any knowledge you have done so. The Afghan war . . . well done indeed."

"I am gratified to be of service."

"Good night, Watson," he called out, turning down the oil lamp and stuffing his pipe with shag. "I must beg you not to avail yourself of my razor come morning. Unshaven will do far better, I think. And Watson?" he added. I could hear from his tone he had largely recovered his good humour.

"Yes?"

"I shouldn't venture into the near right-hand corner. I am afraid it leaves something to be desired in the structural sense. Sleep well."

CHAPTER TWENTY-FIVE

Bonfire Night

I awoke the next morning to find Sherlock Holmes standing over me in his pea jacket and rough red scarf, tossing a heap of worn clothing in the corner. He was distressingly energized, and I knew from the deep arcs under his eyes that his night had been a sleepless one.

"What is the time?"

"Close upon eight."

"You have been out?"

"I have been rambling about town and took the liberty of making a few purchases on your behalf."

"Indeed? Have you eaten?"

"A cup of coffee. Now, Watson, I trust you won't mind exercising a small precaution I've been forced to employ when traveling in these circles. I would appreciate your donning the exceedingly shabby attire to your immediate left, topped with that old coat. Forgive me for having torn it in a few places. Just at the moment, you appear far too affluent to be associated with Jack Escott, but that hearty fellow will meet you downstairs in ten minutes' time, and we will take our morning wet at the Ten Bells public house, preceded by a good brisk walk."

In less than the time specified, I met Holmes (or rather, Holmes in the guise of the seafaring type I took to be called Jack Escott) downstairs, and we struck off in the coarse beige light of morning.

Twenty minutes had passed before the tavern appeared on the corner of Church Street, its doorway flanked by simple columns and its sign, black with "The Ten Bells" marked out in white lettering, swaying gently in the breeze. The single room inside was littered with chairs and knife-scarred tables, while the walls boasted pictorial tiling degraded nearly to ruins by a tenacious layer of grit.

"You are wondering what our intent may be," Holmes responded softly, though I had said nothing. "Never fear—just be sure to agree with me at every turn, and we'll soon come out all right."

The bar was far busier than I would ever have guessed at that hour, the locals industriously draining their cups before setting off to accomplish the labours or leisures of their respective days. A knot of bedraggled half-pay soldiers soon spied Holmes and waved us lazily over to their table.

"Where'd you pick up this one, then, Escott?" hailed a short fellow of middle years, with regulation side-whiskers and the peering red gaze of a man who is seldom if ever free from the influence of strong drink.

"This is Middleton, an old mate of mine just back in town. Murphy! A round of porter for the table."

"How are you, Middleton?" asked the soldier as more brews were poured. I was formulating a reply when my friend interjected.

"Oh, never mind him, Kettle. He was in Afghanistan, you know. Saw more of life than any of us should, or so I've gathered. Only talks when he's had a drop too many, and even then it's of Ghazis, bless him."

"What was it, then? Kandahar?"

Holmes laughed, wiping his mouth with the back of his hand. "Nothing so pleasant as that. Maiwand.* You'd best leave him be."

The former guardsmen squinted sympathetically. "Well, then, what about you, Escott? Back to the Three Cobras tonight?"

---

* Dr. Watson did indeed serve in the Battle of Maiwand, returning to England after having been severely wounded in action.

Holmes's eyes narrowed dreamily. "It had crossed my mind. Middleton here's a ruddy connoisseur of the stuff. We've been rambling about all night. Stumbled onto that fellow Blackstone, what was in Egypt a few years back."

"Johnny Blackstone? Haven't run into him for over a week now. Your friend here may keep mum more than is usual, but it's a sight more peaceful than that Blackstone's balmy talk."

"That'll be the black drop. He means no harm."

"I daresay you're right. But he was in a dark mood last I laid eyes on him."

"I meant to stop by his digs last week—he allowed as he'd be the better for company, but damned if there weren't a pipe in my hand when I said it. It was as much as I could do to recall it were in Spitalfields, let alone the address."

"He lives in Sandy's Row, over Widegate Street area. Keeps himself to himself for the most part, but I dropped in for a nightcap, last month it must have been, though I've not been back since. There he is up at the back of the building, windows all stopped up with scraps. Small wonder he's so few folk looking in."

"Maybe he likes it that way. At any rate, I've Middleton to share a morning pipe if Blackstone's too deep in the dumps to crawl out of 'em." My friend shrugged, finishing the last of his beer.

"You don't mean to stop by now, do you?" Kettle asked. "Lord knows what den he's holed up in. He's that cracked—sets off at one or two in the morning on his rambles and never thinks of his rooms till late the next day. If you want to find him there, look in tonight before midnight."

We said our good-byes and ambled outdoors. I could see the bustling eastern side of Spitalfields Market across the road from us, and the smell of livestock and freshly unearthed onions wafted along the street. My friend was a taut whipcord of suppressed vitality as we set off aimlessly down the road.

"That's done it," Holmes said quietly, but with the thrill of the chase in his clipped tenor. "I had the house number yesterday from a fellow called Wicks over three cups of gin."

"Have you all this while been seeking out Blackstone's lodgings?"

"Indeed yes. It is no joke to infiltrate a network of people and, through expert maneuvering, convey the impression that you have existed on the periphery for far longer than anyone can recall."

"I was astonished at their manner toward you. You might have known them for years."

"For the first five days, I divided no less than eighteen hours a day amongst the most popular dens between Whitechapel and Lime-house, my brain nothing more than a massive sponge. I flatter myself I had the lay of the land fairly quickly, deducing as much as I observed. Patterns began to emerge. When I felt confident enough, and these fellows had grown used to the sight of me, I began dropping names— a brother who'd reenlisted, a friend who'd died, a girl who hadn't been seen in years. I established undisputed, unprovable connections. At last my own story came out. Where had I been? At sea, these four years. Soon I was so universally trusted that I could elicit information with very little fear of being caught.

"When Mr. Li conveyed the message that Blackstone was at the Three Cobras, I arrived mere minutes too late, but his departure easily occasioned talk of him amongst his associates. Slowly, as if I were piecing together a smashed Abyssinian urn, an image emerged. He has not lived long in the area, and no one knew him before August. He resides alone, more often than not going about in a uniform in spite of his discharge. He is a mass of contradictions: despite his rugged good looks and cynical charm, he shuns the company of women. Though his mood is nearly always black and his temper violent, he is well liked by the other lads for his clever speech and free purse.

"I desired nothing more than to find out his lodgings, but it soon became clear that the slippery devil hardly ever receives guests. It could not have been more taxing, Watson—it was a more delicate combination of deductive reasoning and guarded conversation than I ever anticipated, but the final link you witnessed yourself, and the end of the search lies before us. I confess that I feared when you arrived, your presence would disrupt my little fiction. Thankfully, I had nearly reached my goal, and a trusty comrade will now be of inestimable use."

"No one else could have accomplished so much, and without arousing the slightest suspicion," I declared warmly.

Holmes waved away my compliment, but the gesture was a gentle one. "Your envelope is cause for the greatest concern. It was postmarked Saturday, the twentieth of October. Tavistock has had more damning information in his hands for over two weeks now. At any moment, he may publish another stylishly phrased defamation. Then there is the Ripper himself to consider; since he set out to terrorize the unfortunates of Whitechapel, he has never paused this long in his ungodly work. If the pattern of dates continues, he will strike again no later than the eighth of November."

"May we run the villain down tonight, for their sakes."

"For all of London, my dear fellow," he replied grimly. "But above all, for their sakes."

We passed the day easily in the ramshackle room, Holmes chatting desultorily of violins and their origins in sixteenth-century Italy until the sun had fallen. After a bowl of stew and tumbler of whiskey in a nearby tavern, we set off under the clearest night sky we had seen in some time. My friend steered us immediately north, and I quickly recognized our path as we passed the railway depot and crossed Aldgate High Street. A group of street urchins were setting off a riot of firecrackers in an old cistern, and I recalled as a shower of golden sparks fell upon the roofs of the warehouses that it was Guy Fawkes Day, the fifth of November.

"I cannot express how galling it was to have the house number from a semidelirious sot moments before he lost any pretense at consciousness," Holmes remarked as the crack and hiss of gunpowder faded into the distance. "However, despite the delay, it was as well we learned of the street from Kettle, for he knows more of Blackstone's habits than anyone."

"What do you imagine will happen, Holmes?"

"Suffice it to say we had best prepare for anything. In any event, I don't suppose either of us will ever again fail to remember the fifth of November."

We strode down a slick side street littered with whimsical configurations of rubbish gathered into heaps, which I gradually perceived were actually for sale. Broken pipes, cracked cookware, split boots, rusted keys, and twisted cutlery spilled onto the cobbles, and all the smells of the thrice-mended clothing permeated the air. Through this purgatory of lost objects Holmes picked his way easily, until we emerged onto an open byway, edged with warehouses whose smoke-stacks churned black exhalations into the night. Here numerous bonfires blazed, with crude Guy Fawkes effigies roasting above them, and the locals turned spitted potatoes over the coals as they cheered the roar of distant detonations.

My friend stopped at a corner and pointed without hesitation to a rickety structure which leaned against its neighbour for succour in its extreme old age. Though the street was unmarked at that juncture, I had no doubt but that Holmes's encyclopedic knowledge had led us directly to Blackstone's dwelling place.

"You have your weapon about you, I trust?"

"My service revolver is in my pocket."

"Very good." He plunged off the pavement, such as it was, and we approached the sagging grey door. The detective's knock produced nothing more than a hollow thumping which died away the instant it was produced.

"There seems to be no one on the ground floor," he whispered, cracking the lens of his dark lantern. "Let us see if there is any sign of life on the upper levels."

We tried the door and found it latched, but with the aid of his pocketknife, Holmes had it open in a few seconds. A mouse squeaked in the corner and then fled through shafts of lunar illumination to its sanctuary under the stair. My friend crept toward the staircase and ascended, I at his heels, each of us straining our ears for any indication that the floor we approached was occupied.

Two doors, each slightly ajar, presented themselves upon the next landing. The further one sat in shadow, the nearer lashed with bars of silver light from the cracked roof high above us. Without a sound, Holmes moved through the closer door and into the room.

Inside stood a perfect representation of a family's living quarters, with a pot on the stove, a pile of clothing half folded on the floor, even a string of carefully collected, brightly coloured bits of broken glass hung over a tiny basket draped with blankets in the corner. A thin film of dust lay over the entire room. I caught Holmes by the wrist.

"Out. Quickly," I ordered, and in a few steps we were back in the hallway. Holmes's searching expression swiftly cleared when he had deduced the cause behind the uncanny scene that I, as a doctor, had once encountered before.

"Cholera or smallpox?"

"It seems to be no longer worth finding out."

My friend nodded and immediately diverted his attention to the other door, which he opened with a gentle push before poking his head inside.

"This one is uninhabitable, at least in the winter. A fire seems to have eaten away the outer wall some years ago. Our man resides upstairs on the second floor."

Grasping the butt of my revolver firmly, I advanced up the final set of stairs behind Holmes. Though dustier and fallen into further disrepair, I did not need his finely honed senses to inform me that someone was in the habit of passing this way.

A single unmarked door appeared at the end of the second-floor corridor. My friend strode forward without a backward glance and threw open the final unlatched portal.

I saw at once, despite the poverty of light caused by strips of cloth hanging over the two tiny windows, that no one was there. Holmes opened the full flood of the lantern's brilliance and handed it to me. Remaining just outside lest I trample some fragment vital to his investigation, I replaced my revolver in my pocket and examined the room from the hallway. Filth encrusted every surface and a sickly sweet smell, like burnt sugar that had been allowed to decay, permeated the very walls of the place.

Holmes set instantly to exploring every inch of the chamber with an expression of the utmost gravity, and I very soon determined why. Apart from a blanket and a broken chair, not a single object remained in the room. And despite the noxious atmosphere, I failed to spy either pipe or bag which might have contained any opium.

"There has been some deviltry at work here," Holmes said in his coldest, most impassive tone. "Come in—there's nothing to be learned from the floor."

"Our bird appears to have flown," I commented.

"But in heaven's name, why? I was meticulous. I am prepared to swear that no one has the least idea I am even searching for him." Holmes gestured dispiritedly with a wide sweep of his lean arm. "A blanket, and a chair. They tell us nothing. And yet . . . in a sense, it is very peculiar. He has clearly taken all he possessed. Why should the blanket remain? No holes, no mice . . . Everything else is gone. Why leave this behind?"

"Perhaps he was determined to lighten his load."

"That is possible. But there is something about it I do not like. Let us leave this wretched place."

My friend's expression was set and neutral as we retraced our steps, yet somehow it was as dejected as I had ever seen. But our time in that house would not end so quickly as we had imagined, for as we descended the last set of stairs, the outer door swung forward to reveal a hollow-eyed woman, thin and spindly but with fiery red hair, accompanied by two children whose paper-thin complexions loudly declared their ill health.

Holmes, to his credit, held the lamp so that she could clearly see us and relapsed immediately into the charming seafarer whose identity he had laboured so long to establish.

"Oh, dear God!" the woman cried at seeing two strangers in what were, presumably, her rooms.

"Now, don't take on so," Holmes began in his most hypnotic tones. "We've come to see a friend, but we mean you no harm. He ain't here, so we're making our way back out again."

"What on earth do y' mean skulking about in here at night?"

"We made a poor job of it—please accept our apologies, ma'am. My name is Escott, and this here is Middleton."

"Timothy, Rebecca, go along to the room, now," she breathed in the lilting tones of the northern Irish native. "Take yer bundle, and eat yer share." When the children had run off clutching a small rag, she returned her gaze to my friend. "What's yer business, then?"

"We only wished to see your lodger."

"He owes you money, does he?"

"Nothing of the sort, ma'am."

She crossed her arms. "You truly are friends o' his, then? Or are you kin?"

My friend smiled. "I promise you we neither of us would dream of breaking into your house meaning any harm. We wanted a word with him, and that's the end of it."

"Well, you won't be having a word with him now."

"So it seemed to us upstairs," Holmes acknowledged, his eyes as sharp as knife points in the moonlight. "And why not?"

"Because," she said flatly, "if your friend is Johnny Blackstone, there's not a soul as can speak to him this side of the grave. Johnny Blackstone is dead."

CHAPTER TWENTY-SIX

The Lie

It was a great blessing for Holmes and me that we appeared in the character of Blackstone's friends, for the stunned expression that flitted across both our faces thus required no explanation.

The woman's thin lips parted sympathetically. "My name is Mrs. Quinn. I've naught to offer you for refreshment, as we've fallen lately upon some hard times. But if you've no objection to sitting a moment, I'll make it all as clear to ye as I can."

We thus found ourselves seated upon a pew in the well-kept but achingly bare room the Quinns shared. Similar pews lined the other three walls, scorched in places as if rescued from a fire, and a statue of the Virgin Mary whose cloak had half burned away sat majestically in a corner.

"Yer wondering at my furnishings," Mrs. Quinn observed. "There was a great fire at one of the chapels hereabouts some years ago, when Mr. Quinn was still alive. Much of it was piled up for burning, but my Colin, he said the Lord would be grieved to see us wi'out so much as a stone to sit on, and here He's provided us wi' benches that would remind us of His goodness every day.

"Wi'out Mr. Quinn these five years, times has gotten steadily worse, and I'd taken the notion of bringing in extra lodgers. God forgive me for saying since his death this house has seemed as cursed as any I've ever heard tell of back home. The first family lived happily enough upstairs before their eldest daughter took sick. The Connellys they were called, the six of 'em. Wasn't long before Katie'd spread the pox to the others, and it was all I could do to keep 'em supplied with hot water and linens wi'out exposing our family to the sickness. After four of 'em had died, the other two just disappeared into the night. I've been wanting to rent the room again, for it's months since they've gone, but the notion of cleaning it is a hard one, for I've more knowledge of how these things are passed than most, and I've a mortal terror of taking sick with Tim and Rebecca to think of.

"The other chamber was near enough destroyed when a kerosene lamp fell from a table, but I still had the attic room, and last August I rented it to yer friend, Johnny Blackstone, just after the Connellys all vanished. I think he liked this house, for it was so easy for him to be alone, and I hardly ever saw him from one day to the next. Whenever we did meet, often as not I'd have the little ones in tow, and he'd laugh at the sight of 'em. He'd leave treats for 'em at the foot of the stairs—harmless things, boats he'd made, and paper dolls and the like. But he always seemed in a hurry to be quit of us and would strike off for one of his dens, or run upstairs to smoke that foul pipe of his, and so it was that when he died last week, I never noticed for well-nigh three days' time. God forgive me for it."

"How did he die, Mrs. Quinn?"

"He hanged himself, Mr. Escott," she replied, her round hazel eyes brimming with tears.

Holmes and I regarded her with unfeigned horror, but she swiftly recovered her self-possession.

"The parish men took his body and performed a pauper's burial. I cast about a bit for any as knew him, but when none did, I came to think how he'd been behind in his rent, and the washing I take in hasn't been near enough, and winter just beginning. I pawned the lot of his things today when I'd done delivering my washing, Mr. Escott. All but the blanket, for we need another one."

"Mrs. Quinn, though I don't like asking you to think on such things, was there any sign of why a young fellow like Blackstone might have taken his own life? Something in the lot you pawned, for instance?"

"There was nothing like that save for a letter. I believe it's for his sister. I'd have mailed it sooner, but I've only just gotten the postage from the goods I pawned."

She brought the letter and placed it upon the table. Holmes did not so much as glance at it but regarded Mrs. Quinn with an admirable display of buried grief.

"Forgive me—Blackstone's death has come as a powerful blow to us, you must understand. That he had fallen upon evil days I knew, but that he ever entertained the notion of taking his own life . . . well, my mate may be beyond help, Mrs. Quinn, but I can at least set his affairs in order. What did he owe you beyond what you took in from pawning his goods?"

"Three and sixpence, Mr. Escott."

"Here is a crown, then, for his rent and the interest. As for his goods, you've saved us from dealing with them." As we arose and shook hands with Mrs. Quinn, Holmes's eyes at last fell upon the letter. "Might I have the honour of posting this, Mrs. Quinn? Surely all the proceeds from his kit ought to be your own."

"I should be glad if you would do so. Thank you both for yer kindness. I am sure Mr. Blackstone sees it and is grateful."

We took our leave of Mrs. Quinn's ruinous house, the outside air tinged with spent powder and woodsmoke. My friend tucked the letter in his inner pocket, and we marched without a word exchanged between us back to Scarborough Street and up the precarious stairs to Holmes's room.

Though I could see from the detective's first glance at the address that something deeply troubled him, he proceeded with mechanical aplomb, carefully slitting it open only after he had exhausted the envelope. He glanced at the handwriting within, then promptly passed it to me and sat upon the orange crate with the tips of his fingers pressed before his nearly closed eyes.

"Read it."

The message, written in a great, driving script on four one-sided sheets, went as follows:

My dearest Lily,

You must be very angry with me for having hidden myself away all this time, but I fear once I have told you the reason for it, you'll be glad enough never to lay eyes on your brother again. How I've missed you, and Peter, and the little ones. Whatever you do, please don't tell the children of this letter. Say I had to go back to war. Say anything. I couldn't bear it if they were afraid of their uncle, even after the evil I've done. The thought that they will remember me as the man I wished to be always—but you won't tell them, Lily. That's a comfort to me. Maybe it's the only one I have left.

You remember, when we were young ourselves, once in a great while I lost my wits a little. I even struck you, my darling sister, as hard as ever I could, and you only six at the time. Can you remember it still? Your lip bled and you hid from me, and after father dealt with me, I spent every spare hour in the barn for a week making you dolls out of straw so that you would forgive me. I swore I'd never fall into such a rage again.

There was a fellow in Egypt—never mind him, he came out of it all right, but we had been mates and it was never the same afterwards. And another chap after we'd come back to Plymouth who tried to cheat me at cards. I thought the opium helped make me quieter, but soon enough I saw it wasn't any real good.

I've come to the part I would rather cut off my arm than tell you, but if you're ever to forgive me and still think of me with kindness when I'm gone, you have to know the whole truth of it, for I can't bear any more of this sham. There was a girl. We'd walked down an alley together and had hardly been there ten minutes before it happened. She said something wicked to me—no woman ought to say such a thing to a man. I was drunk, and all I could feel was that black rage burning a hole in my chest, and by the work of some devil, my bayonet was in my hand. It was over in a moment. She looked almost sad at what I'd done. I heard the sound of footsteps coming

toward us, and I didn't stop running until I fell in a ditch, where I lay until
morning, and a ditch is where I've lived, body and soul, ever since.

I don't deserve to see you again, and I can't be trusted with the girls.
Maybe I've spent time enough in a deep enough Hell since it happened that
God will forgive me—or maybe there'll be nothing anymore, just quiet, and
maybe I want that most of all.

Johnny

We sat in silence for some time. I knew nothing of what Holmes was thinking, but my own mind was in a whirl. It was a terrible admission, a nightmare of guilt and self-recrimination, but knowing as much as Holmes and I did, also grossly inaccurate. Could Blackstone have fallen into such a murderous trance that he had forgotten stabbing Martha Tabram beyond all bounds of sanity? I reminded myself that his sister's opinion was paramount to him, but it beggared belief that he would admit to a murder and then promptly obscure the manner of it.

And where, if his deranged mind even knew of them, was mention of the other killings? My friend had hinted at every opportunity that he thought this man Blackstone to be none other than Jack the Ripper. His insistence that the Tabram case was our starting point, his preoccupation with uniforms, his tolerance of Dunlevy's spying, the very weeks he had spent in the East-end: all pointed irrevocably to Blackstone's assumed guilt. But if he had been the culprit, were our troubles now at an end? If all five grisly murders were upon his shoulders, the confession I still held listlessly in my hand was nothing more than a monstrous lie, or else the ravings of a man so delusional that he had forgotten the bulk of his wrongdoing. So much was clear to me and yet allowed room for still one more intolerable scenario to present itself. Suppose that Sherlock Holmes had been wrong?

I stirred myself to regard my friend, who remained in the exact posture he had assumed when I began the letter. Relaxed and immobile, he could have remained perfectly still, perhaps for hours, outwardly catatonic while his mind grappled rarefied data into hard fact. Instead, he spoke.

"You know what it means, don't you?" he asked, his tone still reflecting the distant, incisive diction of the pure reasoner.

"I can hardly make head or tail of it. It complicates things immensely."

"On the contrary, it simplifies them a thousand times over."

"But my dear Holmes, how can that be possible?"

"Because now we know," he said softly, "that someone is lying."

I could think of nothing to say. Holmes fell back into thought, drumming his long fingers against one another until a startled expression darted across his features.

"A killing stab with a bayonet, and thirty-eight more wounds with a common pocketknife. Dear God, it is as clear as day. Where is Miss Monk?"

"I do not know. Dunlevy escorted her home yesterday. He is more taken with her than ever."

"Is she likely to be with Dunlevy still?"

"I could not tell you. Her loathing of the fellow certainly seems to have lessened somewhat. But Holmes—"

Holmes, already in his coat, his muffler a whirl of red as he made for the door, made no reply. His haste sent a sharp sliver of unease shooting down my spine as I scrambled after him.

We set off at a rapid pace down the street, dappled everywhere with the orange light of exultant bonfires, but whether we made for Stephen Dunlevy's abode or Miss Monk's rooms I could not say. As we walked, Holmes stared unseeingly with his head sunk upon his chest whilst I fought to prevent myself picturing Miss Monk lying cold and open-eyed in an alleyway. Within a few minutes, we passed the now familiar sight of the Leman Street police station, its stoic lights casting icy blue shafts through their casements of marine-coloured glass. Excepting the Bow Street station, which Her Majesty considered too close to the opera house to broadcast its existence so palpably, each Metropolitan outpost proclaimed itself a haven by its shimmering cobalt lamps.

"When one considers the police presence in the East-end, it is positively unthinkable that so many lives have been lost to this madman."

To my utmost surprise, for I had hardly noted my muttered remark had been made aloud, Holmes stopped dead in his tracks.

"What do you mean, Watson?"

"Well," I faltered, "the security in Whitechapel must be at its most stringent in history. Every available man has been diverted to guard the area. There ought to be dozens of them at any given time—though of course I've no notion of how they organize their beats."

"Beats are between one and one-and-one-half miles long, generally requiring a minimum of ten and a maximum of fifteen minutes to traverse, barring any time-consuming incident. They do not overlap, though their routes do bring them into contact at their perimeters with other constables. Stopping for any reason other than suspicion a crime has been committed is expressly forbidden, though many officers keep a flask of tea warming at a gas lamp somewhere along their path."

He began to pace slowly beside the police station, one hand lightly beating against the adjacent brick wall. "Watson, a deranged man kills five separate women, all in the same small area of London. Instead of fleeing the scene, he remains with the corpses in a state of perfect calm and goes about the business of cutting them open. Once finished with his task, he makes his way to safety as invisibly as a ghost . . . No, no, no. As I have stated it, it is impossible. Fool that I am!" he cried. "Why did I not see at once that it is impossible? The alleys, the byways, the holes in the fences, the cat's meat and the blood-strewn butcheries and the wretched light, all these factors seemed to have allowed this madman to work with impunity. And yet the acts he has committed cannot have been enabled simply by his environment. Once or twice, perhaps, luck may have been on his side, but his success at this late date beggars belief. He is cunning and ruthless. Why would he risk everything to chance?"

He was off again, at a run this time. Boarded shop windows blurred into one another as we rushed headlong up tapering corridors, finally emerging into the pulsating spectacle of Whitechapel Road on the night of the fifth of November.

Dodging past hawkers waving crude effigies labeled with the names of Guy Fawkes and Jack the Ripper, we plunged into traffic, narrowly skirting the drays, hansoms, and carts which choked the thoroughfare. Just when I began to despair of maintaining the break-neck pace my friend had set, he turned sharply left and I recognized the wooden door of the chambers Miss Monk had taken. Holmes strode to the entrance, his brow etched with disquiet.

"We face two possibilities. One is very nearly proven, and the other almost untenable. However, as it should be exorbitantly clear now even to you, my dear Watson, I have been wrong before."

He knocked twice, then swiftly entered. Though the door was unlocked, we saw by the low firelight in the grate that the tidy room was empty.

"She could be anywhere, Holmes," said I, more to myself than to my friend. "After all, it is—"

"The fifth of November." He touched the top of the wide candle sitting on her table. "The wax is still soft. She left within thirty minutes."

"What is the time?"

"Nearly two, by my watch."

"Is she in danger, Holmes?"

"If my hypothesis is correct, she is in no more danger than you or I. However, I have not a shred of hard evidence to back me, and the only logical alternative is not a pleasant one."

I tried with all my might to recall the name of the tavern Miss Monk had mentioned as being the first stop on many of her reconnaissance forays. "There is a pub, Holmes, around the corner from her house."

"The Knight's Standard, on Old Montague Street. An excellent notion, Doctor."

The pub in question was a cheery enough watering hole with two fireplaces, one at either end of an elongated rectangle of a room with an impossibly low beamed ceiling. Through the haze of tobacco fumes, I spied a couple seated in shabby armchairs on either side of a simple table, and the female appeared to be blessed with a halo of black curls.

"There she is! She is all right," I exclaimed.

"Thank God for that."

"I believe that is Dunlevy," I added forcefully, unable to forget Holmes's interest in his proximity to Miss Monk and chafing at the fact that I could not see what was inside my friend's mind.

"Everything is as I thought, then," said Holmes, but the jubilation I had expected was entirely missing from his toneless voice. I had no time to question him, for Miss Monk had spied us and was peering our way as if unsure whether to hail or ignore us.

"Shall we speak to them?"

"It can hardly matter now," he replied with the same chillingly blank inflection.

When we had started toward them, Miss Monk's pleasure could no longer contain itself as she rushed up to us and threw her arms around Holmes.

"Oh, Mr. Holmes, I was that worried! Where the devil have you been hiding yourself? But you look awfully pale, Mr. Holmes. Don't tell me there's been another murder done—"

My friend stepped back with surprised civility and cleared his throat. "Nothing of that nature, Miss Monk." He had dropped, I noted, all pretense of an assumed dialect.

"We are very relieved to see you in one piece, Mr. Holmes. You've found Blackstone, haven't you?" asked Dunlevy, his clear blue eyes searching our faces with concern. "What has happened?"

My friend resumed staring into the fire while I related, briefly and hesitantly, what had occurred. Miss Monk's face slowly grew more hopeful.

"Then . . . then, do you mean . . . if he really is dead, is it the end of this horrid business?"

"I suppose it is the end," I answered, my eyes fixed on Holmes. "After all, he may not have known what he was doing. And the guilt must have been unspeakable; perhaps the trauma simply unhinged his mind."

"But that isn't what Mr. Holmes thinks, is it?" asked Dunlevy, offering us two cigarettes.

The detective accepted the stimulant mechanically and drew a pocketbook from the lining of his pea jacket, handing it to Dunlevy with a stub of lead pencil. "Write something."

Stephen Dunlevy took the items without protest, but eyed Holmes questioningly. "What shall I write?"

"Anything. 'Remember, remember the fifth of November, Gunpowder Treason and plot.'"

When Dunlevy had finished, he tore out the page and passed it to my friend. "Is this of any use to you?"

After glancing at it, Holmes balled it up and threw it in the fire. "It is conclusive. If you will excuse me, I must see what can be done."

"But Mr. Holmes—"

"I've a task for you and Miss Monk, if you would be so kind. Go at once to George Lusk's residence in Mile End. Tell him to meet with his men. They are already arranged into beats, and equipped with police whistles and truncheons, but convey my assertion that they must be flawlessly organized and on the most stringent alert. Afterwards, Miss Monk, do please stay indoors."

Once outside, Holmes made for Whitechapel Road. I touched my friend on the shoulder predicting resistance, but he paused at once and regarded me expectantly.

"You anticipate another murder."

"I am in hopes of preventing it. It will require an extraordinary effort. I need Lestrade's assistance, but . . . I must think of a way. Perhaps my brother can—I do not know. Perhaps it is impossible."

I stared at Holmes in astonishment, for never had I seen him look so completely cowed by his own knowledge.

"You feared it could be Dunlevy."

"He was one possibility. We are left with the other."

"Then you do know who the killer is."

"I do. It is perfectly clear now. But pray God that I am wrong."

"But why?"

As he passed a hand over his eyes, I recalled that he could not have slept more than twenty hours in the last seven days. For the first time since I had known him, Sherlock Holmes appeared to be exhausted by work rather than by inaction.

"Because if I am right," he murmured, "I haven't the first idea what to do."

CHAPTER TWENTY-SEVEN

The Killer

I have always been struck by my friend Sherlock Holmes's temerity in the face of adversity. In all our long years of association, I have never once known his courage to fail him, and his actions later that night, or rather early the next morning, reflected the dauntless tenacity I had come to expect of him. It is a brave man who awakens Mycroft Holmes at four o'clock in the morning.

We stopped at Baker Street for a wash and a change of clothes, but Holmes, on the instant he emerged from his bedroom, announced his intention of going out again.

"You will hardly find it a reflection on you, friend Watson, when I suggest that the fewer individuals storming my dear brother's rooms at this hour, the better for Queen and country. In any event, I trust he will know better than I what steps should be taken."

"Can I do anything in your absence?"

"Read all my correspondence the instant it arrives; I shall stop by the post office when it opens to redirect my mail. And get some rest, my dear fellow. You'll need it, if I have not completely lost my mind."

The notion of resting initially struck me as ludicrous, yet a hot bath and the reflection that I would be as good as useless that night without some respite soon convinced me to follow Holmes's advice.

I awoke near nine o'clock that morning and rang for breakfast, little expecting Mrs. Hudson to appear in my doorway in a far more severe fit of temper than I would ever have given the kindly woman credit for. I was told that the mysterious disappearance of two lodgers, during a time when they are known to be in danger, is unspeakably vexing to an affectionate landlady. I soon forged the appropriate truces.

Knowing Holmes's obsession with presenting a complete case, I was not in the least surprised that I remained in the dark. It was as unlike him to explain a problem before its conclusion as it was for him to leave unfinished threads at the end of one. Something of the detachment of my days in combat entered my bones; there was a war on, and Holmes was the general leading the assault. Even if I could not propose a strategy, now that my friend had returned, I could at least follow orders.

The first telegram for Holmes arrived at half past one in the afternoon and stated, "The officers in question patrol an area bordering Whitechapel and Spitalfields north of Wentworth Street and south of Spital Square. Map follows by post. Abberline."* The second was from Mr. Vandervent of the News Agency, demanding an immediate interview at his offices, with me alone if Holmes still could not be found.

Vandervent's caveat proved unnecessary, as my friend arrived home at slightly after three in the afternoon in an exceedingly bad temper.

"I believe it is the sole business of government to invent elaborate impediments to swift action," he snapped, flinging his hat on the settee emphatically.

"Your brother has been taking you round, I see."

"To hell and back. It is no wonder they depend upon him so. He at once set about notifying the proper channels, which I need hardly tell you took three hours longer than it ought to have done. Mr. Matthews was not without a certain grasp of the problem, however."

---

* Inspector Frederick Abberline was heavily involved in the Ripper investigation and was ultimately promoted to the position of chief inspector in 1890.

"The Home Secretary!" I exclaimed. "Is it truly as bad as that?"

"I am afraid so. Are there any messages?"

Holmes read his telegrams gravely, then jotted down another. I caught a glimpse of George Lusk's address on the form.

"Holmes, you really must eat something."

"No doubt I must. But we must also find a cab, for you do not wish to entertain the notion of inciting Mr. Vandervent's wrath. I have seen it before."

"I should like to know what good you think you'll be to anyone lying helpless in hospital."

He ignored me. "Come along now, my dear Watson, for in light of the notes you discovered, we've every reason to believe Vandervent's news is no trifling affair."

The Central News Agency's offices were located in New Bridge Street in the City, and though I had never seen them, I had been prepared by the air of barely harnessed chaos in the offices of the *London Chronicle* for the thunderous atmosphere within. Pressmen, tweed jackets rumpled and collar ends loosened, flew to and fro throughout the large chamber, comparing papers and smoking endless cigarettes. Few amid the general hubbub glanced our way initially, but those who did so arrested conversations in midsentence as they paused to stare.

"I say, Mr. Holmes—" one began, but he was interrupted by the advent of a whirling dervish wielding a crutch as if it were a pikestaff.

"If you so much as form the thought that this is an opportunity to pose questions to Mr. Sherlock Holmes, I shall explore the potential of the typewriter as a deadly weapon," Mr. Vandervent declared. With a jerk of his white-crowned head, he led us to a private office and elbowed the door shut.

"Thank heaven you've returned, Mr. Holmes," he remarked, relocating stacks of news clippings from the chairs to the floor. "I had determined to meet with Dr. Watson, but it is far better that you both are here. Sit down, gentlemen."

"Mr. Vandervent, I am afraid we haven't much time. There have been some recent developments—"

"I wish to inform you of a development, as you call them, which has not yet come to pass. And despite my best efforts to smash it, including the employment of favours, pleas, threats, and my own considerable personal charm, it will nevertheless come to pass early tomorrow morning."

Mr. Vandervent located what appeared to be the final draft of an article. Seating himself on the edge of his desk with a deft hop, he read it to us.

In a most distressing turn of events, it has become clear that, directly after suspicions lobbied against him by the official police came to light through this publication, Mr. Sherlock Holmes, the aberrant private detective, has fled from his Baker Street dwelling. He had been observed to be spending a great deal of time in the East-end just prior to his unannounced departure, allegedly seeking out Jack the Ripper and further constructing his case. It has been noted by specialists that, in the interim since Mr. Holmes met with highly debilitating injuries on the night of the horrifying double murder, no further crimes have taken place, although such strong negative evidence can hardly be considered conclusive proof against so public a figure as Mr. Holmes. Nevertheless, it seems the clear duty of the Yard to ascertain the unorthodox vigilante's whereabouts as quickly as possible, for the timing of his desertion appears from certain viewpoints to be an admission of the most damning variety.

Holmes whistled appreciatively. I recall a mad desire to use the paper as kindling to burn down its author's residence.

"I've arranged to be kept well apprised of the cur's pet projects, you see," Vandervent continued. "This gem has no doubt already gone to the printer's. I thought to be forewarned is better than nothing."

"I shall have to take care not to end up in the dock at this rate."

"The nerve of the scoundrel!" I fumed. "It is no worse than I expected, but it is hardly less vexing for that."

Vandervent's brows shot up in surprise. "You have been expecting another attack from this bounder?"

"Dr. Watson and I thought it highly improbable that Tavistock would cease his efforts once he had discovered so very fertile a ground for self-expression," Holmes explained.

"Ha," said Vandervent, skeptically. "Well, I have no doubt but that the pure venom of this beauty is due in large part to that caper pulled in his office Saturday night."

"How extraordinary. And what caper might that be?" the detective asked serenely.

"Surely you've heard by now. Chaps ought to be given a knighthood, for my money. Broke untraceably into Tavistock's office under cover of darkness and left a hailstorm of snowy white chicken feathers. The source of the feathers, a scrawny plucked little fellow, was found sitting in Tavistock's desk chair presiding over his foul projects."

A peal of laughter from Holmes caused me very quickly to examine the state of my shoes as he clapped me upon the shoulder. "So he has been shown the white feather. I shall make a point of thanking the culprit. That is, of course, if his identity is ever discovered."

"Well, as we're all plagued with troubles, I shan't take any more of your time," Vandervent dismissed us. "If you require any special assistance escaping the building, do let me know. There's nothing those jackals outside would like better than to sink their teeth into Sherlock Holmes an hour or two before his incarceration. Just mention the word *chicken* on your way out if you'd care for a round of applause."

Tavistock's article blazed forth from the front page of our *London Chronicle* the next day. However phlegmatically Holmes had taken the news in Vandervent's office, the sight of such personal vituperation in our morning mail was enough to make him fling the entire periodical into our fireplace.

"I must leave you for a time, Watson, but I beg that you will be here this evening," he said after coffee, toast, and his morning pipe. "I'd planned we should visit Lestrade at the Yard tonight, but upon further reflection it seems best to avoid tempting them with my actual presence upon their threshold. The inspector will be here by eight, and we shall see what can be done."

"I am very glad of it. We have been bullied by a shadow for far too long."

"He is flesh and blood enough. I assure you, Watson, I don't mean to hold you in suspense, but I've had to be very sure of my facts. Tonight I shall make everything as clear as I can."

"I will be here."

"You've been both constant and fearless over this wretched business, my dear Watson. It makes you quite invaluable, you know." I raised my eyes to attempt a response to this unprecedented display of esteem, but he had already risen abruptly and secured his hat. "Tell Mrs. Hudson there will be five for supper. If I am not back by eight, I will have no doubt been arrested. In that case, of course, there will be four."

As I glanced at my watch for the second time to assure myself it was only a quarter to eight, I heard the clatter of four hooves below our window. Energized by the tension of long-stifled curiosity, I threw open the sitting room door long before our bell rang, and I smiled at the sight of Miss Monk and Stephen Dunlevy climbing the stairs.

When I had ushered them in, I noted that Miss Monk, under her usual dark blue fitted coat, wore a simply tailored linsey* dress of deep

---

* A thin linen cloth.

beige, narrowly striped with a vivid emerald green the shade of her wide-set eyes.

"Miss Monk, you look lovely."

"Oh. It's warmer, over the old skirt. I mean—thank you."

"He's right, you know," Dunlevy observed innocently.

"I believe as I recall your saying so. In the growler. Or was it outside my lodgings? Both, I think."

"The point bore repeating." He shrugged cheerily.

"Where's Mr. Holmes?" Miss Monk inquired.

"He's due to return at any moment. Ah, Lestrade! Come in, Inspector."

The doughty Lestrade stood in our doorway as if he had all that week been pursued by rabid dogs and had only just taken the time to change his collar. He shook my hand and nodded to our guests.

"Miss Monk, was it? I'm not likely to forget a single moment of that night. And you are, sir?"

"Mr. Dunlevy is a journalist," I explained.

"Is he indeed?" Lestrade questioned, with a cold eye.

"He has been assisting us. He was in Whitechapel the night of Martha Tabram's murder in August."

"Martha Tabram! It's a wonder Mr. Holmes doesn't start investigating the Drebber* case again, for all it has to do with Jack the Ripper. I suppose he'll be here soon?"

"I certainly hope so," I replied.

As if by magic Sherlock Holmes flung open the door and hung his hat on the peg. "Good evening to you all! I see that Mrs. Hudson has outdone herself. Please do sit down."

"Here's the author of this charming note: 'Whatever you are doing, cease by seven thirty so as to be at Baker Street by eight,'" the inspector pronounced.

"Lestrade, you look very much in need of a drink."

"Mr. Holmes," said Inspector Lestrade impatiently, "I've no doubt

---

* Recorded by Dr. Watson in the novel *A Study in Scarlet.*

that whatever you have to say to us is of great importance, but I've enough work at the Yard to keep me there all night through as it is. Apart from the heightened patrols, we have the honour of keeping the peace at the Lord Mayor's Show on Friday. From Guildhall to the Courts of Justice and back again, we are expected to maintain order, prevent demonstration, and repress rioting, all while policing a meat tea for three thousand destitute in the heart of Whitechapel. Suffice it to say that neither of us should be here. We ought by rights to be at the Yard, with me outside the bars and you behind them."

"Shall we have a bite of supper, then, or shall I begin at once?"

"At once, if you would." Lestrade seated himself with an expectant air and we all followed suit excepting Holmes, who procured his pipe from the mantelpiece and then leaned against the sideboard as he lit it.

"Very well, then. In the first place, Lestrade, you are going to have to redraw the beats in the northwest corner of Whitechapel abutting Spitalfields, to be implemented tomorrow."

"Do not toy with me."

"I am deadly serious."

"But why?"

"Because the man who calls himself Jack the Ripper is intimately acquainted with them—their exact layout, the constables posted, and the time required for each circuit."

"That is the most preposterous statement I have ever heard you pronounce."

"How many other preposterous statements have you known me to make?"

"A great many."

"And how many of them were true?"

"I've no intention of redrawing the beats simply because you imagine someone has stolen the duty roster."

"He had no need of stealing the duty roster. The person of whom I speak is a Metropolitan police officer."

A terrible silence settled over the room. Holmes sighed heavily.

272 ❋ Lyndsay Faye

"Will you pour the inspector a drink, Watson? I think you will agree he is in need of one.

"What I intend to say to you all must go no further than this room. I am telling you what I know because I require your help. When I have said my piece, you are welcome to pose any questions you wish, but I had better lay our cards on the table in my own fashion so that you will be able to see the matter as I do.

"It really all began with Stephen Dunlevy here. Not long after Miss Monk consented to serve as our contact in Whitechapel, she met Mr. Dunlevy, who confessed to her that he was the soldier who had awaited his friend's return on the night of Tabram's murder. Because the circumstances cast a great deal of suspicion upon this other guardsman, and no less owing to my own doubts regarding Mr. Dunlevy's chosen career, his story arrested my immediate interest, especially as other women began meeting equally inexplicable and violent ends. I endeavoured to learn more by venturing myself into Whitechapel, which is why Dr. Watson and I happened, through purest coincidence, to catch the Ripper at his foul work. A deduction based on the pony's behaviour led me into Dutfield's Yard; the Ripper escaped, as you know, to kill again after he failed in his attempt to dispatch me.

"After this fifth murder, it became obvious to me that we were dealing with no ordinary criminal. He was not a raving lunatic, for if he were, who would ever agree to accompany him with so many unfortunates already dead? Neither was he a thief, nor did he seek calculated revenge, for try as I might to link the poor souls, his victims followed no pattern other than that they were all, as I have said, unfortunates. Thankfully, because I have records of two or three earlier cases matching these particulars—bizarrely motiveless slaughter of anonymous victims—I was able to conclude that the man calling himself Jack the Ripper is a severely diseased monomaniac whose habitual demeanour remains nonetheless perfectly genial."

"That's the most atrocious notion I've ever heard," Lestrade muttered, but Holmes took no notice.

"My mention of the name Jack the Ripper brings me to the letters. When he described in exact detail my own cigarette case, and Mr. Lusk received half a human kidney, I had final proof that the man who had murdered five women was writing these letters to bait us. I have no doubt that another note sent to Dr. Watson purporting to be from me was also the Ripper's work. At first these letters helped us in no way. But finally, I discovered a curious series of numbers which had made an impression on the page beneath. These proved far from negotiable without any context, and so I filed them at the back of my mind until such time as their meaning could be determined.

"After I ascertained his true vocation, Mr. Dunlevy confessed that, while he may have been dressed as a private on the night of Bank Holiday, he was in actuality a journalist whose candid stories were often aided by disguise. He informed me that he had observed Johnny Blackstone, for that was the other soldier's name, lead Martha Tabram into an alley a mere half hour before the time the medical examiners assured us she met her death. Mr. Dunlevy revisited the pub, but he returned to await his acquaintance and while doing so met with Constable Bennett. Finally giving up on Blackstone, Mr. Dunlevy returned to his home and only later discovered that any foul play had taken place.

"I had the strongest intuition that this terrible series of murders had begun the night of Martha Tabram's death, and thus locating the elusive Johnny Blackstone became of the utmost importance. He disappeared following his relief from service for erratic and disturbing behaviour, and he was reportedly hiding in Whitechapel, all of which made me very eager to lay my hands on him. After all, any man who would stab a woman thirty-nine times and then coolly walk away was no doubt a very dangerous individual."

"Dangerous enough," Miss Monk put in darkly.

"Then another, rather oblique clue fell into my lap. Matthew Packer had heard Elizabeth Stride remark that the man she was with, the man who all evidence suggests was her killer, was not clad in his habitual attire. Now, the notion that Blackstone considered himself in a sort of negative disguise when he was not in uniform was a very attractive one. Most people identify casual acquaintances through dress and bearing as much as their faces, and if Blackstone could shed his uniform, changing one or two other significant details about his person, he would be well on his way to traveling invisibly through his neighbourhood."

Holmes's eyes darted to the charred remains of Tavistock's latest attack in our fireplace. "By this time, the now notorious Mr. Leslie Tavistock had begun his deeply disquieting press campaign. While I worried that his information was far too close to the mark, much of his accuracy could be blamed upon Mr. Dunlevy here sharing what he knew of my movements to friends within the London press. I had very nearly convinced myself that any other hypothesis would be irrational when, as a result of an expedition masterminded by my associates, Dr. Watson informed me that not only did Tavistock's source possess information about me that no one but my allies could know without tailing me (and I observed no such person), but that he also had access to my handwriting, and that he and the letter writer, and by extrapolation the Ripper, were one and the same person."

"Dear God," Stephen Dunlevy exclaimed softly. "So the same individual who proclaims himself down on whores has endeavoured to lay the blame for his crimes at your doorstep."

"You see that it is small wonder such an outlandish theory did not attract me before," Holmes stated grimly. "However, in retrospect, it was damnably clever of this fiend to ferret out an unscrupulous journalist, dangle the temptation of a career-making scandal before him, and thus so oppress my movements that I have at times been in danger of my very life.

"Soon after I made the connection between the Ripper, the letter writer, and Tavistock's source, Dr. Watson and I discovered what had become of Johnny Blackstone. He was dead by his own hand, unable to live with the weight of his guilt bearing down upon him."

"Then surely he was the culprit, and our troubles are over!" cried Lestrade. "If I were capable of such acts, I should lose no time in ending my life."

"Therein lies an inherent logical fallacy, my good Lestrade," Holmes said kindly. "You are *not* capable of committing such acts. Neither, in fact, was Johnny Blackstone. In a letter to his sister, which I have since posted, he admitted stabbing Mrs. Tabram with his bayonet in a convulsion of rage, then confessed himself wholly wracked by the crime."

"But monomania is a very poorly understood malady; there is no reason for us to assume he remembers aught of his disgusting actions."

"At first, I thought as you do," my friend continued, packing more shag tobacco into his pipe. "But it is the maximal error, the unpardonable sin, if you will, to twist facts to suit theories rather than twisting theories to suit facts. I asked myself what it would mean if Blackstone's letter were entirely true. The moment I did so, everything was as clear to me as if I had seen it with my own eyes.

"Consider the accounts. Blackstone states that some few minutes after he entered the alley with Tabram, he stabbed her with his bayonet—a fact corroborated by the coroner—and then, hearing footsteps approach, he ran. Mr. Dunlevy told me he stepped back into the bar for a few minutes, and Constable Bennett told you, Lestrade, that he saw nothing in the alley; a man approached him some hours later with news of the body. Surely Mrs. Tabram was not dead instantaneously from a single, hastily delivered stab wound, and just as surely, she would have been in a panicked and highly vocal state. No one saw anything. And yet Blackstone ran because he heard footsteps. Someone was lying, and I knew immediately that the key was to discover who, if not Blackstone, that could be. I am afraid, Mr. Dunlevy, though you were a very long shot indeed, I could not count you out. I made haste to see that Miss Monk was safe, for if you had been the one plaguing me with accusations of murder as you wreaked havoc in

Whitechapel, I would not be overpersonalizing the matter to say your next victim ought to have been Miss Monk."

He continued steadily, his eyes fixed on the journalist. "To my great relief, Miss Monk was in impeccable health, but I put you to a further test by obtaining a sample of your handwriting. I found you had *not* written any of the letters, which meant that, despite your initial false pretenses, you could not be the Ripper. I knew, therefore, that Bennett was lying when he said he had seen nothing in the alley, for however much like a pile of rags a slain body may appear in the dead of night in Whitechapel, just before Constable Bennett approached you, Mr. Dunlevy, Martha Tabram was still very much alive."

CHAPTER TWENTY-EIGHT

A Hunting Party

Holmes paused to draw upon his pipe reflectively. It was a mark of his severely analytical nature that the whole harrowing case was laid before us in the abstracted tone of a chemist expounding upon a breakthrough in alkaloids.

"Why would Constable Bennett lie about his experience in the alley?" Holmes asked with perfect composure. "He had emerged from the shadows in which a terribly wounded woman must have been seeking help. I do not pretend to know what happened between them, whether they were once lovers, or what triggered the demon that had lain dormant heretofore. All I can say for certain is that when Bennett happened upon Martha Tabram, she had been stabbed once with a bayonet, and when he left her, only to walk into the arms of Stephen Dunlevy, she had been stabbed thirty-eight times with another weapon entirely—a pocketknife, such as any constable, or indeed any Londoner, might carry about his person.

"What other indications could inform me I was on the right path? The writing in Goulston Street, for one. I expressed surprise at the time that the killer should happen to have chalk in his pockets. Chalk is used by Scotland Yard officers to brighten the white stripes on their sleeves throughout the course of a shift, to avoid the wrath of their superior officers."

"Of course!" Miss Monk exclaimed. "He carried some in his trousers."

"Then there was the matter of the uniform. I had imagined the apparel Stride missed seeing upon her killer to be military in nature. What if, instead, she had been used to seeing him in a police uniform and customary high helmet? He would look vastly different in street clothes, and her curious remark would thus make perfect sense.

"I attended the funeral of Elizabeth Stride, for the crimes had been so vile and so public that I reasoned her killer might well wish to gauge the effect of his deeds. I saw no one I did not expect to be there, save for a lone police constable who informed me that you, Lestrade, assigned him to keep the peace at Stride's ceremony, such as it was."

Lestrade's distraught features drew together in puzzlement. "I gave no such order."

"I know that now. Your department confirmed as much."

The inspector closed his eyes. "I suppose we must hear the rest of it."

"I had already wasted many hours pondering how the devil any reporter could know what befell me on the night of the double event, not to mention that I attended the funerals of the deceased, or that an irrelevant, discarded knife was found near Eddowes's body, or that I had quit Baker Street to conduct researches in the East-end. The Yard knew every one of these facts."

"And so he held abundant material," I remarked.

"Precisely—he used Tavistock as a conduit to spread his calumnies. Add the fact that I often jot down short missives to you, Lestrade, as well as to a dozen or more other detective inspectors, and the mystery of my forged handwriting was solved in an instant. He could easily have stolen such a note from any one of many offices. But the final, most conclusive inference still eluded me until a profound remark made by you, Watson, at last sparked the long-dormant flames of deductive reasoning."

"I can scarcely recall what I said," I admitted.

"You simply observed, as I should have done in the first place if I were the perfectly honed logical mechanism you present in your tales, that it was astonishing that the Ripper could operate so seamlessly in a district swarming with constables. The perfectly obvious reason for his success was that he knew when they would pass, and on what streets. But when I asked myself what had happened on the night of the extraordinary double murder, yet another seemingly irrelevant fact fell neatly into place," Holmes expounded, his already rapid speech increasing to match his enthusiasm.

"The Ripper killed Elizabeth Stride without a thought of interruption, for he knew Constable Lamb's beat would not take him into Dutfield's Yard. When we disturbed him, he took flight in the direction of the City, and in order to halt my pursuit made an attempt on my life. Then, quite unfathomably, and at enormous risk, he proceeded to slit the throat of yet another girl, presumably because the mutilation, the unholy impetus behind all his thoughts and deeds, had been thwarted by our intervention. He could not be so prescient as to know at all times, on any street, whether or not he would encounter a fellow officer of the law. But members of Lusk's Vigilance Committee mentioned in passing that Eddowes had been killed, senselessly, across the square from the very residence of a Metropolitan police officer. Bennett lives in those buildings. He knew the routes around his own home, of course. How could he not know them?"

Lestrade shook his head with the heavy calm of a man who knows the worst. "He was in such a rage at you that encountering Eddowes must have seemed like a gift from above."

"But what are we to do?" cried Miss Monk in great distress. "You're right, Mr. Holmes. It all fits, every bit of it. But what's the use of talking about it when at any moment, he could—"

"I desire nothing more than to have the villain at our mercy, Miss Monk," he assured her gravely. "However, Constable Edward Bennett resigned from his service, citing overwork and fatigue, and disappeared on Monday, the fifth of November."

"Did he?" I exclaimed bitterly. "The very day Tavistock discovered that his office had been compromised."

"Well done indeed, Watson. I have reached the same conclusion. Whether Tavistock merely bewailed his misfortune to his friend the police constable, or urged Bennett to identify those who had humiliated him, the results were the same: Bennett was warned off. He could not take the chance that his relation to the *London Chronicle* had been discovered."

"But Mr. Holmes," ventured Miss Monk, "if Bennett hadn't run off, what would have happened?"

My friend crossed to the window and looked down into the street. "In all likelihood, complete disaster. In my responsibility to lay hands on him immediately, I would have unleashed all the fury of hell upon the good men of Scotland Yard. Imagine it—the killer in their midst all the while, slaughtering five women in two short months without exciting the least suspicion. Worse still, I have not a scrap of hard proof against the man. It's ten thousand to one we could have convicted him. As much data points to me as it does Bennett, which well illustrates the value of circumstantial evidence. Name the calamity and it would no doubt have befallen us—riots against the force, chaos in the streets. Even now, Sir Charles Warren has already tendered his resignation; Mr. Matthews will accept it at any moment. The case has ruined him. Bennett has ruined him."

Holmes turned to face Lestrade. "I shall not permit him to ruin the Yard itself."

Some moments passed in silence. "Well, then," said the little inspector simply, "what are we to do?"

Unexpectedly, Holmes laughed. "I'd nearly convinced myself that you would not believe a word of it."

"Now, Mr. Holmes," chided Lestrade, "I've always known you to take an odd line, but you do occasionally stumble upon the truth."

"Quite so." My friend smiled. "As to our plans, we have one, and I am afraid only one, advantage at the moment. The paper I mentioned to you, as I have said, revealed an impression. I've the original here, marked over with lead pencil." He passed it to Lestrade and we both examined it.

245	— 11:30
1054	— 14
765	— 12:15

"What the deuce are these meant to indicate?"

"They are nearly as good as a map, my dear Inspector. These are the collar numbers of three police constables, followed by the time it takes them to complete their beats."

"Wonderful!" cried Lestrade. "You've worked out who they are, I hope? There are nearly five hundred constables in Whitechapel's division alone, not including those who have been reassigned."

"My dear Lestrade, of course I have. They are Sample, Leather, and Wilding, and their beats proscribe quite a small area, half in Spital-fields and half in Whitechapel. After I found out their names, I wired Inspector Abberline, who was kind enough to send me a map."

"Did you tell him why?"

Holmes shook his head emphatically. "With the exception of my brother, and the high officials he has chosen to consult, we five are the only ones who know the identity of this madman. Whitehall has every wish to avoid a monumental scandal, and they are aware of my discretion in such cases. I want to impress upon you all that aside from the weeks following the double murder, which must have rattled his nerve, the Ripper has followed a pattern of dates in his crimes. I cannot promise you that he will attack again tomorrow, in time for the Lord Mayor's Show, exposed and on the run as he is. But neverthe-less I believe that he will. He has shown a contempt for the Yard and a hatred for me that will not cease simply because he has abandoned his former persona. You and I, Lestrade, are the last line of defense. With any luck, if we keep our hand close, Bennett will never know the alarm has been raised against him."

"When do those Yard fellows begin work?" Miss Monk asked.

"All three have the night shift, from ten until six. I wired George Lusk the moment Abberline related their territory to me. Lusk has shifted half his Vigilance Committee to assist the official force this evening and the next. Anonymously, of course, Inspector."

"Mr. Holmes, I am beyond the capacity to protest anything you may do."

"That is an appalling admission, Lestrade," my friend noted amusedly. "I very much hope that you may recover swiftly from all the shocks to which I've subjected you."

"As do I." Lestrade smiled. "Have you anything further to tell us?"

Holmes shook his head. "You know all that I do."

"Then I will set myself back to work," he said, rising. "I've beats to redraft now, on top of everything."

"If you will not dine with us, I wish you luck back at the Yard. I shall see you in Whitechapel at ten tomorrow, no doubt, Lestrade?" Holmes asked, shaking his colleague's hand.

"It is an honour to go hunting with you, Mr. Holmes," the inspector returned. "I would not miss it. Good night to you all."

The four of us sat down to supper, although Holmes refused to say another word about the case until after the dishes had been cleared, brandies had been savoured, and Miss Monk had sleepily allowed Dunlevy to drape a wrap over her. We had already said our farewells when Dunlevy squared his shoulders and approached my friend.

"Mr. Holmes, I am very grateful to have been told the truth about these terrible crimes, and I thank you for it. But I am still curious— why did you ask me here this evening? Miss Monk is an ally, no doubt, and I hope you know you may rely on me, but all the same . . . You don't seem one for idle confidences."

"Nor am I, I promise you."

"Then I cannot understand it."

"No? Well, I do hope you will accompany us to Whitechapel

tomorrow, where we intend to defend its inhabitants tooth and nail, if necessary."

"Of course, but—"

"You wish me to be clearer. Very well," said he, assuming an air of command. "I require you, Miss Monk, without unduly alarming the district, to warn as many of your acquaintances as you can that there is likely to be trouble tomorrow night. No dark alleys. No lonely rendezvous. I know you cannot reach everyone, as they are great in number and are already saturated with wild conjecture, but do your best."

"I'll start in tonight, Mr. Holmes."

"Thank you. As for you, Mr. Dunlevy, you are a rather rare commodity, you know. Tomorrow night we shall attempt to prevent a murder with the aid of a vast force, not one of whom can be allowed to know the identity of the man we are seeking. Watson and I saw him at Elizabeth Stride's funeral. That leaves Inspector Lestrade, and finally you, Mr. Dunlevy, who have ever seen the face of our quarry. Call it a whim on my part, but I rather think having three people who are fully apprised of the facts on my side will not be excessively cautious."

The next evening was wet and cold, with dark spears of rain striking our windows, and feeling chilled from within as well as without, I piled more coal upon our innocent fire than was necessary or reasonable. Peering out the bow window into the street below, my vision obscured by the glasslike curtain before me, I thought with apprehension that the odds of being able to see faces with any clarity in the gloom of Whitechapel were astronomically against us.

My friend entered near eight o'clock, dripping wet and deeply fatigued, but his entire hawklike visage fired with zealous determination. When he had emerged from his bedroom, he was clad once more in the shabby garb of Jack Escott. Recognizing the wisdom of this precaution, I wordlessly made my way upstairs to follow suit.

From my bedroom, I could hear the strains of Holmes's violin as they rose and fell, a hauntingly austere melody in a minor key, which I knew to be one of his own compositions from its quavering heights and deceptively simple twists of phrase. When I came down again, Holmes had replaced the Stradivarius in its case and was slipping his revolver in his rough woolen coat pocket.

"That was beautiful, Holmes."

"Do you like it? I am not satisfied with the middle cadence, but the portamento in the final phrase is rather effective. If you are ready, we can set off for the East-end. I've arranged for a cab."

"Holmes?"

"Yes, Middleton," he replied with a twinkle of amusement.

"If we should identify the former police constable Bennett tonight, I am at a loss to know what we should do with him."

"We shall arrest him and give him to Lestrade, who this morning met with Mr. Matthews himself."

"And if we cannot find him?" I pressed him.

"Then I shall run him down."

"And if—"

"I have no intention of allowing that to happen. Come, Watson. We must bear all. Hard condition is twin-born with greatness. You've your revolver?"

"And a clasp knife in my pocket."

Holmes threw his head back with laughter, wrapping a thick cravat about his neck. "Then my mind is entirely at ease."

We met by arrangement with Lestrade at the Ten Bells, near the center of the region delineated on Abberline's map. The staunch fellow looked quite as haggard and absorbed in his draught of ale as any of the labourers filling the surrounding tables.

"Has it all been arranged?" asked Holmes rather feverishly, pitching his voice low beneath the rumble of conversation.

Lestrade looked up from his pint with the greatest reluctance. "Fifty men in plain clothes from F Division, Paddington District, none

of whom Bennett is likely to know, in addition to the expanded com-
plement. I've redrawn the routes. If you are mistaken about this wild
tale, Mr. Holmes, I promise to arrest you myself."

"If I am mistaken, you are welcome to do so."

"You say these Vigilance chaps have police whistles?"

"Assuredly."

"It's just as well that these amateurs are here," the inspector sighed.
"I lose half my force at four this morning, for they're needed again at
the Lord Mayor's procession at eight."

Holmes's fist came down upon the table in an outraged display of
disbelief. "Am I to understand that preventing rotten vegetation from
striking that hideous gilded monstrosity in which the Lord Mayor
will be nestled tomorrow is of greater import than preventing Jack the
Ripper from adding any further organs to his collection?" he hissed.

"I shouted myself hoarse this morning. It can't be helped. There's
that Dunlevy fellow at the door," Lestrade added doubtfully. "Bit thick
to trust a journalist so far, isn't it, Mr. Holmes?"

"I see your usual healthful skepticism has returned in full measure,"
my friend returned archly. "I was concerned I'd deeply unsettled your
mind."

"On with it, then," the inspector grunted. "I've a man stationed
here all night through as a touchstone, if you will. The constables
have been instructed to whistle like mad if they spy anything suspicious, for I didn't like the look of you, Mr. Holmes, the last time you
went hand to hand with him." Holmes bristled visibly at this but for-
bore reply. "I'm with the journalist up Brick Lane, and the two of you
over Bishopsgate. We meet every hour at this pub. I've two lanterns
here without which we should scarcely see our own feet in front of
us. Best of luck, gentlemen all."

The inspector and I took up the lanterns. Nodding to Dunlevy as
we passed, we made our way out into the pouring rain.

CHAPTER TWENTY-NINE

The Case and the Heart

Within half an hour we were soaked and chilled, and my leg ached dully as we made our way down rain-washed alleyways, the sound of our footsteps obscured by the storm. Fewer locals were about in that night's elements than was usual, though people did continue to hurry past, shawls and scarves wrapped tight about their heads, sloshing the eddying mud beneath their feet.

"Curse this weather," Holmes muttered fiercely after our first rendezvous with Lestrade and Dunlevy had ended, propelling us back into the rain. "It is hardly possible to identify a man at three yards in this wet, let alone that the garb necessitated by such conditions lends itself perfectly to concealment."

"There are plainclothesmen enough to cover every passage. He can do nothing without being seen, if he ventures out on such a night at all."

"He will be here."

"But taking into account this gale—"

"I said he will be here," Holmes repeated fervently. "No more words. We must have all our wits about us."

Four o'clock came and went, marked by a lessening of loiterers as the weary plainclothesmen made their way home for a bath and an hour or two of sleep before the Lord Mayor's Show recalled them to duty. The streets began to fill with scattered workmen and unfortunates, ducking into gin shops before the break of day.

Holmes and I met with Lestrade and Dunlevy at the Ten Bells for the final time at six o'clock that morning. We each allowed ourselves a glass of whiskey, clutched in fingers stiff from the cold. No one spoke for a time. Then my friend rose from the table.

"We must search every alley and courtyard."

"We have missed nothing, Mr. Holmes," moaned Lestrade. "If anything, we have stopped him entirely."

"Nevertheless, I will satisfy myself that it is so. The shifts he indicated are over; we may as well go together. If anything has happened, it is too late to prevent it."

We stepped out of the Ten Bells into Church Street and made our way down the road. Holmes strode avidly into passages, but Dunlevy, Lestrade, and I were by then so disheartened that we made scant effort to follow his every darting movement. Dawn's cold grey light had just begun to soften the edges of the gleaming brick buildings when we passed a whitewashed entrance to yet another anonymous courtyard. My friend plunged into its depths while we waited on the street.

"I shall need a warm breakfast and a cup of tea if I'm ever to make it through this day," Lestrade lamented.

"You're to be in attendance at the Lord Mayor's Show?" I commiserated.

"I am indeed."

"My sympathies, Inspector."

"It's not the first sleepless night I've had on account of Mr. Sherlock Holmes."

"Quite probably we have foiled an evil design by it. I can at least remind you that Holmes is the last man to mire himself in chimera."

"That may be so, Dr. Watson," Lestrade muttered sourly, "but he mires himself deep enough in theory that it's a wonder he finds his way out again."

"What's keeping him, I wonder," Dunlevy yawned.

"Holmes!" I called out. There was no reply. I passed through the shabby arch leading to the court, where entrances to tenements lined the constrictive corridor. The second door on the right stood open, and when I saw no sign of the detective at the end of the passage, I entered it.

In all my ensuing years of friendship with Sherlock Holmes, excepting that particular morning, we have never once spoken to each other of that room. On the rare occasions since that day I have pictured hell, I have seen that chamber. Cracks in the masonry showed through the dank walls. There was a candle resting on a broken wineglass, a fire dying in the grate, and a plain wooden bedstead standing in the corner. The metallic smell of blood and offal saturated the air, for on that bed lay a body. More accurately, on the bed and on the table lay various pieces of what had once been a body.

Holmes was leaning with his back against the wall, his countenance deathly white. "The door was open," he said incongruously. "I was passing by, and the door was open."

"Holmes," I whispered in horror.

"The door was open," he said once more, and then buried his face in his hands.

I registered footsteps behind me. "What the devil are you two—" Lestrade began, and then a choked cry escaped his throat when he saw what had been done.

"He could not work out of doors," I stated. "And so, he took her to her room." I forced myself to stare at what had once been her face, but very little apart from the eyes had been left intact.

The inspector gripped the wood of the doorframe unsteadily, all the blood draining from his features.

Dunlevy entered slowly, like a man sleepwalking. "Dear God in heaven," he whispered in a breaking voice. "He has torn her apart."

"You must go," said my friend without moving, his face still covered by his hands.

"What?"

"You must send a telegram to my brother. His name is Mycroft Holmes. Tell him what has happened. He lives at one eighty-seven Pall Mall. Tell him what you see."

"Mr. Holmes—"

"Go quickly, for God's sake! The stakes are incalculable!"

Dunlevy ran off into the rain.

My friend forcibly pushed himself away from the wall and commenced examining the contents of that abominable bedchamber. I stood stupidly by the door for several moments longer before making my way to the body and staring at the various piles of flesh which had been removed and rearranged.

Lestrade joined me. "What do you make of it, Dr. Watson?"

"It is impossible to know where to begin," I replied dully. "I saw something like it once, in a gas explosion."

"The door was open, you say, Mr. Holmes?"

"Yes. It has been open for perhaps twenty minutes."

"How can—"

"The amount of rain which has saturated the floorboards."

"Ah. Anything of interest in the fireplace?"

Holmes turned from his work with an expression of furious impatience, but a second sharp cry from Lestrade arrested whatever rebuke hovered upon his lips.

The inspector had unthinkingly plucked a gleaming silver object out of the tissue heaped on the table. The thickened blood dripped from his hand as he stared at it.

"What is it, Lestrade?"

Lestrade merely shook his head and continued peering at the thing.

"I believe it is your cigarette case, Mr. Holmes," he said in a very small voice.

Holmes released a short breath as if he had been struck in the chest. The inspector began absently polishing the blood off with his pocket handkerchief. "Initials S. S. H., I see. Yes, it is undoubtedly yours. You lost it the night of the double murder, is that not so?" He offered it to Holmes on his right palm. "Take it." Wiping his hands mechanically, Lestrade furrowed his brow in thought. My friend turned the case over in his delicate fingers as if he had never seen it before.

At length, Lestrade spoke more forcefully. "Have you nearly finished in here, Mr. Holmes?"

My friend shook himself. "I require a few minutes more."

The inspector nodded. "Very good. Then, Mr. Holmes, I think you had better leave. Yes, I must ask you to leave very quickly. That is most important. And you as well, of course, Doctor. Then I will just lock this outer door if I can manage to, or shut it at any rate, and make my way to the procession route. I've duties to attend to there. And then, soon enough we shall hear of this matter."

"You cannot be serious!" I cried in wonderment. "Do you honestly suggest that we leave this poor wretch here, as she is, and wait for someone else to discover her?"

"I do. If she is not found by this afternoon, I shall arrange something, but Mr. Holmes must have time to—" My friend glanced up sharply at the inspector. "That is to say, who's to know what else may have been planted in this room. We can't very well look under every piece of remains, disturbing the evidence as we do so. Dr. Watson, I know it is difficult, but when do you imagine this . . . butchery . . . took place?"

"The usual rigor mortis would have been wholly altered by the damage to her body. I would hazard a guess at four in the morning. If the door has been open for only twenty minutes, then he was with her for approximately two hours."

Lestrade nodded, fidgeting with his watch. "Nearly through, Mr. Holmes?"

"I can learn nothing more here," my friend replied, getting up from his hands and knees, in which posture he had been examining the floor.

"You have finished with the fireplace?"

"Quite finished."

"Dr. Watson, you've nothing further?"

"There is nothing to be done in a matter of minutes. Perhaps you could send the complete report of her injuries on to Baker Street?"

"Certainly."

"You must also find out when you are able if the neighbours heard anything, and determine who if any of our number was in a position to observe this girl enter her room," said Holmes.

"Naturally, I will do so. Anything else?"

"There is nothing," my friend replied in a very soft voice. He took the cigarette case from his pocket and regarded it once more. "I have seen enough, Lestrade. We have all of us seen more than enough."

"Then for God's sake, please disappear," Lestrade said calmly. "It's a police matter now. Not a word of that cigarette case, and I shall see to the rest."

The rain continued to strike our faces as we began our return to the west of London, but I do not believe Holmes or I felt it any longer. Indeed, I found it a struggle to feel anything at all, once we had collapsed into a cab. Even so early, straggling crowds began to gather along the anticipated parade route, where labourers struggled on the slick cobblestones to erect heavy cloth banners dripping with water.

"Holmes," I said at length, "have we any hope of success?"

"On which front do you mean, Watson?"

"On any of them, I suppose."

My friend would have appeared perfectly composed at that moment to anyone save myself, but to a man intimate with his habits, his appearance was cause for the greatest trepidation. His eyes shone as hectically as quicksilver, and there were spots of frantic colour on his high cheekbones. He began ticking off points on deceptively steady fingers.

"Do I harbour hopes of running down Jack the Ripper? Undoubtedly. Am I at all likely to be prosecuted for his disgusting crimes? I am not, though such an ordeal would be no worse than I deserve, imbecile that I have proven myself. Do we near the end of our quest for this demon? I am certain of it. Will it matter to that poor girl, whose body has been strewn about that room like so much compost? Will it do her a trace of good, not merely dead as she is, which is tragedy enough, but dead solely so that her corpse could be desecrated beyond recognition by a depraved freak?"

"My dear fellow—"

"No," he finished. "It will do her not the smallest particle of good. And I am to blame for that."

"That is outrageous, Holmes!" I protested. "You cannot seriously assume any fault upon your own shoulders. You, who have done so much . . ."

"I, who have failed so utterly that the end of this case ought by rights to mark the end of this preposterous career."

"Holmes, be logical—"

"I have *done* so!" he lashed out in fury. "See where it has gotten us! Driver!" He struck the roof of the cab with his stick and leapt out.

"Stay here, Watson. I shan't be long."

Looking about in confusion, I saw that Holmes had led us to Pall Mall and, I could only assume, the rooms of his brother. He was inside one of the stately cream-coloured buildings for nearly half an hour, and when he emerged again from the heavy door, his countenance was positively unreadable.

Wordlessly, I extended a hand and helped him back into the cab. I peered at him curiously, but we continued down the few remaining blocks to our rooms in silence. The hansom had barely paused across the street from 221 when Holmes jumped out of it, then stood rooted to the pavement.

"Well, well!" he drawled as an expression of withering contempt flooded his features. "What in the name of all that is loathsome and diseased is standing upon our doorstep?"

I glanced up and nearly lost my footing as I set my boot on the metal support to descend from the cab. Leaning on our door, with his arm upraised as if to ring the bell, was Leslie Tavistock. My companion fleetly crossed the street, stopping on the kerb some few feet beyond our front step.

"What the devil do you think you are doing, Tavistock?" he demanded. The rumpled fellow whirled around to face us, then rushed down with his arms outstretched and his brown eyes wild with fear.

"Oh, Mr. Holmes, is that you? Of course it is. Dr. Watson—Mr. Holmes—you must help me! I can hardly overstate the urgency of my visit."

Holmes brushed past him to the door, his key already in his hand. "I am afraid I am professionally rather busy just now. My schedule could not possibly accommodate you."

"But you must, Mr. Holmes! My very life is in danger. It is horrible, too horrible to contemplate!"

"Is it indeed? I'm afraid I do not find the idea of your life being threatened horrible in the smallest degree. *De gustibus non disputandum,**you know." He threw open the door.

"You must feel as if I've wronged you," Tavistock pleaded, rubbing his hands together desperately. "Never mind about that. I am prepared to pay any price so long as you agree to save me!"

"I tell you for the last time, you ask the impossible."

"I'll print a retraction, Mr. Holmes—your work on this case will be trumpeted from every street corner!"

"Remove yourself from my stairs or you will regret it," Holmes said inexorably, turning as if to go inside.

"Mr. Holmes!" Tavistock cried once more, and seized his left shoulder in an effort to detain him. In an instant, my friend had shifted his weight, whirled upon his left foot, and delivered the journalist a powerful blow to the side of his face. Tavistock fell backward down the

---

* "There is no disputing taste."

steps and landed prostrate upon the pavement gasping for air, the wind knocked from his lungs. Holmes promptly resumed his journey up the stairs to our rooms.

I wished very badly simply to follow him, slamming the door he had left open for me emphatically as I did so. However, my medical instincts prevailed, and I approached the pathetic figure lying splayed beneath our windows.

"Your nose appears to be broken. Can you stand?" I offered him a hand and half lifted him to a sitting position on our steps.

"Oh, I am ruined!" he gasped, fumbling for his handkerchief.

"Here." I offered my own. "I must say, after the way you've treated Sherlock Holmes, I hardly think you deserve any less."

"Deserve! It was in the interests of my profession, nothing more," he whimpered, attempting to stem the tide of blood from his nose. "And now the source of all my information is revealed to be a degenerate lunatic, and Mr. Holmes will not consent to—"

"Stop a moment," I interrupted him. "You would reveal nothing of your source to us before—indeed, you as much as declared undying fealty—and now you refer to him as a lunatic?"

"He is the lowest sort of aberration. I know it, I have seen! I followed him, you realize. I tracked him to his home."

"And what did you discover?" I asked carefully.

"There were jars upon—no, no, it is far too revolting to speak of. I will be pilloried! My character decimated, my career ended."

"What a pity," said I, rising deliberately. "By the by, whatever possessed you to follow your source?"

"I was suspicious. I wish to heaven I had never thought to trail him, but I wanted to know how he'd got his miraculous information." He commenced sobbing bloodily into his coat sleeve. "If he finds me out, he will kill me, I know it!"

"When did you follow him?"

"Last night. After he stopped by my office to ask for his letters back. He said the force would come after him if they discovered he had spoken to the press."

"The force?" I repeated, praying my tone was as casual as I hoped. "What have they to do with it?"

"He is a police constable. His name is Edward Bennett. You cannot know how horrible it was, Dr. Watson. God help me! I am done for." His head collapsed once more upon his arm.

"Come upstairs at once," I said.

"Oh, bless you, bless you, Dr. Watson!"

"Get a hold of yourself, and follow me." I advanced up the stairs and into our sitting room with the thrill of new-sparked hope shining in my breast.

"Watson!" called Holmes when he heard me enter. He had divested himself of his mud-bespattered clothing and was as immaculate as ever, though he rubbed at his shoulder gingerly. "Where on earth have you put the—by the Lord!" he growled when he saw who stood beside me.

"He has discovered the identity of his source, Holmes. He knows where Bennett lives."

"Bennett has abandoned his City dwelling," Holmes shot back, still casting about for I knew not what. "If he hadn't, I would not now be forced to scour his bank accounts, his former office, his family tree, and his preferred tobacconist. There was a stub in the dog grate—"

"He knows where Bennett stayed *last night*, Holmes. Before—before it had been done," I added lamely.

"Ha. Here they are." Grasping the matchbox, the detective stopped to light a cigarette and regarded the pressman with wintry disdain. "What a very interesting twist of events. Curiosity got the better of you, did it? You wanted to see what sort of line Bennett was investigating? You dogged him to his abode and then watched as he left again, which, equipped as you were, was as good as an invitation to break into his house. You've a cut under your right wrist just where an amateur cracksman would nick it on the windowpane, which tells me you used a glass cutter rather than a lock pick. Then you lit a candle stub without a holder and took a look round. The wax has dripped onto your sleeve in two places. Next, I imagine you laid eyes on a relic or two from Bennett's past adventures, and his odd prescience became a trifle clearer to you. The red weal on the back of your hand from hot wax dripping upon bare flesh without remark proves your discovery was an unusual one, whatever it was. You then fled the premises. Am I close to the truth?"

Our visitor's eyes were open and staring in awe. "It's as you say. For God's sake, help me, Mr. Holmes. It is more than a man can bear."

I had never seen such an expression of loathing on Sherlock Holmes's face before, and I hope I never will again. But just as quickly, his brow cleared and he approached our visitor with measured steps.

"Do you know, Mr. Tavistock, I do have a mind to help you. I shall just outline my little proposition. If you tell me where this rat is hiding, I will not tell all of London you are an ally of Jack the Ripper, I will not see that you are arrested for breaking and entering, and I will not throw you out of that window onto the pavement below."

Leslie Tavistock gaped at Holmes, then whispered, "I do not know where he is."

"Come, sir," said Holmes, and his voice was deadly quiet.

"That is to say—I mean—I followed him, yes, but I've no notion where I was! The alleys all twisted and turned—"

"Mr. Tavistock," my friend interrupted, "you will now tell me absolutely everything you can recall about your journey to Bennett's house. Please bear in mind that you see before you a man who has squandered the last vestiges of his patience."

The coward hid his still-bleeding face from us by turning to the window while shutting his eyes in desperate concentration.

"It was a dark, dirty place. The houses were short and very old."

"Brick or wood?"

"They were made of wood."

"Individual doors, or halls leading to multiple entrances like the rookeries around Flower and Dean?"

"There were many doors and corridors. No freestanding houses save Bennett's."

"Any warehouses?"

"No, just those horrible residences."

"Were there any vendors or open markets?"

"No, nothing like that."

"What sort of traffic was it?"

"I beg your—"

"Carriages, ambulances, hay-wains, dogcarts?" Holmes snapped.

"No ambulances, but there were carts."

"Then you were not near the hospital. Could you hear any trains?"

"No, I do not think—"

"Could you hear bells?"

"Yes, Mr. Holmes!" he cried. "Yes, I could hear bells! Very loud, nearly on top of us."

"Then you were adjacent to Christ Church and far from the railway. Did you pass any landmarks?"

"There was a pub with shabby gold lettering above the door, on a sharply angled corner. It had a picture of a girl—"

"That is the Princess Alice, and it is on Commercial Street and Wentworth Street. Which way were you walking?"

"I do not know—"

"Was it on the right, or the left?" Holmes demanded with his teeth clenched.

"The right."

"Did you pass the narrower street corner side of the building first, or the wider part further down the block?"

"The—the narrow, I am sure."

"Then you were walking north. Did you stay on that road?"

"We turned right, as I recall."

"Had you passed another pub before you turned?"

"I do not think so."

"Then you did not pass the Queen's Head, and you were either in Thrawl Street or Flower and Dean Street. Was there an apothecary shop on the corner?"

"No, sir—I think it was a stable yard."

"Where horses are kept?"

"Yes—the house he entered was the only one of its kind, with an area before and a separate entrance. As I walked, it stood to the left."

"Then he resides at either number twenty-six or twenty-eight Thrawl Street." Holmes made a note of it in his pocketbook. "Very well, then. Now, Mr. Tavistock?"

"Yes, Mr. Holmes?"

"I suggest that you forget what you know. If you make an effort to forget this affair, then I will make an effort to forget as well. Do I make myself clear?"

"Perfectly clear, Mr. Holmes."

"Now," said my friend, his voice dangerously low, "get the hell out of my rooms."

Tavistock gasped something incoherent and fled.

"Holmes," I breathed, "that was marvelous."

"Nonsense," he retorted, inhaling a deep draught of smoke. "It was an elementary series of deductions."

"No, not the inferences. The right cross."

"Oh, that," he said, looking down at his knuckles, which were beginning to bruise. "Thank you. That was rather marvelous, wasn't it?"

Not long after we had dug through the early morning papers and sipped exhaustedly at hot coffee strongly fortified with spirits, a telegram arrived for Holmes. The thin yellow slip read as follows:

New murder discovered in Miller's Court, Spitalfields. No clue as to killer's identity. Preliminary medical examination completed; cause of death slit throat. Injuries to corpse too numerous to list. In all likelihood, same six-inch double-bladed knife as used previously. Her heart is gone. God help us all.

Lestrade.

My fist closed over the writing of its own volition. I dropped the paper upon the fire. As I turned away from the hearth, it must have been a trick of the moisture in my own eyes that made me imagine the same expression mirrored upon the face of my friend.

CHAPTER THIRTY

The Gift

For much of that afternoon Holmes sat in his armchair, perfectly still save for the minuscule movements required to smoke his pipe. The rain cleared in the midmorning, the skies wiped clean of their mists while the mud in Baker Street below scattered from the wheels of the cabs and lorries.

At long last, as evening approached, the pageboy entered with a yellow slip on his salver. Glancing at Holmes, I could not tell whether he might, in his utter weariness, have fallen asleep. I shook his shoulder gently.

"Just read it to me, will you, Watson?"

I tore open the telegram. "'I am sorry, Sherlock. It cannot be helped. You have full discretion. Godspeed, my dear boy. Mycroft.'"

Holmes remained silent for a moment, pressing at his shoulder absently. "Then that is final."

"Holmes," I asked somberly, as he unfurled himself from his chair and rang for his boots, "what does 'full discretion' mean?"

"I am afraid I have been requested to undertake a small service by the highest levels of government."

"I see," said I. "May I inquire whether the task they wish you to perform is a criminal one?"

Holmes looked startled but soon recovered. "You and I have several times apprehended a culprit only to discover that justice lay entirely upon the side of the lawbreaker. In those instances, we could do nothing more equitable than to let him go. We acted outside of the British courts. This is . . . similar."

"So the word 'discretion' is used in place of 'pardon,'" I affirmed.

"My dear Watson—"

"They no longer wish for us to arrest him."

"No," he said shortly, and then crossed to the desk in which our revolvers were stored and slipped his gun in his pocket. "My dear fellow, I cannot in any sort of conscience wish you to accompany me."

"I see. It is possible that you are being selfless, and also possible that you are being merely solitary."

"I must do what I must, but I refuse to ask the same of you." He looked me in the face as he leaned back against the mantel. I waited quietly.

"They want me to kill him."

I nodded in silent sympathy.

"And will you?"

"I haven't the slightest notion," he said softly. "Logic appears to have failed me. Among other failings."

"Holmes, it isn't remotely your fault," I stated firmly. "But will you do what they've asked?"

"I suppose if we were to look up the dueling codes, the wretch has certainly given me ample cause. And yet, I can't simply . . . My dear Watson, surely you've no wish to be associated with what is bound to be an altogether ungodly enterprise?"

Though I had never seen Sherlock Holmes so determined, I had also never seen him so at sea. For that reason among a great many others, I could not easily imagine abandoning him in his hour of need.

"I cannot in good faith remain behind," I considered. "If the evening goes as powers beyond our control desire it to, one or more people will require medical attention before the night is out."

Holmes smiled gravely and then shook me by the hand.

Squaring his shoulders, my friend strode to the door and tossed me my hat from its peg. "They've a valid position, you know. We cannot conceivably leave him to roam the streets, and so we shall at least deprive him of his liberty. Arm yourself as you were, but I do not think we need affect any disguise this evening. For an investigator, a charade is often of the greatest use, but for an assassin, it smacks of skulduggery. I cannot be expected to lose all my self-respect in a single day. I should never be able to take on another case."

Of Holmes's pursuit of the world-renowned killer known as Jack the Ripper, little remains to be told. And yet, as the circumstances were so very remarkable, and the outcome so dramatic, I must proceed in my own way. Holmes may decry colour and life in my tales all he likes, but when a winter's evening prevents our embarkation from Baker Street and he has exhausted his agony columns, still he reads them. But I digress, as he has so often had occasion to remark. I shall do my best to keep to the point.

The cab deposited us at the corner of Thrawl Street, deep in the convoluted warren just south of the notorious Flower and Dean Street. Evening had deepened the skies above us to a hazy sapphire. We walked down a side passage into a small mews with bits of wastepaper dancing in the dark breezes.

"There—I believe that is the den in question." The detective nodded at a sagging wooden doorframe; an adjacent window patched with greasy paper was illuminated from within by the light of a yellow lamp. "Are you ready, Doctor?"

Edging to the door, my friend placed his hand upon the latch. He threw it open, and we stepped into the room.

A very old woman sat wrapped in a shawl before the fire, the embers of which, though dying, still cast a considerable heat into the room. I feared briefly that we would cause her grave shock by bursting into the room with weapons drawn as they were, but a glance at her fixed, clouded gaze immediately informed me she was entirely blind.

"Who are you?" she demanded. "What are you doing here?"

"My name is Sherlock Holmes, ma'am," my friend replied, casting his eyes about the room.

"I don't know you. But of course, you must have business with my son. Come near the fire; it is wonderful." The tiny room was so stifling as to be nearly suffocating. "I live upstairs, as a rule. There's a girl who comes up with food. But the windows have all been breaking, you see, in the night."

"Have they?" Holmes inquired.

"Yes. My son patched the one on this floor but said the upstairs would require more careful handling."

"I hope no harm came of it."

"Oh, no, I don't imagine a little thing like that could hurt Edward." She smiled. "Another man, perhaps, but my son is quite remarkable."

"I have no doubt that is true. Does he happen to be at home, Mrs. Bennett?"

"He's stepped out for a moment. But who is with you?"

"This is Dr. Watson. We are both very anxious to speak with your son."

I looked around the room from where I stood by the door. There was a filthy stove with a few pots and pans lying atop it, an ancient sofa, and bookshelves filled with dusty tomes and several glass jars. Lying in a gap between volumes was an ancient, tailless cat whose eyes flicked from one to the other of us in limpid yellow pools.

"Bless you for looking for him here. He doesn't live here, you know, not even after his father died. He lives in the City. But he has been staying in my rooms more often of late."

Holmes also noted the shelving and approached it, leaving his revolver on the table. When he reached out a hand for the jar beside the cat, the creature screamed in a hoarse, pining tone and fled to the middle of the stairs.

"Never mind the Admiral," the old woman said, laughing. "He ought not to be frightened of you. He is safe enough, after all."

"Why do you say the cat is safe?" asked Holmes intently.

"Well, that is obvious, isn't it? He hasn't any tail."

My friend methodically returned the jar to its space beside the imposing bound volumes while stating, "Your son is a scholar." I could just make out the contours of what the glass vessel contained, and concluded that Leslie Tavistock's horror had not been quite as unmanly as I had assumed.

"Are you gentlemen friends of Edward's?"

"Our respective occupations have thrown us very much together in the past few weeks."

"I see—I thought perhaps you knew him. My son is not a scholar. The books belonged to my late husband."

"And his studies held no interest for Edward?"

"Just so. The two of them could not have been more different, if you wish to know the truth of it."

"That is very interesting. I have always thought fathers and sons are often alike."

I little knew why Holmes was so intrigued by the tiny crone's conversation, but his soothing tones and the sweltering heat of the room were beginning to have a soporific effect on me.

"I have heard that said also. But not in this case. My husband was a scholar, as you said. That is one difference. He was physically very imposing, which is another. And also my husband had a very weak temperament."

"In what way?"

"If you must know, he had no ability whatever to master himself. I suffered for his weaknesses, when he was still alive."

"But Edward did not?"

"Oh, no," she said proudly.

"Then he was away at school?"

"No indeed. He was here for the worst of it. But that was of no consequence. Edward cannot be hurt, you see."

"I am not sure that I understand you, ma'am."

"He is blessed that way. Oh, he would cry at first, when he was very, very young, but he soon acquired his gift of strength, and there was an end to his suffering. I prayed every day for him to be blessed with the gift, and finally my greatest desire was granted me. He was eight, I believe—a terrible day that had been, I remember. I think it was the day the Admiral lost the first bit of his tail. But Edward has the gift now, and he can never suffer again.

"I sometimes wish I had prayed so much for the Admiral," she mused. "It would have spared him a great deal to have the gift too. But as I said, the dear creature needn't worry now."

She laughed contentedly at this and held her hands out toward the dying fire.

Her movement drew my friend's attention to the scuttle, which was brimful with fuel. "Have you another coal hod, Mrs. Bennett?"

"No indeed. What would I want with another coal hod?"

"Did your son refill it for you before he left?"

"I don't believe so. He's lit quite a blaze for us, as you can tell. But if we need more coal, there's a supply down in the basement. You just go through that trap under the staircase, you see."

Holmes knelt down to touch the floor and then recoiled as if he had been burned.

"What has he done?" he cried. "Open the door, Watson, quickly!"

My friend lifted Mrs. Bennett from her chair, and the three of us flew outside under the chilling night sky. We had not gotten five strides from the chamber when a sound like the roar of a crashing wave over the side of a storm-tossed ship washed over us and I was thrown to the bitter ground.

It seemed that I could not move for several minutes, but I was in no position to judge time accurately. I know I heard my name spoken three times, each with increasing violence and urgency, but from very far away. Perhaps only seconds passed before I managed to sit up, but when I did so, I felt a sudden splintering pain at my side, and my eyes flew open with the shock of it.

When I looked around me, I faintly noted that the courtyard was flushed with a flickering light. I met the eyes of Holmes, who lay several feet from me and had not yet managed to raise himself from the ground. Mrs. Bennett lay sprawled on her back upon the stones and did not move.

"Are you all right, my friend?" Holmes breathed.

"I think so," I returned. I began to crawl toward them. "Holmes, you are not hurt?"

"Nothing to signify," said he, raising himself on his forearms, though I could see in the eerie light that his head bled in a slow trickle, and either he had touched it with his hand or that appendage was bleeding as well.

"What happened?"

"The basement was on fire. When the trapdoor disintegrated . . ."

"What the devil has he done, Holmes? He has destroyed his own refuge."

"He has indeed," my friend replied hollowly. "From which we can draw only one conclusion."

An icy chill of despair engulfed me at the inevitable inference.

"He no longer has any use for it."

Holmes's lids descended hopelessly for a moment, and then he turned his attention to the lady. "Mrs. Bennett?" he said, touching her shoulder. Her glassy eyes were open, but she gave no sign. "Mrs. Bennett, can you hear me?"

She shuddered slightly. "Where are we?" she asked.

"There was an explosion. Can you move at all?"

"I do not like to try," she murmured.

"Then do not attempt it."

"I wonder if the girl is all right."

"What girl?" my friend asked.

"Gently, Holmes," I whispered. "She is quite mad, after all. We must not alarm her."

"Can you tell me what girl you mean, Mrs. Bennett?"

"I can hardly say exactly," she sighed. "My son had a friend. I don't know what they were doing. There is little enough to see upstairs. He was going to show her the stars, perhaps, through the broken window. They would look different through a broken window."

My friend staggered to his feet and made at once for the door, which I now saw had been blown partially off its hinges. The walls of the chamber within were painted with orange flame, and smoke poured from the now glassless front window.

"Holmes!" I shouted. I managed to stand, but only with a tremendous effort. My friend had tied his scarf over his face, but just as I reached him, he spun around to face me and arrested my movement with a forceful hand on my chest.

"Go to the window!" he cried. He turned and walked into the flames.

One petrifying glance at that room told me Sherlock Holmes was entirely correct. No matter what he found in the upstairs chamber, there could be no return the way he had come. I looked about the yard for a ladder or anything else of use, but saw nothing save a forlorn water barrel. I stumbled desperately toward the rotting object and dragged it with considerable difficulty to the alleyway on the other side of the house.

There, my prospects proved more promising. In addition to the barrel, there were several bales of hay at my disposal, and in a flash I recalled, as if from another decade, that Holmes had predicted a stable next to the site where one of the Ripper's letters had been penned. I could see the window, entirely free of glass and billowing smoke, many feet above my head, and a water pipe running down the side of the building into a tall cistern perhaps a yard distant. Shoving two bales of hay together beside the tank and placing a third on top of them so as to form a makeshift staircase, I heaved the water barrel on top of all, ignoring as best I could the fiery pain in my side.

A moment later, my friend's dark head appeared through the hole in the wall far above.

"The pipe, Holmes!" I cried. "It is the only way!"

He disappeared. Seconds passed, masquerading as hours. I was fighting desperately not to fall but could not understand why. I leaned against the opposite wall and somehow remained standing. *If you remain standing,* I thought madly, *he will come out.*

At last Holmes reappeared, with something tied around his neck. He leaned head and shoulders out the window and barely managed, with his arm fully extended, to reach the water pipe. Using it as an anchor to pull himself out, he swung himself over to it and, when nearing the cistern, jumped to the water barrel and the hay and then fell to the ground. I do not recall, in my entranced state, that I was at all surprised to see Miss Monk hanging limply from his shoulders.

I fumbled at the knot binding her hands and so disentangled them. They had been tied with Holmes's scarf. When I lifted Miss Monk and laid her gently upon the ground, her head lolled backward. Her neck was entirely unmarked.

"Is she alive?" Holmes gasped raggedly.

At first, I could not tell, so shallow was her breath, but at last I identified a sluggish pulse.

"There is life in her still. She has been drugged. Holmes? Holmes, for heaven's sake, lie back and breathe deeply. You've been poisoned by the smoke."

He collapsed against the wall. "Surprising," he managed through shuddering breaths. "I would have thought myself entirely inured to the substance."

I laughed and felt an itching sensation at the back of my neck. I reached behind my head to touch it and my fingers returned clotted with blood.

"Holmes, we must get away from this place. The building is still burning."

"Then let us—" Holmes began, and then his eyes fixed upon a point behind me and above our heads.

"You aren't meant to be here yet," said a soft voice.

I turned around, intending to rise, but managed only to fall to the stones beside my comrades.

"I doused the basement with kerosene. Then I brought Mother downstairs with an excuse about a broken window," Edward Bennett continued thoughtfully, for I knew him from the funeral that seemed an age ago and in another country. "How could you have known the girl was missing so quickly? It ought to have been burned to the ground when you arrived."

"Tavistock led us here," said Holmes after a struggle for air.

"Oh, I see. I didn't know who had broken the window. He has been of the greatest use to me. He is clever enough in his own way. Not as clever as you, of course, Mr. Holmes."

"No, he isn't."

"You were the only real threat to my work, you know," Bennett remarked. His face and figure were strikingly, disarmingly neutral. He had blond hair and queerly pensive blue eyes. Even with him standing before us, I could scarcely describe him to myself, though that may well have been the effect of the explosion upon my senses. "I was with you on the Baron Ramsden case, if you recall. The missing patch of grass. Gregson didn't see it as we did. Of course, you lied to him. You lied to everyone. You think yourself the final seat of judgment, don't you? Astonishing arrogance. I can't abide arrogance. Admit that you lied."

"I cannot think what you mean," Holmes exhaled coldly. "Then again, the world is rather hazy just now."

"That is a pity. I do not think I can allow you to remain in it much longer."

"Your mother—"

"Oh, you got her out as well, did you?" Bennett's face changed entirely as his mouth curved downward in a witheringly cruel contortion. The features twisted into the personification of hatred. I saw the letter writer staring back at us, the man who had written the words

From hell. In an instant the look was gone. "You think of distracting me, but it won't work, Mr. Holmes. You understand everything now."

"I don't," Holmes coughed, retching slightly. "I never pretended to. I never understood any of it."

"Come, now. You know far more than I ever intended you should."

"I don't know why you killed Martha Tabram."

"Martha Tabram?" he repeated wonderingly. "Martha Tabram. I remember. The first girl. She had so much blood on her. She was crying out as she walked down the street. It reminded me of something." He paused to consider. "They have all reminded me of something. I don't know what it was. She was crying and I made her still. And the last girl, when you forced me off the streets—she was singing, and then all at once she was crying. I made her still too. Yes, I think that was part of it."

"Now, Mr. Holmes, I believe we should stop talking."

It was becoming increasingly impossible to concentrate. My eyelids closed of their own accord. I forced them open again.

"You're a fool," Holmes murmured in a terrible, rasping voice. My friend still could not seem to breathe properly. "It will only be a moment before the police—"

"I am not a fool, and the police are a confused lot of imbeciles," came the sharp reply. "I ought to know it. Running about like ants in their absurd circles. Take that message in the street I wrote, for example. I leave a note for them. And what do they do? They erase it." He laughed pleasantly. "I thought they would. I couldn't be sure until I had tried. I meant to write it in Dutfield's Yard, next to the hall where all those Jews hold their meetings. That would have been something to see. But you arrived too soon that time as well."

Bennett drew a knife from his coat. "I don't like to finish it, Mr. Holmes, but I fear I must. I have to leave, you see. I do not believe I can stay in London any longer. But I promise not to hurt you. I never hurt any of them," he whispered as he leaned down slowly toward us.

Two revolver shots went off. Bennett fell, his knife clattering beside him. It glinted in the light of the flames pouring out of the window above. I looked down at the gun in my hand and thought, *It will have to be cleaned.* Then I felt myself falling just as Bennett had, and the world grew swiftly dark.

CHAPTER THIRTY-ONE

With the Respects of the Yard

I awoke in my own room to the sight of pale November light falling on the plane tree outside my window. I touched the bandage upon my head in confusion. I was extraordinarily hungry, and there was a violin playing somewhere.

When I tried to sit up, my left side flooded with a searing pain. I felt the area gently with my fingertips. No bandage had been applied, but there was a compress—a broken rib, then, or two perhaps. Using my elbow as a prop, I gradually managed to ease myself upward, until I was seated on the edge of my bed. No sooner had I accomplished this feat than I saw that it had been entirely unnecessary, for a bell had been placed within arm's reach upon my side table.

The bell rested on a page from the *London Chronicle*. The most prominently placed article's title blared out, "AN HEROIC RESCUE."

In a striking and dramatic turn of events, a courageous rescue has been effected by the dauntless private investigator Mr. Sherlock Holmes, whose unflagging vigilance in connection with the Whitechapel murders once caused spurious doubts to be cast upon his activities in the district. A terrifying fire set in the basement of a building on Thrawl Street speedily led to the destruction of the entire house, a development which could well have caused many fatalities if Mr. Holmes and his partner and biographer Dr. John Watson had not been present at the scene. In a daring display of valour, Mr. Holmes carried two women from the inferno, one of whom had been trapped helpless upon an upper floor. Such evidence of gallantry is welcome indeed in times such as these, when the women of the district have been given so much cause for fear and discouragement. Both Mr. Holmes and Dr. Watson sustained grave injuries at the scene, and though both the ladies to whom they proffered aid lived to see the hospital, the elder, a Mrs. Bennett, regretfully passed on as a result of internal wounds sustained during the blast. The conflagration, which was swiftly contained by that adept firefighting force we have all come to admire so universally, caused only one other casualty: that of ex–Scotland Yard officer Mr. Edward Bennett, who sustained extensive chest injuries during the explosion caused by the sudden movement of the fire from the basement to the ground floor. No doubt he wished to ascertain that his mother was no longer within the deadly structure. It is fervently to be hoped that Mr. Holmes's recovery is a speedy one, that his energies may be directed once more to that protection and defense of the populace for which he is justly famous.

I threw my head back and laughed heartily at this account, though I was forced to stop when the pain in my ribs grew greater than the joy afforded me. Replacing the page under the bell, I abandoned the bed. Dressing proved such an ordeal that I stopped after my trousers, shirtsleeves, and dressing gown, and thus fractionally clad, I made my way downstairs.

Sherlock Holmes was perched on the edge of his desk, improvising a version of a Paganini air so intricate as to be nearly unidentifiable. When he laid eyes on me, the chords shifted at once to a triumphal ode ending in a dizzyingly quick flourish of exultation as he leapt to his feet.

314 * Lyndsay Faye

"Thank heaven. My dear fellow, I am indescribably happy to see you about."

"No more than I am to see you," I returned warmly.

"I shall lose no time in sacking the nurse. These two days have been a trial. She drones comforting platitudes and whistles popular music-hall tunes in unlikely keys."

"Then I am grateful to have only just awoken," I said with a laugh.

"And some time you have been about it too," Holmes added severely. "You have a concussion, you know, and Dr. Agar was rather of the opinion your ribs were broken."

"I am of the same opinion. I read that you were also cruelly injured." Apart from the deeply furrowed circles beneath his eyes and a small gash on his hand, Holmes appeared the picture of health.

"Oh, so you did see that? Leslie Tavistock has been affecting a sort of servile allegiance, but he has not yet added veracity to his brief list of virtues."

"No indeed, for he said Edward Bennett was killed by the explosion."

"That inspired falsehood was Lestrade's notion, as a matter of fact."

"Was it?" I murmured.

Holmes's grey eyes searched my face solicitously. "Here, sit down, my dear fellow. The blast, though it was terribly hard on you, served one higher purpose in the end. Every relic and artifact was burned in the house; I know, for I had searched the other rooms myself, and there was nothing in them."

"And Mrs. Bennett is dead," I reflected. "And her son—"

"He is already buried," my friend said quickly. "Returned to the dust whence he came. There isn't a trace left of the man we knew as Jack the Ripper."

"I cannot believe it is over."

"You must give it a little time. You've only been conscious ten minutes."

"And it seems there are only five people outside the British government who will ever know the truth of the matter."

Holmes's eyes had been dancing merrily at me, but at this remark their fires dimmed.

"Just at the moment, there are four people."

"Four? There are yourself, Lestrade, Dunlevy, Miss Monk, and I. Five."

My friend suddenly concentrated very hard on the ceiling. His jaw was working, but it was some time before he could bring himself to speak.

"There are four. I am afraid that Miss Monk is not herself."

"What do you mean?" I cried. "She was alive. She is alive!"

"Calm yourself, my dear Watson."

"The article said nothing—"

"Bennett drugged her deeply to allow him to spirit her to his mother's rooms. I believe he found her in a pub, doctored her drink, and, under the pretense that she was intoxicated, made away with her. That opiate dosage, whatever it may have been, in combination with inhalation of the polluted atmosphere and the nervous strain of it all, had a profound effect."

"Do not tell me she is—"

"Watson, cease overtaxing yourself, I beg of you. She is not mad. Her memory has been affected. There are gaps. She knows many of those around her, and she understands perfectly, but she is very quiet and frequently confused."

Holmes and I had already suffered too much at the Ripper's hands. This news, however, struck me as I have hardly ever been struck in my life.

"It is cruel, Holmes," I whispered through the catch in my throat. "It is far too cruel. Where is she now?"

"She left hospital yesterday and is living with Mr. George Lusk and his family in their spare room."

"They wished to extend their charity to her?"

"Not at all. I arranged it."

"You feel responsible," I said numbly. "I do not blame you."

To this day, I do not know why I said it. It was an unforgivable remark. My companion did not reply, and I cannot imagine how he could have. He merely steepled his fingers and closed his eyes.

"My dear fellow, forgive me. What you have accomplished is nothing short of miraculous. You could not have—Holmes, don't look like that, please." In my confusion, my eyes rested on the side table. A syringe lay where it had dropped from careless fingers, and the bottle of seven-percent cocaine solution, habitually shut in a drawer, sat beside it in plain view and empty. Nearby rested a large, official-looking envelope with a rich seal and embossed coat of arms.

"Who has written you, Holmes?" I asked in an anguish to shift the subject.

"It is nothing. My brother's whim. He took it into his head that I deserved a knighthood."

"But that is wonderful!" I gasped. "There is not a man in England who could deserve it more. My deepest congrat—"

"I have refused it." He rose from his chair to procure his pipe and tobacco.

I stared at him in blank disbelief.

"You refused a knighthood."

"Don't be obtuse, my dear fellow. I said I refused it, and that is what I have done. Respectfully, I need hardly add," he pronounced, stuffing his pipe with shag.

"But in heaven's name, why? You have single-handedly run to ground the most notorious criminal in modern British history, and no one will ever know of it. At the very least you deserve—"

"If I deserved a knighthood even by the standards of the most vermiculate logic, I would no doubt have accepted it," he snapped viciously.

Then, more gently, Holmes added, "I told Mycroft you ought to have one. I was rather eloquent upon the subject. But I don't think he was listening." He withdrew his watch. "It is now a quarter to one. Miss Monk will arrive two doors down for the first of her continuing sessions with Dr. Agar, at my behest, at half past two this afternoon. He entertains hopes that she will recover. I can think of no reason, if you feel strong enough, you should not walk over to visit her. It would please her, I am certain."

"I would like nothing better. But surely you will accompany me?"

"Not unless you require my assistance. She doesn't know me, you see." He swept the evidence of his drug use into the voluminous pocket of his dressing gown. "Dunlevy will be there, no doubt. He is a most fixated chap—not to say monomaniacal."

"Most would refer to it as love, Holmes."

"Your theory is not without merit. But my dear Watson, you must be famished." He threw open the door and advanced to the top of the stairs. "Mrs. Hudson! A cold luncheon for two and a bottle of claret, if you please!" I heard the distant sound of a joyful exclamation followed quickly by remonstrance. "My dear lady, what is it to me that I have already sent a meal back?" I hid a smile as Mrs. Hudson's voice rose in conviction and force.

Holmes sighed. "I'll be back in a moment, Watson. I think in this case capitulation is the better part of valour."

On an evening flecked with snow some three weeks later, when the groups of crass thrill seekers and vulpine pressmen had disappeared from the former residence of Mary Kelly—the final unfortunate to fall victim to Jack the Ripper—I ambled gingerly down the stairs and out our front door. The air's bite had scarcely accomplished more than to send a feeling of invigoration through my shoulders by the time I had knocked at Dr. Agar's residence and been shown into the immaculately clean vestibule. Even if I required direction, I could hardly have avoided the peals of merriment emanating from the good doctor's consulting room. When I pushed open the door, I observed Miss

Monk in heady conversation with Dr. Agar while beside her on the sofa sat Stephen Dunlevy, whose eyes, after glancing genially in my direction, snapped back to the object of their affection.

"That's the cure for hysteria, and you'll swear to it?" she was demanding, her hand tracing her brow in disbelief.*

"Not at this clinic, I assure you," Dr. Agar said with a laugh.

"I granny why they'd enjoy it, make no mistake, but it's a sight cheaper in the Chapel—Oh! Dr. Watson," she interrupted herself, leaping to her feet and darting over to grasp me by the hand. "Have you ever treated a woman for hysteria?"

"Not as such," I demurred as she seated herself once more. "Miss Monk, you are looking ten times better. I congratulate you, as well as your groundbreaking physician."

"She is doing all the work and I am collecting all the credit." Dr. Agar smiled. "It is quite shameful, but many careers are built so, after all."

"You do yourself a disservice," Dunlevy interjected. "Dr. Watson is right, and may I seize the opportunity to say that I have never been so grateful to anyone in my life. Apart from Mr. Holmes, of course," he added with a grave look in my direction.

"How is Mr. Holmes, Doctor?" Dr. Agar inquired.

I must have hesitated over the question, for Miss Monk stated gamely, "I've recalled summat else about the fellow. He'll think me a right nickey for having ever forgotten so much at this rate, but hasn't he a trick of treating more or less anything in the room as if it's a chair?"

"Yes, he has." I smiled.

"I'm on the point of it, and then it's—" She made a whistling sound and waved a hand in the air. "But I have the best of help." She then looked, to my inner delight, not at Dr. Agar but directly and unmistakably at Stephen Dunlevy.

---

* The treatments for feminine hysteria were varied, but many were highly sexual in nature.

My hat in hand, I declared, "I merely wished to say hello. Holmes will be very relieved to learn how well you are doing, Miss Monk."

"Has he left your flat yet, Dr. Watson?" Dr. Agar asked softly.

"No," I returned, "but he will."

"I know he will," Dr. Agar assured me. "He has an excellent physician."

Glaring at our front door with perhaps more dissatisfaction than the object deserved, I turned my key in the lock. However, as it happened, I was not destined for an evening of attempting to elicit speech from a companion submerged in the worst of reflections, who to my great distress had been subsisting on tobacco, tea, and narcotics. Just as I opened the door to our sitting room, I accidentally nudged the leg of Inspector Lestrade, who appeared to have arrived moments before and was facing my haggard friend with an attitude of determined cheer.

"You are looking far better than when last I saw you, Dr. Watson, and I am heartily glad to say it," he exclaimed, shaking my hand.

Holmes waved us in from his armchair and tossed the prim little detective a matchbox in a graceful arc. "There are cigars on the side table and spirits in the decanter."

"Thank you."

"So you were there that night?" I prompted Lestrade, for I had my own questions to ask, Holmes or no Holmes. I'd not had the heart to force my friend into reliving that hour of painful memory, nor to ask how we had managed to escape.

"To be sure," the inspector answered readily. "By the time the fire brigade arrived, Mr. Holmes had moved you and Miss Monk back to the courtyard. You were out of danger there, at least temporarily. Mr. Holmes here alerted the force to the existence of a body at the side of the house, and you were all taken by police ambulance to London Hospital. The constables on the scene called me in immediately. You could have knocked me over with a feather when I saw who it was, considering the chase he had led us on the night before."

"I read that he was injured in the explosion."

"Quite so." The inspector coughed. "I was able to spirit the brute to the morgue quickly enough. The coroner was not inclined to disagree with my idea that shards of glass from the exploding window struck Bennett fatally. Of course, we are still investigating the murder."

Holmes, who had been regarding the bearskin rug, roused himself briefly at my expression of dismay. "Not you, my dear Watson. That could hardly be called a murder by any standards. Lestrade refers to Mary Kelly."

"Oh, I see," I said in relief.

"It's difficult to keep my heart in it, knowing you sent her killer to hell already, Doctor," Lestrade said placidly, sipping his spirits. "But it's the duty of the Yard to promote a feeling of safety."

"I do not envy you that duty," Holmes said grimly. "It will take some time before anyone can be convinced the Ripper has vanished."

"On the contrary, there is a rumour among the detective inspectors to that very effect," Lestrade retorted. "They are saying that Sherlock Holmes does not run into burning buildings without cause."

My friend appeared abashed. "That is potentially a very dangerous notion."

"You likely think it best for me to quash that bit of gossip," Lestrade nodded. "Well, I won't. I've been approached by a good many of the other inspectors. They seem to think if anyone's likely to know aught of the matter, I'm their man. Well, I haven't told them anything. But if they've suggested that you've put an end to this wretched affair, Mr. Holmes, I've as good as shaken their hands and winked a friendly eye."

Holmes sat up in his chair in indignation.

"Listen here, Mr. Holmes, and see it from my side for a moment. From what we know of Bennett, he hated the force and everything it stood for. Mad he may well have been, but this is a man who actually performed the most evil acts he could conjure up, and then used them against us. We won't ever understand why, but he did his utmost to make us look like fools, gentlemen, to make us all look like fools, and if you ask my opinion, he would have succeeded if not for you, Mr. Holmes. I'm under no illusions about the business. You did an extraordinary thing, and the more at the Yard who work out you had a hand in it, so much the better. All London is in your debt, sir, and I will be damned if I lift one finger to keep it secret."

"Hear, hear," said I.

Lestrade stood. "In fact, we inspectors have taken it upon ourselves to give you a token of our appreciation. I rather thought you might have done with the old one. But we hope this one serves."

My friend opened a small box which Lestrade had produced. Inside lay a beautiful silver cigarette case monogrammed with Holmes's initials, underneath which ran the words, "With the Respects of Scotland Yard, November 1888."

Sherlock Holmes sat with his lips parted, but no sound emerged.

"Thank you," he managed at length.

Lestrade nodded firmly. "It's our honour, Mr. Holmes. Well, I've said my piece. I'm afraid I must be off."

The inspector strode purposefully to our door but stopped upon reaching it. "I hope if anything out of the ordinary comes up, I may call on you?" he asked.

"I have not felt much inclined to take any cases of late," my friend replied hesitantly. "However, you know that should you ever require assistance, you are welcome to consult me."

Lestrade smiled. "You do occasionally stumble on the truth, I've always said that much in your favour. Well, as it's late, I won't keep you."

He had stepped outside the door when my friend called out, "Lestrade!"

The inspector's head reemerged. "Yes, Mr. Holmes?"

"That housebreaking business in Hounslow—it is obvious that there was no break-in at all. You must lay your hands on the nephew."

Lestrade grinned at me broadly.

"I'll pass the word along. Thanks for the tip. Good night, Mr. Holmes."

My friend rose from his chair and threw the curtains back from the bow window. The air outside was crisp and clean, and the wind had died. Holmes glanced back at me.

"What do you think of a ramble through London?"

I smiled cautiously. "Do you mean a silent trek, or an explication of every passerby we happen to encounter?"

"I leave it to you."

I considered the question. "Your deductions are always of the greatest interest to me."

"In that case, I have no choice but to hone my skills," he replied with a shrug.

"Will a bite of supper be involved? For the both of us, mind," I added emphatically.

"It is entirely possible," he granted. "If we are agreed, let us be off. 'Beneath is all the fiends'. There's hell, there's darkness, there's the sulfurous pit . . .'"

"My dear fellow, I don't imagine Shakespeare intended that speech to describe the view from our window. He had never seen it, after all."

"Hadn't he?" Holmes smiled. "Then I suppose you'll have to do in his stead; you've a penchant for the dramatic as well. Let me know when you've worked out something better. Come along, my dear fellow." He disappeared down the stairs.

Acknowledgments

My thanks are first owed to my parents, John and Vicki Farber, whose interest in literature in general and the Sherlock Holmes mysteries in particular led directly to my having the gall to write this book in the first place. They should also be credited with my having the gall to think I can do any thing I set my mind to, which is uncommonly kind of them. Key credit must also be given to my late uncle Michael Dobbins, who once gave a ten-year-old girl his hardback red suede copy of the *Adventures* and the *Returns*. He is missed and will be remembered.

Credit for Fight Choreographer, and President of the Department of Sticking to the Plot for the Love of All That's Decent, goes to Johnny Farber: my brother, my first editor, and my first collaborator. I would pay him, but I probably couldn't afford him.

To my actual editor, Kerri Kolen, and all the team at Simon & Schuster including Victoria Meyer and the band of talent who have made my book what it is, thank you from the bottom of my heart. My vague notions of the concept "editor" were blown to smithereens by Kerri, who is unfailingly kind while she is being critical. I couldn't have asked for a more sensitive and forthright commander in chief.

Dan Lazar's dedication is, as far as I am concerned, the gold standard for agents. If he ever sleeps, I haven't seen it, or at least he sleeps about as much as Sherlock Holmes does. Josh Getzler, also of Writers House, was the first person who ever laid eyes on my book who felt inclined to do something about it. They are both impossibly good to me, and Dan deserves a medal.

My love of Sherlockiana is deep-rooted, but a few scholars must be singled out for mention. William S. Baring-Gould's annotated collection was an invaluable staple, drawing from Sherlockian luminaries too numerous for me to list. Likewise Leslie Klinger's *New Annotated Sherlock Holmes* provided answers of all varieties, and I am grateful for his scholarship, as well as that of all those authors cited in his work.

My most grateful thanks are due to the Estate of Dame Jean Conan Doyle, and in particular its representative Jon Lellenberg, for their invaluable assistance and support. As a lifelong admirer of the world of Sherlock Holmes, their blessing is a prodigious honor. I hold the highest respect and love for Sir Arthur Conan Doyle's characters, and the Estate's encouragement of my project has meant more to me than I can express. In addition, I am in debt to the vast international web of Sherlock Holmes enthusiasts, whose generosity and heartfelt enthusiasm continually astonish me. They share their lives with me, and that is what writing new tales of the Great Detective is about. As John le Carré said, no one writes of Sherlock Holmes without love.

There are a great many Ripper scholars whose research was mined for this volume, and they deserve far more than my thanks. To be specific where specificity is due, Stewart Evans is the sole reason this book appears remotely free of error, and any remaining mistakes fall squarely on my own head. Donald Rumbelow, Martin Fido, Paul Begg, Keith Skinner, Philip Sugden, Stephen Knight, Philip Rawlings, Peter Underwood, Peter Vronsky, Scott Palmer, Roger Wilkes, Patricia Cornwell, James Morton, Harold Schechter, Jan Bondeson, Colin Wilson, Andrew Maunder, Brian Marriner, Paul H. Feldman, Melvin Harris, Paul West, Peter Costello, Nathan Braund, Maxim Jakubowski, Eduardo Zinna, and the press reports archives of the comprehensive www.casebook.org were critically helpful to me in grasping the details of these still-harrowing crimes.

I would like to thank the New York City restaurant Osteria Laguna for firing me, leading to a series of events without which I would never have written this book.

Finally, thank you, Gabriel. You inspire me. Your willingness to expand the realm of the possible makes me fight all the harder. Thank you for believing in this book.

"Moore's cockeyed view of th[...]rns of his disparate characters—from his ability to capture the sp[...]iosity to a creepy goth-girl enamored a bum suffering illusions [...]mes hilarious." with death—and his writi[...] [...]amusing on its own, but add to that

—*St. Louis Post-Dispatch*

"A raunchy slapstick co[...]hed all the way through this page-turner. En- form, and this review[...]d." thusiastically recomm[...] [...] young vampires in love. . . . Moore is in top

—*Library Journal*

"[Moore] glides com[...]bly through the book's loony little corner of San Francisco and thr[...] drastic changes of mood. . . . As with his best work, there's a fundam[...]al sweetness beneath the antics."

—*New York Times*

"Moore hand[...] [the] goofier-than-thou plot adroitly. . . . Think of a collabo- ration among Anne Rice, S. J. Perelman, and Pedro Almodóvar. In other words, Moore in the usual vein (jugular, that is)."

—*Kirkus Reviews*

"Moore makes fun of just about everything, especially the cobwebby genre of vampire fiction. He creates a bizarre alternate world with enough an- chors in reality that crazy things seem normal. Which is why I try not to think about it too hard, but just go with it. Moore is the insane conductor, and I'm just along for the ride. And I really enjoy the ride."

—*Palm Beach Post*

"Few things get the blood moving like a Christopher Moore tale about vam- pires. . . . As he does in earlier work, Moore is telling us about the frailties of the human condition. Take away the fangs and the nighttime binges and Moore describes young love. The joys, the awkwardness, the fears, the lust. . . . Tommy's journey through first love is one we all take. Moore makes this trip a joy, filled with absurd characters who allow people in the dark to laugh and see the light."

—*Cleveland Plain Dealer*

© Charlee Rodgers

About the Author

CHRISTOPHER MOORE is the author of *A Dirty Job, The Stupidest Angel, Fluke, Lamb, The Lust Lizard of Melancholy Cove, Island of the Sequined Love Nun, Bloodsucking Fiends, Coyote Blue,* and *Practical Demonkeeping.* He invites readers to e-mail him at BSFiends@aol.com.

YOU SUCK

A LOVE STORY

CHRISTOPHER MOORE

HARPER

NEW YORK · LONDON · TORONTO · SYDNEY

HARPER

This book is a work of fiction. The characters, incidents, and dialogue are drawn from the author's imagination and are not to be construed as real. Any resemblance to actual events or persons, living or dead, is entirely coincidental.

A signed limited hardcover edition has been privately printed by Charnel House. www.charnelhouse.com

A hardcover edition of this book was published in 2007 by William Morrow, an imprint of HarperCollins Publishers.

HarperCollins books may be purchased for educational, business, or sales promotional use. For information please write: Special Markets Department, HarperCollins Publishers, 10 East 53rd Street, New York, NY 10022.

FIRST HARPER PAPERBACK PUBLISHED 2008.

Designed by Betty Lew

The Library of Congress has catalogued the hardcover edition as follows:

Moore, Christopher.
    You suck: a love story / Christopher Moore. —1st ed.
        p.cm.
ISBN: 978-0-06-059029-1
ISBN-10: 0-06-059029-7
1. Vampires—Fiction. I. Title.

PS3563.O594Y682007
813'.54—dc22   2006047083

ISBN: 978-0-06-059030-7 (pbk.)

08 09 10 11 12 WBC/RRD 10 9 8 7 6 5 4 3 2

For my readers,
by request

ACKNOWLEDGMENTS

Thanks, again, to the usual suspects: my agent, Nick Ellison, and Sarah Dickman, Arija Weddle, and Marissa Matteo at Nicholas Ellison, Inc.; Jennifer Brehl, Kate Nintzel, Lisa Gallagher, Michael Morrison, Mike Spradlin, Jack Womack, Debbie Stier, Lynn Grady, and all my friends at William Morrow; and, of course, to Charlee Rodgers, for putting up with the frozen turkey bowling.

Get Over It, a Lot of People Are Dead

"You bitch, you killed me! You suck!"

Tommy had just awakened for the first time as a vampire. He was nineteen, thin, and had spent his entire life between states of amazement and confusion.

"I wanted us to be together." Jody: pale, pretty, long red hair hanging in her face, cute swoop of a nose in search of a lost spray of freckles, a big lipstick-smeared grin. She'd only been undead herself for a couple of months, and was still learning to be spooky.

"Yeah, that's why you spent the night with *him*." Tommy pointed across the loft to the life-sized bronze statue of a man in a tattered suit. Inside the bronze shell was the ancient vampire who had turned Jody. Another bronze of Jody stood next to him. When the two of them had gone out at sunrise, into the sleep of the dead, Tommy had taken them to the sculptors who lived on the ground floor of his building and had the vampires bronzed. He'd thought it would give him time to think of what to do, and keep Jody from running off with the old vampire. Tommy's mistake had been drilling ear holes in Jody's sculpture so she could hear him. Somehow, during the night, before the bronzing, the old vampire had taught her to turn to mist, and she'd streamed out of the ear holes into the room, and—well—here they were: dead, in love, and angry.

"I needed to know about what I am, Tommy. Who else was going to tell me if not him?"

"Yeah, but you should have asked me before you did *this*," Tommy said. "You shouldn't just kill a guy without asking. It's inconsiderate." Tommy was from Indiana, and his mother had raised him to have good manners and to be considerate of other people's feelings.

"You had sex with me while I was unconscious," Jody said.

"That's not the same," Tommy said. "I was just being friendly, like when you put a quarter in someone else's parking meter when they aren't there—you know they appreciate it later, even if they don't thank you personally."

"Yeah, wait until you go out in your jammies and wake up all sticky in a cheerleader outfit and see how grateful you are. You know, Tommy, when I'm out, technically, I'm dead. Guess what that makes you?"

"Well—uh—yeah, but you're not even human. You're just some foul dead thing." Tommy immediately regretted saying it. It was hurtful and mean, and although Jody was, indeed, dead, he didn't find her foul at all—in fact, he was pretty sure he was in love with her, he was just a little embarrassed about the whole necrophilia/cheerleader thing. Back in the Midwest people didn't mention that sort of thing unless a dog dug up a pom-pom in some guy's backyard and the police eventually discovered the whole human pyramid buried under the swing set.

Jody sniffled, completely for effect. Actually she was relieved that Tommy was now on the defensive. "Well, welcome to the Foul, Dead Thing Club, Mr. Flood."

"Yeah, you drank my blood," Tommy said. "A lot."

Damn, she should have pretended to cry. "You let me."

"Again, being considerate," Tommy said. He stood up and shrugged.

"You just let me because of the sex."

"That's not true, it was because you needed me." He was lying, it was because of the sex.

"Yes, I did," Jody said. "I still do." She held her arms out to him. "I really do."

He walked into her arms and held her. She felt amazing to him, even more amazing than she had before. It was as if his nerves had been dialed up to eleven. "Okay, it was because of the sex."

Great, she thought, *in control once again.* She kissed his neck. "How do you feel about it now?"

"Maybe in a minute, I'm starving." He let go of her and

stormed across the loft to the kitchen, where he pulled a burrito out of the freezer, threw it into the microwave, and hit the button, all in one smooth motion.

"You don't want to eat that," Jody said.

"Nonsense, it smells great. It's like every little bean and pork piece is sending out its own delicious miasma of flavor vapor." Tommy used words like "miasma" because he wanted to be a writer. That's why he'd come to San Francisco in the first place—to take life in big bites and write about it. Oh, and to find a girlfriend.

"Put the burrito down, and back away, Tommy," Jody said. "I don't want you to get hurt."

"Ha, that's cute." He took a big bite and grinned at her as he chewed.

Five minutes later, because she felt responsible, Jody was helping him clean bits of masticated burrito off the kitchen wall and the front of the refrigerator. "It's like every bean was storming the gates of repressive digestion to escape."

"Yeah, well, being refried will do that to you," Jody said, stroking his hair. "You okay?"

"I'm starving. I need to eat."

"Not so much eat," Jody said.

"Oh my God! It's the hunger. I feel like my insides are caving in on themselves. You should have told me about this."

She knew how he felt—actually, she had felt worse

when it happened to her. At least he knew what was happening to him. "Yeah, sweetie, we're going to have to make a few adjustments."

"Well, what do I do? What did you do?"

"I mostly fed off of you, remember?"

"You should have thought this through before you killed me. I'm fucked."

"*We're* fucked. Together. Like Romeo and Juliet, only we get to be in a sequel. Very literary, Tommy."

"Oh, that's a comfort. I can't believe you just killed me like that."

"And turned you into a superbeing, thank you very much."

"Oh, crap, there's burrito spooge all over my new sneakers."

"You can see in the dark, now," Jody said cheerfully. "Wanna try it? I'll get naked. You can look at me in the dark. Naked. You'll like it."

"Jody, I'm starving over here."

She couldn't believe that he didn't respond to the naked persuasion. What kind of monster had she created? "Okay, I'll find you a bug or something."

"A bug?! A bug!? I'm not eating a bug."

"I said there'd have to be some adjustments."

Tommy had been dealing with more than a few adjustments since he'd come west from his hometown of Incontinence, Indiana—not the least of which had been finding a girlfriend, who, while smart, sexy, and quick-witted, drank his blood and tended to fall unconscious at the exact moment of sunrise. He'd always suspected that she might have just picked him because he worked nights and could walk around during the day, especially since she'd once said, "I need someone who works nights and can walk around during the day," but now that he was a vampire, he could close the door on that insecurity and open another onto a whole new world of insecurities he'd never even considered before. The appropriate age for a vampire is four hundred years old—he should be a world-weary and sophisticated creature, his human anxieties long since overcome or evolved into macabre perversions. The problem with a nineteen-year-old vampire is that he drags all of his adolescent insecurities into the dark with him.

"I'm really pale," Tommy said, staring at himself in the bathroom mirror. They'd figured out early on that vampires do, indeed, cast a reflection in a mirror, just like they could tolerate proximity to crucifixes and garlic. (Tommy had run experiments on Jody while she slept, including many involving cheerleader outfits and personal lubricants.) "And not just winter in Indiana pale. I'm, like, pale like you."

"Yeah," said Jody, "I thought you liked the pale."

"Sure, it looks good on you, but I look ill."

"Keep looking," Jody said. She was leaning against the door frame, dressed in tight black jeans and a half shirt, her hair tied back and streaming down her back like a flaccid red comet tail. She was trying not to appear too amused.

"Something's missing," Tommy said. "Something besides color."

"Uh-huh." Jody grinned.

"My skin cleared up! I don't have a single zit."

"Ding, ding, ding," Jody onomatopeed, signaling that Tommy had hit on the correct answer.

"If I had known my skin would clear up, I'd have asked you to change me a long time ago."

"I didn't know how to a long time ago," Jody said. "That's not all, take off your shoes."

"I don't understand, I—"

"Just take off your shoes. "

Tommy sat on the edge of the tub and took off his sneakers and socks.

"What?"

"Look at your toes."

"They're straight. My little toe isn't bent anymore. It's like I've never worn shoes."

"You're perfect," Jody said. She remembered finding out this condition of vampirism and being both delighted and horrified because now she felt that she'd always need to lose five pounds—five pounds that were preserved for eternity.

Tommy pulled up the leg of his jeans and studied his shin. "The scar where I hit myself with a hatchet, it's gone."

"And it always will be," Jody said. "You'll always be perfect, just like you are now. My split ends even went away."

"I'll always be the same?"

"Yes."

"Just like I am now."

"As far as I know," Jody said.

"But I was going to start working out. I was going to be buff. I was going to have abs of steel."

"No, you weren't."

"I was. I was going to be an awesome hunk of muscular man-meat."

"No, you weren't. You wanted to be a writer. You were going to have little stick arms and get winded when you hit the back-space key more than three times consecutively. You're in great shape from working in the grocery store. Wait until you see how you can run."

"You really think I'm in great shape?"

"Yes, I thought I made that clear."

Tommy flexed his chest in the mirror, which showed not at all through his flannel shirt. He unbuttoned his shirt and tried it again, with little effect, then shrugged. "What about the writer thing? Will my brain always be like this? I mean, will I get any smarter, or is that stuck in time, too?"

"Well, yeah, but that's because you're a man, not because you're a vampire."

"You spiteful harpy."

"I think I've made my point," Jody said.

Jody had put on a red leather jacket, even though she could no longer feel discomfort from the cold fog coming in off the Bay. She liked the way it looked with her black jeans and a low-cut black lace camisole she'd rescued from a Nordstrom Rack Store before some slut got hold of it. "Come on, Tommy, we need to go find something for you to eat before we run out of night."

"I know, but I have something I have to do. Give me a minute." He was in the bathroom again, this time with the door shut.

Jody heard the zipper of his jeans go down, then a slightly breathless man-scream. The bathroom door flew open and Tommy, his pants and underwear around his ankles, bunny-hopped in two great leaps across the bedroom.

"Look at this. What's happening to me. Look at this!" He was pointing furiously to his penis. "It's like I'm some radioactive mutant freak."

Jody went to him and grabbed his hands—held him steady, looked him in the eyes. "Tommy, calm down. It's just your foreskin."

"I don't have a foreskin. I'm circumcised."

"Not anymore," Jody said. "Evidently, when you turned, it grew back, just like your toes straightened and your scars all went away."

"Oh. You don't find it creepy, then?"

"No. It's fine."

"You want to touch it?"

"Thanks. Maybe later."

"Oh, sorry, I freaked. Didn't realize. I—uh—I still feel like I have to finish what I was going to do."

"That's fine," Jody said. "You're fine. You go finish up. I'll wait."

"You're sure you don't want to give it a quick fondle?"

"If I do, can we get out of here?"

"Probably not."

"Well then, back in the bathroom you go." She spun him around and gave him a gentle shove. He bunny-hopped his newly recovered foreskin back into the bathroom and closed the door.

Jody shuddered at the sound of the door closing. She hadn't thought about whether or not Tommy would retain his incessant horniness after he turned, she had just wanted a companion who could understand what she was, what she felt, what the world looked like through vampire eyes. If it turned out that he was going to be nineteen forever, she might end up having to kill him for real.

The Last Poop

"So that was it?"

"Yep."

"Never again?"

"Nope."

"Not ever?"

"Nope."

"I feel like I should save them or something."

"Would you just flush and come out of there."

I Am Poor and My Cat Is Huge

Jody walked a step or two behind Tommy, just watching him, as they made their way up Third Street toward Market. She was watching his reaction to his new senses, giving him some room to look around, whispering hints about what he was experiencing. She'd gone through this herself only a couple of months ago, and she'd done it without a guide.

"I can see the heat coming off the streetlamps," Tommy said, looking up and spinning as he walked. "Every window in every building is a different color."

"Try to just look at one thing at a time, Tommy. Don't let it overwhelm you." Jody was waiting for him to comment on the aura that each person was giving off. Not a heat aura, more of a life force. So far they'd only seen healthy red and pink ones—not what she was looking for.

"What's that noise, like running water?" Tommy asked.

"That's the sewers running under the street. All that stuff will fade after a while—you'll still hear it, but you won't notice it unless you focus."

"It's like a thousand people are talking in my head." He looked around at the few pedestrians who were out on the street.

"Televisions and radios, too," Jody said. "Try to focus on one thing, let the rest fall back."

Tommy stopped, looked up at an apartment window four floors up. "There's a guy up there having phone sex."

"Figures you'd zero in on that," Jody said. She focused on the window. Yes, she could hear the guy panting and giving instructions to someone on the phone. Evidently he felt the caller was a dirty little slut and therefore needed to apply varieties of hot salsa to her body. Jody tried to hear the voice on the other end of the phone, but it was too faint—the guy must have been wearing a headset.

"What a freak," Tommy said.

"Shhhh," Jody said. "Tommy, close your eyes and listen. Forget the salsa guy. Don't look."

Tommy closed his eyes and stood in the middle of the sidewalk. "What?"

Jody leaned against a "No Parking" sign and smiled. "What's just to the right of you?"

"How do I know? I was looking up."

"I know. Focus. Listen. Two feet from your right hand, what is it?"

"This is dumb."

"Just listen. Listen to the shape of the sound coming from your right."

"Okay." Tommy squinted, showing he was concentrating.

A couple of androgynous students dressed in black with severe hair, probably from the Academy of Art on the next block, walked by and barely gave them a look until Tommy said, "I can hear a box. A rectangle."

"Acid noob," said one of the students, who sounded like it might be a guy.

"I remember my first trip," said the other, who was probably a girl. "I wandered into the men's room at the Metreon and thought I was in a Marcel Duchamp installation."

Jody waited for them to pass then asked, "Yes, a rectangle, solid, hollow, what?" She was a little giddy now, bouncing on the balls of her feet. This was better than buying shoes.

"It's hollow." Tommy tilted his head. "It's a newspaper machine." He opened his eyes, looked at the newspaper box, then at Jody, his face lit up like a toddler who has just discovered chocolate for the first time.

She ran into his arms and kissed him. "I have so much to show you."

"Why didn't you tell me?" Tommy asked.

"How could I? Do you have words for what you're hearing? For what you're seeing?"

Tommy let her go and looked around, took a deep breath through his nose, as if checking the bouquet of a wine. "No. I don't know how to say these things."

"See, that's why I had to share this with you."

Tommy nodded, but looked a little forlorn. "This part is good. But the other part . . ."

"What other part?"

"The foul, dead, blood-drinking part. I'm still starving."

"Don't whine, Tommy. Nobody likes a whiner."

"Hungry," he said.

She knew how he felt, she was feeling some of it herself, but she didn't know how to solve the feeding problem. Tommy had always been her go-to blood guy; now they were going to have to hunt. She could do it, she had done it, but she didn't want to do it. "Come on, we'll figure this out. Don't pout. Let's go watch people on Market Street. You'll like it." She took his hand and dragged him up the street toward Market, where rivers of tourists, shoppers, and freaks were flowing up and down the streets and sidewalks. Rivers of blood.

Everyone smells like whiz and feet," Tommy said, standing on the sidewalk in front of a Walgreens drugstore. It was still early in the evening and the convention crowd from the hotels was flowing down the sidewalks like a great migrating herd, looking for dinner or a watering hole. Out on the edges, hustlers, homeless, and hangers-on worked their angles, playing the secret path of eye contact to the pocket, while the herd defended itself by paying rapt attention to their companions, their cell phones, or a spot on the sidewalk twelve feet ahead.

"Feet and pee," Tommy continued.

"You get used to it," Jody said.

"Is there a clean pair of underwear anywhere on this street?" Tommy shouted. "You people are disgusting!"

"Would you settle down," Jody said. "People are looking. They think you're crazy."

"Which makes me different, how?"

She looked up the street—for the three blocks she could see there were about three people per block shouting at passersby, wild-eyed and angry, and obviously bat shit. She nodded. He had a point, but then she snatched his shirt collar and pulled his ear down to lip level. "The difference is that you aren't living anymore and it's not a good idea to attract attention to yourself."

"Which is why you chose to wear that delightful ensemble from the skank-wear collection at Hoes-N-Thangs?"

"You said you liked it." Jody had become a little more provocative in her dress since becoming a vampire—but she saw it more as an expression of confidence, not a means to attract attention. Was it a predator thing? A power thing?

"I did—do like it, but every guy who passes is staring at your cleavage. I can hear their heartbeats go up. Did you have to turn to mist to get into those jeans? You did, didn't you?"

A tap on Tommy's shoulder. A young man in a white, short-sleeved dress shirt and a black tie had sidled up to him, holding out a pamphlet. "You sound troubled, brother.

Maybe this will help." The pamphlet proclaimed REJOICE! on the cover in big green letters.

Jody covered her mouth and turned away so the guy wouldn't see her giggling.

"What?!" Tommy said, turning on the guy. "What? What? What? Can't you see I'm trying to discuss my girlfriend's— uh—well, those." Tommy gestured to Jody's shoulder, which was now where those had just been. "Show him, Jody," Tommy said.

Jody shook her head and started to walk away, her shoulders shaking with laughter.

"There's a message here," said the tie guy. "It can bring you comfort—and joy."

"Yeah, well, I was trying to show you some examples of that, but there she goes with them."

"But this is a joy that goes beyond physical—"

"Yeah, like you'd know," Tommy said, cupping his nose and mouth as if covering a sneeze. "Listen, I'd love to discuss this with you, buddy, but right now you have to GO HOME AND WASH YOUR ASS! You smell like you're smuggling a stockyard back there!"

Tommy turned and strode after Jody, leaving the tie guy blushing and crumpling his pamphlet.

"It's not funny," Tommy said.

Jody was trying so hard not to laugh, she snorted. "Yes, it is."

"Can't they see we're damned? You'd think they could tell. At least you. We are damned, aren't we? "

"No idea," Jody said. She hadn't really thought about it.

"Didn't cover that in your advanced vampire course with the old guy?"

"Forgot to ask."

"No problem," Tommy said, with no effort at all to suppress sarcasm. "Minor detail. Anything else you might have forgotten to ask?"

"I thought I'd have more time, for follow-up," Jody said. "I didn't realize that the man I love was going to bronze us that first night."

"Yeah—well—okay. Sorry."

"Where's the trust?" Jody said.

"You killed me," Tommy said.

"Oh, there you go again."

"Please, folks. I need a dollar," said a voice from the left. Jody looked down to see a guy sitting against the granite wall of a closed bank. He was dirty beyond age or race, sort of grimy to the point of shine, and on his lap was an enormous long-haired cat. There was a cup on the sidewalk in front of him and beside it a hand-printed sign that read I AM POOR AND MY CAT IS HUGE.

Tommy, who was still fairly new to the city and hadn't learned to look past this sort of thing, stopped and started digging in his pocket. "That is sure a huge cat."

"Yeah, he eats a lot. It's all I can do to keep him fed."

Jody nudged Tommy, trying to get him back into the pedestrian flow. She liked that he was a nice guy, but it could really be irritating sometimes. Especially when she

was trying to teach him the profundities of being a creature of the night.

"Mostly fur, though, right?" Tommy asked.

"Mister, this cat weighs thirty-five pounds."

Tommy whistled and handed the guy a dollar. "Can I
touch him?"

"Sure," the guy said. "He doesn't care."

Tommy knelt down and poked the cat gently, then
looked up at Jody. "This is a huge cat."

She smiled. "Huge. Let's go."

"Touch him," Tommy said.

"No thanks."

"So," Tommy said to the cat guy, "why don't you give
him to a shelter or something?"

"Then how am I supposed to make a living?"

"You could print up a sign that says 'I'm poor and I lost
my huge cat'? That would work on me."

"You may not be the best sample," said the cat guy.

"Look," Tommy said, standing now and digging into his
pocket. "I'll buy the cat. I'll give you, uh, forty—"

The cat guy shook his head.

"Sixty—"

Furious head shaking . . .

Tommy untangled bills from a wad he'd pulled out of
his pocket, "One hundred—"

"No."

"And thirty . . . two—"

"No."

"And thirty-seven cents."

"No."

"And a paper clip."

"No."

"That's a great offer," Tommy insisted. "That's like four bucks a pound!"

"No."

"Well screw you, then," Tommy said. "I don't feel sorry for you and your huge cat."

"You can't have your dollar back."

"Fine!" Tommy said.

"Fine!" said the cat guy.

Tommy took Jody by the arm and started to walk away. "That's a huge cat," he said.

"Why were you trying to buy it? We're not supposed to have pets in the loft."

"Duh," Tommy said. "Dinner."

"Yuck."

"It's a stopgap," Tommy said. "You know that the Masai of Kenya drink the blood of their cattle with no apparent ill effect to the cow."

"Well, I'm sure it violates our lease if we get a cow."

"That's it."

"What's it?"

"A lease."

Tommy swung her around and brought her back to the cat guy.

"I want to rent the cat," Tommy said. "You could use a

break and I want to show the huge cat to my aunt who is an invalid and can't come down here."

"No."

"One night. One hundred and thirty-two dollars and thirty-seven cents."

The cat guy raised an eyebrow, the grime over that eye cracked a little. "One fifty."

"I don't have one fifty, you know that."

"Then I want to see the redhead's hooters."

Tommy looked at Jody, then back at the cat guy, then back at Jody.

"No," Jody said calmly.

"No," Tommy said indignantly. "How dare you suggest it?"

"One hooter," countered the cat guy.

Tommy looked at Jody. She gave him the wide, green-eyed expression that she would have described as *I will slap you so far into next week that it will take a team of surgeons just to get Wednesday out of your ass.*

"No way," Tommy said. "The redhead's hooters are not on the table." He grinned, looked back at Jody, then looked away, really fast.

The cat guy shrugged. "I'll need some kind of security deposit, like your driver's license—"

"Sure," Tommy said.

"And a credit card."

"No," Jody said, pulling her jacket closed and zipping it up to her neck.

"Nothing kinky," said the cat guy. "I'll know."

"Going to show him to my aunt, and I'll have him back tomorrow, this time."

"Deal," said the cat guy. "His name is Chet."

Y̧ou first," Tommy said. They stood in the great room of their loft on either side of the futon, where the huge cat, a crossbreed between a Persian, a dust mop, and possibly a water buffalo, was actively shedding. Tommy had decided that he was going to be very cool about the whole blood-drinking thing, despite the fact that he was so amped he felt as if he could run up and down the walls. In fact, he wasn't sure that he couldn't run up and down the walls, that was part of what was freaking him out. Still, since coming to San Francisco a couple of months ago, he had spent entirely too much time overreacting, and he wasn't going to do it now—not in front of his girlfriend. Not at all, if he could help it.

"You should go first," Jody said. "You've never fed before."

"But you gave the old vampire some of your blood," Tommy said. "You need it." It was true, she had given the vampire her blood to help heal him from the damage Tommy and his friends had caused by blowing up his yacht and so forth, but he hoped she would say no again.

"No, no, no, after you," Jody said, with a very bad French accent. "I insist."

"Well, if you insist."

Tommy leapt to the futon and bent over the huge cat. He wasn't sure how he was supposed to go about this, but he could see the healthy red life aura around Chet, and he could hear his little kitty heart pounding. There was a crackling noise inside of his head, like someone was popping bubble wrap in his ear canal, and then there was pressure on the roof of his mouth, painful pressure, and more crackling. He felt something give and two sharp points poking his lower lip. He pushed back from the cat and grinned at Jody, who yelped and jumped back a step.

"Fangth," Tommy said.

"Yes, I can see that," Jody said.

"Why'd you jump? Do they look thupid?"

"You startled me, is all," Jody said, looking away from him like he was an arc welder or a total eclipse and full eye contact might blind her. She waved him on. "Go, go, go. Be careful. Not too hard."

"Right," Tommy said. He grinned again and she shied away.

Tommy turned back, braced the cat, who seemed much less freaked by this process than the two vampires in the room, and bit.

"Thuppt, thuppt, ack!" Tommy stood up and started brushing at his tongue to remove cat hair. "Yuck!"

"Hold still," Jody said, going to him and brushing the loose, damp cat hair away from his face. She went to the kitchen counter and came back with a glass of water and a paper towel, which she used to wipe at Tommy's tongue.

"Just use the water to rinse. Don't swallow it. You won't be able to keep it down."

"I'm not going to thwollow it, my mouf is full of cat hair."

Once he had rinsed, Jody picked the last of the hairs from his mouth, and in doing so, she pricked one of her fingers on Tommy's right fang.

"Ouch." She pulled her finger away and put it in her mouth.

"Oh, jeez," Tommy said. He pulled her finger out of her mouth and put it in his. His eyes rolled back in his head and he moaned through his nose.

"Oh, I don't think so," Jody said. She grabbed his hand and bit into his forearm, attaching herself to him like a remora to a shark.

Tommy growled, flipped her around, and threw her facedown on the futon, his arm still in her mouth. She flipped her hair to the side and he sank his teeth into her neck. She screamed, but the shriek was muted, bubbling out on Tommy's bloody forearm. Chet, the huge cat, hissed and bolted across the room, through the bedroom door, to wedge himself under the bed, as the sounds of straining leather, tearing denim, and screaming predators filled the loft.

The irony, that it sounded like a huge catfight, was completely lost on the huge cat.

Red and White and Dead All Over

Kapoc stuffing and chicken feathers lay in great, fluffy drifts across the room, along with the shreds of their clothing, the futon cover, pieces of a fuzzy, Muppet-skin rug, and the crushed remains of a couple of cheap-ass Pier 1 paper lanterns. Sparks crackled from the bare wires over the breakfast bar, where the pendulum light fixtures used to hang. The loft looked as if someone had thrown a hand grenade into the middle of a teddy-bear orgy and the only survivors had had their fur blown off.

"Well, that was different," Jody said, still a little breathless. She was lying across the coffee table, looking out the window at a streetlight from an upside-down angle, naked except for one sleeve of her red leather jacket. She was smeared with blood from head to toe, and even as Tommy watched, the scratches and fang marks on her skin were healing over.

"If I'd known," Tommy said, panting, "I'd have grown a foreskin a long time ago." He lay across the room where she had thrown him, sprawled on a pile of books and kindling that had once been a bookshelf, also smeared with blood and covered in scratches—wearing only a sock.

As he pulled a pencil-sized splinter of bookcase out of his thigh, Tommy thought that he might have been a little hasty about yelling at Jody for turning him into a vampire. Although he couldn't really remember much of it, he was pretty sure he'd just had the most amazing sex ever. Apparently what he had read about vampire sex being all about drinking the blood and nothing else—it was just another myth like the changing into a bat and the inability to cross running water.

"Did you know that was going to happen?" Tommy asked.

"I had no idea," Jody said, still on the coffee table, and looking more to Tommy every minute like a murder victim, except that she was talking, and smiling. "I was going to make you buy me dinner and take me to a movie first."

Tommy chucked the bloody bookcase splinter at her. "I don't mean did you know we were going to do it, I mean did you know that it was going to be like that?"

"How would I know that?"

"I thought maybe the night you spent with the old vampire . . ."

Jody sat up. "I didn't *do* him, Tommy, I just spent the

night with him trying to find out about how to be a vampire. And his name is Elijah."

"Oh, so now you're on a first-name basis."

"Oh, for the love of God, Tommy, would you stop thinking? You're taking what was an amazing experience and sucking all the life out of it."

Tommy fidgeted on his pile of rubble and started to pout, but winced when he tried to push out his lower lip and it caught on his fangs. She was right. He'd always been like that, always overthinking, overanalyzing. "Sorry," he said.

"You have to just be part of the world now," Jody said softly. "You can't put everything into categories, separate yourself from experience by putting words on it. Like the song says, *let it be*."

"Sorry," Tommy said again. He tried to push the thoughts out of his head, closed his eyes, and listened to his heartbeat, and Jody's heartbeat coming from across the room.

"It's okay," Jody said. "Sex like that does sort of beg for a postmortem."

Tommy smiled, his eyes still closed. "So to speak."

Jody stood up and crossed the room to where he was sitting. She offered him her hand to help him up. "Careful, the back of your head is kind of stuck in the drywall."

Tommy turned his head and heard plaster cracking. "I'm still starving."

She pulled him to his feet. "I'm feeling a little drained myself."

"My bad," Tommy said. He could remember now, her

blood pulsing into him, at the same time that his was pulsing into her. He rubbed a place on his shoulder where the
punctures from her fangs hadn't quite healed yet.

She kissed the spot he was rubbing. "You'll heal faster
when you've had fresh blood."

Tommy felt an ache, like a sudden cramp in his stomach. "I really need to eat."

Jody led him into the bedroom, where Chet the huge
cat was cowering in the corner, hiding unsuccessfully behind the wicker hamper.

"Wait," Jody said. She padded back out into the great
room and came back a few seconds later wearing what was
left of her red leather jacket (really more of a vest now) and
her panties, which she had to hold together on one side
where they'd been torn off. "Sorry," she said, "I'm not comfortable being naked in front of strangers."

Tommy nodded. "He's not a stranger, Jody. He's dinner."

"Uh-huh," Jody said, nodding and shaking her head at
the same time, making her appear like a bloodstained,
bobble-head doll. "You go. You're new."

"Me? Don't you know some superanimal hypnotism to
call him to you?"

"Nope. Go get him. I'll wait."

Tommy looked at her. On top of the blood that streaked
and smeared her pale skin, there were gobs of futon stuffing stuck to her here and there, as well as white chicken
feathers in her hair from one of the exploded cushions. He

had feathers and cat hair stuck to his chest and legs. "We're going to have to shave him first, you know?"

Jody nodded, not looking away from the huge cat. "Maybe a shower first."

"Good idea." Tommy put his arm around her.

"But just washing. No sex!"

"Why, we already lost the cleaning deposit?"

"Those shower doors are glass."

"Okay. But can I wash your—"

"No," she said. She took his hand and dragged him into the bathroom.

It turned out that superhuman vampire strength came in handy when shaving a thirty-five-pound cat. After a couple of false starts, which had them chasing Chet the huge shaving-cream-covered cat around the loft, they discovered the value of duct tape as a grooming tool. Because of the tape, they weren't able to shave his feet. When they were finished, Chet looked like a big-eyed, potbellied, protohuman in fur-lined, duct-tape space boots—the feline love child of Gollum and Dobby the house-elf.

"I'm not sure we needed to shave all of him," Tommy said, sitting on the bed next to Jody as they considered the bound and shaven Chet on the floor before them. "He looks creepy."

"Pretty creepy," Jody said. "You'd better drink. Your

wounds aren't healing." All her scratches, bruises, and love bites were completely healed, and except for a fleck of shaving cream here and there in her hair, she was as good as new.

"How?" Tommy asked. "How do I know where to bite him?"

"Try the neck," Jody said. "But sort of feel around for a vein with your tongue before you bite, and don't bite hard." She was trying to sound confident in her instructions, but she was in unexplored territory as much as he was. She was enjoying teaching Tommy about the particulars of vampirism, just as she enjoyed teaching him how to do grown-up human things like how to get the power and phone turned on in the loft—it made her feel sophisticated and in charge, and after a series of boyfriends for whom she had been little more than an accoutrement, whose lifestyles she had affected, from heavy-metal anarchists to financial-district yuppies, she liked being the pacesetter for a change. Still, when it came to teaching him about feeding on animals, she couldn't have been winging it more if she really could turn into a bat. The only time she'd ever considered drinking animal blood was when Tommy had brought her two large, live snapping turtles from Chinatown. She hadn't been able to bring herself to even try biting into the armored reptiles. Tommy had named them Scott and Zelda, which hadn't helped. Now Zelda was functioning as a lawn ornament in Pacific Heights and Scott was encased in bronze and standing next to the old vampire in the great room. The biker sculptors downstairs had bronzed them, which is what had given Tommy the idea to bronze Jody and the old vampire in the first place.

"Are you sure this is okay?" Tommy said, bending over Chet the huge shaved cat. "I mean, you said that we were only supposed to hunt the sick and the weak—the black auras. Chet's aura is shiny and pink."

"It's different with animals." She had no idea if it was different with animals. She'd eaten a moth once, whole—snatched it out of the air and downed it before she could think about it. She realized now that there were a lot more questions she should have asked Elijah when she had had the chance. "Besides, you're not going to kill him."

"Right," Tommy said. He put his mouth on Chet's kitty neck. "Like thith?"

Jody had to turn away to keep from laughing. "Yeah, that looks good."

"He tathes like thaving cream."

"Just go," Jody said.

"'Kay." Tommy bit and started to moan almost immediately. Not a moan of pleasure, but the moan of someone who has his tongue stuck on the ice-cube tray in the freezer. Chet seemed strangely calm, not even struggling against his kitty bonds. Maybe there was something to the vampire's power over his victims, Jody thought.

"Okay, that's enough," Jody said.

Tommy shook his head while still feeding on the huge shaved cat.

"Tommy, let off. You need to leave some."

"Nu-ih," Tommy said.

"Stop sucking the huge cat, Tommy," Jody said sternly. "I'm not kidding." She *was* kidding, a little bit.

Tommy was breathing hard now, and a little color had come into his skin. Jody looked around for something to get his attention. She spotted a vase of flowers on the nightstand.

She pulled out the flowers and tossed the water on Tommy and the huge cat. He kept feeding. The cat shuddered but otherwise remained immobile.

"Okay, then," Jody said. It was a heavy, stoneware vase, something Tommy had picked up to hold some apology flowers he'd brought her from the grocery store where he worked. He'd been good that way, sometimes bringing home apology flowers before he'd even done anything to apologize for. Really, you couldn't ask for more than that from a guy—which is why Jody slowed to half speed as she brought the vase around in a wide arc that ended with it smacking Tommy in the forehead and knocking him back about six feet. Chet the huge shaved cat yowled. Miraculously, the vase did not break.

"Thanks," Tommy said, wiping the blood from his mouth. There was a crescent-moon-shaped dent in his forehead that was rapidly filling in, healing.

"Sure," Jody said, staring at the vase. *Great vase,* she thought. Elegant, fragile porcelain was all well and good for the collector's case or the tea party, but for the girl who finds herself in need of a vessel that can deliver a wallop, Jody was suddenly sold on the sturdy value of stoneware.

"Tastes like cat breath," Tommy said, pointing to Chet. The punctures from Tommy's fangs had already healed. "Is it supposed to?"

Jody shrugged. "What's cat breath taste like?"

"Like tuna casserole left out in the sun for a week." Being from the Midwest, Tommy thought everyone knew what tuna casserole tasted like. Having been born and raised in Carmel, California, Jody knew it only as something eaten by the extinct people on *Nick at Nite*.

"I think I'm going to pass," Jody said. She was hungry, but not cat-breath hungry. She wasn't sure what she was going to do about feeding. She couldn't very well try to live off Tommy anymore, and regardless of the rush and the sense that she was serving nature's cause by taking only the weak and the sick, she didn't like the idea of preying on humans—strangers anyway. She needed time to think, to figure out what their new life was going to be like. Things had been happening too quickly since Tommy and his friends had taken down the old vampire. She said, "We should get Chet back to his owner tonight if we can. You don't want to lose your driver's license—we may need a valid ID to rent a new place."

"A new place?"

"We have to move, Tommy. I told Inspectors Rivera and Cavuto that I would leave town. You don't think they'll check?" There had been two homicide detectives who had

followed the trail of bodies to the old vampire, and ultimately the discovery of Jody's delicate condition. She'd
promised them that she'd take the old vampire and leave
town if they'd let her go.

"Oh yeah," Tommy said. "That means I can't go back to
work at the Safeway either?"

He wasn't stupid, she knew he wasn't stupid, so why was
he so slow to see the obvious? "No, I don't think that would
be a good idea," Jody said. "Since you're going to pass out
cold at sunrise, just the way I do."

"Yeah, that'd be embarrassing," Tommy said.

"Especially when sunlight hits you and you burst into
flames."

"Yeah, there's got to be company policy against that."

Jody screamed in frustration.

"Jeez, kidding," Tommy said, cringing.

She sighed, realizing that he'd been goofing on her. "Get
dressed, cat breath, we don't want to run out of dark. We're
going to need some help."

Out in the great room, the vampire Elijah Ben Sapir was
trying to figure out exactly what was going on around him.
He knew he had been constrained—bound inside a vessel,
and whatever held him was immovable. He'd even turned
to mist, which relieved his anxiety somewhat—there was
an ethereal mind-set that accompanied the form, it took
concentration to not let yourself just float off in a daze—but

the bronze shell was airtight. He could hear them talking, but their comments told him little except that his fledgling had betrayed him. He smiled to himself. What a foolishly human mistake to let hope triumph over reason. He should have known better.

It would be days before the hunger was on him again, and even then, without any movement, he could last indefinitely without blood. He could live a very, very long time constrained like this, he realized—it was his sanity that would suffer. He decided to stay in mist form—drift as in a dream at night, sleep like the dead during the day. This way, he would wait, and when the time came, and it would come (if nothing else, living for eight hundred years had taught him patience), he would make his move.

The Emperor of San Francisco

Two in the morning. Normally, the Emperor of San Francisco would have been tucked in behind a Dumpster with the royal guard snuggled around him for warmth, snoring like a congested bulldozer, but tonight he had been undone by the generosity of a Starbucks froth slave in Union Square who had donated a bucket-sized Holiday Spice Mochaccino to the cause of royal comfort, thus leaving the Emperor and his two companions jangled, wandering the wee hours on a nearly deserted Market Street, waiting for breakfast time to roll around.

"Like crack with cinnamon," said the Emperor. He was a great, boiler tank of a man, an ambling meat locomotive in a wool overcoat, his face a firebox of intensity, framed with a gray tempest of hair and beard such as are found only on gods and lunatics.

Bummer, the smaller of the troops, a Boston terrier,

snorted and tossed his head. He'd lapped up some of the rich coffee broth himself, and felt ready to tear ass out of any rodent or pastrami sandwich that might cross his path. Lazarus, normally the calmer of the two, a golden retriever, pranced and leapt at the Emperor's side as if it might start raining ducks any minute—a recurring nightmare among retrievers.

"Steady, gents," the Emperor chided. "Lets us use this inopportune alertness to inspect a less frantic city than we find in the day, and determine where we might be of service." The Emperor believed that the first duty of any leader was to serve the weakest of his people, and he made an effort to pay attention to the city around him, lest someone fall through the cracks and be lost. Clearly he was a loon. "Calm, good fellows," he said.

But calm was not coming. The smell of cat was tall in the air and the men were jacked on java. Lazarus barked once and bolted down the sidewalk, followed closely by his bug-eyed brother-in-arms, the two descending on a dark figure that lay curled up around a cardboard sign on the traffic island at Battery Street, beneath a massive bronze statue that depicted four muscular men working a metal press. It had always looked to the Emperor like four guys molesting a stapler.

Bummer and Lazarus sniffed the man beneath the statue, sure that he had to have a cat concealed among his rags somewhere. When a cold nose hit a hand, the Emperor saw the man move, and breathed a sigh of relief. With a closer look, the Emperor recognized him as William with the Huge Cat. They knew each other to nod hello, but because of racial tensions between their respective canine and feline companions, the two had never become friends.

The Emperor knelt on the man's cardboard sign and jostled him. "William, wake up." William groaned and an empty Johnny Walker Black bottle slid out of his overcoat.

"Dead drunk, perhaps," said the Emperor, "but fortunately, not dead."

Bummer whimpered. Where was the cat?

The Emperor propped William up against the concrete base of the statue. William groaned. "He's gone. Gone. Gone. Gone."

The Emperor picked up the empty scotch bottle and sniffed it. Yes, it had recently held scotch. "William, was this full?"

William grabbed the cardboard sign off the sidewalk and propped it in his lap. "Gone," he said. The sign read I AM POOR AND SOMEONE STOLE MY HUGE CAT.

"My deepest sympathies," said the Emperor. He was about to ask William how he had managed to procure a fifth of top-shelf scotch, when he heard a long, feline yowl echo down the street, and looked up to see a huge shaved cat, in a red sweater, heading their way. He managed to catch hold of Bummer and Lazarus's collars before they darted after the cat, and dragged them away from William. The huge cat leapt into William's lap and the two commenced a drunken reunion embrace that involved quantities of purring, baby talk, and drool, enough that the Emperor had to fight down a little nausea at the sight of it.

Even the royal hounds had to look away, the two realizing instinctively that a maudlin and shaved, thirty-five-pound cat in a red sweater was clearly above their pay grade. There was just no doggy protocol for it, and presently they began to turn in circles on the sidewalk, as if looking for a good place to feign a nap.

"William, I believe someone has shaved your cat," said the Emperor.

"That would be me," said Tommy Flood as he came around the side of the traffic island, scaring the bejeezus out of everyone there. A pale and delicate hand reached out from behind the island, grabbed the collar of Tommy's coat, and snatched him back around the corner as if he were a rag doll.

"Tommy?" called the Emperor. The big man stalked around the concrete art bunker. Bummer and Lazarus had headed back down the street toward the waterfront, as if they had just seen a particularly fetching porterhouse steak hopping around down there that needed to be investigated. The Emperor found his friend C. Thomas Flood, held tight in the clutches of his girlfriend, Jody Stroud, the vampire, who had her hand pressed tightly over Tommy's mouth and was furiously giving him noogies with the knuckle of her other hand. There was a hollow popping each time she connected, and muted cries from Tommy.

"Jody, I must insist that you unhand the young man," insisted the Emperor.

And she did. Tommy twisted out of her grasp.

"Ow!" Tommy said, rubbing his head.

"Sorry," Jody said. "Couldn't be helped."

"I thought you were going to leave the city with that fiend," said the Emperor. He had been there, with the royal hounds and Tommy's crew from the Safeway, when they'd done battle with the old vampire at the St. Francis Yacht Club.

"Well, yes, of course. He left already and I'm going to join him," Jody said. "Just like I promised Inspector Rivera. But I wanted to make sure that Tommy was going to be all right before I left."

The Emperor liked Jody, and had been a little disappointed when he found that she was a bloodsucking fiend, but she was a pleasant girl nonetheless, and had always been generous with treats for the men, despite Bummer's dropping into yapping fits in her presence. "Well then, I suppose that will have to do," said the Emperor. "It appears that our young writer does require some adult supervision before being set loose on the City."

"Hey, I do okay," Tommy said.

"You shaved the cat," said the Emperor, raising a wild eyebrow that looked like a gray squirrel with a Mohawk.

"I—uh, we were testing him out, to see if I should get a cat to keep me company after Jody leaves." He looked at Jody, who nodded enthusiastically while trying to look wide-eyed and sincere.

"And . . . and," Tommy continued, "I was chewing some

bubble gum, you know, the kind that you can blow really big bubbles with—well, long story short, before I knew it, Chet had lunged at one of my bubbles and was completely covered with bubble gum."

Jody quit nodding and just stared at him.

"So you shaved him," the Emperor added.

Now it was Tommy's turn to nod and look sincere. "Regrettably."

Jody was nodding again, too. "Regrettably," she echoed.

"I see," said the Emperor. They certainly seemed sincere. "Well, the sweater was considerate."

"My idea," Jody said. "You know so he doesn't get chilled. It's actually my sweater. Tommy washed it and put it in the dryer, so it's a little too small for me."

"And don't think it was easy getting a cat that size into a sweater," Tommy said. "It was like trying to dress a ball of razor wire. I'm cut to ribbons." He pushed his sleeves up to expose his forearms, which were distinctly not cut to ribbons. They were, in fact, unmarked, if a little pale.

"Well, good show, then," the Emperor said, backing away. "The men and I will be on our way, then."

"Do you guys need anything, Your Majesty?" Jody asked.

"No, no, we have been most fortunate this evening. Most fortunate indeed."

"Well, take care, then," Jody said, even as the Emperor backed around the corner and headed up the street.

She can be deceptively pleasant for a blood-drinking agent of evil, the Emperor thought.

Bummer and Lazarus were almost out of sight, four blocks ahead. They had known, the rascals. The Emperor was disgusted with himself, leaving William there like that, at the mercy of the fiends. There was no telling what they might do, the two of them, but he felt fear chilling his spine and he couldn't make himself turn around. Perhaps they wouldn't hurt poor William. After all, they had been sweet children in life, both of them. And even in her current state, Jody had shown a certain quality of mercy by waiting until now to turn Tommy. Still, he had a city he was responsible for, and he could not shirk that responsibility.

It was a long walk to the Marina Safeway, but he had to reach it before the night crew left. As knavish as they might be, they were the only people in his city who actually had experience hunting vampires.

Bite him," Tommy said. He was standing over the huge cat guy, who had passed out again under the statue.

Jody shook her head and shuddered. "He's filthy. Don't tell me you can't smell that." Since she'd become a vampire, she'd only experienced nausea when she tried to eat real food, but she was nauseated now, despite the hunger grating in her core.

"Here, I'll clean off a spot." Tommy fished a tissue out of his coat pocket, licked it, and cleaned a spot on William's neck. "There. Go for it."

"Yuck."

"I bit the cat," Tommy said. "You said yourself that you were starving."

"But he's hammered." Jody said. She was taking little steps in place like a little kid who has to pee.

"Bite him."

"Quit saying 'bite him.' I don't think of it like that."

"How do you think of it?"

"I don't really think of it. It's sort of an animal thing."

"Oh, I see," Tommy said. "Bite him before some cops come along and take him away and you miss your chance."

"Ewww," Jody said, kneeling beside William. Chet the huge cat looked up at her from William's lap, then put his head down and closed his eyes. (Blood loss had mellowed him.) Jody pushed William's head aside and reared back with her mouth open wide as her fangs extended. She closed her eyes and bit.

"See how easy that was," Tommy said.

Jody glared at him without letting go, her breath rasping through her nose as she fed. She thought, *I should have hit him harder when I had the chance.* Finally, when she felt she'd taken enough to sustain her, but not enough to hurt the huge cat guy, she pulled away, sat down, and looked up at Tommy.

"You've got a little—" Tommy gestured to the corner of her mouth.

She wiped her mouth with her hand, came away with a little lipstick and a little blood. She looked at William's neck. It was sort of a dirt-gray color, with a white spot rimmed in lipstick. The punctures from her fangs had already healed, but the lipstick sort of stood out like a target. She reached over and wiped the lipstick off with her palm, then wiped her palm off on the huge cat's sweater. Chet purred. William snored. Jody climbed to her feet.

"How was it?" Tommy asked.

"How do you think it was? It was necessary."

"Well, I mean, when you used to bite me it was kind of a sexual thing."

"Oh, right," Jody snapped. "I planned all this because I wanted to fuck the huge cat guy." She was feeling a little light-headed for some reason.

"Sorry. We should get him off of Market Street," Tommy said, "before he gets robbed or arrested. He's got to have some of the money left. That much alcohol would have killed him."

"The hell do you care, writer boy? You shaved and ate his cat. Or was that a sexual thing?" She was definitely feeling light-headed.

"That was a mutual—"

"Oh, bullshit. Bite him. See how sexual it is. Get a taste of that down-home human hemoglobin goodness, Tommy. Don't be a wuss," Jody said. Well, he *was* being a wuss.

Tommy stepped back. "You're drunk."

"And you're being a wuss," Jody said. "Wuss, wuss, wuss."

"Help me. Take his feet. There's a sheltered alcove over

by the Federal Reserve building across the street. He can sleep it off there."

Jody bent to take the guy's feet, but they seemed to move as she reached for them, and when she corrected, she missed, and fell forward, catching herself so that she was on all fours with her ass in the air.

"Yeah, that worked," Tommy said. "How about you take Chet and I'll carry the huge cat guy?"

"Whadever, Mr. Wussyman," Jody said. Maybe she was a little tipsy. In the old days, prevampire days, she'd tried to stay away from alcohol, because it turned out that she was sort of an obnoxious drunk. Or that's what her ex-friends had told her.

Tommy picked up Chet the huge cat, who squirmed as he held him out to Jody. "Take him."

"You are not the head vampire here," Jody said.

"Fine," Tommy said. He slung Chet under his arm and, in a single movement, scooped up the huge cat guy and threw him over his shoulder with the other arm. "Careful crossing the street," Tommy called back to her as he crossed.

"Ha!" Jody said. "I am a finely tuned predator. I am a superbeing. I—" And at that point she bounced her forehead off a light pole with a dull twang and was suddenly lying on her back looking at the streetlights above her, which kept going out of focus, the bastards.

"I'll be back to get you," Tommy called.

He's so sweet, Jody thought.

Do Animals Get the Blues?

Clint was the only one of the Animals still left at the Marina Safeway. He was tall, with a wild mop of dark hair and thick, horn-rimmed glasses that were held together with medical tape, and he had a look of deep panic on his face. He'd been trying to keep the store together for nearly a week with only a couple of stock boys from the day crew, and a porter from a temp service (even Gustavo, the Mexican porter with five kids, had taken off with the Animals), but now a huge order had come in on the truck and he knew he needed professionals. He dialed Tommy's number for the fifth time that night. It was four in the morning, but Tommy was their leader—and perhaps the best frozen-turkey bowler the world had ever known. He knew what it meant to be an Animal; he would be awake.

The machine beeped. Clint said, "Dude, they're all gone. I need your help. It's just me, some temps, and the Lord tonight." Clint had been recently reborn after five years in a drug-induced haze. He swore that the Lord would forever be on his night crew. "The guys took off for Vegas. Call me. No, just bring your box cutter and come to work. I'm buried."

Once they had been nine strong, the Animals. Nine men, all under the age of twenty-five, left alone in a grocery store for eight hours with only Tommy to supervise them. They'd been given their name by the day manager, who had come in one morning to find them drunk, hanging from the giant Safeway letters on the front of the store, pelting one another with marshmallows. Tommy had recruited them to fight the old vampire. They'd found the vampire, sleeping inside a vault on his yacht, and they had also found his art collection. After selling it for ten cents on the dollar, each of them had netted a hundred thousand dollars. Tommy went home with Jody, Clint went home to pray for the vampire's soul. Simon had been killed. The rest of the Animals headed for Vegas.

Clint hung up the phone, then sat down hard in the manager's chair. It was too much responsibility. The weight of it would drive him over the edge. Even now he could hear dogs barking in his head.

"Front door," the temp night porter called over the half wall of the office.

Clint stood up to see the Emperor and his dogs at the double electric doors. He grabbed the keys, disarmed the alarm, and opened the door. The Boston terrier shot by him, heading for the beef-jerky display.

48   CHRISTOPHER MOORE

"Your Majesty," Clint said. "You're out of breath."

The big man held his chest as he panted. "Gather the troops, young man. C. Thomas Flood has been turned to a bloodsucking fiend. Gather your weapons, we must charge again into the breach."

"It's just me and noobs," Clint said. "Did you say that Tommy's a vampire?"

"Indeed. I saw him not two hours ago. As pale as death."

"Well, that's not good."

"Your talent for stating the obvious is unprecedented, young man."

"Come in." Clint stepped away from the door. "We are going to need to pray on this."

"Well, there's a start," said the Emperor.

"Then I need to call Tommy and tell him to never mind about coming to work," Clint said.

"Splendid," said the Emperor, without a hint of sarcasm. "I believe we've achieved a new level of doomed."

Y ou've always been good to me," Jody said.

"Well, I try," Tommy said.

He was going up the narrow stairway to their loft. She was slung over his shoulder, her forehead bounced off his belt with every step. She seemed so light. Tommy was still amazed at his newfound strength. He'd carried her ten blocks already and he wasn't even feeling it. Well, he was a little tired of listening to her, but physically he wasn't fatigued at all.

"I can be such a bitch sometimes."

"That's not true," Tommy said. Yes, it was.

"Yes it is, yes it is. Yes I am. I am a total bitch sometimes."

Tommy stopped at the top of the steps and dug in his pocket for his keys.

"Well, maybe a little, but—"

"So I am a bitch? You're saying I'm a bitch?"

"Oh my God, is the sun never going to come up?"

"Listen, you're lucky to have me, you wuss."

"Yes I am," Tommy said.

"You are?"

He swung her over to her feet, then caught her before she went over backwards into the wall. She had a big goofy smile on her face. Sometime during the evening, blood had dripped down the front of her blouse and there was some smeared on her lip. She looked a little like she'd been punched out. Tommy tried to rub away the blood with his thumb. The cloud of alcohol breath she let go on him made him wince.

"I love you, Tommy." She fell into his arms.

"Right back at you, Jody."

"I'm sorry I gave you noogies. I'm still learning to harness my powers, you know."

"That's okay."

"And called you a wuss."

"No problem."

She licked the side of his neck, nipped at him. "Let's make love before the sun comes up."

Tommy looked over her shoulder at the destruction they had wrought on the loft the last time they'd done it, and he said something he never thought he would hear coming out of his own mouth. "I think I've had enough for tonight. Maybe we should just lock down."

"You think I'm fat, don't you?"

"No, you're perfect."

"It's because I'm fat." She pushed him away and stumbled into the bedroom, then tripped and tumbled face-first into the shredded remains of their bed. "And old," she added, although it was only through his acute vampire hearing that Tommy understood this, since she was speaking directly into the mattress. "Fat and old," she said.

"You're going to get whiplash from those mood swings, Red," Tommy said quietly as he climbed into bed with his clothes on.

Then he lay there beside her thinking about all that they had to do, about how they were going to have to find a place and move without going out during the day, and beyond that, just exactly how were they going to survive and stay hidden? The Emperor could tell. Tommy could tell he could tell. And as much as he liked the Emperor, it wasn't a good sign. And so even as he worried, and listened to his girlfriend yell at him, C. Thomas Flood became the first vampire in history to actually pray for the sun to come up.

A few minutes later, his prayers were answered, and the two of them went out.

Since becoming a vampire, Jody had always hated the way consciousness came on at dusk like the streetlights coming on. There was no groggy twilight between sleep and wakefulness, just "bam, welcome to the night, here's your to-do list." Not tonight. Tonight she got her twilight, her grogginess, and a headache as well. She sat upright in bed so fast she nearly somersaulted off the end, then, when her head didn't seem to follow her, she lay back down with such force that her pillow exploded, sending out a snowstorm of feathers to whirl around the room. She moaned and Tommy came bounding into the room.

"Hey," he said.

"Ouch," Jody said, grabbing her forehead with both hands as if to hold her brains in.

"That's new, huh? Vampire hangover?" Tommy waved some feathers out of the air in front of him.

"I feel like death warmed over," Jody said.

"Cute. I'll bet you're missing coffee right now."

"And aspirin. I've fed off of you when you'd been drinking. Why did it affect me now?"

"I think maybe the huge cat guy had a little more in his blood than I did. Anyway, I have a theory about that. We can test it later, when you feel better, but right now we have a ton of stuff we have to do. We've got to figure out the move. Clint called me from the store last night. Wanting me to work. Then he called back all freaked out, saying I shouldn't come in."

Tommy played the message for her. Twice.

"He knows," Jody said.

"Yeah, but how does he know?"

"Doesn't matter. He knows."

"Fuck!"

"Little bit softer now," Jody said, holding her hair like it was hurting her.

"Too loud?"

Jody nodded. "You know, for your notebook, Tommy. Vampire senses when you're hungover? Not so good."

"Really? That bad?"

"Your breath is nauseating me from across the room."

"Yeah, we need toothpaste."

"There's someone at the door?" Jody covered her ears. She could hear sneakers scraping the sidewalk from all the way downstairs.

"There is?"

The door buzzer sounded.

"Yep," she said.

Tommy ran to the front windows and looked down to the street.

"There's a Humvee limo out there that's about a block long."

"You'd better answer it," Jody said.

"Maybe we should just hide. Pretend we're not home."

"No, you need to get it," Jody said. She could hear the shuffling at the door, the rock and roll playing in the limo, the bong bubbling, lines being chopped on a CD case, and a male voice repeating the phrase "sweet blue titties" over and over like a mantra. She grabbed the pillow from Tommy's side of the bed and pulled it over her head. "Answer it, Tommy. It's the fucking Animals."

Dude," said Lash Jefferson, a wiry black man with a newly shaved scalp, wearing mirror shades. He pulled Tommy out of his doorway and hugged him furiously—crazed, back-slamming, good-to-see-you guy hugs. "We are so fucked, dude," Lash continued.

Tommy pushed away, trying to reconcile that he was glad to see his friend with the fact that Lash smelled like a beer-bar urinal filled with mackerel.

"I thought you guys went to Vegas," Tommy said.

"Yeah. Yeah. We did. Everyone's in the limo. It's just that I need to talk to you. Can we go inside?"

"No." Tommy almost said that Jody was sleeping, which had been his excuse for keeping the Animals out of his loft in the past, but Jody was supposed to have left town. "Step in the stairway, I've got something happening upstairs."

Lash nodded and looked over the top of his shades and bounced his eyebrows. His eyes were bloodshot and glazed over. Tommy could hear his heart racing. Coke or fear, he guessed. Both maybe.

"Look, dude," Lash said. "First thing, we need to borrow some money."

"What? You guys have over a hundred grand each from the art we sold."

"Yeah, we did. We had a big weekend."

Tommy figured in his head. "You guys blew over six hundred grand in what—four days?"

"No," Lash said. "No, not all of it. We're not completely broke."

"Then why do you need to borrow money?"

"Just twenty grand or so, to get us through to tomorrow," Lash said. "Luckily I almost have my MBA and have mad business skills. Otherwise we'd have been broke yesterday."

Tommy nodded. Twenty grand was about six months' salary for him at the Safeway. He'd been a little intimidated by Lash's almost-MBA up until now. Now he was just worried that Lash would be able to tell he had changed. He said, "So, like you were saying, you're fucked."

"We were doing fine, only down like ten grand each, until we met Blue." Lash looked at the ceiling wistfully, like it was a distant memory he was trying to conjure, instead of something that had happened a couple of nights ago.

"Blue?"

"You know that group they have in Vegas? The Blue Men?"

"Yeah, the guys who paint themselves blue and pound on pipes and stuff?" Tommy was lost.

"Yeah," Lash said. "Well, it turns out there are blue women, too. Or at least there's one. And dude, she's sucking us dry."

In the back seat of the limo, Blue held Barry's face between her boobs, snugly enough to keep him under control, but not so snug that he couldn't breathe. While the other Animals had drunk, smoked, and fucked themselves into a zombielike stupor—and now lay sprawled about the glittery interior of the limo—Barry had opted to do two hits of XTC, a line of coke, and a bong load of sticky skunk weed, which had put his brain into some sort of redundant tribal loop that had him kneeling naked before her, chanting "sweet blue titties" for the last twenty minutes. She just couldn't take it anymore, so she had grabbed his curl-fringed bald head and pulled his face into her cleavage just to shut him up. Mercifully, he had gone quiet, because she really didn't want to suffocate him as long as he still had money.

It takes a meandering road of wrong turns to take a girl from being the milky-skinned Cheddar princess of Fond du Lac, Wisconsin, to a blue-dyed call girl turning tricks at downtown casinos in Vegas, but Blue would be damned if she'd add yet another wrong turn by smothering a golden goose between her proportionally improbable silicon joy orbs. The Animals were her way out, and if she had to stay in character as an Alien Pleasure Unit or a blueberry muffin to keep them on the hook, she would.

Blue was a method hooker. Early in her adventures, after she'd left cocktailing due to a propensity for spilling drinks, and before she'd begun stripping, where her lack of balance was mitigated by the presence of a sturdy pole, she had a short career acting in low-budget porn. She befriended a promising actress named Lotta Vulva, who gave her a book on the Stanislavski Method. "If you can find your sense memory," Lotta said, "it will keep you from barfing on the actors. Directors hate that." The "Method" had served Blue well since then, as it allowed her to calculate betting odds or figure her checkbook while her character was performing acts that she herself would have found unpleasant or outright disgusting. (How much better to reside in her sense memory of the budding Cheddar princess, coaxing the hearty, whole-milk goodness from the udders of a Holstein, than to face the harshly lit reality of her actions?)

After six months Blue was driven out of the film business by a "defect" one director called "not enough tits to fill a shot glass," which no amount of Method was able to remedy. She returned to cocktailing, albeit at a strip club, where she seldom had to carry more than one ten-dollar beer at a time, until she saved enough money for breast-augmentation surgery and made her way to the pole. She danced her way through her twenties, before she was driven off the stage by younger, more gravity-resistant girls, and because she had skipped personal typing class in high school and had therefore besmirched her permanent record, she landed in the employ of an outcall escort service.

"I feel like I'm doing Domino's delivery blow jobs," Blue told her roommate. "Satisfaction in twenty minutes or less or your money back. And the agency is taking most of the money. I'll never get out of this business at this rate."

"You need a gimmick," said her roommate, a cocktail waitress at the Venetian. "Like those Blue Men guys in the show. I swear they'd just be a bunch of frat boys beating on garbage cans if they weren't painted blue."

And so it began. The fallen Cheddar princess of Fond du Lac found some semipermanent skin dye, opened credit-card deposit accounts, had some pictures taken, placed ads in all the free sleaze rags around the city, and Blue was born. It wasn't as if she wouldn't have been able to make a living without the gimmick—most guys will shag a snake if you hold it steady for them. But it turned out they would pay a lot for the exotica of a blue woman.

She worked as much as she could handle, and her savings had climbed to the point where she could actually see the possibility of an exit. But about that same time, she realized that by going blue, she had opted out of the pipe dream of every hooker, stripper, and telemarketer: the rich guy who would take her away from it all. The whale who would drop a fortune on her to become his personal pet. There would be no big score for the blue chick, or so she thought, until the Animals called her in for a combination strip show and fuckfest. Where they got the money didn't matter. What mattered was that they had a lot of it, and it appeared that they would keep giving it to her until it was all gone. She had nearly half a million dollars in her makeup case, and Blue—the *character* Blue—could put up with a lot of attention from the Animals while *she* hid in the back of her mind and formulated an investment strategy. The tall, skinny one, Drew, had opened the hotel-room door and said, "Hi. We discussed it and agreed that when we were kids, we all really wanted to bone a Smurf."

"I get that a lot," said Blue.

We just wanted to bone a Smurf," Lash said.

"Understandably," said Tommy.

"She's really nice," Lash said.

"Important quality in a ho," said Tommy.

"But now we can't seem to quit."

"So you want me to do what—hold an intervention?"

"No, you're our leader. We look to you for other things. So we want you to give us money so we can keep partying, and pay our rents and stuff."

"And when all of *my* money is gone, then I can intervene."

"Sure, if you feel you have to," said Lash. "How's your credit?"

"Lash, are you high?"

"Of course."

"Right. Of course. What was I thinking?" Tommy was relaxing now about Lash noticing that he was a vampire. Clearly the former stewards of Safeway night stock, in addition to being wasted, had gone collectively out of their minds. "Lash, I don't almost have an MBA like you, but isn't there sort of some business principle that you're violating? I mean, isn't there a class about not spending your rent money on hookers or something?"

"Step off, Flood," Lash said. "You hooked up with a vampire."

"She was cute," Tommy said.

"An important quality in a vampire," Lash said, looking over the top of his shades.

"She had sex with me," Tommy countered. He wanted to say that she was nice, but Lash had already used "nice" for his blue hooker.

"I think I've made my point," Lash said. "Give me your money."

"You haven't made your point. You completely haven't made your point." Tommy reared back as if to punch Lash in the chest, as the Animals did to one another all the time, but remembered that now he might crush some of the Animals' ribs. Instead, he said, "Don't make me cave in your skinny chest, bee-yotch."

"Your redheaded vampire kung fu is no match for the fearsome blue booty kung fu." Lash made a howling chicken noise and waved his hands around as he fell back into a fighting stance, then went right back onto his ass on the steps. He laughed until he choked, then coughed and said, "Seriously, dude, if you don't give us money, we're going to be totally broke in about six hours. I did the math."

"You could go back to work," Tommy said. "Clint called here last night. They're buried at the store. They need night stockers."

"No?" Lash said, pulling down his sunglasses.

"Yes," Tommy said.

"Then we're not fired?"

"Evidently not," Tommy said.

"That's it. We could go back to work. That's what we'll tell her. We have to go back to work."

"Why didn't you just tell her to go away before she did you all the way here from Vegas."

"We didn't want to be rude."

"Oh, right. Well then, off you go."

Lash pushed to his feet and steadied himself on the banister long enough to look Tommy in the eye. "You okay? You look pale."

"I'm heartbroken and shit," Tommy said. He hated it, but Lash's bloodshot eyes peering over the sunglasses had actually given him a twinge of hunger.

"Right." Lash went through the security door.

Tommy watched him as he paused at the rear door of the limo and turned back.

"You need some blue nooky to cheer you up?" Lash asked. "Our treat."

"No, I'm good," Tommy said.

"All for one, and whatnot," Lash said.

"Appreciate it." Tommy shrugged. "Heartbroken."

"Okay." Lash threw open the limo's door and two of the

Animals, Drew and Troy Lee, rolled out onto the pavement, followed by a great storm cloud of pot smoke.

"Fuck, dude. Did you know there was a door there?" said Drew, the scruffy thin one.

"Look," said Troy Lee, the Asian guy who actually did know kung fu. "Hey, look, it's fearless leader."

"Go to work," Tommy said. "It's only seven. You guys can get sobered up and be completely ready for your shift at eleven." *Not a chance,* Tommy thought.

"Yeah, we can do it," Lash said, peeking into the limo. "Hey, Barry, climb off, motherfucker, I'm up next, then it's Jeff's turn. I put it on the board. Blue, don't let him do that to your ear, baby, you won't hear for a month."

Tommy closed the security door and sat down hard on the steps, hiding his face in his hands to try to make it all go away. The Animals had been his friends, his crew. They had taken him in when he was alone in the city, made him their leader, and if he got the tone of Clint's second message right, in about four hours, when they got to the store, they were going to turn on him.

The List

Ⱳhile Jody showered, Tommy made a list.

Feed
Laundry
New Apartment
Toothpaste
Sweet Monkey Love
Windex
Dispose of Vampire
Minion

"What do we need an onion for?" Jody asked. She was having a little trouble getting her vision to focus.

"Minion, minion," Tommy said.

"Mint-flavored onion? Why do we need that?"

"A minion! Someone who can move around during the day who can help us out. Like I was for you."

"Oh, my bitch."

Tommy dropped his list. "Nuh-uh."

Jody picked it up and walked over to the kitchen counter where the coffee machine stood. "I would sell my soul for a big cup of joe."

"I was not your bitch," Tommy said.

"Right, right, right. Whatever. So how long do we have to do this list?"

"I checked the almanac. Sunrise is at six fifty-three, so we have about twelve hours. It's almost the solstice, so we get a lot of darkness."

"Solstice? Oh my God, it's almost Christmas."

"So?"

"Hello? Shopping?"

"Hello? We have an excuse. We're dead."

"My mother doesn't know that. I have to find something for her that she'll disapprove of. And your family—"

"Oh my God! Christmas. I was supposed to go home to Indiana for Christmas. We need to redo the list."

"You do it. I'm going to dry my hair," Jody said.

The new list read:

Christmas Presents
Call Home
Feed

Minion (not our Bitch)
Hot Monkey Love
Windex
Write Literature
Dispose of Creepy Old Vampire
New Apartment
Laundry
Toothpaste

"I think you should take monkey love off of the list," Jody said. "What if we lose the list and someone finds it?"

"Well I think 'dispose of Creepy Old Vampire' would be a little more embarrassing, don't you?"

"You're right, cut monkey love and change 'vampire' to 'Elijah.'" Jody tapped the list with a pen. "And take off Windex and put in 'buy coffee.'"

"We can't drink coffee."

"We can smell it. Tommy, I desperately need coffee. It's like the blood hunger, only, you know, more civilized."

"Speaking of blood hunger—"

"Yeah, you'd better move that up the list."

"And add a bottle of whiskey. You're going to have to buy it."

"Sorry, writer boy, but we're doing this stupid list together."

"I'm not old enough to buy liquor."

Jody stepped away from him and shuddered. "That's right. Isn't it?"

"Yep," Tommy said, nodding—trying to look wide-eyed and innocent.

"Well, okay then. I should have checked IDs before picking my bitch."

"Hey!"

"Kidding. What are you going to do with a bottle of whiskey anyway?"

"Check something else off the list," Tommy said. "I have an idea. Get your purse."

"What did the Animals want, anyway?"

"Twenty grand."

"I hope you told them to fuck themselves."

"They did that already."

"Did they suspect, you know, about what you are now?"

"Not yet. Lash said I looked a little pale. I sent them to the store. If Clint knows, well—"

"Oh, good move. Maybe we should just take out an ad. 'Young vampire couple seeks angry village people to hunt them down and kill them.'"

"Ha. Village people. Funny. Put self-tanning lotion on the list. I think the pale thing is giving me away."

At seven in the evening, three days before Christmas, Union Square was awash in shoppers. There was a Santa's Village set up in the raised square, with a line of children and parents that wound five hundred deep through a labyrinth of red velvet cattle gates. Around the square, the street performers, who would normally have knocked off around five, lined the granite steps up to the square. A juggler here, a sleight-of-hand guy there, a half-dozen "robots"—people painted silver and gold who would move in machine-jerk rhythm for the drop of a coin or a bill—and even a couple of human statues. Jody's favorite was a gold guy in a business suit, who stood motionless for hours on end, as if he'd been frozen in midstep on the way to work. There was a small hole in his briefcase into which people stuffed bills and dropped coins after photographing him or trying to make him flinch.

"This guy used to freak me out," Tommy whispered. "But now I can see him breathing and the aura thing."

"I watched him for a whole lunch hour one time and he never moved," Jody said. "In the summer, you know he has to be suffering in that painted suit." Suddenly she shuddered at the thought of Elijah, the old vampire, still encased in bronze back at the loft. Yes, he had killed her, technically, but in a way he'd just opened a door for her, a door that, no matter how bizarre, was immediate, vital, and passionate. And yes, he'd done it for his amusement, he'd said, but also because he was lonely.

She wound her arm into Tommy's and kissed him on the cheek.

"What was that for?"

"Because you're here," she said. "What's first on the list?"

"Christmas presents."

"Skip down."

"Sweet monkey love."

"Yeah, we'll do it in the Santa's Workshop window at Macy's."

"Really?"

"No, not really."

"Okay, then we need liquor."

Jody snatched the list out of his hand so quickly that most people wouldn't have even seen her move. "You are no longer in charge of the list. We're getting me a new leather jacket."

I AM HOMELESS AND SOMEONE SHAVED MY HUGE CAT. William had changed his sign. Chet the huge cat was still wearing Jody's sweater. He eyed the two vampires suspiciously as they approached.

Tommy held the bottle of Johnny Walker out to William. "Merry Christmas."

William took the liquor and squirreled it away in his coat. "Most people just give money," he said.

"We're cutting out the middleman," Jody said. "How are you feeling today?"

"Great, why? Really good, you know, considering that I'm homeless and you guys shaved my cat."

"You were pretty hammered last night."

"Yeah, but I feel great today."

"That's how it used to affect me," Tommy said. "Remember. Kind of energizing."

Jody waved Tommy away. "You didn't get light-headed or anything?" Jody asked.

"I was a little hungover when I woke up, but I was fine after a couple of cups of coffee."

"Fuck!" Jody spat. Then she held her head.

"Calm," Tommy said, patting her shoulder. "Dr. Flood will make it all better. Maybe."

Jody growled, just loud enough for Tommy to hear.

"Ya know," said William, when there was a break in the pedestrian traffic and he didn't have to concentrate on looking pathetic, "I'm flush for cash, but since you're in the Christmas spirit, I'd still go for a look at Red's hooters."

"Bite me, dirtbag," Jody said as she rolled up on William.

"Honey." Tommy caught the back of her newly purchased red leather jacket, just in case. They'd never know if his idea was going to work if Jody snapped the bum's neck.

"I will not be sexually harassed by the entrée."

"Something you ate isn't agreeing with you?" Tommy grinned at her when she looked back at him, but the fire went out of her eyes.

"You can just cross sweet monkey love right off your list," Jody said.

"Jeez, what a bitch," said William. "Her time of the month?"

Tommy quickly wrapped his arms around Jody, lifted her off her feet, and carried her a few steps around the corner, even as she squirmed.

"Let me go, I'm not going to hurt him."

"Good."

"Much."

"That's what I thought," Tommy said, still holding her tight. "Why don't you head over to the Walgreens and I'll finish up with the huge cat guy?"

A family of Christmas shoppers smiled as they passed them, thinking they were young lovers indulging in a public display of affection. The father whispered "Get a room" under his breath to his wife, which a normal person wouldn't have heard.

"Count your lucky stars, buddy, we almost did it in the Santa's Workshop window. Hot, sweaty elf sex—in front of the kids. The kids would have liked that, huh?"

The father hurried his family on down the street.

"Nice," Jody said. "Way to stay under the radar."

"Well, you know, I like to stay sharp," Tommy said. Because he was nineteen and had only started having sex regularly since he met Jody, he still thought he had some sort of secret knowledge that was unavailable to other people. *How can they possibly be thinking about anything else?* he thought in the private part of his mind.

"I'll bet it smells like peppermint," Tommy said.

"What?"

"Elf sex."

"Would you please put me down."

"Okay, but don't hurt the huge cat guy."

"I'm fine. I'll meet you at the drugstore in five minutes. This had better work."

"Five minutes," Tommy said. "Cinnamon. Maybe it smells like cinnamon."

The pale couple stalked the aisles of the Walgreens, having a great time dismissing the crass accoutrements of bourgeois American life, and generally scoffing at all the conventions of traditional culture. They were elite, after all. Special. Chosen—if you will—if only by the nature of their heightened sensitivities and superior sensibilities. They both claimed the ability to look past the facade put on by most people, and see the very depths of the human soul. Strange, then, that they didn't see it coming when the skinny guy in a flannel shirt popped around the corner in front of them.

"Let's ask these guys," Flannel said. "They look like heroin addicts."

Jared White Wolf and Abby Normal backpedaled from the eyeliner display where they'd been looking for something hypoallergenic. Abby's eyes had been watering all night, causing her makeup to run and giving her more of a sad-clown-of-life look than she was going for.

Jared hid behind Abby, just a little, which was awkward, since he was nearly a foot taller than she. The guy in flannel was joined by a beautiful, pale redhead, carrying an armload of toiletries. *What amazing hair,* Abby thought, looking at the long red tresses. *I'd give anything for hair like that.*

"Tommy, leave these poor people alone," said the redhead.

"No, wait." Flannel turned to Abby and smiled. "Do you guys know where they keep the syringes?"

Abby looked at Jared, who looked at the guy in flannel. "Well, you can't just buy them," Jared said. He was fiddling with the leather straps on his bondage pants, looking coy. Abby slapped his hand.

"You need a prescription to buy syringes," Abby said.

"Do you really think I look like a heroin addict?" Jared threw his bangs out of his face dramatically. His head was shaved except for his bangs, which reached to his chin, specifically so he could throw them out of his face dramatically. "I was, like, thinking that maybe I should bulk up. You know, eat and stuff, but—"

"Well, thanks," said Flannel Shirt. The redhead moved off down the aisle. "I was going to try some heroin, but if you can't buy needles, well, there you go. See you guys. Nice shirt, by the way."

Abby looked down at her T-shirt, black, of course, with the image of a poet taken from a nineteenth-century etching. "Like you even know who it is."

" 'She walks in beauty, like the night,' " quoted the flannel-shirt guy. He winked at her, then grinned. "Byron's a hero of mine. See ya."

He turned and started to walk away. Abby reached out and snagged his sleeve. "Hey, there are needle exchange programs all over town. They're listed in the *Bay Guardian*."

"Thanks," said flannel. He turned and Abby grabbed him again.

"We're going to be at the Glas Kat. There's a Goth club tonight. Five-hundred block of Fourth Street. I know a dealer there. You know, for your heroin."

The flannel-shirt guy nodded, and looked at Byron's picture on her shirt again, then at her face. *Fucksocks. He's so looking at my streaking eye makeup.*

"Thanks, milady," said Flannel Shirt. And he was gone, off over the dark moors of the tampon aisle.

"What was that about?" whined Jared. "He's so, so *Happy Days*." Jared White Wolf spent a lot of time watching *Nick at Nite* when he wasn't brooding or fussing with his appearance.

Abby walked into the flap of Jared's black duster and pounded his slight chest with her palms. "Didn't you see. Didn't you see?"

"What, you acting like a complete ho?"

"He had fangs," Abby said.

"Well, so do I," Jared said, reaching into his pocket and pulling out a pair of perfect, dentistry-quality vampire fangs. "Duh, everybody does."

"Yeah, but his grew! I saw them. Let's go," Abby said, pulling Jared White Wolf by his great bat-wing lapels. "I have to change into something hot before we go to the club."

"Wait, I want to get some Halls. My throat is raw from all the cloves we smoked last night."

"Hurry." The buckles of Abby's black platform boots

jangled as she dragged her friend past the lipsticks and hair products before he could get interested.

"Okay," said Jared, "but if I don't meet a cute guy to-night, you have to stay up all night and hold me while I cry."

You should try black lipstick sometime," Tommy said to Jody as they approached their building, their arms loaded with packages. He was still thinking about the kids at the drugstore. It was the first time since tenth grade that he'd used his knowledge of Romantic poetry. For a while he'd tried molding himself into the tragic Romantic hero, brooding and staring clench-jawed off into space as he composed dark verse in his head. But it turned out that trying to appear tragic in Incontinence, Indiana, was re-dundant, and his mother kept shouting at him and making him forget his rhymes. "Tommy, if you keep grinding your teeth like that, they'll wear away and you'll have to have dentures like Aunt Ester." Tommy only wished his beard was as heavy as Aunt Ester's—then he could stare out over the moors while he stroked it pensively.

"Yeah," Jody said, "because I need to make it more ob-vious that I'm an undead creature that feeds on the blood of the living."

"You make it sound so sordid."

"No, I meant it in a nice way."

"Oh."

"Because it's not like people wouldn't understand if they found out we were vampires, because we slipped up and, oh, I don't know, UNSHEATHED OUR FANGS IN THE FUCKING DRUGSTORE!"

Tommy almost dropped his packages. She hadn't said a word about that all night. He'd hoped she hadn't noticed. "It was an accident."

"You called that girl 'milady.'"

"She was impressed with my Byron."

"Yeah, well, your Byron was probably sticking out a little, too, wasn't he?"

"It wasn't like that."

"You drooled." Jody paused at their security door and dug into her jacket for her key.

Tommy stepped around her. "I'm still new at this. I think I'm doing pretty well. My ghastly pallor obviously impressed the lady at the needle exchange." He reached into his bag and fanned out a handful of sterile-wrapped and capped syringes.

"Congratulations, you can now pass as an HIV-positive heroin addict."

"*Très chic.*" He grinned like he imagined a sexy Italian man-whore might.

"Who drools in public," Jody said.

Damn, she's immune to my sexy Italian man-whore grin, Tommy thought. He said, "Be nice, I'm new. My lips don't fit together right when my fangs are out."

She turned the key and swung the door open. There,

passed out on the landing, was William the huge cat guy
and sleeping on his chest, Chet the huge cat.

"I told you it would work," Tommy said.

Jody stepped into the stairwell and closed the door behind her. "You go first."

Fifteen minutes later, as he placed five syringes full of
blood in their refrigerator, Tommy said, "This vampire
thing is going to be great."

He'd had a moment when he'd bitten William—not just
getting over the idea of being that close to someone who
smelled that nasty, but also being close to another man
period. But after cleaning William's neck with an alcohol
swab they'd gotten from the drugstore, and consoling himself that most literary vampires seemed sexually ambivalent
anyway, the blood hunger pushed him through.

He was feeling more relaxed, now that they had the
food problem solved—for a while, anyway. If his friends
didn't kill them in the next couple of days, he might even
enjoy life as a vampire. Then he turned to Jody and frowned.
"But I can't help but think that it may be wrong, taking
advantage of a homeless alcoholic."

"We could just hunt and kill people," Jody said cheerfully. She had a little crust of William's blood in the corner
of her mouth. Tommy licked his thumb and wiped it away.

"We did give him a nice sweater for his huge shaved
cat," Tommy said.

"I loved that sweater," Jody said. "And we are giving him a warm landing to sleep on," she added, diving onto Tommy's rationalization dog pile.

"And if we only take a little bit each day, he'll actually feel better. I know I did."

"And we won't become alcoholics ourselves."

"How are you feeling, by the way?" Tommy said.

"Better. Hair of the dog. You?"

"Two-beer buzz, max. I'll be fine. You want to try the experiment?"

Jody checked her watch. "No time. We'll do it tomorrow night."

"Right. So, on to the list. Looks like hot monkey love."

"Tommy, we need to find a daytime person to help us. We have to move out of this place."

"I've been thinking about Alaska."

"Okay, good for you, but we still need to find a place to live where the Animals and Inspector Rivera can't find us."

"No, I'm thinking we should move to Alaska. For one thing, in the winter, it's dark for like twenty hours a day, so we'd have plenty of time. And I read somewhere that Eskimos put their old people out on the ice when they are ready to die. It would be like people were leaving snacks out for us."

"You're kidding."

"Eskimo Pies?" He grinned.

Jody put her hand on her hip and looked at him, her

mouth hanging open a little, as if she was waiting for something more. When it didn't come, she said, "Okay then, I'm going to change."

"Into a wolf?"

"Clothes, cadaver breath."

"I didn't know. I thought maybe you'd learned."

Tommy thought Alaska was a great idea. Just because she was a few years older, she always acted like his ideas were stupid. "The thing with William worked," he said defensively as he put away the supplies they'd bought at the drugstore.

"That was a good idea," Jody said from inside the closet.

Now what? "Well, Alaska isn't a bad idea."

"Tommy, there's like nine people in all of Alaska. We'll stand out, don't you think?"

"No, everyone is pale there. They don't have sun for most of the year."

She came out of the closet wearing her little black cocktail dress and her strappy come-fuck-me pumps. "I'm ready," she said.

"Wow," Tommy said. He'd forgotten what they were talking about.

"You think the Ferrari-red lipstick would be too much?"

"No, I love the Ferrari-red lipstick on you." *Hot, sweet monkey love,* he thought. This was exactly why he loved her. In the midst of all of the pressure, the danger, really—she still took time to think of his feelings.

She lifted her breasts until they threatened to spill out of the plunging neckline of the dress. "Too much?"

"Perfect," Tommy said, walking toward her with his hands out. "Gimme."

She breezed past him into the bathroom. "Not for you. I need to get going."

"No, no, no," Tommy said. "Hot monkey love."

While Tommy watched from the doorway, Jody applied the Ferrari-red lipstick, checked it, then frowned and wiped it off, then grabbed a different tube off the vanity. "When I get back."

"Where?" Tommy said. Sexual frustration had reduced him to single syllables.

She turned to him with the new coat of maroon lipstick. "To get your minion."

"Not like that, you're not," Tommy said.

"This is how it works, Tommy. This is how I got you."

"Nuh-uh, you weren't wearing that when I met you."

"No, but the reason you pursued me is because you were interested in me sexually, wasn't it?"

"Well, that's how it started, but it's more than that now." And it was more, but that was no reason to leave him here all aroused and stuff.

She walked over to him and put her arms around him. He let his hands slip inside the low back of her dress. His pants were getting tight and he could feel the pressure of his fangs coming out.

"When I get back," she said. "I promise. You're my guy, Tommy. I picked you as my guy, forever. I'm going to find someone to help us move and do things for us in the daytime."

"They're just going to want to bone you, and when you don't do them, they'll turn on you."

"Not necessarily."

"Of course they will. Look at you."

"I'll figure it out, okay. I don't know how else to go about it."

"We could put an ad on Craig's List." (Craig's List was a classified Web site that had started in the Bay Area and was now the first place people checked for jobs, apartments, or nearly everything.)

"We're not putting an ad on Craig's List. Look, Tommy, we have more things to do than we have time. You can clean the loft and go get the laundry done and I'll get us an onion."

"Minion," he corrected.

"Whatever. I love you," she said.

Bitch! He was vanquished. *Unfair.* "I love you, too."

"I'll take one of the disposable cell phones you bought. You can call me anytime."

"They're not even activated yet."

"Well, get on that, buddy. The sooner I get out there and find someone, the sooner I can get back here for some hot monkey love."

She has absolutely no sense of ethics, he thought. *She's a monster. And yet, there she is, only a few dress straps from being naked.*

"Okay," he said. "Don't step on the huge cat on the way out."

Jody had only been gone twenty minutes before Tommy decided that cleaning and laundry sucked and that he could find a minion as well as she could, even if he didn't look as hot in a little black dress. He was careful not to wake Chet and William on his way out.

She Walks in Beauty

Jody moved down Columbus Avenue with long, runway-model strides, feeling the windblown fog brush by her like the chill ghosts of rejected suitors. What she could never teach Tommy, what she could never really share with him, was what it felt like to move from being a victim—afraid of attack, the shadow around the corner, the footsteps behind—to being the hunter. It wasn't the stalking or the rush of taking down prey—Tommy would understand that. It was walking down a dark street, late at night, knowing that you were the most powerful creature there, that there was absolutely nothing, no one, that could fuck with you. Until she had been changed and had stalked the city as a vampire, she never realized that virtually every moment she had been there as a woman, she had been a little bit afraid. A man would never understand. That was the reason for the dress and the shoes—not to attract a minion, but to throw her sexuality out there on display, dare some underevolved male to make the mistake of seeing her as a victim. Truth be told, although it had come down to confrontation only once, and then she'd been wearing a baggy sweatshirt and jeans, Jody enjoyed kicking ass. She also enjoyed—every bit as much—just knowing that she could. It was her secret.

Without fear, the City was a great sensual carnival. There was no danger in anything she experienced, no anxiety. Red was red, yellow didn't mean caution, smoke didn't mean fire, and the mumbling of the four Chinese guys standing by their car just around the corner was just the click and twang of empty swinging dick talk. She could hear their hearts speed up when they saw her, could smell sweat and garlic and gun oil coming off them. She'd learned the smell of fear and imminent violence, too, of sexual arousal and surrender, although she'd have been hard-pressed to describe any of that. It was just there. Like color.

You know . . .

Try to describe blue.

Without mentioning blue.

See?

There weren't a lot of people out on the street at this time of night, but there were a few, spread up the length of Columbus: barhoppers, late diners just wrapping it up, college boys heading down to the strip clubs on Broadway, the exodus from Cobb's Comedy Club up the street, people giddy and so into the rhythm of laughing that they found one another and everything they saw hilarious—all of them vibrant, wearing auras of healthy pink life, trailing heat and perfume and cigarette smoke and gas held through long dinners. Witnesses.

The Chinese guys weren't harmless, by any means, but she didn't think they'd attack her, and she felt a twinge of regret. One of them, the one with the gun, yelled something at her in Cantonese—something sleazy and insulting, she could tell by the tone. She spun as she walked, smiled her biggest red carpet smile, and without breaking stride, said, "Hey, nano-dick, go fuck yourself!"

There was a lot of bluster and shuffle, the smart one, the one with fear coming off him, held his friend Nano-dick back, thus saving his life. *She must be a cop, or just crazy. Something's wrong.* They clustered around their tricked-out Honda and huffed out great breaths of testosterone and frustration. Jody grinned, and detoured up a side street, away from traffic.

"My night," she said to herself. "Mine."

Now off the main drag, she saw only a single old man shuffling ahead of her. His life aura looked like a burned-out bulb, a spot of dark gray around him. He walked stooped over, with a dogged determination, as if he knew that if he stopped, he would never start again. From what she could tell, he never would. He wore baggy, wide-wale corduroys that made the sound of rodents nesting when he walked. A wisp of breeze off the Bay brought Jody the acrid smell of failing organs, of stale tobacco, of despair, of a deep, rotting sickness, and she felt the ela-tion leave her.

She slipped comfortably into the new slot the night had made for her, like tumblers of a lock slipping into place.

She made sure that she made enough noise so that he could hear her approaching, and when she was beside him, he paused, his feet still moving in tiny steps that turned him to the side, as if his motor was idling.

"Hi," she said.

He smiled. "My, you are a lovely girl. Would you walk with me?"

"Sure."

They walked a few steps together before he said, "I'm dying, you know."

"Yeah, I kind of figured," Jody said.

"I'm just walking. Thinking, and walking. Mostly walking."

"Nice night for it."

"A little cold, but I don't feel it. I got a whole pocketful of painkillers. You want one?"

"No, I'm good. Thanks."

"I ran out of things to think about."

"Just in time."

"I wondered if I'd get to kiss a pretty girl once before the end. I think that would be all I'd want."

"What's your name?"

"James. James O'Mally."

"James. My name is Jody. I'm pleased to meet you." She stopped and offered her hand to shake.

"The pleasure is all mine, I assure you," said James, bowing as best he could.

She took his face in her hands, and steadied him, then kissed him on the lips, softly and for a long time, and when she pulled away they were both smiling.

"That was lovely," James O'Mally said.

"Yes it was," Jody said.

"I suppose I'm finished now," James said. "Thank you."

"The pleasure was all mine," Jody said. "I assure you."

Then she put her arms around his slight frame, and held him, one hand cradling the back of his head like an infant, and he only trembled a little when she drank.

A little later, she bundled his clothes together under her arm, and hooked his old wing tips on two fingers. The dust that had been James O'Mally was spread in a powdery-gray pile on the sidewalk, like a negative shadow, a bleached spot. She brushed it flat with her palm, and wrote, *Nice kiss, James,* with her fingernail.

As she walked away, an hourglass trickle of James trailed out of his clothes behind her and was carried off on the chill bay breeze.

The guy working the door of the Glas Kat looked like a raven had exploded on his head, his hair plastered out in a chaos of black spikes. The music coming from inside sounded like robots fucking. And complaining about it. In rhythmic monotone. European robots.

Tommy was a little intimidated. 'Sploded raven-head guy had better fangs than he did, was paler, and had seventeen silver rings in his lips. (Tommy had counted.)

"Bet it's hard to whistle with those in, huh?" Tommy asked.

"Ten dollars," said 'Sploded.

Tommy gave him the money. He checked Tommy's ID and stamped his wrist with a red slash. Just then a group of Japanese girls dressed like tragic Victorian baby dolls breezed by behind Tommy, waving their wrist slashes like they'd just returned from a joyful suicide party instead of smoking cloves on the street. They, too, looked more like vampires than Tommy did.

He shrugged and entered the club. Everyone, it appeared, looked more like a vampire than he did. He'd bought some black jeans and a black leather jacket at the Levi's store while Jody was off finding something hideous for her mother for Christmas, but evidently he should have been looking for some black lipstick and something cobalt- or fuchsia-colored to weave into his hair. And in retrospect, the flannel shirt may have been a mistake. He looked like he'd shown up at the sacrificial mass of the damned ready to fix the dishwasher.

The music changed to an ethereal female chorus of

Celtic nonsense. With a techno beat. And robots complaining. Grumpy robots.

He tried to listen around it, the way Jody had taught
him. With all the black light, strobes, and black clothing,
his newly heightened senses were overloading. He tried to
focus on people's faces, their life auras, look through the
haze of heat, hairspray, and patchouli for the girl he'd met
at Walgreens.

Tommy had felt alone in a crowd before, even inferior to
everyone in a crowd, but now he felt, well, different. It
wasn't just the clothes and the makeup, it was the humanity.
He wasn't part of it. Heightened senses or not, he felt like he
had his nose pressed against the window, looking in. The
problem was, it was the window of a donut shop.

"Hey!" Someone grabbed his arm and he wheeled
around so quickly that the girl nearly tumbled over backwards, startled.

"Fuck! Dude."

"Hi," Tommy said. "Wow." Thinking, *Ah, jelly donut*. It
was the girl from Walgreens. She was nearly a foot shorter
than he, and a little skinny. Tonight she'd gone with the
waifish look, wearing striped stockings with holes ripped in
them and a shiny red PVC miniskirt. She'd traded in her
Lord Byron shirt for a tank top, black, of course, with dripping red letters that read GOT BLOOD?, and fishnet gloves that
went halfway up her biceps. Her makeup was sad-clown
marionette: black tears drawn streaming down either side

of her face. She crooked her finger to get him to bend down so she could shout into his ear over the music.

"My name's Abby Normal."

Tommy spoke into her ear; she smelled of hairspray and what was that? Raspberry? "My name is Flood," he said. "C. Thomas Flood." It was his pen name. The *C* didn't really stand for anything, he just liked the sound of it. "Call me Flood," he added. Tommy was a stupid name for a vampire, but Flood—ah, Flood—there was disaster and power there, and a hint of mystery, he thought.

Abby smiled like a cat in a tuna cannery. "Flood," she said. "Flood."

She was trying it on, it seemed to Tommy. He imagined that she'd have a black vinyl binder at school and she'd soon be writing *Mrs. Flood* surrounded by a heart with an arrow through it on the cover in her own blood. He'd never seen a girl so obviously attracted to him, and he realized that he had no experience in dealing with it. For a moment he flashed on the three vampire brides of Dracula who try to seduce Jonathan Harker in Stoker's classic novel. (He'd been studying all the vampire fiction he could get his hands on since meeting Jody, since it didn't appear that anyone had written a good how-to book on vampirism.) Could he really deal with three luscious vampire brides? Would he have to bring them a kid in a sack the way Dracula does in the book? How many kids a week would it take to keep them happy? And where did you get kid sacks? And although he hadn't discussed it with Jody, he was pretty sure she was not going to be happy sharing him with two other luscious vampire brides, even if he brought her sacks and sacks full of kids. They'd need a bigger apartment. One with a washer and dryer in the building, because there'd be a lot of bloodstained lingerie to be washed. Vampire logistics were a nightmare. You should get a castle and a staff when you got your fangs. How was he going to do all of this? "This sucks," Tommy finally said, overwhelmed by the enormity of his responsibilities.

Abby looked startled, then a little hurt. "Sorry," she said. "You want to get out of here?"

"Oh, no, I didn't mean—I mean, uh, yes. Let us go."

"Do you still need to get your heroin?"

"What? No, that matter is taken care of."

"You know, Byron and Shelley did opiates," Abby said. "Laudanum. It was like cough syrup."

Then, for no reason that he could think of, Tommy said, "Those scamps, they loved to get wrecked and read ghost stories from the German."

"That is so fucking cool," Abby said, grabbing his arm and hugging his biceps like it was her newest, bestest friend. She started pulling him toward the door.

"What about your friend?" Tommy said.

"Oh, someone made a comment about his cape being gray when we first got here, so he went home to redye all of his blacks."

"Of course," Tommy said, thinking, *What the fuck?*

Out on the sidewalk, Abby said, "I suppose we need to find somewhere private."

"We do?"

"So you can take me," Abby said, stretching her neck to the side, looking more like a stringless marionette than ever.

Tommy had no idea what to do. How did she know? Everyone in that club would have scored higher on the "are you a vampire?" test than he would. There needed to be a book, and this sort of thing needed to be in it. Should he deny it? Should he just get on with it? What was he going to tell Jody when she woke up next to the skinny marionette girl? He hadn't really understood women when he was a normal, human guy, when it seemed that all you had to do was pretend that you didn't want to have sex with them until they would have sex with you, but being a vampire added a whole new aspect to things. Was he supposed to conceal that he was a vampire *and a dork*? He used to read the articles in *Cosmo* to get some clue to the female psyche, and so he deferred to advice he'd read in an article entitled "Think He's Just Pretending to Like You So You'll Have Sex with Him? Try a Coffee Date."

"How 'bout I buy you a cup of coffee instead," he said. "We can talk."

"It's because I have small boobs, isn't it?" Abby said, going into a very practiced pout.

"Of course not." Tommy smiled in a way he thought would be charming, mature, and reassuring. "Coffee won't help that."

• •

As Jody pushed the bundle of clothes into the storm sewer, a silver cigarette case slid out of the jacket pocket onto the pavement. She reached for it and felt a light shock—no, that wasn't it. It was a warmth that moved up her arm. She kicked the clothes into the opening and stood under the streetlight, turning the silver case in her hands. It had his name engraved on it. She couldn't keep it, like she had the folding money from his pockets, but she couldn't throw it away either. Something wouldn't let her.

She heard a buzz, like an angry insect, and looked up to see a neon "Open" sign flickering above a shop called Asher's Secondhand. That was it. That's where the cigarette case had to go. She owed it to James. After all, he'd given her everything, or at least everything he'd had left. She quick-stepped across the street and into the shop.

The owner was working the counter at the back by himself. A thin guy in his early thirties, with a look of pleasant confusion not unlike the one she'd first noticed on Tommy's face. Normally, this guy would be prime minion material, or at least based on her minion recruitment of the past he would, except apparently, he was dead. Or at least not alive like most people. He had no life aura around him. No healthy pink glow, no crusty brown or gray corona of illness. Nothing. The only time she'd ever seen this before was with Elijah, the old vampire.

The shopkeeper looked up and she smiled. He smiled back. She moved to the counter. While he tried not to stare at her cleavage, she looked more closely for some life aura. There was heat, or at least there appeared to be some heat coming off him.

"Hi," said the shopkeeper. "Can I help you?"

"I found this," she said, holding up the cigarette case. "I was in the neighborhood and something made me think that this belonged here." She set the case down on the counter. How could he have no life aura? What the hell was he?

"Touch me," she said. She held out her hand to him.

"Huh?" He seemed a little frightened at first, but he took her hand, then quickly let go.

He was warm. "Then you're not one of us?" But he wasn't one of them either.

"Us? What do you mean us?" He touched the cigarette case and she could tell that this was exactly why she had brought it here. It was supposed to be here. Whatever part of James O'Mally had been left in that cigarette case had led her here. And this thin, confused-looking guy was supposed to have it. He took what was left of people all the time. It's what he did. Jody felt some of the confidence she'd felt earlier draining away. Maybe the night wasn't hers after all.

Jody backed away a step. "No. You don't just take the weak and the sick, do you? You take anyone."

"Take? What do you mean, take?" He was furiously trying to push the cigarette case back to her across the counter.

He didn't know. He was like she was when she'd awakened that first night as a vampire and had no idea what she had become. "You don't even know, do you?"

"Know what?" He picked up the cigarette case again. "Wait a second, can you see this thing glowing?"

"No glow. It just felt like it belonged here." This poor guy, he didn't even know. "What's your name?" She asked.

"Charlie Asher. This is Asher's."

"Well Charlie, you seem like a nice guy, and I don't know exactly what you are, and it doesn't seem like you know. You don't, do you?"

He blushed. Jody could see his face flush with heat. "I've been going through some changes lately."

Jody nodded. He really would have been perfect as a minion—if he hadn't been some bizarre supernatural creature. She'd just gotten used to the idea of vampires being real, and it took some serious blood drinking to drive that reality home, and now there were other—other—things? Still, Jody felt bad for him, "Okay," she said. "I know what it's like, uh, to find yourself thrown into a situation where forces beyond your control are changing you into someone, something you don't have an owner's manual for. I understand what it is to not know. But someone, somewhere, does know. Someone can tell you what's going on." *And hopefully they aren't just fucking with you,* she wanted to add, but thought better of it.

"What are you talking about?" he asked.

"You make people die, don't you Charlie?" She didn't

know why she said it, but as soon as she said it, she knew it was true. Like when all her other senses had been dialed to eleven, she could sense something new, like noise on the line, and it was telling her this.

"But how do you—?"

"Because it's what I do," Jody said. "Not like you, but it's what I do. Find them, Charlie. Backtrack and find whoever was there when your world changed."

She shouldn't have said that, she knew it as she was saying it. She'd just handed him an item that had been owned by someone she'd taken not twenty minutes ago. But even as regret for passing out incriminating evidence hit her, she also realized that she had left Tommy out there to wave in the wind just like this guy. Even if it was only for a few hours, Tommy had no idea how to go about being a vampire—truth be told, he hadn't really been that good at being a human. He was just a doofy guy from Indiana and she'd abandoned him to the merciless city.

She turned and ran out of the shop.

Cocoa?" Tommy said. "You look cold." He'd given her his jacket out on the street.

He's so gallant, Abby thought. *He probably wants me to drink cocoa to get my blood sugar up before he sucks the life from my veins.*

Abby had lived much of her life waiting for something extraordinary to happen. No matter where she had been, there was a world somewhere that was more interesting. She'd progressed from wanting to live in a fantastic, *kawaii*-cute plastic world of Hello Kitty, to being a Day-Glo, Manga lollipop space girl in platform sneakers, and then just a couple of years ago she had moved into the dark gothic world of pseudo vampires, suicidal poets, and romantic disappointment. It was a dark, seductive world where you got to sleep really late on the weekends. She'd been true to her dark nature, too, trying to maintain an aspect of exhausted mopeyness while channeling any enthusiasm she felt into a vehicle for imminent disappointment, and above all, suppressing the deep-seated perkiness that her friend Lily said she'd never shed when she'd refused to throw away her Hello Kitty backpack or let go of her Nintendog virtual beagle puppy.

"He has virtual parvo," Lily had said. "You have to put him down."

"He doesn't have parvo," Abby had insisted. "He's just tired."

"He's doomed, and you're cute, and hopelessly perky," Lily taunted.

"I am not. I'm complex and I'm dark."

"You're perky and your e-dog has i-parvo."

"As Azrael is my witness, I will never be perky again," said Abby, her wrist set tragically to her forehead. Lily stood with her as she threw her Nintendog cartridge under the tire of the 91 midnight express bus.

And now she had been chosen by a real creature of the night, and she would be true to her word: she had shed her perkiness. She sipped her hot chocolate, and studied the vampire Flood across the table. How clever, that he could appear as just a simple, clueless guy—but then, he could probably take many shapes.

"I could be a slave to your darkest desires," Abby said. "I can do things. Anything you want."

The vampire Flood commenced a coughing fit. When he had control again, he said, "Well, that's terrific, because we have a lot of laundry piled up and the apartment is a wreck."

He was testing her. Seeing if she was worthy before bringing her into his world. "Anything you desire, my lord. I can do laundry, clean, bring you small creatures to quench your thirst until I am worthy."

The vampire Flood snickered. "This is so cool," he said. "You'll do my laundry, just like that?"

Abby knew she had to tread carefully here, not fall for his trap. "Anything," she said.

"Have you ever gone apartment hunting?"

"Sure," she lied.

"Okay, you can start tomorrow first thing. You need to find us an apartment."

Abby was horrified. She hadn't really tried on the idea of leaving her old life so quickly. But all that would mean nothing when she became immortal, and ran with the children of the night. But her mom was going to be pissed. "I can't move in right away, my lord. I have affairs to put in order before I make the change."

The vampire Flood smiled, his fangs barely visible now.

"Oh, it's not for you. There's another." He paused and leaned across the table. "An elder," he whispered.

There was another? Was she to become the sacrifice to a whole coven of the undead? Well, whatever. Lily would be so jealous. "As you please, my lord," she said.

"You might want to chill with the 'my lord' stuff," Flood said.

"Sorry."

"It's okay. You know this all has to be completely secret, right?"

"Right. Secret."

"I mean, I'm okay with it, but the other, the elder, she has a terrible temper."

"She?"

"Yeah, you know, an Irish redhead."

"A Celtic countess, then? The one who was with you at Walgreens?"

"Exactly."

"Sweet!" Abby blurted out. She couldn't help it. She immediately tried to hide her latent perkiness by biting the edge of her cocoa cup.

"You've got chocolate, here." The vampire Flood gestured to her lip. "Kind of a marshmallow mustache."

"Sorry," Abby said, wiping her mouth furiously with the back of her fishnet glove, smearing her black lipstick across the side of her face.

"It's okay," said the vampire Flood. "It's cute."

"Fuck!" Abby said.

It's Like Time Travel, Only, You Know, Slower...

THE CHRONICLES OF ABBY NORMAL:
Tortured Victim of the Daylight Dwellers

So here I am again, to open my veins and spill my pain onto your pages. My dark friend, after sixteen years of totally boring existence, I come to you at last with a glimmer of hope to break through the gloomth that is my miserable life. OMG! I have found him! Or I should say, he has found me.

That's right, my Dark Lord has found me. A for-real vampyre. He is called the vampyre Flood, and he didn't say, but I think he is descended from European royalty—a viscount or a discount or one of those.

I was in Walgreens with Jared when we saw him—and OMFG he's so hot, in a totally stealth way. I would have thought he was just a totally mainstream geek or something, with his flannel shirt and jeans, but he asked us about buying syringes and I totally saw his fangs come out. So, I was like, "I can hook you up with my dealer," like that, and then he looked at my T-shirt and saw Byron's picture on it and he quoted "She Walks in Beauty," which is like my favorite poem next to the one by Baudelaire about his girlfriend being nothing but worm food, except that Lily called that one first because Baudelaire is her fave poet and so she got the shirt with him on it, even though Byron is way more scrumptious and I would do him on sharp gravel if I had the chance.

So I went home and changed my clothes and fixed my makeup, and when we got to Glas Kat we breezed by the door like we were twenty-five or something. Jared made our IDs himself at Kinkos and we both look so mature in our pictures, although I think he overdid it with the mustache. Anyway, we were there like ten minutes, and this song came on that I really like—"Boning You in the Ossuary," by Dead Can Dub—which is so cool and macabre. And I tried to get Jared to dance, but this guy comes by and grabs Jared's cape and says, "Blacks fade much?" and that was it. Jared went into a level-five freak-out, and turned into a total fuckwit, trying to get me to hide him and stuff, and then just saying he couldn't take it anymore and he had to go home and redye right then. So he abandoned me to the dank loneliness that is the night and I bought a bottle of water and some chips and got ready to grieve my lost youth, when HE showed up. OMG!

Check it, he actually knew Byron and Shelley! He used to party with them in Switzerland when they were all young. They all did laudanum and read ghost stories and stuff, and then they actually invented Goth, right there in this villa on some lake. He is like THE SOURCE! He took me for coffee and I wanted to give myself to him right there in Starbucks. Lily will be totally jealous.

So he said I have to wait. He is connected to some ancient Celtic vampire countess and I'm supposed to find them an apartment in the morning. He even gave me the name of a rental agent to call and a big wad of cash. I have to prove myself worthy of his trust, otherwise there's like no way he'll bestow the dark gift on me, and I'll totally have to finish my sophomore year and probably end up in junior college or working at Old Navy or something.

So, since we're off for Christmas break, I'm going to call this woman and go find an apartment for the vampyre Flood and the Celtic vampyre countess. And when Flood rises from the grave at sunset, I will get my reward.

I'm totally freaked about meeting the Celtic vampyre countess. Flood says she has a temper. What if she hates me? Flood says he's not really into her—it's not like that. It's like, she's his vampyre sire, and they've been together for like five hundred years, so, you know, they have history, and I can respect that.

NOTE: Make sure to find out if I need to move their native soil to the new apartment before we move their coffins.

NOTE: Do I need to have a coffin made? Is it okay if it's purple?

Oh yeah, my sister Ronnie has head lice.

Red, White, and Blue,
Not Necessarily in That Order

*S*now White, thought Blue.

With the seven to look after me, and me them, I could be just like Snow White. Granted, the Animals weren't exactly dwarves, Jeff Murray, the ex-high-school-basketball star was at least six five, and Drew, their resident pharmacologist, was pretty close to that height, but she wasn't exactly Snow White either. Still, they were all kind to her, considerate, and basically respectful of her, within their limits as a bunch of pot-head punani hounds. They did seem to have a decent work ethic, were loyal, didn't fight among themselves, and were relatively clean, as guys this age went.

In a few days, she'd have the rest of their money, she knew it, and they knew it, but then what? It was a ton of money, to be sure, but it wasn't fuck-you money. (Defined as having so much money that you can say "fuck you" to anyone, anywhere, anytime, and not have to worry about the consequences.) She'd have to find something to do, somewhere to go. As the possibility of her getting out of the life finally loomed large, she realized that she was going to need a new life to live, and frankly, it was scaring the hell out of her. Time isn't kind to a girl living on her looks, and she'd already extended her sell-by date by going blue, but what now? Who knew that the future she'd been hoping for would show up with such sharp teeth. So Blue asked herself the question . . .

Can a fallen Cheddar princess of Fond Du Lac make a life with seven perpetually adolescent party animals from the Bay Area? Maybe it could happen, but she had her misgivings about dwarf number seven: Clint.

In her experience, it took a lot of work to fuck the Jesus out of a guy, and even then, he was prone to come down with a bad case of the guilts a day or two later. Not really a problem when you were working outcall, but if you were going to high-ho a whole pack of dwarves on a semipermanent basis, one of them having a high-maintenance, holy-ghost haunting was going to be a problem.

"Whore of Babylon," Clint said as the Animals led her into the Safeway like they were presenting her at the palace.

She paused in the automatic doors, despite the fact that she felt like she was turning blue under her blue, dressed as she was in a silver lamé minidress and six-inch clear Lucite heels, none of it protecting her from the frigid wind coming off the Bay, whipping through the Marina

Safeway parking lot. Thinking she'd probably spend most of her time naked, she hadn't packed for San Francisco weather.

"I've never even been to Babylon," she said. "But I'm open to new experiences." She licked her lips and stepped to where her breasts were within an inch of Clint's chest.

He turned and bolted to the office, chanting, "Get thee behind me, get thee behind me, get thee behind me," the whole way.

"However you want it, baby," said Blue. She decided she'd think of him as Freaked, the paranoid dwarf.

"Barry will show you to the break room," Lash said. He'd become the new leader of the Animals, mainly because he tended to be the most sober. "Jeff, send the limo back and lock the doors. Drew, make some coffee. Gustavo, see what the situation is on the floors. We may need you to throw stock on the shelves."

They stood there, looking at him. Stoned. Drunk. Baffled. Blue would think of Barry, the little, prematurely bald guy, as her special dwarf, Baffled. She smiled.

Clint peeked over the three-quarter wall of the office. "Hey, you guys. You should know that the Emperor was here last night. He says that Tommy Flood is a vampire."

"Huh?" Lash said.

"He's a vampire. That girl of his, she didn't leave town. She changed him."

"Get the fuck outta here," said Jeff.

Clint nodded furiously. "It's true."

"Well, fuck," said the others, in an unsynchronized chorus.

"Meeting," Lash announced. "Gentlemen, take your seats." He looked apologetically to Blue. "This shouldn't take long."

"I'll make coffee," she said.

"Uh . . ." Lash seemed concerned. "Blue, we're kind of on a budget from here on out."

"Coffee's free," Blue said. She turned and started heading to the back of the store. "I'll find it."

The Animals watched Blue walk away and, when she turned the corner, gathered by the registers. Clint unlocked the office door and came out. "So, we have to notify those cops, so they can help us hunt him down."

Lash looked at the Animals, who looked back. Lash raised an eyebrow. The others nodded. Lash put his arm around Clint's shoulders. "Clint, the guys and I have discussed it, and we'd all like to do something for you."

Clint ran back in the office and slammed the door. "No! We have to destroy the agents of Satan."

"Right. Of course. We'll get right on that. But first I'd like you to ask yourself something, Clint. And I'd like you to answer not as the born-again man that you are now, but from that little boy that's inside of all of us."

"Okay," Clint said, peeking over the office door.

"Clint, haven't you ever wanted to bone a Smurf?"

. .

Jody heard Tommy come in the security door downstairs and met him on the stairs with a big hug and a backbreaking kiss.

"Wow," Tommy said.

"Are you okay?"

"I'm really good now. I was just checking on William. I think he pooped himself."

"I'm so sorry, Tommy. I shouldn't have left you on your own this soon."

"It's okay. I'm okay. Hey, you have something on your dress."

Jody was still wearing the little black dress. Some of the dust that was James O'Mally was still clinging to it near the hemline. "Oh, I must have bumped up against something."

"Let me get that for you," Tommy said, brushing at her thigh, then starting to raise the dress up past her waist.

Jody caught his hand. "Horndog!"

Chet the huge shaved cat looked up for a second, then put his head back down on William's chest and went back to sleep.

"But you left me on my own," Tommy said, trying to sound sad, but smiling too much to make it work.

"You're fine." She looked at her watch. "We only have about forty minutes till sunup. We can talk while we get ready for bed."

"I'm ready for bed now," Tommy said.

She led him up the stairs into the loft, through the great room, the bedroom, and into the bathroom. She grabbed her toothbrush off the sink and tossed Tommy his. She pasted, then chucked the tube to him.

"Do we still have to floss?" Tommy asked. "I mean, what's the point of being immortal if we have to floss?"

"Yeah," Jody said, through a mouthful of pinkish foam, "you should just go lie in the sun and get it over with, rather than suffer the torture of flossing."

"Don't be sarcastic. I didn't think we could get sick at all, but your hangover proved that to be wrong."

Jody nodded and spit. "Don't swallow any when you rinse. The water will come right back up."

"How come your foam is pink? My foam isn't pink. And I went last."

"My gums might be bleeding," Jody said.

Jody wasn't ready to tell him that she'd taken someone tonight. She would tell him, just not now. So, to change the subject, she summoned her superhuman strength and pantsed him.

"Hey!"

"When did you get skull-and-crossbones boxers?"

"I bought them tonight, when you were getting Christmas presents. I thought they would seem dangerous."

"You bet," Jody said, nodding furiously to keep from laughing. "And you'll blend in—in case you're ever caught with your pants down in the pirate locker room."

"Yeah, there's that," Tommy said, a little toothpaste

foam dribbling down his chest as he looked at his boxers. "I have the whitest legs in the universe. My legs are like great white carrion worms."

"Stop, you're making me horny."

"I've got to use that tanning lotion we bought. Where is it?"

Jody moved with catlike speed out to the kitchen, snatched the lotion off the counter, and was back sitting on the edge of the bed in only a couple of seconds. If she could just keep Tommy from asking any questions until sunup, she was sure she'd figure out a way to tell him about the old man. "Come over here, worm legs, let me put some lotion on you." To emphasize her commitment to lotionization, she stood, pulled the straps of her dress off her shoulders, and let it fall to the floor at her feet. She stepped out of her dress and stood there, in just her pumps and a silver necklace with a tiny heart that he had given her.

Tommy hopped out of the bathroom—his pants still around his ankles—one long hop, and he stood in front of her. Jody smiled. Give a geek supernatural agility and speed, and what you get is a superagile, speedy geek.

"You went out commando, in that dress?"

"Never again," Jody said, grabbing the waistband of his boxers and pulling him toward her. "These are mine, now. I want to be dangerous."

"That's so, so slutty," he said, lisping a little, his fangs coming out now.

"Yep. Where do you want to start with the lotion?"

He pulled her close and kissed her neck. "We have to be careful not to break the furniture this time."

"Fuck it, less to move," she said, her own fangs coming out now. She raked them down his chest. "If we figure out a way to get a place before someone kills us."

"Oh, yeah, I found us a minion," he said as she bit into his side and tore his boxers off in a single swift pull.

"What?"

But Tommy was finished talking for a while.

Blue watched as the Butterball rocketed by her and slammed into a triangle of two-liter soft-drink bottles—the front bottle burst, sending a cola-brown eruption of foam across the floor by the meat case.

"Strike!" Barry shouted. He danced in a tight circle among the Animals, pointing and chanting, "I own you, and you, and you," to each as he passed.

Blue looked to Lash, and raised a cobalt eyebrow.

Lash shrugged. "It happens. That's why we use diet soda. It's not as sticky." He had decided that they all needed to sober up some more before they started stocking the shelves; thus the turkey bowling.

"Can someone bring a mop?" Clint said. Because he would not gamble, he was the designated pin setter. He was scrambling around trying to retrieve soda bottles even as Jeff Murray was warming up at the other end of the aisle, swinging a Foster's Fresh Frozen Homestyle in each hand. He be-

lieved that he got better pin action off the Foster's because of
the savory gravy packet stuffed in its center. He claimed
that Foster's had mastered superior poultry technology, and
was, in fact, working on an oversized titanium turkey. The
other Animals were forced to point out to him that he was
completely full of shit as they sprayed root beer on him.

"So you guys hunted vampires?" Blue asked Lash. She
had come back to the front with coffee for everyone just in
time to hear Lash lay out the scenario for the Animals.
She'd held off asking any questions until now. A Fresh
Frozen meat missile zipped down the aisle between them.
Lash didn't even blink.

"Yep. We didn't kill him. We just blew up his yacht and
took his art. That's where we got the money."

"Yeah, right," said Blue. "I got that part. It's the vampire
part I'm not clear on. Like a real vampire. A real, blood-
drinking, can't-go-out-in-the-day, live-forever vampire."

"We figured he had to be at least six hundred years old,"
Troy Lee added, joining in the conversation. "Blue, you
wanna skid the buzzard?" He nodded to the end of the aisle,
where Jeff was offering his spare Fresh Frozen turkey like a
sacrifice.

"So you guys, who work in a grocery store, have seen a
vampire?"

"Two of them," Lash said. "Our night-crew leader,
Tommy, was living with one of them."

"She was hot," Troy Lee added.

"Vampire hunters?" Blue couldn't believe it.

"Well, not anymore," Lash said.

"Yeah," Troy Lee said. "Clint says that Tommy's a vampire now. We're not going to mess with him."

"Spawn of Satan!" Clint shouted from the end of the aisle.

Drew, who Blue had decided to think of as Doc, because he always carried the pot, ran down the aisle and shot-putted a twelve-pound self-basting at Clint's head. "Shut the fuck up!" Clint ducked and covered. The turkey went over the meat counter and stuck in the drywall by the window at the back of the meat department. To Blue, Drew said, "Sorry, couldn't be helped."

"Well, that's gonna take all night to patch," said Clint.

Lash looked at Troy Lee. "Could you kill him?"

"On it," Troy Lee said, falling into a fighting stance, before taking off and chasing Clint around the corner. "Prepare to die, White Devil!"

"So," said Blue. "You were saying?"

"Well, Clint says Tommy is a vampire now, and we should go stake him out or something, but he's one of us, so we've decided to pursue a policy of Buddhist tolerance."

Just then Troy Lee dragged Clint back around the corner in a headlock. Despite being six inches shorter and forty pounds lighter than Clint, he'd studied martial arts since he was six and that took size out of the equation.

"Should I hypnotize the chicken?" Troy asked.

"Make it so," said Lash.

Troy Lee adjusted his chokehold on Clint. The larger

man's eyes bugged out, his mouth moved like a gasping fish out of water, and he went limp in Troy's arms, who then dropped him in the puddle of diet soda on the floor.

"He'll come around in a second or two." Lash leaned into Blue to explain. "We used to call it *choke* the chicken, but that sounded kind of gayish."

"Of course," said Blue. That trick would come in handy in her work. She'd have to ask Troy Lee to teach it to her.

"And you think that your friend and this girl are really vampires."

"I suppose. Clint said he heard it from the Emperor, and he was the one that turned us on to the old vampire guy in the first place. Either way, they're not our problem."

"What if I said they were?" Blue said. Her mind was putting it together like a sewing machine on crack. It was insane, but for once she could see a future stretching out before her, welcoming her. "What if I said I wanted you to go after them?"

Lash blinked at her like she was speaking Klingon. "Huh?" He looked at the other Animals, who had stopped bowling and moved into range of the conversation. They stood there with frosty gobblers steaming in their hands like they were on wet-nurse duty for a group of headless infant snowmen.

"Flood is our friend," Lash said.

"I don't want you to kill him," Blue said. "Just catch him."

Lash looked to the others, who looked away—at the

floor, at the cabbage and lettuce counter, at the turnips, at their frozen charges.

"I'll make it worth your while," Blue said.

Jody lay on the bed watching Tommy turn slowly, back and forth in the air like a pale white-boy mobile. The loft had twenty-foot ceilings with open, industrial-style beams, and sometime during their lovemaking, they had both ended up hanging from them. Jody dropped to the bed after she came, but Tommy still hung by one hand. The bright side was that with the exception of the set of shredded sheets upon which she lay, they had kept the destruction to a minimum. The downside—well, she really could have gone a couple of lifetimes without seeing him from this angle.

"We did good," Jody said. "Hardly anything broken."

"You think that monkeys really do it that way?" Tommy replied.

"I always thought you were just using that as an expression." She'd thought she could remain detached enough about their lovemaking to stay in control—to enjoy it, but to use it, as it were—but since Tommy had changed, it wasn't like that anymore. She lost herself in it, she didn't just make love with him, she fucked him like a crazed monkey girl. It was good, but disconcerting. She had liked being in control.

"You look amazing from this angle," Tommy said.

"You look like a man-shaped fluorescent lightbulb," Jody said, grinning at him, then noticing a change. "Do not get wood, Thomas Flood. You will not get wood, do you hear me?"

"You sound like my mom," Tommy said.

"Ewwwww," Jody said, shuddering and covering her eyes.

"Ewwwww," Tommy said, realizing what he had just said and about what and whom.

He dropped to the bed and bounced. "Sorry. Quick, put the self-tanning lotion on me, we only have a few minutes before sunup."

"Okay, but just the lotion."

"Right, go."

Jody took the lotion and squirted some on her hands. "Turn around, I'll get your back."

"But—"

"Just point that thing the other way, writer boy, you have had all the monkey love you're going to get tonight." She said it, but she didn't mean it—she'd go another round if he wanted, if they had time before sunrise. Then she remembered.

"Did you say you found us a minion?"

"Yeah, I did. She's going to start tomorrow—er, today. I gave her money to get us an apartment. Told her what we needed."

"Her?"

"Yeah, you remember that girl we saw in the drugstore?"

Jody stopped rubbing, grabbed his shoulders, and spun him around. "You gave our deposit money to a nine-year-old?"

"She's not nine. She's sixteen."

"Still, Tommy. You trusted our secret to a sixteen-year-old girl?"

"She already knew."

"Yes, because you let your fangs show like some doofus of the night. You could have explained that somehow, or better yet, never seen her again."

"Look, she's smart, and she'll be loyal. I promise."

"You could have just gotten us killed."

"What would you have done? Huh? You have to trust someone."

"But a sixteen-year-old kid?"

"I'm only nineteen, and I was a great minion. Besides, she thinks I'm her dark lord."

"Did you even tell her about me?"

"Of course, she knows all about you. Knows that you're my sire—that's what they call the vampire who made you. I even told her that you were older, that you had vast experience."

"Vast? Vast experience sounds like I'm a slutty old divorcée. How old does she think I am?"

"Five hundred."

"What?"

"But you look great for five hundred. I mean, look, you got my attention. Do my front."

"Do your own front." She threw the lotion bottle at him and he snatched it out of the air.

"Love you," Tommy said, slathering self-tanning goo all over his face and chest.

"I'm going to lock the bedroom door," Jody said as the alarm on their watches started beeping, signaling ten minutes before sunrise. She'd gotten the alarm watches for both of them, just in case. "You didn't give her keys, did you?"

"Not to the bedroom."

"Great. What if she finds William in the stairwell and stakes him out? You could have given our key to a Buffy wannabe—"

"This stuff is supposed to take like eight hours to work, so by sundown I'll be sexy bronze."

"There's a bronze vampire in the living room. Why don't you go ask him how that's working out for him?"

"He's impersonal bronze, not sexy bronze like I'll be."

"Come to bed. And put on a T-shirt. I don't want a sexy bronze stain on the sheets, even if they are torn up."

Tommy sniff-tested a half-dozen shirts, finally decided on one, climbed into bed, and was kissing Jody good morning when the sunrise put them out.

Then, When They Woke Up

"Oh my God, that stuff turned me completely orange."

"Not completely."

"I look like the Great Pumpkin."

"Good grief, Tommy, you do not."

Blood, Coffee, Sex, Magic—
Not Necessarily in That Order

Just after sundown.

They watched the coffee dripping out of the filter like they were distilling nitroglycerine and the slightest bit of inattention might cause an explosion. "It smells really good," Jody said.

"It's like I never noticed it before," Tommy said.

"You'd think it would smell sickening, since it's indigestible," Jody said. The last time she'd taken a sip of coffee, her vampire system had rejected it so violently that she ended up convulsively dry-heaving on the floor, feeling like forks were twisting inside of her.

"This might work," Tommy said. "You ready?"

"Ready."

He poured a tablespoonful or so of coffee into a glass cup. Then he uncapped one of the syringes that held William's blood and squirted a few drops into the coffee.

"You first," he said, swishing the cup around in front of her.

"No, you," Jody said. As good as the coffee smelled, the memory of her nausea held her back.

Tommy shrugged and threw the coffee back like a tequila shooter, then set the cup down on the counter.

Jody stepped back and snatched a tea towel off the fridge handle in preparation for the coffee's return trip. Tommy rolled his eyes, shuddered, then grabbed his throat and fell to the floor, twitching and choking. "Dying," he croaked. "Suffering and dying."

Jody was barefoot and didn't want to stub her toe, so she pulled the kick to his ribs. "You suck, you know that."

Tommy rolled on the floor giggling, curling himself around her foot. "It works! It works! It works!" He sort of dog-humped her leg in rhythm and tugged at the hem of her robe. "You never have to be grumpy again!"

Jody grinned. "Pour cups, grommet! Full cups."

Tommy climbed to his feet. "We don't even know the blood-to-coffee ratio yet."

"Pour!" Jody was in the fridge in an instant, grabbing another syringe. "We'll wing it."

The she heard the downstairs door open and spun on her heel. "William?"

Tommy listened to the footfalls coming up the steps and shook his head. "Nope, too light."

They could hear the key fitting into the lock. "You said you didn't give her a key," Jody said.

"I said I didn't give her a key to the bedroom," Tommy said.

"Lord Flood, there's a stinky dead guy with a huge cat on your landing," said Abby Normal as she came through the door.

THE CHRONICLES OF ABBY NORMAL:
Dedicated Servant of the Vampyre Flood

I have been to the lair of the vampyre Flood. I am part of the coven! Kinda. Okay, back up. So I like slept till eleven, because we're on Christmas break, only it's called winter break now because Jesus is AN OPPRESSIVE ZOMBIE BASTARD AND WE DO NOT BOW DOWN TO HIS BIRTHDAY! At least not at Allen Ginsberg High School, we don't. (Go, Fighting Beatniks!) But it's all good, 'cause I'm going to have to get used to getting up later if I'm going to be a creature of the night.

So, like first thing, I made some toast, and it burned, as black as my soul, and I was so bummed that my tears of despair fell like cold bits of crystal, to be destroyed on the unforgiving rocks of this miserable life. But then I saw that Mom had left a twenty out on the counter with a note:

Allison (Allison is my day-slave name—my mom named me after some song by some Elvis guy, so I totally refuse to *accept it), here's your lunch money, and please stop at Walgreens and pick up some RID shampoo for Ronnie's head lice.* (Veronica is my sister, who is twelve and a total tumor on the ass of my existence.)

So, I was like, Sweet! Starbucks!

It took forever to pick what I was going to wear, and not just because I'd never rented an apartment before. The lightbulb burned out in my closet and we didn't have any extras, so I had to take everything out in the living room to look at it in the light. Like the song says, I wear black on the outside to reflect the black I feel on the inside, but OMG, it's impossible to tell one thing from another in a dark closet. Since it was going to be a business thing, I decided on my striped tights with my red PVC mini, my skull-and-crossbones hoodie, and my lime Converse All Stars. I went with just a plain stud in my nose, a barbell in my eyebrow, and a simple silver ring in my lip—understated and elegant. I carried my hot-pink biohazard messenger bag.

Ronnie was all, "I wanna come with you, I wanna come with you," but I pointed out that she was a scourge on humanity and that if she came along I would tell everyone on the bus she had lice, so she elected to stay home and watch toons. It was then that I ventured into the undiscovered country, and called the number that the vampyre Flood had given me.

And the woman was totally a bitch.

She was like, "Hello. Blah Blah Property Management."

And I was like, "I need to rent an apartment."

And she was all, "How many bedrooms and did you have an area in mind?"

And I was all, "What's with all the questions, bitch? Are you some kind of thought police or something?"

And she was like, "I'm just trying to help."

"Right, help. Like tuberculosis."

So she's all, "I beg your pardon," like the queen of freakin' France or something.

And then I remembered that I was supposed to ask for a specific person, so I was like, "Oh, I need to speak to Alicia DeVries, Is she there?"

And the bitch connected me.

So it turns out that Alicia DeVries is this crusty hippie who is like as old as my grandma, but wants to be all Earth Mother and everything, which I'm not against, because old hippies have the best pot and they'll just give it to you if you pretend not to notice that they're crusty and old. So Alicia picks me up in her crust-mobile rainbow peace-and-love Jeep CJ and I give her the requirements of the vampyre Flood, which were bedroom with no windows, a washer and dryer, private entrance with lockout, and, at least above the ground floor, windows looking down on the street.

And she's all, "We have to have a Social Security number and driver's license number for the paperwork—you have to be eighteen."

So I'm, "My client will provide all the information you need, it's just that he's very busy and can't deal with pissant details during the day." Then I waved the cash that Flood gave me and she went all spacey, overmeditated, *"namaste"* on me, like it's not about the money when it's really about the money. Then she takes me to this loft, which it turns out is only like a half a block from the address where Flood said to meet him at sundown. Sweet!

So I'm all, "Excellent, the master will be pleased."

And she's like, "I'll make you out a receipt."

Then she starts to lecture me about respecting myself as a woman, and not allowing myself to be subjugated to the desires of an older man and shit—like I'm this corporate fuck-puppet for some creepy businessman or something. I didn't want her to get suspicious and try to rescue me, so I'm like, "No, you misunderstand, I call him the master because he's the sensei of my jujitsu dojo—he's not boning me or anything."

Luckily I have an extensive martial-arts background from watching anime with Jared and I knew that one must never bone the sensei.

So she like reaches over and pats my knee. All, "That's okay, sweetheart."

And I'm like, "Step off, rug-muncher!" I mean, I'm as bi as the next person, but not with some crusty old hippie—I need music and some X, and then only if some guy has rejected me and thrown my heart into the gutter like an abandoned vegetarian burrito—and even then I draw the line at making out.

So she gave me the keys and took my money and just,

like, left me there. So I called Lily, who came over with a two-liter of Diet Green Tea, a bag of Cheese Newts (I still hadn't had breakfast), and some book she found called *The Big Book of Death*. So we looked at the book, which is this how-to thing with great art, and drank tea and ate Cheese Newts until she had to go to work. I wanted to tell her about the vampyre Flood, but I promised that I would keep his secret, so all I told her was that I had discovered my Dark Lord, and he would soon satisfy my every desire and I couldn't tell her anything else. So she was all, "whatever, ho," which is what I like about her—Lily is *très noir*.

So I walked over to the Sony Metreon and watched the flat-screens until it started to get dark. I was already about ready to pee with nervousness when I got to Flood's door, but then, just as I get my key in the door, this big Hummer limo pulls up, and these three college-age guys climb out followed by this blue woman in a silver dress with ginormous fake boobs. And they're all, "Where is Flood? We need to find Flood?" And she's all, "Where did you get the key? You need to let us in before it gets dark."

I'm not intimidated—because I know that her boobs are fake. And it's so obvious that they hunt the nosferatu that it's not even funny. Inside, I was like: "Ha, suck my spiky rubber strap-on, vampyre hunter!"

But on the outside I was totally chill. And I'm like, "I don't know who you're talking about. This is my apartment." Then I opened the door and inside, lying on the landing, there's this dead guy with a huge bald cat in a red sweater on his chest. And the cat hissed at me and I screamed just a little bit and slammed the door. "You have to go," I said. "My boyfriend is naked and he gets mad if strangers see his enormous unit." I looked right at the blue bitch when I said that, like: *Oh yeah, some of us are confident enough in our own femininity that we don't need fake tits to get a guy with a huge unit.*

And the black guy is like, "I just talked to Flood here last night."

And I was like, "Yeah, he moved."

Then the Asian guy checked his watch and was like, "Dude, too late, it's officially sunset."

And it was like it was on cue or something, the cat on the dead guy let out a long scary yowl, and even the blue skank backed away toward the limo.

"You'd better go now," I said, all ominous and full of foreboding and dread.

And she was all, "We'll be back."

And I was like, "So?"

So they went. But then I had to get past the cat and the dead guy and go up the steps. I have to say, that as much as I'm all about the peace of the grave and the glorious gloomth of the nonliving and all, it's different when there's a real dead guy you have to walk over, not to mention a really big, angry cat in a sweater.

NOTE TO SELF: Always carry Kitty Treats for Self-Defense (because evidently they don't like Skittles, which I tried).

. .

Since I didn't have any kitty treats, I got by the preternaturally big-ass cat by opening the door wide and yelling, "Hey, kitty, go away!" Much to my amazement, the cat ran out of the doorway and hid under a parked car. It was like I already had vampyre powers to command the Children of the Night. Then I had to get past the dead guy on the landing, which was sort of like dead-guy hopscotch, but I got up the stairs and managed only to step on one of his arms. I was hoping he really was dead, and not one of the nosferatu, because then he might be pissed off when he rose. He certainly smelled dead, the fetid stench of the charnel house emanated from him like a foul miasma of evil, as they say in the books.

So I opened the door, and I go, "Lord Flood, there's a stinky dead guy with a huge cat on your landing." Thinking that I would get total loyal-servant brownies.

Then I saw her, the ancient vampyre mistress—her skin like alabaster, or you know, no zits at all, and she seemed to glow with inner power. I could see why even a powerful vampyre like Flood might be helpless under her awesome strengths, gathered over the ages by sucking the lifeblood of thousands of helpless victims, probably kids. And she was like, drinking a cup of coffee out of a Garfield mug, as if flaunting her immortality in the face of us petty, insignificant mortals. She had on only a bathrobe, which was partly open in front, so you could see that she had like great cleavage, ancient total skank that she was.

So I'm like, "Hi."

And she's like, "So, Wednesday, you know Buffy's not a real person, right?"

Bitch.

Ψhat do you mean, dead?" Tommy said. He ran to the door and flung it open. "He's not here." He bolted down the steps in his bare feet, leaving Jody standing across the breakfast bar from Abby. "I'm going to look for him," Tommy called. The downstairs door closed, the lock clicked.

Jody pulled her robe closed when she saw Abby Normal staring. She could hear the girl's heart pounding, could see her pulse beating in her neck, could smell nervous sweat, clove cigarettes, and some kind of cheese snack.

They stared at each other.

"I found you an apartment, Mistress," Abby said. She dug into the pocket of her hoodie and came out with a rent receipt.

"Call me Jody," Jody said.

Abby nodded conspiratorially, like she was acknowledging it was only a code name. She was a cute kid, in a scary, will-probably-poison-the-dog-and-then-molest-him kind of way. Jody had never really had a problem with younger women as competition. After all, she was only twenty-six, and with the extreme antiaging treatment she'd gained from her vampirism, right down to her baby toes straightening out and every freckle she'd ever had disappearing, she felt superior, even a tad maternal toward Abby, who was a little knock-kneed in her red plastic skirt and green sneakers.

"I'm Abby," Abby said, and she curtsied.

Jody choked, sprayed coffee out her nose, and turned quickly so as not to laugh in Abby's face.

"Are you okay, Mistress—I mean, Jody?"

"No, I'm fine." It was strange just how sensitive the vampire sinus is to hot liquids. Jody was sure that she might never smell anything but bloody French roast again, and her eyes were watering, or so she thought, but when she turned back around, Abby jumped back six feet and yelped.

"Holy shit!" Abby had backed against the futon frame and was about to tumble over backwards.

Jody was around the breakfast bar, steadying the girl in less than a tenth of a second—which caused Abby to jump straight into the air about three feet.

Jody could tell the girl was going to fall. Abby was going to come down with one foot on the back of the futon frame, one in midair, and she was going to tumble over and land on her shoulder and head on the hardwood floor. Jody saw this coming, could have caught Abby and set her gently on her feet, but instead, she felt that maternal instinct kick in—the realization that if the child didn't take a knock or two, she'd never learn—so Jody stepped back into the kitchen, where she picked up her coffee and watched as the kid hit.

"Ouch!" Said Abby, now a black-and-red heap on the floor.

"Boy, that looked like it hurt," Jody said.

Abby was on her feet, limping and rubbing her head. "What the fuck, Countess? I thought you had my back."

"Yeah, sorry," Jody said. "Why the freak-out?"

"There's blood running down your face. I guess it startled me."

Jody dabbed at her eyes with the sleeve of her robe, leaving little red spots on the white terry cloth. "Well, would you look at that?" She was trying to be casual, trying to act like someone four or five hundred years old might behave, but the blood tears were disturbing her more than a little.

Change the subject. "So, this apartment you found, where is it?"

"Don't you want to wait for Flood?" Abby asked.

"Flood? What Flood?"

"Flood, the orange-colored vampire who just ran out the door."

"Oh, him," Jody said. Tommy and his tanning lotion. He was out running around on the street with no shirt or shoes. Orange. "Was he orange?"

Abby threw out her nearly nonexistent hip. "Hello? You're crying blood and your partner is orange and you didn't notice? Do you guys get senile over the years or what?"

Jody set her cup down on the counter, just to make sure that it didn't shatter in her hand. She drew on her experience working in the claims department at Transamerica, where her immediate supervisor was a complete ass-bag, and it took everything she could do, every minute of the day, not to bang the woman's skull repeatedly in a filing drawer. She liked to think of it as her professional face. So instead of snapping Abby's pale little neck, she smiled, counting to ten as she did. At ten, she said, "Go get him. Bring him back." Another smile. "Okay, sweetie?"

"But why is he orange?"

"The shedding is upon him," Jody said. "Every hundred years or so, we shed our skin, and a few weeks prior we turn orange. It's a very dangerous time for us. So please, go find him."

Abby nodded furiously and backed away toward the door. "Really?"

"Really," Jody said, nodding gravely. "Quick, away with you, the time of the shedding is upon him." She waved toward the door the way she thought a five-hundred-year-old countess might. (*Where did the countess thing come from, anyway?*)

"Right," Abby said, and she took off out the loft door and down the steps after Tommy.

Jody went to the bathroom and used a damp washcloth to wash the blood tears off her face. *I may actually be evil,* she thought. She knew it should bother her more, being evil and all, but after she put on a little mascara and some lipstick and poured herself another cup of blood-laced coffee, she found that she was okay with it.

Moving Day

Jody sipped her coffee and sighed, satisfied, like she'd just had a gentle coffee orgasm, the sort of pleasurable release you only see people have in commercials for froufrou coffee and hemorrhoid cream. This blood-beverage phenomenon added a whole new twist to their lives. A glass of wine? A diet cola maybe—wait, screw diet—a sugary, teeth-rotting cola. What about solid food? Sure, being a godlike creature of the night was great, but what about a jelly donut? French fries? She was Irish, she felt a deep-seated need for potatoes.

She was musing on the idea of heading up to McDonald's on Market Street and spooging a syringe full of William's blood all over a supersized box of deep-fried nirvana when the phone rang. The caller ID number was blocked, it just said *mobile*. It might be Tommy. He'd activated the disposable mobile phones they'd bought, but he probably hadn't written down the numbers.

"Hey, pumpkin," Jody said.

She heard a clattering at the other end of the line. "Sorry, I dropped the phone."

Oops. Not Tommy. "Who is this?"

"Uh, it's, uh, it's Steve. I'm the med student who called you about your condition."

He'd found her when she'd gone to a Blood Drinkers Anonymous meeting in Japan Town, which turned out to be a bunch of nerds with problems distinguishing fantasy from reality. Had watched her from a distance and called her on a pay phone from blocks away, ready to jump in his car and bolt if she came near him. He knew what she was.

He'd said that he had examined one of the bodies left by the old vampire. Elijah had snapped their necks so the bodies would be found, instead of turning to dust.

"What do you want?"

"Well, like I said, I'm a med student at Berkeley. Actually, I'm in research. Gene therapy."

"Yeah, next lie, please." Jody's mind was going ninety miles and hour. Too many people knew about her. Maybe she and Tommy *should* have left town.

"What lie?" Steve asked.

"Berkeley doesn't have a med school," Jody said. "So what do you want?"

"I don't want anything. I've been trying to tell you, I've studied the blood of the victims. I think I may be able to reverse your condition. Turn you back. I just need some time in the lab with your blood."

"Bullshit, Steve. This isn't biology."

"Yes it is. I told your boyfriend the night you turned him."

"How did you know . . . ?"

"I was on the phone with him when you told him you were going to be together for a very long time."

"Well, that was rude, just listening like that."

"Sorry. I've managed to get cloned cells from the throats of victims to revert to their natural human state."

"Which is dead," Jody said.

"No, living cells. I just need to meet with you."

He'd pressed this before, and Jody had been willing to meet with him, but unfortunately, while she was sleeping, Tommy had put her in the freezer for a few days and she'd missed the appointment. "No meeting, Steve. Forget you know anything about this. You'll have to write your dissertation on something else."

"Well, take my number if you change your mind, okay?"

He gave her the number and Jody wrote it down.

"It's a burner cell phone," Steve said, "So you can't find me through it."

"I don't want to find you, Steve."

"I promise I won't reveal your—your condition to anyone, so you don't need to find me."

"Don't worry," Jody said. "I don't want to find you." *Get over yourself,* she wanted to add.

"What about the other one you warned me about?"

Jody looked at the bronze statue that held Elijah Ben Sapir. "He won't bother you either."

"Oh, good."

"Steve?"

"Yeah?"

"If you tell anyone, I'll find you, and I'll slowly snap every bone in your body before I kill you." Jody tried to make it sound cheerful, but the threat sort of cut through the bright, friendly lilt in her voice.

"Okay then. Bye."

"Yeah," Jody said. "You take care."

The shedding?" Tommy said as he came through the door. Jody stood at the counter in her new red leather jacket, boots, and mist-tight black jeans.

Jody could hear Abby locking the downstairs door, so they had a few seconds alone.

"Look, did you want me to tell her you were just a big orange doofus?"

"I guess not. Hey—"

"She calls you Flood?"

"I couldn't tell her 'Tommy.' I'm her dark lord. Your dark lord can't be named Tommy. 'Flood' has an air of power."

"And dampness."

"Yeah, it's got the dampness thing going for it, too."

Abby came in, breathing hard. She'd been sweating and

her eyeliner was running in two black streaks down her cheeks. "We didn't find him. I could have sworn he was dead. He smelled like it."

"You got something against dead people?" Jody said— tough-guy voice. "Are you saying there's something wrong with dead people? Is that what you're saying? Are you saying you're too good for the dead, is that what you're saying?"

Abby stepped behind Tommy and peeked around. The kid was still out of breath from trying to keep up with Tommy, and now she was frightened, too. "No, Mistress, I think the nonliving are great. I'm all about dead people. I have a 'I Fuck the Dead' T-shirt even. I can wear it tomorrow if you want. I didn't mean . . ."

"It's okay, Abby," Jody said, waving it off. "Just fucking with you."

"Jody!" Tommy said, scolding. "Don't scare the minion."

"Sorry," Jody said, thinking, once again, that she might be evil. "What about the new apartment. Did you look at it?"

"We went by it. It's only a few doors down. We don't even have to cross the street."

"You think that's far enough? They won't find us there?"

"Well, at least they won't find us *here*. I don't think anyone's going to think that we'd only move a few doors down. They'll think we've at least left the City. What kind of idiot would only move a few doors away? It's brilliant."

"Plus an easy move," Jody said. "You guys can do it without a truck."

"You guys?"

"Well, I've got to find William, and you can't exactly run around until the shedding has subsided. Abby, do you have enough makeup to cover his face and hands?"

"Tons," Abby said. She held up her messenger bag. "But I can only help for a little while. I have to get home."

"Why?" Tommy asked. "We require your services." He meant to sound sophisticated and European, but it came out sounding lecherous.

"He means moving," Jody said. "I've got his other services covered."

"I can't," Abby said. "My sister has lice."

So," Abby said, "the countess is kind of a bitch."

"No, she's just a dark creature of unspeakable evil," Tommy said. He had the futon on his back and was making his way down the street as Abby followed him with a lamp in one hand and a blender in the other. "In a nice way," he added—thinking that maybe he'd already made enough of an impression on Abby.

Although it was early in the evening, and it was a little unusual to see a guy walking down the street carrying a futon, followed by a Goth girl carrying a lamp and a blender, it was just unusual enough that people would have felt stupid if they asked what was going on and someone pointed out it was modern dance, or performance art, or people robbing an apartment. San Francisco is a city of sophisticates,

and except for a homeless guy who remarked on the tacki-
ness of Tommy's Pier 1 Imports decor, they had moved half
of the furniture and clothing without comment.

"Do you need to feed?" Abby asked when they got back
to the old loft. They were standing in the living room,
where there was little left except some bookcases and the
three bronze statues.

"Huh?" Tommy replied.

"I'm guessing that you need to feed," Abby said, pulling
her hoodie aside and offering up her neck. "And I have to get
going. I have to get to Walgreens and catch the bus home
before the parental unit goes critical. Go ahead. I'm ready."

She closed her eyes and started breathing hard, as if
bracing for the pain. "Take me, Flood. I'm ready."

"Really?" Tommy said.

Abby opened one eye. "Well yeah."

"You're sure?" Tommy hadn't bitten another woman.
He wasn't sure if it might not be cheating. What if the
whole sex thing went off the way it did with Jody? That
kind of activity would kill a normal human woman, plus,
he was pretty sure that Jody would not approve. "Maybe a
little from the wrist," Tommy said.

Abby opened her eyes and pulled up her sleeve. "Of
course, so you don't leave the mark of *nosferatu*." She said it
with a hiss—*nasss*—*sssss*—*fer-a-too*—like she was speaking
snake.

"Oh, it won't leave any marks," Tommy said. "You'll
heal up like instantly." He was starting to feel the hunger

rise in him, he could feel his fangs pressing down from the roof of his mouth.

"Really?"

"Oh yeah, Jody bit me almost every night before I changed over, and no one ever noticed down at the store."

"The store?"

Oops. "The ye olde porridge and leeches store, where I worked, in the ye old days."

"I thought you were a lord?"

"Well, yeah, I mean, I owned the store, and some serfs, and scullery maids—couldn't get enough of the scullery maids—but I put in a shift now and then. You know, help to stir the porridge and inventory the leeches. Serfs will steal you blind if you don't watch them. Well, enough business, let's get to that feeding."

He took her wrist and pulled it to his mouth, then stopped. She was looking at him, one eyebrow sort of cocked in the air, and there was a silver ring in it, so it felt more incredulous than a normal eyebrow.

He dropped her arm.

"You know, maybe you should get home before you get in trouble. I wouldn't want my minion on restriction."

Abby looked hurt now. "But, Lord Flood, have I offended you? Am I not deserving?"

"You were looking at me like you thought I was fucking with you," Tommy said.

"Weren't you?"

"Well no. This is a two-way street, Abby. I can't ask for

your loyalty if I don't give you trust in return." He couldn't believe the bullshit that was coming out of his mouth.

"Oh, okay then."

"Tomorrow night," Tommy said. "I'll bleed you within an inch of your life, I promise." The things you never think you'll hear yourself say.

Abby rolled down her sleeve. "Okay then. Will you be able to get the rest by yourself?"

"Sure. Vampire powers. Duh." He laughed, waving at the heavy bronze statues like they were nothing.

"You know," Abby said, "the man and the turtle are cool, but that woman statue, you should get rid of that. She looks kind of skanky."

"You think?"

Abby nodded. "Yeah. Maybe there's some church or something that you could donate it to. Like, to show how you don't want your daughter to grow up. Oh, sorry, Lord Flood, I didn't mean to say church."

"No, I'm okay," Tommy said. "I'll walk you out."

"Thanks," Abby said.

He followed her downstairs and held the door to the street, then at the last minute, as she was walking away, she turned and kissed him quickly on the cheek. "I love you, Lord Flood," she whispered in his ear. Then she turned and ran up the sidewalk.

Tommy felt himself blush. Dead as he was, he felt heat rise in his cheeks. He turned and trudged back up the steps, feeling the full weight of his four, maybe five hundred years of life. He needed to talk to Jody. How long could it take to find one drunk guy with a giant cat?

He dug his cell phone out of his pocket and dialed the number of the phone he'd given Jody. He could hear it ringing on the kitchen counter where she had left it.

Powers for Good

The Emperor was sitting on a black marble bench just around the corner from the great opera house, feeling small and ashamed, when he saw the striking redhead in jeans coming toward him. Bummer lapsed into a barking fit and the Emperor snatched the Boston terrier up by the scruff of the neck and stuffed him into the oversized pocket of his coat to quiet him.

"Brave Bummer," said the old man. "Would that I could still hold that kind of passion, even if it were fear. But my fear is weak and damp, I've barely the spine for a dignified surrender."

He'd felt like this since he'd seen Jody outside the secondhand store, where she'd warned him away from the owner. Yes, now he knew her to be one of the undead, a bloodsucking fiend—but then, not so much a fiend. She had been a friend, a good one, even after he had betrayed Tommy to the Animals. He could feel the City's eye on him, could feel her disappointment in him. What does a man have, if not character? What is character, if not a man's measure of himself against his friends and enemies? The great city of San Francisco shook her head at him, ashamed. Her bridges slumped in the fog with disappointment.

He remembered a house somewhere and that same look on the face of a dark-haired woman, but mercifully, in an instant that memory was a ghost, and Jody was bending to scratch behind the ears of the steadfast Lazarus, who had never been agitated by her like his bug-eyed brother, who even now squirmed furiously in the woolen pocket.

"Your Majesty," Jody said. "How are you?"

"Worthless and weak," said the Emperor. She really was a lovely girl. He'd never known her to hurt a soul. What a cad he was.

"I'm sorry to hear that. You have plenty to eat? Staying warm?"

"The men and I have this very hour vanquished a corned beef on a sourdough roll the size of a healthy infant, thank you."

"Tommy's Joynt?" Jody said with a smile.

"Indeed. We are not worthy, yet my people provide."

"Don't be silly, you're worthy. Look, Emperor, have you seen William?"

"William of the huge and recently shaven cat?"

"That's the one."

"Why yes, we crossed his path not long ago. He was at

the liquor store at Geary and Taylor. He seemed very enthusiastic about purchasing some scotch. More energetic than I've seen him in many years."

"That was how long ago?" She stopped petting Lazarus and stood.

"Little more than an hour ago."

"Thank you, Your Majesty. You don't know where he was going?"

"I should think to find a safe place to drink his dinner. Although I can't claim to know him well, I don't think William passes the evening in the Tenderloin often."

Jody patted the Emperor's shoulder, and he took her hand.

"I'm so sorry, dear."

"Sorry? About what?"

"When I saw you and Thomas the other night, I noticed. It's true, isn't it? Thomas has changed."

"No, he's still a doofus."

"I mean he is one of your kind now?"

"Yes." She looked up the street. "I was alone," she said.

The Emperor knew exactly how she felt. "I told one of his crew from the Safeway, Jody. I'm sorry, I was frightened."

"You told the Animals?"

"The born-again one, yes."

"And how did he react?"

"He was worried for Thomas's soul."

"Yeah, that would be Clint's reaction. You don't know if he told the other Animals?"

"I would guess yes, by now."

"Okay, don't worry, then, Your Highness. It's okay. Just don't tell anyone else. Tommy and I are leaving the City just like we promised those police detectives. We just have to get things in order."

"And the other—the old vampire?"

"Yes. Him, too."

She turned and strode away, heading into the Tenderloin, her boot heels clacking on the sidewalk as she kept her pace just below a run.

The Emperor shook his head and rubbed Lazarus behind the ears. "I should have told her about the detectives. I know that, old friend." There was only so much weakness he could confess to at one time—that, too, a fault. The Emperor resolved to sleep somewhere cold and damp tonight, perhaps in the park by the Maritime Museum, as penance for his weakness.

There was no way she was going to remember his new mobile number. It was five in the morning before Tommy had finished moving all of the furniture, books, and clothes. Now the new loft looked almost exactly like the old loft had looked, except that it didn't have a working phone line. So Tommy sat on the counter of the old loft, looking at the three bronze statues and waiting for Jody to call.

Just the three statues left to move: Jody, the old vampire, and the turtle. The old vampire looked fairly natural.

He'd been unconscious when he'd been bronzed, but Tommy had the biker sculptors downstairs pose him as if he was in midstep, out for a stroll. Jody was posed with her hand on her hip, her head thrown back as if she'd just tossed her long hair over her shoulder, smiling.

Tommy turned his head to the side, getting perspective. She didn't look skanky. What made Abby say the statue was skanky? Sexy, well yes. Jody had been wearing some very low-cut jeans and a crop top when he'd posed her for the electroplating, and the bikers had insisted upon exposing more of her cleavage than was probably decorous, but what could you expect from a couple of guys who specialized in making high-end garden gnomes acting out the Kama Sutra?

Okay, she looked a little skanky, but he didn't see how that was a bad thing. He had actually been delighted when she came streaming out of the ear holes to materialize, stark naked, in front of him. If she hadn't killed him, it would have been the fulfillment of a sexual fantasy he'd nurtured for a long time. (There had been this old TV show he'd watched as a kid, about a beautiful genie who lived in a bottle—well, Tommy had done some serious bottle polishing over that one.)

So the Jody statue stayed. But the old vampire, Elijah, that was a different story. There was a real creature in there. A real scary creature. Whatever bizarre events had brought them to this spot had been set off by Elijah Ben Sapir. He was a reminder that neither he—Tommy—nor

Jody had chosen to be vampires. Neither had chosen to live out the rest of their days in the night. Elijah had taken their choices away from them, and replaced them with a whole new set of scarier, bigger choices. The first of which was how the hell do you deal with the fact that you have imprisoned a sentient, feeling being in a shell of bronze, even if he is an evil dick-weed from the Dark Ages? But they couldn't let him out. He'd kill them for sure if they did. Really kill them, too, a complete death, the kind with no nooky.

Suddenly Tommy was angry. He'd had a future. He might have been a writer, a Nobel Prize winner, an adventurer, a spy. Now he was just a foul dead thing, and the furthest his ambition would reach was his next victim. Okay, that wasn't really true, but still, he was pissed off. So what if Elijah was trapped in a bronze shell forever. He'd trapped them in these monstrous bodies. Maybe it was time to do something monstrous.

Tommy picked up Jody's statue and threw it over his shoulder and, despite his great vampire strength, followed it over backward as it clanged against the floor. Okay, it had taken the two bikers and a refrigerator dolly to get the statues up here, maybe a little planning was in order.

It turned out he could move the statue pretty efficiently if he slung it over his back and let one of her feet drag, and so he did, down the steps, half a block down the sidewalk, and back up the steps of the new loft. Bronze Jody looked happy in the new place, he thought. The turtle took half as long. She, too, looked pleased with the surroundings.

As for Elijah, Tommy figured what was the point of being
in a city on a peninsula if you didn't take advantage of the
water now and then. And Elijah evidently liked the ocean,
since he'd come to the City on his yacht, which Tommy and
the Animals had managed to blow to smithereens.

The vampire statue was even heavier that Jody's, but
Tommy felt energized by the idea of getting rid of it. Just a
short twelve blocks to the sea and that would be that.

"From the sea ye came, and to the sea ye shall return,"
Tommy said, thinking that he might be quoting Coleridge,
or maybe a Godzilla movie.

As Tommy dragged the bronzed vampire down Mission Street, he considered his future. What *would* he do? He
had a lot of time to fill, and after a while, figuring out new
ways to jump Jody would only fill up a part of his nights.
He was going to have to find a purpose. They had money—
cash the vampire had given Jody when he turned her—and
what was left of the money from the sale of Elijah's art, but
eventually that would run out. Maybe he should get a job.
Or become a crime fighter.

That's it, he would use his powers for good. Maybe get
an outfit.

After a few blocks Tommy noticed that Elijah's toe, the
one that was dragging on the sidewalk, was starting to wear
away. The bikers had warned Tommy that the bronze shell
was pretty thin. It wouldn't do to unleash a claustrophobic
and hungry ancient vampire when you were the guy who
had imprisoned him, so Tommy stood the vampire on the

corner for a minute while he dug through a trash bin until he found some heavy-duty plastic Big Gulp cups, which he fitted on the vampire's dragging foot as skid protection.

"Ha!" Tommy said. "Thought you had me."

A couple of guys in hip-hop wear walked by as Tommy was fitting the cups on the vampire's feet. Tommy made the mistake of making eye contact and they paused.

"Stole it from a building on Fourth," Tommy said.

The two nodded, as if they were saying, *Of course, we were just wondering,* and proceeded to move down the sidewalk.

They must sense my superior strength and speed, Tommy thought, *so they wouldn't dare mess with me.* In fact, the two had confirmed that the white boy in the ghost makeup was crazy—and what would they do with a four-hundred-pound statue anyway?

Tommy figured he'd drag the statue to the Embar-cadero and toss it off the pier by the Ferry Building. If there was anyone around, he'd just stand at the rail like he was there with his gay lover, then shove the statue in when no one was looking. He felt enormously sophisticated about the plan. No one would ever think a guy from Indi-ana was pretending to be gay. That kind of thing just wasn't done. Tommy had known a kid once in high school who had gone up to Chicago to see the musical *Rent* and was never heard from again. Tommy reckoned he'd been dis-appeared by the local Kiwanis Club.

When he got to the Embarcadero, which ran all along

the waterfront, Tommy was tempted to just chuck Elijah in the Bay right there and call it a night, but he had a plan, so he dragged the vampire that last two blocks to the promenade at the end of Market Street, where the antique streetcars, the cable cars, and the cross-bay ferries all converged in a big paved park and sculpture garden. Here, away from the buildings, the night seemed to open up to his vampire senses, take on a new light. Tommy stopped for moment, stood Elijah by a fountain, and watched heat streaming out of some grates by the streetcar turnaround. Perfect. There was absolutely no one around.

Then the beeping started. Tommy looked at his watch. Sunrise in ten minutes. The night hadn't opened up to him, it had been shutting him down. Ten minutes, and the loft was a good twenty blocks away.

Jody was quickstepping along the alleyway that came out in front of their old loft. She still had twenty minutes until sunrise, but she could see the sky lightening, and twenty minutes was cutting it too close. Tommy would be freaked. She should have taken the cell phone with her. She shouldn't have left him alone with the new minion.

She'd finally found William, passed out in a doorway in Chinatown, with Chet the huge cat sleeping on his chest. They'd have to remember not to leave William with any money from now on, if he was going to be their food source. Otherwise he'd go elsewhere for his alcohol, and that wasn't going to work. He was making his staggering way home on his own. Maybe she'd let him take a shower at the old loft—they weren't going to get their deposit back anyway.

There was still a light on in the loft. Great, Tommy was home. She'd forgotten to get a key for the new place. She was about to step out of the alley when she smelled cigar smoke and heard a man's voice. She stopped and peeked around the corner.

There was a brown Ford sedan parked across the street from their old loft, and in it sat two middle-aged men. Cavuto and Rivera, the homicide detectives that she'd made a deal with the night they'd blown up Elijah's yacht. They'd moved just in time, but then, maybe not quite. She couldn't get to the new place either. It was only a half a block away, and she'd have to cross in the open. And even then, what if it was locked?

She jumped four feet straight up when the alarm on her watch went off.

It was toward the end of their second shift after returning to the Safeway that the Animals sobered up. Lash was sitting by himself in the wide backseat of the Hummer limo, his head cradled in his hands, hoping desperately that the despair and self-loathing he was feeling was only the effect of a hangover, instead of what it really was, which was a big flaming enema of reality. The reality was, they had spent more than a half a million dollars on a blue hooker. He let the hugeness of it roll around in his head, and looked up at the other Animals, who were sitting around the perimeter of the limo, similarly posed, trying not to make eye contact with one another. They'd had nearly two semi trucks of stock to put up that night, and they'd known it was coming because they'd ordered it to make up for the time they'd been away and Clint had let the shelves get low. So they'd sobered up, put their heads down, and thrown stock like the Animals that they were. Now it was getting close to dawn and it was dawning on all of them that they might have severely fucked up.

Lash risked a sideways glance at Blue, who was sitting between Barry and Troy Lee. She'd taken Lash's apartment on Northpoint, and made him sleep on the couch at Troy Lee's, where there were about seven hundred Chinese family members, including Troy's grandmother, who, every time she passed through the room during the day, when Lash was trying to sleep, would screech, "What's up, my nigga!" and try to get him to wake up and give her a pound or a high five.

Lash had been explaining to her that it's impolite to refer to an African American as a nigga, unless one was another African-American, when Troy Lee came in and said, "She only speaks Cantonese."

"She does not. She keeps coming in and saying, 'What's up, my nigga?'"

"Oh yeah. She does that to me, too. Did you give her a pound?"

"No, I didn't give her a pound, motherfucker. She called me a nigga."

"Well, she's not going to quit unless you give her a pound. It's just the way she rolls."

"That's some bullshit, Troy."

"It's her couch."

Lash, exhausted and already hungover, gave the wizened old woman a pound.

Granny turned to Troy Lee. "What's up, my nigga!" She offered and received a pound from her grandson.

"That shit is not the same!" Lash said.

"Get some sleep. We have a big load tonight."

Now half a million dollars was gone. His apartment was gone. The limo was costing them a thousand dollars a day. Lash looked out the blackout windows at the moving patchwork of shadows thrown by the streetlights, then turned to Blue

"Blue," he said. "We have to get rid of the limo."

Everyone looked up, shocked. No one had said anything to her since they'd finished stocking. They'd brought her coffee and juice, but no one had said anything.

Blue looked at him. "Get me what I want." Not a hint of malice, not even a demand, really, just a statement of fact.

"Okay," Lash said. Then to the driver he said, "Take a right up here. Head back to that building where we went last night."

Lash crawled over the divider into the front passenger seat. He couldn't see shit out the blackened windows. They'd only gone about three blocks into the SOMA district when he saw someone running. Running way, way too fast for a jogger. Running—like he was on fire—running.

"Pull up alongside of that guy."

The driver nodded.

"Hey, guys, is that Flood?"

"Yeah, it is," Barry, the bald one, said.

Lash rolled down the window. "Tommy, you need a ride, man?"

Tommy, still running, nodded like a bobble-head on crack.

Barry threw open the back door, and before the limo could even slow down, Tommy leapt in, landing across Drew and Gustavo's laps.

"Man, am I glad you guys came along," Tommy said. "In about a minute, I'm going to—"

He passed out in their laps as the sun washed over the hills of San Francisco.

Broken Clowns

Inspector Alphonse Rivera watched the broken clown girl—black-and-white-striped stockings and green sneakers—come out of Jody Stroud's apartment and head up the street, then turn and look back at their brown, unmarked sedan.

"We're made," said Nick Cavuto, Rivera's partner, a broad-shouldered bear of a man, who longed for the days of Dashiell Hammett, when cops talked tough and there were very few problems that couldn't be solved with your fists or a smack from a lead sap.

"We're not made. She's just looking. Two middle-aged guys sitting in the car on the city street—it's unusual."

If Cavuto was a bear, then Rivera was a raven—a sharp-featured, lean Hispanic, with just a touch of gray at the temples. Lately he'd taken to wearing expensive Italian suits, in raw silk or linen when he could find them. His partner was in rumpled Men's Wearhouse. Rivera often wondered if

Nick Cavuto might not be the only gay man on the planet who had no fashion sense whatsoever.

The knock-kneed kid with the raccoon eye makeup was making her way across the street toward them.

"Roll up your window," Cavuto said. "Roll up your window. Pretend like you don't see her."

"I'm not going to hide from her," Rivera said. "She's just a kid."

"Exactly. You can't hit her."

"Jesus, Nick. She's just a creepy kid. What's wrong with you?"

Cavuto had been on edge since they'd pulled up an hour ago. They both had, really, since the guy named Clint, one of the night crew from the Marina Safeway, had left a message on Rivera's voice mail that Jody Stroud, the redheaded vampire, had not left town as she had promised, and that her boyfriend, Tommy Flood, was now also a vampire. It was a very bad turn of events for the two cops, both of whom had taken a share of the money from the old vampire's art collection in return for letting them all go. It had seemed like the only option, really. Neither of the cops wanted to explain how the serial killer they'd been chasing had been an ancient vampire, and how he'd been tracked down by a bunch of stoners from the Safeway. And when the Animals blew up the vampire's yacht—well, the case was solved, and if the vampires had left, it would have all been good. The cops had planned to retire early and open a rare-book store. Rivera thought he might learn to golf.

Now he was feeling it all float away on an evil breeze. A cop for twenty years, without ever so much as fixing a traffic ticket, then the one time you take a hundred thousand dollars and let a vampire go, the whole world turns on you like you're some kind of bad guy. Rivera was raised a Catholic, but he was starting to believe in karma.

"Pull out. Pull out," Cavuto said. "Go around the block until she goes away."

"Hey," said the broken clown girl. "You guys cops?"

Cavuto hit the window button on his door but the ignition was off, so the window didn't budge. "Go away, kid. Why aren't you in school? Do we need to take you in?"

"Winter break, brain trust," said the kid.

Rivera couldn't hold the laugh in and he snorted a little trying to.

"Move along, kid. Go wash that shit off your face. You look like you fell asleep with a Magic Marker in your mouth."

"Yeah," said the kid, examining a black fingernail, "well, you look like someone pumped about three hundred pounds of cat barf into a cheap suit and gave it a bad haircut."

Rivera slid down in his seat and turned his face toward the door. He couldn't look at his partner. He was sure that if it was possible for steam to come out of someone's ears, that might be happening to Cavuto, and if he looked, he'd lose it.

"If you were a guy," Cavuto said, "I'd have you in handcuffs already, kid."

"Oh God," Rivera said under his breath.

"If I were a guy, I'll bet you would. And I'll bet I'd have to send you to the S and M ATM, because the kinky shit is extra." The kid leaned down so she was eye level with Cavuto, and winked.

That was it. Rivera started giggling like a little girl—tears were creeping out the corners of his eyes.

"You're a big fucking help," Cavuto said. He reached over, flipped the ignition key to "accessory," then rolled up his window.

The kid came over to Rivera's side of the car.

"So, have you seen Flood?" she asked. "Cop?" She added "cop" with a high pop on the *p*, like it was a punctuation mark, not a profession.

"You just came out of his apartment," Rivera said, trying to shake off the giggles. "You tell me."

"Place is empty. The douche nozzle owes me money," said the kid.

"For what?"

"Stuff I did for him."

"Be specific, sweetheart. Unlike my partner, I don't threaten." It was a threat, of course, but he thought he might have hit pay dirt, the kid's eyes opened wide enough to see light.

"I helped him and that redheaded hag load their stuff into a truck."

Rivera looked her up and down. She couldn't have weighed ninety pounds. "He hired you to help him move?"

"Just little crap. Lamps and stuff. They were like, in a hurry. I was walking by, he flagged me down. Said he'd give me a hundred bucks."

"But he didn't?"

"He gave me eighty. He said it was all he had on him. To come back this morning for the rest."

"Did either of them say where they were going?"

"Just that they were going to leave the City this morning, as soon as they paid me."

"You notice anything unusual about either of them—Flood or the redhead?"

"Just day dwellers, like you. Bourgeois four-oh-fours."

"Four-oh-Fours?"

"Clueless—Pottery Barn fucktards."

"Of course," Rivera said. He could hear his partner snickering now.

"So you haven't seen them?" the kid said.

"They're not coming, kid."

"How do you know that?"

"I know that. You're out twenty dollars. Cheap lesson. Go away and don't come back here, and if either of them contact you, or you see them, call me."

Rivera handed the kid a business card. "What's your name?"

"My day-slave name?"

"Sure, let's try that one."

"Allison. Allison Green. But on the street I'm known as Abby Normal."

"On the street?"

"Shut up, I have street cred." Then she added, "Cop!" like the chirp of a car alarm arming.

"Good. Take your street cred and run along, Allison."

She shuffled off, trying to swivel nearly nonexistent hips as she went.

"You think they left the City?" Cavuto asked.

"I want to own a bookstore, Nick. I want to sell old books and learn to golf."

"So that would be no?"

"Let's go talk to the born-again Safeway guy."

Four robots and one statue guy worked the Embarcadero by the Ferry Building. Not every day. Some days, when it was slow, there were only two robots and a statue guy, or on rainy days, none of them worked, because the silver or gold makeup they used to color their skin didn't hold up well in the rain, but as a rule, it was four robots and one statue guy. Monet was the statue guy—the ONLY statue guy. He'd staked his territory three years ago, and if some poseur ever showed up, he had to meet Monet on the field of stillness, where they would clash in the motion-free battle of doing absolutely nothing. Monet had always prevailed, but this guy—this new guy—was really good.

The challenger had been there when Monet arrived in the late morning, and he hadn't even blinked for two hours. The guy's makeup was perfect, too. He looked as if he had really been bronzed, so it was beyond Monet why he would choose to get his collections in Big Gulp cups that he'd jammed his feet into. Monet carried a small portfolio case, with a hole cut in it where tourists could stuff their bills. He had primed his money hole with a five today, just to show the challenger that he wasn't intimidated, but the truth was, after two hours, he hadn't made half of what he saw the newcomer take in, and he *was* intimidated. And his nose itched.

His nose itched and the new statue guy was kicking his ass. Normally Monet would change positions every half hour or so, then stand motionless while the tourists taunted him and tried to make him flinch, but with the new competition, he had to stay still as long as it took.

The robots on the promenade had all assumed poses from which they could watch. They only had to hold still until someone dropped cash into their cup, then they would do the robot dance. It was boring work, but the hours were good and you were outside. It looked like Monet was going down.

Sundown.

He felt like his ass was on fire.

Tommy came to to the sound of a riding crop being smacked against his bare butt and the rough bark of a woman's voice.

"Say it! Say it! Say it!"

He tried to pull away from the pain but couldn't move

his arms or legs. He was having trouble focusing his vision—waves of light and heat were rocketing around his brain and all he could really see was a bright red spot with waves of heat coming off of it and a figure moving around the edges. It was like staring into the sun through a red filter. He could feel the heat on his face.

"Ouch!" Tommy said. "Dammit!" He pulled against his bonds and heard a metallic rattling, but nothing gave.

The red hot light went away and was replaced by the blurry form of a female face, a blue face, just inches away from his own. "Say it," she whispered harshly, spitting a little on the "it."

"Say what?"

"Say it, vampire!" she said. She whipped the riding crop across his stomach and he howled.

Tommy squirmed against his bonds and heard the rattling again. With the spotlight moved away, he could see that he was suspended by very professional-looking nylon restraints to a brass, four-poster bed frame that had been stood on end. He was completely naked and evidently the blue woman, who was dressed in a black vinyl bustier, boots, and nothing else, had been whaling on him for some time. He could see welts across his stomach and thighs, and well, his ass felt like it was on fire.

She wound up to smack him again.

"Whoa, whoa, whoa, whoa," Tommy said, trying not to screech. He only realized then that his fangs were extended and he'd bitten his own lips.

The blue woman held up. "Say it."

Tommy tried to keep his voice calm. "I know you've been doing this for a while now, but I've only been awake for about a minute of it, so I have no idea what you are asking me. If you slow down and repeat the whole question, I'll be happy to tell you whatever I know."

"Your safety word," said the blue woman.

"Which is?" Tommy said. He noticed for the first time that she had enormous boobs spilling out of that bustier and it occurred to him that he had never seen big blue boobs before. They were kind of mesmerizing. He wouldn't have been able to look away even if he weren't strapped down.

"I told you," she said, letting the riding crop fall to her side.

"You told me what a safety word is?"

"I just told you what *it* is."

"So you know it, then?"

"Yes," she said.

"Then why are you asking?"

"To see if you're at your breaking point." She seemed to be pouting a little now. "Don't be a dick, this isn't my specialty."

"Where am I?" Tommy asked. "You're Lash's Smurf, aren't you? Are we at Lash's?"

"I'm asking the questions here." She snapped the riding crop against his thigh.

"Ouch! Fuck! Stop that. You have issues, lady."

"Say it!"

"What is it? I was asleep when you told me, you stupid bitch!" He was wrong, he *was* able to look away from the blue boobs. He snarled at her, something coming up from deep inside him that he didn't even recognize—something that felt wild and on the verge of out of control—like when he first made love with Jody as a vampire, only this felt— well, lethal.

"It's Cheddar."

"Cheddar? Like the cheese?" He was getting a beating because of cheese?

"Yes."

"So I said it. Now what?"

"You're broken."

"'Kay," Tommy said, straining against the heavy nylon straps, understanding now what he was feeling. He was going to kill her. He didn't know how yet, but he was as certain of it as of anything he had ever known. Grass was green, water was wet, and this bitch was dead.

"So now you have to turn me," she said.

"Turn you?" he said. His fangs ached, like they were going to leap out of his mouth.

"Make me like you," she said.

"You want to be orange? Is this another Cheddar thing? Because—"

"Not orange, you nitwit, a vampire!" she said, and she snapped the riding crop across his chest.

He bit his lips again and felt the blood running down

his chin. "So for that you needed all the hitting?" He said. "Come over here."

She leaned up and kissed him, then pushed away hard and came away with his blood on her mouth. "I guess I'm going to have to get used to this," she said, licking her lips.

"Closer," Tommy said.

Being the Chronicles of Abby Normal: Completely Fucked Servant of the Vampyre Flood

OMFG-W00T! I have failed, left my duty undone, like so much dog poop on the gloaming sidewalk of the tragedy that is my life. Even as I sit here at the Metreon Starbucks, writing this, the froth slaves seem to move like silver-eyed zombies and my nonfat, soy Amaretto Mochaccino has gone as bitter as snake bile. (Which is like the bitterest bile you can get.) If there wasn't a totally hot guy two tables away, acting like he doesn't notice me, I would weep—but real tears make your mascara run, so I'm staying chilly in my despair. Your loss, cute guy, for I have been chosen. Suffer, bitch!

I had to leave Lord Flood to his own devices last night, but before I left, I confessed my undying love for him. I am a hopeless hose beast. All I had to do was say good-bye, but no, I just barked it out. It's like he has this power over me—like I have an eating disorder and he's a package of

Oreo Double Stuff cookies. (I don't have an eating disorder, I'm just skinny because I enjoy eating mass quantities and then yakking it back up. It's not a body-image problem. I think my system has always wanted to live on a liquid diet, and until I'm brought into my Dark Lord's loving embrace, then it's Starbucks for me.)

I have been trying to call my Dark Lord and the Countess all day on their cells, but I kept getting voice mail. Well, duh—they're vampires. They won't be answering the phone. I'm such a tard sometimes.

So I went to the old loft early this morning, in fact even before dawn. I should be, like, made a Brontë sister for coming up with a story to get out of the house that early, but I wanted to talk to the master before his slumber. Thing was, the scary drunk guy and his huge cat were gone, but so were my master and the Countess. Everything had been moved except the statue of the turtle and the Countess.

So I rolled out, headed for the new loft I rented, when I spotted two cops sitting in a POS brown car. I knew they were vampyre hunters right away. It must be the master's dark powers rubbing off on me. There was a big fat gay cop and a sharp-faced Hispano-cop.

So I was like, "Could you guys look any more like cops?"

And they were like, "Move along, little lady."

So I was forced to point out to them that they were not the boss of me and then I proceeded to humiliate them by verbally bitch-slapping them until they cried. What is it about the crusties? Their minds work so slowly that you have to, like, prompt them to stand up so you can slap them again until they faint like the little wuss-bags that they are. I never want to be crusty. And I won't be, because my Lord will bring me into the fold and I shall stalk the night for eternity, my beauty forever preserved as it is, except I'd like a little bigger boobs.

Anyway, I wandered around on Market Street and up in Union Square to give the cops enough time to slink off to lick their wounds, then I returned to the master's street to check the new loft. This time there was this Asian guy sitting across the street in a Honda, looking all Manga-cool, but it was obvious that he was watching the loft door. He didn't look like a cop, but he was definitely watching, so I stopped and pretended to watch the sculptors work who have the space under the master's old loft. They are these two crusty biker guys, but they do some amazing shit. They'd left the garage door open so I stepped in.

They were putting dead chickens on wires and dipping them in silver paint, then hanging them on sticks by the wires.

So I was all, "What the fuck, biker? What are you doing?"

And one of them was like, "It's almost the year of the cock."

And I was all, "Don't be gross, you crustacious fuck. You pull that thing out and I'll pepper-spray you until you fry." (You have to be stern with weenie waggers—I've been exposed to on the bus over seventeen times, so I know.)

And he was like, "No, it's the year of the cock in the Chinese zodiac."

Which I knew, of course.

"We're making statues," said the bigger biker, who was named Frank. (The other one's name was Monk. He didn't talk much, which might explain the name.)

So they showed me how they took real dead roosters they bought in Chinatown, ran wires through them to pose them, then dipped them in a thin metallic paint, then put them in this big tank and attached electric clips to them. They pass some current through the clips and the current attracts bronze molecules or something to the metallic paint. It's like instant bronze rooster. I thought about the statue of the Countess upstairs and got a little creeped out.

So I'm all, "You ever do a person?"

And they were like, "No way, that would be wrong. You'd better go now, because we're behind and don't you have school and stuff?"

So walking out, I saw the Asian guy checking me out and I was like, "Hey, it's almost the year of the cock. Shouldn't you be out shopping for one?"

He looked really nervous, but he kinda grinned. Then started his car and drove off, but he wants me, I can tell, so he'll be back. I hope he wants me. He was so cute—in that Final Fantasy Thirty-Seven way. What I'm saying is, the Sex Fu is strong with this one.

So there was no sign of my Dark Lord or the Countess at the new place. I wonder if they have crawled under the earth in some park and satisfied their perverse desires with each other among the worms and the tree roots. Eww!

Oh well, almost dark. I'd better go back to the loft and wait for them.

Addendum: The lice shampoo didn't work on my sister. Looks like we might have to shave her head. I'm going to try to talk her into getting a pentagram tattooed on her scalp. I know a guy in the Haight who will do it for free if you verbally abuse him while he's tattooing. More later.

Sundown. Jody awoke to pain and the smell of cooking meat. She rolled away from the source of the pain and went crashing through the acoustical ceiling tiles to land in a commercial sink full of dishes and soapy water. A Mexican guy was backing across the dish room crossing himself and invoking saints in Spanish as Jody climbed out of the sink and brushed suds off her jacket and jeans. When she touched the front of her thighs she nearly leapt back through the ceiling the pain was so sharp.

"Mother-fuck-that-hurts!" she said, hopping around on one foot, because that will generally help all manner of pain, regardless of where it's located on the body. Her boot heel clicking against the tiles sounded like a limping flamenco dancer.

The dishwasher turned and bolted out of the dish room into the bakery.

The bakery. When the alarm on her watch had threatened dawn she ran down the alley checking doors as she went, and the only one she found unlocked led into the stockroom of a bakery. She needed a place to hide where she'd be undisturbed while she slept, and although she considered hiding under a couple of the fifty-pound bags of flour, she had no way of knowing if the bakers would be using them today. She'd already awakened in a morgue once before (when Tommy had frozen her), and finding a rotund necrophiliac morgue attendant rubbing his hands and other bits over her seminaked body while she thawed had soured her to the whole morgue experience. No, she had to find someplace more secluded.

One of the bakers had been coming into the stockroom, she could hear his voice and footfalls outside the door. She looked around for somewhere to hide, then spotted the grimy acoustic ceiling tiles suspended above. She leapt onto the pallet of flour, lifted a tile to see that the ceiling was suspended a full four feet below the structural ceiling. Bless old buildings. She grabbed a water pipe, pulled herself through the ceiling, jackknifed her legs up and around the pipe, then used her free hand to pull the ceiling tile back in place, all in less than two seconds.

She listened as the man moved around below her, then scooped up one of the big bags of flour and left the room. That was a good call.

She checked her watch. Less than a minute before she'd go out. She spotted four pipes running together parallel to the floor. They were slightly warm, which was why she could see them at all in the darkness, but each was two inches around and braced to the ceiling every few feet. They'd hold her.

She scrambled over to the pipes, squirmed out of her leather jacket, and put it across the pipes, then lay facedown on top of it. This way, even if one of her legs slipped off, it wouldn't pull her off the pipes. She was trying to wedge the toes of her boots into the gap between the pipes when she went out.

The problem was that the pipes weren't used that early in the morning. As the building awoke, hot water began coursing through them, and Jody had been subjected to the heat all day. Her jacket had protected her face and torso, but her thighs had been slow-cooked inside her jeans.

She gritted her teeth and bolted through the dish room door into the back room of the bakery. So *now* it's deserted. Of course, bakers work in the middle of the night and the early morning. At sundown the dishwasher would be the only guy still in the building.

She found her way to the stockroom, then out into the alley. She could see the entries to both of their lofts from the end of the alley, and fortunately, no one appeared to be watching from the street. There were lights on in the new loft and she made her way to the door, her legs burning with every step.

She listened at the door—did what she thought of as "reaching out." If she focused she could almost hear shapes, depending on the ambient noise. There was someone in the loft—she could hear the heartbeat, industrial music

playing in headphones, the shuffling of a body—a light
body dancing. It was the kid, Abby Normal. Where in the
hell was Tommy? He couldn't be far from the loft—the sun
had gone down only five minutes ago.

Jody pounded on the door, but the shuffling sounds upstairs didn't change rhythm, and she pounded again, this
time leaving a dent in the metal door. *Fuck, the kid has the
headphones cranked and can't hear a thing.*

Jody shivered, although not because of the cold, but
because the hunger was rising in her. Her body telling her
she needed to feed so she could heal.

She'd only done it once before, and wasn't sure she could
pull it off again, but she needed to get into the loft and leave
a lockable door intact. She concentrated as the old vampire
had taught her, and gradually, she felt herself fading—going
to mist.

Monet was no longer dressed as the statue guy, no longer
in character—not *that* character, anyway. Now he was the
masta-blasta, gansta-rappa, full-ninja-badass and a bag of mo-
thafuckin' chips, bi-yatch—bent on revenge and whatnot.
He'd given up midafternoon on making any money and had
gone home to remove his makeup and lick his wounds. He'd
taken a vicious ass-whuppin' today, even if it was only to his
ego. But now he was rolling with his homies, P.J. and Fly,
they would put that bronze muthafucka down—if he was
still around. If he didn't run away like a little bitch.

"You strapped?" Fly said, adjusting his do-rag as he drove his ten-year-old Honda Civic with rims worth more than the rest of the car.

"Huh?" Monet inquired.

"Do you have a weapon?" Fly said, enunciating all Royal Shakespeare Company precise.

"Oh, yeah." Monet pulled the Glock out of his waistband and showed it to Fly.

"Nigga, put that shit down," said P.J., who was in the backseat, wearing a Phat Pharm tracksuit that was four sizes too big for him.

"Sorry," Monet said, tucking the gun back into the waistband of his jeans. He'd borrowed the Glock—rented it, really—from a real gangsta in Hunter's Point, who needed it back in two hours or he'd charge another twenty-five bucks. Before he gave Monet the gun, he made him swear that no one would be wearing gang colors, so nothing Monet did could come back on him. Monet had made the assurance, then, after P.J. did a Google search for gang colors, they settled on orange do-rags, since no gang seemed to claim that one.

"Highway Safety Posse, yo," Monet had said.

"Yo, Stone Tangerine Thugs, yo," suggested Fly.

"Yo, yo, yo, check it out," said P.J., with enough hand gestures that any deaf person watching would have thought he had ASL Tourette's syndrome. "Cheesy Goldfish Crew."

"Yo, dog, that's so stupid it's not stupid," Monet said.

"Is that good?" asked Fly.

"Yo, dog, get in character." Fly was a bad actor. They were all in the same acting class.

He should have just hired real gangsters to do this. P.J. was probably going to trip over the legs of his track pants and completely ruin their intimidation.

"This is it," Fly said, pulling off the street, right up onto the sidewalk of the Embarcadero by the Ferry Building. "That him?"

"That's him," Monet said. There was no one around but the occasional passing car, but the new statue guy still stood there.

"Remember," Fly said. "Walk. Don't run up. Just walk, like you got all the time in the world. Use your sense memories."

"Right, right, right," Monet said. He and P.J. got out of the car and quickstepped across the bricks to where the statue guy was running his game. Damn, he was good, didn't even flinch.

As he reached the statue guy, Monet raised the Glock and the barrel connected with the statue's forehead. "Bi-yatch!" There was a dull clank.

"Whoa," P.J. said. "Nigga really is a statue."

Monet tapped the statue, three dull clanks. "Yep."

"But he got all that money in his shoes," P.J. said.

"Well, take it, stupid," Monet said.

"Yo, step off, Monet. I'm not the one that got upstaged by a statue."

"Shut up," Monet said.

P.J. was grabbing handfuls of bills out of the Big Gulp cups at the statue's feet and shoving them into his pockets. "Must be a G here, G."

"Yo," Monet said. "Help me get the statue into the car."

P.J. stood and got one shoulder under the statue and tried to lift it, while Monet tucked the gun in his pants and got under the other. They dragged the statue only a couple of feet before they had to set it down and catch their breath.

"Motherfucker heavy," P.J. said.

"Would you guys come on!" Fly screamed from the car, totally out of character now.

"Fuck this," Monet said. This whole thing was just too embarrassing. He'd paid rent on the gun, hadn't he? He drew the Glock from his waistband and squeezed one off at the statue.

"Shit," P.J. said, ducking. "Are you crazy?"

"Bi-atch need to learn a—" Monet's comment was choked off.

P.J. stood up and looked back. There was smoke streaming out of the bullet hole in the statue, and in the second he watched, it had formed into a hand and grabbed Monet by the throat. P.J. turned to run, but something caught the hood of his tracksuit and yanked him back off his feet. He could hear Monet gagging and choking. Then he felt a sharp pain in the side of his neck and he felt suddenly light-headed.

The last thing he saw was Fly peeling away in the Honda.

Being the Chronicles of Abby Normal: Newly Baptized Minion of the Children of the Night

Bow before me, skeezy mortals, for now I see you for the pathetic little rodents that you are. Scurry before my dazzling darkness, daysters, for I am your mistress, your queen, your goddess—I have been brought into the fold—I am Abigail Von Normal, NOSFERATU, bitches!

Sort of.

OMG. It was so fucking cool—like coming twice with Skittles and a Coke. I was in the loft, spacing into my jams on my MP3 player. I had downloaded the latest Dead Can Dub CD (*Death Boots Badonka Mix*) at the Starbucks and it was totally transcendent. I was transported to an ancient Romanian castle, where everyone had done X and was dancing totally chill and sensuous (with perfect hair). I was grinding a free-form booty dance on the armchair—perfecting my dance gestalt—when I saw some smoke coming in under the door.

(I can't wait to dance with Jared to this new CD. He's so going to love this move I do. That's what I love about dancing with gay guys. If they get wood during a booty dance, you can just take it as a compliment, not an agenda. Jared said that if I was a guy, he would totally suck my dick. He can be so sweet.)

So I pulled out one of my headphones and I was like, "Whoa, fire in the staircase—sucks to be me." There's only one exit, so, you know, blackened Abby coming up.

But the smoke formed into a pillar, and then it started growing arms and legs. When I saw it had eyes I ran into the bedroom and shut the door. I wasn't trippin' or anything, just totally calm. But it wasn't like when your friends hold your hair while you puke and tell you it's just the drugs and you'll be okay—so I went for the safe thing of locking the door so I could assess the situation. Then the door just 'splodes into splinters and there's the Countess, totally naked, standing in the doorway with the knob in her hand. And she was totally hot, except that her legs were all fucked up, like they were burned or rotted or something.

So I'm all, "You totally wrecked your deposit."

And the Countess like grabs my hair and pulls me to her and bites my neck, just like that. It didn't really hurt—it was more surprising—like you woke up from getting a root canal to find your dentist going down on you. Well, not exactly like that—more mystical. But still, surprising. (Okay, it hurt, but not as much as the time Lily tried to pierce our nipples with a compass from geometry class and an ice cube. Youch!)

She smelled like burning meat, and I tried to push her away, but it was like my limbs were paralyzed or there was a fat guy sitting on me—like I was buried alive or something, just watching it happen. And then I started to get light-headed and I thought I was going to pass out. That's when the ho dropped me.

She goes, "Go downstairs and get my clothes off the sidewalk. And make coffee."

And I'm like, *Wait a minute, I just lost my mortality virginity, shouldn't I get a cigarette and a fucking towel or something?* But I just said, "Okay," because where the Countess was all burned was healing while I watched, and it was kind of freaking me out to be looking at her naked, burned-up thighs and her totally red pubes anyway. So I went downstairs and just outside the door there was a homeless guy digging through a pile of clothes. Well, really, he was sniffing her panties. And because I don't feel we always do enough to help the homeless, I was like, "Take them, and tell no one what you witnessed here tonight."

(I was already feeling the superiority of my Nosferatitude, so it only seemed appropriate that I go all noblesse oblige on his ass.) So off he went to sniff the lacy crotch of the undead while I went back upstairs to find coffee filters.

So when I get up there the Countess is dressed and hair brushed and she's all, "Where is Tommy? Have you seen Tommy? Did you talk to those cops? And where's Tommy?"

And I was all, "Countess, begging your pardon and shit, but you need to chill. The vampyre Flood was gone when

I got here this morning, and so was that bronze statue from the other side. I thought you guys went off to sleep in the damp womb of your native soil or something."

"Yuck!" goes the Countess. Then she tightens down all of sudden. "Make me a cup of coffee, two sugars, and squeeze one of those vials of blood into it—and call us a cab."

And I was like, "Hey, step off, Countess. I'm one of you and you are not the boss of me and—"

And she said, "I said for *us,* didn't I?"

So I did her bidding—well, *our* bidding, really—and we took a cab over to the Marina Safeway, but why we didn't transform into bats and fly is beyond me. Anyway, we were there in ten minutes. But as we start to pull in, the Countess tells the driver to keep going.

She was all, "It's Rivera and Cavuto. This is not good."

The POS brown cop car was parked in front of the store. I was all, "Cops? Their shit is weak."

She seemed surprised that I knew the cops, but I told her how I had owned them like the little wussy-boys that they are and I could tell that the Countess was feeling pretty good about bringing me into the dark fold of the coven.

Then she was all, "Fucking Clint—he's telling them about Tommy."

But I couldn't even see what she was looking at beyond the big glass front of the Safeway. I guess my powers will develop as time goes on. Five hundred years is a long time to get your vampyre kung fu down.

The Countess had the driver drop us at Fort Mason, so

we could still see the front of the Safeway, and we stood in the fog like the creatures of the night that we were while we waited for the cops to leave.

Then the Countess put her arm around my shoulders and she was all, "Abby, I'm sorry I, uh, attacked you like that. I was hurt really badly and to heal I needed fresh blood. I wasn't really in control of myself. It won't happen again."

"No worries," I told her. "I'm honored to be promoted. Besides, it was kind of hot." Which it was, you know, except for the smell of burning flesh and stuff.

And she was all, "Well, thanks for looking out for us."

And I was all, "Pardon, Countess, but why are we at the Safeway?" Because it's not like we needed groceries.

And she was all, "These guys used to work with Tommy, and one of them knows that he is, uh, one of the children of the night. I think they might know something about where he is now."

Then, over at the Safeway, we saw this goofy-looking guy with frizzy hair and glasses unlock the front door and let the cops out. They got in their car and the frizzy guy locked the front door behind them.

"Showtime," said the Countess. She zipped up her leather jacket, took a pair of sunglasses out of her jacket pocket, and put them on. She goes, "Stay back, Abby. I'll be right back." Then she started across the parking lot toward the Safeway, taking big strides and looking all angel of vengeance, with her red hair flying out behind her, and the lights shining down on her through the fog.

I was like, "Oh shit!"

She didn't even slow down. When she got about ten feet from the front window she snatched up one of the steel-reinforced trash cans like it was made of cardboard and flung it through the window. And she just kept walking! Little cubes of safety glass rained down on her and she just walked through the front of the store like she owned it and everyone in it—which she did.

Before I even got in the store, she was coming back around the corner, dragging the frizzy-haired guy by the throat. She threw him up against a rack of wine bottles, which shattered, spilling red all over the floor and splattering the registers and stuff.

I was all, "Oh, dog, Countess gonna crack open a forty of whup-ass on you now. Oh, you in the shit now, wigga!" (I am not inclined to use hip-hop vernacular often, but there are times when, like French, it just better expresses the sentiment of the moment.)

Just then the whole crowd of guys I'd seen in the limo came running around the corner. The Countess snatched a wine bottle off the rack, and without a second of hesitation, she threw it and it hit the first guy, a tall, hippie-looking guy, right in the middle of the forehead and he went down like he was shot.

She goes, "Back!" and they all headed back around the corner the way they came, except the hippie-looking guy, who was out cold.

Then the Countess picked up the guy with glasses by

the throat. And even though he was like a foot taller than her, she whipped him around like a rag doll until he was screaming stuff about Satan and Jesus and telling her to get behind him and shit. And the Countess was all, "Where is Tommy?"

And he was all, "I don't know. I don't know."

And the Countess grabbed him by the hair and held his head steady against the wine rack. Real chilly, she says, "Clint, I'm going to take your right eye now. Then if you don't tell me where Tommy is, I'm going to take your left. Ready. On three. One . . . Two . . ."

Then he's all, "I didn't have anything to do with it. She's the spawn of Satan, I told them that."

"Three!" goes the Countess.

"He's in Lash's apartment on Northpoint. I don't know the number."

And the Countess just yells "Number?" out to the whole store.

And the black guy pops up from behind a display of Cheerios and is all, "Six ninety-three Northpoint, Apartment 301." And one of the other guys pulls him back down.

Then the Countess is all, "Thank you. If he's hurt, I'll be back." And she throws the Clint guy through a rack of Doritos, which exploded their nacho cheesy goodness all over the place.

Then she's all, "Well, that's a nice surprise."

And I'm all, "That Lord Flood is in an apartment on Northpoint?"

"I didn't think they would really know. I just didn't know where else to start."

"Probably your senses attuned to Lord Flood's presence over the eons," I said, like a total tard.

And she's all, "Let's go, Abby."

And I don't know why, I guess because I had like low blood sugar or something from blood loss, but I was like, "Can I get some gum?"

And she was all, "Sure. Grab some coffee, too. Whole beans. We're almost out."

So I did. And when I caught up with her, she was halfway across the parking lot, headed back toward Ghirardelli Square, and little pieces of safety glass were still shining in her hair and she smiled at me when I caught up and I just couldn't help myself, because that was the coolest thing I'd ever seen. Ever! And I was all, "Countess, I love you."

And she put her arm around me and kissed me on the forehead and goes, "Let's get Tommy."

I guess I'll start feeling my vampyre powers tomorrow night, but right now I feel like a total fucking loser. But I am so going to rule when school starts again.

Nobody Likes a Dead Whore

Finding her boyfriend tied naked to an upright bed frame, covered in blood, with a dead, blue dominatrix at his feet would be enough to rattle some women's confidence in the stability of their relationship. Some women might even take it as a sign of trouble. But Jody had been single for a number of years—she'd dated rock musicians and stockbrokers—and was conditioned to unusual bumps on the road of romance, so she simply sighed and kicked the hooker in the ribs—more as a conversation opener than a confirmation that the ho was dead—and said, "So, rough night?"

"Awk-ward," Abby sang, peeking in the door, then immediately swinging back into the hallway.

"I forgot my safety word," Tommy said.

Jody nodded. "Well, that had to be embarrassing."

"She beat me."

"You okay?"

"Yeah. But it hurt. A lot." Tommy looked past Jody toward the door. "Hi, Abby!"

Abby swung around the corner. "Lord Flood," she said, with a nod and a little grin. Then she looked down at the body, her eyes went wide, and she swung back out into the hall.

"How're your sister's lice?" Tommy said.

"Shampoo didn't work." Abby called, without looking in. "We had to shave her head."

"Sorry about that."

"It's okay. She looks kind of cool, in a 'Make a Wish kid' kind of way."

Jody said. "Abby, why don't you come in and shut the door? If someone walks by and looks in, it might, oh, I don't know, freak them out a little."

" 'Kay," said Abby. She stepped in and palmed the door shut behind her, as if the clicking of the door latch might actually be the thing that would attract attention.

"I think I killed her," Tommy said. "She was beating me, and she wanted me to bite her, so I did. I think I drained her dry."

"Well, she's dead all right." Jody reached down and tossed the blue hooker's arm up. It fell back to the floor. "But you didn't drain her."

"I didn't?"

"She'd be dust if you did. Heart attack or stroke or something. Looks like most of her blood went on you and the carpet."

"Yeah, I sort of tore her throat out and she fell before I could finish."

"Well, what did she expect? You were tied up."

"You don't seem that bothered by it. I thought you'd be jealous."

"Did you ask her to bring you here and beat you until you snapped and killed her?"

"Nope."

"Did you encourage her to beat you until you snapped and killed her?"

"Of course not."

"And you didn't get off on her beating you until you snapped and killed her."

"Honestly?"

"You're naked and chained to a bed frame, and I'm just inches away from both a riding crop and your genitals. I think honesty would be a good policy."

"Well, honestly, the killing part was kind of a turn-on."

"But not sexual."

"No way. It was totally homicidal lust."

"Then we're okay."

"Really, you're not mad?"

"I'm just glad you're okay."

"I should feel bad about it, I know, but I don't."

"That happens."

"Some bitches just need killing," Abby said, looking briefly at Tommy, then realizing he was naked under all that blood, looking away quickly.

"There you go," Jody said. She stepped up and began to undo his restraints. They were double bands of fleece and nylon, with heavy metal shackles locked over them. "What did she buy these for, to handcuff a grizzly bear? Abby, check the body for a key."

"Nuh-uh," Abby said, staring down at the dead blue hooker.

Jody noticed that the kid was focused on the breasts, which were defying gravity, and apparently death itself, by standing there at complete attention. "Those aren't real," Jody said.

"I knew that."

"She was a very mean woman," Tommy said, trying to help. "With really big but insincere boobs. Don't be afraid."

Abby tore her gaze from the dead woman's chest and looked from Tommy, to Jody, to Jody's chest, and back to the body. "Fucksocks! Does everybody have big boobs but me? God, I hate you guys!" She ran out the door and slammed it behind her.

"I *do not* have big boobs," Jody said.

"Perfectly proportioned," Tommy said. "Perfect, really."

"Thanks, sweetie," Jody said, kissing him on the lips lightly so as not to get a taste of the whore's blood.

"I think I saw her hang the key in Lash's Forty-Fucking-Niners hat rack by the door."

"I really need to teach you how to go to mist," Jody said, retrieving the key.

"Yeah, that would have helped me avoid a lot of this."

"You know the Animals sold you out, right?"

"I can't see them doing that. She must have blackmailed them or something."

"Clint told the cops, too. Rivera and Cavuto had our loft staked out."

"Clint doesn't really count, though. He traded in all his moral credibility in this world when he committed to live forever."

"Amazing how badly the promise of immortality makes people behave."

"Like it doesn't matter how you treat people," Tommy said.

"There!" Jody finally got the shackle on Tommy's right wrist unlocked and started working on the left. They were heavy, but she thought that given the motivation of torture, she could have broken loose, or at least torn apart the bed frame. "You couldn't just snap these?"

"I guess I need to work out." He scratched his nose furiously. "So, should we hide the body or something?"

"No, I think it's a good warning for your buddies."

"Right."

"What about the cops?"

"Not our problem," she said as she twisted the key in the lock and snapped the restraint off his left wrist. "We don't have a dead blue hooker in *our* apartment."

"That's an excellent point," Tommy said, rubbing his wrist. "Thank you for rescuing me, by the way. I love you." He grabbed her and pulled her to him, nearly tumbling over on his face when she stepped back and he encountered the resistance of his ankle restraints.

"I love you, too," she said, palming his forehead and pushing him back on balance, "but you are covered with skank oil and you will not get it on my new leather jacket."

In the cab, Abby pouted—sticking out her lower lip far enough that pink was showing above her black lipstick, making her look vaguely like a cat eating a plum.

"Just drop me at my house."

Tommy, who sat in the middle, wearing one of Lash's Forty-Niners jerseys, put his arm around Abby's shoulders to comfort her.

"It's okay, kid. You did great. We are most pleased with you."

Abby snorted and looked out the window. Jody, in turn, put her arm around Tommy's neck and dug her nails into his shoulder. "Shut up," she whispered, so soft that only Tommy would be able to hear it. "You're not helping."

"Look, Abby," Jody said, "it's not something that happens all at once, like in the movies. Sometimes you have to eat bugs for years before you become one of the chosen."

"I know I did," Tommy said. "Beetles, bugs, spiders, mice, rats, snakes, marmosets, OUCH! Stop that, I've been tortured already tonight."

"You two are just into each other," Abby said. "You don't care about anyone else. We're like cattle to you."

The cabdriver, who was a Hindu, looked in the rear-view mirror.

"So what's your point?" Jody said.

Tommy elbowed her in the ribs.

"Kidding. Jeez. Abby, we care very deeply about you. We've trusted you with everything. In fact, you may have saved my life tonight."

Tommy reared back and looked at Jody.

"Long story," the redhead said. Then to Abby again: "Get some rest and come to the loft tomorrow at dusk. We'll talk about your future."

Abby crossed her arms. "Tomorrow is Christmas. I'm trapped with the family."

"Tomorrow is Christmas?" Tommy said.

"Yeah," Jody said. "So?"

"The Animals won't be working. I have some issues with them."

"You were thinking revenge?"

"Well, yeah."

Jody patted the flight bag on the seat, which held all of the money that the Animals had paid to Blue, almost six hundred thousand dollars. "I think you have that covered."

Tommy frowned. "I'm beginning to doubt the steadiness of your moral compass."

"Sure, I'm the one with skewed ethics, when you spent the whole night tied up and beaten by a blue dominatrix and then ripping her throat out."

"You make everything sound so sleazy."

Abby put her fingers in her mouth and whistled—shrill and nearly deafening in the enclosed space. "Hello, there's a cabdriver here. Would you two shut the fuck up."

"Hey," Jody said.

"Hey," Tommy said.

"Hey, you, little creepy girl," said the cabdriver, "you will not be whistling in my cab again or I will be putting you out on the curb."

"Sorry," Abby said.

"Sorry," Tommy and Jody said in unison.

With the exception of the odd serial killer, and car salesmen who think of them as the perfect unit for measuring trunk space, nobody likes a dead whore. ("Yeah, you can get five-maybe six dead hookers in this baby.")

"She looks so natural," said Troy Lee, looking down on Blue. "Except for the way her arm is bent under her—and the riding crop—and the blood everywhere, I mean."

"And she's blue," said Lash.

The other Animals nodded mournfully.

It was turning out to be a stressful morning for the Animals: cleaning up the mess that Jody had made of the store, getting Drew to the emergency room to get his forehead sewn up where the wine bottle had hit him (they immediately passed around the painkillers he was prescribed, which help to take the edge off), then explaining the broken front window to the manager when he came in, and now this—

"You're the one with almost an MBA," Barry, the short balding one, said to Lash. "You should know what to do."

"They don't cover what to do with a dead hooker," Lash countered. "That's a whole different program. Political science, I think."

Despite the dulling they'd given themselves with the painkillers and a case of beer they'd shared in the parking lot at the Safeway, they were all feeling sad, and a little frightened.

"Gustavo is the porter," Clint said. "Shouldn't he do the cleanups?"

"Ahhhhh!" said Jeff, the tall ex-jock, as he thumped Clint on the head with a protruding knuckle. Feeling like the knuckle might not quite be enough, he snatched off Clint's horn-rimmed glasses and threw them to Troy Lee, who snapped them into four neat pieces and handed them back to Clint.

"This is all your fault," Lash said. "If you hadn't ratted Flood out to the cops, this wouldn't have happened."

"I just told them that Tommy was a vampire," Clint whined. "I didn't tell them he was here. I didn't tell them about your whore of Babylon."

"You didn't know her like we did," Barry added, his voice breaking a little. "She was special."

"Expensive," Drew said.

"*Sí*, expensive," added Gustavo.

"She probably could finally afford to go to Babylon," said Lash.

"Forgive them, for they know not what they do," Clint said.

Troy Lee bent and examined Blue, careful not to touch her. "It's hard to see bruising through the blue dye, but I guess she broke her neck. The blood must be Flood's. I don't see any marks on her."

"No bite marks, you mean," said Clint.

"Of course that's what I mean, nit wit. You know Flood's girlfriend did this, right?"

"How do you know?" Lash asked. "It could have been Flood."

"I don't think so," said Troy Lee. "Tommy was tied up here—see the orange crap all over the restraints. And these were unlocked, not broken."

"Maybe when Blue let him go he killed her."

Troy Lee picked something off of Blue's face, as delicately as if he were taking her ghost. "Except for this."

He held a long red hair up where Lash could see it. "No reason for her to be here, if Flood was loose."

"Dude, you're like one of those *CSI* guys," Drew said.

"We should call those two homicide cops," Barry said, like he was the first who might have thought of it.

"And tell them to come help us with our dead hooker," Lash said.

"Well they know about the vampires," Barry said. "Maybe they'll help us."

"How 'bout we move her to your apartment, and then call them?"

"Well, what are we going to do with her?" Barry said, standing feet apart, hands behind his back, a brave Hobbit ready to face a dragon.

Troy Lee shrugged. "Wait until dark, then drop her in the Bay?"

"I can't bear to touch her," Barry said. "Not after the moments we shared."

"You little *putas*," Gustavo said, stepping up and beginning to roll up the bloodstained rug. He had a wife and five children, and although he had never disposed of a dead hooker before, he thought that it couldn't be any worse than changing the diaper on a gloopy infant.

The other Animals all looked at one another, embarrassed, until Gustavo growled at them and they jumped to move the heavy bed frame out of his way.

"I never really liked her that much, anyway," Barry said.

"She really did take advantage of us," Jeff said.

"I just went along with you guys so I didn't ruin the party," said Troy Lee. "I didn't enjoy even half of those blow jobs."

"Let's just put her in my closet until tonight, then a couple of us can sneak the bitch out to Hunter's Point and drop her off."

"On Christmas?" Drew asked.

"Can't believe she took all our money and now she's going to ruin Christmas," said Troy Lee.

"Our money!" said Lash. "That bitch!"

Nobody likes a dead whore.

. .

I do like a dead whore now and then," said the vampire Elijah Ben Sapir, derailing a perfectly good theme. He'd snapped the whore's neck right before she was completely drained so there would be a body. "But one doesn't want to be too obvious." He dragged the whore's body behind a Dumpster, and watched as the wounds on her neck healed over. He'd taken her in an alley near Tenth and Mission streets. He'd had the hood up on the oversized tracksuit he was wearing, so she'd been surprised when they'd ventured down the alley and he threw it back to reveal a very pale Semitic man.

"Look at-chew. Thought baby was a playa—" the whore had said, her last words. She'd only had a hundred dollars on her, which, along with the tracksuit and a pair of Nikes, were the complete resources the ancient vampire had at his disposal.

He'd come to the city in a yacht worth millions, filled with art worth millions more, and now he was reduced to making kills for petty cash. Of course he owned several homes around the world, and had stashes of cash put away in a dozen cities, but it would take some time to access it. And perhaps it wasn't so bad to have the wolf at the door, for a change. After all, he'd come to the City and taken a new fledgling in order to alleviate his boredom. (It's very hard to feel alive when you've been dead for eight hundred years.) And she had done that. He was not bored—and he felt very much alive.

He walked out of the alley and checked the sky. Dawn was threatening—he had perhaps twenty minutes until sunup. "Where does the time go?" He crossed the street and was buzzed into a hotel with a sign that read FOR RENT. BY HOUR, DAY, OR WEEK. He could smell the cigarettes, sweat, and heroin on the desk clerk, and he kept his head down so the hood covered his face.

"Do you have a room without a window?"

"Twenty-five bucks, like all the others," the clerk said. "You want sheets? Sheets are five more."

The vampire smiled. "No, I don't want to spoil myself."

He paid the clerk, took the key, and trudged up the steps. Yes, he felt very much alive. One really can't appreciate what one has until it's gone. And without a significant loss, how would one enjoy the process of revenge?

Our Dead Homeys

The vampires sat side by side on the bare futon frame, watching as a five-legged bug limped up the big front window of the loft.

Tommy thought that the rhythm of the bug's steps made for a danceable backbeat—thought he might be able to set music to it, if he knew how to write music. *Suite for Angst and Limping Bug,* he'd call it.

"Nice bug," Tommy said.

"Yeah," Jody said.

We should save it for Abby, Jody thought. She was feeling guilty about having bitten the girl—not so much because of the violation, because obviously the kid had been willing, but because she felt as if she really didn't have any choice. She had been injured and her predator nature told her to survive, whatever the cost, which is what bothered her. Was her humanity drifting away?

"The Animals are going to come for us now," Tommy said. He was feeling angry, betrayed by his old crew, but most of all he felt separate from them now. He felt separate from everyone. Tomorrow was Christmas and he didn't even want to call his parents because they were a different species now. What do you buy for an inferior species?

"It's just the Animals," Jody said. "We'll be safe."

"I'll bet that's what Elijah thought, too, and they got him."

"We should go get him," Jody said. She imagined Elijah Ben Sapir, standing in the full sun by the Ferry Building, tourists passing him, wondering why someone would put a statue there. Would the brass protect him?

Tommy checked his watch. "We'd never get there and back in time. I tried that yesterday."

"How could you do that to him, Tommy? He was one of us."

"One of us? He was going to kill us, if you remember. He kind of did kill us. I resent that. Besides, if you're covered in bronze, what does it matter if you're underwater? I was just trying to get him out of sight so we could think about our future without him being part of it."

"Right. Okay," Jody said. "Sorry." Future? She'd lived with a half-dozen guys, none had ever willingly talked about the future before. And she and Tommy had a supersized buttload of future ahead of them as long as someone didn't catch them sleeping. "Maybe we really should leave the City," she said. "No one would know about us in a new city."

"I was thinking we should get a Christmas tree," Tommy said.

Jody looked away from the bug. "That's a thought, or we could put some mistletoe up, put on Christmas carols, and stand outside waiting for Santa until the sun comes up and incinerates us. How's that sound?"

"Nobody appreciates your sarcasm, missy. I'm just trying to get a handle on normal. Three months ago I was stocking groceries in Indiana, looking at community college, driving around in my crappy car, wishing I had a girlfriend, and wishing that there was some potential for something to happen beyond getting a job with benefits and living the same life as my dad. Now I have a girlfriend, and superpowers, and a bunch of people want to kill me, and I don't know how to act. I don't know what to do next. And it's going to be that way forever. Forever! I'm going to be scared out of my mind forever! I can't deal with forever."

He'd been barking at her, but she resisted the urge to snap back. He was nineteen, not a hundred and fifty—he didn't even have the tools for being an adult, let alone being immortal. "I know," she said. "Tomorrow night, first thing, we'll hire a car, go get Elijah, and pick up a Christmas tree on the way back. How's that sound?"

"Hiring a car? That sounds exotic."

"It'll be like prom." Was she being too patronizing?

"You don't have to do that," he said. "I'm sorry I'm acting like a weenie."

"But you're my weenie," Jody said. "Take me to bed."

Still holding her hand, he stood, then pulled her up into his arms. "We'll be okay, right?"

She nodded and kissed him, feeling for just a second like a girl in love instead of a predator. She immediately felt a resurgence of shame over feeding on Abby.

The doorbell rang.

"Did you know we had a doorbell?"

"Nope."

"Y̶ou can't beat a dead whore in the morning," said Nick Cavuto cheerfully, because apparently, everyone loves a dead hooker, despite what certain writer types might think. They were standing in the alley off Mission Street.

Dorothy Chin—short, pretty, and whip-smart—snorted a laugh and checked the thermometer probe she'd stuck in the deceased's liver like a meat thermometer into a roast. "She hasn't been dead four hours, guys."

Rivera rubbed his temples and felt his bookstore slipping away, along with his marriage. He'd known the marriage had been going for a while, but he was feeling a little brokenhearted about the bookstore. He figured he knew, but he asked anyway. "Cause of death?"

"Toothy blow job," Cavuto said.

"Yes, Alphonse," said Dorothy with a tad too much sincerity, "I'd have to concur with Detective Cavuto, she died of a toothy blow job."

"It just pisses some guys off," Cavuto added, "a professional without skills."

"Guy just snapped her neck and took his money back," said Dorothy with a big grin.

"So a broken neck?" said Rivera, mentally waving good-bye to a whole set of first-edition Raymond Chandlers, ten-to-six workdays, golfing on Mondays.

Cavuto snorted this time. "Her head's turned around the wrong way, Rivera. What did you think it was?"

"Seriously," Dorothy Chin said, "I have to do the autopsy to be sure, but offhand that's the obvious cause. I'd also say she's probably lucky to go that way. She's HIV positive and it looks like the disease had developed into full-blown AIDS."

"How do you know that?"

"See these sarcomas on her feet."

Chin had removed one of the hooker's shoes—she pointed to open sores on the corpse's foot and ankle.

Rivera sighed. He didn't want to ask, but he asked anyway, "What about blood loss?"

Dorothy Chin had done the autopsies on two of the previous victims and cringed a little. It was a pattern. They'd all been terminally ill, they'd all died of a broken neck, and they'd all shown evidence of extreme blood loss, but no external wounds—not even a needle mark.

"Can't tell out here."

Cavuto had lost his cheery manner now. "So we spend Christmas day canvassing dirtbags to see if anyone saw anything?"

At the end of the alley, uniforms were still talking to the grimy homeless man who had called in the murder. He was trying to get them to spring for a bottle of whiskey—because it was Christmas. Rivera didn't want to go home, but he didn't want to spend a day trying to find out what he already knew. He checked his watch.

"What time was sunrise this morning?" he asked.

"Oh, wait," Cavuto said, patting down his pockets, "I'll check my almanac."

Dorothy Chin snorted again, then started giggling.

"Dr. Chin," Rivera said, tightening down now, "could you be more precise about the time of death?"

Chin picked up on Rivera's tone and went full professional. "Sure. There's an algorithm for the cooling time of a body. Get me the weather from last night, let me get her back to the morgue and weigh her, and I'll get you a time within ten minutes."

"What?" Cavuto said to Chin. "What?" This time to Rivera.

"Winter solstice, Nick," Rivera said. "Christmas was originally set at the winter solstice, the shortest day of the year. It's eleven-thirty now. I'm betting that four hours ago the sun was just coming up."

"Uh-huh," Cavuto said. "Prostitutes have shitty hours—is that what you're saying?"

Rivera raised an eyebrow. "Our guy didn't travel far after sunrise, is what I'm saying. He's going to be around here."

"I was afraid that's what you were saying," Cavuto said. "We're never going to get the bookstore open, are we?"

"Tell the uniforms to look anywhere it's dark: under Dumpsters, in crawl spaces, attics—anywhere."

"Getting warrants on Christmas day might be a problem."

"You won't need warrants if you get permission from the owners—we're not looking to bust anyone living here, we're looking for a murder suspect."

Cavuto pointed to the eight-story brick building that composed one wall of the alley. "This building has something like eight hundred ministorage units in it."

"Then you guys had better get started."

"Where're you going?"

"There was a missing person report on an old guy in North Beach a couple of days ago. I'm going to check it out."

"Because you don't want to go Dumpster diving for v—"

"Because," Rivera cut him off before he could say the V-word, "he had terminal cancer. His wife assumed he just wandered off and got lost. Now I'm not so sure. Call me if you find anything."

"Uh-huh." Cavuto turned to the three uniforms who were interviewing the bum. "Hey, guys, have I got a merry Christmas detail for you."

The Animals decided to hold a small memorial service for Blue in Chinatown. Troy Lee was already there, as was Lash, who wouldn't go home to his apartment until Blue's body was removed, and Barry, who was Jewish, would be coming there for dinner with his family, as was the tradition in his faith. Plus, the liquor stores in Chinatown were open on Christmas, and if you slipped some money under the counter, you could get firecrackers. The Animals were fairly sure that Blue would have wanted firecrackers at her funeral.

The Animals stood in a semicircle, beers in hand, on a playground off Grant Street. The deceased was being honored in absentia—in her place was a half-eaten pair of edible panties. From a distance, they looked like a bunch of wastrels mourning a Fruit Roll-Up.

"I'd like to start, if I may," said Drew. He wore a long overcoat and his hair was tied back with a black ribbon, revealing the target-shaped bruise on his forehead where Jody had hit him with the wine bottle. Out of his coat he pulled a bong the size of a tenor sax, and using a long lighter designed for lighting fireplaces, he sparked that magnificent mama-jama up and bubbled away like a scuba diver having an asthma attack. When he could hold no more, he raised the bong, poured some water on the ground, and croaked, "To Blue," which came out in a perfect smoke ring, the sight of which brought tears to everyone's eyes.

"To Blue," everyone repeated as they placed one hand on the bong and tipped a bit out of their beers.

"To Broo, my nigga," said Troy Lee's grandma, who had insisted upon joining the ceremony once she realized there would be firecrackers.

"She will be avenged," said Lash.

"And we'll get our fucking money back," said Jeff, the big jock.

"Amen," the Animals said.

They had decided on a nondenominational ceremony, as Barry was a Jew, Troy Lee was a Buddhist, Clint was an Evangelical, Drew was a Rastafarian, Gustavo was a Catholic, and Lash and Jeff were heathen stoners. Gustavo had been called in to work that day because someone had to be in the store as long as the front was only boarded up with plywood, so in deference to his beliefs, they had bought some incense and holders and placed a picket fence of smoldering joss sticks around the edible panty. The incense also worked within Troy and Grandma's Buddhist tradition, and Lash pointed out during the ceremony that although they have their differences otherwise, all gods like a good-smellin' ho.

"Amen!" said the Animals again.

"And they're handy for lightin' firecrackers off of," added Jeff as he bent over an incense stick and set a string cracking.

"Hallelujah!" said the Animals.

Each offered to share some kind of memory of Blue, but all of their stories quickly degenerated to orifices and squishiness, and no one wanted to go there in front of Troy's grandma, so instead they threw firecrackers at Clint while he read from the Twenty-third Psalm.

Before they cracked the second case of beer, it was decided that after dark, three of them—Lash, Troy Lee, and Barry—would take Bluc from Lash's apartment, load her into the back of Barry's station wagon, and take her out in the middle of the Bay in Barry's Zodiac. (Barry was the diver of the bunch, and had all the cool aquatic stuff. They'd used his spearguns to help take down the old vampire.)

Lash braced himself as he opened the apartment door, but to his surprise, there was no smell. He led Barry and Troy into the bedroom, and together they wrestled the rolled-up rug out of the closet.

"It's not heavy enough," Barry said.

"Oh shit, oh shit, oh shit," Troy said, trying furiously to unroll the rug.

Finally Lash reached down, grabbed the edge of the rug, and whipped it up over his head. There was a thudding sound against the far wall, followed by the jingle of metal, like coins settling.

The three Animals stood and stared.

"What are those?" Asked Barry.

"Earrings," answered Troy. Indeed, there were seven earrings settling on the hardwood floor.

"Not those. Those!" Barry nodded toward two clear, cantaloupe-sized, gelatinous lozenges that quivered on the floor like stranded jellyfish.

Lash shivered. "I've seen them before. My brother used to work in a plant in Santa Barbara that made them."

"What the fuck are they?" Said Troy, squinting through a drunken haze.

"Those are breast implants," Lash said.

"What are those wormy things?" asked Barry. There were two translucent sluglike blobs of something stuck to the rug near the edge.

"Looks like window caulk," said Lash. He noticed that there was a fine blue powder near the edge of the rug. He ran his hand over it, pinched some on his fingers, and sniffed it. Nothing.

"Where'd she go?" asked Barry.

"No idea," said Lash.

It's a Wonderful Life

Gustavo Chavez had been born the seventh child of a brick maker in a small village in the state of Michoacan, Mexico. At eighteen he married a local girl, the daughter of a farmer, herself a seventh child, and at twenty, with his second child on the way, he crossed the border into the United States, where he lived with a cousin in Oakland, along with a score of other relatives, and worked grueling, twelve-hour days as a laborer, making enough to feed himself and send more money home to his family than he could possibly have made in his father's brickyard. He did this because it was the responsible and right thing to do, and because he had been raised a good Catholic man who, like his father, would provide for his family and no more than two or three mistresses. Each year, about a month before Christmas, he would sneak back across the border to celebrate Christmas with his family, meet any new children that might have been born, and make love with his wife, Maria, until they were both so sore it hurt to walk. In fact, the vision of Maria's inviting thighs would often begin haunting him around Halloween and the hapless night porter would find himself in a state of semi-arousal as he swung his soapy mop, to and fro, across fifteen thousand square feet of linoleum every night.

Tonight he was in the store alone, and he was feeling far from aroused, for it was Christmas night, and he could not go to mass or take Communion until he confessed. He was feeling deeply ashamed. Christmas night and he hadn't even called Maria—hadn't spoken to her for weeks, because like the rest of the Animals, he had gone to Las Vegas, and had given all his money to the blue whore.

He had called, of course, after they'd first taken the vampire's art and sold it for so much money, but since then, his life had been a fog of tequila and marijuana and the evil attentions of the blue one. He, a good man, who cared for his family, had never hit his wife, had only cheated with a second cousin and never with a white woman, had been undone by the curse of the blue devil's pussy. *La maldición de la concha del diabla azul.*

This is the saddest, loneliest Christmas ever, thought Gustavo as he dragged his mop past the canvas doors leading into the produce-department cooler. *I am like the poor ca-*brón *in that book* The Pearl, *where by simply trying to take advantage of some good fortune, I have lost all that I care about. Okay, I did get drunk for a week and my* pearl *was a blue whore who fucked the* chimichangas *out of me, but still, pretty sad.* He thought these things in Spanish, so they sounded infinitely more tragic and romantic.

Then there came a noise from the cooler, and he was startled for a second. He wrung out his mop, so as to be ready for anything. He didn't like being in the store by himself, but with the front windows broken out, someone had to be here, and because he was far from home, had nowhere else to go, and the union would see that he was paid double time, Gustavo had volunteered. Perhaps if he sent home a little extra, Maria might forget the hundred thousand dollars he'd promised.

There, something was moving behind the plastic doors of the cooler, which were waving slightly. The stout Mexican crossed himself and backed out of the produce department, swinging his mop now in quick swaths, leaving barely a hint of dampness on the linoleum. He was by the dairy case now, and a stack of yogurts fell over inside the glass doors, as if someone had shoved them out of the way to look through.

Gustavo dropped the mop and ran to the back of the store, saying a Hail Mary peppered with swearwords as he went, wondering if those were footsteps he heard behind him, or the echoes of his own footfalls resounding through the deserted store.

Out the front door and away, he chanted in his head. *Out the front door and away.* He nearly fell rounding the turn at the meat case, his shoes still wet from the mop water. He caught himself on one hand and came up like a sprinter, while reaching back on his belt for his keys as he went.

There were footfalls behind him—light, slapping—bare feet on linoleum, but fast, and close. He couldn't stop to unlock the door when he got there, he couldn't look back, he couldn't turn to look—a second of hesitation and he would be lost. He exhaled a long wail and ran right through a rack of candy and gum by the registers. He tumbled over the first register in an avalanche of candy bars and magazines, many of which displayed headlines like I MARRIED BIGFOOT, or SPACE ALIEN CULT TAKES OVER HOLLYWOOD, or VAMPIRES HUNT OUR STREETS, and other such nonsense.

Gustavo scrambled out of the pile and was crawling on his belly like a desert lizard scrambling to get across hot sand, when a heavy weight came down on his back, knocking the air out of him. He gasped, trying to get his breath, but something grabbed him by the hair and yanked his head backwards. He heard crackling noises in his ear, smelled something like rotten meat, and gagged. He saw the fluorescent lights, some canned hams, and a very happy cardboard elf making cookies as he was dragged down the aisle and through the doors into the dark back room of the deli like so much lunch meat.

Feliz navidad.

Our first Christmas together," Jody said, kissing him on the cheek—giving his butt a little squeeze through his pj bottoms. "Did you get me something cute?"

"Hi, Mom," Tommy said into the phone. "It's Tommy."

"Tommy. Sweetheart. We've been calling all day. It just rang and rang. I thought you were going to come home for Christmas."

"Well, you know, Mom, I'm in management at the store now. Responsibilities."

"Are you working hard enough?"

"Oh yeah, Mom. I'm working ten—sixteen hours a day sometimes. Exhausted."

"Well good. And you have insurance?"

"The best, Mom. The best. I'm nearly bulletproof."

"Well, I suppose that's good. You're not still working that horrible night shift, are you?"

"Well, sort of. In the grocery business, that's where the money is."

"You need to get on the day shift. You're never going to meet a nice girl working those hours, son."

It was at this point, having heard Mother Flood's admonition, that Jody lifted her shirt and rubbed her bare breasts against him while batting her eyelashes coquettishly.

"But I have met a nice girl, Mom. Her name is Jody. She's studying to be a nun—er, teacher. She helps the poor."

It was then that Jody pantsed him, then ran into the bedroom giggling. He caught himself on the counter to keep from tumbling over.

"Whoa."

"What, son? What's the matter?"

"Nothing, nothing, Mom. I just had a little eggnog with the guys and started to feel it."

"You're not on the drugs, are you, honey?"

"No, no, no, nothing like that."

"Because your father has rehab benefits on you until you're twenty-one. We can have one of those interventions if you can find a cheap flight home. I know that Aunt Esther would love to see you, even if you are strung out on the crack."

"And I her, and I her, Mom. Look, I just called to say Merry Christmas, I'll let you—"

"Wait, honey, your father wants to say hi."

"—go."

"Hey, Skeeter. Frisco turned you into an ass bandit yet?"

"Hi, Dad. Merry Christmas."

"Glad you finally called. Your mother was worried sick about you."

"Well, you know, the grocery business."

"You working hard enough?"

"Trying. They're cutting back on our OT—union will only let us work sixty hours a week."

"Well, as long as you're trying. How's that old Volvo running?"

"Great. Like a top." The Volvo had burned to the wheels his first day in the City.

"Swiss sure can build some cars, can't they? Can't say much for those little red pocketknives they make, but sons-abitches can build a car."

"Swedes."

"Yeah, well, I love the little meatballs too. Look, kid,

your mother's got me deep-frying a turkey out in the driveway. It's starting to smoke a little. I probably oughta should
go check on it. Took an hour to get the oil up to speed—it's
only about ten degrees here today."

"Yeah, it's a little chilly here, too."

"Looks like it's starting to catch the carport on fire a
little. Better go."

"Okay. Love you, Dad."

"Call your mother more often, she worries. Holy cats,
there goes the Oldsmobile. Bye, son."

A half hour later they were sipping coffee laced with William's blood when the doorbell rang again. "This is getting
irritating," Jody said.

"Call your mom," Tommy said. "I'll get it."

"We should get some sleeping pills—knock him out so
he doesn't have to drink all that booze before we bleed
him."

The doorbell rang again.

"We just need to get him a key." Tommy went to the
console by the door and pushed the button. There was a
buzz and the click of the lock at street level. The door
opened—William coming in to settle on the stairs for the
night. "I don't know how he sleeps on those steps."

"He doesn't sleep. He passes out," said the undead redhead. "Do you think if we gave him peppermint schnapps
the coffee would have a minty holiday flavor?"

Tommy shrugged. He went to the door, threw it open, and called down. "William, you like peppermint schnapps?"

William raised a grimy eyebrow, looking suspicious. "You got something against scotch?"

"No, no, I don't want to mess up your discipline. I was just thinking of a more balanced diet. Food groups, you know."

"I had some soup and some beer today," William said.

"Okay then."

"Schnapps gives me mint farts. They scare the hell out of Chet."

Tommy turned to Jody and shook his head. "Sorry, no way, minty farts." Then to William again: "Okay then, William. I gotta get back to the little woman. You need anything? Food, blanket, toothbrush, a damp towelette to freshen up?"

"Nah, I'm good," William said. He held up a fifth of Johnny Walker Black.

"How's Chet doing?"

"Stressed. We just found out our friend Sammy got murdered in the hotel on Eleventh." Chet looked up the stairwell with sad kitty eyes, which he sort of always seemed to have since he'd been shaved.

"Sorry to hear that," Tommy said.

"Yeah, on Christmas, too," William said. "Hooker got killed across the street last night, same way. Neck was snapped. Sammy has been sick for a while, so he splurged on a room for the holiday. Fuckers killed him right there in bed. Just goes to show you."

Tommy had no idea what it meant to show you. "Sad," Tommy said. "So how come Chet's stressed but you're not?"

"Chet doesn't drink."

"Of course. Well then, Merry Christmas to you guys."

"You, too," said William, toasting with his bottle. "Any chance of a Christmas bonus, now that I'm a full-time employee?"

"What'd you have in mind?"

"I'd sure like a gander at Red's bare knockers."

Tommy turned to Jody, who was shaking her head, looking pretty determined.

"Sorry," Tommy said. "How about a new sweater for Chet?"

William scowled. "You just can't bargain with *The Man*." He took a drink from his bottle and turned away from Tommy as if he had something important to discuss with his huge shaved cat and couldn't be bothered with management.

"Okay then," Tommy said. He closed the door and returned to the counter. "I'm *The Man*," he said with a big grin.

"Your mom would be so proud," Jody said. "We need to go see about Elijah."

"Not until you call your mom. Besides, he's waited this long, it's not like he's going anywhere."

Jody got up and came around the breakfast bar and took Tommy's hand. "Sweetie, I need you to play what William just said back in your mind, really slowly."

"I know, I'm *The Man!*"

"No, the part about his friend being killed by a broken neck, and how he has been sick, and how someone else was killed the night before, also by broken neck. I'll bet she was sick, too. Sound like a pattern you've heard before?"

"Oh my God," Tommy said.

"Uh-huh," Jody said. She held his hand to her lips and kissed his knuckles. "I'll get my jacket while you fluff up your little brain for traveling, 'kay?"

"Oh my God, you'll do anything to get out of calling your mom."

Ladies and Gentlemen, Presenting the Disappointments

He was the best one-handed free-throw shooter in the Bay Area, and that Christmas night he had sunk sixty-four in a row in his driveway hoop, shooting the new leather Spaulding ball his dad had left under the tree for him. Sixty-seven in a row, without ever setting down or spilling his beer. His record was seventy-two, and he would have broken it, had he not been dragged off into the bushes to be slaughtered.

Jeff Murray was not the smartest of the Animals, nor the most well-born, but when it came to squandering potential, he was the hands-down winner. Jeff had been a star power forward through his sophomore, junior, and senior years in high school, and he had been offered a full-boat ride to Cal, Berkeley—there had even been talk of his going pro after a couple of years in college, but Jeff had decided to impress his prom date by showing her he had enough vertical leap to clear a moving car.

It was a minor misjudgment, and he would have cleared the car had he not drunk most of a case of beer before the attempt, and had the car's height not been eight inches enhanced by the light bar on the roof. The light bar just caught Jeff's left sneaker, and somersaulted him four times in the air before he landed upright in a James Brown split on the tarmac. He was pretty sure that his knee wasn't supposed to bend that way, and a team of doctors would later agree. He'd wear a brace forever and he'd never play competitive basketball again. Although he was a smokin' one-handed H.O.R.S.E. player, and he might have even been a champion if it weren't for that slaughtered-in-the-bushes thing.

He liked the new leather ball, and he knew he shouldn't be using it on the asphalt, and especially this late at night, when the sound of his dribbling might disturb his neighbors.

He lived in a garage apartment in Cow Hollow, and the fog was blowing in damp streams up his street, making the basketball sound lonely and ominous, so no one complained. It was Christmas—if all some poor bastard had was some hoops, then you'd have to be a special kind of heartless to call the cops on him. A car turned at the end of the street; blue halogens swept through the fog like sabers, then went out. Jeff squinted into the fog, but couldn't make out what kind of car it was, only that it had stopped a couple of doors down and it was a dark color.

He turned to take his record-breaking shot, but distracted, he put a little too much backspin on the ball and it jumped out of the hoop. He ran it down at the junipers by the garage, but was only able to tip it, so that it went into the bushes. He set his beer down on the driveway and went in after it, and—well, you know . . .

Francis Evelyn Stroud answered the phone on the second ring, as she always did, as it was proper to do. "Hello."

"Hi, Mom, It's Jody. Merry Christmas."

"And to you, darling. You're calling rather late."

"I know, Mom. I was going to call earlier, but had a thing." *I was a thing,* Jody thought.

"A thing? Of course. Did you get the package I sent?"

It would be expensive and completely inappropriate, a cashmere business suit, or something in a houndstooth or a herringbone, something worn only by matronly academics or matronly spies with stout poison-dart shoes. And Mother Stroud would have sent it to the old address. "Yes, I got it. It's lovely. I can't wait to wear it."

"I sent a leather-bound set of the complete works of Wallace Stegner," Mother Stroud said.

Fuck! Jody kicked at Tommy for making her call. He skipped out of range, waving a scolding finger at her.

Of course. Stegner, the Stanford paragon. Mother was one of the first coeds to graduate from Stanford and she never missed an opportunity to point out that Jody hadn't gone there. Jody's father had also gone to Stanford. She was born to Stanford, and yet she had disgraced them by going to

San Francisco State, and not finishing. "Yeah, those will be great, too. I guess they just haven't caught up with me yet."

"You've moved again?" Mrs. Stroud had lived in the same house in Carmel for thirty years. Carpet and draperies never survived more than two years, but she'd been in the same house.

"Yeah, we needed a little more space. Tommy's working at home now."

"We? Then you're still with that writer boy?"

Mom said "writer" like it was a fungus.

Jody scribbled on a Post-it at the counter: *Note: Break Tommy's arms off. Beat him with them.*

"Yes. I'm still with Tommy. He's been nominated for a Fulbright. So, did you have a nice Christmas?"

"It was fine. Your sister brought that man."

"Her *husband,* Bob, you mean?" Mother Stroud did not care for men since Jody's father had left her for a younger woman.

"Well, whatever his name is."

"It's Bob, Mom. He went to school with us. You've known him since he was nine."

"Well, I had a smoked turkey delivered, and a lovely foie-gras-and-wild-mushroom appetizer."

"You had Christmas catered?"

"Of course."

"Of course." Of course. Of course. It would never occur to her that by having Christmas dinner catered, she was making other people work on Christmas. "Well, I put my present in the mail, Mom. I'd better go. Tommy's being honored at a dinner tonight because of his massive intellect."

"On Christmas?"

Oh, what the fuck. "He's Jewish."

She could hear the intake of breath on the other end of the phone. *This is the light version, Mom, imagine how scandalized you be if I told you he was dead and that I killed him.*

"You didn't tell me that."

"Sure I did. You must be losing details. Gotta go, Mom. I gotta help Tommy get his penis piercing in before the dinner. Bye." She hung up.

Tommy had been dancing naked in front of her for most of the phone call. When she hung up he stopped. "Did I mention that I worry about your ethical equilibrium?"

"Said the guy who was just playing *buff the scrotum* with my red scarf while I was making the merry Christmas call to my mother?"

"Admit it. You're a little turned on."

Dr. Drew—Drew McComber, the Ohm-budsman, the resident pharmacist and medical adviser to the Animals, was afraid of the dark. The fear had crept up on him, like a hash brownie, and coldcocked him with an inescapable paranoia after four years on the night crew at the Marina Safeway. Thing was, he awoke in the evening, to the pervasive grow lights in his garage apartment in the Marina, then drove four blocks under the streetlights to the brightly lit Safeway, then got off work in the morning when the sun was well off the horizon, to return to his grow-lit apartment, to sleep with a satin mask in place. He encountered darkness so infrequently that it seemed like a menacing stranger when he did.

On Christmas night, round midnight, Drew sat among a jungle of five-foot-tall pot plants in his living room, wearing sunglasses and watching a movie on cable about the special relationship between the lady of an English manor and her chimney sweep. (Because of his work schedule, and the constant demand to stay wasted, Drew found it difficult to keep a girlfriend. Until the Animals found Blue, his sex life had been a largely solitary affair, and (sigh) apparently had become so once again.) Each time the chimney sweep's sooty hand smacked the powdered bottom of the lady of the manor, Drew grieved a little—that dusky handprint on alabaster flank falling like a shadow on his erotic soul. There was arousal, but no joy. Sad and lonely wood did tent his hemp-fiber cargo pants.

Then, as if scripted by *Erecto, the Generously Endowed Pizza Delivery God of Improbable Trysts,* there was a knock at Drew's door. Rather than answer the door directly, Drew adjusted himself and ambled through the ganja forest to a small video screen in his kitchenette—a video peephole. He'd installed it in the days before his doctor had given him the prescription that made him a quasilegal medical marijuana grower *(patient complains that reality harshes his mellow—prescribe 2 grams cannabis every three hours by inhalation, ingestion, or suppository).*

Sure enough, as if he had called in an order, the video screen revealed a pale but pretty blonde standing on his doorstep in a conservative blue cocktail dress and heels. She might have just come from a party or a dinner out—her hair was pinned up with tiny blue bows. She might have shown up to audition for the role of the lady of the manor.

Drew keyed the intercom. "Hi. Are you sure you have the right house?"

"I think so," said the girl. "I'm looking for Drew." She smiled into the camera. Perfect teeth.

"Jeez," Drew said, then realizing that he had said it aloud, he cleared his throat and said, "I'll be right there."

He smoothed his erection down, pushed his hair behind his ears, and in five long strides he was through the forest and at the front door. At the last second he remembered the sunglasses, pushed them up on his head, smiled broadly, and threw open the door, releasing a wide beam of ultraviolet light into the night fog.

The pretty blonde dropped her smile, then screamed as she burst into flames and leapt out of the light. Drew ran out into the dark to save her.

Being the Chronicles of Abby Normal:
Pathetic Nosferatu Noobsicle

Well, except for the murder, Christmas was like a slow drag over broken glass—I now truly know the ennui of passing eternity in total boredom—eating and hurling to-furky all day, stuck with Ronnie and Mom until like six, when Jared came over. His father has a fresh family with little crumb-snatcher stepsisters, so they like forget about him as soon as the squealing and presents start in the morning. He spent the whole day rewatching *The Nightmare Before Christmas* disc in his room and smoking cloves. His room is totally sacrosanct since he told his 'rents that he couldn't guarantee that he wouldn't be masturbating to gay porn if anyone came in. (He's so lucky sometimes—I could stand on my head and flick the bean right there at the dinner table and my mom would be all, "Honey, Christmas is family time, we should be together" and make me finish in front of everyone.)

So, we like watched *The Nightmare Before Christmas* disc with Mom and Ronnie until they fell asleep on the couch— then Jared and I drew some really cool tribal tattoos on Ronnie's shaved head with Magic Marker, but only like in red and black, so they look real.

Then he was all, "We should go get some coffee— my aunt gave me a hundred-dollar Starbucks gift card for Christmas."

And I hate it when people brag about their Christmas presents, because it's completely shallow and materialistic. So, I was all, "Yeah, well, I'd love to, but I am now one of the chosen, so I have duties."

And he was all, "No way, you're Jewish?"

And I was all, "No, I am nosferatu."

And he was all, "You are not."

And I was all, "Remember that sexylicious guy from Walgreens. It was him. Well, actually it's the Countess who brought me into the sacred circle of sanguinity."

And he was all, "You didn't even call me?"

"I'm sorry, Jared, but you are of an inferior species now."

So he goes, "I know, I totally suck."

And I know he's going to go all tragico-emo on me. So I say, "Buy me a Mochaccino and I'll reveal to you our dark ways and stuff."

We leave a note saying that Jared has impregnated me and we're running off together to join a satanic cult, so my mother won't panic when she wakes up, because she's totalitarian about leaving notes. Then we head to the SOMA.

But apparently, the entire fucking country shuts down on Christmas, slammed under the oppressive iron fist of the baby Jesus, so out of nine Starbucks we try, all are closed.

And Jared is all, "Take me to meet them. I want to be in the dark fold, too."

And I was all, "No way, loser, your hair is totally flat." Which it was. He only had the one spike in front, and his sculpting gel had like failed hours ago, so in his PVC raincoat, he kinda looked like a black lacquer coatrack like you see in Chinatown, but that wasn't why I couldn't take him to see the Countess and my Dark Lord. I just couldn't. I knew the Countess would freak out if she saw I was exploiting her exquisite gift to show off for a friend, so I was all, "It's very secret." But Jared started to pout and brood at the same time, which he can totally pull off because he practices, so I started to feel like a malodorous soupçon of mashed assholes, as Lautréamont so aptly put it. (*Shut up, Lily says it sounds more romantic in French*.)

So I let him come, but I told him he had to stay outside across the street. But when we came around the corner of the Dark Lord's block, there was a guy in a yellow tracksuit standing in the middle of the street. Just standing there, with his hood up and his head down, looking like he was going to stand there forever. And he turned really slow in our direction.

Jared was all, "*Wanksta rappa,*" in my ear, and he giggled that high-pitched little-girl giggle he does sometimes that's like violence catnip to other guys. (Which is why Jared has to carry a foot-long double-edged dagger in his boot, which he calls his Wolf-fang. Fortunately it doesn't give him any false confidence and he is still a total puss, but he likes the attention he gets when doormen take it away from him at clubs.)

Anyway, I think my vampyre senses were, like, on edge, because I could just tell that this wasn't your normal hip-hop guy standing in the middle of a deserted street in a three-hundred-dollar tracksuit at midnight on Christmas night, so I grabbed Jared's arm and pulled him back around the corner.

And I'm all, "Dude. Shields up. Creep. Stealth. Lowest profile."

So we peek around the corner, totally cloaked this time, and the tracksuit guy is like over by the door of the loft, and someone is coming out. It's the crusty old drunk guy with the huge shaved cat, and he has his unit out, like he's going to take a leak, which I could have gone another sixteen years without seeing. And Tracksuit grabs him like he's a rag doll and pulls his head back by the hair, and bites him on the neck. And when he does, I can see that it's not a hip-hop guy at all, but some crusty white vampyre, his fangs were like visible from space. So the huge cat guy is thrashing and screaming and spraying whiz all over the place and I can hear the huge cat hissing behind the door, and Jared grabs me by my messenger bag and starts pulling me away, down the street. So that's all I saw.

And Jared was all, "Whoa."

And I was all, "Yeah."

And as soon as we got a few blocks away, I pulled out my cell and called the Countess's cell, but it went right to voice mail. So now we're at a special midnight showing of *The Nightmare Before Christmas* at the Metreon, drinking a huge Diet Coke to calm our nerves while we wait for a return call from my vampyre coven. (Jared forgot his inhaler and has been gasping since we saw the attack. It's so embarrassing. People are like looking, and I've moved a couple of seats over so they won't think I'm giving him a hand job or something.) I am totally overcome with dread and foreboding, and the time passes like a seeping infection on a bad eyebrow piercing. So we wait. I wish we had some pot. More later.

Oh yeah, and Mom got me a green Care Bear for Christmas! I totally love it.

"You're sure this is where you left it?" Jody was looking up and down the Embarcadero. There were no people out on the street—the performers and hustlers were long gone. She could hear the Bay Bridge humming in the distance, a foghorn started to low over in Alameda. A BART train burped out of a tunnel onto the street a block away, headed toward the ballpark, empty. A police cruiser turning out of Market Street strafed them with its headlights before heading past the Ferry Building toward Fisherman's Wharf. Tommy waved to the cops.

"Yeah. I was right here and my watch went off. He weighed a ton. It would have taken a bunch of guys to move him."

Jody saw something shining on the bricks near her feet and crouched down to touch the source. Metal filings of some sort. She licked her finger and came up with a coating of yellowish metallic particles on her fingertip. "Unless someone cut it up."

"Who would do that? Who would cut a statue up and steal the pieces?"

"Doesn't matter. Maybe thieves, maybe city workers. If someone cut that bronze shell, one of two things happened. If it was daytime, Elijah fried out here in the sun. If it was dark, he's free."

"It wasn't light, was it?"

Jody shook her head. "I'm guessing no." She saw a light pattern among the bricks a few steps away and crouched down again. There was a fine, grayish powder between the bricks. She pinched some between her fingers and shook her head. "For sure no."

"What? What is that?"

She brushed her finger off on her jeans and dug into her jacket pocket. "Tommy, remember I told you that you didn't drink the whore dry because she wouldn't have been there if you had?"

"Yeah."

"Well, that's because when a vampire drains someone—when *we* drain someone, they turn to a fine gray powder.

I can't explain why, but it looks like that. Feels like that."
She pointed to the mortar lines between the bricks.

Tommy knelt down and touched the powder, looked
up. "How do you know that?"

"You know how I know that?"

"You've killed people."

She shrugged. "Just a couple. And they were sick. Terminal. They were asking for it, sort of."

"So that's why you weren't upset about the hooker?"

She pulled her cell phone out of her jacket pocket, then
held it behind her back and twisted back and forth looking
at her feet, like a little girl being interrogated about how
Mommy's lamp got broken. "Are you mad?"

"I'm a little disappointed."

"Really? I'm really sorry. You would have done the same
thing if you'd been there."

"I'm just disappointed that you didn't feel that you could
trust me."

"You were having a hard time with your change. I didn't
want to bother you."

"But it wasn't sexual or anything, right?"

"Absolutely not. Purely nutritional." She didn't think it
necessary to tell him about kissing the old man. It would
just confuse things.

"Well, I guess it's okay, then. I guess if you had to."

He stood and she ran to him and kissed him. "I can't tell
you how glad I am to have that off my chest."

"Yeah, well . . ."

"Hang on." She held up a finger and hit the power button on her phone.

"Calling your mom to tell her she was right about your being a tramp?"

"I'm calling the kid."

"Abby?"

"Yeah. I need to tell her to stay away from our place. Elijah is going to start messing with us like before."

Jody watched as the little icons on her phone showed that it was searching for a signal. "But she said she wasn't coming by tonight. It's Christmas."

"I know she said that, but I think she may come by anyway."

"Why?"

"Well, she has a thing for me, I think. I bit her last night."

"You bit Abby?"

"Yeah. I told you, I was hurt. I needed—"

"God, you're such a blood slut."

"I knew you'd be mad."

"Well, it's Abby, for fuck's sake. I'm her dark lord."

"Look, a voice mail."

Elijah Ben Sapir cast the twitching, pee-spraying alcoholic across the street, where he bounced off the metal garage door of the foundry and back out to the curb, where his head knocked the side mirror off an illegally parked Mazda.

Then the vampire walked with exaggerated steps, his arms held out from his sides like a bad stage monster to try to keep the urine-sotted velour fabric of his tracksuit from contacting his skin. Although he had experienced all manner of filth and gore in his eight hundred years, and had, in fact, spent whole days hiding naked under loamy soil to escape the sun, he didn't remember being quite so put off as he was at being pissed on by his lunch. Perhaps it was that he only had one set of clothes now, and there was no luxurious yacht with a full wardrobe to retire to, or perhaps it was that he had spent the day between two urine-stained mattresses under an unconscious junkie while police searched the hotel around him. He'd just hit his limit, that's all.

He'd known the desk clerk would give him up to the police, so as soon as he had gone to his room, the vampire had hidden his tracksuit in the corner of the closet, gone to mist, then slipped under the door into the next room and in between the mattress and box springs of a semiconscious junkie. He'd gone back to solid just as sunrise put him out for the day.

At sundown, he was surprised at how elated he was to find the tracksuit still in the closet, after he fed off the junkie (just a sip) and snapped his neck. (Leaving more or less a greeting card to the homicide inspectors who had attacked him with the others at the yacht club.) Now his precious tracksuit was all covered in whiz and he was furious.

He stalked over to where he'd thrown the bum and snatched him up by the ankle. Elijah was not tall by modern standards, but he found that if he held the bum's ankle high above his head, he could shake him sufficiently to get the job done.

"You're not even her minion, are you?" Elijah banged the bum's head against the sidewalk to punctuate his question.

"Please," said the bum. "My huge cat—"

Thud, thud, thud on the sidewalk. A little shake. Change, a few bills, a lighter, and a bottle of Johnny Walker rained out of the bum's pockets.

"You're just her little moo cow, aren't you? I tasted her on you."

"There's a kid," said the moo cow. "A spooky little girl. She takes care of them."

"Them?"

Elijah flung the bum against the garage and proceeded to pick up the change and the bills on the sidewalk. The steel door next to the garage door opened and a burly bald man in overalls stepped out on the sidewalk, smacking a lead-tipped tire thumper on his palm. "You motherfuckers making enough noise out here?"

Elijah bared his fangs and hissed at the biker, then leapt to the wall over the garage door and clung there, facedown, above the biker's head.

The biker looked up at the vampire, down at the prostrate bum, then at the damaged Mazda. "Well, okay then," he said. "I can see you fellas still have some shit to work out." He slipped back into the foundry and slammed the door.

Elijah dropped to his feet and headed up the street, not

even bothering to stop to snap the moo cow's neck. How could he have been so stupid? He wasn't going to terrorize her by killing a food source. He needed to threaten her minion, just as he had with the boy. How could he have known that she'd actually betray him and choose the boy? Turn the boy? It wouldn't happen again.

Amid all the anger, the hunger, and the excitement at having a purpose, Elijah Ben Sapir felt a twinge of heartache. He had begun this adventure thinking himself the puppet master; now he was all entangled in the strings. Making mistakes.

No worry. He cocked his head and focused. Past the rasping breath of the moo cow, the buildings settling, the Bay Bridge humming, and a thousand hearts beating in the lofts around him, he could hear the retreating steps of the little girl and her friend.

Being the Chronicles of Abby Normal: The Hunted

Apparently I am the Hunted, which, I want to note here, I am totally not qualified for. Here I sit, perched in the rafters (I think these things are rafters) of the Oakland Bay Bridge like a crippled night bird, waiting for doom to descend on me in the form of an ancient, undead thing, to wrench the very limbs from my delicate body. So that sucks.

Fortunately I have some sustenance until my Dark Lord and Lady rise from their diurnal slumber to kick some fucking ass. I know I should be eating bugs and spiders and stuff to facilitate my vampyrism, but as a vegetarian, I haven't developed the hunting skills, so I've started with some Gummi Bears I got at the theater. (Supposedly they are made out of beef pectin or extract of horse hooves or something, so I think they make a good transition to the nosferatu diet. And I like biting off their tiny heads.)

Here, high above the City—well, actually, we're about

ten feet above some homeless people who live under the bridge—I feel like the guardian of an ancient tomb, willing to face any attacker to protect my master and mistress, who are wrapped in tarps, lying on the next beam or rafter or whatever.

OMFG, there are fucking pigeons everywhere! Sorry, one just pooped on my notebook. Never mind. Move along. I'm over it. But ewwww!

Jared has gone to his dad's house in the Noe Valley to get the lawn cart and minivan so we can transport my masters to safety. He left me his dagger, which I've only had to brandish once, against a woman who wanted to take the tarp from over my Dark Lord. Then I used it to scrape off my old nail polish, which was totally chipped and stuff from doing minion manual labor.

So, my masters like met up with us outside the Museum of Modern Art and they were all, "Are you okay? Did he hurt you?" And they were being all secretive around Jared, like he didn't know we were vampyres. And I was all, "Just chill, he's assistant minion." So they relaxed.

Then Flood pulls this bronze hand out of his bag and he's all, "Abby, do you know what this is?"

And I was all, "Why yes, Lord Flood," because I speak *obvious* as a second language. "It's a bronze hand, correct?"

So the Countess took the hand from him. "Abby, this is what's left of the shell of the vampyre who turned me."

So I'm all, "Begging your pardon and whatnot, Countess, but that's a statue hand."

And she's all, "That's what I'm saying." Which is not what the fuck she was saying at all.

So it turns out that the bronze statue that used to be in the loft was actually the vampyre who turned the Countess, and then the Countess turned the vampyre Flood, except he was just Flood then. So the old vampyre, whose name is Elijah, got all PMS and started fucking with the Countess by leaving dead bodies all over town with evidence pointing toward her, and threatening to kill her minion, who was Flood at the time, and it got completely out of hand, with some cops and the geeks from the Safeway blowing up Elijah's yacht and really pissing him off, and then the Countess pretending to save Elijah when in fact she was extracting his ancient vampyry secrets, and Flood bronzing them both, but letting the Countess out because she is the love of his life and whatnot. So Flood, who is not a mysterious and ancient creature of the night at all, but has been a vampyre like a week longer than I have, took the statue down to the waterfront to drop it in the Bay, so it wouldn't remind the Countess of her heart being torn asunder by the yearning for two lovers and stuff. But the sun came up and Flood left the statue on the Embarcadero, and when they went back it was gone, and it turns out that Elijah is loose and he was the crusty vampyre in the yellow tracksuit I saw shaking the huge cat guy and he is now stalking me to get back at the Countess for being a duplicitous ho.

So Jared was all, "Fuck. That's awesome."

And I was all, "You lied to me."

And the Countess was all, "Yeah, sunshine, that's why I'm telling you this now." Which was completely unnecessary sarcasm on her part.

And Jared was like, "This is the best Christmas ever."

And I was all, "Shut up, gay-bait. I've been betrayed."

And the Countess was all, "You'll get over it. We have to go see if William is okay."

And I see now that she was right, but I brooded as we went back to the loft, just to make a point, because I hate it when people take me for granted. When we got to the Countess's block, there was an ambulance there and cops all over the place, so Flood and the Countess hung back and sent me over to get the 411. I could see that the huge cat guy was on a stretcher and they were strapping oxygen on him.

And I was all, "Let me through, this man is my father."

And the EMTs were all, "No way."

And I was all, "Who called you, anyway?"

And they were like, "The guy in the building. A sculptor or something."

And then the cat guy was all, "Let her through."

So they let me through.

So I blew by the EMT to the huge cat guy, and I was all, "Are you okay?"

And he was like, "Well, my head hurts like hell, and I think my leg is broke."

And I was all, "Is there anything I can do?" Because I was under orders of the Countess to gain information and offer assistance.

And he was like, "If you could take care of Chet. He's in the stairwell. He'll be hungry."

And I was all, "You got it."

So then he like pulled the oxygen mask off and had me bend over so he could whisper, and I was all, "Yes, Dad," for the EMTs who were watching.

And he whispered like, "Before they take me away, could I see your tits."

So I kicked him in the ribs. And the EMTs went all by-zerk and shit, and told me to get away, but they were totally overreacting, because I had on my red Converse All Stars, which will hardly even bruise you.

So they loaded him into the ambulance, and just as they were shutting the doors, he reached out his hand, like he was a drowning man reaching for the last spark of his mortality before the inky waves of death swept him away—so I flashed my boobs for him, just a quick lift of my bra and top at the same time, because I don't think we do enough to help the homeless, and I wanted him to die a happy man. And besides, they're small and I don't get that many requests.

So I got Chet out of the stairway of the old loft and was carrying him kid-style when I saw the two cops from before—the ones the Countess said helped blow up Elijah—so I went up to the Hispano-cop and I was all, "So, what's up, cop?"

And he was all, "You need to get home, and you have no business out at this hour, and we should take you to the station and call your parents and blah, blah, blah, threat,

threat, disapproval, and fascist dogma all up in your darkly delicious grille." (I'm paraphrasing. Although I do have a delicious grille as I had to wear braces for three years when I was a kid, and now my teeth are like my most acceptable feature. I hope my fangs come in straight.)

And the big gay cop was all, "What are you doing here?"

And I was all, "I live here, bone-smoker, what are you doing here? Aren't you guys homicide cops?"

And he was all, "Let's see some ID blah, blah, bluster, bluster, Oh My God I am so full of shit."

And I was like, "I guess you wouldn't have to deal with this shit if you had properly blowed up that old vampyre when you stole his art collection."

So all of a sudden the Hispano-cop and his big gay partner were all, "Whaaa—?"

And I'm like, "Just so we know where we stand. How long you bitches going to be here?"

And they were like, "Just a half hour or so longer, miss. We need to interview some witnesses and go clean out our boxers where we have just completely shit ourselves. Do you need a ride somewhere?" (Again paraphrasing.)

So I walked off, while they were still stunned, let Chet into the new loft down the street like it was mine, then ran around the block and reported to the Countess and Flood. Jared was just staring at them like he was hypnotized or something. I was like, "Hey, Boo," to remind him what a tard he was being and Jared snapped out. (Lily and Jared and I watched the *To Kill a Mockingbird* DVD like six times together and our favorite part is when Scout sees Boo Radley behind the door and goes, "Hey, Boo." It's like thanking the universe for sending you a benevolent retard to help you out, which is how I often feel about Jared.) So I was like, "Buy me a coffee." And the Countess and Flood look at each other and shake their heads. No money.

So I was like, "You guys are so fucking lame. You have piles of cash and you roll with no money. You are no longer the Dark Lord and Lady of me." Which I totally didn't mean, but I was stressed and starting to get a low-on-caffeine headache. But Jared goes, "Hey, Boo" at me, and he's holding a ten-dollar bill. And I pretended to find a snag in my fishnets so everyone would quit looking at me.

The Countess said she knew of a Chinese diner off Fremont Street that was open all night on Christmas and we could hang out there until the cops left. Jared and I had cups of coffee and an order of fries, which FYI, taste a little like shrimp in a Chinese diner. And Flood and the Countess are watching us, looking all sad. So I'm like, "What? What? What?"

And the Countess is all, "Nothing."

Which I know is totally something, because I say it all the time. And I watch her eyes follow Jared's cup as he sips his coffee and I'm all, "Oh, fucksocks, Countess, cowboy the fuck up, would you?" Then I slipped Jared's dagger out of his boot, grabbed his hand, and poked him in the thumb.

I'd like to say right here that the screaming was totally unnecessary. And whatever the Chinese guy was saying at me from behind the counter was a total overreaction and how does he expect me to understand him when he's talking that fast AND in Chinese? Anyway, after I squeezed Jared's thumb into his cup, then a little into my own and gave it to Flood, everyone calmed down, even the Chinese guy after Jared paid him for two more coffees—and the meeting of the Immortal SOMA Drama Queens officially came to order.

It seemed like we waited forever, and the Countess and Flood wouldn't answer any of my questions about the *way of the nosferatu*. It was like they had no idea what they were doing. Like last year I took Advanced Foods class (which is like cooking for nerds) after lunch, and so I usually took a nap. Which was fine, because I'm not even thrilled about regular foods, so, you know, what do I need with like advanced digital HD wi-fi foods and whatnot—so I took the course pass-fail and slept. But then, at the end of the semester, my mom springs this trap on me, like—"Oh, Allison, I've bought ingredients and you can prepare dinner for Ronnie and me to show what you learned in your Advanced Foods class. It'll be fun."

You can pretty much bet that anytime Mom uses the phrase "it'll be fun," she is about to drive a stake in fun's heart so that it may never rise again. Which is what happened. Artichokes? Who eats something like that? I thought it was a weapon.

So anyway, after nine eternities in the diner, we went back to the loft, where the Countess said she had my Christmas present waiting. When we got to the block, the cops and EMTs were gone and it looked like the coast was clear, but when the Countess opened the security door to the loft, there, sitting on the steps, was the old vampyre, naked.

Well, the Countess and Flood jumped about eighteen feet in the air and I'm pretty sure I peed a little. Yes, I definitely peed. Jared just started an asthma attack, not the whole attack, just the first gasp. He just stopped breathing after that.

So Elijah is all, "I needed to do some laundry."

Let me say right here, if I haven't made it clear, that I have seen as many pale, naked old-man parts in the last twenty-four hours to bruise my delicate psyche for a lifetime, so don't be surprised if you someday find me wandering the moors at midnight, a crazed look in my eye, babbling about albino Tater Tots nesting in Brillo pads and being pursued by sagging man ass, because that shit can happen when you've been traumatized.

Then Flood threw himself against the door and screamed for us to run as he bravely held the door against our ancient vampyre ancestor's assaults. I was beginning to doubt Flood's ability to fulfill his duties as my Dark Lord until he stepped up and saved us—valiant vampyre hero that he is—because I was starting to think he was just a geek with a passing knowledge of poetry.

As we ran I could hear Elijah saying, "He peed on my tracksuit," as he threw himself against the door, or I guessed he did, because I didn't turn around until we were two blocks away.

The Countess was all, "I've got to go back for him." But before she even turned around, my Dark Lord came running around the corner.

And he was all, "Go, go, go!" waving at us.

And we were all, "Where? Where? Where?"

And then as the Countess threw her arms around Flood and started to squeeze the bejeezus out of him, and Jared was all, "Gasp, get a room, gasp," her watch started beeping. Then Flood's watch was beeping, too. And they were all, "Uh-oh."

So we had like ten minutes to find someplace dark to hide them, and no one had any money for a hotel, even if we had the time to check in and whatnot. So they ran toward a big construction site under the Bay Bridge. And I was thinking, *I do not want to bury my masters in the construction site. What if they got paved?* It would totally freak them out to get paved.

And the Countess was all, "How did you get away?"

And the vampyre Flood was all, "The dryer buzzer went off."

And she was all, "He let you live because his laundry was done?"

And Flood goes, "Lucky, huh?" Totally not out of breath, even with the running.

So when we got to the construction site, everything was either open or would be when everyone came to work. And the Countess looked up into the rafters or whatever of the bridge and goes, "There."

So there is where we went. I grabbed some tarps that were covering this generator thing by the construction site and Jared and I climbed up into the rafters with our vampyre sires and helped tuck them in just in time for them to go out.

But as it got lighter, and we saw all the homeless people around, Jared and I realized that our masters would not be safe here when all the homeless people who lived under the bridge noticed the tarps and our delicate youth or smelled my Gummi Bears and came after us. So Jared went to get the garden cart, some trash bags and duct tape, and hopefully his stepmom's minivan so we can move our masters to a safer realm.

Oh, check it, before the Countess passed into the inky sleep of the undead, I was like, "So what did you get me for Christmas?"

And she was all, "Ten thousand dollars."

And I was like, "I didn't get you guys anything."

And she was like, "That's okay. You are our most special favorite minion and it's all good."

Which is why I love her and will guard her to the death. Then she like kissed the vampyre Flood and passed out. I'm sure their love will span the ages, if Jared and I don't fuck up and fry them during transport.

OMG! I just remembered, we forgot to feed Chet!

The Half-Life of American Cheese

The Cheddar Princess of Fond du Lac was toasted. It wasn't just the bursting into flames that had crispied her up more than somewhat physically, it was that Drew's blood tasted like bong water, and she was still a little mentally baked from feeding on him. She'd made the mistake of trying to get the taste out of her mouth with some orange juice and had been rewarded with five minutes of the dry heaves.

She brushed at her arms and great black flakes of burned skin came away, revealing fresh, unscarred skin below. Drew's blood was healing her, but it appeared that the process was going to take time and, like life in general, was going to be messy.

Maybe a bath.

She padded naked into the bathroom, which was done all in slabs of granite and green glass, and ran her bath. While the tub filled, she picked the last few burned tatters of her dress away from her skin and dropped them into the toilet. There was a swath of gray dust across the black tile, the remains of the original owner, and she was tracking him all over the bathroom and bedroom suite, so she stopped to sweep him into the corner with a towel. That had sort of been a surprise (in what was turning out to be a long line of surprises) when her first victim had disintegrated in her arms two nights ago, just as she was getting the hang of blood drinking.

"Oops."

He had been so nice, too. Had picked her up in his Mercedes not two minutes after she'd stumbled out of Lash's apartment building wearing nothing but a leather bustier and thigh-high platform boots. It wasn't the first time she'd been on the street with her ass hanging out—that wasn't what had thrown her. It was waking up feeling like her tits were on fire to see her body rejecting the giant silicone globes she had spent so much money having implanted. Even as she tried to push them back in with her hands, the implants pushed through her skin, opening her up like they were aliens hatching out of her. She screamed as they broke through and rolled to the floor, then lay there, quivering on the carpet. As she watched, her skin mended, her breasts tightened and lifted, the pain had turned to a tingling, but now she felt a squirming in her face—her lips specifically, and she wiped her mouth and came away with two sluglike lines of silicone that had been injected years ago. It was only then, in looking at the grotesque globs of lip filler on her hand, that Blue realized she wasn't blue at all. Her palms were baby white. Her arms, her legs—she ran to the bathroom and looked in the mirror. An old familiar stranger looked back at her—the Cheddar Princess of Fond du Lac. She hadn't seen this person since high school; the milky-white skin, hair almost white blond, still in the severe cut of the blue call girl, but looking somewhat like a pageboy cut now. Even the tattoos she'd had done in her early days in Vegas were gone.

I'm alive, she thought. Then: *And I'm going to be alive forever.* Then: *And I'm going to need some fucking money.*

She ran to Lash's bedroom to where she'd left her makeup case. It was gone. Her money was gone!

She ran out of the apartment and down the steps like she might see a green trail of bills blowing in the wind in the direction her money had escaped, but once on the street, she headed for the only place she knew, toward the Marina Safeway. She got half a block before the Mercedes pulled up and the electric window rolled down.

"Hey, you need a ride? It's a little chilly out here for that outfit."

His name had been David, and he did something that had to do with moving money around. Whatever it was, it must have paid well. He was wearing a two-thousand-dollar suit and his penthouse apartment on Russian Hill looked out on Golden Gate Bridge and the massive dome at the Palace of Fine Arts.

He'd given her his coat to wear up in the elevator. It was in the elevator that the hunger had come upon her. Poor David. They hadn't even talked price before she'd had him bent over the green glass vanity in the bathroom, drinking his life away.

"Oops." The difference, she realized, between what had happened to her and what had happened to David had been the bloody kiss she'd taken from Tommy. But for a kiss, she, too, would be a pile of dust. *There should be a song like that,* she thought. At least she'd learned before she took her victims.

Now she swept the last of David into the corner, then scraped him up with a piece of cardboard from his shirt drawer and dumped him into the wastebasket. Then she slipped into the tub full of bubbles and began to scrub off her charred skin.

She wouldn't be able to stay long. David had been married or had a girlfriend. Blue had found a whole closet full of women's clothes—expensive clothes, and the woman would probably be back. Of course, this would make a great base of operations, maybe she could just wait for the wife to return and sweep her into the wastebasket with David.

Blue leaned back and closed her eyes, listened to the bubbles popping, the wires humming through the building, the traffic out on the streets, to fishing boats leaving the wharf—then a sudden intake of breath from the living room, then another, deeper gasp as the second one found life, then a long man-scream. The dead Animals she'd collected were coming back to life.

"Sit tight, boys," Blue said. "Mama's just going to get cleaned up and put on a new dress, then we'll go get you something to eat and pick up my money."

She ran a sponge over her arm and smiled. She really could be Snow White now. *One dwarf at a time,* she thought.

Elijah Ben Sapir had roamed the planet for eight hundred and seventeen years. In that time he had seen empires rise and fall, miracles and massacres, ages of ignorance and ages of enlightenment: the full spectrum of mankind's cruelty and kindness. He had seen all manner of freakishness, from the perversions of nature to the perversions of mind, twisted, beautiful, terrifying: he thought he had seen it all. But for all of his years, and all the acuity of perception enabled by his vampire senses, he had never seen a huge shaved cat in a red sweater, and sitting there in his newly washed yellow tracksuit, still warm from the dryer and smelling of soap and fabric softener, he smiled.

"Hey, kitty," the old vampire said.

The huge cat eyed him suspiciously from across the loft. The cat could sense that he was a predator, just as Elijah could sense that the cat had been prey to a vampire. Kitty treat.

"I'm not going to eat you, kitty. I've fed quite enough."

It was true. Elijah was feeling a little bloated from trying to keep the body count up. Perhaps he should just kill the next few, not feed. But no, the police wouldn't know it was a vampire then, and there'd be no joy in terrorizing the fledgling. He just wasn't ready to feed yet. There was someone in the stairwell right now, he could hear her breathing and smell patchouli and clove cigarette odor wafting under the door. *Soon enough,* he thought.

"Perhaps we'll find something for you to eat, hey, kitty?"

Elijah vaulted off the bar stool and began opening cupboards. In the third one he found pouches of Tender Vittles. He took a bowl from the cupboard that looked as if it had never been used, dumped in the meatish nuggets, and shook them around.

"Come, kitty."

Chet padded a few steps toward the kitchenette, then stopped. Elijah put the bowl down and stepped away. "I understand, kitty. I don't like to eat in front of witnesses either. But sometimes—"

The vampire heard a car pull up outside, a car that hadn't been tuned in a while. He cocked his head and listened as the doors opened and slammed. Four got out. He heard their steps on the concrete, a female voice, hissing at the other three. In an instant he was at the window looking down, and in spite of himself, he smiled again. There was no vivid life aura around the four down on the sidewalk. No healthy pink glow, no black shadow of death. The visitors below were not human.

Vampires. On one hand, an indication of an enormous problem—one that just might attract attention that he could ill afford—but on the other, exciting in a way that he hadn't felt in a hundred years.

"Four against one. Oh my, kitty, how ever will I prevail?"

The old vampire ran his tongue over his fangs. For all the rage, frustration, and discomfort he'd endured since choosing the redhead as his fledgling, he was, for the first time in decades, not bored. He was having the time of his very long life.

"Killing time, kitty," he said, slipping into a pair of Tommy's Nikes.

Jody awoke to the smell of clove cigarettes and the crunching of Cheese Newts. There was music screeching, too—a whiny guy singing about some girl named Ligeia, who apparently he missed a great deal because he was talking about dragging her worm-worn corpse from the earth and caressing her cheek on a cliff above the sea before throwing himself off, with her in his arms. The singer sounded a little down, and like he could have used a throat lozenge.

She opened her eyes and was initially blinded until she adjusted to the black light, then she yelped. Jared White Wolf was sitting on the bed about two feet away from her, shoving handfuls of crunchy Cheese Newts into his mouth. There was a brown rat on his shoulder.

"Hi." Newt crumbs sprayed and fluoresced on the black sheets and clothing.

"Hi," Jody said, turning her head to avoid the crumbs.

"This is my room. Do you like it?"

Jody looked around, for once not really that thrilled with her vampire night-vision abilities. There were disturbing stains glowing on the sheets, and almost everything else in the room was black with a patina of vibrant blacklightenhanced dust or lint—there was even lint on the rat.

"It's swell," she said. *Interesting,* she thought. She was no longer afraid of gang members and street criminals, and would even throw down with an eight-hundred-year-old vampire if need be, but rodents still sort of gave her the willies. The rat's eyes were glowing silver in the black light.

"This is Lucifer Two." Jared scooped the animal off his shoulder and held him out.

Despite an attempt at self-control, Jody climbed backwards halfway up the wall, shredding a Marilyn Manson poster with her nails in the process.

"Lucifer One went on to his dark reward when I tried to dye him black."

"Sad," Jody said.

"Yeah." Jared turned the rat and rubbed noses with him. "I was hoping we could turn him to nosferatu when you bring Abby and me into the fold."

"Yeah, sure, that'll happen. Why am I in your room, Jared?"

"It was the only place we could think to bring you. It wasn't safe under the bridge. Abby had to go, so I'm in charge."

"Good for you. Where's Tommy?"

"Under the bed."

She would have known that—would have heard him breathing if the music wasn't cranked up to coffin-splitting volume.

"Could you turn the music down a little, please?"

" 'Kay," Jared said. He tucked Lucifer Two in his pocket and spidered across the bed, getting a little tangled in his black duster, then rolled to the floor and across the room in a commando-under-fire move until he got to the stereo, where he twisted the dial, putting the keening Emo singer out of his misery, or at least shutting him the fuck up.

"Where are we?" Tommy's voice from under the bed. "It smells like gym socks stuffed with ground-up hippies."

"We're in Jared's room," Jody said. She let a hand drop off the edge of the bed. Tommy took it and she pulled him out. He was still partially wrapped in duct tape and garbage bags.

"Was I a hostage again?"

"We had to cover you up to keep you from burning in the sun."

"Well, thanks."

Tommy looked at Jody, who shrugged.

"I was unwrapped when I woke up," she said.

"That's because Abby says you're the Alpha vamp. Do you guys want to play Xbox or watch a DVD? I have *The Crow Special Collector's Edition.*"

"Gee," Jody said, "that would be great, Jared, but we'd better be going."

Tommy had already picked up the Xbox controller, but set it down with marked disapproval, as if he'd notice a little botulism there on the trigger button.

"Oh, you can't go until the 'rents go to bed." Jared giggled, high and girlish. "The door is right by where they watch TV."

"We'll go out a window," Jody said.

Jared giggled again, then snorted a little, then started to honk, then took a hit from the inhaler that hung around his neck before he went on. "There's no window. This basement is totally windowless. Like we've been walled up in here with our own grotesque despair. Isn't it sweet?"

"We could go to mist," Tommy said. "Go out under the door."

"That would be so cool," Jared said, "but my dad put rubber gaskets around the door to contain my disgusting Goth stench. That's what he calls it: my 'disgusting Goth stench.' Although I don't think I'm really Goth, more like death punk. He just doesn't like cloves. Or pot. Or patchouli. Or gay people."

"Philistine," Tommy said.

"Oh, would you guys like some Cheese Newts?" Jared picked the box up off the floor and held it out. "I can open a vein on them if you need me to." He waved the thumb Abby had stabbed to prepare their coffee the night before, now wrapped in a ragged ball of gauze and medical tape the size of a racquetball.

"I'm good," Tommy said.

Jody nodded in agreement; although she would love a cup of coffee, she didn't think she should ask the kid to stab himself quite so soon.

She checked her watch. "What time do your parents go to bed?"

"Oh, around ten. You'll have plenty of time to stalk the

night and whatnot. Would you like to wash up or something? There's a bathroom down here. And a washing machine. My room was the wine cellar, then my dad crashed his car and started twelve-stepping, so I got this sweet room for my own. Abby says it's dank and disgusting—and she says it like it's a bad thing! I think it's just her perky side manifesting. I love her, but she really can be perky sometimes—don't tell her I said so."

Jody shook her head, then nudged Tommy, who shook his head in agreement. "We won't tell." The kid was sort of giving her the creeps. She thought she might have lost that ability with blood drinking and the sleep of the undead and all, but nope, she was getting completely creeped out.

"Jared, when is Abby coming back?"

"Oh, she should be here any minute. She went to your loft to feed the cat."

"She went to our loft? The loft where Elijah was?"

"No, it's okay. She went during daylight so he couldn't hurt her."

"It's not daylight anymore," Jody said.

"How do you know?" Jared said "No windows, duh."

Tommy Stooge-smacked his forehead with enough force to render a mortal man unconscious. "Because we're awake, you fucking moron!"

"Oh yeah, ha," Jared said. The trilling giggle again. "That's bad, huh?"

They Know Not What They Do

When Rivera and Cavuto arrived at the Safeway, they found that the remaining Animals had crucified Clint on a stainless-steel chip rack and were shooting him with paintball guns. Lash unlocked the door to let them in. The Emperor and his men followed. Clint's screaming sent Bummer into a barking fit and the Emperor snatched him up and stuffed him headfirst into the pocket of his overcoat.

"That really necessary?" Rivera asked, pointing to the paint-splattered martyr.

"We think so," Lash said. "He ratted us out." Lash turned, sighted down the pass-through of register three, and fired a quick volley of electric-blue paintballs into the center of Clint's chest. "Did he call you again?"

Rivera threw a thumb over his shoulder at the Emperor.

The Emperor bowed. "You needed help, my son."

Lash nodded, considering that the Emperor might be

right, then reeled and fired three quick shots into Clint's groin. "Just the same, motherfucker!"

"Stop that!" Rivera said. He snatched the paintball gun out of Lash's hand.

"It's cool. He's wearing a cup."

"And he's saved," said Barry, who had been firing from register four.

"Well, he is now," Cavuto said. As he approached the paint-sodden Evangelical, he pulled a serrated-edge pocket knife from his back pocket and flicked it open. "And just so you know," Cavuto added when his back was to them, "if I turn and there's a single paintball gun pointed in this direction, I will be forced to mistake it for a real weapon and unleash lead Disneyland on your pathetic asses."

Barry and Troy Lee immediately dropped their weapons onto the counter.

"So, the Emperor tells us that you guys have been up to some shit. I thought we all agreed that we were going to keep it on the down-low until things calmed down."

Lash looked at his shoes. "We just had a little party in Vegas."

Rivera nodded. "And you kidnapped Tommy Flood?"

Lash glared over Rivera's shoulder at the Emperor. "That was a secret. Really we were saving him from the daylight."

"So the redhead did turn him?"

"Looked like it. He was unconscious at dawn. Just a little sunlight hit his leg when we were moving him and it started to smoke."

"So you geniuses did what?"

"Well, we tied him to a bed at my apartment and left."

"You left?"

"We had to work."

Cavuto had cut the zip ties that held Clint to the chip rack and helped him to the register, where he sat him down, careful not to get any paint on his sport coat.

"Forgive them, they know not what they do," Clint said, wincing as he touched his paint-spattered shoulder.

"Because they're fucking idiots," Cavuto said, handing him a roll of paper towels.

Rivera ignored the scene at the register. "So you just left him there. So I'll find him there now, right?"

"That was a couple of nights ago," Lash said.

"Go on." Rivera looked at his watch.

"Well, in the morning he was gone."

"And?"

"It's awkward." For variety, Lash looked at Barry's shoes.

"Yeah, tying up your friends and torturing them can be that way," Rivera said.

"We didn't torture him. That was her."

"Her?" Rivera raised an eyebrow.

"Blue. A hooker we rented in Vegas."

"Now we're talkin'," Cavuto said.

"She came back with us. She wanted us to kidnap Tommy or his girlfriend."

"Why did she want that? To get their share of the art money?"

"No, she had plenty of money. I think she wanted to be a vampire."

Rivera tried to hide his surprise. "And?"

"When we went back to the apartment in the morning, Tommy was gone and Blue was dead."

"We had nothing to do with it," Barry added.

"But we didn't think you'd believe it," Troy Lee said.

Rivera felt a tension headache starting to throb in his temples. He closed his eyes and rubbed his forehead. "So you found a dead woman in your apartment. And you didn't think that *then* might be a good time to call the police?"

"Well, you know, dead hooker in your house—embarrassing," Troy Lee said. "I think we've all been there. Can I get a high five—" Apparently, he couldn't, and was thus left hanging.

"That's the weird thing," Barry said. "When we went to move her body, it was gone. But the rug we wrapped her in was still there."

"Yeah, that's the weird thing," Cavuto said, nudging his partner in the arm.

"Heinous fuckery most foul," said the Emperor.

"Ya think?" said Cavuto.

Bummer growled from his pocket sanctuary.

"You guys are not helping," Rivera said. Then to Lash again: "You have a description of this hooker?"

Lash described Blue, glossing quickly over the fact that

she was blue, and spending entirely too much time describing her breasts.

"They were outstanding," Barry said. "I kept them."

Rivera turned to Troy Lee, who seemed the most rational of these insane bastards.

"Explain, please."

"We found silicone implants wrapped up in the rug where we had left Blue."

"Uh-huh," Rivera said. "Intact?"

"Huh?" Troy inquired.

"Were they all cut up?"

"You think someone cut them out of her and took the body?" Troy asked.

"No," Rivera said. "So now you've lost three of your buddies?"

"Yeah. Drew, Jeff, and Gustavo didn't show up tonight."

Rivera had Lash get the addresses of the missing Animals from the office and wrote them down in his notebook.

"And you don't think that they might just be out partying?"

"We called all the phones, checked their houses," Lash said. "The door was hanging open at Drew's, and Jeff had left half a beer in the driveway, which he would never do. Besides, Jeff and Drew might flake, but Gustavo wouldn't. We even went to his cousin's house in Oakland looking for him."

"And he did not *está en la biblioteca* either," said Barry, who, for some reason, believed that all Spanish-speaking people spent a lot of time in the library and had therefore checked there for the intrepid night porter.

"No more bodies that you might have forgotten to mention?"

"Nuh-uh," Lash said. "Our money was gone, though. But we'd given it all to Blue anyway."

"I didn't," Clint said. "Mutual funds, less ten percent for the church."

"You gave six hundred thousand dollars to a hooker?" Rivera almost slapped the kid. Almost.

"Well"—Lash looked at Barry and Troy Lee, then, trying to suppress a grin—"yeah."

Rivera shook his head. "Keep the door locked and don't report this to anyone else."

"That's it?" Lash said. "You aren't going to arrest us or anything?"

"For what?" Rivera flipped his notebook closed and tucked it into the inside pocket of his suit coat.

"Uh, I don't know."

"Me either," said Rivera. "Emperor, you stay inside tonight with these guys. Okay?"

"As you wish, Inspector." The Emperor scratched behind Lazarus's ears.

"That okay?" Rivera said to Lash.

Lash nodded. "Are we going to be safe?" he asked.

Rivera stopped, looked around at the Animals and the Emperor and his dogs. "Nope," he said. "Let's go, Nick." He turned and walked out the door.

The foghorn was lowing across the Bay as the detectives walked back to their car. Fort Mason, just across the street, was barely visible in the rolling cloud of gray mist.

"You think the old vampire is hunting the Animals?" Cavuto asked.

"Someone is," Rivera said. "But I'm not sure it's him."

"You think it might be the redhead and the kid?"

"Could be, but I don't think so. You know, even with the vampire, we always had an identifiable MO—broken neck and massive blood loss, on a victim who turned out to be terminally ill, right?"

"Yeah."

"So if he went after these kids, why no bodies?"

"So it's Flood and the redhead. And they hide their bodies."

"I think it could be worse than that."

"Like worse in a way that we'll never be able to open the bookstore and may in fact end up doing time for taking the vampire's art collection?"

"Like worse in that the hooker and the missing Animals aren't dead at all."

"How is that worse?" Then Cavuto realized how that was worse.

They climbed into the car and stared at the windshield for a while without saying anything.

Finally, after a full minute, Cavuto said, "We're fucked."

"Yep," Rivera said.

"The whole city is fucked."

"Yep."

Being the Chronicles of Abby Normal: Star-Crossed Lover and Tragic Femme Fatale

OMG! We are doomed by our forbidden love! We are like from different feuding families, from the wrong side of the tracks, he is like year of the Rabbit and I am a Leo, so we are even star-crossed, and it's a well-known fact that rabbits and lions have a strained relationship. OMFG! He's so hot! He rocks my stripy socks. If we had moors, I would so be off brooding upon one, my delicate jaw muscles clenched as I stared off into the mist, feeling my profound missingness for him. (I can't believe that San Francisco doesn't have a moor. Everywhere you go we have automated, coin-operated robotic bathrooms, or Frisbee golf courses, or some new stainless-steel epileptic razor-blade public-art thingy, you'd think the least they could do would be to install a decent moor—because there are a lot more people who like brooding than like Frisbee golf. I'm pretty sure moors can be used for other purposes, too, like hauntings and hiding bodies and family picnics and whatnot.) Thus I am forced to do my brooding at Tulley's Coffee on Market Street.

It took most of the day for us to move the Countess and the vampyre Flood to Jared's room. First we had to wrap them up in duct tape and garbage bags to protect them from the sun, then get them down the hill from the Bay Bridge in the garden cart, which was totally physically hard, and not like taking X and dancing or playing DDR all night, more like work. Then, when we were loading them into the minivan, these two cops come by.

And they're all, "So, what are you doing with your piercings and your magenta-on-black hair, and what can we do to further repress your creativity? Bluster-blah-blah."

And Jared was all, "Nothing." All wussy and guilty-sounding. He had the front end of the Countess at the time and he totally just dropped her headfirst on the floorboard of the van.

So I was like, "Fucktard! The Countess is going to rip your nads off when she awakens!" (And she might, too, although when we unwrapped her she seemed unbruised.)

And the cop was all, "Hold it right there, kid." With his hand on his gun like I was going to go all Columbine on his ass or something. So I knew it was time for some strategy.

So I stepped over to the cop, and I started whispering like I didn't want Jared to hear. And I'm all, "Officer, I'm really embarrassed to even be seen like this. I'm a Kappa

Kappa Delta pledge and we're doing this hazing thing. I wouldn't be caught dead dressed like this, but it's like the most popular and powerful sorority on campus."

And the cop is all, "What about the guy? He's not in your sorority."

And I was all, "Shhhhhhh. God, you want to hurt her feelings? They made her shave her head like that and she's having a hard enough time with that and being totally flat-chested. Frankly, I don't think she's going to make it. Everyone knows that KKDs are pretty. Hello." I batted my eyelashes and sort of pushed my basically invisible boobs together with my arms, as I have often seen done in music videos.

And the cop was all, "Can I see your student ID?"

And I was like, FUCK, because I didn't know which college would be most likely to have a sorority, so I went with my Berkeley student ID, because Berkeley is a well-known bastion of hippie behavior and higher learning in which a sorority girl would probably have to blow like a hundred football players just to keep her GPA up. And cops like football.

So he was all, "Okay, but make sure there's plenty of airholes so your friends can breathe."

And I was all, "Sure thing. See ya later, cop."

So when we got the masters to Jared's house, his step-mom was all, "So, I see you have your little friend with you."

And Jared had to play chilly, so he was like, yeah, we

have a school project. And stepmonster was so proto-orgasmic that Jared was with a girl that she didn't even say much when we dragged the bodies through the den. Jared was all, "They're for social studies. We're doing replicas of Egyptian mummies."

Despite the complete embarrassment for me as a fellow woman, I'm grateful that when fathers pick their trophy wives, they don't check résumés or SAT scores, because you couldn't get away with that shit with a woman of normal intelligence. But Jared's stepmonster was all, "Oh, how nice for you. Would you like some juice?" Fortunately she wasn't around in sixth grade when Jared and I actually did our mummy project. We got in trouble for charging three hundred dollars' worth of Ace bandages on my mom's Visa, and my sister Ronnie has never fully recovered the feeling in her feet (and has an anxiety attack whenever she's in an enclosed space). But there was no gangrene or amputations like the doctors threatened, and we got a B, so I don't see what all the noise and counseling was about.

Anyway, after we unwrapped the Countess, I knew I had to go back and feed Chet, like I promised the disgusting huge cat guy, and since we had now shared a moment of intimacy, I felt obligated. So we shoved the vampyre Flood under Jared's bed, because Jared wanted to sit on the bed and play Xbox and it's a single bed. So, anyway, I caught the bus on Twenty-fourth Street, and got back to the SOMA with just enough time to feed Chet before the old naked vampyre awakened from his undead slumber. And I took

Jared's dagger with me in my biohazard messenger bag, because I thought I would dispatch Elijah by decapitation as, like, an extra-credit thing for the Countess.

Shut up. It wasn't like I went down in the basement in my nightgown to check on a blown fuse when the radio clearly had stated that there was a psycho killer on the loose and he was probably in the basement. I'm not stupid. I put on Jared's motocross boots and his leather jacket and spiked dog collar, and tied my hair back, so I was totally Thunderdome-ready. How hard could it be to feed the cat and cut the head off a sleeping old guy, anyway? It's not like they wake up. I mean, we bonked Flood's head on the steps going to Jared's room like eight times and he didn't even groan.

So I would have been all good and totally in line to be Princess of Darkness or at least Assistant Manager of Darkness, except when I was going up the steps I heard the dryer open. And I was all, *Uh-oh*. Since when is sundown like at five-o'clock? What am I, nine years old that I should have sunset at five o'clock? Sunset shouldn't be until like eight or nine o'clock, right? Right?

So, I'm like, WHOA. And I froze. And I stood there for like a half an hour, not moving at all, because I didn't buckle like the top buckles of Jared's motocross boots, to show my casual badassness, so it was like I was wearing fucking sleigh bells. (I know, I'm a tard.) So I couldn't move.

Then, after about a year, I hear this car pull up outside and the doors open, and I'm thinking—*Hello, Diversion, my old friend*. And I ran out the security door and right into this tall blond ho. And she's dressed all couture and shit, like it's fashion week at church or something, except she's with three of the guys from the Hummer limo, and she's pale as albino monkey cum. And I don't mean in a good way either. I mean in a sort of *"Hey, Myrtle Joe Cornfed, y'all let go your stepdaddy's penis and get over here and turn the channel to NAS-CAR"* kind of way. I mean, she had no mascara on at all!

Then she just picks me up by the arms and it hurt a lot, and I'm like kicking and thrashing and all, and she throws back her head and here come the fangs.

And I'm all, "No way. They'll just let any-fucking-body into the coven."

And she's all, "Not you. Unless you know where my money is."

And I'm all, "Step off, skank."

And she goes to bite me, and something yanks her back off her feet and I go flying.

Next thing, I'm looking up at the old vampyre in his yellow tracksuit, who is holding the blond ho by the hair, and the pale limo guys are like coming in on him. And Tracksuit is all, "Against the rules, pet. You can't go willy-nilly turning everyone you meet. It attracts the wrong kind of attention."

And wham, he smacks her face on the hood of her Mercedes, leaving a face print on the paint, I swear on the crusty hippie grave of my mother.

So I'm all, "Owned! Bee-yatch! Dog fucking owned you!" Doing a minor booty dance of ownage, perhaps, in retrospect, a bit prematurely. (I believe hip-hop to be the appropriate language for taunting, at least until I learn French.)

So they all turn on me. And I'm all, "awkward." So I started backing across the street. And crusty old vampyre bounces monkey cum's face off the hood of the Mercedes a couple of more times, then drops her and comes for me. The limo guys are all sort of standing by the car like they are waiting for instructions or something. Then one of them says, "Hey," and starts coming my way, too.

So I'm at the wall across the street, and I know I can't run, so I reach into my bag and pull Jared's dagger. And Tracksuit starts laughing—like really stoner laughing, pointing at my ensemble.

And I was all, "Shut up, fuckface, this knife and boots totally go with fishnets." Except for the Countess, I realize now that vampyres lose all fashion sense at death.

But then I hear this really loud thumper coming from down the alley, like club music you can feel in your breastbone, and this totally race-pimped yellow Honda comes screaming out of the alley. Who knew you could even get a car down that alley.

So the old vampyre has to jump back to avoid being run over and the limo guys jump back, and I was kind of hiding my head in my arms, but I hear, "Get in," and it's the cool Manga-haired Asian guy who I'd seen outside the loft before.

And I'm all, "What?" Because the music is really loud.

And he's all, "Get in."

And I'm all, "What?"

And by this time the old vampyre has jumped over the hood of the Honda and is about to grab me when there's this flash. Really more than a flash, because it stayed on. But there was this blinding light. And the music goes down and I hear, "Get in."

So I look into the light, and I'm like, "Grandma, is that you?"

Okay, I didn't say that. I'm totally fucking with you. I looked into the light and saw the Manga-haired guy, wearing sunglasses, and he's waving for me to get in his car. And then I see that the old vampyre is charred like Wile E. Coyote after a bad rocket shoes test. And so are the limo guys, and they're smoking and limping away from the Honda, which is shining like a star or something.

And Manga is all, "Now!"

And I'm all, "Shut up, you're not the boss of me." But I got in the Honda and we totally drifted around the corner, and when we're a block or two away Steve (that's his name, Steve) kills the ginormous floodlights in the backseat and I can sort of see again.

And he's all, "High-intensity ultraviolet."

And I'm, "You, too."

And he's like, "What are you talking about?"

I'm like, "I thought it was a compliment."

Then he smiled, like the cutest smile, although he was still driving *muy* intense and totally badass, and he goes,

"No, that light back there was high-intensity ultraviolet. It burns them."

And I was all, "I knew that."

And he was like, "You know that those three guys were vampyres, too, right?"

And I'm all, "Duh." But I didn't know. So I'm like, "How did *you* know?"

Then he takes off his shades and puts on these binocular robot-glasses things, like they wear in Siphon Assassin Six for Xbox, which I am against because it glorifies violence in the minds of adolescent boys and because it's totally impossible to get a decent head shot when your squad mates are bumping into you, which needs to be fixed in the next version if I'm going to be able to do the "gray spray" on the sentry tower glass.

So Steve is all, "Yeah, they're infrared. You can see heat with them, and there was no heat coming off anyone back there but you."

And I'm like, "Who the fuck are you?"

And he's like, "My name's Steve. I'm working on my biochem masters at S.F. State."

"Stop," I said. "Please do not further endorken youself to me. You have great hair and a car that is most fly, and you have just saved me with your mad ninja driving skills, so do not sully your heroic hottie image in my mind by further reciting your nerdy scholastic agenda. Don't tell me what you're studying, Steve, tell me what's in your soul. What haunts you?"

And he was like, "Dude, you need to cut back on the caffeine."

Which was fair, and I know that he was only saying it out of concern for my welfare and whatnot, because I think he knew even then that we were destined to be together, soul mates.

So while he drives, Steve tells me that he was doing some experiments on some bodies for his master's thingy, and he found that the cells of the victims were regenerating when you added blood to them, and he thinks he can turn them back to normal human cells by using some gene therapy or something. And he's been talking to the Countess and Lord Flood about turning them back, but the Countess is all, "No way, hot Manga-haired science guy."

So I was all, "Why would she want to give up immortality and superpowers and whatnot?"

And he was all, "I don't know."

And I was all, "We should discuss it over coffee."

And he was like, "I would love to do that, but I'm already late for work."

And I was like, "I thought you were a mad scientist."

And he was all, "I work at Stereo City."

And I was like, "Dude, you should get a job at Metreon selling the big-screens, because they have like the best test couches."

And he was like, "Okay." Just like that, "Okay."

So he wanted to give me a ride home, so I would be safe,

which is so sweet, but I needed double-soy Mochaccino to calm my nerves, so here I am at Tulley's, totally brooding.

But before I got out of the car, I was like, "Steve, do you have a girlfriend?"

And he was like, "No, I put a lot of time into my studies, and I sort of always have."

And I was like, "So would you be in the market for a Gaijin princess?"

And he was like, "That's Japanese. I'm Chinese."

And I'm like, "Don't change the subject, Kung Pao, what I want to know is if you're ready to spend some up-close and personal time with ninety pounds of barbarian woman-flesh! Sorry, I don't know how much that is in kilos."

I don't know what came over me. I was just fizzing over with adrenaline and passion and whatnot, I guess. I usually don't throw myself at guys, but he was so mysterious and smart and hot.

So he got this big grin and he was like, "My parents would freak out if they saw you."

And I was like, "You live at home?"

And he was all, "Well, uh, yeah, uh, kinda, uh—"

So I grabbed the pen out of his pocket and wrote my cell number on his arm while he stuttered, then when I put the pen back I kissed him sort of hard and totally passionately, which I could tell he liked a lot, so I pushed him away and slapped him so he wouldn't think I was a slut. But not very hard, so he wouldn't think I wasn't interested.

And I was all, "Call me."

And he was all, "I will."

So I was like, "Do not fuck with your hair."

And he was all, "Okay."

And I was all, "Be careful."

And he was all, "I will. You, too."

And I was all, "Oh, yeah, thanks for the rescue and whatnot."

And he was all, "Sure. Thanks for the kiss."

And so I am his shameless White Devil Juliet and he is my sweet Ninja Romeo (unless Ninjas are also Japanese, in which case I will have to look some shit up for metaphors because the only thing Chinese I can think of right now is Dim Sum, and I believe it's disrespectful to refer to your soul mate in terms of finger food).

Fucksocks! My cell. Jared. L8rz.

Well, That Was Fucked Up

"Then, Lucifer Two attains the blood sword and takes Jared the White as his consort, and they hold dominion over all of the Kindred for ever and ever," said Jared White Wolf, concluding the hour-long plot synopsis of his unwritten epic vampire adventure novel. "So what do you think?"

"I really liked it, but I think you may need to work on the characters more," Tommy said, flexing his writer muscles a little. It helped him to not think about the thirst that was rising in him.

Jared looked to Jody, and raised a drawn-on eyebrow.

"I think we must get out of this basement right now," Jody said, "and if that means murdering your parents and little sisters, well, you don't make an omelet—"

"But what did you think of my novel?" Jared said.

"I think it's not a novel, it's a sexual fantasy about you and your rat."

"It is not. That's just the characters' names."

"Try Abby's cell again, Jared." Jody was gritting her teeth.

"Tell her to get back here," Tommy said. He was starting to get cramps from the blood thirst.

"Hold on, I get shit reception down here." Jared took his cell and his rat and headed out the door and up the steps.

When he was gone, Tommy turned to Jody. "I'm really feeling the hunger."

"Me, too."

"Should we maybe just, you know, sample Jared?"

"I don't think that's a good idea."

"Well," Tommy said. "William is in the hospital, and we don't know where Abby is, and I don't see as we have that many options."

"Tommy, let's just walk out of here. What's the worst that can happen? We shock Jared's parents? I get the feeling they may be desensitized."

"That's fine, but then where do we go tomorrow? A hotel? I guess, if we get the money, we can have Abby guard the door to keep the maid from coming in and frying us." Tommy brightened. "Hey, maybe Abby grabbed some money from the loft?"

"Abby might not even be alive," Jody said, more than just irritation in her voice now. "You know how Elijah was going to kill you to fuck with me? If he's been watching us, he has to know about Abby. She'll be next. We should have left here right away. I feel horrible for leaving her out there alone."

"She went right to him." Tommy cradled his head in hands. "I hate this, Jody. Why did you do this to me? It could have worked. I could have looked out for you and had a real life. Now I just live from feeding to feeding, putting people in danger. Everyone wants to kill us or take something from us. I'm from Indiana, they don't prepare us for this kind of thing in the Midwest."

Jody slid off the bed to the floor and sat next to him, put her arm around his shoulders. "It's not like that, Tommy. We're like gods. Sure, we have to hunt, but if you let go to the predator part of you, you'll lose that anxious feeling. You have to feel the power of it."

"Power? What power? I was ready to have the rat as a snack."

"Well, you can have the rat if you need him, because that little fucker is creepy."

Tommy pulled away from her. "Don't."

Jared came through the door then, pumping his inhaler. "Oh my God! Oh my God! She met the hottest guy who is a ninja, and they're like totally into each other. And those guys you told us about, that kidnapped you, a bunch of them are vampires now. And there's a tall woman vampire, too, who tried to bite Abs. And Abby totally took them all on and burned them up with some kind of portable sunlight. Oh my God, she's so awesome. I wish I had balls like her."

"Where is she now?" Jody asked.

"She's having a Mochaccino at Tulley's on Market. I loaned her like twenty dollars. Which she's going to pay me back out of her Christmas bonus you're giving her. Hey, do I get a Christmas bonus, because—"

"Call her and tell her to stay right where she is," Jody said. "We're on our way."

"We are?" Tommy said. *They could get out of here, find a—a donor!*

"No, not you," Jody said. "We are." She patted Jared on the shoulder, careful not to get her hand near the rat.

"We are?" Jared said.

"Yes, Jared, you have to come out to your parents. You have to confess that you've had a girl in your room all day. We'll walk up and you can just introduce me as your girl-friend."

"Okay. I guess. You might want to borrow some eyeliner and touch up your lipstick a little first, okay?"

"I will slap the gloom off of you, rat shagger," Jody said with a smile that was just a few degrees below being warm.

Over his very long life, Elijah Ben Sapir had been hunted, beaten, tortured, drowned, impaled, imprisoned, and even burned on two occasions—tolerance for those who live off the lifeblood of others being what it is—but in eight centuries, this was the first time he had been flash-fried by a tricked-out Honda. Despite the novelty of it, when novelty had just become his new joy, he figured that if he went an-other eight hundred years before it happened again, he'd be okay.

Creeping down a SOMA alley, snatching rats from behind Dumpsters and draining them to dust just so he could heal himself enough to hunt a real victim, was serving as an abject lesson as to why he and his kind were sworn to remain concealed. It was bound to happen: the application of new technology for the detection and destruction of vampires. Hadn't he adopted technology to protect himself? His self-piloting yacht with its sensors and sealed vault had served him as well as any guarded castle. But he'd forgotten the rule—not forgotten, really, but ignored it—deciding to indulge in hope, to the point of faith, that he would always prevail. So some clever cow had figured out how to package sunlight and unleash it upon his arrogant carcass. The cow would never have found the solution had the vampire not shown him the problem. Humbled was Elijah, and angry, and hungry, and a little sad, because he had loved his yellow tracksuit, and now it was but beads of blackened polyester burned into his skin.

He picked at them as he listened for prey, tucked between a Dumpster and a white step-van full of bread racks. Here came one now—fat enough to complete the healing, Elijah could tell by the weight of his step. The back door of the bakery opened and the rotund baker stepped out and shook a cigarette out of his pack. His life aura was pink and healthy, his heart thumped strong, and would for a long time if Elijah did not suck it dry. Normally he only took the sick and the weak, those who were short for the grave anyway, but this was a desperate time. He leapt on the big man's back and rode him to the ground, catching his scream in one hand, using the other to hit pressure points in his neck that had the baker unconscious in two seconds.

Elijah drank, listening to his blackened skin crackle, slough, and heal, even as the baker still breathed. There would be no neck snap, no body to find this time. He dumped the dust from the baker's clothes and slipped into them. His white Nikes were the only survivors of his previous outfit, so he threw the baker's clogs into the Dumpster along with his wallet, pocketed the cash, and took off, dressed in white from head to foot.

The vampire smiled to himself, not with joy, but with the grim irony of the situation. People often speak of things coming to them in a flash of inspiration, but the cliché held new meaning for Elijah. The flash meant that the game was over, that his foray into human desire, even for revenge, had gone far enough, and now it was time for damage control. They all had to die. He wouldn't enjoy killing her. Not her.

After being burned up for the second time in two days, Blue was ready for a healing massacre—a bloodbath—but the Animals had stopped her, citing sissy ethical reasons like murder was, you know, wrong.

"You're burned up!" Blue said. "This is no time to develop a conscience. Where was your conscience when you were making me do you a dozen times a day, huh?"

"That's different," said Drew. "You were in on it."

"Yeah," added Jeff. "And we paid you."

"No one was hurt, *amiga*," Gustavo added.

Blue broke off some charred crust coming over the seat of the Mercedes at Gustavo, who was in the passenger seat. Drew dragged her back into her seat by her hips. She crossed her arms and pouted, huffing out little flakes of ash in exasperation. They were supposed to be doing her bidding. They were supposed to be her seven—well, *three*—dwarves.

"You shut the fuck up, bean town. I was hurt. I *am* hurt. Look at me."

They didn't look at her. They were all burnt black from the waist up, in the front at least. Their shirts hung on them in charred shreds. The linen dress that Blue had been wearing had incinerated almost completely. She was wearing only her panties and a severely singed bra. Her face was still a bit lopsided from where Elijah had banged it on the car hood.

"We didn't do this, Blue," Drew said.

Blue smacked him repeatedly in the head a half-dozen times, knocking off most of one of his charred ears and all of the carbon strands that were what was left of his hair. The tip of her little finger broke off in the process, at which point she sat back and growled like a beaten dog.

"We need blood to heal," Blue said. "Lots of it."

"I know," Jeff said. The charred power forward was driving. "I'm takin' care of it."

"You just passed five perfectly good teenagers," Blue said. "Where the fuck are you going?"

"Somewhere where the donors can handle our action," Jeff said.

"Well, we're broke until you get my money back, so your donors better have some fucking cash."

"We can't exactly go into a bar in the financial district," Drew said. "Not looking like this."

"Oh, like they'd let you dirtbags in at your best." Blue found that being burnt up put her on edge more than normal. She'd tried taking a Valium left by the Mercedes guy, just like Drew and the other had downed handfuls of his painkillers, only to find their vampire systems rejected them with extreme violence.

"We're here," Jeff said, pulling the Mercedes into a wide public parking lot.

"You're fucking kidding me," Blue said. "The zoo?"

Tommy waited half an hour before he called Jody's cell, only to get a dropped signal, then voice mail. He called three more times in the next half hour, played two rounds of Gunning for Nuns Xtreme on Jared's Xbox, called Abby's cell only to get voice mail, then made his first sincere attempt at turning to mist. Jody had said it was a mental thing, you just had to see yourself as mist, force yourself to mist, "like flexing a muscle," she had said. "Once you've done it once, you just know how it feels and you can do it again. Like getting up on water skis."

It wasn't that he could get out of the basement undetected, it was what Jody had said about being in the mist state—that time sort of just glided, like you were in a dream. It was the only reason, she said, that she hadn't beaten him senseless for having her bronzed. When you were mist, it just wasn't all that bad. Maybe if he could turn to mist, he could pass the time without driving himself nuts with worry.

For all his mental flexing, all he got was a flatulent toot that sent him diving for the door and fanning the room out with it. He was truly a foul dead thing—fouler than he'd even guessed. He looked for paint peeling off the walls.

That was it. He was not a kid hiding in his friend's basement, he was a—what did Abby call it?—he was one of the anointed, a prince of the night. He was going to walk out of here, right past the family, and if he had to take them out, well, so be it. That would teach Jody for leaving him behind and turning her phone off. *How do you feel now, Red? Huh? Massacred, dismembered family? Huh? Glad you saved your any-time minutes now?!*

He tramped up the steps and into Jared's parents' family room.

"Hi," Jared's father said.

Tommy had expected a bit of a monster based on Jared's description of his father. Instead what he saw was a bit of an accountant. He was about forty-five, in pretty good shape, holding a little girl on his lap who was coloring a picture of a pony. Another little girl, who looked about the same age, was coloring on the floor at his feet.

"Hi," Tommy said.

"You must be the vampire Flood," Jared's dad said, with a bit of a knowing smile.

"Uh. Well. Kinda." It showed. He could no longer hide among the humans. It must be because it had been so long since he had fed.

"Sort of a weak ensemble, don't you think?" Jared's dad said.

"Weak," repeated the little girl without looking up from her pony.

"Huh?" Tommy inquired.

"For a vampire. Jeans, sneakers, and flannel?"

Tommy looked at his clothes. "Black jeans," he pointed out. Shouldn't this guy be cowering in fear, maybe begging Tommy not to put his little daughter in a sack for his vampire brides?

"Okay, I suppose times change. You know that Jared and his girlfriend went up to Tulley's on Market to meet Abby, right?"

"His girlfriend, Jody?"

"Right," said Dad. "Cute girl. Not as many piercings as I expected, but we're just happy she's a girl."

An attractive blond woman in her late twenties came into the room carrying a tray with carrot and celery sticks on it. "Oh, hi," she said, dazzling a smile at Tommy. "You must be the vampire Flood. Hi, I'm Emily. Would you like some crudités? You're welcome to stay for dinner. We're having mac and cheese, it was the girls' night to pick."

I should drink her blood and put her kids in a sack, Tommy thought. But his vicious predator nature was overcome by his Midwestern upbringing, so instead he said, "Thank you very much, Emily, but I really should be going if I'm going to catch up to Jared and Jody."

"Well, okay then," said the woman. "Girls, say good-bye to the vampire Flood."

"Good-bye, the vampire Flood," the girls sang in chorus.

"Uh, bye." Tommy bolted out of the room, then back in again. "Where's the door?"

Everyone pointed through the kitchen, whence Jared's stepmonster had just come.

He ran through the kitchen and out the door, then stood with his back against the minivan in the drive, trying to catch his breath. "That was fucked up," he gasped, then realized that he wasn't out of breath from exertion at all. He was having an anxiety attack. "That was really, really fucked up."

Wallflowers of the Night

It was a lot like trying to get your courage up to ask a girl to dance, except that in this case it wasn't so much the fear of rejection, or that you'd be awkward and embarrass yourself, although that was a consideration, but that whoever you picked was going to be reduced to dust, which was somewhat more significant than trampling her toes.

Tommy stood on Castro Street looking for his next victim. His *first* victim, really. He was tired of being the apprentice. If Jody was going to just leave him in the basement because he wasn't vampire enough for her, then maybe he'd have to become like her. Maybe he'd learn about this predator nature she talked about. Maybe, like that guy in the basement in *The Phantom of the Opera*, he would have to hear "The Music of the Night." He wasn't sure what had happened to the basement guy. He'd gone to see the movie with a girl from his high school, but had to leave halfway through to keep from taking his own life. It hadn't been a good date.

There were plenty of people out on the street, even at this hour, but none of them screamed victim. There were no women in low-cut dresses who had just turned an ankle. There were no girls in negligees running down the street, glancing back over their shoulders. There were, in fact, not many girls at all. Lots of guys. Lots.

He reckoned that it wasn't really necessary that he pick a woman. After all, he'd fed off of William and Chet, both of whom were male, but this was different. This was really becoming the hunter, and despite his hunger, there was no little bit of revenge in his decision to bite someone. So it had to be a girl. He had to get back at Jody for ditching him at Jared's. He had to show her that she wasn't the only vein in the circulatory system. Or whatever.

The few women he saw were so healthy, with big bright pink life auras around them, and weren't alone either. He had to get someone alone.

Frustrated, he backed down the alley and started pacing back and forth. After a short time he took a run at the wall, ran up ten feet or so, then turned and ran back across the alley and up the other wall about ten feet, then back, and up the wall fifteen feet—like a skateboarder working a half-pipe, he ran back and forth, feeling the strength and speed of what he was—feeling his confidence rise.

I am a superior being, he thought. *I am a friggin' god!*

Then his foot went through a window and he sank up

to his crotch into the building, then dangled over the alley upside down, three stories up, flailing.

Stupid place for a window, he thought. Then he saw her.

She was sort of tall, but dressed in a red evening gown, with athletic curves, and long red hair that had been lacquered into ringlets. She was perfect, and she was coming down the alley. It was like he'd ordered her from an old Hammer film to be the hapless victim. Sweet!

So he was hanging upside down by one leg. That could be a tactic. He felt his fangs extending and he drooled a little, which hit her on the shoulder.

She started a little, and that's when he made his move. He'd always loved the scene in *Dracula* where Jonathan Harker sees the Count climbing, facedown, down the castle walls and thinks, *Hey, something is up here.* Tommy had pleaded with Jody to try it, but she never would, so this was his chance. He pulled himself out of the window, hooked his fingers between the bricks, and began his climb.

And dropped thirty feet to the alley, landing flat on his back.

"Ouch."

Upon Tommy's impact, his intended victim had let out a very masculine scream, jumped three feet straight up, and came down sideways on her high heels. She knelt over him rubbing her ankle.

"Cheesy Christ on a cracker, darlin'. Where did you come from?" Southern, and deep.

"Slipped," Tommy said. "You're a man, huh?"

"Well, let's say that is a street which I have walked, to which I do not wish to return."

"You're very pretty," Tommy said.

"Sweet of you to say." He tossed his hair a bit. "You want I should call an ambulance?"

"No, no. Thanks. I'll be okay."

"What were you doing up there, anyway?"

Conveniently, Tommy was still staring straight up at the sky, framed by the buildings, and he could see that she thought he'd fallen from the roof. "Listening for 'the music of the night.'"

"Were you watching the DVD? I heard people tried to kill themselves rather than sit through it."

"Something like that."

"Honey, just push pause. Just push pause."

"I'll remember that. Thanks."

"You sure you don't want me to call someone?"

"No, no. I'll call someone as soon as I catch my breath." Tommy reached into his back pocket and pulled out a hand-ful of broken plastic and wires that had once been his cell phone.

"Okay then, y'all take care." She stood, turned, and walked slowly out of the alley, trying not to limp.

"Hey, miss," Tommy called after him. "I'm not gay."

"'Course you aren't, darlin'."

"I rule the night!"

She waved without looking as she rounded the corner.

"Redheads," he growled.

He could feel his broken ribs knitting together. It wasn't pleasant. As soon as they were healed enough, it was back to Jared's house to eat the rat. Move up the food chain slowly, maybe.

An hour later the torn and tattered vampire Flood limped up the driveway to Jared's house. Abby and Jared were smoking in the driveway.

"Lord Flood," Abby said. "What are you doing here?"

"You look like someone opened a whole six-pack of whup-ass on you," Jared said.

"You shut up. How did your family know I was a vampire?"

"Well, certainly not from your wardrobe."

"Jared, I am all busted up, and I'm feeling hungry, and a little fragile. Now answer my question or I will go inside and murder your family, feed on their blood, step on your rat, and break your Xbox."

"Whoa, drama queen much?"

"Fine," Tommy said. He shrugged, which hurt, and headed for the kitchen door. "Find me a sack big enough for your two little sisters."

Jared jumped in front of him. "I told them we were playing Vampire the Masquerade and that your part was the Vampire Flood."

Abby nodded. "We used to play all the time before we actually became minions."

"It's like Dungeons and Dragons but way cooler," Jared said.

"Okay." Tommy nodded. Which hurt. There they were, two perfectly healthy donors from whom he could feed, who would be willing. And he *was* hurt, and he needed to feed in order to heal. Still, he couldn't ask. He was staring at Abby's neck, then looked away when she appeared to notice.

"Where's Jody?"

"She'll be here soon," Abby said. "She sent us back to find you. We called but your cell wasn't on."

"Where is she?"

"She went to the new loft. She said she'd bring some money and what was left of William's blood back for you. You can stay in a hotel. Jared and I can guard you."

"She went to the loft? Where Elijah is?"

"Oh, that's not a problem," Abby said. "My Samurai prince burned him up while rescuing me from the blond vampire ho and her grocery-store vamplets."

Tommy looked at Jared. " 'Splain please."

Just knock," Drew said. "They'll unlock it for you. You're al-most naked." They stood by the front door of the Marina Safeway. Drew had healed a little from his burns, but was still bald and covered with a dusting of soot. Blue was completely healed, but wore only her charred underwear and the beige high heels that had looked so lovely with her linen dress.

Since the first time she took the stage in high heels and a bikini back in her first Fond du Lac beauty pageant, right through her career stripping and then bonking for dollars, she thought the whole idea of high heels and underwear patently absurd. Yet here she was, rich, powerful, and immortal—yet still standing around wearing high heels and underwear. This time, however, there was some rationale for the outfit beyond that it floated some horndog's hormonal boat. At the zoo, while the Animals had pursued their prey among animals, she had found two night watchmen, each isolated on his rounds, and took them down. Unfortunately, she hadn't taken their clothing because she didn't want to have to explain to the Animals why she was dressed like a night watchman, since they had suddenly decided to take the moral high ground on slaughter.

The Animals had not fared so well. Drew was the only one in better shape than when they'd first been burned. He'd gone for a llama, because he'd always thought they were cute. He was able to feed only a little, however, before he was bitten and spat upon, and decided to call it a night. Gustavo had gone for a zebra, under the mistaken assumption that his experience with horses as a boy in Mexico would somehow give him an edge in handling the African equine. Consequently, he had been summarily stomped, and now had several broken bones, including a nasty compound fracture of one leg, in addition to being burned up. Jeff, the basketball failure, was still embarrassed about having been taken down by a girl, and so picked a jungle cat as his victim, thinking that he would take on the strength and speed of his donor. His right arm was attached only by a few muscles and much of that shoulder was gone altogether. His skin was still crusty black from the waist up.

"Fuck knocking," said Blue. The big front window had only that day been replaced, but she was going to lead her charge right through it. "Get in, find them, and take them." She found she was falling back on her dominatrix experience a lot lately, which was not a skill in which she had complete confidence, having only recently been killed while performing it.

She took three quick steps up, snatched up the steel-reinforced trash can that Jody had used on the window only days ago, and flung it underhanded with all her strength. The can rocketed through the air, bounced off the new, double-impact-resistant Plexiglas window, and knocked Blue on her ass.

Blue climbed to her feet without making any eye contact with her undead posse, dusted off her bottom, then snapped her newly broken nose back into place.

"Well, knock then, fuckstick," she said to Drew. "Knock, knock, knock. We don't have all night."

Don't You Hate Running into Your Ex?

As soon as she unlocked the new loft's security door from the street, Jody smelled blood, burned flesh, and shampoo. A case of the willies that felt like an electric serpent slithered up her spine. She went up the stairs, light on the balls of her feet, ready. She heard every tick in the apartment, the refrigerator motor, floorboards shifting, the huge cat Chet snoring in the bedroom, and, of course, someone breathing.

The lights were off. He was sitting in a canvas sling-back chair, barefoot, in a pair of Tommy's jeans and a T-shirt, drying his hair with a towel. Jody stopped by the kitchen.

"Fledgling," said the vampire. "I'm always pleasantly surprised when I am reminded of how lovely you are. Surprises are rare at my age."

"Must have surprised the fuck out of you to have that Honda toast you, then, huh?" She felt herself tightening down, the electric jangle channeling itself into an awareness, an edge. It wasn't fear anymore, it was readiness.

"An unpleasant one, yes. I assume your little servant is safe for now."

"Well, you know, she was winded for a few minutes from kicking your ass, but she *is* just a little girl."

The vampire laughed, and Jody couldn't help but smile. She went to the windows at the front of the loft and opened them. "Smells like burned meat in here."

"She'll have to go, you know," said the vampire, still smiling.

"No, she won't," Jody turned on her heel. Faced him.

"Of course she will. All of them but you. I'm quite tired of being alone, little one. You can come away with me, just as we planned."

Jody was stunned at his density. "I was lying to you, Elijah. I never intended to go away with you. I was just pretending to find out how to be a vampire."

"What were you going to do the next night, then—if your pet hadn't bronzed us, I mean?"

"I thought I'd send you away."

"No you didn't."

"I thought I'd let the Animals kill you, like they were going to anyway."

"No you didn't."

"I don't know." The edge was slipping. "I don't know." Maybe she was going to go with him. She had felt so alone, so lost.

"Ah, so here we are again. Let's pretend like all this unpleasantness hasn't happened, and it's the next night, and here we are, just the two of us. The only ones of our kind. What will you do, Jody?"

"But we aren't the only ones of our kind."

"We are the only ones you need worry about. You do know that you are the first new vampire in a hundred years?"

Jody tried not to show her surprise. "How lucky for me," she said.

"Oh, you're not the only one I've turned. I've turned many. You're the only one who could weather the change with her mind intact. The others had to be, well, decommissioned."

"You killed them?"

"Yes. But not you. Help me clean up and then we'll leave, together."

"Clean up?"

"There are certain rules, love. Rules that I set down myself, and the first of them is make no more vampires. Yet you've let loose a storm of fledglings, and they all have to be cleaned up, including your boy pet."

"*Make no more?* What about me? You made me."

"I didn't expect you to survive, love. I thought you would be an amusement, a break in monotony, an interlude, but you distinguished yourself."

"And now you want me to run off with you."

"We'll live like royalty. I have resources you couldn't imagine."

"You're wearing stolen jeans, sugar daddy."

"Well, yes, I will have to make my way to one of my caches."

"I have an idea," Jody said, and this was really the reason she had come here, by herself, knowing that he would be here. Or at least hoping. "How about I give you enough money to get you out of town and you do that, just like we promised Rivera and Cavuto? You leave me alone, you leave Tommy alone, you just leave."

Elijah stood now, tossed the towel on the chair, and moved to her so quickly that she could barely even see him move. "Art, music, literature," said Elijah. "Desire, passion, power—the best of man and the best of beast. Together. You would say no to that?"

He put his hand on her cheek and she let him.

"Love?" Jody said, looking into his eyes—they reflected like drops of mercury in her night vision.

"For fairy tales. We are the stuff from which nightmares are made. Make nightmares with me."

"Wow, nice offer. Can't imagine why you haven't had any takers for a hundred years." Jody grabbed his wrist. If he wouldn't leave, she could take him. She was a vampire, too.

The vampire had been smiling, but his smile changed aspect, going from pleased to predatory. "So be it, then."

His hand was at her neck in an instant, she didn't see

him move or have a chance to react. Suddenly she couldn't move her arms or legs, and there was an intense pain behind her ear and under her jaw. She screamed, releasing a sound she couldn't imagine coming out of a human, more like something you'd hear from a tortured cat. He clamped his other hand over her mouth.

"I didn't teach you everything in our one night together, love."

She watched helplessly as he tossed his head back and his fangs unsheathed.

Troy Lee squared off against Drew at the end of the dog-food aisle, two short fighting swords in hand.

"Bring it, stoner," Troy Lee said. He spun the swords. Drew fell into a crouch by the dishwashing liquids.

"I'm fast now," Drew said.

"Uh-huh," Troy said. He whipped the swords through the air in a deadly fanning motion. He'd been training since he was a child; he wasn't afraid, especially of Drew.

"Hey," came a woman's voice from right beside him. Troy Lee looked over, lightning quick, just in time to register what looked like a full moon coming at his face.

There was a loud clang and Troy was nearly flipped over backwards when the iron skillet hit him in the forehead. Blue let it drop to her side and grinned at Drew. "I've always wanted to do that."

"Housewares used to be my aisle," Drew said.

"Take him," said Blue. "Let him drink some of your blood before he dies." She headed toward a commotion in the can aisle. "Save some, boys. Mama's got a broken nose that needs to heal."

Jody felt her own fangs extend and her kneecaps quiver as Elijah fed on her, but otherwise she couldn't move. How could she have been so stupid? He was eight hundred years old—of course he hadn't taught her everything. Of course he was stronger than she was—she was stronger than Tommy, and she had only been a vampire a couple of months longer than he had.

If she could stay conscious, maybe when he stopped feeding she could make her move. Could he reduce her to dust like a human, or would he have to do something else? Stupid. Stupid. Stupid. Why didn't she know all of this? Why wasn't she acting on instinct? Where was the predator mind when you needed it?

Her vision started to tunnel down—she was losing conciousness. She could hear rapid footsteps outside, though. First below, then across the street, then below again. Elijah heard them, too, and he loosened his grip for an instant, but before she could twist away, his fingers dug into her neck and jaw again. Then a black blur flew through the window and she heard something thud on the floor over by the kitchen. There was another loud thud and Elijah released her and she fell to the floor. She tried to push herself up, but something was thrown over her and she heard a buzzing sound. She heard screaming and smelled burning flesh, glass breaking, then someone was lifting her, carrying her. She couldn't move or even fight anymore. She let go, let herself float away, but the last thing she heard was a girl's voice saying, "Did you feed Chet?"

The Emperor sat on the dock of the St. Francis Yacht Club, watching the fog wash over the breakwater. He'd gone against the advice of the homicide detectives and had left the grocery store. It was his city, and it was his place to take the battle to its attackers. He had cowered in fear long enough. His wickedly pointed sword lay on the dock at his side. The men, Bummer and Lazarus, were sleeping in a fuzzy pile at his back.

"Ah, gentle warriors, how do we engage in battle when our enemy moves with such elegant stealth? Perhaps we should return to the Safeway and help defend."

Bummer's left ear twitched, and he let out a muffled *ruff* in his sleep.

A thick bank of fog was moving down from the opening in the breakwater and it caught the Emperor's attention because it appeared to be moving across the wind from the west. Yes, it was indeed—the cold breeze was coming straight over the breakwater from the north. The fog bank bubbled thick as it moved, tendrils reached out and then were reabsorbed like the false feet of some crawling creature.

The Emperor climbed to his feet and roused the men, snatched Bummer up before the sleepy terrier could get his bearings, and headed toward the clubhouse with Lazarus at his heels. He crouched in a shadow by the entrance to the restrooms, holding the hounds as he watched.

The fog bank enveloped the end of the dock, paused, then dissipated as if a fan had been turned on it, and three tall figures stood on the dock, a man and two women. They wore long coats, cashmere, the Emperor thought, but he couldn't for the life of him remember why he might know that. They moved down the dock toward him as if they were floating. The Emperor could see their outlines in the moonlight—jawlines and cheekbones that looked as if they'd been chiseled, square shoulders, and narrow hips. They might have been brother and sisters, except one of the women was of African descent, the other looked like she might be Italian or Greek. The man was a head taller than the women and looked Nordic, perhaps German, with close-cropped white hair. All were as pale as bleached bone.

As they passed him the Emperor pulled the hounds closer and Bummer let out a threatening *ruff*.

They stopped. The man turned. "How long have you been here?" he asked.

"Forever, I think," said the Emperor.

The man smiled and nodded, then turned and was on his way. "I know how you feel," he said without looking back.

. .

Gustavo and Jeff found Barry hiding in the shelves among the toilet-paper packages. When they got close, Barry burst out of the TP and made a run for the end of the aisle, pulling napkins, aluminum foil, garbage bags, and plastic silverware off the shelves as he went to slow his pursuers. Gustavo went down first, slipping on a package of plastic forks. Jeff high-stepped through the obstacles and was right on Barry's ass until he was almost to the end of the aisle and Lash stepped out holding one of Barry's spearguns.

"Down!" Lash barked, and Barry hit the tile on his chest and slid.

There was a pneumatic hiss and the heavy stainless spear thudded into Jeff's sternum and blew him back off his feet.

"Ow, goddammit," said the power forward, clutching at the spear and trying to pull it out of his chest.

Gustavo climbed to his feet, ran to Jeff, and started yanking on the spear.

Lash handed Barry a four-foot-long stick with a blunt metal tip on it and fitted another spear into the gun.

"That the last one?" Barry asked.

Lash nodded. "Where's Clint?"

Just then the tall blond woman appeared at the far end of the aisle, dragging an unconscious Clint by his collar. A wide bloodstain ran from her chin to her crotch and they could see her fangs even from this distance. "Bad boys.

Leaving your born-again lying on the floor where people can trip over him."

She dropped Clint on his face, and headed up the aisle toward them, in long, slow strides.

Lash bolted, Barry right behind him, through the canvas doors into the back room, and into the walk-in dairy cooler. It was like a long hallway with plastic milk boxes stacked on one side and the glass dairy cases on the other. They pushed stacks of heavy one-gallon milk boxes in front of the door, then leaned with their backs against the back of the cooler, watching the store through the clear cooler doors in the dairy case, over the cartons of yogurt and cottage cheese.

"What's that she's carrying?" Barry asked.

"A frying pan," Lash said.

"Oh," Barry said "Sorry I let her in. She was almost naked."

"How could you have known?"

"Well, when she claimed she had a nooky-gram for my birthday, I should have figured something was up."

"Your birthday's like in March, isn't it?"

"Yeah."

Lash slapped Barry hard once on his bare scalp, then re-aimed the speargun over the yogurts.

"I deserved that," Barry said.

"Think that spear hit Jeff's heart?"

"Had to. It's a foot through his sternum."

"He doesn't seem dead."

"Guess that means head shot." Barry shook his head. "You want me to try?"

"Nah, if I miss, you have the bang stick." Lash nodded at the long stick Barry was holding at port arms. Essentially it was a twelve-gauge shotgun shell on the end of a stick, used for killing sharks. You poked them with it and the shotgun shell fired into them at point-blank range.

"I'll bet she doesn't even know what it is."

"Get it right," Lash said. "Blow her fucking brains out."

They looked at each other as they heard the refrigeration compressors and fans wind down. Then the lights went out.

"We're fucked," Lash said.

"Yep," Barry agreed.

Being the Chronicles of Abby Normal: Dark and Mysterious Goddess of Forbidden Love

Don't judge me. I have looked death in the face and made him my bitch! I did what I did out of love, and I don't want to sound conceited, but OMG, we are heroes! And when I say we, I mean us.

Had I told you before, you would have called me "losah!," pronounced me perky and cute beyond redemption, but now that I am secure in my own nefarious love lair and whatnot, I can at last confess, that in my naive youth, my favorite literary character was not the tentacled horror Cthulu from Lovecraft as I previously stated in AP English 235, but, in fact, Pippi Longstocking. Before you condemn me for my Pippism, check it out:

Pippi drank a lot of coffee. (Because, like me, she was wise.)

Pippi had unnaturally red hair (as I, myself have had, upon occasion).

Pippi often wore long, stripy socks (as yours truly has been known to do).

Pippi had superhuman strength. (It could happen.)

Pippi kicked ass. (Not unlike your humble narrator.)

Pippi was a kid who lived without parents in her own house. (Go, girl!)

With a monkey. (Haven't you always wanted a monkey?)

What Longstockings did not have, was the coolest cyber-ninja-sex-magic boyfriend to ever save the world and whatnot. (Props to Pip, but girlfriend needed some yang to rock her yin.)

> Steve. My darling, my love,
> My heart is aflame
> But OMFG, Steve,
> I grieve,
> That your name
> Is so fucking lame.

I call him Foo Dog, because he guards the gate of my temple, if you know what I mean. I'm wearing the jacket he made me right now. I had it on when they came for me, but that's not the thing. The thing is, I didn't save myself, I saved love.

So, that night, after I told the Countess how my sweet Foo Dog saved me from the vampyre, the Countess said she was going to go back to the loft to get some money and feed Chet and get the last of William's blood for Lord Flood, for their love is truly eternal. And Jared and I were like, "We'll go, too," but the Countess sent us back to liberate the vampyre Flood from Jared's basement and his hideous family. So we were all, "Well, okay."

But when we got to Jared's house, Flood was totally gone. And then Steve—I mean Foo Dog—called me and he was all, "I'm getting off work early, I don't want to leave you out there unprotected."

So I told him where we were. Then Lord Flood comes walking out of the dark and he's all, "What? What? What?"

And I'm all, "The Countess went back to the loft."

And he's all, "She is in danger. We must away."

And I was like, "Chill thee thus, for my sweet love-ninja is on the way in his fly ride."

So Flood was like, " 'Kay."

I see now that my attraction to the vampyre Flood was nothing more than childish infatuation, never to be requited, because he had eyes only for the Countess.

So it was a little awkward when Steve showed up and I had to chill the Lord Flood and make him sit in the backseat to show that my real affections were with Foo Dog, who was formerly known as Steve.

And when we got to the loft, the windows were open, but there were no lights on. And Flood had us drive a block past, then we got out and he walked back. Then he runs up and he's like, "Elijah's up there. He's got her."

And I'm all, "Then go get her."

And Steve is like, "No, I'll go get her." And he pulls this long coat out of the trunk.

It's all covered with warts or something, and I'm like, "Nice coat, but you know, vampyre . . ."

And Steve is like, "They're UV LEDs. Like the lights we burned the vampires with before."

And I'm like, "Sweet!"

So Steve starts to put the coat on and Flood stops him and goes, "He'll hear you coming up the stairs. I'll go."

And Steve is all, "You can't. It will burn you, too."

And Flood is all, "No it won't."

So they are like five minutes behind the car putting together this über-cool ensem of like an old gas mask, and a hoodie, and full-on gloves and everything, until Flood is totally covered, wearing the long coat with the glass warts all over it, looking like one of the cenobites from *Hellraiser*.

And Steve is like, "Don't hit the switch until you know she's covered." And he hands Flood like a black rubber tarp and a baseball bat, which totally sucked the cool right out of the ensem, but I guess was necessary.

Then, just when I'm about to ask how he's going to get in without being heard, we hear the Countess scream, and Flood runs across the street and about halfway up the side of the building, then turns and runs down it, then across the street, up the side of his building, and goes through the window feet fucking first.

And I'm like, "Whoa."

And Steve and Jared are like, "Whoa."

And a second later we hear a thumping, and purple light comes on in the loft windows and the old vampyre comes crashing through the windows on fucking fire, falling like a comet! And he lands on his feet in the middle of the street, hisses once and looks at us, and that's when Steve holds up one of his UV floodlights, and the vampyre fucking scrams down the alley across the street so fast that he was just a blur.

Next thing, Flood is coming out of the building carrying the Countess, who is wrapped in the black rubber tarp and is totally roofied like a limp rag. And Steve's all, "Get her in the car."

And I'm like, "Did you feed Chet?"

And Jared is like, "Hello, Abby, the other vampyres."

So I'm like, "Shut up. I know." So we all piled into Steve's car and we took Flood and the Countess to a hotel off up on Van Ness, which Steve paid for with his Visa, which was generous and mature of him.

It was one of those motels where you have your own entrance to the parking lot so they don't see you in the hallway, so Flood carried the Countess up to the room, and we carried some stuff that Steve had packed up in the trunk of his car.

It was so sad. Flood just stroked the Countess's cheek and tried to get her to wake up, but she wouldn't. And he was all, "Abby, she needs to feed. I wouldn't ask, but he's done something to her, she's hurt."

And I would have totally done it, but Steve pulled me back, and he picks up this playmate cooler that he had us bring up, and he pulls out these pouches of blood.

And he hands them to Flood and says, "I took them from the university hospital. They could kick me out of school for this."

And Flood is all, "Thanks." And he bites a hole in one of the pouches and squeezes it on the Countess's lips and that's when I started to cry.

There were like four pouches, and when he was going for the last one, Steve was like, "You need to drink that one."

And Flood was like, "No way, it's for her."

And Steve was like, "You know you do."

So Flood like nodded and drank the last one himself, and then he just sat there by her, stroking her hair.

Then Steve was like, "Tommy, you know I can reverse your vampirism. I'm pretty sure the process works."

And Flood just looked at him and nodded. It was so sad. And then the Countess started to moan, and she opened her eyes and she saw the vampyre Flood and she was all, "Hey, baby." Just like that. And I started crying again like a big wuss and Steve took Jared and me out to the car to give them some space.

And Steve was like, "I made this for you from my jacket." And he put this leather motorcycle jacket on me that was covered with those glass LED thingies. It was kinda heavy, because there were batteries built into the padding, but cool. And he was all, "This will keep you safe. The switch is in the snap on the left cuff. Just squeeze it and the lights will come on. They won't hurt you, but you should wear sunglasses to protect your retinas." Then he put a pair of totally cyber wraparound sunglasses on me and kissed me. And I kissed him back, hard, with major tongue, and finally he pulled away, as gentle as a butterfly. So then I slapped him, so he wouldn't think I was a slut. But so he wouldn't think I was being frigid, I sort of jumped on him and wrapped my legs around him and sort of accidentally rode him to the ground and was accidentally kind of dry-humping him on the pavement when the lights on my jacket came on and people looked out their hotel windows and whatnot, so Jared ended our special romantic moment by hitting my light switch and dragging me off.

And I was all, "You are *THE MAN*, Foo!"

And he was all, "Huh?" Because I hadn't told him yet that his new name was Foo Dog.

But then he said he actually had to get home and check in or his parents would freak out. And said to watch the masters until I got back, if I got a chance try to talk them into being converted. So we made out on the hood of the Honda for a while and he drove off into night's cold loneliness like the superhero that he is. (The effect was ruined, kind of, in that Jared caught a ride with him.)

So I went back upstairs and sat at the foot of the masters' bed, keeping guard and listening to them.

They were talking softly, but I could hear them.

The vampyre Flood was all, "Maybe we should give it a try."

And the Countess was all, "What, the cure? Tommy, it can't work. You've seen what I can do, you know what you can do. This isn't biology, this is magic."

"Maybe it's not. Maybe it's science we don't know yet."

"It doesn't matter. We don't even know if it works."

"We should try."

"Why would we try, Tommy? You've only been immortal for a couple of weeks. Do you want to give up the power, the—I don't know—the command over your world?"

"Well—yes."

"You do?"

"Yeah. I don't like it, Jody. I don't like being afraid all the time. I don't like being alone. I don't like being a killer."

"That woman was torturing you, Tommy. That's never going to happen again."

"That's wasn't the problem. I'd get over her. The problem was that I liked it. I *liked* it."

Then the Countess was quiet for a while, and I thought it might be dawn or something, but I peeked over the edge of the bed and she was just staring into his eyes. She looked over at me.

"Hey, girlie girl," the Countess said, and she smiled at me and it felt like a gift or something. It was like, real. Then she took her watch off and threw it to me at the end of the bed. "That has an automatic almanac in it—how about you set the alarm to go off about twenty minutes before sunset, so you don't get caught out again, okay?" And I was going to tell her about the jacket that Foo made for me, but I kind of couldn't talk, so I just nodded and put the watch on and slid back down to the floor.

Then I heard the Countess go, "You aren't alone. I'm here. We can go where no one knows us, no one is chasing us, and I'll always be here for you."

And he goes, "I know. I mean alone from everyone else. Separate. I want to be human, not some foul dead thing."

"I thought you wanted to be special."

"I do, but I want to be human special—because of something I did."

Then it was quiet for a while, and finally the Countess goes, "I love it, Tommy. I'm not afraid all the time like you; just the opposite. I didn't realize how afraid I used to be until I became like this. I like walking the street knowing that I'm the Alpha animal, hearing and seeing and smelling everything, being part of everything. I like it. I wanted to share that with you"

"It's okay. You couldn't have known."

"I don't want to be alone either. That's why I turned you. I love you."

Then the alarm went off on Lord Flood's watch, and he shut it off.

Then he's all, "We can't go back to the way it was, before, I mean? Where I look after you?"

"It's not the same world, Tommy. You know that now. We were in the same room in different worlds."

"Okay then. I love you, Jody."

"I love you, too," goes the Countess.

Then they didn't say anything for a long time, and when my new watch showed that the sun was up, I looked, and they were lying there, holding each other, and I could see the red stains on the pillow from their tears.

And I was like, "Oh, hell no!"

Being the Chronicles of Abby Normal: Not Unlike the Toaster, I Control the Darkness

So I slept a little that day, and talked to my sweet love-ninja, Foo, a couple of times on the phone, then he came over and we left Jared with some blood for Lord Flood and the Countess when they awoke, and motored to the loft. It took like an hour to clean up all the broken glass and ash and stuff from the night before. We had just finished cleaning and counting the money and making out and whatnot when the alarm went off on the Countess's watch.

And I was like, "Dude, I'm not ready."

And he was all, "Dude, you are more ready than anyone I've ever known."

And I was all, "OMG, I am so going to sex you to death if we live through this."

And then he was all bashful and pretended to be doing something technical so we were ready.

Then, like an hour after sundown, I heard them coming. I was at the kitchen counter when the security door
downstairs opened, and when I turned around they were
just, like there. Lord Flood called them the Animals, but
now they were kind of the *roadkill*. And I like touched the
snap on my UV jacket, just to make sure it was there.

So I was all, "Hey, vampyre scum."

And the formerly black and now gray one, who was like
their leader, was all up in my grille, like, "We need the
money, where is the money?"

And I was like, "Step off, undead-tard. There's no
money."

And he was like, "Don't fuck with us. Flood and the
redhead took like six hundred grand from my apartment."

And I was all, "Actually, its like five hundred and eighty-
three thousand eight hundred and fifty-eight."

And he was all, "Give it!"

And all seven of them were like gathering around me—
even the born-again one the Countess had thrashed—like
they were going to do the massive gang-suck on me, so I had
my finger on my light button all the time, in case I needed to
flash-fry the motherfuckers. But I stayed chilly and I was
like, "Are you high?"

And he was all, "No, I'm not high. No one is high."

And they all started whining and whatnot, all, "We
can't even take a bong hit. We can't drink a beer. Our systems won't take it. Being sober sucks. We are useless undead stoners."

So I was all, "Step back and behold, bi-atches."

And I'm all taking a bottle of Stoli out of the freezer, and mixing in a glass with some of the blood from the pouches, just like the ones we left for the Countess and Lord Flood, and they're all drooling when they see the blood, so I was thinking, *Don't make me fry you.*

But then I give the glass to the gray vamp, and he's all, "Sweet."

And the others are like, "Me, me, me."

So I'm like mixing Bloody Marys all around, and the greasy hippyish one is like, "Can we dunk pot cookies in this?"

And I'm like, "Of course, stoner vamp."

And they're all, "You are a goddess. And we are not worthy. And oh please, may we have some more?" Until they started to drop.

So like two minutes later there's like this big pile of passed-out vampyres in the kitchen, and I'm all, "Yo, Foo, I got your shit ready."

And Foo comes out of the bedroom, all cute, holding his UV floodlight like he's going to save me, then sees that they are all out cold and gives me a big kiss and is like, "You rock."

And I'm like, "You have no idea, my Manga-haired love toy."

And he was like, "The sedative in the blood, blah, blah, four hours, blah, blah, nerdspeak, geektalk—"

And I'm like, "Whateva, studmuffin. Handle it."

So it took like two hours for Foo to do all his medical stuff with the Animals, taking some blood and doing
various medical nerdism stuff to it, then putting it back
in, but finally he was done and I called Jared to tell him
that we were on our way to get Lord Flood and the
Countess.

So I like made the other call to make sure everything
was all in order and whatnot, and Foo was all, "Are you
sure this is what you want to do?"

And I was all, "Foo, theirs is the greatest love of all time.
It's the only thing to do."

And he was all, "Okay, as long as you're sure. Because
we can do them the same as we did the others."

And I was all, "No, that won't work. They have to be
together. And you don't have to live at home anymore.
We'll have a completely sweet love lair."

So we did it.

Blue watched from the alley across the street as the Animals came out the security door, empty-handed, and stumbled into the street. She knew she should have gone herself,
but that whole getting-burned-up thing had taught her that
perhaps it was better to delegate. That they didn't have her
money was bad enough, but that they didn't have her
money and heat was coming off of them was disastrous.
"Those dumbfucks can't get anything right," she said to
herself. "I'm going to have to kill them all over again."

"I don't think so," said a voice from behind her. She whipped around, leading with her long fingernails in a swipe that would have taken off half a man's face.

Elijah caught her hand. He'd found another tracksuit, this one powder blue. "It's time to let it go. The genie must go back in the bottle, I'm afraid."

"Let me go, I need to go get my money."

"No, my dear, you don't want to do that. The residents of that loft have recently developed a very unpleasant fashion sense."

"You're fucking with my income, paleface."

"You don't need to worry about that anymore."

"Meaning what?"

"It ends here. Come with me, my dear."

"You want me to come with you? I don't even know you."

"Yes, but we share a special relationship."

"Special? You beat my face into the hood of a Mercedes."

"Well, yes. Sorry. To the innocent my behavior can sometimes be distasteful."

"Yeah? *Innocent.* I've fucked thousands of guys."

"Yes, well, I've killed enough to fill a city."

Blue shrugged. "Okay, you win."

"Revenge is a dish best served cold anyway, don't you think?"

"Or not at all," said a male voice behind Elijah.

Elijah and Blue turned. Three of them stood there in

their long coats, looking like sculptures, looking eternal, like they could wait forever.

"Can just anyone sneak up on me now?" said Blue.

"Time to go, Elijah," said the African woman.

"None of you would be here if it weren't for me," Elijah said.

"Yes, and we would have been hunted down and killed a long time ago if we hadn't adhered to your rules."

"Ah, my rules," Elijah said, looking down now.

"How many left to clean?"

Elijah looked across the street to the loft windows, then at Blue. She raised an eyebrow, smiled a little.

"She's the only one left." He lied.

"Then finish it."

"I'd rather not," Elijah said.

The Emperor of San Francisco wept for his city. He had done what he could, called the police, alerted the newspapers, even tried to take to battle himself, but by the time he'd gathered the courage to return to the Marina Safeway, it had been finished, and he could do nothing more than speculate to the uniformed police officers how the window had been broken and why the store was empty. They'd tried to track down the night crew, but none of them seemed to be home. And his city was plagued by vampires.

Now the Emperor wept and consoled the troops, rubbing Bummer behind the ears and gently patting Lazarus on the ribs as he lay sleeping on the dock. The fog was coming slow off the Bay tonight, not windblown like it was so often here.

He heard footsteps before he saw them, then there were five of them. The fiend, the three in the long coats he had seen come in the night before, and a blond woman in a blue party dress. They walked past, and only the fiend turned and paused. The Emperor held Bummer tight, afraid that he would burst into one of his barking fits and all would be lost.

"Old man," said Elijah. "The City is yours again." Then he joined the others at the end of the dock.

The Emperor could see their motor yacht waiting outside the breakwater—it had to be two hundred feet long, far too big to enter the marina.

"Very well, then, shall we go?" said Elijah.

"Can I get a coat like that?" asked Blue, nodding toward the tall blond man.

The blond man said, "You'll get one when you learn the secret handshake and get your decoder ring."

Blue looked at Elijah. "Is he fuckin' with me?"

"Yes," said Elijah. He offered her his arm. She took it, and stepped down into the longboat.

The Emperor watched the vampires disappear into the fog.

Rivera had six uniforms in SWAT gear with a battering ram ready to take down the door, so he and Cavuto were more than somewhat surprised when it opened almost as soon as they knocked. A shirtless, sleepy-looking Chinese guy with spiky hair stood in the doorway.

"Yes, can I help you?"

Rivera held up the warrant. "I have a warrant to search this apartment."

" 'Kay," said the Chinese guy. "Abby, cops are here."

The skinny broken clown girl appeared at the top of the stairs in a kimono.

"Hey, cops," said Abby Normal.

"What are you doing here?" Rivera said.

"I live here, cop." She popped the *p*. Rivera hated that.

"Actually, it's my apartment," said the Chinese guy. "Do you need to see ID?"

"Yeah, that would be nice, kid," said Cavuto. He whipped the kid around and marched him up the stairs as the kid read the warrant.

"Do not bruise the Foo, cop," said the broken clown girl.

Rivera turned to the uniforms and shrugged apologetically. "Sorry, guys, I guess we got this one." They shuffled away.

"What are you guys looking for?" asked the Chinese kid. "Maybe we could speed this up."

"We're looking for Thomas Flood and Jody Stroud. He's the one on the lease for this apartment and the one down the street."

"Oh, yeah. I'm subletting," said the Chinese kid.

"Steven Wong," Cavuto read off the kid's license.

Rivera was feeling very, very bad about this. They had found one more body in the Mission with the blood-loss-and-broken-neck MO—the guy had been naked, supposedly someone had stolen his powder-blue tracksuit, so they logged it as robbery, but then, a week ago, the killings stopped. That didn't mean it was over. He'd made the mistake of thinking it was over with these two before. Rivera had finally gotten the Christian kid at the Safeway to file charges on the redhead for assault. After a long talk with the other stoners, they'd gotten the Flood kid on the arrest warrant for conspiracy. They'd also implied that somehow Flood and the redhead had gotten their share of the old vampire's money. Maybe they *had* left town. If they had, well, good, but he still had a slew of unsolved murders.

"You're subletting from Thomas Flood?"

"I never met him, actually," said Steve. "We arranged it through the rental agent."

"Yeah, so step off, cop," said the skinny girl.

Rivera looked around the apartment. There was no need to tear the place apart. Obviously everything in here was new. Mostly decorated in Pier 1 Imports cheap wicker motif and some punky Urban Outfitter flair, which he guessed was the input of the creepy little girl.

The bronze sculptures were out of character, though. A life-sized nude of a young woman, a large snapping turtle, and a life-sized bronze of a couple posed as if in Rodin's *The Kiss*.

"These must have been expensive," Rivera said.

"Not really. I know the artists," the Chinese kid said. "Some biker guys down the street."

"Foo's in biotech," said the broken clown girl. "He makes like stupid money, cop."

"Yeah, that's swell," said Rivera. He'd watched this neighborhood turn from a rust slum of repair shops and the odd ethnic restaurant to a gentrified hive of hipster professionals in remodeled lofts during the dot-com boom, and it had never turned back. The whole neighborhood was full of kids who spent the equivalent of Rivera's annual salary on a car they wouldn't drive a dozen times a year. This kid apparently was just another one.

"So you don't know these people?" Rivera said, pointing to the warrant.

Steven Wong shook his head. "Sorry, I've never met them. I send my rent directly to the rental agency. You might check with them."

"Okay then. Sorry to bother you."

"Okay then?" Cavuto said. "That's it?"

"They're not here, Nick. These two don't know where they are."

"But, that's not enough."

"Yeah? You want to spend some time talking to Allison here, see what you can find out?" Rivera nodded toward the broken clown girl.

Cavuto had tried to keep someone between himself and the skinny girl since they'd come upstairs, but now he looked at her full on and shuddered. "No, I guess that's it." He turned and lumbered down the steps.

"You need to check your girlfriend's ID," Rivera said to Steve. "You may not be old enough for her." Then he turned and left as well.

Chill, Foo," Abby said. "They're gone. They won't be back. Let's go shopping."

"Abby, are you sure about this? It seems cruel." He patted the life-sized sculpture of the couple embraced in a kiss.

"I heard the Countess say once that it was like being in a dream. They just sort of float, all peaceful and dreamy. The main thing is they're together."

"You're sure?"

"Theirs is the greatest love of all time. It would be wrong for them to be apart, Foo."

"Well, I think we should just change them back. Now that we know the process works."

"Someday."

"Now."

"The Countess doesn't want that."

"It's wrong."

"How can it be wrong? It's my idea, and I am their dedicated minion and whatnot. I control the dark." She ran and jumped into his arms.

"I guess you do," he said. "Okay, let's go shopping for stuff for our most fly apartment."

. .

Ψilliam arrived back at the loft just after dark, feeling very much rested and well fed from his hospital stay, but craving a sip or two of the good stuff, and terribly worried about Chet. He let himself into the stairway with his key, but when he rang the bell, no one answered, so he sat down to wait for the redhead and that guy to bring his bottle.

He hadn't been there ten minutes before he heard the meowing at the door, and his heart leapt as he opened the outer door to find Chet, his red sweater still intact, purring outside.

"Come on, boy. I missed you, buddy."

William scooped up his kitty and carried him into the stairwell. As soon as the door closed, Chet, the huge shaved vampire cat, was upon him.

TURN THE PAGE FOR *YOU SUCK* EXTRAS, INCLUDING

THE EMPEROR AND
HIS DOGS

AN AUTHOR'S NOTE

You Suck is the third of my books in which the Emperor and his dogs appear, and over the years I've gotten hundreds of letters asking about them. "Are they real or did you make them up?" is the question asked most often, and the answer is, simply, "Yes, they were real and I did make them up."

The Emperor is based on a historical figure named Joshua Norton, an English businessman from the 1840s who came to California to make his fortune and, instead, ended up losing it, supposedly in a lawsuit over a rice futures contract. (Norton, seeing the huge population in San Francisco's Chinatown, was trying to corner the market on rice.) Whether he was mad before or the deal sent him over the edge, Norton ended up living on the streets of San Francisco and soon issued a proclamation declaring himself the Emperor of the United States and Protector of Mexico. That a homeless fellow might indulge in delusions of grandeur is not unusual; that an entire city would be complicit in the delusion is.

The tailors of San Francisco supplied Norton with top hats and grand tailcoats with gold braiding and epaulets.

Restaurants allowed the Emperor to eat for free, and print-
ers not only printed and posted Norton's proclamations,
they created currency with his image on it, which was accepted from him by local businesses. Papers covered Norton as if he were a legitimate politician, despite some of his
more insane proclamations: that a bridge be built across
the Golden Gate, that another be built across the bay to
Oakland, and that a league of nations be formed to resolve
disputes without war.

The people of the city treated Norton with great respect, and he them, as if they were indeed his subjects and
he a benevolent ruler. There is a story that Emperor Norton
even diverted a race riot in Chinatown when, after a crop
failure in California's Central Valley, jobless men blamed
the Chinese for their fate and stormed the neighborhood
bent on burning it to the ground. Supposedly, Norton
stopped them by putting himself between the workers and
Chinese and reciting the Lord's Prayer.

When Emperor Norton died in 1880, more than 30,000
people marched in his funeral procession. But his legacy
lives on in the work of Mark Twain, who based his character of the King in Huckleberry Finn on Emperor Norton, as
well as in the work of Robert Louis Stevenson and Neil
Gaiman, and in a number of Western movies and television
programs.

Bummer and Lazarus are the real names of two stray
dogs that lived in San Francisco contemporaneous to Emperor Norton, and while it's rumored that they were the

4

Emperor's dogs, such was not the case. They were similarly adopted by the city of San Francisco, fed and cared for, but remained strays living on the street, and when Bummer died in 1865, his obituary was written by Mark Twain and it appeared in the *Californian*. There is a plaque commemorating Bummer and Lazarus in the small park at the base of the Transamerica Pyramid.

JODY

A CAΠEΦ
An Excerpt from *A Dirty Job*

"Outstanding . . . ingeniously unpredict-able . . . and the dialogue follows a zany illogic worthy of the Marx Brothers."

—*Washington Post Book World*

A Dirty Job, Christopher Moore's ninth novel, centers around Charlie Asher, a pretty normal guy with a normal life. He and his wife—a bright and pretty woman who actually loves him for his normalcy—live in San Francisco, in an apartment over the thrift shop Charlie owns. They're even about to have their first child. Yes, Charlie's doing okay—until people start dropping dead around him, and everywhere he goes a dark presence whispers to him from under the streets. Charlie Asher, it seems, has been recruited for a new job . . .

But, as we readers know, Charlie Asher isn't the only one in San Francisco who's recently found himself on the other side of normal. Read on for an excerpt from *A Dirty Job* featuring C. Thomas Flood's favorite redhead.

That evening Charlie was watching the store, wondering why he had lied to his employees, when he saw a flash of red passing by the front window. A second later, a strikingly pale redhead came through the door. She was wearing a short, black cocktail dress and black fuck-me pumps. She strode up the aisle like she was auditioning for a music video. Her hair cascaded in long curls around her shoulders and down her back like a great auburn veil. Her eyes were emerald green, and when she saw him looking, she smiled, and stopped, some ten feet away.

Charlie felt an almost painful jolt that seemed to emanate from somewhere in the area of his groin, and after a second he recognized it as an autonomic lust response. He hadn't felt anything like that since Rachel had passed, and he felt vaguely ashamed.

She was examining him, looking him over like you would examine a used car. He was sure he must be blushing.

"Hi," Charlie said. "Can I help you?"

The redhead smiled again, just a little, and reached into a small black bag that he hadn't noticed she'd been carrying. "I found this," she said, holding up a silver cigarette case. Something Charlie didn't see very often anymore, even in the secondhand business. It was glowing, pulsating like the objects in the back room. "I was in the neighborhood and something made me think that this belonged here."

She moved to the counter opposite Charlie and set the cigarette case down in front of him.

Charlie could barely move. He stared at her, not even conscious that to avoid her eyes he was staring at her cleavage, and she appeared to be looking around his head and shoulders as if following the path of insects that were buzzing around him.

"Touch me," she said.

"Huh?" He looked up, saw she was serious. She held out her hand; her nails were manicured and painted the same deep red as her lipstick. He took her hand.

As soon as she touched him she pulled away. "You're warm."

"Thanks." In that moment he realized that she wasn't. Her fingers had been ice-cold.

"Then you're not one of us?"

He tried to think of what "us" might be? Irish? Low blood pressure? Nymphomaniac? Why did he even think that? "Us? What do you mean, 'us'?"

She backed away a step. "No. You don't just take the weak and the sick, do you? You take anyone."

"Take? What do you mean, 'take'?"

"You don't even know, do you?"

"Know what?" Charlie was getting very nervous. As a Beta Male, he found it difficult enough to function under the attention of a beautiful woman, but she was just plain spooky. "Wait. Can you see this thing glowing?" He held out the cigarette case.

"No glow. It just felt like it belonged here," she said. "What's your name?"

"Charlie Asher. This is Asher's."

"Well, Charlie, you seem like a nice guy, and I don't know exactly what you are, and it doesn't seem like you know. You don't, do you?"

"I've been going through some changes," Charlie said, wondering why he felt compelled to share this at all.

The redhead nodded, as if confirming something to herself. "Okay. I know what it's like to, uh, find yourself thrown into a situation where forces beyond your control are changing you into someone, something you don't have an owner's manual for. I understand what it is to not know. But someone, somewhere, does know. Someone can tell you what's going on."

"What are you talking about?" But he knew what she was talking about. What he didn't know was how she could possibly know.

"You make people die, don't you, Charlie?" She said it like she had worked up the courage to tell him that he had some spinach in his teeth. More of a service to him than an accusation.

"How do you—?" How did she—

"Because it's what I do. Not like you, but it's what I do. Find them, Charlie. Backtrack and find whoever was there when your world changed."

Charlie looked at her, then at the cigarette case, then at the redhead again, who was no longer smiling, but was stepping backward toward the door. Trying to stay in touch with normal, he focused on the cigarette case and said, "I suppose I can do an appraisal—"

He heard the bell over the door jingle, and when he looked up she was gone.

He didn't see her moving by the windows on either side of the door; she was just gone. He ran to the front of the store and out the door onto the sidewalk. The Mason Street cable car was just topping the hill up by California Street and he could hear the bell, there was a thin fog coming up from the Bay that threw colorful halos around the neon signs of the other businesses, but there was no striking redhead on the street. He went to the corner and looked down Vallejo, but again no redhead, just the Emperor, sitting against the building with his dogs.

"Good evening, Charlie."

"Your Majesty, did you see a redhead go by here just now?"

"Oh yes. Spoke to her. I'm not sure you have a chance there, Charlie, I believe she's spoken for. And she did warn me to stay away from you."

"Why? Did she say why?"

"She said that you were Death."

"I am?" Charlie said. "Am I?" His breath caught in his throat as the day played back in his head. "What if I am?"

"You know, son," the Emperor said, "I am not an expert in dealing with the fairer sex, but you might want to save that bit of information until the third date or so, after they've gotten to know you a little."

STRAP YOURSELVES IN, LADIES AND GENTLEMEN,

IT'S CHRISTOPHER MOORE TIME!

YOU SUCK: A Love Story
ISBN 978-0-06-059030-7 (paperback) • ISBN 978-0-06-122718-9 (unabridged CD)

C. Thomas Flood (better known as Tommy) has just awakened. He and the girl of his dreams, Jody, have just shared a physical intimacy unlike any Tommy has known before. He opens his eyes, sees Jody smiling down at him, opens his mouth, and says, "You bitch, you killed me. You suck!" For Jody is a vampire. And now Tommy's one, too. They're still a couple, but they've got some things to work through. Tommy has new powers to explore. Jody doesn't know how much she should teach him, and how much she should let him discover for himself.

A DIRTY JOB: A Novel
ISBN 978-0-06-059028-4 (paperback) • ISBN 978-0-06-087259-5 (unabridged CD)

Charlie Asher has survived in the gene pool by doggie-paddling in the shallow end. But Charlie's safe life is about to take a really weird detour when his daughter, Sophie, is born—minutes before his wife dies of a freak medical condition. As if being a widower and the single parent of a newborn aren't enough, soon people begin to drop dead around Charlie, and he discovers that his worst fears were molehills compared to the mountain of poo he's in.

FLUKE: Or, I Know Why the Winged Whale Sings
ISBN 978-0-06-056668-5 (paperback) • ISBN 978-0-06-123879-6 (unabridged CD)

Every winter, whale researchers Nate Quinn and Clay Demolocus, partners in the Maui Whale Research Foundation, ply the warm Pacific waters, trying to solve an age-old mystery: Just why do humpback whales sing? Then one day a whale moons Nate, lifting its tail to display a cryptic scrawled message: Bite Me. But no one else saw a thing—not Clay, not fetching research assistant Amy, not even spliff-puffing white-boy Rastaman Kona (née Preston Applebaum). The weirdness only gets weirder when Nate gets a call telling him a whale has made contact—by phone.

ISLAND OF THE SEQUINED LOVE NUN
ISBN 978-0-06-073544-9 (paperback)

A wonderfully crazed excursion into the demented heart of a tropical paradise—a world of cargo cults, cannibals, mad scientists, ninjas, and talking fruit bats. Our bumbling hero is Tucker Case, a hopeless geek trapped in a cool guy's body, who makes a living as a pilot for the Mary Jean Cosmetics Corporation. But when he demolishes his boss's pink plane, Tuck must make a run for his life.

LAMB: The Gospel According to Biff, Christ's Childhood Pal
ISBN 978-0-380-81381-0 (paperback) • ISBN 978-0-06-123878-9 (unabridged CD)

The birth of Jesus has been well-chronicled, as have his glorious teachings, acts, and divine sacrifice after his thirtieth birthday. But no one knows about the early life of the Son of God—"the missing years"—except Biff. Ever since the day he came upon six-year-old Joshua of Nazareth resurrecting lizards in the village square, Levi bar Alphaeus, a.k.a. "Biff," had the distinction of being the Messiah's best bud. That's why the angel Raziel has resurrected Biff from the dust of Jerusalem and brought him to America to write a new gospel, one that tells the real, untold story.

THE LUST LIZARD OF MELANCHOLY COVE
ISBN 978-0-06-073545-6 (paperback)

The town psychiatrist has decided to switch everybody in Pine Cove, California from their normal antidepressants to placebos, so naturally—well, to be accurate, artificially—business is booming at the local blues bar. Trouble is, those lonely slide-guitar notes have also attracted a colossal sea-beast with a thing for explosive oil tanker trucks. Suddenly, morose Pine Cove turns libidinous and is hit by a mysterious crime wave, and a beleaguered constable has to fight off his own gonzo appetites to find out what's wrong and what, if anything, to do about it.

PRACTICAL DEMONKEEPING
ISBN 978-0-06-073542-5 (paperback)

Moore's ingenious debut novel introduces the reader to one of the most memorably mismatched pairs in the annals of literature. The good-looking one is one-hundred-year-old ex-seminarian and "roads" scholar Travis O'Hearn. The green one is Catch, a demon with a nasty habit of eating most of the people he meets. Behind the fake Tudor façade of Pine Cove, California, Catch sees a four-star buffet. Travis, on the other hand, thinks he sees a way of ridding himself of his toothy traveling companion. The winos, neo-pagans, and deadbeat Lotharios of Pine Cove, meanwhile, have other ideas.

THE STUPIDEST ANGEL: A Heartwarming Tale of Christmas Terror
ISBN 978-0-06-084235-2 (hardcover) • ISBN 978-0-06-073874-7 (unabridged CD)

Ah, Christmas—the hap-hap-happiest season of all! Except for Pine Cove Constable Theo Crowe, who's looking for the local evil developer who disappeared after playing Santa at the Caribou Lodge Christmas party. Meanwhile the town braces for the annual onslaught of holiday tourists and the storm of the century. Oh, and did we mention the tall blonde stranger with supernatural strength—a clueless angel sent to Earth on a mysterious mission—who arrives looking for "a child"? Yikes! Pass the eggnog.

www.ChrisMoore.com